A MISS MARPLE QUARTET

Agatha Christie

A
MISS MARPLE
QUARTET

THE BODY IN THE LIBRARY
A POCKET FULL OF RYE
A MURDER IS ANNOUNCED
THE MOVING FINGER

COLLINS
8 Grafton Street, London W1
1985

William Collins Sons & Co. Ltd
London · Glasgow · Sydney · Auckland
Toronto · Johannesburg

BRITISH LIBRARY CATALOGUING IN PUBLICATION DATA

Christie, Agatha
A Miss Marple quartet.
I. Title
823'.912[F]   PR6005.H66

ISBN 0-00-231469-X

First published 1985
© Agatha Christie 1942, 1953, 1950, 1943

Photoset in Linotron Sabon by
Rowland Phototypesetting Ltd, Bury St Edmunds, Suffolk
Made and printed in Great Britain by
William Collins Sons & Co. Ltd, Glasgow

CONTENTS

The Body in the Library   7

A Pocket Full of Rye   151

A Murder is Announced   311

The Moving Finger   509

THE BODY IN THE LIBRARY

CHAPTER 1

I

Mrs Bantry was dreaming. Her sweet peas had just taken a First at the flower show. The vicar, dressed in cassock and surplice, was giving out the prizes in church. His wife wandered past, dressed in a bathing-suit, but as is the blessed habit of dreams this fact did not arouse the disapproval of the parish in the way it would assuredly have done in real life. . . .

Mrs Bantry was enjoying her dream a good deal. She usually did enjoy those early-morning dreams that were terminated by the arrival of early-morning tea. Somewhere in her inner consciousness was an awareness of the usual early-morning noises of the household. The rattle of the curtain-rings on the stairs as the housemaid drew them, the noises of the second housemaid's dustpan and brush in the passage outside. In the distance the heavy noise of the front-door bolt being drawn back.

Another day was beginning. In the meantime she must extract as much pleasure as possible from the flower show — for already its dream-like quality was becoming apparent. . . .

Below her was the noise of the big wooden shutters in the drawing-room being opened. She heard it, yet did not hear it. For quite half an hour longer the usual household noises would go on, discreet, subdued, not disturbing because they were so familiar. They would culminate in a swift, controlled sound of footsteps along the passage, the rustle of a print dress, the subdued chink of tea-things as the tray was deposited on the table outside, then the soft knock and the entry of Mary to draw the curtains.

In her sleep Mrs Bantry frowned. Something disturbing was penetrating through to the dream state, something out of its time. Footsteps along the passage, footsteps that were too hurried and too soon. Her ears listened unconsciously for the chink of china, but there was no chink of china.

The knock came at the door. Automatically from the depths of her dream Mrs Bantry said: 'Come in.' The door opened — now there would be the chink of curtain-rings as the curtains were drawn back.

But there was no chink of curtain-rings. Out of the dim green light Mary's voice came – breathless, hysterical: 'Oh, m'am, oh, m'am, *there's a body in the library.*'

And then with a hysterical burst of sobs she rushed out of the room again.

II

Mrs Bantry sat up in bed.

Either her dream had taken a very odd turn or else – or else Mary had really rushed into the room and had said (incredible! fantastic!) that there was a body in the library.

'Impossible,' said Mrs Bantry to herself. 'I must have been dreaming.'

But even as she said it, she felt more and more certain that she had not been dreaming, that Mary, her superior self-controlled Mary, had actually uttered those fantastic words.

Mrs Bantry reflected a minute and then applied an urgent conjugal elbow to her sleeping spouse.

'Arthur, Arthur, wake up.'

Colonel Bantry grunted, muttered, and rolled over on his side.

'Wake up, Arthur. Did you hear what she said?'

'Very likely,' said Colonel Bantry indistinctly. 'I quite agree with you, Dolly,' and promptly went to sleep again.

Mrs Bantry shook him.

'You've got to listen. Mary came in and said that there was a body in the library.'

'Eh, what?'

'A *body* in the *library*.'

'Who said so?'

'Mary.'

Colonel Bantry collected his scattered faculties and proceeded to deal with the situation. He said:

'Nonsense, old girl; you've been dreaming.'

'No, I haven't. I thought so, too, at first. But I haven't. She really came in and said so.'

'Mary came in and said there was a body in the library?'

'Yes.'

'But there couldn't be,' said Colonel Bantry.

'No – no, I suppose not,' said Mrs Bantry doubtfully.

Rallying, she went on:

'But then why did Mary say there was?'

'She can't have.'

'She did.'

'You must have imagined it.'

'I didn't imagine it.'

Colonel Bantry was by now thoroughly awake and prepared to deal with the situation on its merits. He said kindly:

'You've been dreaming, Dolly, that's what it is. It's that detective story you were reading – *The Clue of the Broken Match*. You know – Lord Edgbaston finds a beautiful blonde dead on the library hearthrug. Bodies are always being found in libraries in books. I've never known a case in real life.'

'Perhaps you will now,' said Mrs Bantry. 'Anyway, Arthur, you've got to get up and see.'

'But really, Dolly, it *must* have been a dream. Dreams often do seem wonderfully vivid when you first wake up. You feel quite sure they're true.'

'I was having quite a different sort of dream – about a flower show and the vicar's wife in a bathing-dress – something like that.'

With a sudden burst of energy Mrs Bantry jumped out of bed and pulled back the curtains. The light of a fine autumn day flooded the room.

'I did *not* dream it,' said Mrs Bantry firmly. 'Get up at once, Arthur, and go downstairs and see about it.'

'You want me to go downstairs and ask if there's a body in the library? I shall look a damned fool.'

'You needn't ask anything,' said Mrs Bantry. 'If there *is* a body – and of course it's just possible that Mary's gone mad and thinks she sees things that aren't there – well, somebody will tell you soon enough. *You* won't have to say a word.'

Grumbling, Colonel Bantry wrapped himself in his dressing-gown and left the room. He went along the passage and down the staircase. At the foot of it was a little knot of huddled servants, some of them were sobbing. The butler stepped forward impressively.

'I'm glad you have come, sir. I have directed that nothing should be done until you came. Will it be in order for me to ring up the police, sir?'

'Ring 'em up about what?'

The butler cast a reproachful glance over his shoulder at the tall young woman who was weeping hysterically on the cook's shoulder.

'I understood, sir, that Mary had already informed you. She said she had done so.'

Mary gasped out:

'I was so upset I don't know what I said. It all came over me again and my legs gave way and my inside turned over. Finding it like that – oh, oh, oh!'

She subsided again on to Mrs Eccles, who said: 'There, there, my dear,' with some relish.

'Mary is naturally somewhat upset, sir, having been the one to make the gruesome discovery,' explained the butler. 'She went into the library as usual, to draw the curtains, and – and almost stumbled over the body.'

'Do you mean to tell me,' demanded Colonel Bantry, 'that there's a dead body in my library – *my* library?'

The butler coughed.

'Perhaps, sir, you would like to see for yourself.'

III

'Hallo, 'allo, 'allo. Police station here. Yes, who's speaking?'

Police-Constable Palk was buttoning up his tunic with one hand while the other held the receiver.

'Yes, yes, Gossington Hall. Yes? Oh, good morning, sir.' Police-Constable Palk's tone underwent a slight modification. It became less impatiently official, recognizing the generous patron of the police sports and the principal magistrate of the district.

'Yes, sir? What can I do for you? – I'm sorry, sir, I didn't quite catch – a *body*, did you say? – yes? – yes, if you please, sir – that's right, sir – young woman not known to you, you say? – quite, sir. Yes, you can leave it all to me.'

Police-Constable Palk replaced the receiver, uttered a long-drawn whistle and proceeded to dial his superior officer's number.

Mrs Palk looked in from the kitchen whence proceeded an appetizing smell of frying bacon.

'What is it?'

'Rummest thing you ever heard of,' replied her husband. 'Body of a young woman found up at the Hall. In the Colonel's library.'

'Murdered?'

'Strangled, so he says.'

'Who was she?'

'The Colonel says he doesn't know her from Adam.'

'Then what was she doing in 'is library?'

Police-Constable Palk silenced her with a reproachful glance and spoke officially into the telephone.

'Inspector Slack? Police-Constable Palk here. A report has just come in that the body of a young woman was discovered this morning at seven-fifteen —'

IV

Miss Marple's telephone rang when she was dressing. The sound of it flurried her a little. It was an unusual hour for her telephone to ring. So well ordered was her prim spinster's life that unforeseen telephone calls were a source of vivid conjecture.

'Dear me,' said Miss Marple, surveying the ringing instrument with perplexity. 'I wonder who that can be?'

Nine o'clock to nine-thirty was the recognized time for the village to make friendly calls to neighbours. Plans for the day, invitations and so on were always issued then. The butcher had been known to ring up just before nine if some crisis in the meat trade had occurred. At intervals during the day spasmodic calls might occur, though it was considered bad form to ring up after nine-thirty at night. It was true that Miss Marple's nephew, a writer, and therefore erratic, had been known to ring up at the most peculiar times, once as late as ten minutes to midnight. But whatever Raymond West's eccentricities, early rising was not one of them. Neither he nor anyone of Miss Marple's acquaintance would be likely to ring up before eight in the morning. Actually a quarter to eight.

Too early even for a telegram, since the post office did not open until eight.

'It must be,' Miss Marple decided, 'a wrong number.'

Having decided this, she advanced to the impatient instrument and quelled its clamour by picking up the receiver. 'Yes?' she said.

'Is that you, Jane?'

Miss Marple was much surprised.

'Yes, it's Jane. You're up very early, Dolly.'

Mrs Bantry's voice came breathless and agitated over the wires.

'The most awful thing has happened.'

'Oh, my dear.'

'We've just found a body in the library.'

For a moment Miss Marple thought her friend had gone mad.

'You've found a *what*?'

'I know. One doesn't believe it, does one? I mean, I thought they only happened in books. I had to argue for hours with Arthur this morning before he'd even go down and see.'

Miss Marple tried to collect herself. She demanded breathlessly: 'But whose body is it?'

'It's a blonde.'

'A what?'

'A blonde. A beautiful blonde – like books again. None of us has ever seen her before. She's just lying there in the library, dead. That's why you've got to come up at once.'

'You want *me* to come up?'

'Yes, I'm sending the car down for you.'

Miss Marple said doubtfully:

'Of course, dear, if you think I can be of any comfort to you –'

'Oh, I don't want comfort. But you're so good at bodies.'

'Oh no, indeed. My little successes have been mostly theoretical.'

'But you're very good at murders. She's been murdered, you see, strangled. What I feel is that if one has got to have a murder actlly happening in one's house, one might as well enjoy it, if you know what I mean. That's why I want you to come and help me find out who did it and unravel the mystery and all that. It really *is* rather thrilling, isn't it?'

'Well, of course, my dear, if I can be of any *help* to you.'

'Splendid! Arthur's being rather difficult. He seems to think I shouldn't enjoy myself about it at all. Of course, I do know it's very sad and all that, but then I don't know the girl – and when you've seen her you'll understand what I mean when I say she doesn't look *real* at all.'

V

A little breathless, Miss Marple alighted from the Bantrys' car, the door of which was held open for her by the chauffeur.

Colonel Bantry came out on the steps, and looked a little surprised.

'Miss Marple? – er – very pleased to see you.'

'Your wife telephoned to me,' explained Miss Marple.

'Capital, capital. She ought to have someone with her. She'll crack up otherwise. She's putting a good face on things at the moment, but you know what it is –'

At this moment Mrs Bantry appeared, and exclaimed:

'Do go back into the dining-room and eat your breakfast, Arthur. Your bacon will get cold.'

'I thought it might be the Inspector arriving,' explained Colonel Bantry.

'He'll be here soon enough,' said Mrs Bantry. 'That's why it's important to get your breakfast first. You need it.'

'So do you. Much better come and eat something, Dolly –'

'I'll come in a minute,' said Mrs Bantry. 'Go on, Arthur.'

Colonel Bantry was shooed back into the dining-room rather like a recalcitrant hen.

'*Now!*' said Mrs Bantry with an intonation of triumph. 'Come on.'

She led the way rapidly along the long corridor to the east of the house. Outside the library door Constable Palk stood on guard. He intercepted Mrs Bantry with a show of authority.

'I'm afraid nobody is allowed in, madam. Inspector's orders.'

'Nonsense, Palk,' said Mrs Bantry. 'You know Miss Marple perfectly well.'

Constable Palk admitted to knowing Miss Marple.

'It's very important that she should see the body,' said Mrs Bantry. 'Don't be stupid, Palk. After all, it's *my* library, isn't it?'

Constable Palk gave way. His habit of giving in to the gentry was lifelong. The Inspector, he reflected, need never know about it.

'Nothing must be touched or handled in any way,' he warned the ladies.

'Of course not,' said Mrs Bantry impatiently. 'We know *that*. You can come in and watch, if you like.'

Constable Palk availed himself of this permission. It had been his intention, anyway.

Mrs Bantry bore her friend triumphantly across the library to the big old-fashioned fireplace. She said, with a dramatic sense of climax: 'There!'

Miss Marple understood then just what her friend had meant when she said the dead girl wasn't real. The library was a room very typical of its owners. It was large and shabby and untidy. It had big sagging arm-chairs, and pipes and books and estate papers laid out on the big table. There were one or two good old family portraits on the walls, and some bad Victorian water-colours, and some would-be-funny hunting scenes. There was a big vase of Michaelmas daisies in the corner. The whole room was dim and mellow and casual. It spoke of long occupation and familiar use and of links with tradition.

And across the old bearskin hearthrug there was sprawled something new and crude and melodramatic: The flamboyant figure of a girl. A girl with unnaturally fair hair dressed up off her face in elaborate curls and rings. Her thin body was dressed in a backless evening-dress of white spangled satin. The face was heavily made-up, the powder standing out grotesquely on its blue swollen surface, the mascara of the lashes lying thickly on the distorted cheeks, the scarlet of the lips looking like a gash. The fingernails were enamelled in a deep blood-red and so were the toenails in their cheap silver sandal shoes. It was a cheap, tawdry, flamboyant figure – most incongruous in the solid old-fashioned comfort of Colonel Bantry's library.

Mrs Bantry said in a low voice:

'You see what I mean? It just isn't *true!*'

The old lady by her side nodded her head. She looked down long and thoughtfully at the huddled figure.

She said at last in a gentle voice:

'She's very young.'

'Yes – yes – I suppose she is.' Mrs Bantry seemed almost surprised – like one making a discovery.

Miss Marple bent down. She did not touch the girl. She looked at the fingers that clutched frantically at the front of the girl's dress, as though she had clawed it in her last frantic struggle for breath.

There was the sound of a car scrunching on the gravel outside. Constable Palk said with urgency:

'That'll be the Inspector. . . .'

True to his ingrained belief that the gentry didn't let you down, Mrs Bantry immediately moved to the door. Miss Marple followed her. Mrs Bantry said:

'That'll be all right, Palk.'

Constable Palk was immensely relieved.

VI

Hastily downing the last fragments of toast and marmalade with a drink of coffee, Colonel Bantry hurried out into the hall and was relieved to see Colonel Melchett, the Chief Constable of the county, descending from a car with Inspector Slack in attendance. Melchett was a friend of the Colonel's. Slack he had never much taken to – an energetic man who belied his name and who accompanied his bustling manner with a good deal of disregard for the feelings of anyone he did not consider important.

'Morning, Bantry,' said the Chief Constable. 'Thought I'd better come along myself. This seems an extraordinary business.'

'It's – it's –' Colonel Bantry struggled to express himself. 'It's *incredible – fantastic!*'

'No idea who the woman is?'

'Not in the slightest. Never set eyes on her in my life.'

'Butler know anything?' asked Inspector Slack.

'Lorrimer is just as taken aback as I am.'

'Ah,' said Inspector Slack. 'I wonder.'

Colonel Bantry said:

'There's breakfast in the dining-room, Melchett, if you'd like anything?'

'No, no – better get on with the job. Haydock ought to be here any minute now – ah, here he is.'

Another car drew up and big, broad-shouldered Doctor Haydock, who was also the police surgeon, got out. A second police car had disgorged two plain-clothes men, one with a camera.

'All set – eh?' said the Chief Constable. 'Right. We'll go along. In the library, Slack tells me.'

Colonel Bantry groaned.

'It's incredible! You know, when my wife insisted this morning that the housemaid had come in and said there was a body in the library, I just wouldn't believe her.'

'No, no, I can quite understand that. Hope your missus isn't too badly upset by it all?'

'She's been wonderful – really wonderful. She's got old Miss Marple up here with her – from the village, you know.'

'Miss Marple?' The Chief Constable stiffened. 'Why did she send for her?'

'Oh, a woman wants another woman – don't you think so?'

Colonel Melchett said with a slight chuckle:

'If you ask me, your wife's going to try her hand at a little amateur detecting. Miss Marple's quite the local sleuth. Put it over us properly once, didn't she, Slack?'

Inspector Slack said: 'That was different.'

'Different from what?'

'That was a local case, that was, sir. The old lady knows everything that goes on in the village, that's true enough. But she'll be out of her depth here.'

Melchett said dryly: 'You don't know very much about it yourself yet, Slack.'

'Ah, you wait, sir. It won't take me long to get down to it.'

VII

In the dining-room Mrs Bantry and Miss Marple, in their turn, were partaking of breakfast.

After waiting on her guest, Mrs Bantry said urgently:

'Well, Jane?'

Miss Marple looked up at her, slightly bewildered.

Mrs Bantry said hopefully:

'Doesn't it *remind* you of anything?'

For Miss Marple had attained fame by her ability to link up trivial village happenings with graver problems in such a way as to throw light upon the latter.

'No,' said Miss Marple thoughtfully, 'I can't say that it does – not at the moment. I was reminded a little of Mrs Chetty's youngest – Edie, you know – but I think that was just because this poor girl bit her nails and her front teeth stuck out a little. Nothing more than that. And, of course,' went on Miss Marple, pursuing the parallel further, 'Edie was fond of what I call cheap finery, too.'

'You mean her dress?' said Mrs Bantry.

'Yes, a very tawdry satin – poor quality.'

Mrs Bantry said:

'I know. One of those nasty little shops where everything is a guinea.' She went on hopefully:

'Let me see, what happened to Mrs Chetty's Edie?'

'She's just gone into her second place – and doing very well, I believe.'

Mrs Bantry felt slightly disappointed. The village parallel didn't seem to be exactly hopeful.

'What I can't make out,' said Mrs Bantry, 'is what she could possibly be doing in Arthur's study. The window was forced, Palk tells me. She might have come down here with a burglar and then they quarrelled – but that seems such nonsense, doesn't it?'

'She was hardly dressed for burglary,' said Miss Marple thoughtfully.

'No, she was dressed for dancing – or a party of some kind. But there's nothing of that kind down here – or anywhere near.'

'N-n-o,' said Miss Marple doubtfully.

Mrs Bantry pounced.

'Something's in your mind, Jane.'

'Well, I was just wondering –'

'Yes?'

'Basil Blake.'

Mrs Bantry cried impulsively: 'Oh, no!' and added as though in explanation, 'I know his mother.'

The two women looked at each other.

Miss Marple sighed and shook her head.

'I quite understand how you feel about it.'

'Selina Blake is the nicest woman imaginable. Her herbaceous borders are simply marvellous – they make me green with envy. And she's frightfully generous with cuttings.'

Miss Marple, passing over these claims to consideration on the part of Mrs Blake, said:

'All the same, you know, there has been a lot of *talk*.'

'Oh, I know – I know. And of course Arthur goes simply livid when he hears Basil Blake mentioned. He was really *very* rude to Arthur, and since then Arthur won't hear a good word for him. He's got that silly slighting way of talking that these boys have nowadays – sneering at people sticking up for their school or the Empire or that sort of thing. And then, of course, the *clothes* he wears!

'People say,' continued Mrs Bantry, 'that it doesn't matter what you wear in the country. I never heard such nonsense. It's just in the country that everyone notices.' She paused, and added wistfully: 'He was an adorable baby in his bath.'

'There was a lovely picture of the Cheviot murderer as a baby in the paper last Sunday,' said Miss Marple.

'Oh, but Jane, you don't think *he* –'

'No, no, dear. I didn't mean that at all. That would indeed be jumping to conclusions. I was just trying to account for the young woman's presence down here. St Mary Mead is such an unlikely place. And then it seemed to me that the only possible explanation was Basil Blake. He *does* have parties. People came down from London and from the studios – you remember last July? Shouting and singing – the most *terrible* noise – everyone very drunk, I'm afraid – and the mess and the broken glass next morning simply unbelievable – so old Mrs Berry told me – and a young woman asleep in the bath with practically *nothing on!*'

Mrs Bantry said indulgently:

'I suppose they were film people.'

'Very likely. And then – what I expect you've heard – several weekends lately he's brought down a young woman with him – a platinum blonde.'

Mrs Bantry exclaimed:

'You don't think it's *this* one?'

'Well – I wondered. Of course, I've never seen her close to – only just getting in and out of the car – and once in the cottage garden when she was sunbathing with just some shorts and a brassière. I never really saw her *face*. And all these girls with their make-up and their hair and their nails look so alike.'

'Yes. Still, it *might* be. It's an idea, Jane.'

CHAPTER 2

I

It was an idea that was being at that moment discussed by Colonel Melchett and Colonel Bantry.

The Chief Constable, after viewing the body and seeing his subordinates set to work on their routine tasks, had adjourned with the master of the house to the study in the other wing of the house.

Colonel Melchett was an irascible-looking man with a habit of tugging at his short red moustache. He did so now, shooting a perplexed sideways glance at the other man. Finally, he rapped out:

'Look here, Bantry, got to get this off my chest. Is it a fact that you don't know from Adam who this girl is?'

The other's answer was explosive, but the Chief Constable interrupted him.

'Yes, yes, old man, but look at it like this. Might be deuced awkward for you. Married man – fond of your missus and all that. But just between ourselves – if you *were* tied up with this girl in any way, better say so *now*. Quite natural to want to suppress the fact – should feel the same myself. But it won't do. Murder case. Facts bound to come out. Dash it all, I'm not suggesting *you* strangled the girl – not the sort of thing you'd do – *I* know that. But, after all, she came here – to this house. Put it she broke in and was waiting to see you, and some bloke or other followed her down and did her in. Possible, you know. See what I mean?'

'Damn it all, Melchett, I tell you I've never set eyes on that girl in my life! I'm not that sort of man.'

'That's all right, then. Shouldn't blame you, you know. Man of the world. Still, if you say so – Question is, what was she doing down here? She doesn't come from these parts – that's quite certain.'

'The whole thing's a nightmare,' fumed the angry master of the house.

'The point is, old man, what was she doing in your library?'

'How should I know? *I* didn't ask her here.'

'No, no. But she *came* here, all the same. Looks as though she wanted to see you. You haven't had any odd letters or anything?'

'No, I haven't.'

Colonel Melchett enquired delicately:

'What were you doing yourself last night?'

'I went to the meeting of the Conservative Association. Nine o'clock, at Much Benham.'

'And you got home when?'

'I left Much Benham just after ten – had a bit of trouble on the way home, had to change a wheel. I got back at a quarter to twelve.'

'You didn't go into the library?'

'No.'

'Pity.'

'I was tired. I went straight up to bed.'

'Anyone waiting up for you?'

'No. I always take the latchkey. Lorrimer goes to bed at eleven unless I give orders to the contrary.'

'Who shuts up the library?'

'Lorrimer. Usually about seven-thirty this time of year.'

'Would he go in there again during the evening?'

'Not with my being out. He left the tray with whisky and glasses in the hall.'

'I see. What about your wife?'

'I don't know. She was in bed when I got home and fast asleep. She may have sat in the library yesterday evening or in the drawing-room. I forgot to ask her.'

'Oh well, we shall soon know all the details. Of course, it's possible one of the servants may be concerned, eh?'

Colonel Bantry shook his head.

'I don't believe it. They're all a most respectable lot. We've had 'em for years.'

Melchett agreed.

'Yes, it doesn't seem likely that they're mixed up in it. Looks more as though the girl came down from town – perhaps with some young fellow. Though why they wanted to break into this house –'

Bantry interrupted.

'London. That's more like it. We don't have goings on down here – at least –'

'Well, what is it?'

'Upon my word!' exploded Colonel Bantry. 'Basil Blake!'

'Who's he?'

'Young fellow connected with the film industry. Poisonous young brute. My wife sticks up for him because she was at school with his mother, but of all the decadent useless young jackanapes! Wants his behind kicked! He's taken that cottage on the Lansham Road – you know – ghastly modern bit of building. He has parties there, shrieking, noisy crowds, and he has girls down for the weekend.'

'Girls?'

'Yes, there was one last week – one of these platinum blondes –'

The Colonel's jaw dropped.

'A platinum blonde, eh?' said Melchett reflectively.

'Yes. I say, Melchett, you don't think –'

The Chief Constable said briskly:

'It's a possibility. It accounts for a girl of this type being in St Mary Mead. I think I'll run along and have a word with this young fellow – Braid – Blake – what did you say his name was?'

'Blake. Basil Blake.'

'Will he be at home, do you know?'

'Let me see. What's today – Saturday? Usually gets here some time Saturday morning.'

Melchett said grimly:
'We'll see if we can find him.'

II

Basil Blake's cottage, which consisted of all modern conveniences enclosed in a hideous shell of half timbering and sham Tudor, was known to the postal authorities, and to William Booker, builder, as 'Chatsworth', to Basil and his friends as 'The Period Piece', and to the village of St Mary Mead at large as 'Mr Booker's new house.'

It was little more than a quarter of a mile from the village proper, being situated on a new building estate that had been bought by the enterprising Mr Booker just beyond the Blue Boar, with frontage on what had been a particularly unspoilt country lane. Gossington Hall was about a mile farther on along the same road.

Lively interest had been aroused in St Mary Mead when news went round that 'Mr Booker's new house' had been bought by a film star. Eager watch was kept for the first appearance of the legendary creature in the village, and it may be said that as far as appearances went Basil Blake was all that could be asked for. Little by little, however, the real facts leaked out. Basil Blake was *not* a film star – not even a film actor. He was a very junior person, rejoicing in the title of about fifteenth in the list of those responsible for Set Decorations at Lenville Studios, headquarters of British New Era Films. The village maidens lost interest, and the ruling class of censorious spinsters took exception to Basil Blake's way of life. Only the landlord of the Blue Boar continued to be enthusiastic about Basil and Basil's friends. The revenues of the Blue Boar had increased since the young man's arrival in the place.

The police car stopped outside the distorted rustic gate of Mr Booker's fancy, and Colonel Melchett, with a glance of distaste at the excessive half timbering of Chatsworth, strode up to the front door and attacked it briskly with the knocker.

It was opened much more promptly than he had expected. A young man with straight, somewhat long, black hair, wearing orange corduroy trousers and a royal-blue shirt, snapped out: 'Well, what do you want?'

'Are you Mr Basil Blake?'

'Of course I am.'

'I should be glad to have a few words with you, if I may, Mr Blake?'

'Who are you?'

'I am Colonel Melchett, the Chief Constable of the County.

Mr Blake said insolently:

'You don't say so; how amusing!'

And Colonel Melchett, following the other in, understood what Colonel Bantry's reactions had been. The toe of his own boot itched.

Containing himself, however, he said with an attempt to speak pleasantly:

'You're an early riser, Mr Blake.'

'Not at all. I haven't been to bed yet.'

'Indeed.'

'But I don't suppose you've come here to enquire into my hours of bedgoing – or if you have it's rather a waste of the county's time and money. What is it you want to speak to me about?'

Colonel Melchett cleared his throat.

'I understand, Mr Blake, that last weekend you had a visitor – a – er – fair-haired young lady.'

Basil Blake stared, threw back his head and roared with laughter.

'Have the old cats been on to you from the village? About my morals? Damn it all, morals aren't a police matter. *You* know that.'

'As you say,' said Melchett dryly, 'your morals are no concern of mine. I have come to you because the body of a fair-haired young woman of slightly – er – exotic appearance has been found – murdered.'

'Strewth!' Blake stared at him. 'Where?'

'In the library at Gossington Hall.'

'At Gossington? At old Bantry's? I say, that's pretty rich. Old Bantry! The dirty old man!'

Colonel Melchett went very red in the face. He said sharply through the renewed mirth of the young man opposite him: 'Kindly control your tongue, sir. I came to ask you if you can throw any light on this business.'

'You've come round to ask me if I've missed a blonde? Is that it? Why should – hallo, 'allo, 'allo, what's this?'

A car had drawn up outside with a scream of brakes. Out of it tumbled a young woman dressed in flapping black-and-white pyjamas. She had scarlet lips, blackened eyelashes, and a platinum-blonde head. She strode up to the door, flung it open, and exclaimed angrily:

'Why did you run out on me, you brute?'

Basil Blake had risen.

'So there you are! Why shouldn't I leave you? I told you to clear out and you wouldn't.'

'Why the hell should I because you told me to? I was enjoying myself.'

'Yes – with that filthy brute Rosenberg. You know what *he's* like.'

'You were jealous, that's all.'

'Don't flatter yourself. I hate to see a girl I like who can't hold her drink and lets a disgusting Central European paw her about.'

'That's a damned lie. You were drinking pretty hard yourself – and going on with the black-haired Spanish bitch.'

'If I take you to a party I expect you to be able to behave yourself.'

'And I refuse to be dictated to, and that's that. You said we'd go to the party and come on down here afterwards. I'm not going to leave a party before I'm ready to leave it.'

'No – and that's why I left you flat. I was ready to come down here and I came. I don't hang round waiting for any fool of a woman.'

'Sweet, polite person you are!'

'You seem to have followed me down all right!'

'I wanted to tell you what I thought of you!'

'If you think you can boss me, my girl, you're wrong!'

'And if you think you can order me about, you can think again!'

They glared at each other.

It was at this moment that Colonel Melchett seized his opportunity, and cleared his throat loudly.

Basil Blake swung round on him.

'Hallo, I forgot you were here. About time you took yourself off, isn't it? Let me introduce you – Dinah Lee – Colonel Blimp of the County Police. And now, Colonel, that you've seen my blonde is alive and in good condition, perhaps you'll get on with the good work concerning old Bantry's little bit of fluff. Good morning!'

Colonel Melchett said:

'I advise you to keep a civil tongue in your head, young man, or you'll let yourself in for trouble,' and stumped out, his face red and wrathful.

CHAPTER 3

I

In his office at Much Benham, Colonel Melchett received and scrutinized the reports of his subordinates.

'. . . so it all seems clear enough, sir,' Inspector Slack was concluding: 'Mrs Bantry sat in the library after dinner and went to bed just before ten. She turned out the lights when she left the room and, presumably, no one entered the room afterwards. The servants went to bed at half-past ten and Lorrimer, after putting the drinks in the hall, went to bed at a quarter to eleven. Nobody heard anything out of the usual except the third housemaid, and she heard too much! Groans and a blood-curdling yell and sinister footsteps and I don't know what. The second housemaid who shares a room with her says the other girl slept all night through without a sound. It's those ones that make up things that cause us all the trouble.'

'What about the forced window?'

'Amateur job, Simmons says; done with a common chisel – ordinary pattern – wouldn't have made much noise. Ought to be a chisel about the house but nobody can find it. Still, that's common enough where tools are concerned.'

'Think any of the servants know anything?'

Rather unwillingly Inspector Slack replied:

'No, sir, I don't think they do. They all seemed very shocked and upset. I had my suspicions of Lorrimer – reticent, he was, if you know what I mean – but I don't think there's anything in it.'

Melchett nodded. He attached no importance to Lorrimer's reticence. The energetic Inspector Slack often produced that effect on people he interrogated.

The door opened and Dr Haydock came in.

'Thought I'd look in and give you the rough gist of things.'

'Yes, yes, glad to see you. Well?'

'Nothing much. Just what you'd think. Death was due to strangulation. Satin waistband of her own dress, which was passed round the neck and crossed at the back. Quite easy and

26

simple to do. Wouldn't have needed great strength – that is, if the girl were taken by surprise. There are no signs of a struggle.'

'What about time of death?'

'Say, between ten o'clock and midnight.'

'You can't get nearer than that?'

Haydock shook his head with a light grin.

'I won't risk my professional reputation. Not earlier than ten and not later than midnight.'

'And your own fancy inclines to which time?'

'Depends. There was a fire in the grate – the room was warm – all that would delay rigor and cadaveric stiffening.'

'Anything more you can say about her?'

'Nothing much. She was young – about seventeen or eighteen, I should say. Rather immature in some ways but well developed muscularly. Quite a healthy specimen. She was virgo intacta, by the way.'

And with a nod of his head the doctor left the room.

Melchett said to the Inspector:

'You're quite sure she'd never been seen before at Gossington?'

'The servants are positive of that. Quite indignant about it. They'd have remembered if they'd ever seen her about in the neighbourhood, they say.'

'I expect they would,' said Melchett. 'Any one of that type sticks out a mile round here. Look at that young woman of Blake's.'

'Pity it wasn't her,' said Slack; 'then we should be able to get on a bit.'

'It seems to me this girl must have come down from London,' said the Chief Constable thoughtfully. 'Don't believe there will be any local leads. In that case I suppose, we should do well to call in the Yard. It's a case for them, not for us.'

'Something must have brought her down here, though,' said Slack. He added tentatively 'Seems to me, Colonel and Mrs Bantry *must* know something – of course, I know they're friends of yours, sir –'

Colonel Melchett treated him to a cold stare. He said stiffly:

'You may rest assured that I'm taking every possibility into account. *Every* possibility.' He went on: 'You've looked through the list of persons reported missing, I suppose?'

Slack nodded. He produced a typed sheet.

'Got 'em here. Mrs Saunders, reported missing a week ago, dark-haired, blue eyed, thirty-six. 'Tisn't her – and, anyway, everyone knows except her husband that she's gone off with a fellow from Leeds – commercial. Mrs Barnard – she's sixty-five. Pamela Reeves, sixteen, missing from her home last night, had attended Girl Guide rally, dark brown hair in pigtail, five feet five –'

Melchett said irritably:

'Don't go on reading idiotic details, Slack. This wasn't a school-girl. In my opinion –'

He broke off as the telephone rang. 'Hallo – yes – yes, Much Benham Police Headquarters – what? Just a minute –'

He listened, and wrote rapidly. Then he spoke again, a new tone in his voice:

'Ruby Keene, eighteen, occupation professional dancer, five feet four inches, slender, platinum-blonde hair, blue eyes, *retroussé* nose, believed to be wearing white diamanté evening-dress, silver sandal shoes. Is that right? What? Yes, not a doubt of it, I should say. I'll send Slack over at once.'

He rang off and looked at his subordinate with rising excitement. 'We've got it, I think. That was the Glenshire Police (Glenshire was the adjoining county). Girl reported missing from the Majestic Hotel, Danemouth.'

'Danemouth,' said Inspector Slack. 'That's more like it.'

Danemouth was a large and fashionable watering-place on the coast not far away.

'It's only a matter of eighteen miles or so from here,' said the Chief Constable. 'The girl was a dance hostess or something at the Majestic. Didn't come on to do her turn last night and the management were very fed up about it. When she was still missing this morning one of the other girls got the wind up about her, or someone else did. It sounds a bit obscure. You'd better go over to Danemouth at once, Slack. Report there to Superintendent Harper, and co-operate with him.'

II

Activity was always to Inspector Slack's taste. To rush off in a car, to silence rudely those people who were anxious to tell him things, to cut short conversations on the plea of urgent necessity. All this was the breath of life to Slack.

In an incredibly short time, therefore, he had arrived at Dane-mouth, reported at police headquarters, had a brief interview with a distracted and apprehensive hotel manager, and, leaving the latter with the doubtful comfort of – 'got to make sure it *is* the girl, first, before we start raising the wind' – was driving back to Much Benham in company with Ruby Keene's nearest relative.

He had put through a short call to Much Benham before leaving Danemouth, so the Chief Constable was prepared for his arrival, though not perhaps for the brief introduction of: 'This is Josie, sir.'

Colonel Melchett stared at his subordinate coldly. His feeling was that Slack had taken leave of his senses.

The young woman who had just got out of the car came to the rescue.

'That's what I'm known as professionally,' she explained with a momentary flash of large, handsome white teeth. 'Raymond and Josie, my partner and I call ourselves, and, of course, all the hotel know me as Josie. Josephine Turner's my real name.'

Colonel Melchett adjusted himself to the situation and invited Miss Turner to sit down, meanwhile casting a swift, professional glance over her.

She was a good-looking young woman of perhaps nearer thirty than twenty, her looks depending more on skilful grooming than actual features. She looked competent and good-tempered, with plenty of common sense. She was not the type that would ever be described as glamorous, but she had nevertheless plenty of attraction. She was discreetly made-up and wore a dark tailor-made suit. Though she looked anxious and upet she was not, the Colonel decided, particularly grief-stricken.

As she sat down she said: 'It seems too awful to be true. Do you really think it's Ruby?'

'That, I'm afraid, is what we've got to ask you to tell us. I'm afraid it may be rather unpleasant for you.'

Miss Turner said apprehensively:

'Does she – does she – look very terrible?'

'Well – I'm afraid it may be rather a shock to you.' He handed her his cigarette-case and she accepted one gratefully.

'Do – do you want me to look at her right away?'

'It would be best, I think, Miss Turner. You see, it's not much good asking you questions until we're sure. Best get it over, don't you think?'

'All right.'

They drove down to the mortuary.

When Josie came out after a brief visit, she looked rather sick.

'It's Ruby all right,' she said shakily. 'Poor kid! Goodness, I do feel queer. There isn't' – she looked round wistfully – 'any gin?'

Gin was not available, but brandy was, and after gulping a little down Miss Turner regained her composure. She said frankly:

'It gives you a turn, doesn't it, seeing anything like that? Poor little Rube! What swine men are, aren't they?'

'You believe it was a man?'

Josie looked slightly taken aback.

'Wasn't it? Well, I mean – I naturally thought –'

'Any special man you were thinking of?'

She shook her head vigorously.

'No – not me. I haven't the least idea. Naturally Ruby wouldn't have let on to me if –'

'If what?'

Josie hesitated.

'Well – if she'd been – going about with any one.'

Melchett shot her a keen glance. He said no more until they were back at his office. Then he began:

'Now, Miss Turner, I want all the information you can give me.'

'Yes, of course. Where shall I begin?'

'I'd like the girl's full name and address, her relationship to you and all you know about her.'

Josephine Turner nodded. Melchett was confirmed in his opinion that she felt no particular grief. She was shocked and distressed but no more. She spoke readily enough.

'Her name was Ruby Keene – her professional name, that is. Her real name was Rosy Legge. Her mother was my mother's cousin. I've known her all my life, but not particularly well, if you know what I mean. I've got a lot of cousins – some in business, some on the stage. Ruby was more or less training for a dancer. She had some good engagements last year in panto and that sort of thing. Not really classy, but good provincial companies. Since then she's been engaged as one of the dancing partners at the Palais de Danse in Brixwell – South London. It's a nice respectable place and they look after the girls well, but there isn't much money in it.' She paused.

Colonel Melchett nodded.

'Now this is where I come in. I've been dance and bridge hostess at the Majestic in Danemouth for three years. It's a good job, well paid and pleasant to do. You look after people when they arrive – size them up, of course – some like to be left alone and others are lonely and want to get into the swing of things. You try to get the right people together for bridge and all that, and get the young people dancing with each other. It needs a bit of tact and experience.'

Again Melchett nodded. He thought that this girl would be good at her job; she had a pleasant, friendly way with her and was, he thought, shrewd without being in the least intellectual.

'Besides that,' continued Josie, 'I do a couple of exhibition dances every evening with Raymond. Raymond Starr – he's the tennis and dancing pro. Well, as it happens, this summer I slipped on the rocks bathing one day and gave my ankle a nasty turn.'

Melchett had noticed that she walked with a slight slimp.

'Naturally that put the stop to dancing for a bit and it was rather awkward. I didn't want the hotel to get someone else in my place. That's always a danger' – for a minute her good-natured blue eyes were hard and sharp; she was the female fighting for existence – 'that they may queer your pitch, you see. So I thought of Ruby and suggested to the manager that I should get her down. I'd carry on with the hostess business and the bridge and all that. Ruby would just take on the dancing. Keep it in the family, if you see what I mean?'

Melchett said he saw.

'Well, they agreed, and I wired to Ruby and she came down. Rather a chance for her. Much better class than anything she'd ever done before. That was about a month ago.'

Colonel Melchett said:

'I understand. And she was a success?'

'Oh, yes,' Josie said carelessly, 'she went down quite well. She doesn't dance as well as I do, but Raymond's clever and carried her through, and she was quite nice-looking, you know – slim and fair and baby-looking. Overdid the make-up a bit – I was always on at her about that. But you know what girls are. She was only eighteen, and at that age they always go and overdo it. It doesn't do for a good-class place like the Majestic. I was always ticking her off about it and getting her to tone it down.'

Melchett asked: 'People liked her?'

'Oh, yes. Mind you, Ruby hadn't got much comeback. She was a bit dumb. She went down better with the older men than with the young ones.'

'Had she got any special friend?'

The girl's eyes met his with complete understanding.

'Not in the way *you* mean. Or, at any rate, not that *I* knew about. But then, you see, she wouldn't tell me.'

Just for a moment Melchett wondered why not – Josie did not give the impression of being a strict disciplinarian. But he only said: 'Will you describe to me now when you last saw your cousin.'

'Last night. She and Raymond do two exhibition dances – one at 10.30 and the other at midnight. They finished the first one. After it, I noticed Ruby dancing with one of the young men staying in the hotel. I was playing bridge with some people in the lounge. There's a glass panel between the lounge and the ball-room. That's the last time I saw her. Just after midnight Raymond came up in a terrible taking, said where was Ruby, she hadn't turned up, and it was time to begin? I *was* vexed, I can tell you! That's the sort of silly things girls do and get the management's backs up and then they get the sack! I went up with him to her room, but she wasn't there. I noticed that she'd changed. The dress she'd been dancing in – a sort of pink, foamy thing with full skirts – was lying over a chair. Usually she kept the same dress on unless it was the special dance night – Wednesdays, that is.

'I'd no idea where she'd got to. We got the band to play one more foxtrot – still no Ruby, so I said to Raymond I'd do the exhibition dance with him. We chose one that was easy on my ankle and made it short – but it played up my ankle pretty badly all the same. It's all swollen this morning. Still Ruby didn't show up. We sat about waiting up for her until two o'clock. Furious with her, I was.'

Her voice vibrated slightly. Melchett caught the note of real anger in it. Just for a moment he wondered. The reaction seemed a little more intense than was justified by the facts. He had a feeling of something deliberately left unsaid. He said:

'And this morning, when Ruby Keene had not returned and her bed had not been slept in, you went to the police?'

He knew from Slack's brief telephone message from Danemouth that that was not the case. But he wanted to hear what Josephine Turner would say.

She did not hesitate. She said: 'No, I didn't.'

'Why not, Miss Turner?'

Her eyes met his frankly. She said:

'*You* wouldn't – in my place!'

'You think not?'

Josie said:

'I've got my job to think about. The one thing a hotel doesn't want is scandal – especially anything that brings in the police. I didn't think anything had happened to Ruby. Not for a minute! I thought she'd just made a fool of herself about some young man. I thought she'd turn up all right – and I was going to give her a good dressing down when she did! Girls of eighteen are such fools.'

Melchett pretended to glance through his notes.

'Ah, yes, I see it was a Mr Jefferson who went to the police. One of the guests staying at the hotel?'

Josephine Turner said shortly:

'Yes.'

Colonel Melchett asked:

'What made this Mr Jefferson do that?'

Josie was stroking the cuff of her jacket. There was a constraint in her manner. Again Colonel Melchett had a feeling that something was being withheld. She said rather sullenly:

'He's an invalid. He – he gets all het up rather easily. Being an invalid, I mean.'

Melchett passed on from that. He asked:

'Who was the young man with whom you last saw your cousin dancing?'

'His name's Bartlett. He'd been there about ten days.'

'Were they on very friendly terms?'

'Not specially, I should say. Not that *I* knew, anyway.'

Again a curious note of anger in her voice.

'What does he have to say?'

'Said that after their dance Ruby went upstairs to powder her nose.'

'That was when she changed her dress?'

'I suppose so.'

'And that is the last thing you know? After that she just –'

'Vanished,' said Josie. 'That's right.'

'Did Miss Keene know anybody in St Mary Mead? Or in this neighbourhood?'

'I don't know. She may have done. You see, quite a lot of young men come in to Danemouth to the Majestic from all round about. I wouldn't know where they lived unless they happened to mention it.'

'Did you ever hear your cousin mention Gossington?'

'Gossington?' Josie looked patently puzzled.

'Gossington Hall.'

She shook her head.

'Never heard of it.' He tone carried conviction. There was curiosity in it too.

'Gossington Hall,' explained Colonel Melchett, 'is where her body was found.'

'Gossington Hall?' She stared. 'How extraordinary!'

Melchett thought to himself: 'Extraordinary's the word!' Aloud he said:

'Do you know a Colonel or Mrs Bantry?'

Again Josie shook her head.

'Or a Mr Basil Blake?'

She frowned slightly.

'I think I've heard that name. Yes, I'm sure I have – but I don't remember anything about him.'

The diligent Inspector Slack slid across to his superior officer a page torn from his note-book. On it was pencilled:

'Col. Bantry dined at Majestic last week.'

Melchett looked up and met the Inspector's eye. The Chief Constable flushed. Slack was an industrious and zealous officer and Melchett disliked him a good deal. But he could not disregard the challenge. The Inspector was tacitly accusing him of favouring his own class – of shielding an 'old school tie.'

He turned to Josie.

'Miss Turner, I should like you, if you do not mind, to accompany me to Gossington Hall.'

Coldly, defiantly, almost ignoring Josie's murmur of assent, Melchett's eyes met Slack's.

CHAPTER 4

I

St Mary Mead was having the most exciting morning it had known for a long time.

Miss Wetherby, a long-nosed, acidulated spinster, was the first to spread the intoxicating information. She dropped in upon her friend and neighbour Miss Hartnell.

'Forgive me coming so early, dear, but I thought, perhaps, you mightn't have heard the *news*.'

'What news?' demanded Miss Hartnell. She had a deep bass voice and visited the poor indefatigably, however hard they tried to avoid her ministrations.

'About the body in Colonel Bantry's library – a *woman's* body –'

'In Colonel Bantry's *library?*'

'Yes. Isn't it *terrible?*'

'His *poor* wife.' Miss Hartnell tried to disguise her deep and ardent pleasure.

'Yes, indeed. I don't suppose she had any idea.'

Miss Hartnell observed censoriously:

'She thought too much about her garden, and not enough about her husband. You've got to keep an eye on a man – all the time – all the time,' repeated Miss Hartnell fiercely.

'I know. I know. It's really too dreadful.'

'I wonder what Jane Marple will say. Do you think she knew anything about it? She's so sharp about these things.'

'Jane Marple has gone up to Gossington.'

'What? This morning?'

'Very early. Before breakfast.'

'But really! I do think! Well, I mean, I think that is carrying things *too* far. We all know Jane likes to poke her nose into things – but I call this – indecent!'

'Oh, but Mrs Bantry sent for her.'

'Mrs Bantry *sent* for her?'

'Well, the car came – with Muswell driving it.'

'Dear me! How very peculiar. . . .'

They were silent a minute or two digesting the news.

'Whose body?' demanded Miss Hartnell.

'You know that dreadful woman who comes down with Basil Blake?'

'That terrible peroxide blonde?' Miss Hartnell was slightly behind the times. She had not yet advanced from peroxide to platinum. 'The one who lies about in the garden with practically nothing on?'

'Yes, my dear. There she was – on the hearthrug – *strangled!*'

'But what do you men – at *Gossington?*'

Miss Wetherby nodded with infinite meaning.

'Then – Colonel Bantry *too* –?'

Again Miss Wetherby nodded.

'Oh!'

There was a pause as the ladies savoured this new addition to village scandal.

'What a wicked woman!' trumpeted Miss Hartnell with righteous wrath.

'Quite, quite abandoned, I'm afraid!'

'And Colonel Bantry – such a nice quiet man –'

Miss Wetherby said zestfully:

'Those quiet ones are often the worst. Jane Marple always says so.'

II

Mrs Price Ridley was among the last to hear the news.

A rich and dictatorial widow, she lived in a large house next door to the vicarage. Her informant was her little maid Clara.

'*A woman*, you say, Clara? *Found dead on Colonel Bantry's hearthrug.*'

'Yes, mum. And they say, mum, as she hadn't anything on at all, mum, not a stitch!'

'That will do, Clara. It is not necessary to go into details.'

'No, mum, and they say, mum, that at first they thought it was Mr Blake's young lady – what comes down for the weekends with 'im to Mr Booker's new 'ouse. But now they say it's quite a different young lady. And the fishmonger's young man, he says he'd never have believed it of Colonel Bantry – not with him handing round the plate on Sundays and all.'

'There is a lot of wickedness in the world, Clara,' said Mrs Price Ridley. 'Let this be a warning to you.'

'Yes, mum. Mother, she never *will* let me take a place where there's a gentleman in the 'ouse.'

'That will *do*, Clara,' said Mrs Price Ridley.

III

It was only a step from Mrs Price Ridley's house to the vicarage.

Mrs Price Ridley was fortunate enough to find the vicar in his study.

The vicar, a gentle, middle-aged man, was always the last to hear anything.

'Such a *terrible* thing,' said Mrs Price Ridley, panting a little, because she had come rather fast. 'I felt I must have your advice, your counsel about it, dear vicar.'

Mr Clement looked mildly alarmed. He said:

'Has anything happened,

'Has anything *happened*?' Mrs Price Ridley repeated the question dramatically. 'The most terrible scandal! None of us had any idea of it. An abandoned woman, completely unclothed, strangled on Colonel Bantry's hearthrug.'

The vicar stared. He said:

'You – are you feeling quite well?'

'No wonder you can't believe it! *I* couldn't at first. The hypocrisy of the man! All these years!'

'Please tell me exactly what all this is about.'

Mrs Price Ridley plunged into a full-swing narrative. When she had finished Mr Clement said mildly:

'But there is nothing, is there, to point to Colonel Bantry's being involved in this?'

'Oh, dear vicar, you are so unworldly! But I must tell you a little story. Last Thursday – or was it the Thursday before? well, it doesn't matter – I was going up to London by the cheap day train. Colonel Bantry was in the same carriage. He looked, I thought, very abstracted. And nearly the whole way he buried himself behind *The Times*. As though, you know, he didn't want to *talk*.'

The vicar nodded with complete comprehension and possible sympathy.

'At Paddington I said goodbye. He had offered to get me a taxi, but I was taking the bus down to Oxford Street – but he got into one, and I distinctly heard him tell the driver to go to – *where do you think?*'

Mr Clement looked enquiring.

'An address in *St John's Wood!*'

Mrs Price Ridley paused triumphantly.

The vicar remained completely unenlightened.

'That, I consider, *proves* it,' said Mrs Price Ridley.

IV

At Gossington, Mrs Bantry and Miss Marple were sitting in the drawing-room.

'You know,' said Mrs Bantry, 'I can't help feeling glad they've taken the body away. It's not *nice* to have a body in one's house.'

Miss Marple nodded.

'I know, dear. I know just how you feel.'

'You can't,' said Mrs Bantry; 'not until you've had one. I know you had one next door once, but that's not the same thing. I only hope,' she went on, 'that Arthur won't take a dislike to the library. We sit there so much. What are you doing, Jane?'

For Miss Marple, with a glance at her watch, was rising to her feet.

'Well, I was thinking I'd go home. If there's nothing more I can do for you?'

'Don't go yet,' said Mrs Bantry. 'The fingerprint men and the photographers and most of the police have gone, I know, but I still feel something might happen. You don't want to miss anything.'

The telephone rang and she went off to answer. She returned with a beaming face.

'I told you more things would happen. That was Colonel Melchett. He's bringing the poor girl's cousin along.'

'I wonder why,' said Miss Marple.

'Oh, I suppose, to see where it happened and all that.'

'More than that, I expect,' said Miss Marple.

'What do you mean, Jane?'

'Well, I think – perhaps – he might want her to meet Colonel Bantry.'

Mrs Bantry said sharply:

'To see if she recognizes him? I suppose – oh yes, I suppose they're bound to suspect Arthur.'

'I'm afraid so.'

'As though Arthur could have anything to do with it!'

Miss Marple was silent. Mrs Bantry turned on her accusingly.

'And don't quote old General Henderson – or some frightful old man who kept his housemaid – at me. Arthur isn't like that.'

'No, no, of course not.'

'No, but he *really* isn't. He's just – sometimes – a little bit silly about pretty girls who come to tennis. You know – rather fatuous and avuncular. There's no harm in it. And why shouldn't he? After all,' finished Mrs Bantry rather obscurely, 'I've got the garden.'

Miss Marple smiled.

'You must not worry, Dolly,' she said.

'No, I don't mean to. But all the same I do a little. So does Arthur. It's upset him. All these policemen prowling about. He's gone down to the farm. Looking at pigs and things always soothes him if he's been upset. Hallo, here they are.'

The Chief Constable's car drew up outside.

Colonel Melchett came in accompanied by a smartly dressed young woman.

'This is Miss Turner, Mrs Bantry. The cousin of the – er – victim.'

'How do you do,' said Mrs Bantry, advancing with outstretched hand. 'All this must be rather awful for you.'

Josephine Turner said frankly: 'Oh, it is. None of it seems *real*, somehow. It's like a bad dream.'

Mrs Bantry introduced Miss Marple.

Melchett said casually: 'Your good man about?'

'He had to go down to one of the farms. He'll be back soon.'

'Oh –' Melchett seemed rather at a loss.

Mrs Bantry said to Josie: 'Would you like to see where – where it happened? Or would you rather not?'

Josephine said after a moment's pause:

'I think I'd like to see.'

Mrs Bantry led her to the library with Miss Marple and Melchett following behind.

'She was there,' said Mrs Bantry, pointing dramatically, 'on the hearthrug.'

'Oh!' Josie shuddered. But she also looked perplexed. She said, her brow creased: 'I just *can't* understand it! I *can't*!'

'Well, *we* certainly can't,' said Mrs Bantry.

Josie said slowly:

'It isn't the sort of place –' and broke off.

Miss Marple nodded her head gently in agreement with the unfinished sentiment.

'That,' she murmured, 'is what makes it so very interesting.'

'Come now, Miss Marple,' said Colonel Melchett good-humouredly, 'haven't you got an explanation?'

'Oh yes, I've got an *explanation*,' said Miss Marple. 'Quite a feasible one. But of course it's only my own *idea*. Tommy Bond,' she continued, 'and Mrs Martin, our new schoolmistress. She went to wind up the clock and a frog jumped out.'

Josephine Turner looked puzzled. As they all went out of the room she murmured to Mrs Bantry: 'Is the old lady a bit funny in the head?'

'Not at all,' said Mrs Bantry indignantly.

Josie said: 'Sorry; I thought perhaps she thought she *was* a frog or something.'

Colonel Bantry was just coming in through the side door. Melchett hailed him, and watched Josephine Turner as he introduced them to each other. But there was no sign of interest or recognition in her face. Melchett breathed a sigh of relief. Curse Slack and his insinuations!

In answer to Mrs Bantry's questions Josie was pouring out the story of Ruby Keene's disappearance.

'Frightfully worrying for you, my dear,' said Mrs Bantry.

'I was more angry than worried,' said Josie. 'You see, I didn't know then that anything had happened to her.'

'And yet,' said Miss Marple, 'you went to the police. Wasn't that – excuse me – rather *premature*?'

Josie said eagerly:

'Oh, but I didn't. That was Mr Jefferson –'

Mrs Bantry said: 'Jefferson?'

'Yes, he's an invalid.'

'Not *Conway* Jefferson? But I know him well. He's an old friend of ours. Arthur, listen – Conway Jefferson. He's staying at the Majestic, and it was he who went to the police! Isn't that a coincidence?'

Josephine Turner said:

'Mr Jefferson was here last summer too.'

'Fancy! And we never knew. I haven't seen him for a long time.' She turned to Josie. 'How – how is he, nowadays?'

Josie considered.

'I think he's wonderful, really – quite wonderful. Considering, I mean. He's always cheerful – always got a joke.'

'Are the family there with him?'

'Mr Gaskell, you mean? And young Mrs Jefferson? And Peter? Oh, yes.'

There was something inhibiting Josephine Turner's usual attractive frankness of manner. When she spoke of the Jeffersons there was something not quite natural in her voice.

Mrs Bantry said: 'They're both very nice, aren't they? The young ones, I mean.'

Josie said rather uncertainly:

'Oh yes – yes, they are. I – we – yes, they are, *really*.'

V

'And what,' demanded Mrs Bantry as she looked through the window at the retreating car of the Chief Constable, 'did she mean by that? "They are, *really*." Don't you think, Jane, that there's something –'

Miss Marple fell upon the words eagerly.

'Oh, I do – indeed I do. It's quite *unmistakable*! Her manner changed *at once* when the Jeffersons were mentioned. She had seemed quite natural up to then.'

'But what do you think it *is*, Jane?'

'Well, my dear, *you* know them. All I feel is that there is *something*, as you say, about them which is worrying that young woman. Another thing, did you notice that when you asked her if she wasn't anxious about the girl being missing, she said that she was *angry*! And she *looked* angry – *really* angry! That strikes me as *interesting*, you know. I have a feeling – perhaps I'm wrong – that that's her main reaction to the fact of the girl's death. She didn't care for her, I'm sure. She's not grieving in any way. But I do think, very definitely, that the thought of that girl, Ruby Keene, makes her *angry*. And the interesting point is – *why?*'

'We'll find out!' said Mrs Bantry. 'We'll go over to Danemouth and stay at the Majestic – yes, Jane, you too. I need a change for my nerves after what has happened here. A few days at the Majestic – that's what we need. And you'll meet Conway Jefferson. He's a dear – a perfect dear. It's the saddest story imaginable. Had a son and a daughter, both of whom he loved dearly. They were both married, but they still spent a lot of time at home. His wife, too, was the sweetest woman, and he was devoted to her. They were flying home one year from France and there was an accident. They were all killed: the pilot, Mrs Jefferson, Rosamund and Frank. Conway had both legs so badly injured they had to be amputated. And he's been wonderful – his courage, his pluck! He was a very active man and now he's a helpless cripple, but he never complains. His daughter-in-law lives with him – she was a widow when Frank Jefferson married her and she had a son by her first marriage – Peter Carmody. They both live with Conway. And Mark Gaskell, Rosamund's husband, is there too most of the time. The whole thing was the most awful tragedy.'

'And now,' said Miss Marple, 'there's another tragedy –'

Mrs Bantry said: 'Oh yes – yes – but it's nothing to do with the Jeffersons.'

'Isn't it?' said Miss Marple. 'It was Mr Jefferson who went to the police.'

'So he did. . . . You know, Jane, that *is* curious. . . .'

CHAPTER 5

I

Colonel Melchett was facing a much annoyed hotel manager. With him was Superintendent Harper of the Glenshire Police and the inevitable Inspector Slack – the latter rather disgruntled at the Chief Constable's wilful usurpation of the case.

Superintendent Harper was inclined to be soothing with the almost tearful Mr Prestcott – Colonel Melchett tended towards a blunt brutality.

'No good crying over spilt milk,' he said sharply. 'The girl's dead – strangled. You're lucky that she wasn't strangled in your hotel. This puts the enquiry in a different county and lets your establishment down extremely lightly. But certain enquiries have got to be made, and the sooner we get on with it the better. You can trust us to be discreet and tactful. So I suggest you cut the cackle and come to the horses. Just what exactly do you know about the girl?'

'I knew nothing of her – nothing at all. Josie brought her here.'

'Josie's been here some time?'

'Two years – no, three.'

'And you like her?'

'Yes, Josie's a good girl – a nice girl. Competent. She gets on with people, and smoothes over differences – bridge, you know, is a touchy sort of game –' Colonel Melchett nodded feelingly. His wife was a keen but an extremely bad bridge player. Mr Prestcott went on: 'Josie was very good at calming down unpleasantnesses. She could handle people well – sort of bright and firm, if you know what I mean.'

Again Melchett nodded. He knew now what it was Miss Josephine Turner had reminded him of. In spite of the make-up and the smart turnout there was a distinct touch of the nursery governess about her.

'I depend upon her,' went on Mr Prestcott. His manner became aggrieved. 'What does she want to go playing about on slippery rocks in that damn fool way? We've got a nice beach here. Why couldn't she bathe from that? Slipping and falling and breaking her ankle. It wasn't fair on *me*! I pay her to dance and play bridge and keep people happy and amused – not to go bathing off rocks and breaking her ankle. Dancers ought to be careful of their ankles – not take risks. I was very annoyed about it. It wasn't fair to the hotel.'

Melchett cut the recital short.

'And then she suggested this girl – her cousin – coming down?'

Prestcott assented grudgingly.

'That's right. It sounded quite a good idea. Mind you, I wasn't going to pay anything extra. The girl could have her keep; but as for salary, that would have to be fixed up between her and Josie. That's the way it was arranged. *I* didn't know anything about the girl.'

'But she turned out all right?'

'Oh yes, there wasn't anything wrong with her – not to look at, anyway. She was very young, of course – rather cheap in style, perhaps, for a place of this kind, but nice manners – quiet and well-behaved. Danced well. People liked her.'

'Pretty?'

It had been a question hard to answer from a view of the blue swollen face.

Mr Prestcott considered.

'Fair to middling. Bit weaselly, if you know what I mean. Wouldn't have been much without make-up. As it was she managed to look quite attractive.'

'Many young men hanging about after her?'

'I know what you're trying to get at, sir.' Mr Prestcott became excited. '*I* never saw anything. Nothing special. One or two of the boys hung around a bit – but all in the day's work, so to speak. Nothing in the strangling line, I'd say. She got on well with the older people, too – had a kind of prattling way with her – seemed quite a kid, if you know what I mean. It amused them.'

Superintendent Harper said in a deep melancholy voice:

'Mr Jefferson, for instance?'

The manager agreed.

'Yes, Mr Jefferson was the one I had in mind. She used to sit with him and his family a lot. He used to take her out for drives sometimes. Mr Jefferson's very fond of young people and very good to them. I don't want to have any misunderstanding. Mr Jefferson's a cripple; he can't get about much – only where his wheelchair will take him. But he's always keen on seeing young people enjoy themselves – watches the tennis and the bathing and all that – and gives parties for young people here. He likes youth – and there's nothing better about him as there well might be. A very popular gentleman and, I'd say, a very fine character.'

Melchett asked:

'And he took an interest in Ruby Keene?'

'Her talk amused him, I think.'

'Did his family share his liking for her?'

'They were always very pleasant to her.'

Harper said:

'And it was he who reported the fact of her being missing to the police?'

He contrived to put into the words a significance and a reproach to which the manager instantly responded.

'Put yourself in my place, Mr Harper. *I* didn't dream for a minute anything was wrong. Mr Jefferson came along to my office, storming, and all worked up. The girl hadn't slept in her room. She hadn't appeared in her dance last night. She must have gone for a drive and had an accident, perhaps. The police must be informed at once! Enquiries made! In a state, he was, and quite high-handed. He rang up the police station then and there.'

'Without consulting Miss Turner?'

'Josie didn't like it much. I could see that. She was very annoyed about the whole thing – annoyed with Ruby, I mean. But what could she say?'

'I think,' said Melchett, 'we'd better see Mr Jefferson. Eh, Harper?'

Superintendent Harper agreed.

II

Mr Prestcott went up with them to Conway Jefferson's suite. It was on the first floor, overlooking the sea. Melchett said carelessly:

'Does himself pretty well, eh? Rich man?'

'Very well off indeed, I believe. Nothing's ever stinted when he comes here. Best rooms reserved – food usually *à la carte*, expensive wines – best of everything.'

Melchett nodded.

Mr Prestcott tapped on the outer door and a woman's voice said: 'Come in.'

The manager entered, the others behind him.

Mr Prestcott's manner was apologetic as he spoke to the woman who turned her head at their entrance from her seat by the window.

'I am so sorry to disturb you, Mrs Jefferson, but these gentlemen are – from the police. They are very anxious to have a word with Mr Jefferson. Er – Colonel Melchett – Superintendent Harper, Inspector – er – Slack – Mrs Jefferson.'

Mrs Jefferson acknowledged the introduction by bending her head.

A plain woman, was Melchett's first impression. Then, as a slight smile came to her lips and she spoke, he changed his opinion. She had a singularly charming and sympathetic voice and her eyes, clear hazel eyes, were beautiful. She was quietly but not unbecomingly dressed and was, he judged, about thirty-five years of age.

She said:

'My father-in-law is asleep. He is not strong at all, and this affair has been a terrible shock to him. We had to have the doctor, and the doctor gave him a sedative. As soon as he wakes he will, I know, want to see you. In the meantime, perhaps I can help you? Won't you sit down?'

Mr Prestcott, anxious to escape, said to Colonel Melchett: 'Well – er – if that's all I can do for you?' and thankfully received permission to depart.

With his closing of the door behind him, the atmosphere took on a mellow and more social quality. Adelaide Jefferson had the power of creating a restful atmosphere. She was a woman who never seemed to say anything remarkable but who succeeded in stimulating other people to talk and in setting them at their ease. She struck now the right note when she said:

'This business has shocked us all very much. We saw quite a lot of the poor girl, you know. It seems quite unbelievable. My father-in-law is terribly upset. He was very fond of Ruby.'

Colonel Melchett said:

'It was Mr Jefferson, I understand, who reported her disappearance to the police?'

He wanted to see exactly how she would react to that. There was a flicker – just a flicker – of – annoyance? concern? – he could not say what exactly, but there was *something*, and it seemed to him she had definitely to brace herself, as though to an unpleasant task, before going on.

She said:

'Yes, that is so. Being an invalid, he gets easily upset and worried. We tried to persuade him that it was all right, that there was some natural explanation, and that the girl herself would not like the police being notified. He insisted. Well' – she made a slight gesture – 'he was right and we were wrong.'

Melchett asked: 'Exactly how well did you know Ruby Keene, Mrs Jefferson?'

She considered.

'It's difficult to say. My father-in-law is very fond of young people and likes to have them round him. Ruby was a new type to him – he was amused and interested by her chatter. She sat with us a good deal in the hotel and my father-in-law took her out for drives in the car.'

Her voice was quite non-committal. Melchett thought to himself: 'She could say more if she chose.'

He said: 'Will you tell me what you can of the course of events last night?'

'Certainly, but there is very little that will be useful, I'm afraid. After dinner Ruby came and sat with us in the lounge. She remained even after the dancing had started. We had arranged to play bridge later, but we were waiting for Mark, that is Mark Gaskell, my brother-in-law – he married Mr Jefferson's daughter, you know – who had some important letters to write, and also for Josie. She was going to make a fourth with us.'

'Did that often happen?'

'Quite frequently. She's a first-class player, of course, and very nice. My father-in-law is a keen bridge player and whenever possible liked to get hold of Josie to make the fourth instead of an outsider. Naturally, as she has to arrange the fours, she can't always play with us, but she does whenever she can, and as' – her eyes smiled a little – 'my father-in-law spends a lot of money in the hotel, the management are quite pleased for Josie to favour us.'

Melchett asked:

'You like Josie?'

'Yes, I do. She's always good-humoured and cheerful, works hard and seems to enjoy her job. She's shrewd, though not well educated, and – well – never pretends about anything. She's natural and unaffected.'

'Please go on, Mrs Jefferson.'

'As I say, Josie had to get her bridge fours arranged and Mark was writing, so Ruby sat and talked with us a little longer than usual. Then Josie came along, and Ruby went off to do her first solo dance with Raymond – he's the dance and tennis professional. She came back to us afterwards just as Mark joined us. Then she went off to dance with a young man and we four started our bridge.'

She stopped, and made a slight insignificant gesture of helplessness.

'And that's all I know! I just caught a glimpse of her once dancing, but bridge is an absorbing game and I hardly glanced through the glass partition at the ballroom. Then, at midnight, Raymond came along to Josie very upset and asked where Ruby was. Josie, naturally, tried to shut him up but –'

Superintendent Harper interrupted. He said in his quiet voice: 'Why "*naturally,*" Mrs Jefferson?'

'Well' – she hesitated, looked, Melchett thought, a little put out – 'Josie didn't want the girl's absence made too much of. She considered herself responsible for her in a way. She said Ruby was probably up in her bedroom, said the girl had talked about having a headache earlier – I don't think that was true, by the way; Josie just said it by way of excuse. Raymond went off and telephoned up to Ruby's room, but apparently there was no answer, and he came back in rather a state – temperamental, you know. Josie went off with him and tried to soothe him down, and in the end she danced with him instead of Ruby. Rather plucky of her, because you could see afterwards it had hurt her ankle. She came back to us when the dance was over and tried to calm down Mr Jefferson. He had got worked up by then. We persuaded him in the end to go to bed, told him Ruby had probably gone for a spin in a car and that they'd had a puncture. He went to bed worried, and this morning he began to agitate at once.' She paused. 'The rest you know.'

'Thank you, Mrs Jefferson. Now I'm going to ask you if you've any idea who could have done this thing?'

She said immediately: 'No idea whatever. I'm afraid I can't help you in the slightest.'

He pressed her. 'The girl never said anything? Nothing about jealousy? About some man she was afraid of? Or intimate with?'

Adelaide Jefferson shook her head to each query.

There seemed nothing more that she could tell them.

The Superintendent suggested that they should interview young George Bartlett and return to see Mr Jefferson later. Colonel Melchett agreed, and the three men went out, Mrs Jefferson promising to send word as soon as Mr Jefferson was awake.

'Nice woman,' said the Colonel, as they closed the door behind them.

'A very nice lady indeed,' said Superintendent Harper.

III

George Bartlett was a thin, lanky youth with a prominent Adam's apple and an immense difficulty in saying what he meant. He was in such a state of dither that it was hard to get a calm statement from him.

'I say, it is awful, isn't it? Sort of thing one reads about in the Sunday papers – but one doesn't feel it really happens, don't you know?'

'Unfortunately there is no doubt about it, Mr Bartlett,' said the Superintendent.

'No, no, of course not. But it seems so rum somehow. And miles from here and everything – in some country house, wasn't it? Awfully county and all that. Created a bit of a stir in the neighbourhood – what?'

Colonel Melchett took charge.

'How well did you know the dead girl, Mr Bartlett?'

George Bartlett looked alarmed.

'Oh, n-n-not well at all, s-s-sir. No, hardly at all – if you know what I mean. Danced with her once or twice – passed the time of day – bit of tennis – *you* know.'

'You were, I think, the last person to see her alive last night?'

'I suppose I was – doesn't it sound awful? I mean, she was perfectly all right when I saw her – absolutely.'

'What time was that, Mr Bartlett?'

'Well, you know, I never know about time – wasn't very late, if you know what I mean.'

'You danced with her?'

'Yes – as a matter of fact – well, yes, I did. Early on the evening, though. Tell you what, it was just after her exhibition dance with the pro. fellow. Must have been ten, half-past, eleven, I don't know.'

'Never mind the time. We can fix that. Please tell us exactly what happened.'

'Well, we danced, don't you know. Not that *I'm* much of a dancer.'

'How you dance is not really relevant, Mr Bartlett.'

George Bartlett cast an alarmed eye on the Colonel and stammered:

'No – er – n-n-no, I suppose it isn't. Well, as I say, we danced, round and round, and I talked, but Ruby didn't say very much and she yawned a bit. As I say, I don't dance awfully well, and so girls – well – inclined to give it a miss, if you know what I mean. She said she had a headache – I know where I get off, so I said righty ho, and that was that.'

'What was the last you saw of her?'

'She went off upstairs.'

'She said nothing about meeting anyone? Or going for a drive? Or – or – having a date?' The Colonel used the colloquial expression with a slight effort.

Bartlett shook his head.

'Not to me.' He looked rather mournful. 'Just gave me the push.'

'What was her manner? Did she seem anxious, abstracted, anything on her mind?'

George Bartlett considered. Then he shook his head.

'Seemed a bit bored. Yawned, as I said. Nothing more.'

Colonel Melchett said:

'And what did you do, Mr Bartlett?'

'Eh?'

'What did you do when Ruby Keene left you?'

George Bartlett gaped at him.

'Let's see now – what *did* I do?'

'We're waiting for you to tell us.'

'Yes, yes – of course. Jolly difficult, remembering things, what? Let me see. Shouldn't be surprised if I went into the bar and had a drink.'

'*Did* you go into the bar and have a drink?'

'That's just it. I *did* have a drink. Don't think it was just then. Have an idea I wandered out, don't you know? Bit of air. Rather stuffy for September. Very nice outside. Yes, that's it. I strolled around a bit, then I came in and had a drink and then I strolled back to the ballroom. Wasn't much doing. Noticed what's-her-name –

Josie – was dancing again. With the tennis fellow. She'd been on the sick list – twisted ankle or something.'

'That fixes the time of your return at midnight. Do you intend us to understand that you spent over an hour walking about outside?'

'Well, I had a drink, you know. I was – well, I was thinking of things.'

This statement received more incredulity than any other.

Colonel Melchett said sharply:

'What were you thinking about?'

'Oh, I don't know. Things,' said Mr Bartlett vaguely.

'You have a car, Mr Bartlett?'

'Oh, yes, I've got a car.'

'Where was it, in the hotel garage?'

'No, it was in the courtyard, as a matter of fact. Thought I might go for a spin, you see.'

'Perhaps you did go for a spin?'

'No – no, I didn't. Swear I didn't.'

'You didn't, for instance, take Miss Keene for a spin?'

'Oh, I say. Look here, what are you getting at? I didn't – I swear I didn't. Really, now.'

'Thank you, Mr Bartlett, I don't think there is anything more at present. *At present*,' repeated Colonel Melchett with a good deal of emphasis on the words.

They left Mr Bartlett looking after them with a ludicrous expression of alarm on his unintellectual face.

'Brainless young ass,' said Colonel Melchett. 'Or isn't he?'

Superintendent Harper shook his head.

'We've got a long way to go,' he said.

CHAPTER 6

I

Neither the night porter nor the barman proved helpful. The night porter remembered ringing up to Miss Keene's room just after midnight and getting no reply. He had not noticed Mr Bartlett leaving or entering the hotel. A lot of gentlemen and ladies were strolling in and out, the night being fine. And there were side doors off the corridor as well as the one in the main hall. He was fairly certain Miss Keene had not gone out by the main door, but if she had come down from her room, which was on the first floor, there was a staircase next to it and a door out at the end of the corridor, leading on to the side terrace. She could have gone out of that unseen easily enough. It was not locked until the dancing was over at two o'clock.

The barman remembered Mr Bartlett being in the bar the preceding evening but could not say when. Somewhere about the middle of the evening, he thought. Mr Bartlett had sat against the wall and was looking rather melancholy. He did not know how long he was there. There were a lot of outside guests coming and going in the bar. He had noticed Mr Bartlett but he couldn't fix the time in any way.

II

As they left the bar, they were accosted by a small boy of about nine years old. He burst immediately into excited speech.

'I say, are you the detectives? I'm Peter Carmody. It was my grandfather, Mr Jefferson, who rang up the police about Ruby. Are you from Scotland Yard? You don't mind my speaking to you, do you?'

Colonel Melchett looked as though he were about to return a short answer, but Superintendent Harper intervened. He spoke benignly and heartily.

'That's all right, my son. Naturally interests you, I expect?'

'You bet it does. Do you like detective stories? I do. I read them all, and I've got autographs from Dorothy Sayers and Agatha Christie and Dickson Carr and H. C. Bailey. Will the murder be in the papers?'

'It'll be in the papers all right,' said Superintendent Harper grimly.

'You see, I'm going back to school next week and I shall tell them all that I knew her — really knew her *well*.'

'What did you think of her, eh?'

Peter considered.

'Well, I didn't like her much. I think she was rather a stupid sort of girl. Mum and Uncle Mark didn't like her much either. Only

Grandfather. Grandfather wants to see you, by the way. Edwards is looking for you.'

Superintendent Harper murmured encouragingly:

'So your mother and your Uncle Mark didn't like Ruby Keene much? Why was that?'

'Oh, I don't know. She was always butting in. And they didn't like Grandfather making such a fuss of her. I expect,' said Peter cheerfully, 'that they're glad she's dead.'

Superintendent Harper looked at him thoughtfully. He said: 'Did you hear them – er – say so?'

'Well, not exactly. Uncle Mark said: "Well, it's one way out, anyway," and Mums said: "Yes, but such a horrible one," and Uncle Mark said it was no good being hypocritical.'

The men exchanged glances. At that moment a respectable, clean-shaven man, neatly dressed in blue serge, came up to them.

'Excuse me, gentlemen. I am Mr Jefferson's valet. He is awake now and sent me to find you, as he is very anxious to see you.'

Once more they went up to Conway Jefferson's suite. In the sitting-room Adelaide Jefferson was talking to a tall, restless man who was prowling nervously about the room. He swung round sharply to view the newcomers.

'Oh, yes. Glad you've come. My father-in-law's been asking for you. He's awake now. Keep him as calm as you can, won't you? His health's not too good. It's a wonder, really, that this shock didn't do for him.'

Harper said:

'I'd no idea his health was as bad as that.'

'He doesn't know it himself,' said Mark Gaskell. 'It's his heart, you see. The doctor warned Addie that he mustn't be over-excited or startled. He more or less hinted that the end might come any time, didn't he, Addie?'

Mrs Jefferson nodded. She said:

'It's incredible that he's rallied the way he has.'

Melchett said dryly:

'Murder isn't exactly a soothing incident. We'll be as careful as we can.'

He was sizing up Mark Gaskell as he spoke. He didn't much care for the fellow. A bold, unscrupulous, hawk-like face. One of those men who usually get their own way and whom women frequently admire.

'But not the sort of fellow I'd trust,' the Colonel thought to himself.

Unscrupulous – that was the word for him.

The sort of fellow who wouldn't stick at anything. . . .

III

In the big bedroom overlooking the sea, Conway Jefferson was sitting in his wheelchair by the window.

No sooner were you in the room with him than you felt the power and magnetism of the man. It was as though the injuries which had left him a cripple had resulted in concentrating the vitality of his shattered body into a narrower and more intense focus.

He had a fine head, the red of the hair slightly grizzled. The face was rugged and powerful, deeply sun-tanned, and the eyes were startling blue. There was no sign of illness or feebleness about him. The deep lines on his face were the lines of suffering, not the lines of weakness. Here was a man who would never rail against fate but accept it and pass on to victory.

He said: 'I'm glad you've come.' His quick eyes took them in. He said to Melchett: 'You're the Chief Constable of Radfordshire? Right. And you're Superintendent Harper? Sit down. Cigarettes on the table beside you.'

They thanked him and sat down. Melchett said:

'I understand, Mr Jefferson, that you were interested in the dead girl?'

A quick, twisted smile flashed across the lined face.

'Yes – they'll all have told you that! Well, it's no secret. How much has my family said to you?'

He looked quickly from one to the other as he asked the question.

It was Melchett who answered.

'Mrs Jefferson told us very little beyond the fact that the girl's chatter amused you and that she was by way of being a protégée. We have only exchanged half a dozen words with Mr Gaskell.'

Conway Jefferson smiled.

'Addie's a discreet creature, bless her. Mark would probably have been more outspoken. I think, Melchett, that I'd better tell you some facts rather fully. It's important, in order that you should understand my attitude. And, to begin with, it's necessary that I go back to the big tragedy of my life. Eight years ago I lost my wife, my son and my daughter in an aeroplane accident. Since then I've been like a man who's lost half himself – and I'm not speaking of my physical plight! I was a family man. My daughter-in-law and my son-in-law have been very good to me. They've done all they can to take the place of my flesh and blood. But I've realized – especially of late, that they have, after all, their own lives to live.

'So you must understand that, essentially, I'm a lonely man. I like young people. I enjoy them. Once or twice I've played with the idea of adopting some girl or boy. During this last month I got very friendly with the child who's been killed. She was absolutely natural – completely naïve. She chattered on about her life and her experiences – in pantomime, with touring companies, with Mum and Dad as a child in cheap lodgings. Such a different life from any I've known! Never complaining, never seeing it as sordid. Just a natural, uncomplaining, hard-working child, unspoilt and charming. Not a lady, perhaps, but thank God, neither vulgar nor – abominable word – "lady-like".'

'I got more and more fond of Ruby. I decided, gentlemen, to adopt her legally. She would become – by law – my daughter. That, I hope, explains my concern for her and the steps I took when I heard of her unaccountable disappearance.'

There was a pause. Then Superintendent Harper, his unemotional voice robbing the question of any offence, asked: 'May I ask what your son-in-law and daughter-in-law said to that?'

Jefferson's answer came back quickly:

'What could they say? They didn't, perhaps, like it very much. It's the sort of thing that arouses prejudice. But they behaved very well – yes, very well. It's not as though, you see, they were dependent on me. When my son Frank married I turned over half my worldly goods to him then and there. I believe in that. Don't let your children wait until you're dead. They want the money when they're young, not when they're middle-aged. In the same way when my daughter Rosamund insisted on marrying a poor man, I settled a big sum of money on her. That sum passed to him at her death. So, you see, that simplified the matter from the financial angle.'

'I see, Mr Jefferson,' said Superintendent Harper.

But there was a certain reserve in his tone. Conway Jefferson pounced upon it.

'But you don't agree, eh?'

'It's not for me to say, sir, but families, in my experience, don't always act reasonably.'

'I dare say you're right, Superintendent, but you must remember that Mr Gaskell and Mrs Jefferson aren't, strictly speaking, my *family*. They're not blood relations.'

'That, of course, makes a difference,' admitted the Superintendent.

For a moment Conway Jefferson's eyes twinkled. He said: 'That's not to say that they didn't think me an old fool! That *would* be the average person's reaction. But I wasn't being a fool. I know character. With education and polishing, Ruby Keene could have taken her place anywhere.'

Melchett said:

'I'm afraid we're being rather impertinent and inquisitive, but it's important that we should get at all the facts. You proposed to make full provision for the girl – that is, settle money upon her, but you hadn't already done so?'

Jefferson said:

'I understand what you're driving at – the possibility of someone's benefiting by the girl's death? But nobody could. The necessary formalities for legal adoption were under way, but they hadn't yet been completed.'

Melchett said slowly:

'Then, if anything happened to you –?'

He left the sentence unfinished, as a query. Conway Jefferson was quick to respond.

'Nothing's likely to happen to me! I'm a cripple, but I'm not an invalid. Although doctors *do* like to pull long faces and give advice about not overdoing things. Not overdoing things! I'm as strong as a horse! Still, I'm quite aware of the fatalities of life – my God, I've good reason to be! Sudden death comes to the strongest man – especially in these days of road casualties. But I'd provided for that. I made a new will about ten days ago.'

'Yes?' Superintendent Harper leaned forward.

'I left the sum of fifty thousand pounds to be held in trust for Ruby Keene until she was twenty-five, when she would come into the principal.'

Superintendent Harper's eyes opened. So did Colonel Melchett's. Harper said in an almost awed voice:

'That's a very large sum of money, Mr Jefferson.'

'In these days, yes, it is.'

'And you were leaving it to a girl you had only known a few weeks?'

Anger flashed into the vivid blue eyes.

'Must I go on repeating the same thing over and over again? I've no flesh and blood of my own – no nieces or nephews or distant cousins, even! I might have left it to charity. I prefer to leave it to an individual.' He laughed. 'Cinderella turned into a princess over-night! A fairy-godfather instead of a fairy-godmother. Why not? It's *my* money. *I* made it.'

Colonel Melchett asked: 'Any other bequests?'

'A small legacy to Edwards, my valet – and the remainder to Mark and Addie in equal shares.'

'Would – excuse me – the residue amount to a large sum?'

'Probably not. It's difficult to say exactly, investments fluctuate all the time. The sum involved, after death duties and expenses had been paid, would probably have come to something between five and ten thousand pounds net.'

'I see.'

'And you needn't think I was treating them shabbily. As I said, I divided up my estate at the time my children married. I left myself, actually, a very small sum. But after – after the tragedy – I wanted something to occupy my mind. I flung myself into business. At my house in London I had a private line put in connecting my bedroom with my office. I worked hard – it helped me not to think, and it made me feel that my – my mutilation had not vanquished me. I threw myself into work' – his voice took on a deeper note, he spoke more to himself than to his audience – 'and, by some subtle irony, everything I did prospered! My wildest speculations succeeded. If I gambled, I won. Everything I touched turned to gold. Fate's ironic way of righting the balance, I suppose.'

The lines of suffering stood out on his face again.

Recollecting himself, he smiled wryly at them.

'So you see, the sum of money I left Ruby was indisputably mine to do with as my fancy dictated.'

Melchett said quickly:

'Undoubtedly, my dear fellow, we are not questioning that for a moment.'

Conway Jefferson said: 'Good. Now I want to ask some questions in my turn, if I may. I want to hear – more about this terrible business. All I know is that she – that little Ruby was found strangled in a house some twenty miles from here.'

'That is correct. At Gossington Hall.'

Jefferson frowned.

'Gossington? But that's –'

'Colonel Bantry's house.'

'Bantry! *Arthur Bantry?* But I know him. Know him and his wife! Met them abroad some years ago. I didn't realize they lived in this part of the world. Why, it's –'

He broke off. Superintendent Harper slipped in smoothly:

'Colonel Bantry was dining in the hotel here Tuesday of last week. You didn't see him?'

'Tuesday? Tuesday? No, we were back late. Went over to Harden Head and had dinner on the way back.'

Melchett said:

'Ruby Keene never mentioned the Bantrys to you?'

Jefferson shook his head.

'Never. Don't believe she knew them. Sure she didn't. She didn't know anybody but theatrical folk and that sort of thing.' He paused and then asked abruptly:

'What's Bantry got to say about it?'

'He can't account for it in the least. He was out at a Conservative meeting last night. The body was discovered this morning. He says he's never seen the girl in his life.'

Jefferson nodded. He said:

'It certainly seems fantastic.'

Superintendent Harper cleared his throat. He said:

'Have you any idea at all, sir, who can have done this?'

'Good God, I wish I had!' The veins stood out on his forehead. 'It's incredible, unimaginable! I'd say it couldn't have happened, if it hadn't happened!'

'There's no friend of hers – from her past life – no man hanging about – or threatening her?'

'I'm sure there isn't. She'd have told me if so. She's never had a regular "boy-friend". She told me so herself.'

Superintendent Harper thought:

'Yes, I dare say that's what *she* told you! But that's as may be!'

Conway Jefferson went on:

'Josie would know better than anyone if there had been some man hanging about Ruby or pestering her. Can't she help?'

'She says not.'

Jefferson said, frowning:

'I can't help feeling it must be the work of some maniac – the brutality of the method – breaking into a country house – the whole thing so unconnected and senseless. There are men of that type, men outwardly sane, but who decoy girls – sometimes children – away and kill them. Sexual crimes really, I suppose.'

Harper said:

'Oh, yes, there are such cases, but we've no knowledge of anyone of that kind operating in this neighbourhood.'

Jefferson went on:

'I've thought over all the various men I've seen with Ruby. Guests here and outsiders – men she'd danced with. They all seem harmless enough – the usual type. She had no special friend of any kind.'

Superintendent Harper's face remained quite impassive, but unseen by Conway Jefferson there was still a speculative glint in his eyes.

It was quite possible, he thought, that Ruby Keene might have had a special friend even though Conway Jefferson did not know about it.

He said nothing, however. The Chief Constable gave him a glance of enquiry and then rose to his feet. He said:

'Thank you, Mr Jefferson. That's all we need for the present.'

Jefferson said:

'You'll keep me informed of your progress?'

'Yes, yes, we'll keep in touch with you.'

The two men went out.

Conway Jefferson leaned back in his chair.

His eyelids came down and veiled the fierce blue of his eyes. He looked suddenly a very tired man.

Then, after a minute or two, the lids flickered. He called: 'Edwards?'

From the next room the valet appeared promptly. Edwards knew his master as no one else did. Others, even his nearest, knew only his strength. Edwards knew his weakness. He had seen Conway Jefferson tired, discouraged, weary of life, momentarily defeated by infirmity and loneliness.

'Yes, sir?'

Jefferson said:

'Get on to Sir Henry Clithering. He's at Melborne Abbas. Ask him, from me, to get here today if he can, instead of tomorrow. Tell him it's urgent.'

CHAPTER 7

I

When they were outside Jefferson's door, Superintendent Harper said:

'Well, for what it's worth, we've got a motive, sir.'

'H'm,' said Melchett. 'Fifty thousand pounds, eh?'

'Yes, sir. Murder's been done for a good deal less than that.'

'Yes, but –'

Colonel Melchett left the sentence unfinished. Harper, however, understood him.

'You don't think it's likely in this case? Well, I don't either, as far as that goes. But it's got to be gone into all the same.'

'Oh, of course.'

Harper went on:

'If, as Mr Jefferson says, Mr Gaskell and Mrs Jefferson are already well provided for and in receipt of a comfortable income, well, it's not likely they'd set out to do a brutal murder.'

'Quite so. Their financial standing will have to be investigated, of course. Can't say I like the appearance of Gaskell much – looks a sharp, unscrupulous sort of fellow – but that's a long way from making him out a murderer.'

'Oh, yes, sir, as I say, I don't think it's *likely* to be either of them, and from what Josie said I don't see how it would have been humanly possible. They were both playing bridge from twenty minutes to eleven until midnight. No, to my mind there's another possibility much more likely.'

Melchett said: 'Boy-friend of Ruby Keene's?'

'That's it, sir. Some disgruntled young fellow – not too strong in the head, perhaps. Someone, I'd say, she knew before she came here. This adoption scheme, if he got wise to it, may just have put the lid on things. He saw himself losing her, saw her being removed to a different sphere of life altogether, and he went mad and blind with rage. He got her to come out and meet him last night, had a row with her over it, lost his head completely and did her in.'

'And how did she come to be in Bantry's library?'

59

'I think that's feasible. They were out, say, in his car at the time. He came to himself, realized what he'd done, and his first thought was how to get rid of the body. Say they were near the gates of a big house at the time. The idea comes to him that if she's found there the hue and cry will centre round the house and its occupants and will leave him comfortably out of it. She's a little bit of a thing. He could easily carry her. He's got a chisel in the car. He forces a window and plops her down on the hearthrug. Being a strangling case, there's no blood or mess to give him away in the car. See what I mean, sir?'

'Oh, yes, Harper, it's all perfectly possible. But there's still one thing to be done. *Cherchez l'homme.*'

'What? Oh, very good, sir.'

Superintendent Harper tactfully applauded his superior's joke, although, owing to the excellence of Colonel Melchett's French accent he almost missed the sense of the words.

II

'Oh – er – I say – er – c-c-could I speak to you a minute?'

It was George Bartlett who thus waylaid the two men.

Colonel Melchett, who was not attracted to Mr Bartlett and who was anxious to see how Slack had got on with the investigation of the girl's room and the questioning of the chambermaids, barked sharply:

'Well, what is it – what is it?'

Young Mr Bartlett retreated a step or two, opening and shutting his mouth and giving an unconscious imitation of a fish in a tank.

'Well – er – probably isn't important, don't you know – thought I ought to tell you. Matter of fact, can't find my car.'

'What do you mean, can't find your car?'

Stammering a good deal, Mr Bartlett explained that what he meant was that he couldn't find his car.

Superintendent Harper said:

'Do you mean it's been stolen?'

George Bartlett turned gratefully to the more placid voice.

'Well, that's just it, you know. I mean, one can't tell, can one? I mean someone may just have buzzed off in it, not meaning any harm, if you know what I mean.'

'When did you last see it, Mr Bartlett?'

'Well, I was tryin' to remember. Funny how difficult it is to remember anything, isn't it?'

Colonel Melchett said coldly:

'Not, I should think, to a normal intelligence. I understood you to say just now that it was in the courtyard of the hotel last night –'

Mr Bartlett was bold enough to interrupt. He said:

'That's just it – was it?'

'What do you mean by "was it"? You said it *was*.'

'Well – I mean I *thought* it was. I mean – well, I didn't go out and look, don't you see?'

Colonel Melchett sighed. He summoned all his patience. He said:

'Let's get this quite clear. When was the last time you saw – actually *saw* your car? What make is it, by the way?'

'Minoan 14.'

'And you last saw it – when?'

George Bartlett's Adam's apple jerked convulsively up and down.

'Been trying to think. Had it before lunch yesterday. Was going for a spin in the afternoon. But somehow, you know how it is, went to sleep instead. Then, after tea, had a game of squash and all that, and a bathe afterwards.'

'And the car was then in the courtyard of the hotel?'

'Suppose so. I mean, that's where I'd put it. Thought, you see, I'd take someone for a spin. After dinner, I mean. But it wasn't my lucky evening. Nothing doing. Never took the old bus out after all.'

Harper said:

'But, as far as you knew, the car was still in the courtyard?'

'Well, naturally. I mean, I'd put it there – what?'

'Would you have noticed if it had *not* been there?'

Mr Bartlett's shook his head.

'Don't think so, you know. Lot of cars going and coming and all that. Plenty of Minoans.'

Superintendent Harper nodded. He had just cast a casual glance out of the window. There were at that moment no fewer than eight Minoan 14s in the courtyard – it was the popular cheap car of the year.

'Aren't you in the habit of putting your car away at night?' asked Colonel Melchett.

'Don't usually bother,' said Mr Bartlett. 'Fine weather and all that, you know. Such a fag putting a car away in a garage.'

Glancing at Colonel Melchett, Superintendent Harper said: 'I'll join you upstairs, sir. I'll just get hold of Sergeant Higgins and he can take down particulars from Mr Bartlett.'

'Right, Harper.'

Mr Bartlett murmured wistfully:

'Thought I ought to let you know, you know. Might be important, what?'

III

Mr Prestcott had supplied his additional dancer with board and lodging. Whatever the board, the lodging was the poorest the hotel possessed.

Josephine Turner and Ruby Keene had occupied rooms at the extreme end of a mean and dingy little corridor. The rooms were small, faced north on to a portion of the cliff that backed the hotel, and were furnished with the odds and ends of suites that had once, some thirty years ago, represented luxury and magnificence in the best suites. Now, when the hotel had been modernized and the bedrooms supplied with built-in receptacles for clothes, these large Victorian oak and mahogany wardrobes were relegated to those rooms occupied by the hotel's resident staff, or given to guests in the height of the season when all the rest of the hotel was full.

As Melchett saw at once, the position of Ruby Keene's room was ideal for the purpose of leaving the hotel without being observed, and was particularly unfortunate from the point of view of throwing light on the circumstances of that departure.

At the end of the corridor was a small staircase which led down to an equally obscure corridor on the ground floor. Here there was a glass door which led out on to the side terrace of the hotel, an unfrequented terrace with no view. You could go from it to the main terrace in front, or you could go down a winding path and come out in a lane that eventually rejoined the cliff road farther along. Its surface being bad, it was seldom used.

Inspector Slack had been busy harrying chambermaids and examining Ruby's room for clues. He had been lucky enough to find the room exactly as it had been left the night before.

Ruby Keene had not been in the habit of rising early. Her usual procedure, Slack discovered, was to sleep until about ten or half-past and then ring for breakfast. Consequently, since Conway Jefferson had begun his representations to the manager very early, the police had taken charge of things before the chambermaids had touched the room. They had actually not been down that corridor at all. The other rooms there, at this season of the year, were only opened and dusted once a week.

'That's all to the good as far as it goes,' Slack explained gloomily. 'It means that if there *were* anything to find we'd find it, but there isn't anything.'

The Glenshire police had already been over the room for finger-prints, but there were none unaccounted for. Ruby's own, Josie's, and the two chambermaids – one on the morning and one on the evening shift. There were also a couple of prints made by Raymond Starr, but these were accounted for by his story that he had come up with Josie to look for Ruby when she did not appear for the midnight exhibition dance.

There had been a heap of letters and general rubbish in the pigeonholes of the massive mahogany desk in the corner. Slack had just been carefully sorting through them. But he had found nothing of a suggestive nature. Bills, receipts, theatre programmes, cinema stubs, newspaper cuttings, beauty hints torn from magazines. Of the letters there were some from 'Lil,' apparently a friend from the Palais de Danse, recounting various affairs and gossip, saying they 'missed Rube a lot. Mr Findeison asked after you ever so often! Quite put out, he is! Young Reg has taken up with May now you've gone. Barny asks after you now and then. Things going much as usual. Old Grouser still as mean as ever with us girls. He ticked off Ada for going about with a fellow.'

Slack had carefully noted all the names mentioned. Enquiries would be made – and it was possible some useful information might come to light. To this Colonel Melchett agreed; so did Superintendent Harper, who had joined them. Otherwise the room had little to yield in the way of information.

Across a chair in the middle of the room was the foamy pink dance frock Ruby had worn early in the evening with a pair of pink satin high-heeled shoes kicked off carelessly on the floor. Two sheer silk stockings were rolled into a ball and flung down. One had a ladder in it. Melchett recalled that the dead girl had had bare feet and legs. This, Slack learned, was her custom. She used make-up on her legs instead of stockings and only sometimes wore stockings for dancing, by this means saving expense. The wardrobe door was open and showed a variety of rather flashy evening-dresses and a row of shoes below. There was some soiled underwear in the clothes-basket, some nail-parings, soiled face-cleaning tissue and bits of cotton wool stained with rouge and nail polish in the waste-paper basket – in fact, nothing out of the ordinary! The facts seemed plain to read. Ruby Keene had hurried upstairs, changed her clothes and hurried off again – *where?*

Josephine Turner, who might be supposed to know most of Ruby's life and friends, had proved unable to help. But this, as Inspector Slack pointed out, might be natural.

'If what you tell me is true, sir – about this adoption business, I mean – well, Josie would be all for Ruby breaking with any old friends she might have and who might queer the pitch, so to speak. As I see it, this invalid gentleman gets all worked up about Ruby Keene being such a sweet, innocent, childish little piece of goods. Now, supposing Ruby's got a tough boy-friend – that won't go down so well with the old boy. So it's Ruby's business to keep that dark. Josie doesn't know much about the girl anyway – not about her friends and all that. But one thing she wouldn't stand for – Ruby's messing up things by carrying on with some undesirable fellow. So its stands to reason that Ruby (who, as I see it, was a sly little piece!) would keep very dark about seeing any old friend. She wouldn't let on to Josie anything about it – otherwise Josie would say: "No, you don't, my girl." But you know what girls are – especially young ones – always ready to make a fool of themselves over a tough guy. Ruby wants to see him. He comes down here, cuts up rough about the whole business, and wrings the girl's neck.'

'I expect you're right, Slack,' said Colonel Melchett, disguising his usual repugnance for the unpleasant way Slack had of putting things. 'If so, we ought to be able to discover this tough friend's identity fairly easily.'

'You leave it to me, sir,' said Slack with his usual confidence. 'I'll get hold of this "Lil" girl at that Palais de Danse place and turn her right inside out. We'll soon get at the truth.'

Colonel Melchett wondered if they would. Slack's energy and activity always made him feel tired.

'There's one other person you might be able to get a tip from, sir,' went on Slack, 'and that's the dance and tennis pro. fellow. He must have seen a lot of her and he'd know more than Josie would. Likely enough she'd loosen her tongue a bit to him.'

'I have already discussed that point with Superintendent Harper.'

'Good, sir. I've done the chambermaids pretty thoroughly! They don't know a thing. Looked down on these two, as far as I can make out. Scamped the service as much as they dared. Chambermaid was in here last at seven o'clock last night, when she turned down the bed and drew the curtains and cleared up a bit. There's a bathroom next door, if you'd like to see it?'

The bathroom was situated between Ruby's room and the slightly larger room occupied by Josie. It was unilluminating. Colonel Melchett silently marvelled at the amount of aids to beauty that women could use. Rows of jars of face cream, cleansing cream, vanishing cream, skin-feeding cream! Boxes of different shades of powder. An untidy heap of every variety of lipstick. Hair lotions and 'brightening' applications. Eyelash black, mascara, blue stain for under the eyes, at least twelve different shades of nail varnish, face tissues, bits of cotton wool, dirty powder puffs. Bottles of lotions – astringent, tonic, soothing, etc.

'Do you mean to say?' he murmured feebly, 'that women use all these things?'

Inspector Slack, who always knew everything, kindly enlightened him.

'In private life, sir, so to speak, a lady keeps to one or two distinct shades, one for evening, one for day. They know what suits them and they keep to it. But these professional girls, they have to ring a change, so to speak. They do exhibition dances, and one night it's a tango and the next a crinoline Victorian dance and then a kind of Apache dance and then just ordinary ballroom, and, of course, the make-up varies a good bit.'

'Good Lord!' said the Colonel. 'No wonder the people who turn out these creams and messes make a fortune.'

'Easy money, that's what it is,' said Slack. 'Easy money. Got to spend a bit in advertisement, of course.'

Colonel Melchett jerked his mind away from the fascinating and age-long problem of women's adornments. He said to Harper, who had just joined them:

'There's still this dancing fellow. Your pigeon, Superintendent?'

'I suppose so, sir.'

As they went downstairs Harper asked:

'What did you think of Mr Bartlett's story, sir?'

'About his car? I think, Harper, that that young man wants watching. It's a fishy story. Supposing that he did take Ruby Keene out in that car last night, after all?'

IV

Superintendent Harper's manner was slow and pleasant and absolutely non-committal. These cases where the police of two counties had to collaborate were always difficult. He liked Colonel Melchett and considered him an able Chief Constable, but he was nevertheless glad to be tackling the present interview by himself. Never do too much at once, was Superintendent Harper's rule. Bare routine enquiry for the first time. That left the persons you were interviewing relieved and predisposed them to be more unguarded in the next interview you had with them.

Harper already knew Raymond Starr by sight. A fine-looking specimen, tall, lithe and good-looking, with very white teeth in a deeply-bronzed face. He was dark and graceful. He had a pleasant, friendly manner and was very popular in the hotel.

'I'm afraid I can't help you much, Superintendent. I knew Ruby quite well, of course. She'd been here over a month and we had practised our dances together and all that. But there's really very little to say. She was quite a pleasant and rather stupid girl.'

'It's her friendships we're particularly anxious to know about. Her friendships with men.'

'So I suppose. Well, *I* don't know anything! She'd got a few young men in tow in the hotel, but nothing special. You see, she was nearly always monopolized by the Jefferson family.'

'Yes, the Jefferson family.' Harper paused meditatively. He shot a shrewd glance at the young man.

'What did you think of that business, Mr Starr?'

Raymond Starr said coolly: 'What business?'

Harper said: 'Did you know that Mr Jefferson was proposing to adopt Ruby Keene legally?'

This appeared to be news to Starr. He pursed up his lips and whistled. He said:

'The clever little devil! Oh, well, there's no fool like an old fool.'

'That's how it strikes you, is it?'

'Well – what else can one say? If the old boy wanted to adopt someone, why didn't he pick upon a girl of his own class?'

'Ruby Keene never mentioned the matter to you?'

'No, she didn't. I knew she was elated about something, but I didn't know what it was.'

'And Josie?'

'Oh, I think Josie must have known what was in the wind.

Probably she was the one who planned the whole thing. Josie's no fool. She's got a head on her, that girl.'

Harper nodded. It was Josie who had sent for Ruby Keene. Josie, no doubt, who had encouraged the intimacy. No wonder she had been upset when Ruby had failed to show up for her dance that night and Conway Jefferson had begun to panic. She was envisaging her plans going awry.

He asked:

'Could Ruby keep a secret, do you think?'

'As well as most. She didn't talk about her own affairs much.'

'Did she ever say anything – anything at all – about some friend of hers – someone from her former life who was coming to see her here, or whom she had had difficulty with – you know the sort of thing I mean, no doubt.'

'I know perfectly. Well, as far as I'm aware, there was no one of the kind. Not by anything she ever said.'

'Thank you, Mr Starr. Now will you just tell me in your own words exactly what happened last night?'

'Certainly. Ruby and I did our ten-thirty dance together –'

'No signs of anything unusual about her then?'

Raymond considered.

'I don't think so. I didn't notice what happened afterwards. I had my own partners to look after. I do remember noticing she wasn't in the ballroom. At midnight she hadn't turned up. I was very annoyed and went to Josie about it. Josie was playing bridge with the Jeffersons. She hadn't any idea where Ruby was, and I think she got a bit of a jolt. I noticed her shoot a quick, anxious glance at Mr Jefferson. I persuaded the band to play another dance and I went to the office and got them to ring up to Ruby's room. There wasn't any answer. I went back to Josie. She suggested that Ruby was perhaps asleep in her room. Idiotic suggestion really, but it was meant for the Jeffersons, of course! She came away with me and said we'd go up together.'

'Yes, Mr Starr. And what did she say when she was alone with you?'

'As far as I can remember, she looked very angry and said: "Damned little fool. She can't do this sort of thing. It will ruin all her chances. Who's she with, do you know?"

'I said that I hadn't the least idea. The last I'd seen of her was dancing with young Bartlett. Josie said: "She wouldn't be with *him*. What *can* she be up to? She isn't with that film man, is she?"'

Harper said sharply: '*Film man?* Who was he?'

Raymond said: 'I don't know his name. He's never stayed here. Rather an unusual-looking chap – black hair and theatrical-looking. He has something to do with the film industry, I believe – or so he told Ruby. He came over to dine here once or twice and danced with Ruby afterwards, but I don't think she knew him at all well. That's why I was surprised when Josie mentioned him. I said I didn't think he'd been here tonight. Josie said: "Well, she must be out with *someone*. What on earth am I going to say to the Jeffersons?" I said what did it matter to the Jeffersons? And Josie said it *did* matter. And she said, too, that she'd never forgive Ruby if she went and messed things up.

'We'd got to Ruby's room by then. She wasn't there, of course, but she'd been there, because the dress she had been wearing was lying across a chair. Josie looked in the wardrobe and said she thought she'd put on her old white dress. Normally she'd have changed into a black velvet dress for our Spanish dance. I was pretty angry by this time at the way Ruby had let me down. Josie did her best to soothe me and said she'd dance herself so that old Prestcott shouldn't get after us all. She went away and changed her dress and we went down and did a tango – exaggerated style and quite showy but not really too exhausting upon the ankles. Josie was very plucky about it – for it hurt her, I could see. After that she asked me to help her soothe the Jeffersons down. She said it was important. So, of course, I did what I could.'

Superintendent Harper nodded. He said:

'Thank you, Mr Starr.'

To himself he thought: 'It was important, all right! Fifty thousand pounds!'

He watched Raymond Starr as the latter moved gracefully away. He went down the steps of the terrace, picking up a bag of tennis balls and a racket on the way. Mrs Jefferson, also carrying a racket, joined him and they went towards the tennis courts.

'Excuse me, sir.'

Sergeant Higgins, rather breathless, stood at Harper's side.

The Superintendent, jerked from the train of thought he was following, looked startled.

'Message just come through for you from headquarters, sir. Labourer reported this morning saw glare as of fire. Half an hour ago they found a burnt-out car in a quarry. Venn's Quarry – about two miles from here. Traces of a charred body inside.'

A flush came over Harper's heavy features. He said:

'What's come to Glenshire? An epidemic of violence? Don't tell me we're going to have a Rouse case now!'

He asked: 'Could they get the number of the car?'

'No, sir. But we'll be able to identify it, of course, by the engine number. A Minoan 14, they think it is.'

CHAPTER 8

I

Sir Henry Clithering, as he passed through the lounge of the Majestic, hardly glanced at its occupants. His mind was preoccupied. Nevertheless, as is the way of life, something registered in his subconscious. It waited its time patiently.

Sir Henry was wondering as he went upstairs just what had induced the sudden urgency of his friend's message. Conway Jefferson was not the type of man who sent urgent summonses to anyone. Something quite out of the usual must have occurred, decided Sir Henry.

Jefferson wasted no time in beating about the bush. He said:

'Glad you've come. Edwards, get Sir Henry a drink. Sit down, man. You've not heard anything, I suppose? Nothing in the papers yet?'

Sir Henry shook his head, his curiosity aroused.

'What's the matter?'

'Murder's the matter. I'm concerned in it and so are your friends the Bantrys.'

'Arthur and Dolly Bantry?' Clithering sounded incredulous.

'Yes, you see, the body was found in their house.'

Clearly and succinctly Conway Jefferson ran through the facts. Sir Henry listened without interrupting. Both men were accustomed to grasping the gist of a matter. Sir Henry, during his term as Commissioner of the Metropolitan Police, had been renowned for his quick grip on essentials.

'It's an extraordinary business,' he commented when the other had finished. 'How do the Bantrys come into it, do you think?'

'That's what worries me. You see, Henry, it looks to me as though possibly the fact that I know them might have a bearing on the case. That's the only connection I can find. Neither of them, I gather, ever saw the girl before. That's what they say, and there's no reason to disbelieve them. It's most unlikely they *should* know her. Then isn't it possible that she was decoyed away and her body deliberately left in the house of friends of mine?'

Clithering said:

'I think that's far-fetched.'

'It's possible, though,' persisted the other.

'Yes, but unlikely. What do you want *me* to do?'

Conway Jefferson said bitterly:

'I'm an invalid. I disguise the fact – refuse to face it – but now it comes home to me. I can't go about as I'd like to, asking questions, looking into things. I've got to stay here meekly grateful for such scraps of information as the police are kind enough to dole out to me. Do you happen to know Melchett, by the way, the Chief Constable of Radfordshire?'

'Yes, I've met him.'

Something stirred in Sir Henry's brain. A face and figure noted unseeingly as he passed through the lounge. A straight-backed old lady whose face was familiar. It linked up with the last time he had seen Melchett. . . .

He said:

'Do you mean you want me to be a kind of amateur sleuth? That's not my line.'

Jefferson said:

'You're *not* an amateur, that's just it.'

'I'm not a professional any more. I'm on the retired list now.'

Jefferson said: 'That simplifies matters.'

'You mean that if I were still at Scotland Yard I couldn't butt in? That's perfectly true.'

'As it is,' said Jefferson, 'your experience qualifies you to take an interest in the case, and any co-operation you offer will be welcomed.'

Clithering said slowly:

'Etiquette permits, I agree. But what do you really want, Conway? To find out who killed this girl?'

'Just that.'

'You've no idea yourself?'

'None whatever.'

Sir Henry said slowly:

'You probably won't believe me, but you've got an expert at solving mysteries sitting downstairs in the lounge at this minute. Someone who's better at it than I am, and who in all probability *may* have some local dope.'

'What are you talking about?'

'Downstairs in the lounge, by the third pillar from the left, there sits an old lady with a sweet, placid, spinsterish face, and a mind that has plumbed the depths of human iniquity and taken it as all in the day's work. Her name's Miss Marple. She comes from the village of St Mary Mead, which is a mile and a half from Gossington, she's a friend of the Bantrys – and where crime is concerned she's the goods, Conway.'

Jefferson stared at him with thick, puckered brows. He said heavily:

'You're joking.'

'No, I'm not. You spoke of Melchett just now. The last time I saw Melchett there was a village tragedy. Girl supposed to have drowned herself. Police quite rightly suspected that it wasn't suicide, but murder. They thought they knew who did it. Along to me comes old Miss Marple, fluttering and dithering. She's afraid, she says, they'll hang the wrong person. She's got no evidence, but she knows who did do it. Hands me a piece of paper with a name written on it. And, by God, Jefferson, she was right!'

Conway Jefferson's brows came down lower than ever. He grunted disbelievingly:

'Woman's intuition, I suppose,' he said sceptically.

'No, she doesn't call it that. Specialized knowledge is her claim.'

'And what does that mean?'

'Well, you know, Jefferson, *we* use it in police work. We get a burglary and we usually know pretty well who did it – of the regular crowd, that is. We know the sort of burglar who acts in a particular sort of way. Miss Marple has an interesting, though occasionally trivial, series of parallels from village life.'

Jefferson said sceptically:

'What is she likely to know about a girl who's been brought up in a theatrical milieu and probably never been in a village in her life?'

'I think,' said Sir Henry Clithering firmly, 'that she might have ideas.'

II

Miss Marple flushed with pleasure as Sir Henry bore down upon her.

'Oh, Sir Henry, this is indeed a great piece of luck meeting you here.'

Sir Henry was gallant. He said:

'To me it is a great pleasure.'

Miss Marple murmured, flushing: 'So kind of you.'

'Are you staying here?'

'Well, as a matter of fact, we are.'

'We?'

'Mrs Bantry's here too.' She looked at him sharply. 'Have you heard yet? Yes, I can see you have. It is terrible, is it not?'

'What's Dolly Bantry doing here? Is her husband here too?'

'No. Naturally, they both reacted quite differently. Colonel Bantry, poor man, just shuts himself up in his study, or goes down to one of the farms, when anything like this happens. Like tortoises, you know, they draw their heads in and hope nobody will notice them. Dolly, of course, is *quite* different.'

'Dolly, in fact," said Sir Henry, who knew his old friend fairly well, 'is almost enjoying herself, eh?'

'Well – er – yes. Poor dear.'

'And she's brought you along to produce the rabbits out of the hat for her?'

Miss Marple said composedly:

'Dolly thought that a change of scene would be a good thing and she didn't want to come alone.' She met his eye and her own gently twinkled. 'But, of course, your way of describing it is quite true. It's rather embarrassing for me, because, of course, I am no use at all.'

'No ideas? No village parallels?'

'I don't know very much about it all yet.'

'I can remedy that, I think. I'm going to call you into consultation, Miss Marple.'

He gave a brief recital of the course of events. Miss Marple listened with keen interest.

'Poor Mr Jefferson,' she said. 'What a very sad story. These terrible accidents. To leave him alive, crippled, seems more cruel than if he had been killed too.'

'Yes, indeed. That's why all his friends admire him so much for the resolute way he's gone on, conquering pain and grief and physical disabilities.'

'Yes, it is splendid.'

'The only thing I can't understand is this sudden outpouring of affection for this girl. She may, of course, have had some remarkable qualities.'

'Probably not,' said Miss Marple placidly.

'You don't think so?'

'I don't think her qualities entered into it.'

Sir Henry said:

'He isn't just a nasty old man, you know.'

'Oh, no, no!' Miss Marple got quite pink. 'I wasn't implying that for a minute. What I was trying to say was – very badly, I know – that he was just looking for a nice bright girl to take his dead daughter's place – and then this girl saw her opportunity and played it for all she was worth! That sounds rather uncharitable, I know, but I have seen so many cases of the kind. The young maid-servant at Mr Harbottle's for instance. A *very* ordinary girl, but quiet with nice manners. His sister was called away to nurse a dying relative and when she got back she found the girl completely above herself, sitting down in the drawing-room laughing and talking and not wearing her cap or apron. Miss Harbottle spoke to her very sharply and the girl was impertinent, and then old Mr Harbottle left her quite dumbfounded by saying that he thought she had kept house for him long enough and that he was making other arrangements.

'Such a scandal as it created in the village, but poor Miss Harbottle had to go and live *most* uncomfortably in rooms in Eastbourne. People *said* things, of course, but I believe there was no familiarity of any kind – it was simply that the old man found it much pleasanter to have a young, cheerful girl telling him how clever and amusing he was than to have his sister continually pointing out his faults to him, even if she *was* a good economical manager.'

There was a moment's pause, and then Miss Marple resumed.

'And there was Mr Badger who had the chemist's shop. Made a lot of fuss over the young lady who worked in his toilet section. Told his wife they must look on her as a daughter and have her to live in the house. Mrs Badger didn't see it that way at all.'

Sir Henry said: 'If she'd only been a girl in his own rank of life – a friend's child –'

Miss Marple interrupted him.

'Oh! but that wouldn't have been nearly as satisfactory from his point of view. It's like King Cophetua and the beggar maid. If you're really rather a lonely, tired old man, and if, perhaps, your own family have been neglecting you' – she paused for a second – 'well, to befriend someone who will be overwhelmed with your magnificence – (to put it rather melodramatically, but I hope you see what I mean) – well, that's much more interesting. It makes you feel a much greater person – a beneficent monarch! The recipient is more likely to be dazzled, and that, of course, is a pleasant feeling for you.' She paused and said: 'Mr Badger, you know, bought the girl in his shop some really fantastic presents, a diamond bracelet and a most expensive radio-gramophone. Took out a lot of his savings to do it. However, Mrs Badger, who was a much more astute woman than poor Miss Harbottle (marriage, of course, *helps*), took the trouble to find out a few things. And when Mr Badger discovered that the girl was carrying on with a *very* undesirable young man connected with the racecourses, and had actually pawned the bracelet to give him the money – well, he was completely disgusted and the affair passed over quite safely. And he gave Mrs Badger a diamond ring the following Christmas.'

Her pleasant, shrewd eyes met Sir Henry's. He wondered if what she had been saying was intended as a hint. He said:

'Are you suggesting that if there had been a young man in Ruby Keene's life, my friend's attitude towards her might have altered?'

'It probably would, you know. I dare say, in a year or two, he might have liked to arrange for her marriage himself – though more likely he wouldn't – gentlemen are usually rather selfish. But I certainly think that if Ruby Keene had had a young man she'd have been careful to keep very quiet about it.'

'And the young man might have resented that?'

'I suppose that *is* the most plausible solution. It struck me, you know, that her cousin, the young woman who was at Gossington this morning, looked definitely *angry* with the dead girl. What you've told me explains *why*. No doubt she was looking forward to doing very well out of the business.'

'Rather a cold-blooded character, in fact?'

'That's too harsh a judgement, perhaps. The poor thing has had to earn her living, and you can't expect her to sentimentalize because a well-to-do man and woman – as you have described Mr Gaskell and Mrs Jefferson – are going to be done out of a further large sum of money to which they have really no particular moral right. I should say Miss Turner was a hard-headed, ambitious young woman, with a good temper and considerable *joie de vivre*. A little,' added Miss Marple, 'like Jessie Golden, the baker's daughter.'

'What happened to her?' asked Sir Henry.

'She trained as a nursery governess and married the son of the house, who was home on leave from India. Made him a very good wife, I believe.'

Sir Henry pulled himself clear of these fascinating side issues. He said:

'Is there any reason, do you think, why my friend Conway Jefferson should suddenly have developed this "Cophetua complex," if you like to call it that?'

'There might have been.'

'In what way?'

Miss Marple said, hesitating a little:

'I should think – it's only a suggestion, of course – that perhaps his son-in-law and daughter-in-law *might* have wanted to get married again.'

'Surely he couldn't have objected to that?'

'Oh, no, not *objected*. But, you see, you must look at it from *his* point of view. He had a terrible shock and loss – so had they. The three bereaved people live together and the *link* between them is the loss they have all sustained. But Time, as my dear mother used to say, is a great healer. Mr Gaskell and Mrs Jefferson are young. Without knowing it themselves, they may have begun to feel restless, to resent the bonds that tied them to their past sorrow. And so, feeling like that, old Mr Jefferson would have become conscious of a sudden lack of sympathy without knowing its cause. It's usually that. Gentlemen so *easily* feel neglected. With Mr Harbottle it was Miss Harbottle going away. And with the Badgers it was Mrs Badger taking such an interest in Spiritualism and always going out to séances.'

'I must say,' said Sir Henry ruefully, 'that I do dislike the way you reduce us all to a General Common Denominator.'

Miss Marple shook her head sadly.

'Human nature is very much the same anywhere, Sir Henry.'

Sir Henry said distastefully:

'Mr Harbottle! Mr Badger! And poor Conway! I hate to intrude the personal note, but have you any parallel for *my* humble self in your village?'

'Well, of course, there is Briggs.'

'Who's Briggs?'

'He was the head gardener up at Old Hall. *Quite* the best man they ever had. Knew *exactly* when the under-gardeners were slacking off – quite uncanny it was! He managed with only three men and a boy and the place was kept better than it had been with six. And took several firsts with his sweet peas. He's retired now.'

'Like me,' said Sir Henry.

'But he still does a little jobbing – if he likes the people.'

'Ah,' said Sir Henry. 'Again like me. That's what I'm doing now – jobbing – to help an old friend.'

'Two old friends.'

'Two?' Sir Henry looked a little puzzled.

Miss Marple said:

'I suppose you meant Mr Jefferson. But I wasn't thinking of him. I was thinking of Colonel and Mrs Bantry.'

'Yes – yes – I see –' He asked sharply: 'Was that why you alluded to Dolly Bantry as "poor dear" at the beginning of our conversation?'

'Yes. She hasn't begun to realize things yet. *I* know because I've had more experience. You see, Sir Henry, it seems to me that there's a great possibility of this crime being the kind of crime that never *does* get solved. Like the Brighton trunk murders. But if that happens it will be absolutely disastrous for the Bantrys. Colonel Bantry, like nearly all retired military men, is really *abnormally* sensitive. He reacts very quickly to public opinion. He won't notice it for some time, and then it will begin to go home to him. A slight here, and a snub there, and invitations that are refused, and excuses that are made – and then, little by little, it will dawn upon him and he'll retire into his shell and get terribly morbid and miserable.'

'Let me be sure I understand you rightly, Miss Marple. You mean that, because the body was found in his house, people will think that *he* had something to do with it?'

'Of course they will! I've no doubt they're saying so already. They'll say so more and more. And people will cold-shoulder the Bantrys and avoid them. That's why the truth has got to be found out and why I was willing to come here with Mrs Bantry. An open accusation is one thing – and quite easy for a soldier to meet. He's indignant and he has a chance of fighting. But this other *whispering* business will break him – will break them both. So you see, Sir Henry, we've *got* to find out the truth.'

Sir Henry said:

'Any ideas as to why the body should have been found in his house? There must be an explanation of that. Some connection.'

'Oh, of course.'

'The girl was last seen here about twenty minutes to eleven. By midnight, according to the medical evidence, she was dead. Gossington's about eighteen miles from here. Good road for sixteen of those miles until one turns off the main road. A powerful car could do it in well under half an hour. Practically *any* car could average thirty-five. But why anyone should either kill her here and take her body out to Gossington or should take her out to Gossington and strangle her there, I don't know.'

'Of course you don't, because it didn't happen.'

'Do you mean that she was strangled by some fellow who took her out in a car and he then decided to push her into the first likely house in the neighbourhood?'

'I don't think anything of the kind. I think there was a very careful plan made. What happened was that the plan went wrong.'

Sir Henry stared at her.

'Why did the plan go wrong?'

Miss Marple said rather apologetically:

'Such curious things happen, don't they? If I were to say that this particular plan went wrong because human beings are so much more vulnerable and sensitive than anyone thinks, it wouldn't sound sensible, would it? But that's what I believe – and –'

She broke off. 'Here's Mrs Bantry now.'

CHAPTER 9

Mrs Bantry was with Adelaide Jefferson. The former came up to Sir Henry and exclaimed: '*You?*'

'I, myself.' He took both her hands and pressed them warmly. 'I can't tell you how distressed I am at all this, Mrs B.'

Mrs Bantry said mechanically:

'*Don't call me Mrs B!*' and went on: 'Arthur isn't here. He's taking it all rather seriously. Miss Marple and I have come here to sleuth. Do you know Mrs Jefferson?'

'Yes, of course.'

He shook hands. Adelaide Jefferson said:

'Have you seen my father-in-law?'

'Yes, I have.'

'I'm glad. We're anxious about him. It was a terrible shock.'

Mrs Bantry said:

'Let's come out on the terrace and have drinks and talk about it all.'

The four of them went out and joined Mark Gaskell, who was sitting at the extreme end of the terrace by himself.

After a few desultory remarks and the arrival of the drinks Mrs Bantry plunged straight into the subject with her usual zest for direct action.

'We can talk about it, can't we?' she said. 'I mean, we're all old friends – except Miss Marple and she knows all about crime. And she wants to help.'

Mark Gaskell looked at Miss Marple in a somewhat puzzled fashion. He said doubtfully:

'Do you – er – write detective stories?'

The most unlikely people, he knew, wrote detective stories. And Miss Marple, in her old-fashioned spinster's clothes, looked a singularly unlikely person.

'Oh no, I'm not clever enough for *that*.'

'She's wonderful,' said Mrs Bantry impatiently. 'I can't explain now, but she is. Now, Addie, I want to know all about things. What was she really like, this girl?'

'Well –' Adelaide Jefferson paused, glanced across at Mark, and half laughed. She said: 'You're so direct.'

'Did you like her?'

'No, of course I didn't.'

'What was she really like?' Mrs Bantry shifted her enquiry to Mark Gaskell. Mark said deliberately:

'Common or garden gold-digger. And she knew her stuff. She'd got her hooks into Jeff all right.'

Both of them called their father-in-law Jeff.

Sir Henry thought, looking disapprovingly at Mark:

'Indiscreet fellow. Shouldn't be so outspoken.'

He had always disapproved a little of Mark Gaskell. The man had charm but he was unreliable – talked too much, was occasionally boastful – not quite to be trusted, Sir Henry thought. He had sometimes wondered if Conway Jefferson thought so too.

'But couldn't you *do* something about it?' demanded Mrs Bantry.

Mark said dryly:

'We might have – if we'd realized it in time.'

He shot a glance at Adelaide and she coloured faintly. There had been reproach in that glance.

She said:

'Mark thinks I ought to have seen what was coming.'

'You left the old boy alone too much, Addie. Tennis lessons and all the rest of it.'

'Well, I had to have some exercise.' She spoke apologetically. 'Anyway, I never dreamed –'

'No,' said Mark, 'neither of us ever dreamed. Jeff has always been such a sensible, level-headed old boy.'

Miss Marple made a contribution to the conversation.

'Gentlemen,' she said with her old maid's way of referring to the opposite sex as though it were a species of wild animal, 'are frequently not as level-headed as they seem.'

'I'll say you're right,' said Mark. 'Unfortunately, Miss Marple, we didn't realize that. We wondered what the old boy saw in that rather insipid and meretricious little bag of tricks. But we were pleased for him to be kept happy and amused. We thought there was no harm in her. No harm in her! I wish I'd wrung her neck!'

'Mark,' said Addie, 'you really *must* be careful what you say.'

He grinned at her engagingly.

'I suppose I must. Otherwise people will think I actually *did* wring her neck. Oh well, I suppose I'm under suspicion, anyway. If anyone had an interest in seeing that girl dead it was Addie and myself.'

'Mark,' cried Mrs Jefferson, half laughing and half angry, 'you really *mustn't*!'

'All right, all right,' said Mark Gaskell pacifically. 'But I do like speaking my mind. Fifty thousand pounds our esteemed father-in-law was proposing to settle upon that half-baked nitwitted little slypuss.'

'Mark, you mustn't – she's dead.'

'Yes, she's dead, poor little devil. And after all, why shouldn't she use the weapons that Nature gave her? Who am I to judge? Done plenty of rotten things myself in my life. No, let's say Ruby was entitled to plot and scheme and we were mugs not to have tumbled to her game sooner.'

Sir Henry said:

'What did you say when Conway told you he proposed to adopt the girl?'

Mark thrust out his hands.

'What could we say? Addie, always the little lady, retained her self-control admirably. Put a brave face upon it. I endeavoured to follow her example.'

'*I* should have made a fuss!' said Mrs Bantry.

'Well, frankly speaking, we weren't entitled to make a fuss. It was Jeff's money. We weren't his flesh and blood. He'd always been damned good to us. There was nothing for it but to bite on the bullet.' He added reflectively: 'But we didn't love little Ruby.'

Adelaide Jefferson said:

'If only it had been some other kind of girl. Jeff had two godchildren, you know. If it had been one of them – well, one would have *understood* it.' She added, with a shade of resentment: 'And Jeff's always seemed so fond of Peter.'

'Of course,' said Mrs Bantry. 'I always have known Peter was your first husband's child – but I'd quite forgotten it. I've always thought of him as Mr Jefferson's grandson.'

'So have I,' said Adelaide. Her voice held a note that made Miss Marple turn in her chair and look at her.

'It was Josie's fault,' said Mark. 'Josie brought her here.'

Adelaide said:

'Oh, but surely you don't think it was deliberate, do you? Why, you've always liked Josie so much.'

'Yes, I did like her. I thought she was a good sport.'

'It was sheer accident her bringing the girl down.'

'Josie's got a good head on her shoulders, my girl.'

'Yes, but she couldn't foresee —'

Mark said:

'No, she couldn't. I admit it. I'm not really accusing her of planning the whole thing. But I've no doubt she saw which way the wind was blowing long before we did and kept very quiet about it.'

Adelaide said with a sigh:

'I suppose one can't blame her for that.'

Mark said:

'Oh, we can't blame anyone for anything!'

Mrs Bantry asked:

'Was Ruby Keene very pretty?'

Mark stared at her. 'I thought you'd seen —'

Mrs Bantry said hastily:

'Oh yes, I saw her — her body. But she'd been strangled, you know, and one couldn't tell —' She shivered.

Mark said, thoughtfully:

'I don't think she was really pretty at all. She certainly wouldn't have been without any make-up. A thin ferrety little face, not much chin, teeth running down her throat, nondescript sort of nose —'

'It sounds revolting,' said Mrs Bantry.

'Oh no, she wasn't. As I say, with make-up she managed to give quite an effect of good looks, don't you think so, Addie?'

'Yes, rather chocolate-box, pink and white business. She had nice blue eyes.'

'Yes, innocent baby stare, and the heavily-blacked lashes brought out the blueness. Her hair was bleached, of course. It's true, when I come to think of it, that in colouring — artificial colouring, anyway — she had a kind of spurious resemblance to Rosamund — my wife, you know. I dare say that's what attracted the old man's attention to her.'

He sighed.

'Well, it's a bad business. The awful thing is that Addie and I can't help being glad, really, that she's dead —'

He quelled a protest from his sister-in-law.

'It's no good, Addie; I know what you feel. I feel the same. And I'm not going to pretend! But, at the same time, if you know what I mean, I really am most awfully concerned for Jeff about the whole business. It's hit him very hard. I –'

He stopped, and stared towards the doors leading out of the lounge on to the terrace.

'Well, well – see who's here. What an unscrupulous woman you are, Addie.'

Mrs Jefferson looked over her shoulder, uttered an exclamation and got up, a slight colour rising in her face. She walked quickly along the terrace and went up to a tall middle-aged man with a thin brown face, who was looking uncertainly about him.

Mrs Bantry said: 'Isn't that Hugo McLean?'

Mark Gaskell said:

'Hugo McLean it is. Alias William Dobbin.'

Mrs Bantry murmured:

'He's very faithful, isn't he?'

'Dog-like devotion,' said Mark. 'Addie's only got to whistle and Hugo comes trotting from any odd corner of the globe. Always hopes that some day she'll marry him. I dare say she will.'

Miss Marple looked beamingly after them. She said:

'I see. A romance?'

'One of the good old-fashioned kind,' Mark assured her. 'It's been going on for years. Addie's that kind of woman.'

He added meditatively: 'I suppose Addie telephoned him this morning. She didn't tell me she had.'

Edwards came discreetly along the terrace and paused at Mark's elbow.

'Excuse me, sir. Mr Jefferson would like you to come up.'

'I'll come at once.' Mark sprang up.

He nodded to them, said: 'See you later,' and went off.

Sir Henry leant forward to Miss Marple. He said:

'Well, what do you think of the principal beneficiaries of the crime?'

Miss Marple said thoughtfully, looking at Adelaide Jefferson as she stood talking to her old friend:

'I should think, you know, that she was a very devoted mother.'

'Oh, she is,' said Mrs Bantry. 'She's simply devoted to Peter.'

'She's the kind of woman,' said Miss Marple, 'that everyone likes. The kind of woman that could go on getting married again and again. I don't mean a *man's* woman – that's quite different.'

'I know what you mean,' said Sir Henry.

'What you both mean,' said Mrs Bantry, 'is that she's a good listener.'

Sir Henry laughed. He said:

'And Mark Gaskell?'

'Ah,' said Miss Marple, 'he's a downy fellow.'

'Village parallel, please?'

'Mr Cargill, the builder. He bluffed a lot of people into having things done to their houses they never meant to do. And how he charged them for it! But he could always explain his bill away plausibly. A downy fellow. He married money. So did Mr Gaskell, I understand.'

'You don't like him.'

'Yes, I do. Most women would. But he can't take me in. He's a very attractive person, I think. But a little unwise, perhaps, to *talk* as much as he does.'

'Unwise is the word,' said Sir Henry. 'Mark will get himself into trouble if he doesn't look out.'

A tall dark young man in white flannels came up the steps to the terrace and paused just for a minute, watching Adelaide Jefferson and Hugo McLean.

'And that,' said Sir Henry obligingly, 'is X, whom we might describe as an interested party. He is the tennis and dancing pro. – Raymond Starr, Ruby Keene's partner.'

Miss Marple looked at him with interest. She said:

'He's very nice looking, isn't he?'

'I suppose so.'

'Don't be absurd, Sir Henry,' said Mrs Bantry, 'there's no supposing about it. He *is* good looking.'

Miss Marple murmured:

'Mrs Jefferson has been taking tennis lessons, I think she said.'

'Do you mean anything by that, Jane, or don't you?'

Miss Marple had no chance of replying to this downright question. Young Peter Carmody came across the terrace and joined them. He addressed himself to Sir Henry:

'I say, are you a detective, too? I saw you talking to the Superintendent – the fat one is a superintendent, isn't he?'

'Quite right, my son.'

'And somebody told me you were a frightfully important detective from London. The head of Scotland Yard or something like that.'

'The head of Scotland Yard is usually a complete dud in books, isn't he?'

'Oh no, not nowadays. Making fun of the police is very old-fashioned. Do you know who did the murder yet?'

'Not yet, I'm afraid.'

'Are you enjoying this very much, Peter?' asked Mrs Bantry.

'Well, I am, rather. It makes a change, doesn't it? I've been hunting round to see if I could find any clues, but I haven't been lucky. I've got a souvenir, though. Would you like to see it? Fancy, mother wanted me to throw it away. I do think one's parents are rather trying sometimes.'

He produced from his pocket a small matchbox. Pushing it open, he disclosed the precious contents.

'See, *it's a fingernail. Her fingernail!* I'm going to label it *Fingernail of the Murdered Woman* and take it back to school. It's a good souvenir, don't you think?'

'Where did you get it?' asked Miss Marple.

'Well, it was a bit of luck, really. Because, of course, I didn't know she was going to be murdered *then*. It was before dinner last night. Ruby caught her nail in Josie's shawl and it tore it. Mums cut it off for her and gave it to me and said put it in the wastepaper basket, and I meant to, but I put it in my pocket instead, and this morning I remembered and looked to see if it was still there and it was, so now I've got it as a souvenir.'

'Disgusting,' said Mrs Bantry.

Peter said politely: 'Oh, do you think so?'

'Got any other souvenirs?' asked Sir Henry.

'Well, I don't know. I've got something that might be.'

'Explain yourself, young man.'

Peter looked at him thoughtfully. Then he pulled out an envelope. From the inside of it he extracted a piece of brown tapey substance.

'It's a bit of that chap George Bartlett's shoe-lace,' he explained. 'I saw his shoes outside the door this morning and I bagged a bit just in case.'

'In case what?'

'In case he should be the murderer, of course. He was the last person to see her and that's always frightfully suspicious, you know. Is it nearly dinner-time, do you think? I'm frightfully hungry. It always seems such a long time between tea and dinner. Hallo, there's Uncle Hugo. I didn't know mums had asked *him* to come down. I suppose she sent for him. She always does if she's in a jam. Here's Josie coming. Hi, Josie!'

Josephine Turner, coming along the terrace, stopped and looked rather startled to see Mrs Bantry and Miss Marple.

Mrs Bantry said pleasantly:

'How d'you do, Miss Turner. We've come to do a bit of sleuthing!'

Josie cast a guilty glance round. She said, lowering her voice:

'It's awful. Nobody knows yet. I mean, it isn't in the papers yet. I suppose everyone will be asking me questions and it's so awkward. I don't know what I ought to say.'

Her glance went rather wistfully towards Miss Marple, who said:

'Yes, it will be a very difficult situation for you, I'm afraid.'

Josie warmed to this sympathy.

'You see, Mr Prestcott said to me: "Don't talk about it." And that's all very well, but everyone is sure to ask me, and you can't offend people, can you? Mr Prestcott said he hoped I'd feel able to carry on as usual – and he wasn't very nice about it, so of course I want to do my best. And I really don't see why it should all be blamed on me.'

Sir Henry said:

'Do you mind me asking you a frank question, Miss Turner?'

'Oh, do ask me anything you like,' said Josie, a little insincerely.

'Has there been any unpleasantness between you and Mrs Jefferson and Mr Gaskell over all this?'

'Over the murder, do you mean?'

'No, I don't mean the murder.'

Josie stood twisting her fingers together. She said rather sullenly:

'Well, there has and there hasn't, if you know what I mean. Neither of them have *said* anything. But I think they blamed it on me – Mr Jefferson taking such a fancy to Ruby, I mean. It wasn't my fault, though, was it? These things happen, and I never dreamt of such a thing happening beforehand, not for a moment. I – I was quite dumbfounded.'

Her words rang out with what seemed undeniable sincerity.

Sir Henry said kindly:

'I'm quite sure you were. But once it *had* happened?'

Josie's chin went up.

'Well, it was a piece of luck, wasn't it? Everyone's got the right to have a piece of luck sometimes.'

She looked from one to the other of them in a slightly defiant questioning manner and then went on across the terrace and into the hotel.

Peter said judicially:

'I don't think *she* did it.'

Miss Marple murmured:

'It's interesting, that piece of finger-nail. It had been worrying me, you know – how to account for her nails.'

'Nails?' asked Sir Henry.

'The dead girl's nails,' explained Mrs Bantry. 'They were quite *short*, and now that Jane says so, of course it *was* a little unlikely. A girl like that usually has absolute talons.'

Miss Marple said:

'But of course if she tore one off, then she might clip the others close, so as to match. Did they find nail parings in her room, I wonder?'

Sir Henry looked at her curiously. He said:

'I'll ask Superintendent Harper when he gets back.'

'Back from where?' asked Mrs Bantry. 'He hasn't gone over to Gossington, has he?'

Sir Henry said gravely:

'No. There's been another tragedy. Blazing car in a quarry –'

Miss Marple caught her breath.

'Was there someone in the car?'

'I'm afraid so – yes.'

Miss Marple said thoughtfully:

'I expect that will be the Girl Guide who's missing – Patience – no, Pamela Reeves.'

Sir Henry stared at her.

'Now why on earth do you think that, Miss Marple?'

Miss Marple got rather pink.

'Well, it was given out on the wireless that she was missing from her home – since last night. And her home was Daneleigh Vale; that's not very far from here. And she was last seen at the Girl-Guide Rally up on Danebury Downs. That's very close indeed. In fact, she'd have to pass through Danemouth to get home. So it does rather fit in, doesn't it? I mean, it looks as though she might have seen – or perhaps heard – something that no one was supposed to see and hear. If so, of course, she'd be a source of danger to the murderer and she'd have to be – removed. Two things like that *must* be connected, don't you think?'

Sir Henry said, his voice dropping a little:

'You think – a second murder?'

'Why not?' Her quiet placid gaze met his. 'When anyone has committed one murder, they don't shrink from another, do they? Nor even from a third.'

'A third? You don't think there will be a *third* murder?'

'I think it's just possible. . . . Yes, I think it's highly possible.'

'Miss Marple,' said Sir Henry, 'you frighten me. Do you know who is going to be murdered?'

Miss Marple said: 'I've a very good idea.'

CHAPTER 10

I

Superintendent Harper stood looking at the charred and twisted heap of metal. A burnt-up car was always a revolting object, even without the additional gruesome burden of a charred and blackened corpse.

Venn's Quarry was a remote spot, far from any human habitation. Though actually only two miles as the crow flies from Danemouth, the approach to it was by one of those narrow, twisted, rutted roads, little more than a cart track, and which led nowhere except to the quarry itself. It was a long time now since the quarry had been worked, and the only people who came along the lane were the casual visitors in search of blackberries. As a spot to dispose of a car it was ideal. The car need not have been found for weeks but for the accident of the glow in the sky having been seen by Albert Biggs, a labourer, on his way to work.

Albert Biggs was still on the scene, though all he had to tell had been heard some time ago, but he continued to repeat the thrilling story with such embellishments as occurred to him.

'Why, dang my eyes, I said, whatever be that? Proper glow it was, up in the sky. Might be a bonfire, I says, but who'd be having bonfire over to Venn's Quarry? No, I says, 'tis some mighty big fire, to be sure. But whatever would it be, I says? There's no house or farm to that direction. 'Tis over by Venn's, I says, that's where it is, to be sure. Didn't rightly know what I ought to do about it, but seeing as Constable Gregg comes along just then on his bicycle, I tells him about it. 'Twas all died down by then, but I tells him just where 'twere. 'Tis over that direction, I says. Big glare in the sky, I says. Mayhap as it's a rick, I says. One of them tramps, as likely as not, set alight of it. But I did never think as how it might be a car – far less as someone was being burnt up alive in it. 'Tis a terrible tragedy, to be sure.'

The Glenshire police had been busy. Cameras had clicked and the position of the charred body had been carefully noted before the police surgeon had started his own investigation.

The latter came over now to Harper, dusting black ash off his hands, his lips set grimly together.

'A pretty thorough job,' he said. 'Part of one foot and the shoe are about all that has escaped. Personally I myself couldn't say if the body was a man's or a woman's at the moment, though we'll get some indication from the bones, I expect. But the shoe is one of the black strapped affairs – the kind schoolgirls wear.'

'There's a schoolgirl missing from the next county,' said Harper 'quite close to here. Girl of sixteen or so.'

'Then it's probably her,' said the doctor. 'Poor kid.'

Harper said uneasily: 'She wasn't alive when –'

'No, no, I don't think so. No signs of her having tried to get out. Body was just slumped down on the seat – with the foot sticking out. She was dead when she was put there, I should say. Then the car was set fire to in order to try and get rid of the evidence.'

He paused, and asked:

'Want me any longer?'

'I don't think so, thank you.'

'Right, I'll be off.'

He strode away to his car. Harper went over to where one of his sergeants, a man who specialized in car cases, was busy.

The latter looked up.

'Quite a clear case, sir. Petrol poured over the car and the whole thing deliberately set light to. There are three empty cans in the hedge over there.'

A little farther away another man was carefully arranging small objects picked out of the wreckage. There was a scorched black leather shoe and with it some scraps of scorched and blackened material. As Harper approached, his subordinate looked up and exclaimed:

'Look at this, sir. This seems to clinch it.'

Harper took the small object in his hand. He said:

'Button from a Girl Guide's uniform?'

'Yes, sir.'

'Yes,' said Harper, 'that does seem to settle it.'

A decent, kindly man, he felt slightly sick. First Ruby Keene and now this child, Pamela Reeves.

He said to himself, as he had said before:

'What's come to Glenshire?'

His next move was first to ring up his own Chief Constable, and afterwards to get in touch with Colonel Melchett. The disappearance of Pamela Reeves had taken place in Radfordshire though her body had been found in Glenshire.

The next task set him was not a pleasant one. He had to break the news to Pamela Reeves's father and mother. . . .

II

Superintendent Harper looked up consideringly at the façade of Braeside as he rang the front door bell.

Neat little villa, nice garden of about an acre and a half. The sort of place that had been built fairly freely all over the countryside in the last twenty years. Retired army men, retired civil servants – that type. Nice decent folk; the worst you could say of them was that they might be a bit dull. Spent as much money as they could afford on their children's education. Not the kind of people you associated with tragedy. And now tragedy had come to them. He sighed.

He was shown at once into a lounge where a stiff man with a grey moustache and a woman whose eyes were red with weeping both sprang up. Mrs Reeves cried out eagerly:

'You have some news of Pamela?'

Then she shrank back, as though the Superintendent's commiserating glance had been a blow.

Harper said:

'I'm afraid you must prepare yourself for bad news.'

'Pamela –' faltered the woman.

Major Reeves said sharply:

'Something's happened – to the child?'

'Yes, sir.'

'Do you mean she's dead?'

Mrs Reeves burst out:

'Oh no, no,' and broke into a storm of weeping. Major Reeves put his arm round his wife and drew her to him. His lips trembled but he looked enquiringly at Harper, who bent his head.

'An accident?'

'Not exactly, Major Reeves. She was found in a burnt-out car which had been abandoned in a quarry.'

'In a car? In a quarry?'

His astonishment was evident.

Mrs Reeves broke down altogether and sank down on the sofa, sobbing violently.

Superintendent Harper said:

'If you'd like me to wait a few minutes?'

Major Reeves said sharply:

'What does this mean? Foul play?'

'That's what it looks like, sir. That's why I'd like to ask you some questions if it isn't too trying for you.'

'No, no, you're quite right. No time must be lost if what you suggest is true. But I can't believe it. Who would want to harm a child like Pamela?'

Harper said stolidly:

'You've already reported to your local police the circumstances of your daughter's disappearance. She left here to attend a Guides' rally and you expected her home for supper. That is right?'

'Yes.'

'She was to return by bus?'

'Yes.'

'I understand that, according to the story of her fellow Guides, when the rally was over Pamela said she was going into Danemouth to Woolworth's, and would catch a later bus home. That strikes you as quite a normal proceeding?'

'Oh yes, Pamela was very fond of going to Woolworth's. She often went into Danemouth to shop. The bus goes from the main road, only about a quarter of a mile from here.'

'And she had no other plans, so far as you know?'

'None.'

'She was not meeting anybody in Danemouth?'

'No, I'm sure she wasn't. She would have mentioned it if so. We expected her back for supper. That's why, when it got so late and she hadn't turned up, we rang up the police. It wasn't like her not to come home.'

'Your daughter had no undesirable friends – that is, friends that you didn't approve of?'

'No, there was never any trouble of that kind.'

Mrs Reeves said tearfully:

'Pam was just a child. She was very young for her age. She liked games and all that. She wasn't precocious in any way.'

'Do you know a Mr George Bartlett who is staying at the Majestic Hotel in Danemouth?'

Major Reeves stared.

'Never heard of him.'

'You don't think your daughter knew him?'

'I'm quite sure she didn't.'

He added sharply: 'How does he come into it?'

'He's the owner of the Minoan 14 car in which your daughter's body was found.'

Mrs Reeves cried: 'But then he must –'

Harper said quickly:

'He reported his car missing early today. It was in the courtyard of the Majestic Hotel at lunch time yesterday. Anybody might have taken the car.'

'But didn't someone see who took it?'

The Superintendent shook his head.

'Dozens of cars going in and out all day. And a Minoan 14 is one of the commonest makes.'

Mrs Reeves cried:

'But aren't you doing something? Aren't you trying to find the – the devil who did this? My little girl – oh, my little girl! She wasn't burnt alive, was she? Oh, Pam, Pam . . . !'

'She didn't suffer, Mrs Reeves. I assure you she was already dead when the car was set alight.'

Reeves asked stiffly:

'How was she killed?'

Harper gave him a significant glance.

'We don't know. The fire has destroyed all evidence of that kind.'

He turned to the distraught woman on the sofa.

'Believe me, Mrs Reeves, we're doing everything we can. It's a matter of checking up. Sooner or later we shall find someone who saw your daughter in Danemouth yesterday, and saw whom she was with. It all takes time, you know. We shall have dozens, hundreds of reports coming in about a Girl Guide who was seen here, there, and everywhere. It's a matter of selection and of patience – but we shall find out the truth in the end, never you fear.'

Mrs Reeves asked:

'Where – where is she? Can I go to her?'

Again Superintendent Harper caught the husband's eye. He said:

'The medical officer is attending to all that. I'd suggest that your husband comes with me now and attends to all the formalities. In the meantime, try and recollect anything Pamela may have said – something, perhaps, that you didn't pay attention to at the time but which might throw some light upon things. You know what I mean – just some chance word or phrase. That's the best way you can help us.'

As the two men went towards the door, Reeves said, pointing to a photograph:

'There she is.'

Harper looked at it attentively. It was a hockey group. Reeves pointed out Pamela in the centre of the team.

'A nice kid,' Harper thought, as he looked at the earnest face of the pigtailed girl.

His mouth set in a grim line as he thought of the charred body in the car.

He vowed to himself that the murder of Pamela Reeves should not remain one of Glenshire's unsolved mysteries.

Ruby Keene, so he admitted privately, might have asked for what was coming to her, but Pamela Reeves was quite another story. A nice kid, if he ever saw one. He'd not rest until he'd hunted down the man or woman who'd killed her.

CHAPTER 11

A day or two later Colonel Melchett and Superintendent Harper looked at each other across the former's big desk. Harper had come over to Much Benham for a consultation.

Melchett said gloomily:

'Well, we know where we are – or rather where we aren't!'

'Where we aren't expresses it better, sir.'

'We've got two deaths to take into account,' said Melchett. 'Two murders, Ruby Keene and the child Pamela Reeves. Not much to identify her by, poor kid, but enough. That shoe that escaped burning has been identified positively as hers by her father, and there's this button from her Girl Guide uniform. A fiendish business, Superintendent.'

Superintendent Harper said very quietly:

'I'll say you're right, sir.'

'I'm glad it's quite certain she was dead before the car was set on fire. The way she was lying, thrown across the seat, shows that. Probably knocked on the head, poor kid.'

'Or strangled, perhaps,' said Harper.

Melchett looked at him sharply.

'You think so?'

'Well, sir, there are murderers like that.'

'I know. I've seen the parents – the poor girl's mother's beside herself. Damned painful, the whole thing. The point for us to settle is – are the two murders connected?'

'I'd say definitely yes.'

'So would I.'

The Superintendent ticked off the points on his fingers.

'Pamela Reeves attended rally of Girl Guides on Danebury Downs. Stated by companions to be normal and cheerful. Did not return with three companions by the bus to Medchester. Said to them that she was going into Danemouth to Woolworth's and would take the bus home from there. The main road into Danemouth from the downs does a big round inland. Pamela Reeves took a short-cut over two fields and a footpath and lane which would bring her into Danemouth near the Majestic Hotel. The lane, in fact, actually passes the hotel on the west side. It's possible, therefore, that she overheard or saw something – something concerning Ruby Keene – which would have proved dangerous to the murderer – say, for instance, that she heard him arranging to meet Ruby Keene at eleven that evening. He realizes that this schoolgirl has overheard, and he has to silence her.'

Colonel Melchett said:

'That's presuming, Harper, that the Ruby Keene crime was premeditated – not spontaneous.'

Superintendent Harper agreed.

'I believe it was, sir. It looks as though it would be the other way – sudden violence, a fit of passion or jealousy – but I'm beginning to think that that's not so. I don't see otherwise how you can account for the death of the Reeves child. If she was a witness of the actual crime, it would be late at night, round about eleven p.m., and what would she be doing round about the Majestic at that time? Why, at nine o'clock her parents were getting anxious because she hadn't returned.'

'The alternative is that she went to meet someone in Danemouth unknown to her family and friends, and that her death is quite unconnected with the other death.'

'Yes, sir, and I don't believe that's so. Look how even the old lady, old Miss Marple, tumbled to it at once that there was a connection. She asked at once if the body in the burnt car was the body of the missing Girl Guide. Very smart old lady, that. These old ladies are sometimes. Shrewd, you know. Put their fingers on the vital spot.'

'Miss Marple has done that more than once,' said Colonel Melchett dryly.

'And besides, sir, there's the car. That seems to me to link up her death definitely with the Majestic Hotel. It was Mr George Bartlett's car.'

Again the eyes of the two men met. Melchett said:

'George Bartlett? Could be! What do you think?'

Again Harper methodically recited various points.

'Ruby Keene was last seen with George Bartlett. He says she went to her room (borne out by the dress she was wearing being found there), but did she go to her room and change *in order to go out with him*? Had they made a date to go out together earlier – discussed it, say, before dinner, and did Pamela Reeves happen to overhear?'

Melchett said: 'He didn't report the loss of his car until the following morning, and he was extremely vague about it then, pretended he couldn't remember exactly when he had last noticed it.'

'That might be cleverness, sir. As I see it, he's either a very clever gentleman pretending to be a silly ass, or else – well, he is a silly ass.'

'What we want,' said Melchett, 'is motive. As it stands, he had no motive whatever for killing Ruby Keene.'

'Yes – that's where we're stuck every time. Motive. All the reports from the Palais de Danse at Brixwell are negative, I understand?'

'Absolutely! Ruby Keene had no special boy-friend. Slack's been into the matter thoroughly – give Slack his due, he *is* thorough.'

'That's right, sir. Thorough's the word.'

'If there was anything to ferret out, he'd have ferreted it out. But there's nothing there. He got a list of her most frequent dancing partners – all vetted and found correct. Harmless fellows, and all able to produce alibis for that night.'

'Ah,' said Superintendent Harper. 'Alibis. That's what we're up against.'

Melchett looked at him sharply. 'Think so? I've left that side of the investigation to you.'

'Yes, sir. It's been gone into – very thoroughly. We applied to London for help over it.'

'Well?'

'Mr Conway Jefferson may think that Mr Gaskell and young Mrs Jefferson are comfortably off, but that is not the case. They're both extremely hard up.'

'Is that true?'

'Quite true, sir. It's as Mr Conway Jefferson said, he made over considerable sums of money to his son and daughter when they married. That was over ten years ago, though. Mr Frank Jefferson fancied himself as knowing good investments. He didn't invest in anything absolutely wildcat, but he was unlucky and showed poor judgement more than once. His holdings have gone steadily down. I should say the widow found it difficult to make both ends meet and send her son to a good school.'

'But she hasn't applied to her father-in-law for help?'

'No, sir. As far as I can make out she lives with him, and consequently has no household expenses.'

'And his health is such that he wasn't expected to live long?'

'That's right, sir. Now for Mr Mark Gaskell. He's a gambler, pure and simple. Got through his wife's money very soon. Has got himself tangled up rather critically just at present. He needs money badly – and a good deal of it.'

'Can't say I liked the looks of him much,' said Colonel Melchett. 'Wild-looking sort of fellow – what? And he's got a motive all right. Twenty-five thousand pounds it meant to him getting that girl out of the way. Yes, it's a motive all right.'

'They both had a motive.'

'I'm not considering Mrs Jefferson.'

'No, sir, I know you're not. And, anyway, the alibi holds for both of them. They *couldn't* have done it. Just that.'

'You've got a detailed statement of their movements that evening?'

'Yes, I have. Take Mr Gaskell first. He dined with his father-in-law and Mrs Jefferson, had coffee with them afterwards when Ruby

Keene joined them. Then he said he had to write letters and left them. Actually he took his car and went for a spin down to the front. He told me quite frankly he couldn't stick playing bridge for a whole evening. The old boy's mad on it. So he made letters an excuse. Ruby Keene remained with the others. Mark Gaskell returned when she was dancing with Raymond. After the dance Ruby came and had a drink with them, then she went off with young Bartlett, and Gaskell and the others cut for partners and started their bridge. That was at twenty minutes to eleven – and he didn't leave the table until after midnight. That's quite certain, sir. Everyone says so. The family, the waiters, everyone. Therefore *he* couldn't have done it. And Mrs Jefferson's alibi is the same. She, too, didn't leave the table. They're out, both of them – out.'

Colonel Melchett leaned back, tapping the table with a paper cutter.

Superintendent Harper said:

'That is, assuming the girl was killed before midnight.'

'Haydock said she was. He's a very sound fellow in police work. If he says a thing, it's so.'

'There might be reasons – health, physical idiosyncrasy, or something.'

'I'll put it to him.' Melchett glanced at his watch, picked up the telephone receiver and asked for a number. He said: 'Haydock ought to be at home at this time. Now, assuming that she was killed *after* midnight?'

Harper said:

'Then there might be a chance. There was some coming and going afterwards. Let's assume that Gaskell had asked the girl to meet him outside somewhere – say at twenty-past twelve. He slips away for a minute or two, strangles her, comes back and disposes of the body later – in the early hours of the morning.'

Melchett said:

'Takes her by car thirty-odd miles to put her in Bantry's library? Dash it all, it's not a likely story.'

'No, it isn't,' the Superintendent admitted at once.

The telephone rang. Melchett picked up the receiver.

'Hallo, Haydock, is that you? Ruby Keene. Would it be possible for her to have been killed *after* midnight?'

'I told you she was killed between ten and midnight.'

'Yes, I know, but one could stretch it a bit – what?'

'No, you couldn't stretch it. When I say she was killed before midnight I mean before midnight, and don't try to tamper with the medical evidence.'

'Yes, but couldn't there be some physiological what-not? You know what I mean.'

'I know that you don't know what you're talking about. The girl was perfectly healthy and not abnormal in any way – and I'm not going to say she was just to help you fit a rope round the neck of some wretched fellow whom you police wallahs have got your knife into. Now don't protest. I know your ways. And, by the way, the girl wasn't strangled willingly – that is to say, she was drugged first. Powerful narcotic. She died of strangulation but she was drugged first.' Haydock rang off.

Melchett said gloomily: 'Well, that's that.'

Harper said:

'Thought I'd found another likely starter – but it petered out.'

'What's that? Who?'

'Strictly speaking, he's your pigeon, sir. Name of Basil Blake. Lives near Gossington Hall.'

'Impudent young jackanapes!' The Colonel's brow darkened as he remembered Basil Blake's outrageous rudeness. 'How's he mixed up in it?'

'Seems he knew Ruby Keene. Dined over at the Majestic quite often – danced with the girl. Do you remember what Josie said to Raymond when Ruby was discovered to be missing? "She's not with that film fellow, is she?" I've found out it was Blake she meant. He's employed with the Lemville Studios, you know. Josie has nothing to go upon except a belief that Ruby was rather keen on him.'

'Very promising, Harper, very promising.'

'Not so good as it sounds, sir. Basil Blake was at a party at the studios that night. You know the sort of thing. Starts at eight with cocktails and goes on and on until the air's too thick to see through and everyone passes out. According to Inspector Slack, who's questioned him, he left the show round about midnight. At midnight Ruby Keene was dead.'

'Anyone bear out his statement?'

'Most of them, I gather, sir, were rather – er – far gone. The – er – young woman now at the bungalow – Miss Dinah Lee – says his statement is correct.'

'Doesn't mean a thing!'

'No, sir, probably not. Statements taken from other members of the party bear Mr Blake's statement out on the whole, though ideas as to time are somewhat vague.'

'Where are these studios?'

'Lemville, sir, thirty miles south-west of London.'

'Hm – about the same distance from here?'

'Yes, sir.'

Colonel Melchett rubbed his nose. He said in a rather dissatisfied tone:

'Well, it looks as though we could wash him out.'

'I think so, sir. There is no evidence that he was seriously attracted by Ruby Keene. In fact' – the Superintendent coughed primly – 'he seems fully occupied with his own young lady.'

Melchett said:

'Well, we are left with "X", an unknown murderer – so unknown Slack can't find a trace of him! Or Jefferson's son-in-law, who might have wanted to kill the girl – but didn't have a chance to do so. Daughter-in-law ditto. Or George Bartlett, who has no alibi – but unfortunately no motive either. Or with young Blake, who has an alibi and no motive. And that's the lot! No, stop, I suppose we ought to consider the dancing fellow – Raymond Starr. After all, he saw a lot of the girl.'

Harper said slowly:

'Can't believe he took much interest in her – or else he's a thundering good actor. And, for all practical purposes, he's got an alibi too. He was more or less in view from twenty minutes to eleven until midnight, dancing with various partners. I don't see that we can make a case against him.'

'In fact,' said Colonel Melchett, 'we can't make a case against anybody.'

'George Bartlett's our best hope. If we could only hit on a motive.'

'You've had him looked up?'

'Yes, sir. Only child. Coddled by his mother. Came into a good deal of money on her death a year ago. Getting through it fast. Weak rather than vicious.'

'May be mental.' said Melchett hopefully.

Superintendent Harper nodded. He said:

'Has it struck you, sir – that that may be the explanation of the whole case?'

'Criminal lunatic, you mean?'

'Yes, sir. One of those fellows who go about strangling young girls. Doctors have a long name for it.'

'That would solve all our difficulties,' said Melchett.

'There's only one thing I don't like about it,' said Superintendent Harper.

'What?'

'It's too easy.'

'H'm – yes – perhaps. So, as I said at the beginning, where are we?'

'Nowhere, sir,' said Superintendent Harper.

CHAPTER 12

I

Conway Jefferson stirred in his sleep and stretched. His arms were flung out, long, powerful arms into which all the strength of his body seemed to be concentrated since his accident.

Through the curtains the morning light glowed softly.

Conway Jefferson smiled to himself. Always, after a night of rest, he woke like this, happy, refreshed, his deep vitality renewed. Another day!

So for a minute he lay. Then he pressed the special bell by his hand. And suddenly a wave of remembrance swept over him.

Even as Edwards, deft and quiet-footed, entered the room, a groan was wrung from his master.

Edwards paused with his hand on the curtains. He said: 'You're not in pain, sir?'

Conway Jefferson said harshly:

'No. Go on, pull 'em.'

The clear light flooded the room. Edwards, understanding, did not glance at his master.

His face grim, Conway Jefferson lay remembering and thinking. Before his eyes he saw again the pretty, vapid face of Ruby. Only in his mind he did not use the adjective vapid. Last night he would have said innocent. A naïve, innocent child! And now?

A great weariness came over Conway Jefferson. He closed his eyes. He murmured below his breath:

'Margaret . . .'

It was the name of his dead wife. . . .

II

'I like your friend,' said Adelaide Jefferson to Mrs Bantry.

The two women were sitting on the terrace.

'Jane Marple's a very remarkable woman,' said Mrs Bantry.

'She's nice too,' said Addie, smiling.

'People call her a scandalmonger,' said Mrs Bantry, 'but she isn't really.'

'Just a low opinion of human nature?'

'You could call it that.'

'It's rather refreshing,' said Adelaide Jefferson, 'after having had too much of the other thing.'

Mrs Bantry looked at her sharply.

Addie explained herself.

'So much high-thinking – idealization of an unworthy object!'

'You mean Ruby Keene?'

Addie nodded.

'I don't want to be horrid about her. There wasn't any harm in her. Poor little rat, she had to fight for what she wanted. She wasn't bad. Common and rather silly and quite good-natured, but a decided little gold-digger. I don't think she schemed or planned. It was just that she was quick to take advantage of a possibility. And she knew just how to appeal to an elderly man who was – lonely.'

'I suppose,' said Mrs Bantry thoughtfully, 'that Conway *was* lonely?'

Addie moved restlessly. She said:

'He was – this summer.' She paused and then burst out: 'Mark will have it that it was all my fault. Perhaps it was, I don't know.'

She was silent for a minute, then, impelled by some need to talk, she went on speaking in a difficult, almost reluctant way.

'I – I've had such an odd sort of life. Mike Carmody, my first husband, died so soon after we were married – it – it knocked me out. Peter, as you know, was born after his death. Frank Jefferson was Mike's great friend. So I came to see a lot of him. He was Peter's godfather – Mike had wanted that. I got very fond of him – and – oh! sorry for him too.'

'Sorry?' queried Mrs Bantry with interest.

'Yes, just that. It sounds odd. Frank had always had everything he wanted. His father and his mother couldn't have been nicer to him. And yet – how can I say it? – you see, old Mr Jefferson's personality is so strong. If you live with it, you can't somehow have a personality of your own. Frank felt that.

'When we were married he was very happy – wonderfully so. Mr Jefferson was very generous. He settled a large sum of money on Frank – said he wanted his children to be independent and not have to wait for his death. It was so nice of him – so generous. But it was much too sudden. He ought really to have accustomed Frank to independence little by little.

'It went to Frank's head. He wanted to be as good a man as his father, as clever about money and business, as far-seeing and successful. And, of course, he wasn't. He didn't exactly speculate with the money, but he invested in the wrong things at the wrong time. It's frightening, you know, how soon money goes if you're not clever about it. The more Frank dropped, the more eager he was was to get it back by some clever deal. So things went from bad to worse.'

'But, my dear,' said Mrs Bantry, 'couldn't Conway have advised him?'

'He didn't want to be advised. The one thing he wanted was to do well on his own. That's why he never let Mr Jefferson know. When Frank died there was very little left – only a tiny income for me. And I – I didn't let his father know either. You see –'

She turned abruptly.

'It would have felt like betraying Frank to him. Frank would have hated it so. Mr Jefferson was ill for a long time. When he got well he assumed that I was a very well-off widow. I've never undeceived him. It's been a point of honour. He knows I'm very careful about money – but he approves of that, thinks I'm a thrifty sort of woman. And, of course, Peter and I have lived with him practically ever since, and he's paid for all our living expenses. So I've never had to worry.'

She said slowly:

'We've been like a family all these years – only – only – you see (or don't you see?) I've never been Frank's *widow* to him – I've been Frank's *wife*.'

Mrs Bantry grasped the implication.

'You mean he's never accepted their deaths?'

'No. He's been wonderful. But he's conquered his own terrible tragedy by refusing to recognize death. Mark is Rosamund's husband and I'm Frank's wife – and though Frank and Rosamund aren't here with us – they are still existent.'

Mrs Bantry said softly:

'It's a wonderful triumph of faith.'

'I know. We've gone on, year after year. But suddenly – this summer – something went wrong in me. I felt – I felt rebellious. It's an awful thing to say, but I didn't want to think of Frank any more! All that was over – my love and companionship with him, and my grief when he died. It was something that had been and wasn't any longer.

'It's awfully hard to describe. It's like wanting to wipe the slate clean and start again. I wanted to be me – Addie, still reasonably young and strong and able to play games and swim and dance – just a *person*. Even Hugo – (you know Hugo McLean?) he's a dear and wants to marry me, but, of course, I've never really thought of it – but this summer I *did* begin to think of it – not seriously – only vaguely . . .'

She stopped and shook her head.

'And so I suppose it's true. *I neglected Jeff.* I don't mean *really* neglected him, but my mind and thoughts weren't with him. When Ruby, as I saw, amused him, I was rather glad. It left me freer to go and do my own things. I never dreamed – of course I never dreamed – that he would be so – so – *infatuated* by her!'

Mrs Bantry asked:

'And when you did find out?'

'I was dumbfounded – absolutely dumbfounded! And, I'm afraid, angry too.'

'*I'd* have been angry,' said Mrs Bantry.

'There was Peter, you see. Peter's whole future depends on Jeff. Jeff practically looked on him as a grandson, or so I thought, but, of course, he wasn't a grandson. He was no relation at all. And to think that he was going to be – disinherited!' Her firm, well-shaped hands shook a little where they lay in her lap. 'For that's what it felt like – and for a vulgar, gold-digging little simpleton – Oh! I could have killed her!'

She stopped, stricken. Her beautiful hazel eyes met Mrs Bantry's in a pleading horror. She said:

'*What an awful thing to say!*'

Hugo McLean, coming quietly up behind them, asked:

'What's an awful thing to say?'

'Sit down, Hugo. You know Mrs Bantry, don't you?'

McLean had already greeted the older lady. He said now in a slow, persevering way:

'What was an awful thing to say?'

Addie Jefferson said:

'That I'd like to have killed Ruby Keene.'

Hugo McLean reflected a minute or two. Then he said:

'No, I wouldn't say that if I were you. Might be misunderstood.'

His eyes – steady, reflective, grey eyes – looked at her meaningfully.

He said:

'*You've got to watch your step, Addie.*'

There was a warning in his voice.

III

When Miss Marple came out of the hotel and joined Mrs Bantry a few minutes later, Hugo McLean and Adelaide Jefferson were walking down the path to the sea together.

Seating herself, Miss Marple remarked:

'He seems very devoted.'

'He's been devoted for years! One of those men.'

'I know. Like Major Bury. He hung round an Anglo-Indian widow for quite ten years. A joke among her friends! In the end she gave in – but unfortunately ten days before they were to have been married she ran away with the chauffeur! Such a nice woman, too, and usually so well balanced.'

'People do do very odd things,' agreed Mrs Bantry. 'I wish you'd been here just now, Jane. Addie Jefferson was telling me all about herself – how her husband went through all his money but they never let Mr Jefferson know. And then, this summer, things felt different to her –'

Miss Marple nodded.

'Yes. She rebelled, I suppose, against being made to live in the past? After all, there's a time for everything. You can't sit in the house with the blinds down for ever. I suppose Mrs Jefferson just pulled them up and took off her widow's weeds, and her father-in-law, of course, didn't like it. Felt left out in the cold, though I don't suppose for a minute he realized who put her up to it. Still, he certainly wouldn't like it. And so, of course, like old Mr Badger when his wife took up Spiritualism, he was just ripe for what happened. Any fairly nice-looking young girl who listened prettily would have done.'

'Do you think,' said Mrs Bantry, 'that that cousin, Josie, got her down here deliberately – that it was a family plot?'

Miss Marple shook her head.

'No, I don't think so at all. I don't think Josie has the kind of mind that could foresee people's reaction. She's rather dense in that way. She's got one of those shrewd, limited, practical minds that never do foresee the future and are usually astonished by it.'

'It seems to have taken everyone by surprise,' said Mrs Bantry. 'Addie – and Mark Gaskell too, apparently.

Miss Marple smiled.

'I dare say he had his own fish to fry. A bold fellow with a roving eye! Not the man to go on being a sorrowing widower for years, no matter how fond he may have been of his wife. I should think they were both restless under old Mr Jefferson's yoke of perpetual remembrance.'

'Only,' added Miss Marple cynically, 'it's easier for gentlemen, of course.'

IV

At that very moment Mark was confirming this judgement on himself in a talk with Sir Henry Clithering.

With characteristic candour Mark had gone straight to the heart of things.

'It's just dawned on me,' he said, 'that I'm Favourite Suspect No. 1 to the police! They've been delving into my financial troubles. I'm broke, you know, or very nearly. If dear old Jeff dies according to schedule in a month or two, and Addie and I divide the dibs also according to schedule, all will be well. Matter of fact, I owe rather a lot. . . . If the crash comes it will be a big one! If I can stave it off, it will be the other way round – I shall come out on top and be a very rich man.'

Sir Henry Clithering said:

'You're a gambler, Mark.'

'Always have been. Risk everything – that's my motto! Yes, it's a lucky thing for me that somebody strangled that poor kid. I didn't do it. I'm not a strangler. I don't really think I could ever murder anybody. I'm too easy going. But I don't suppose I can ask the police to believe *that*! I must look to them like the answer to the criminal investigator's prayer! I had a motive, was on the spot, I am not burdened with high moral scruples! I can't imagine why I'm not in jug already! That Superintendent's got a very nasty eye.'

'You've got that useful thing, an alibi.'

'An alibi is the fishiest thing on God's earth! No innocent person ever has an alibi! Besides, it all depends on the time of death, or something like that, and you may be sure if three doctors say the girl was killed at midnight, at least six will be found who will swear positively that she was killed at five in the morning – and where's my alibi then?'

'At any rate, you are able to joke about it.'

'Damned bad taste, isn't it?' said Mark cheerfully. 'Actually, I'm rather scared. One is – with murder! And don't think I'm not sorry for old Jeff. I am. But it's better this way – bad as the shock was – than if he'd found her out.'

'What do you mean, found her out?'

Mark winked.

'Where did she go off to last night? I'll lay you any odds you like she went to meet a man. Jeff wouldn't have like that. He wouldn't have liked it at all. If he'd found she was deceiving him – that she wasn't the prattling little innocent she seemed – well – my father-in-law is an odd man. He's a man of great self-control, but that self-control can snap. And then – look out!'

Sir Henry glanced at him curiously.

'Are you fond of him or not?'

'I'm very fond of him – and at the same time I resent him. I'll try and explain. Conway Jefferson is a man who likes to control his surroundings. He's a benevolent despot, kind, generous, and affectionate – but his is the tune, and the others dance to his piping.'

Mark Gaskell paused.

'I loved my wife. I shall never feel the same for anyone else. Rosamund was sunshine and laughter and flowers, and when she was killed I felt just like a man in the ring who's had a knock-out blow. But the referee's been counting a good long time now. I'm a man, after all. I like women. I don't want to marry again – not in the least. Well, that's all right. I've had to be discreet – but I've had my good times all right. Poor Addie hasn't. Addie's a really nice woman. She's the kind of woman men want to marry, not to sleep with. Give her half a chance and she would marry again – and be very happy and make the chap happy too. But old Jeff saw her always as Frank's wife – and hypnotized her into seeing herself like that. He doesn't know it, but we've been in prison. I broke out, on the quiet, a long time ago, Addie broke out this summer – and it gave him a shock. It split up his world. Result – Ruby Keene.'

Irrepressibly he sang:

> '*But she is dead and in her grave,*
> *And, oh, the difference to me!*

'Come and have a drink, Clithering.'

It was hardly surprising, Sir Henry reflected, that Mark Gaskell should be an object of suspicion to the police.

CHAPTER 13

I

Dr Metcalf was one of the best-known physicians in Danemouth. He had no aggressive bedside manner, but his presence in the sick room had an invariably cheering effect. He was middle-aged, with a quiet pleasant voice.

He listened carefully to Superintendent Harper and replied to his questions with gentle precision.

Harper said:

'Then I can take it, Doctor Metcalf, that what I was told by Mrs Jefferson was substantially correct?'

'Yes, Mr Jefferson's health is in a precarious state. For several years now the man has been driving himself ruthlessly. In his determination to live like other men, he has lived at a far greater pace than the normal man of his age. He has refused to rest, to take things easy, to go slow – or any of the other phrases with which I and his other medical advisers have tendered our opinion. The result is that the man is an overworked engine. Heart, lungs, blood pressure – they're all overstrained.'

'You say Mr Jefferson has absolutely refused to listen?'

'Yes. I don't know that I blame him. It's not what I say to my patients, Superintendent, but a man may as well wear out as rust out. A lot of my colleagues do that, and take it from me it's not a bad way. In a place like Danemouth one sees most of the other thing: invalids clinging to life, terrified of over-exerting themselves, terrified of a breath of draughty air, of a stray germ, of an injudicious meal!

'I expect that's true enough,' said Superintendent Harper. 'What it amounts to, then, is this: Conway Jefferson is strong enough, physically speaking – or, I suppose I mean, muscularly speaking. Just what can he do in the active line, by the way?'

'He has immense strength in his arms and shoulders. He was a powerful man before his accident. He is extremely dexterous in his handling of his wheelchair, and with the aid of crutches he can move himself about a room – from his bed to the chair, for instance.'

'Isn't it possible for a man injured as Mr Jefferson was to have artificial legs?'

'Not in his case. There was a spine injury.'

'I see. Let me sum up again. Jefferson is strong and fit in the muscular sense. He feels well and all that?'

Metcalf nodded.

'But his heart is in a bad condition. Any overstrain or exertion, or a shock or a sudden fright, and he might pop off. Is that it?'

'More or less. Over-exertion is killing him slowly, because he won't give in when he feels tired. That aggravates the cardiac condition. It is unlikely that exertion would kill him suddenly. But a sudden shock or fright might easily do so. That is why I expressly warned his family.'

Superintendent Harper said slowly:

'But in actual fact a shock *didn't* kill him. I mean, doctor, that there couldn't have been a much worse shock than this business, and he's still alive?'

Dr Metcalf shrugged his shoulders.

'I know. But if you'd had my experience, Superintendent, you'd know that case history shows the impossibility of prognosticating accurately. People who *ought* to die of shock and exposure *don't* die of shock and exposure, etc., etc. The human frame is tougher than one can imagine possible. Moreover, in my experience, a *physical* shock is more often fatal than a *mental* shock. In plain language, a door banging suddenly would be more likely to kill Mr Jefferson than the discovery that a girl he was fond of had died in a particularly horrible manner.'

'Why is that, I wonder?'

'The breaking of a piece of bad news nearly always sets up a defence reaction. It numbs the recipient. They are unable – at first – to take it in. Full realization takes a little time. But the banged door, someone jumping out of a cupboard, the sudden onslaught of a motor as you cross a road – all those things are immediate in their action. The heart gives a terrified leap – to put it in layman's language.'

Superintendent Harper said slowly:

'But as far as anyone would know, Mr Jefferson's death might easily have been caused by the shock of the girl's death?'

'Oh, easily.' The doctor looked curiously at the other. 'You don't think –'

'I don't know what I think,' said Superintendent Harper vexedly.

II

'But you'll admit, sir, that the two things would fit in very prettily together,' he said a little later to Sir Henry Clithering. 'Kill two birds with one stone. First the girl – and the fact of her death takes off Mr Jefferson too – before he's had any opportunity of altering his will.'

'Do you think he will alter it?'

'You'd be more likely to know that, sir, than I would. What do you say?'

'I don't know. Before Ruby Keene came on the scene I happen to know that he had left his money between Mark Gaskell and Mrs Jefferson. I don't see why he should now change his mind about that. But of course he might do so. Might leave it to a Cats' Home, or to subsidize young professional dancers.'

Superintendent Harper agreed.

'You never know what bee a man is going to get in his bonnet – especially when he doesn't feel there's any moral obligation in the disposal of his fortune. No blood relations in this case.'

Sir Henry said:

'He is fond of the boy – of young Peter.'

'D'you think he regards him as a grandson? You'd know that better than I would, sir.'

Sir Henry said slowly:

'No, I don't think so.'

'There's another thing I'd like to ask you, sir. It's a thing I can't judge for myself. But they're friends of yours and so you'd know. I'd like very much to know just how fond Mr Jefferson is of Mr Gaskell and young Mrs Jefferson.'

Sir Henry frowned.

'I'm not sure if I understand you, Superintendent?'

'Well, it's this way, sir. How fond is he of them as *persons* – apart from his relationship to them?'

'Ah, I see what you mean.'

'Yes, sir. Nobody doubts that he was very attached to them both – but he was attached to them, as I see it, because they were, respectively, the husband and the wife of his daughter and his son. But supposing, for instance, one of them had married again?'

Sir Henry reflected. He said:

'It's an interesting point you raise there. I don't know. I'm inclined to suspect – this is a mere opinion – that it would have altered his attitude a good deal. He would have wished them well, borne no rancour, but I think, yes, I rather think that he would have taken very little more interest in them.'

'In both cases, sir?'

'I think so, yes. In Mr Gaskell's, almost certainly, and I rather think in Mrs Jefferson's also, but that's not nearly so certain. I think he *was* fond of her for her own sake.'

'Sex would have something to do with that,' said Superintendent Harper sapiently. 'Easier for him to look on her as a daughter than to look on Mr Gaskell as a son. It works both ways. Women accept a son-in-law as one of the family easily enough, but there aren't many times when a woman looks on her son's wife as a daughter.'

Superintendent Harper went on:

'Mind if we walk along this path, sir, to the tennis court? I see Miss Marple's sitting there. I want to ask her to do something for me. As a matter of fact I want to rope you both in.'

'In what way, Superintendent?'

'To get at stuff that I can't get at myself. I want you to tackle Edwards for me, sir.'

'Edwards? What do you want from him?'

'Everything you can think of! Everything he knows and what he thinks! About the relations between the various members of the family, his angle on the Ruby Keene business. Inside stuff. He knows better than anyone the state of affairs – you bet he does! And he wouldn't tell *me*. But he'll tell *you*. Because you're a gentleman and a friend of Mr Jefferson's. And something *might* turn up from it. That is, of course, if you don't object?'

Sir Henry said grimly:

'I don't object. I've been sent for, urgently, to get at the truth. I mean to do my utmost.'

He added:

'How do you want Miss Marple to help you?'

'With some girls. Some of those Girl Guides. We've rounded up half a dozen or so, the ones who were most friendly with Pamela Reeves. It's possible that they may know something. You see, I've been thinking. It seems to me that if that girl was really going to Woolworth's she would have tried to persuade one of the other girls to go with her. Girls usually like to shop with someone.'

'Yes, I think that's true.'

'So I think it's possible that Woolworth's was only an excuse. I want to know where the girl was really going. She may have let slip something. If so, I feel Miss Marple's the person to get it out of these girls. I'd say she knows a thing or two about girls – more than I do. And, anyway, they'd be scared of the police.'

'It sounds to me the kind of village domestic problem that is right up Miss Marple's street. She's very sharp, you know.'

The Superintendent smiled. He said:

'I'd say you're right. Nothing much gets past her.'

Miss Marple looked up at their approach and welcomed them eagerly. She listened to the Superintendent's request and at once acquiesced.

'I should like to help you very much, Superintendent, and I think that perhaps I *could* be of some use. What with the Sunday School, you know, and the Brownies, and our Guides, and the Orphanage quite near – I'm on the committee, you know, and often run in to have a little talk with Matron – and then *servants* – I usually have very young maids. Oh, yes, I've quite a lot of experience in when a girl is speaking the truth and when she is holding something back.'

'In fact, you're an expert,' said Sir Henry.

Miss Marple flashed him a reproachful glance and said:

'Oh, *please* don't laugh at me, Sir Henry.'

'I shouldn't dream of laughing at you. You've had the laugh of me too many times.'

'One does see so much evil in a village,' murmured Miss Marple in an explanatory voice.

'By the way,' said Sir Henry, 'I've cleared up one point you asked me about. The Superintendent tells me that there were nail clippings in Ruby's wastepaper basket.'

Miss Marple said thoughtfully:

'There were? Then that's that. . . .'

'Why did you want to know, Miss Marple?' asked the Superintendent.

Miss Marple said:

'It was one of the things that – well, that seemed *wrong* when I looked at the body. The hands were wrong, somehow, and I couldn't at first think *why*. Then I realized that girls who are very much made-up, and all that, usually have very long fingernails. Of course, I know that girls everywhere do bite their nails – it's one of those habits that is very hard to break. But vanity often does a lot of help. Still, I presumed that this girl *hadn't* cured herself. And then the little boy – Peter, you know – he said something which showed that her nails *had* been long, only she caught one and broke it. So then, of course, she might have trimmed off the rest to make an even appearance, and I asked about clippings and Sir Henry said he'd find out.'

Sir Henry remarked:

'You said just now, "*one* of the things that seemed wrong when you looked at the body". Was there something else?'

Miss Marple nodded vigorously.

'Oh yes!' she said. 'There was the dress. The dress was *all* wrong.'

Both men looked at her curiously.

'Now why?' said Sir Henry.

'Well, you see, it was an old dress. Josie said so, definitely, and I could see for myself that it was shabby and rather worn. Now that's all wrong.'

'I don't see why?'

Miss Marple got a little pink.

'Well, the idea is, isn't it, that Ruby Keene changed her dress and went off to meet someone on whom she presumably had what my young nephews call a "crush"?'

The Superintendent's eyes twinkled a little.

'That's the theory. She'd got a date with someone – a boy-friend, as the saying goes.'

'Then why,' demanded Miss Marple, 'was she wearing an old dress?'

The Superintendent scratched his head thoughtfully. He said:

'I see your point. You think she'd wear a new one?'

'I think she'd wear her best dress. Girls do.'

Sir Henry interposed.

'Yes, but look here, Miss Marple. Suppose she was going outside to this *rendezvous*. Going in an open car, perhaps, or walking in some rough going. Then she'd not want to risk messing a new frock and she'd put on an old one.'

'That would be the sensible thing to do,' agreed the Superintendent.

Miss Marple turned on him. She spoke with animation.

'The sensible thing to do would be to change into trousers and a pullover, or into tweeds. That, of course (I don't want to be snobbish, but I'm afraid it's unavoidable), that's what a girl of – of our class would do.

'A well-bred girl,' continued Miss Marple, warming to her subject, 'is always very particular to wear the right clothes for the right occasion. I mean, however hot the day was, a well-bred girl would never turn up at a point-to-point in a silk flowered frock.'

'And the correct wear to meet a lover?' demanded Sir Henry.

'If she were meeting him inside the hotel or somewhere where evening dress was worn, she'd wear her best evening frock, of course – but *outside* she'd feel she'd look ridiculous in evening dress and she'd wear her most attractive sports wear.'

'Granted, Fashion Queen, but the girl Ruby –'

Miss Marple said:

'Ruby, of course, wasn't – well, to put it bluntly – Ruby *wasn't* a lady. She belonged to the class that wear their best clothes however unsuitable to the occasion. Last year, you know, we had a picnic outing at Scrantor Rocks. You'd be surprised at the unsuitable clothes the girls wore. Foulard dresses and patent shoes and quite elaborate hats, some of them. For climbing about over rocks and in gorse and heather. And the young men in their best suits. Of course, hiking's different again. That's practically a uniform – and girls don't seem to realize that shorts are very unbecoming unless they are very slender.'

The Superintendent said slowly:

'And you think that Ruby Keene–'

'I think that she'd have kept on the frock she was wearing – her best pink one. She'd only have changed it if she'd had something newer still.'

Superintendent Harper said:

'And what's your explanation, Miss Marple?'

Miss Marple said:

'I haven't got one – yet. But I can't help feeling that it's important. . . .'

III

Inside the wire cage, the tennis lesson that Raymond Starr was giving had come to an end.

A stout middle-aged woman uttered a few appreciative squeaks, picked up a sky-blue cardigan and went off towards the hotel.

Raymond called out a few gay words after her.

Then he turned towards the bench where the three onlookers were sitting. The balls dangled in a net in his hand, his racket was under one arm. The gay, laughing expression on his face was wiped off as though by a sponge from a slate. He looked tired and worried.

Coming towards them, he said: '*That's* over.'

Then the smile broke out again, that charming, boyish, expressive smile that went so harmoniously with his suntanned face and dark lithe grace.

Sir Henry found himself wondering how old the man was. Twenty-five, thirty, thirty-five? It was impossible to say.

Raymond said, shaking his head a little:

'*She*'ll never be able to play, you know.'

'All this must be very boring for you,' said Miss Marple.

Raymond said simply:

'It is, sometimes. Especially at the end of the summer. For a time the thought of the pay buoys you up, but even that fails to stimulate imagination in the end!'

Superintendent Harper got up. He said abruptly:

'I'll call for you in half an hour's time, Miss Marple, if that will be all right?'

'Perfectly, thank you. I shall be ready.'

Harper went off. Raymond stood looking after him. Then he said: 'Mind if I sit here for a bit?'

'Do,' said Sir Henry. 'Have a cigarette?' He offered his case, wondering as he did so why he had a slight feeling of prejudice against Raymond Starr. Was it simply because he was a professional tennis coach and dancer? If so, it wasn't the tennis – it was the dancing. The English, Sir Henry decided, had a distrust for any man who danced too well! This fellow moved with too much grace! Ramon – Raymond – which was his name? Abruptly, he asked the question.

The other seemed amused.

'Ramon was my original professional name. Ramon and Josie – Spanish effect, you know. Then there was rather a prejudice against foreigners – so I became Raymond – very British –'

Miss Marple said:

'And is your real name something quite different?'

He smiled at her.

'Actually my real name is Ramon. I had an Argentine grandmother, you see –' (And that accounts for that swing from the hips, thought Sir Henry parenthetically.) 'But my first name is Thomas. Painfully prosaic.'

He turned to Sir Henry.

'You come from Devonshire, don't you, sir? From Stane? My people lived down that way. At Alsmonston.'

Sir Henry's face lit up.

'Are you one of the Alsmonston Starrs? I didn't realize that.'

'No – I don't suppose you would.'

There was a slight bitterness in his voice.

Sir Henry said awkwardly:

'Bad luck – er – all that.'

'The place being sold up after it had been in the family for three hundred years? Yes, it was rather. Still, our kind have to go, I suppose. We've outlived our usefulness. My elder brother went to New York. He's in publishing – doing well. The rest of us are scattered up and down the earth. I'll say it's hard to get a job nowadays when you've nothing to say for yourself except that you've had a public-school education! Sometimes, if you're lucky, you get taken on as a reception clerk at an hotel. The tie and the manner are an asset there. The only job I could get was showman in a plumbing establishment. Selling superb peach- and lemon-coloured porcelain baths. Enormous showrooms, but as I never knew the price of the damned things or how soon we could deliver them – I got fired.

'The only things I *could* do were dance and play tennis. I got taken on at an hotel on the Riviera. Good pickings there. I suppose I was doing well. Then I overheard an old Colonel, real old Colonel, incredibly ancient, British to the backbone and always talking about Poona. He went up to the manager and said at the top of his voice:

'"Where's the *gigolo*? I want to get hold of the *gigolo*. My wife and daughter want to dance, yer know. Where is the feller? What does he sting yer for? It's the *gigolo* I want."'

Raymond went on:

'Silly to mind – but I did. I chucked it. Came here. Less pay but pleasanter work. Mostly teaching tennis to rotund women who will never, never, never be able to play. That and dancing with the neglected wallflower daughters of rich clients. Oh well, it's life, I suppose. Excuse today's hard-luck story!'

He laughed. His teeth flashed out white, his eyes crinkled up at the corners. He looked suddenly healthy and happy and very much alive.

Sir Henry said:

'I'm glad to have a chat with you. I've been wanting to talk with you.'

'About Ruby Keene? I can't help you, you know. I don't know who killed her. I knew very little about her. She didn't confide in me.'

Miss Marple said: 'Did you like her?'

'Not particularly. I didn't dislike her.'

His voice was careless, uninterested.

Sir Henry said:

'So you've no suggestions to offer?'

'I'm afraid not. . . . I'd have told Harper if I had. It just seems to me one of those things! Petty, sordid little crime – no clues, no motive.'

'Two people had a motive,' said Miss Marple.

Sir Henry looked at her sharply.

'Really?' Raymond looked surprised.

Miss Marple looked insistently at Sir Henry and he said rather unwillingly:

'Her death probably benefits Mrs Jefferson and Mr Gaskell to the amount of fifty thousand pounds.'

'What?' Raymond looked really startled – more than startled – upset. 'Oh, but that's absurd – absolutely absurd – Mrs Jefferson – neither of them – could have had anything to do with it. It would be incredible to think of such a thing.'

Miss Marple coughed. She said gently:

'I'm afraid, you know, you're rather an idealist.'

'I?' he laughed. 'Not me! I'm a hard-boiled cynic.'

'Money,' said Miss Marple, 'is a very powerful motive.'

'Perhaps,' Raymond said hotly. 'But that either of those two would strangle a girl in cold blood –' He shook his head.

Then he got up.

'Here's Mrs Jefferson now. Come for her lesson. She's late.' His voice sounded amused. 'Ten minutes late!'

Adelaide Jefferson and Hugo McLean were walking rapidly down the path towards them.

With a smiling apology for her lateness, Addie Jefferson went on to the court. McLean sat down on the bench. After a polite enquiry whether Miss Marple minded a pipe, he lit it and puffed for some minutes in silence, watching critically the two white figures about the tennis court.

He said at last:

'Can't see what Addie wants to have lessons for. Have a game, yes. No one enjoys it better than I do. But why *lessons*?'

'Wants to improve her game,' said Sir Henry.

'She's not a bad player,' said Hugo. 'Good enough, at all events. Dash it all, she isn't aiming to play at Wimbledon.'

He was silent for a minute or two. Then he said:

'Who *is* this Raymond fellow? Where do they come from, these pros.? Fellow looks like a dago to me.'

'He's one of the Devonshire Starrs,' said Sir Henry.

'What? Not really?'

Sir Henry nodded. It was clear that this news was unpleasing to Hugo McLean. He scowled more than ever.

He said: 'Don't know why Addie sent for *me*. She seems not to have turned a hair over this business! Never looked better. Why send for me?'

Sir Henry asked with some curiosity:

'When did she send for you?'

'Oh – er – when all this happened.'

'How did you hear? Telephone or telegram?'

'Telegram.'

'As a matter of curiosity, when was it sent off?'

'Well – I don't know exactly.'

'What time did you receive it?'

'I didn't exactly receive it. It was telephoned on to me – as a matter of fact.'

'Why, where were you?'

'Fact is, I'd left London the afternoon before. I was staying at Danebury Head.'

'What – quite near here?'

'Yes, rather funny, wasn't it? Got the message when I got in from a round of golf and came over here at once.'

Miss Marple gazed at him thoughtfully. He looked hot and uncomfortable. She said: 'I've heard it's very pleasant at Danebury Head, and not very expensive.'

'No, it's not expensive. I couldn't afford it if it was. It's a nice little place.'

'We must drive over there one day,' said Miss Marple.

'Eh? What? Oh – er – yes, I should.' He got up. 'Better take some exercise – get an appetite.'

He walked away stiffly.

'Women,' said Sir Henry, 'treat their devoted admirers very badly.'

Miss Marple smiled but made no answer.

'Does he strike you as rather a dull dog?' asked Sir Henry. 'I'd be interested to know.'

'A little limited in his ideas, perhaps,' said Miss Marple. 'But with possibilities, I think – oh, definitely possibilities.'

Sir Henry in his turn got up.

'It's time for me to go and do my stuff. I see Mrs Bantry is on her way to keep you company.'

IV

Mrs Bantry arrived breathless and sat down with a gasp.

She said:

'I've been talking to chambermaids. But it isn't any good. I haven't found out a thing more! Do you think that girl can really have been carrying on with someone without everybody in the hotel knowing all about it?'

'That's a very interesting point, dear. I should say, definitely *not*. *Somebody* knows, depend upon it, if it's true! But she must have been very clever about it.'

Mrs Bantry's attention had strayed to the tennis court. She said approvingly:

'Addie's tennis is coming on a lot. Attractive young man, that tennis pro. Addie's looking quite nice looking. She's still an at-tractive woman – I shouldn't be at all surprised if she married again.'

'She'll be a rich woman, too, when Mr Jefferson dies,' said Miss Marple.

'Oh, don't always have such a nasty mind, Jane! Why haven't you solved this mystery yet? We don't seem to be getting on at all. I thought you'd know *at once*.' Mrs Bantry's tone held reproach.

'No, no, dear. I didn't know at once – not for some time.'

Mrs Bantry turned startled and incredulous eyes on her.

'You mean you know *now* who killed Ruby Keene?'

'Oh yes,' said Miss Marple, 'I know *that*!'

'But Jane, who is it? Tell me at once.'

Miss Marple shook her head very firmly and pursed up her lips.

'I'm sorry, Dolly, but that wouldn't do at all.'

'Why wouldn't it do?'

'Because you're so indiscreet. You would go round telling every-one – or, if you didn't tell, you'd *hint*.'

'No, I wouldn't. I wouldn't tell a soul.'

'People who use that phrase are always the last to live up to it. It's no good, dear. There's a long way to go yet. A great many things that are quite obscure. You remember when I was so against letting Mrs Partridge collect for the Red Cross, and I couldn't say *why*. The reason was that her nose had twitched in just the same way that that maid of mine, Alice, twitched *her* nose when I sent her out to pay the books. Always paid them a shilling or so short, and said "it could go on to the next week's account." which, of course, was *exactly* what Mrs Partridge did, only on a much larger scale. Seventy-five pounds it was *she* embezzled.'

'Never mind Mrs Partridge,' said Mrs Bantry.

'But I had to explain to you. And if you care I'll give you a *hint*. The trouble in this case is that everybody has been much too *credulous* and *believing*. You simply cannot *afford* to believe everything that people tell you. When there's anything fishy about, I never believe anyone at all! You see, I know human nature so well.'

Mrs Bantry was silent for a minute or two. Then she said in a different tone of voice:

'I told you, didn't I, that I didn't see why I shouldn't enjoy myself over this case. A real murder in my own house! The sort of thing that will never happen again.'

'I hope not,' said Miss Marple.

'Well, so do I, really. Once is enough. But it's *my* murder, Jane; I want to enjoy myself over it.'

Miss Marple shot a glance at her.

Mrs Bantry said belligerently:

'Don't you believe that?'

Miss Marple said sweetly:

'Of course, Dolly, if you tell me so.'

'Yes, but you never believe what people tell you, do you? You've just said so. Well, you're quite right.' Mrs Bantry's voice took on a sudden bitter note. She said: 'I'm not altogether a fool. You may think, Jane, that I don't know what they're saying all over St Mary Mead – all over the county! They're saying, one and all, that there's no smoke without fire, that if the girl was found in Arthur's library, then Arthur must know something about it. They're saying that the girl was Arthur's mistress – that she was his illegitimate daughter – that she was blackmailing him. They're saying anything that comes into their damned heads! And it will go on like that! Arthur won't realize it at first – he won't know what's wrong. He's such a dear old stupid that he'd never believe people would think things like that about him. He'll be cold-shouldered and looked at askance (whatever *that* means!) and it will dawn on him little by little and suddenly he'll be horrified and cut to the soul, and he'll fasten up like a clam and just *endure*, day after day, in misery.

'It's because of all that's going to happen to him that I've come here to ferret out every single thing about it that I can! This murder's *got* to be solved! If it isn't, then Arthur's whole life will be wrecked – and I won't have that happen. I won't! I won't! I won't!'

She paused for a minute and said:

'I *won't* have the dear old boy go through hell for something he didn't do. That's the only reason I came to Danemouth and left him alone at home – to find out the truth.'

'I know, dear,' said Miss Marple. 'That's why I'm here too.'

CHAPTER 14

I

In a quiet hotel room Edwards was listening deferentially to Sir Henry Clithering.

'There are certain questions I would like to ask you, Edwards, but I want you first to understand quite clearly my position here. I was at one time Commissioner of Police at Scotland Yard. I am now retired into private life. Your master sent for me when this tragedy occurred. He begged me to use my skill and experience in order to find out the truth.'

Sir Henry paused.

Edwards, his pale intelligent eyes on the other's face, inclined his head. He said: 'Quite so, Sir Henry.'

Clithering went on slowly and deliberately:

'In all police cases there is necessarily a lot of information that is held back. It is held back for various reasons – because it touches on a family skeleton, because it is considered to have no bearing on the case, because it would entail awkwardness and embarrassment to the parties concerned.'

Again Edwards said:

'Quite so, Sir Henry.'

'I expect, Edwards, that by now you appreciate quite clearly the main points of this business. The dead girl was on the point of becoming Mr Jefferson's adopted daughter. Two people had a motive in seeing that this should not happen. Those two people are Mr Gaskell and Mrs Jefferson.'

The valet's eyes displayed a momentary gleam. He said: 'May I ask if they are under suspicion, sir?'

'They are in no danger of arrest, if that is what you mean. But the police are bound to be suspicious of them and will continue to be so *until the matter is cleared up.*'

'An unpleasant position for them, sir.'

'Very unpleasant. Now to get at the truth one must have *all* the facts of the case. A lot depends, *must* depend, on the reactions, the words and gestures, of Mr Jefferson and his family. How did they feel, what did they show, what things were said? I am asking you, Edwards, for inside information – the kind of inside information that only you are likely to have. You know your master's moods. From observation of them you probably know what caused them. I am asking this, not as a policeman, but as a friend of Mr Jefferson's. That is to say, if anything you tell me is not, in my opinion, relevant to the case, I shall not pass it on to the police.'

He paused. Edwards said quietly:

'I understand you, sir. You want me to speak quite frankly – to say things that in the ordinary course of events I should not say – and that, excuse me, sir, *you* wouldn't dream of listening to.'

Sir Henry said:

'You're a very intelligent fellow, Edwards. That's exactly what I *do* mean.'

Edwards was silent for a minute or two, then he began to speak.

'Of course I know Mr Jefferson fairly well by now. I've been with him quite a number of years. And I see him in his "off" moments, not only in his "on" ones. Sometimes, sir, I've questioned in my own mind whether it's good for anyone to fight fate in the way Mr Jefferson has fought. It's taken a terrible toll of him, sir. If, sometimes, he could have given way, been an unhappy, lonely, broken old man – well, it might have been better for him in the end. But he's too proud for that! He'll go down fighting – that's his motto.

'But that sort of thing leads, Sir Henry, to a lot of nervous reaction. He looks a good-tempered gentleman. I've seen him in violent rages when he could hardly speak for passion. And the one thing that roused him, sir, was deceit. . . .'

'Are you saying that for any particular reason, Edwards?'

'Yes, sir, I am. You asked me, sir, to speak quite frankly?'

'That is the idea.'

'Well, then, Sir Henry, in my opinion the young woman that Mr Jefferson was so taken up with wasn't worth it. She was, to put it bluntly, a common little piece. And she didn't care tuppence for Mr Jefferson. All that play of affection and gratitude was so much poppycock. I don't say there was any harm in her – but she wasn't, by a long way, what Mr Jefferson thought her. It was funny, that, sir, for Mr Jefferson was a shrewd gentleman; he wasn't often deceived over people. But there, a gentleman isn't himself in his judgement when it comes to a young woman being in question. Young Mrs Jefferson, you see, whom he'd always depended upon a lot for sympathy, had changed a good deal this summer. He noticed it and he felt it badly. He was fond of her, you see. Mr Mark he never liked much.'

Sir Henry interjected:

'And yet he had him with him constantly?'

'Yes, but that was for Miss Rosamund's sake. Mrs Gaskell that was. She was the apple of his eye. He adored her. Mr Mark was Miss Rosamund's husband. He always thought of him like that.'

'Supposing Mr Mark had married someone else?'

'Mr Jefferson, sir, would have been furious.'

Sir Henry raised his eyebrows. 'As much as that?'

'He wouldn't have shown it, but that's what it would have been.'

'And if Mrs Jefferson had married again?'

'Mr Jefferson wouldn't have liked that either, sir.'

'Please go on, Edwards.'

'I was saying, sir, that Mr Jefferson fell for this young woman. I've often seen it happen with the gentlemen I've been with. Comes over them like a kind of disease. They want to protect the girl, and shield her, and shower benefits upon her – and nine times out of ten the girl is very well able to look after herself and has a good eye to the main chance.'

'So you think Ruby Keene was a schemer?'

'Well, Sir Henry, she was quite inexperienced, being so young, but she had the makings of a very fine schemer indeed when she'd once got well into her swing, so to speak! In another five years she'd have been an expert at the game!'

Sir Henry said:

'I'm glad to have your opinion of her. It's valuable. Now, do you recall any incident in which this matter was discussed between Mr Jefferson and his family?'

'There was very little discussion, sir. Mr Jefferson announced what he had in mind and stifled any protests. That is, he shut up Mr Mark, who was a bit outspoken. Mrs Jefferson didn't say much – she's a quiet lady – only urged him not to do anything in a great hurry.'

Sir Henry nodded.

'Anything else? What was the girl's attitude?'

With marked distaste the valet said:

'I should describe it, sir, as jubilant.'

'Ah – jubilant, you say? You had no reason to believe, Edwards, that' – he sought about for a phrase suitable to Edwards – 'that – er – her affections were engaged elsewhere?'

'Mr Jefferson was not proposing marriage, sir. He was going to adopt her.'

'Cut out the "elsewhere" and let the question stand.'

The valet said slowly: 'There *was* one incident, sir. I happened to be a witness of it.'

'That is gratifying. Tell me.'

'There is probably nothing in it, sir. It was just that one day the young woman, chancing to open her handbag, a small snapshot fell out. Mr Jefferson pounced on it and said: "Hallo, Kitten, who's this, eh?"'

'It was a snapshot, sir, of a young man, a dark young man with rather untidy hair and his tie very badly arranged.

'Miss Keene pretended that she didn't know anything about it.

She said: "I've no idea, Jeffie. No idea at all. I don't know how it could have got into my bag. *I* didn't put it there!"

'Now, Mr Jefferson, sir, wasn't quite a fool. That story wasn't good enough. He looked angry, his brows came down heavy, and his voice was gruff when he said:

'"Now then, Kitten, now then. *You* know who it is right enough."

'She changed her tactics quick, sir. Looked frightened. She said: "I do recognize him now. He comes here sometimes and I've danced with him. I don't know his name. The silly idiot must have stuffed his photo into my bag one day. These boys are too silly for anything!" She tossed her head and giggled and passed it off. But it wasn't a likely story, was it? And I don't think Mr Jefferson quite believed it. He looked at her once or twice after that in a sharp way, and sometimes, if she'd been out, he asked her where she'd been.'

Sir Henry said: 'Have you ever seen the original of the photo about the hotel?'

'Not to my knowledge, sir. Of course, I am not much downstairs in the public apartments.'

Sir Henry nodded. He asked a few more questions, but Edwards could tell him nothing more.

II

In the police station at Danemouth, Superintendent Harper was interviewing Jessie Davis, Florence Small, Beatrice Henniker, Mary Price, and Lilian Ridgeway.

They were girls much of an age, differing slightly in mentality. They ranged from 'county' to farmers' and shopkeepers' daughters. One and all they told the same story – Pamela Reeves had been just the same as usual, she had said nothing to any of them except that she was going to Woolworth's and would go home by a later bus.

In the corner of Superintendent Harper's office sat an elderly lady. The girls hardly noticed her. If they did, they may have wondered who she was. She was certainly no police matron. Possibly they assumed that she, like themselves, was a witness to be questioned.

The last girl was shown out. Superintendent Harper wiped his forehead and turned round to look at Miss Marple. His glance was enquiring, but not hopeful.

Miss Marple, however, spoke crisply.

'I'd like to speak to Florence Small.'

The Superintendent's eyebrows rose, but he nodded and touched a bell. A constable appeared.

Harper said: 'Florence Small.'

The girl reappeared, ushered in by the constable. She was the daughter of a well-to-do farmer – a tall girl with fair hair, a rather foolish mouth, and frightened brown eyes. She was twisting her hands and looked nervous.

Superintendent Harper looked at Miss Marple, who nodded.

The Superintendent got up. He said:

'This lady will ask you some questions.'

He went out, closing the door behind him.

Florence shot an uneasy glance at Miss Marple. Her eyes looked rather like one of her father's calves.

Miss Marple said: 'Sit down, Florence.'

Florence Small sat down obediently. Unrecognized by herself, she felt suddenly more at home, less uneasy. The unfamiliar and terrorizing atmosphere of a police station was replaced by something more familiar, the accustomed tone of command of somebody whose business it was to give orders. Miss Marple said:

'You understand, Florence, that it's of the utmost imortance that everything about poor Pamela's doings on the day of her death should be known?'

Florence murmured that she quite understood.

'And I'm sure you want to do your best to help?'

Florence's eyes were wary as she said, of course she did.

'To keep back any piece of information is a very serious offence,' said Miss Marple.

The girl's fingers twisted nervously in her lap. She swallowed once or twice.

'I can make allowances,' went on Miss Marple, 'for the fact that you are naturally alarmed at being brought into contact with the police. You are afraid, too, that you may be blamed for not having spoken sooner. Possibly you are afraid that you may also be blamed for not stopping Pamela at the time. But you've got to be a brave girl and make a clean breast of things. If you refuse to tell what you know now, it will be a very serious matter indeed – *very* serous – practically *perjury*, and for that, as you know, you can be sent to prison.'

'I – I don't –'

Miss Marple said sharply:

'Now don't prevaricate, Florence! Tell me all about it at once! Pamela wasn't going to Woolworth's, was she?'

Florence licked her lips with a dry tongue and gazed imploringly at Miss Marple like a beast about to be slaughtered.

'Something to do with the films, wasn't it?' asked Miss Marple.

A look of intense relief mingled with awe passed over Florence's face. Her inhibitions left her. She gasped:

'Oh, *yes!*'

'I thought so,' said Miss Marple. 'Now I want all the details, please.'

Words poured from Florence in a gush.

'Oh! I've been ever so worried. I promised Pam, you see, I'd never say a word to a soul. And then when she was found all burnt up in that car – oh! it was horrible and I thought I should *die* – I felt it was all my fault. I ought to have stopped her. Only I never thought, not for a minute, that it wasn't all right. And then I was asked if she'd been quite as usual that day and I said "Yes" before I'd had time to think. And not having said anything then I didn't see how I could say anything later. And, after all, I didn't know anything – not really – only what Pam told me.'

'What did Pam tell you?'

'It was as we were walking up the lane to the bus – on the way to the rally. She asked me if I could keep a secret, and I said "Yes" and she made me swear not to tell. She was going into Danemouth for a film test after the rally! She'd met a film producer – just back from Hollywood, he was. He wanted a certain type, and he told Pam she was just what he was looking for. He warned her, though, not to build on it. You couldn't tell, he said, not until you saw how a person photographed. It might be no good at all. It was a kind of Bergner part, he said. You had to have someone quite young for it. A schoolgirl, it was, who changes places with a revue artist and has a wonderful career. Pam's acted in plays at school and she's awfully good. He said he could see she could act, but she'd have to have some intensive training. It wouldn't be all beer and skittles, he told her, it would be damned hard work. Did she think she could stick it?'

Florence Small stopped for breath. Miss Marple felt rather sick as she listened to the glib rehash of countless novels and screen stories. Pamela Reeves, like most other girls, would have been warned against talking to strangers – but the glamour of the films would obliterate all that.

'He was absolutely businesslike about it all,' continued Florence. 'Said if the test was successful she'd have a contract, and he said that as she was young and inexperienced she ought to let a lawyer look at it before she signed it. But she wasn't to pass on that *he'd* said that. He asked her if she'd have trouble with her parents, and Pam said she probably would, and he said: "Well, of course, that's always a difficulty with anyone as young as you are, but I think if it was put to them that this was a wonderful chance that wouldn't happen once in a million times, they'd see reason." But, anyway, he said, it wasn't any good going into that until they knew the result of the test. She mustn't be disappointed if it failed. He told her about Hollywood and about Vivien Leigh – how she'd suddenly taken London by storm – and how these sensational leaps into fame did happen. He himself had come back from America to work with the Lemville Studios and put some pep into the English film companies.'

Miss Marple nodded.

Florence went on:

'So it was all arranged. Pam was to go into Danemouth after the rally and meet him at his hotel and he'd take her along to the studios (they'd got a small testing studio in Danemouth, he told her). She'd have her test and she could catch the bus home afterwards. She could say she'd been shopping, and he'd let her know the result of the test in a few days, and if it was favourable Mr Harmsteiter, the boss, would come along and talk to her parents.

'Well, of course, it sounded too wonderful! I was green with envy! Pam got through the rally without turning a hair – we always call her a regular poker face. Then, when she said she was going into Danemouth to Woolworth's she just winked at me.

'I saw her start off down the footpath.' Florence began to cry. 'I ought to have stopped her. I ought to have stopped her . . . I ought to have known a thing like that couldn't be true. I ought to have told someone. Oh dear, I wish I was *dead*!'

'There, there.' Miss Marple patted her on the shoulder. 'It's quite all right. No one will blame you. You've done the right thing in telling me.'

She devoted some minutes to cheering the child up.

Five minutes later she was telling the story to Superintendent Harper. The latter looked very grim.

'The clever devil!' he said. 'By God, I'll cook his goose for him. This puts rather a different aspect on things.'

'Yes, it does.'

Harper looked at her sideways.

'It doesn't surprise you?'

'I expected something of the kind.'

Superintendent Harper said curiously:

'What put you on to this particular girl? They all looked scared to death and there wasn't a pin to choose between them as far as I could see.'

Miss Marple said gently:

'You haven't had as much experience with girls telling lies as I have. Florence looked at you very straight, if you remember, and stood very rigid and just fidgeted with her feet like the others. But you didn't watch her as she went out of the door. I knew at once then that she'd got something to hide. They nearly always relax too soon. My little maid Janet always did. She'd explain quite convincingly that the mice had eaten the end of a cake and give herself away by smirking as she left the room.'

'I'm very grateful to you,' said Harper.

He added thoughtfully: 'Lemville Studios, eh?'

Miss Marple said nothing. She rose to her feet.

'I'm afraid,' she said, 'I must hurry away. So glad to have been able to help you.'

'Are you going back to the hotel?'

'Yes – to pack up. I must go back to St Mary Mead as soon as possible. There's a lot for me to do there.'

CHAPTER 15

I

Miss Marple passed out through the french windows of her drawing-room, tripped down her neat garden path, through a garden gate, in through the vicarage garden gate, across the vicarage garden, and up to the drawing-room window, where she tapped gently on the pane.

The vicar was busy in his study composing his Sunday sermon, but the vicar's wife, who was young and pretty, was admiring the progress of her offspring across the hearthrug.

'Can I come in, Griselda?'

'Oh, do, Miss Marple. Just *look* at David! He gets so angry because he can only crawl in reverse. He wants to get to something and the more he tries the more he goes backwards into the coalbox!'

'He's looking very bonny, Griselda.'

'He's not bad, is he?' said the young mother, endeavouring to assume an indifferent manner. 'Of course I don't *bother* with him much. All the books say a child should be left alone as much as possible.'

'Very wise, dear,' said Miss Marple. 'Ahem, I came to ask if there was anything special you are collecting for at the moment?'

The vicar's wife turned somewhat astonished eyes upon her.

'Oh, heaps of things,' she said cheerfully. 'There always are.'

She ticked them off on her fingers.

'There's the Nave Restoration Fund, and St Giles's Mission, and our Sale of Work next Wednesday, and the Unmarried Mothers, and a Boy Scouts' Outing, and the Needlework Guild, and the Bishop's Appeal for Deep Sea Fishermen.'

'Any of them will do,' said Miss Marple. 'I thought I might make a little round – with a book, you know – if you would authorize me to do so?'

'Are you up to something? I believe you are. Of course I authorize you. Make it the Sale of Work; it would be lovely to get some real money instead of those awful sachets and comic pen-wipers and depressing children's frocks and dusters all done up to look like dolls.

'I suppose,' continued Griselda, accompanying her guest to the window, 'you wouldn't like to tell me what it's all about?'

'Later, my dear,' said Miss Marple, hurrying off.

With a sigh the young mother returned to the hearthrug and, by way of carrying out her principles of stern neglect, butted her son three times in the stomach so that he caught hold of her hair and pulled it with gleeful yells. They then rolled over and over in a grand rough-and-tumble until the door opened and the vicarage maid announced to the most influential parishioner (who didn't like children):

'Missus is in here.'

Whereupon Griselda sat up and tried to look dignified and more what a vicar's wife should be.

II

Miss Marple, clasping a small black book with pencilled entries in it, walked briskly along the village street until she came to the crossroads. Here she turned to the left and walked past the *Blue Boar* until she came to Chatsworth, alias 'Mr Booker's new house'.

She turned in at the gate, walked up to the front door and knocked briskly.

The door was opened by the blonde young woman named Dinah Lee. She was less carefully made-up than usual, and in fact looked slightly dirty. She was wearing grey slacks and an emerald jumper.

'Good morning,' said Miss Marple briskly and cheerfully. 'May I just come in for a minute?'

She pressed forward as she spoke, so that Dinah Lee, who was somewhat taken aback at the call, had no time to make up her mind.

'Thank you so much,' said Miss Marple, beaming amiably at her and sitting down rather gingerly on a 'period' bamboo chair.

'Quite warm for the time of year, is it not?' went on Miss Marple, still exuding geniality.

'Yes, rather. Oh, quite,' said Miss Lee.

At a loss how to deal with the situation, she opened a box and offered it to her guest. 'Er – have a cigarette?'

'Thank you so much, but I don't smoke. I just called, you know, to see if I could enlist your help for our Sale of Work next week.'

'Sale of Work?' said Dinah Lee, as one who repeats a phrase in a foreign language.

'At the vicarage,' said Miss Marple. 'Next Wednesday.'

'Oh!' Miss Lee's mouth fell open. 'I'm afraid I couldn't –'

'Not even a small subscription – half a crown perhaps?'

Miss Marple exhibited her little book.

'Oh – er – well, yes, I dare say I could manage that.'

The girl looked relieved and turned to hunt in her handbag.

Miss Marple's sharp eyes were looking round the room.

She said:

'I see you've no hearthrug in front of the fire.'

Dinah Lee turned round and stared at her. She could not but be aware of the very keen scrutiny the old lady was giving her, but it aroused in her no other emotion than slight annoyance. Miss Marple recognized that. She said:

'It's rather dangerous, you know. Sparks fly out and mark the carpet.'

'Funny old Tabby,' thought Dinah, but she said quite amiably if somewhat vaguely:

'There used to be one. I don't know where it's got to.'

'I suppose,' said Miss Marple, 'it was the fluffy, woolly kind?'

'Sheep,' said Dinah. 'That's what it looked like.'

She was amused now. An eccentric old bean, this.

She held out a half-crown. 'Here you are,' she said.

'Oh, thank you, my dear.'

Miss Marple took it and opened the little book.

'Er – what name shall I write down?'

Dinah's eyes grew suddenly hard and contemptuous.

'Nosey old cat,' she thought, 'that's all she came for – prying around for scandal!'

She said clearly and with malicious pleasure:

'Miss Dinah Lee.'

Miss Marple looked at her steadily.

She said:

'This is Mr Basil Blake's cottage, isn't it?'

'Yes, and *I*'m Miss Dinah Lee!'

Her voice rang out challengingly, her head went back, her blue eyes flashed.

Very steadily Miss Marple looked at her. She said:

'Will you allow me to give you some advice, even though you may consider it impertinent?'

'I *shall* consider it impertinent. You had better say nothing.'

'Nevertheless,' said Miss Marple, 'I am going to speak. I want to advise you, very strongly, not to continue using your maiden name in the village.'

Dinah stared at her. She said:

'What – what do you mean?'

Miss Marple said earnestly:

'In a very short time you may need all the sympathy and goodwill you can find. It will be important to your husband, too, that he shall be thought well of. There is a prejudice in old-fashioned country districts against people living together who are not married. It has amused you both, I dare say, to pretend that that is what you are doing. It kept people away, so that you weren't bothered with what I expect you would call "old frumps". Nevertheless, old frumps have their uses.'

Dinah demanded:

'How did you know we are married?'

Miss Marple smiled a deprecating smile.

'Oh, my dear,' she said.

Dinah persisted.

'No, but how *did* you know? You didn't – you didn't go to Somerset House?'

A momentary flicker showed in Miss Marple's eyes.

'Somerset House? Oh, no. But it was quite easy to *guess*. Everything, you know, gets round in a village. The – er – the kind of quarrels you have – typical of early days of marriage. Quite – *quite* unlike an illicit relationship. It has been said, you know (and, I think, quite truly), that you can only really get under anybody's skin if you are married to them. When there is no – no *legal* bond, people are much more careful, they have to keep assuring themselves how happy and halcyon everything is. They have, you see, to *justify* themselves. They dare not quarrel! Married people, I have noticed, quite enjoy their battles and the – er – appropriate reconciliations.'

She paused, twinkling benignly.

'Well, I –' Dinah stopped and laughed. She sat down and lit a cigarette. 'You're absolutely marvellous!' she said.

Then she went on:

'But why do you want us to own up and admit to respectability?'

Miss Marple's face was grave. She said:

'Because, any minute now, *your husband may be arrested for murder*.'

III

For several moments Dinah stared at her. Then she said incredulously:

'Basil? Murder? Are you joking?'

'No, indeed. Haven't you seen the papers?'

Dinah caught her breath.

'You mean – that girl at the Majestic Hotel. Do you mean they suspect Basil of killing her?'

'Yes.'

'But it's nonsense!'

There was the whir of a car outside, the bang of a gate. Basil Blake flung open the door and came in, carrying some bottles. He said:

'Got the gin and the vermouth. Did you –'

He stopped and turned incredulous eyes on the prim, erect visitor.

Dinah burst out breathlessly:

'Is she mad? She says you're going to be arrested for the murder of that girl Ruby Keene.'

'Oh, God!' said Basil Blake. The bottles dropped from his arms on to the sofa. He reeled to a chair and dropped down in it and buried his face in his hands. He repeated: 'Oh, my God! Oh, my God!'

Dinah darted over to him. She caught his shoulders.

'Basil, look at me! It isn't true! I know it isn't true! I don't believe it for a moment!'

His hand went up and gripped hers.

'Bless you, darling.'

'But why should they think – You didn't even *know* her, did you?'

'Oh, yes, he knew her,' said Miss Marple.

Basil said fiercely:

'Be quiet, you old hag. Listen, Dinah darling, I hardly knew her at all. Just ran across her once or twice at the Majestic. That's all, I swear that's all.'

Dinah said, bewildered:

'I don't understand. Why should anyone suspect you, then?'

Basil groaned. He put his hands over his eyes and rocked to and fro.

Miss Marple said:

'What did you do with the hearthrug?'

His reply came mechanically:

'I put it in the dustbin.'

Miss Marple clucked her tongue vexedly.

'That was stupid – very stupid. People don't put good hearthrugs in dustbins. It had spangles in it from her dress, I suppose?'

'Yes, I couldn't get them out.'

Dinah cried: 'But what are you both talking about?'

Basil said sullenly:

'Ask her. She seems to know all about it.'

'I'll tell you what I think happened, if you like,' said Miss Marple. 'You can correct me, Mr Blake, if I go wrong. I think that after having had a violent quarrel with your wife at a party and after having had, perhaps, rather too much – er – to drink, you drove down here. I don't know what time you arrived –'

Basil Blake said sullenly:

'About two in the morning. I meant to go up to town first, then when I got to the suburbs I changed my mind. I thought Dinah might come down here after me. So I drove down here. The place was all dark. I opened the door and turned on the light and I saw – and I saw –'

He gulped and stopped. Miss Marple went on:

'You saw a girl lying on the hearthrug – a girl in a white evening-dress – strangled. I don't know whether you recognized her then –'

Basil Blake shook his head violently.

'I couldn't look at her after the first glance – her face was all blue – swollen. She'd been dead some time and she was *there* – in *my* room!'

He shuddered.

Miss Marple said gently:

'You weren't, of course, quite yourself. You were in a fuddled state and your nerves are not good. You were, I think, panic-stricken. You didn't know what to do –'

'I thought Dinah might turn up any minute. And she'd find me there with a dead body – a girl's dead body – and she'd think I'd killed her. Then I got an idea – it seemed, I don't know why, a good idea at the time – I thought: I'll put her in old Bantry's library. Damned pompous old stick, always looking down his nose, sneering at me as artistic and effeminate. Serve the pompous old brute right, I thought. He'll look a fool when a dead lovely is found on his hearthrug.' He added, with a pathetic eagerness to explain: 'I was a bit drunk, you know, at the time. It really seemed positively *amusing* to me. Old Bantry with a dead blonde.'

'Yes, yes,' said Miss Marple. 'Little Tommy Bond had very much the same idea. Rather a sensitive boy with an inferiority complex, he said teacher was always picking on him. He put a frog in the clock and it jumped out at her.

'You were just the same,' went on Miss Marple, 'only, of course, bodies are more serious matters than frogs.'

Basil groaned again.

'By the morning I'd sobered up. I realized what I'd done. I was scared stiff. And then the police came here – another damned pompous ass of a Chief Constable. I was scared of him – and the only way I could hide it was by being abominably rude. In the middle of it all Dinah drove up.'

Dinah looked out of the window.

She said:

'There's a car driving up now . . . there are men in it.'

'The police, I think,' said Miss Marple.

Basil Blake got up. Suddenly he became quite calm and resolute. He even smiled. He said:

'So I'm for it, am I? All right, Dinah sweet, keep your head. Get on to old Sims – he's the family lawyer – and go to mother and tell her about our marriage. She won't bite. And don't worry. *I didn't do it.* So it's bound to be all right, see, sweetheart?'

There was a tap on the cottage door. Basil called 'Come in.' Inspector Slack entered with another man. He said:

'Mr Basil Blake?'

'Yes.'

'I have a warrant here for your arrest on the charge of murdering Ruby Keene on the night of September 21st last. I warn you that anything you say may be used at your trial. You will please accompany me now. Full facilities will be given you for communicating with your solicitor.'

Basil nodded.

He looked at Dinah, but did not touch her. He said:

'So long, Dinah.'

'Cool customer,' thought Inspector Slack.

He acknowledged the presence of Miss Marple with a half bow and a 'Good morning,' and thought to himself:

'Smart old Pussy, *she's* on to it! Good job we've got that hearthrug. That and finding out from the car-park man at the studio that he left that party at *eleven* instead of midnight. Don't think those friends of his meant to commit perjury. They were bottled and Blake told 'em firmly the next day it was twelve o'clock when he left and they believed him. Well, *his* goose is cooked good and proper! Mental, I expect! Broadmoor, not hanging. First the Reeves kid, probably strangled her, drove her out to the quarry, walked back into Danemouth, picked up his own car in some side lane, drove to this party, then back to Danemouth, brought Ruby Keene out here, strangled her, put her in old Bantry's library, then probably got the wind up about the car in the quarry, drove there, set it on fire, and got back here. Mad – sex and blood lust – lucky *this* girl's escaped. What they call recurring mania, I expect.'

Alone with Miss Marple, Dinah Blake turned to her. She said:

'I don't know who you are, but you've got to understand this – *Basil didn't do it.*'

Miss Marple said:

'I know he didn't. I know who *did* do it. But it's not going to be easy to prove. I've an idea that something you said – just now – may help. It gave me an idea – the *connection* I'd been trying to find – now what *was* it?'

CHAPTER 16

I

'I'm home, Arthur!' declared Mrs Bantry, announcing the fact like a Royal Proclamation as she flung open the study door.

Colonel Bantry immediately jumped up, kissed his wife, and declared heartily: 'Well, well, that's splendid!'

The words were unimpeachable, the manner very well done, but an affectionate wife of as many years' standing as Mrs Bantry was not deceived. She said immediately:

'Is anything the matter?'

'No, of course not, Dolly. What should be the matter?'

'Oh, I don't know,' said Mrs Bantry vaguely. 'Things are so queer, aren't they?'

She threw off her coat as she spoke and Colonel Bantry picked it up carefully and laid it across the back of the sofa.

All exactly as usual – yet not as usual. Her husband, Mrs Bantry thought, seemed to have shrunk. He looked thinner, stooped more; there were pouches under his eyes and those eyes were not ready to meet hers.

He went on to say, still with that affectation of cheerfulness:

'Well, how did you enjoy your time at Danemouth?'

'Oh! it was great fun. You ought to have come, Arthur.'

'Couldn't get away, my dear. Lot of things to attend to here.'

'Still, I think the change would have done you good. And you like the Jeffersons?'

'Yes, yes, poor fellow. Nice chap. All very sad.'

'What have you been doing with yourself since I've been away?'

'Oh, nothing much. Been over the farms, you know. Agreed that Anderson shall have a new roof – can't patch it up any longer.'

'How did the Radfordshire Council meeting go?'

'I – well – as a matter of fact I didn't go.'

'Didn't *go*? But you were taking the chair?'

'Well, as a matter of fact. Dolly – seems there was some mistake about that. Asked me if I'd mind if Thompson took it instead.'

'I *see*,' said Mrs Bantry.

She peeled off a glove and threw it deliberately into the waste-paper basket. Her husband went to retrieve it, and she stopped him, saying sharply:

'Leave it. I hate gloves.'

Colonel Bantry glanced at her uneasily.

Mrs Bantry said sternly:

'Did you go to dinner with the Duffs on Thursday?'

'Oh, that! It was put off. Their cook was ill.'

'Stupid people,' said Mrs Bantry. She went on: 'Did you go to the Naylors' yesterday?'

'I rang up and said I didn't feel up to it, hoped they'd excuse me. They quite understood.'

'They did, did they?' said Mrs Bantry grimly.

She sat down by the desk and absent-mindedly picked up a pair of gardening scissors. With them she cut off the fingers, one by one, of her second glove.

'What *are* you doing, Dolly?'

'Feeling destructive,' said Mrs Bantry.

She got up. 'Where shall we sit after dinner, Arthur? In the library?'

'Well – er – I don't think so – eh? Very nice in here – or the drawing-room.'

'I think,' said Mrs Bantry, 'that we'll sit in the library!'

Her steady eye met his. Colonel Bantry drew himself up to his full height. A sparkle came into his eye.

He said:

'You're right, my dear. We'll sit in the library!'

II

Mrs Bantry put down the telephone receiver with a sigh of annoyance. She had rung up twice, and each time the answer had been the same: Miss Marple was out.

Of a naturally impatient nature, Mrs Bantry was never one to acquiesce in defeat. She rang up in rapid succession the vicarage, Mrs Price Ridley, Miss Hartnell, Miss Wetherby, and, as a last resort, the fishmonger, who, by reason of his advantageous geographical position, usually knew where everybody was in the village.

The fishmonger was sorry, but he had not seen Miss Marple at all in the village that morning. She had not been her usual round.

'Where *can* the woman be?' demanded Mrs Bantry impatiently aloud.

There was a deferential cough behind her. The discreet Lorrimer murmured:

'You were requiring Miss Marple, madam? I have just observed her approaching the house.'

Mrs Bantry rushed to the front door, flung it open, and greeted Miss Marple breathlessly:

'I've been trying to get you *everywhere*. Where have you been?' She glanced over her shoulder. Lorrimer had discreetly vanished. 'Everything's *too* awful! People are beginning to cold-shoulder Arthur. He looks *years* older. We *must* do something, Jane. *You* must do something!'

Miss Marple said:

'You needn't worry, Dolly,' in a rather peculiar voice.

Colonel Bantry appeared from the study door.

'Ah, Miss Marple. Good morning. Glad you've come. My wife's been ringing you up like a lunatic.'

'I thought I'd better bring you the news,' said Miss Marple, as she followed Mrs Bantry into the study.

'News?'

'Basil Blake has just been arrested for the murder of Ruby Keene.'

'Basil Blake?' cried the Colonel.

'But he didn't do it,' said Miss Marple.

Colonel Bantry took no notice of this statement. It is doubtful if he even heard it.

'Do you mean to say he strangled that girl and then brought her along and put her in *my* library?'

'He put her in your library,' said Miss Marple. 'But he didn't kill her.'

'Nonsense! If he put her in my library, of course he killed her! The two things go together.'

'Not necessarily. He found her dead in his own cottage.'

'A likely story,' said the Colonel derisively. 'If you find a body, why, you ring up the police – naturally – if you're an honest man.'

'Ah,' said Miss Marple, 'but we haven't all got such iron nerves as you have, Colonel Bantry. You belong to the old school. This younger generation is different.'

'Got no stamina,' said the Colonel, repeating a well-worn opinion of his.

'Some of them,' said Miss Marple, 'have been through a bad time. I've heard a good deal about Basil. He did ARP work, you know, when he was only eighteen. He went into a burning house and brought out four children, one after another. He went back for a dog, although they told him it wasn't safe. The building fell in on him. They got him out, but his chest was badly crushed and he had to lie in plaster for nearly a year and was ill for a long time after that. That's when he got interested in designing.'

'Oh!' The Colonel coughed and blew his nose. 'I – er – never knew that.'

'He doesn't talk about it,' said Miss Marple.

'Er – quite right. Proper spirit. Must be more in the young chap than I thought. Always thought he'd shirked the war, you know. Shows you ought to be careful in jumping to conclusions.'

Colonel Bantry looked ashamed.

'But, all the same' – his indignation revived – 'what did he mean trying to fasten a murder on *me*?'

'I don't think he saw it like that,' said Miss Marple. 'He thought of it more as a – as a joke. You see, he was rather under the influence of alcohol at the time.'

'Bottled, was he?' said Colonel Bantry, with an Englishman's sympathy for alcoholic excess. 'Oh, well, can't judge a fellow by what he does when he's drunk. When I was at Cambridge, I remember I put a certain utensil – well, well, never mind. Deuce of a row there was about it.'

He chuckled, then checked himself sternly. He looked piercingly

at Miss Marple with eyes that were shrewd and appraising. He said:
'*You* don't think he did the murder, eh?'

'I'm sure he didn't.'

'And you think you know who did?'

Miss Marple nodded.

Mrs Bantry, like an ecstatic Greek chorus, said: 'Isn't she wonderful?' to an unhearing world.

'Well, who was it?'

Miss Marple said:

'I was going to ask you to help me. I think, if we went up to Somerset House we should have a very good idea.'

CHAPTER 17

I

Sir Henry's face was very grave.

He said:

'I don't like it.'

'I am aware,' said Miss Marple, 'that it isn't what you call orthodox. But it *is* so important, isn't it, to be quite *sure* – "to make assurance doubly sure," – as Shakespeare has it. I think, if Mr Jefferson would agree –'

'What about Harper? Is he to be in on this?'

'It might be awkward for him to know too much. But there might be a hint from you. To watch certain persons – have them trailed, you know.'

Sir Henry said slowly:

'Yes, that would meet the case. . . .'

II

Superintendent Harper looked piercingly at Sir Henry Clithering.

'Let's get this quite clear, sir. You're giving me a hint?'

Sir Henry said:

'I'm informing you of what my friend has just informed me – he didn't tell me in confidence – that he proposes to visit a solicitor in Danemouth tomorrow for the purpose of making a new will.'

The Superintendent's bushy eyebrows drew downwards over his steady eyes. He said:

'Does Mr Conway Jefferson propose to inform his son-in-law and daughter-in-law of that fact?'

'He intends to tell them about it this evening.'

'I see.'

The Superintendent tapped his desk with a pen-holder.

He repeated again: 'I see. . . .'

Then the piercing eyes bored once more into the eyes of the other man. Harper said:

'So you're not satisfied with the case against Basil Blake?'

'Are you?'

The Superintendent's moustaches quivered. He said:

'Is Miss Marple?'

The two men looked at each other.

Then Harper said:

'You can leave it to me. I'll have men detailed. There will be no funny business, I can promise you that.'

Sir Henry said:

'There is one more thing. You'd better see this.'

He unfolded a slip of paper and pushed it across the table.

This time the Superintendent's calm deserted him. He whistled:

'So that's it, is it? That puts an entirely different complexion on the matter. How did you come to dig up this?'

'Women,' said Sir Henry, 'are eternally interested in marriages.'

'Especially,' said the Superintendent, 'elderly single women.'

III

Conway Jefferson looked up as his friend entered.

His grim face relaxed into a smile.

He said:

'Well, I told 'em. They took it very well.'

'What did you say?'

'Told 'em that, as Ruby was dead, I felt that the fifty thousand I'd originally left her should go to something that I could associate with her memory. It was to endow a hostel for young girls working as professional dancers in London. Damned silly way to leave your money – surprised they swallowed it. As though *I'd* do a thing like that!'

He added meditatively:

'You know, I made a fool of myself over that girl. Must be turning into a silly old man. I can see it now. She was a pretty kid – but most of what I saw in her I put there myself. I pretended she was another Rosamund. Same colouring, you know. But not the same heart or mind. Hand me that paper – rather an interesting bridge problem.'

IV

Sir Henry went downstairs. He asked a question of the porter.

'Mr Gaskell, sir? He's just gone off in his car. Had to go to London.'

'Oh! I see. Is Mrs Jefferson about?'

'Mrs Jefferson, sir, has just gone up to bed.'

Sir Henry looked into the lounge and through to the ballroom. In the lounge Hugo McLean was doing a crossword puzzle and frowning a good deal over it. In the ballroom Josie was smiling valiantly into the face of a stout, perspiring man as her nimble feet avoided his destructive tread. The stout man was clearly enjoying his dance. Raymond, graceful and weary, was dancing with an anæmic-looking girl with adenoids, dull brown hair, and an expensive and exceedingly unbecoming dress.

Sir Henry said under his breath:

'*And so to bed,*' and went upstairs.

V

It was three o'clock. The wind had fallen, the moon was shining over the quiet sea.

In Conway Jefferson's room there was no sound except his own heavy breathing as he lay, half propped up on pillows.

There was no breeze to stir the curtains at the window, but they stirred. . . . For a moment they parted, and a figure was silhouetted against the moonlight. Then they fell back into place. Everything was quiet again, but there was someone else inside the room.

Nearer and nearer to the bed the intruder stole. The deep breathing on the pillow did not relax.

There was no sound, or hardly any sound. A finger and thumb were ready to pick up a fold of skin, in the other hand the hypodermic was ready.

And then, suddenly, out of the shadows a hand came and closed over the hand that held the needle, the other arm held the figure in an iron grasp.

An unemotional voice, the voice of the law, said:

'No, you don't. I want that needle!'

The light switched on and from his pillows Conway Jefferson looked grimly at the murderer of Ruby Keene.

CHAPTER 18

I

Sir Henry Clithering said:

'Speaking as Watson, I want to know your methods, Miss Marple.'

Superintendent Harper said:

'*I'd* like to know what put you on to it first.'

Colonel Melchett said:

'You've done it again, by Jove! I want to hear all about it from the beginning.'

Miss Marple smoothed the puce silk of her best evening-gown. She flushed and smiled and looked very self-conscious.

She said: 'I'm afraid you'll think my "methods", as Sir Henry calls them, are terribly amateurish. The truth is, you see, that most people – and I don't exclude policemen – are far too trusting for this wicked world. They believe what is told them. I never do. I'm afraid I always like to prove a thing for myself.'

'That is the scientific attitude,' said Sir Henry.

'In this case,' continued Miss Marple, 'certain things were taken for granted from the first – instead of just confining oneself to the facts. The facts, as I noted them, were that the victim was quite

young and that she bit her nails and that her teeth stuck out a little –
as young girls' so often do if not corrected in time with a plate – (and
children are very naughty about their plates and taking them out
when their elders aren't looking).

'But that is wandering from the point. Where was I? Oh, yes,
looking down at the dead girl and feeling sorry, because it is always
sad to see a young life cut short, and thinking that whoever had
done it was a very wicked person. Of course it was all very confusing
her being found in Colonel Bantry's library, altogether too like a
book to be *true*. In fact, it made the wrong pattern. It wasn't, you
see, *meant*, which confused us a lot. The *real* idea had been to plant
the body on poor young Basil Blake (a *much* more likely person),
and his action in putting it in the Colonel's library delayed things
considerably, and must have been a source of great annoyance to
the *real* murderer.

'Originally, you see, Mr Blake would have been the first object of
suspicion. They'd have made enquiries at Danemouth, found he
knew the girl, then found he had tied himself up with another
girl, and they'd have assumed that Ruby came to blackmail
him, or something like that, and that he'd strangled her in a fit of
rage. Just an ordinary, sordid, what I call *night-club* type of
crime!

'But that, of course, *all went wrong*, and interest became focused
much too soon on the Jefferson family – to the great annoyance of *a
certain person*.

'As I've told you, I've got a very suspicious mind. My nephew
Raymond tells me (in fun, of course, and quite affectionately) that I
have a mind like a *sink*. He says that most Victorians have. All I
can say is that the Victorians knew a good deal about human
nature.

'As I say, having this rather insanitary – or surely *sanitary*? –
mind, I looked at once at the *money* angle of it. Two people stood to
benefit by this girl's death – you couldn't get away from that. Fifty
thousand pounds is a lot of money – especially when you are in
financial difficulties, as both these people were. Of course they both
seemed very nice, agreeable people – they didn't seem *likely* people
– but one never can tell, can one?

'Mrs Jefferson, for instance – everyone liked her. But it did seem
clear that she had become very restless that summer, and that she
was tired of the life she led, completely dependent on her father-in-
law. She knew, because the doctor had told her, that he couldn't live

long – so *that* was all right – to put it callously – or it *would* have been all right if Ruby Keene hadn't come along. Mrs Jefferson was passionately devoted to her son, and some women have a curious idea that crimes committed for the sake of their offspring are almost morally justified. I have come across that attitude once or twice in the village. "Well, 'twas all for Daisy, you see, miss," they say, and seem to think that that makes doubtful conduct quite all right. Very *lax* thinking.

'Mr Mark Gaskell, of course, was a much more likely starter, if I may use such a sporting expression. He was a gambler and had not, I fancied, a very high moral code. But, for certain reasons, I was of the opinion that a *woman* was concerned in this crime.

'As I say, with my eye on motive, the money angle seemed *very* suggestive. It was annoying, therefore, to find that both these people had alibis for the time when Ruby Keene, according to the medical evidence, had met her death.

'But soon afterwards there came the discovery of the burnt-out car with Pamela Reeve's body in it, and then the whole thing leaped to the eye. The alibis, of course, were worthless.

'I now had two *halves* of the case, and both quite convincing, but they did not fit. There must *be* a connection, but I could not find it. The one person whom I *knew* to be concerned in the crime hadn't got a motive.

'It was stupid of me,' said Miss Marple meditatively. 'If it hadn't been for Dinah Lee I shouldn't have thought of it – the most obvious thing in the world. Somerset House! Marriage! It wasn't a question of only Mr Gaskell or Mrs Jefferson – there was the further possibilities of *marriage*. If either of those two was married, or even was *likely* to marry, *then the other party to the marriage contract was involved too*. Raymond, for instance, might think he had a pretty good chance of marrying a rich wife. He had been very assiduous to Mrs Jefferson, and it was his charm, I think, that awoke her from her long widowhood. She had been quite content just being a daughter to Mr Jefferson – like Ruth and Naomi – only Naomi, if you remember, took a lot of trouble to arrange a suitable marriage for Ruth.

'Besides Raymond there was Mr McLean. She liked him very much and it seemed highly possible that she would marry him in the end. *He* wasn't well off – and he was not far from Danemouth on the night in question. So it seemed, didn't it,' said Miss Marple, 'as though *anyone* might have done it?

'But, of course, really, in my own mind, I *knew*. You couldn't get away, could you, from those bitten nails?'

'Nails?' said Sir Henry. 'But she tore her nail and cut the others.'

'Nonsense,' said Miss Marple. '*Bitten* nails and close *cut* nails are quite different! Nobody could mistake them who knew anything about girls' nails – very ugly, bitten nails, as I always tell the girls in my class. Those nails, you see, were a *fact*. And they could only mean one thing. *The body in Colonel Bantry's library wasn't Ruby Keene at all.*

'And that brings you straight to the one person who must be concerned. *Josie!* Josie identified the body. She knew, she *must* have known, that it wasn't Ruby Keene's body. She said it was. She was puzzled, completely puzzled, at finding that body where it was. She practically betrayed that fact. Why? Because *she* knew, none better, where it ought to have been found! In Basil Blake's cottage. Who directed our attention to Basil? Josie, by saying to Raymond that Ruby might have been with the film man. And before that, by slipping a snapshot of him into Ruby's handbag. Who cherished such bitter anger against the dead girl that she couldn't hide it even when she looked down at her dead? Josie! Josie, who was shrewd, practical, hard as nails, and *all out for money*.

'That is what I meant about believing too readily. Nobody thought of disbelieving Josie's statement that the body was Ruby Keene's. Simply because it didn't seem at the time that she could have any motive for lying. Motive was always the difficulty – Josie was clearly involved, but Ruby's death seemed, if anything, contrary to her interests. It was not till Dinah Lee mentioned Somerset House that I got the connection.

'Marriage! If Josie and Mark Gaskell were actually married – then the whole thing was clear. As we know now, Mark and Josie were married a year ago. They were keeping it dark until Mr Jefferson died.

'It was really quite interesting, you know, tracing out the course of events – seeing exactly how the plan had worked out. Complicated, and yet simple. First of all the selection of the poor child, Pamela, the approach to her from the film angle. A screen test – of course the poor child couldn't resist it. Not when it was put up to her as plausibly as Mark Gaskell put it. She comes to the hotel, he is waiting for her, he takes her in by the side door and introduces her to Josie – one of their make-up experts! That poor child, it makes me quite sick to think of it! Sitting in Josie's bathroom while Josie bleaches her hair and makes up her face and varnishes her finger-nails and toenails. During all this, the drug was given. In an ice-cream soda, very likely. She goes off into a coma. I imagine that they put her into one of the empty rooms opposite – they were only cleaned once a week, remember.

'After dinner Mark Gaskell went out in his car – to the sea-front, *he* said. That is when he took Pamela's body to the cottage dressed in one of Ruby's old dresses and arranged it on the hearthrug. She was still unconscious, but not dead, when he strangled her with the belt of the frock. . . . Not nice, no – but I hope and pray she knew nothing about it. Really, I feel quite pleased to think of him being hanged. . . . That must have been just after ten o'clock. Then he drove back at top speed and found the others in the lounge where Ruby Keene, *still alive*, was dancing her exhibition dance with Raymond.

'I should imagine that Josie had given Ruby instructions before-hand. Ruby was accustomed to doing what Josie told her. She was to change, go into Josie's room and wait. She, too, was drugged, probably in after-dinner coffee. She was yawning, remember, when she talked to young Bartlett.

'Josie came up later to "look for her" – *but nobody but Josie went into Josie's room*. She probably finished the girl off then – with an injection, perhaps, or a blow on the back of the head. She went down, danced with Raymond, debated with the Jeffersons where Ruby could be, and finally went up to bed. In the early hours of the morning she dressed the girl in Pamela's clothes, carried the body down the side stairs – she was a strong muscular young woman – fetched George Bartlett's car, drove two miles to the quarry, poured petrol over the car and set it alight. Then she walked back to the hotel, probably timing her arrival there for eight or nine o'clock – up early in her anxiety about Ruby!'

'An intricate plot,' said Colonel Melchett.

'Not more intricate than the steps of a dance,' said Miss Marple.

'I suppose not.'

'She was very thorough,' said Miss Marple. 'She even foresaw the discrepancy of the nails. That's why she managed to break one of Ruby's nails on her shawl. It made an excuse for pretending that Ruby had clipped her nails close.'

Harper said: 'Yes, she thought of everything. And the only real proof you had, Miss Marple, was a schoolgirl's bitten nails.'

'More than that,' said Miss Marple. 'People *will* talk too much. Mark Gaskell talked too much. He was speaking of Ruby and he said "her teeth ran down her throat." But the dead girl in Colonel Bantry's library had teeth that stuck *out*.'

Conway Jefferson said rather grimly:

'And was the last dramatic *finale* your idea, Miss Marple?'

Miss Marple confessed. 'Well, it *was*, as a matter of fact. It's so nice to be *sure*, isn't it?'

'Sure is the word,' said Conway Jefferson grimly.

'You see,' said Miss Marple, 'once Mark and Josie knew that you were going to make a new will, they'd *have* to do something. They'd already committed *two* murders on account of the money. So they might as well commit a third. Mark, of course, must be absolutely clear, so he went off to London and established an alibi by dining at a restaurant with friends and going on to a night club. Josie was to do the work. They still wanted Ruby's death to be put down to Basil's account, so Mr Jefferson's death must be thought due to his heart failing. There was digitalin, so the Superintendent tells me, in the syringe. Any doctor would think death from heart trouble quite natural in the circumstances. Josie had loosened one of the stone balls on the balcony and she was going to let it crash down afterwards. His death would be put down to the shock of the noise.'

Melchett said: 'Ingenious devil.'

Sir Henry said: 'So the third death you spoke of was to be Conway Jefferson?'

Miss Marple shook her head.

'Oh no – I meant Basil Blake. They'd have got him hanged if they could.'

'Or shut up in Broadmoor,' said Sir Henry.

Conway Jefferson grunted. He said:

'Always knew Rosamund had married a rotter. Tried not to admit it to myself. She was damned fond of him. Fond of a murderer! Well, he'll hang as well as the woman. I'm glad he went to pieces and gave the show away.'

Miss Marple said:

'She was always the strong character. It was her plan throughout. The irony of it is that she got the girl down here herself, never dreaming that she would take Mr Jefferson's fancy and ruin all her own prospects.'

Jefferson said:

'Poor lass. Poor little Ruby. . . .'

Adelaide Jefferson and Hugo McLean came in. Adelaide looked almost beautiful tonight. She came up to Conway Jefferson and laid a hand on his shoulder. She said, with a little catch in her breath:

'I want to tell you something, Jeff. At once. I'm going to marry Hugo.'

Conway Jefferson looked up at her for a moment. He said gruffly:

'About time you married again. Congratulations to you both. By the way, Addie, I'm making a new will tomorrow.'

She nodded. 'Oh yes. I know.'

Jefferson said:

'No, you don't. I'm settling ten thousand pounds on you. Everything else I have goes to Peter when I die. How does that suit you, my girl?'

'Oh, *Jeff*!' Her voice broke. 'You're *wonderful*!'

'He's a nice lad. I'd like to see a good deal of him – in the time I've got left.'

'Oh, you shall!'

'Got a great feeling for crime, Peter has,' said Conway Jefferson meditatively. 'Not only has he got the fingernail of the murdered girl – one of the murdered girls, anyway – but he was lucky enough to have a bit of Josie's shawl caught in with the nail. So he's got a souvenir of the murderess too! That makes him *very* happy!'

II

Hugo and Adelaide passed by the ballroom. Raymond came up to them.

Adelaide said, rather quickly:

'I must tell you my news. We're going to be married.'

The smile on Raymond's face was perfect – a brave, pensive smile.

'I hope,' he said, ignoring Hugo and gazing into her eyes, 'that you will be very, very happy. . . .'

They passed on and Raymond stood looking after them.

'A nice woman,' he said to himself. 'A very nice woman. And she would have had money too. The trouble I took to mug up that bit about the Devonshire Starrs. . . . Oh well, my luck's out. Dance, dance, little gentleman!'

And Raymond returned to the ballroom.

A POCKET FULL
OF RYE

CHAPTER 1

It was Miss Somers's turn to make the tea. Miss Somers was the newest and the most inefficient of the typists. She was no longer young and had a mild worried face like a sheep. The kettle was not quite boiling when Miss Somers poured the water on to the tea, but poor Miss Somers was never quite sure when a kettle *was* boiling. It was one of the many worries that afflicted her in life.

She poured out the tea and took the cups round with a couple of limp, sweet biscuits in each saucer.

Miss Griffith, the efficient head typist, a grey-haired martinet who had been with Consolidated Investments Trust for sixteen years, said sharply: 'Water not boiling *again*, Somers!' and Miss Somers's worried meek face went pink and she said, 'Oh dear, I *did* think it was boiling *this* time.'

Miss Griffith thought to herself: 'She'll last for another month, perhaps, just while we're so busy. . . . But really! The mess the silly idiot made of that letter to Eastern Developments – a perfectly straightforward job, and always so stupid over the tea. If it weren't so difficult to get hold of any intelligent typists – and the biscuit tin lid wasn't shut tightly last time, either. *Really –*'

Like so many of Miss Griffith's indignant inner communings the sentence went unfinished.

At that moment Miss Grosvenor sailed in to make Mr Fortescue's sacred tea. Mr Fortescue had different tea, and different china and special biscuits. Only the kettle and the water from the cloakroom tap were the same. But on this occasion, being Mr Fortescue's tea, the water boiled. Miss Grosvenor saw to that.

Miss Grosvenor was an incredibly glamorous blonde. She wore an expensively cut little black suit and her shapely legs were encased in the very best and most expensive black-market nylons.

She sailed back through the typists' room without deigning to give anyone a word or a glance. The typists might have been so many blackbeetles. Miss Grosvenor was Mr Fortescue's own special personal secretary; unkind rumour always hinted that she was something more, but actually this was not true. Mr Fortescue had recently married a second wife, both glamorous and expensive, and fully capable of absorbing all his attention. Miss Grosvenor was to Mr Fortescue just a necessary part of the office décor – which was all very luxurious and very expensive.

Miss Grosvenor sailed back with the tray held out in front of her like a ritual offering. Through the inner office and through the waiting-room, where the more important clients were allowed to sit, and through her own ante-room, and finally with a light tap on the door she entered the holy of holies, Mr Fortescue's office.

It was a large room with a gleaming expanse of parquet floor on which were dotted expensive oriental rugs. It was delicately panelled in pale wood and there were some enormous stuffed chairs upholstered in pale buff leather. Behind a colossal sycamore desk, the centre and focus of the room, sat Mr Fortescue himself.

Mr Fortescue was less impressive than he should have been to match the room, but he did his best. He was a large flabby man with a gleaming bald head. It was his affectation to wear loosely cut country tweeds in his city office. He was frowning down at some papers on his desk when Miss Grosvenor glided up to him in her swanlike manner. Placing the tray on the desk at his elbow, she murmured in a low impersonal voice, 'Your tea, Mr Fortescue,' and withdrew.

Mr Fortescue's contribution to the ritual was a grunt.

Seated at her own desk again Miss Grosvenor proceeded with the business in hand. She made two telephone calls, corrected some letters that were lying there typed ready for Mr Fortescue to sign and took one incoming call.

'Ay'm afraid it's impossible just now,' she said in haughty accents. 'Mr Fortescue is in conference.'

As she laid down the receiver she glanced at the clock. It was ten minutes past eleven.

It was just then that an unusual sound penetrated through the almost sound-proof door of Mr Fortescue's office. Muffled, it was yet fully recognizable, a strangled agonized cry. At the same moment the buzzer on Miss Grosvenor's desk sounded in a long-drawn frenzied summons. Miss Grosvenor, startled for a moment into complete immobility, rose uncertainly to her feet. Confronted by the unexpected, her poise was shaken. However, she moved towards Mr Fortescue's door in her usual statuesque fashion, tapped and entered.

What she saw upset her poise still further. Her employer behind his desk seemed contorted with agony. His convulsive movements were alarming to watch.

Miss Grosvenor said, 'Oh dear, Mr Fortescue, are you ill?' and was immediately conscious of the idiocy of the question. There was no doubt but that Mr Fortescue was very seriously ill. Even as she came up to him, his body was convulsed in a painful spasmodic movement.

Words came out in jerky gasps.

'Tea – what the hell – you put in the tea – get help – quick get a doctor –'

Miss Grosvenor fled from the room. She was no longer the supercilious blonde secretary – she was a thoroughly frightened woman who had lost her head.

She came running into the typists' office crying out:

'Mr Fortescue's having a fit – he's dying – we must get a doctor – he looks awful – I'm sure he's dying.'

Reactions were immediate and varied a good deal.

Miss Bell, the youngest typist, said, 'If it's epilepsy we ought to put a cork in his mouth. Who's got a cork?'

Nobody had a cork.

Miss Somers said, 'At his age it's probably apoplexy.'

Miss Griffith said, 'We must get a doctor – *at once*.'

But she was hampered in her usual efficiency because in all her sixteen years of service it had never been necessary to call a doctor to the city office. There was her own doctor but that was at Streatham Hill. Where was there a doctor near here?

Nobody knew. Miss Bell seized a telephone directory and began looking up Doctors under D. But it was not a classified directory and doctors were not automatically listed like taxi ranks. Someone suggested a hospital – but which hospital? 'It has to be the right hospital,' Miss Somers insisted, 'or else they won't come. Because of the National Health, I mean. It's got to be in the area.'

Someone suggested 999 but Miss Griffith was shocked at that and said it would mean the police and that would never do. For citizens of a country which enjoyed the benefits of Medical Service for all, a group of quite reasonably intelligent women showed incredible ignorance of correct procedure. Miss Bell started looking up Ambulances under A. Miss Griffith said, 'There's his own doctor – he must *have* a doctor.' Someone rushed for the private address book. Miss Griffith instructed the office boy to go out and find a doctor – somehow, *anywhere*. In the private address book, Miss Griffith found Sir Edwin Sandeman with an address in Harley Street. Miss Grosvenor, collapsed in a chair, wailed in a voice whose accent was noticeably less Mayfair than usual, 'I made the tea just as usual – reely I did – there couldn't have been anything wrong in it.'

'*Wrong* in it?' Miss Griffith paused, her hand on the dial of the telephone. 'Why do you say that?'

'*He* said it – Mr Fortescue – he said it was the tea –'

Miss Griffith's hand hovered irresolutely between Welbeck and 999. Miss Bell, young and hopeful, said: 'We ought to give him some mustard and water – *now*. Isn't there any mustard in the office?'

There was no mustard in the office.

Some short while later Dr Isaacs of Bethnal Green, and Sir Edwin Sandeman met in the elevator just as two different ambulances drew up in front of the building. The telephone and the office boy had done their work.

CHAPTER 2

Inspector Neele sat in Mr Fortescue's sanctum behind Mr Fortescue's vast sycamore desk. One of his underlings with a notebook sat unobtrusively against the wall near the door.

Inspector Neele had a smart soldierly appearance with crisp brown hair growing back from a rather low forehead. When he uttered the phrase 'just a matter of routine' those addressed were wont to think spitefully: 'And routine is about all *you*'re capable of!' They would have been quite wrong. Behind his unimaginative appearance, Inspector Neele was a highly imaginative thinker, and one of his methods of investigation was to propound to himself fantastic theories of guilt which he applied to such persons as he was interrogating at the time.

Miss Griffith, whom he had at once picked out with an unerring eye as being the most suitable person to give him a succinct account of the events which had led to his being seated where he was, had just left the room having given him an admirable résumé of the morning's happenings. Inspector Neele propounded to himself three separate highly coloured reasons why the faithful doyenne of the typists' room should have poisoned her employer's mid-morning cup of tea, and rejected them as unlikely.

He classified Miss Griffith as (*a*) Not the type of a poisoner, (*b*) Not in love with her employer, (*c*) No pronounced mental instability, (*d*) Not a woman who cherished grudges. That really seemed to dispose of Miss Griffith except as a source of accurate information.

Inspector Neele glanced at the telephone. He was expecting a call from St Jude's Hospital at any moment now.

It was possible, of course, that Mr Fortescue's sudden illness was due to natural causes, but Dr Isaacs of Bethnal Green had not thought so and Sir Edwin Sandeman of Harley Street had not thought so.

Inspector Neele pressed a buzzer conveniently situated at his left hand and demanded that Mr Fortescue's personal secretary should be sent in to him.

Miss Grosvenor had recovered a little of her poise, but not much. She came in apprehensively, with nothing of the swanlike glide about her motions, and said at once defensively:

'I didn't do it!'

Inspector Neele murmured conversationally: 'No?'

He indicated the chair where Miss Grosvenor was wont to place herself, pad in hand, when summoned to take down Mr Fortescue's letters. She sat down now with reluctance and eyed Inspector Neele in alarm. Inspector Neele, his mind playing imaginatively on the themes Seduction? Blackmail? Platinum Blonde in Court? etc., looked reassuring and just a little stupid.

'There wasn't anything wrong with the tea,' said Miss Grosvenor. 'There couldn't have been.'

'*I* see,' said Inspector Neele. 'Your name and address, please?'

'Grosvenor. Irene Grosvenor.'

'How do you spell it?'

'Oh. Like the Square.'

'And your address?'

'14 Rushmoor Road, Muswell Hill.'

Inspector Neele nodded in a satisfied fashion.

'No seduction,' he said to himself. 'No Love Nest. Respectable home with parents. No blackmail.'

Another good set of speculative theories washed out.

'And so it was you who made the tea?' he said pleasantly.

'Well, I had to. I always do, I mean.'

Unhurried, Inspector Neele took her closely through the morning ritual of Mr Fortescue's tea. The cup and saucer and teapot had already been packed up and dispatched to the appropriate quarter for analysis. Now Inspector Neele learned that Irene Grosvenor and only Irene Grosvenor had handled that cup and saucer and teapot. The kettle had been used for making the office tea and had been refilled from the cloakroom tap by Miss Grosvenor.

'And the tea itself?'

'It was Mr Fortescue's own tea, special China tea. It's kept on the shelf in my room next door.'

Inspector Neele nodded. He enquired about sugar and heard that Mr Fortescue didn't take sugar.

The telephone rang. Inspector Neele picked up the receiver. His face changed a little.

'St Jude's?'

He nodded to Miss Grosvenor in dismissal.

'That's all for now, thank you, Miss Grosvenor.'

Miss Grosvenor sped out of the room hurriedly.

Inspector Neele listened carefully to the thin unemotional tones speaking from St Jude's Hospital. As the voice spoke he made a few cryptic signs with a pencil on the corner of the blotter in front of him.

'Died five minutes ago, you say?' he asked. His eye went to the watch on his wrist. *Twelve forty-three*, he wrote on the blotter.

The unemotional voice said that Doctor Bernsdorff himself would like to speak to Inspector Neele.

Inspector Neele said, 'Right. Put him through,' which rather scandalized the owner of the voice who had allowed a certain amount of reverence to seep into the official accents.

There were then various clicks, buzzes, and far-off ghostly murmurs. Inspector Neele sat patiently waiting.

Then without warning a deep bass roar caused him to shift the receiver an inch or two away from his ear.

'Hallo, Neele, you old vulture. At it again with your corpses?'

Inspector Neele and Professor Bernsdorff of St Jude's had been brought together over a case of poisoning just over a year ago and had remained on friendly terms.

'Our man's dead, I hear, doc.'

'Yes. We couldn't do anything by the time he got here.'

'And the cause of death?'

'There will have to be an autopsy, naturally. Very interesting case. Very interesting indeed. Glad I was able to be in on it.'

The professional gusto in Bernsdorff's rich tones told Inspector Neele one thing at least.

'I gather you don't think it was natural death,' he said dryly.

'Not a dog's chance of it,' said Dr Bernsdorff robustly. 'I'm speaking unofficially, of course,' he added with belated caution.

'Of course. Of course. That's understood. He was poisoned?'

'Definitely. And what's more – this is quite unofficial, you understand – just between you and me – I'd be prepared to make a bet on what the poison was.'

'Indeed?'

'Taxine, my boy. Taxine.'

'Taxine? Never heard of it.'

'I know. *Most* unusual. Really delightfully unusual! I don't say I'd have spotted it myself if I hadn't had a case only three or four weeks ago. Couple of kids playing dolls' tea-parties – pulled berries off a yew tree and used them for tea.'

'Is that what it is? Yew berries?'

'Berries or leaves. Highly poisonous. Taxine, of course, is the alkaloid. Don't think I've heard of a case where it was used deliberately. Really *most* interesting and unusual . . . You've no idea, Neele, how tired one gets of the inevitable weed-killer. Taxine is a real treat. Of course, I *may* be wrong – don't quote me, for Heaven's sake – but I don't think so. Interesting for you, too, I should think. Varies the routine!'

'A good time is to be had by all, is that the idea? With the exception of the victim.'

'Yes, yes, poor fellow.' Dr Bernsdorff's tone was perfunctory. 'Very bad luck on him.'

'Did he say anything before he died?'

'Well, one of your fellows was sitting by him with a notebook. He'll have the exact details. He muttered something once about tea – that he'd been given something in his tea at the office – but that's nonsense, of course.'

'Why is it nonsense?' Inspector Neele, who had been reviewing speculatively the picture of the glamorous Miss Grosvenor adding yew berries to a brew of tea, and finding it incongruous, spoke sharply.

'Because the stuff couldn't possibly have worked so soon. I understand the symptoms came on immediately he had drunk the tea?'

'That's what they say.'

'Well, there are very few poisons that act as quickly as that apart from the cyanides, of course – and possibly pure nicotine –'

'And it definitely wasn't cyanide or nicotine?'

'My dear fellow. He'd have been dead before the ambulance arrived. Oh no, there's no question of anything of that kind. I *did* suspect strychnine, but the convulsions were not at all typical. Still unofficial, of course, but I'll stake my reputation it's taxine.'

'How long would that take to work?'

'Depends. An hour. Two hours, three hours. Deceased looked like a hearty eater. If he had a big breakfast, that would slow things up.'

'Breakfast,' said Inspector Neele thoughtfully. 'Yes, it looks like breakfast.'

'Breakfast with the Borgias.' Dr Bernsdorff laughed cheerfully. 'Well, good hunting, my lad.'

'Thanks, doctor. I'd like to speak to my sergeant before you ring off.'

Again there were clicks and buzzes and far-off ghostly voices. And then the sound of heavy breathing came through, an inevitable prelude to Sergeant Hay's conversation.

'Sir,' he said urgently. *'Sir.'*

'Neele here. Did the deceased say anything I ought to know?'

'Said it was in the tea. The tea he had at the office. But the MO says not . . .'

'Yes, I know about that. Nothing else?'

'No, sir. But there's one thing that's odd. The suit he was wearing – I checked the contents of the pockets. The usual stuff – handkerchief, keys, change, wallet – but there was one thing that's downright peculiar. The right-hand pocket of his jacket. It had *cereal* in it.'

'Cereal?'

'Yes, sir.'

'What do you mean by cereal? Do you mean a breakfast food? Farmer's Glory or Wheatifax? Or do you mean corn or barley –'

'That's right, sir. Grain it was. Looked like rye to me. Quite a lot of it.'

'I see . . . Odd . . . But it might have been a sample – something to do with a business deal.'

'Quite so, sir – but I thought I'd better mention it.'

'Quite right, Hay.'

Inspector Neele sat staring ahead of him for a few moments after he had replaced the telephone receiver. His orderly mind was moving from Phase I to Phase II of the enquiry – from suspicion of poisoning to certainty of poisoning. Professor Bernsdorff's words may have been unofficial, but Professor Bernsdorff was not a man to be mistaken in his beliefs. Rex Fortescue had been poisoned and the poison had probably been administered one to three hours before the onset of the first symptoms. It seemed probable, therefore, that the office staff could be given a clean bill of health.

Neele got up and went into the outer office. A little desultory work was being done but the typewriters were not going at full speed.

'Miss Griffith? Can I have another word with you?'

'Certainly, Mr Neele. Could some of the girls go out to lunch? It's long past their regular time. Or would you prefer that we get something sent in?'

'No. They can go to lunch. But they must return afterwards.'

'Of course.'

Miss Griffith followed Neele back into the private office. She sat down in her composed efficient way.

Without preamble, Inspector Neele said:

'I have heard from St Jude's Hospital. Mr Fortescue died at 12.43.'

Miss Griffith received the news without surprise, merely shook her head.

'I was afraid he was very ill,' she said.

She was not, Neele noted, at all distressed.

'Will you please give me particulars of his home and family?'

'Certainly. I have already tried to get into communication with Mrs Fortescue, but it seems she is out playing golf. She was not expected home to lunch. There is some uncertainty as to which course she is playing on.' She added in an explanatory manner, 'They live at Baydon Heath, you know, which is a centre for three well-known golf courses.'

Inspector Neele nodded. Baydon Heath was almost entirely inhabited by rich city men. It had an excellent train service, was only twenty miles from London and was comparatively easy to reach by car even in the rush of morning and evening traffic.

'The exact address, please, and the telephone number?'

'Baydon Heath 3400. The name of the house is Yewtree Lodge.'

'*What?*' The sharp query slipped out before Inspector Neele could control it. 'Did you say *Yewtree* Lodge?'

'Yes.'

Miss Griffith looked faintly curious, but Inspector Neele had himself in hand again.

'Can you give me particulars of his family?'

'Mrs Fortescue is his second wife. She is much younger than he is. They were married about two years ago. The first Mrs Fortescue has been dead a long time. There are two sons and a daughter of the first marriage. The daughter lives at home and so does the elder son who is a partner in the firm. Unfortunately he is away in the North of England today on business. He is expected to return tomorrow.'

'When did he go away?'

'The day before yesterday.'

'Have you tried to get in touch with him?'

'Yes. After Mr Fortescue was removed to hospital I rang up the Midland Hotel in Manchester where I thought he might be staying, but he had left early this morning. I believe he was also going to Sheffield and Leicester, but I am not sure about that. I can give you the names of certain firms in those cities whom he might be visiting.'

Certainly an efficient woman, thought the Inspector, and if she murdered a man she would probably murder him very efficiently, too. But he forced himself to abandon these speculations and concentrate once more on Mr Fortescue's home front.

'There is a second son you said?'

'Yes. But owing to a disagreement with his father he lives abroad.'

'Are both sons married?'

'Yes. Mr Percival has been married for three years. He and his wife occupy a self-contained flat in Yewtree Lodge, though they are moving into their own house at Baydon Heath very shortly.'

'You were not able to get in touch with Mrs Percival Fortescue when you rang up this morning?'

'She had gone to London for the day.' Miss Griffith went on, 'Mr Lancelot got married less than a year ago. To the widow of Lord Frederick Anstice. I expect you've seen pictures of her. In the *Tatler* – with horses, you know. And at point-to-points.'

Miss Griffith sounded a little breathless and her cheeks were faintly flushed. Neele, who was quick to catch the moods of human beings, realized that this marriage had thrilled the snob and the romantic in Miss Griffith. The aristocracy was the aristocracy to Miss Griffith and the fact that the late Lord Frederick Anstice had

had a somewhat unsavoury reputation in sporting circles was almost certainly not known to her. Freddie Anstice had blown his brains out just before an enquiry by the Stewards into the running of one of his horses. Neele remembered something vaguely about his wife. She had been the daughter of an Irish Peer and had been married before to an airman who had been killed in the Battle of Britain.

And now, it seemed, she was married to the black sheep of the Fortescue family, for Neele assumed that the disagreement with his father referred to primly by Miss Griffith, stood for some disgraceful incident in young Lancelot Fortescue's career.

Lancelot Fortescue! What a name! And what was the other son – Percival? He wondered what the first Mrs Fortescue had been like? She'd had a curious taste in Christian names. . . .

He drew the phone towards him and dialled TOL. He asked for Baydon Heath 3400.

Presently a man's voice said:

'Baydon Heath 3400.'

'I want to speak to Mrs Fortescue or Miss Fortescue.'

'Sorry. They aren't in, either of 'em.'

The voice struck Inspector Neele as slightly alcoholic.

'Are you the butler?'

'That's right.'

'Mr Fortescue has been taken seriously ill.'

'I know. They rung up and said so. But there's nothing I can do about it. Mr Val's away up North and Mrs Fortescue's out playing golf. Mrs Val's gone up to London but she'll be back for dinner and Miss Elaine's out with her Brownies.'

'Is there no one in the house I can speak to about Mr Fortescue's illness? It's important.'

'Well – I don't know.' The man sounded doubtful. 'There's Miss Ramsbottom – but she don't ever speak over the phone. Or there's Miss Dove – she's what you might call the 'ousekeeper.'

'I'll speak to Miss Dove, please.'

'I'll try and get hold of her.'

His retreating footsteps were audible through the phone. Inspector Neele heard no approaching footsteps but a minute or two later a woman's voice spoke.

'This is Miss Dove speaking.'

The voice was low and well poised, with clear-cut enunciation. Inspector Neele formed a favourable picture of Miss Dove.

'I am sorry to have to tell you, Miss Dove, that Mr Fortescue died in St Jude's Hospital a short time ago. He was taken suddenly ill in his office. I am anxious to get in touch with his relatives –'

'Of course. I had no idea –' She broke off. Her voice held no agitation, but it was shocked. She went on: 'It is all most unfortunate. The person you really want to get in touch with is Mr Percival Fortescue. He would be the one to see to all the necessary arrangements. You might be able to get in touch with him at the Midland in Manchester or possibly at the Grand in Leicester. Or you might try Shearer and Bonds of Leicester. I don't know their telephone number, I'm afraid, but I know they are a firm on whom he was going to call and they might be able to inform you where he would be likely to be today. Mrs Fortescue will certainly be in to dinner and she may be in to tea. It will be a great shock to her. It must have been very sudden? Mr Fortescue was quite well when he left here this morning.'

'You saw him before he left?'

'Oh yes. What was it? Heart?'

'Did he suffer from heart trouble?'

'No – no – I don't think so – But I thought as it was so sudden –' She broke off. 'Are you speaking from St Jude's Hospital? Are you a doctor?'

'No, Miss Dove, I'm not a doctor. I'm speaking from Mr Fortescue's office in the city. I am Detective-Inspector Neele of the CID and I shall be coming down to see you as soon as I can get there.'

'Detective-Inspector? Do you mean – what *do* you mean?'

'It was a case of sudden death, Miss Dove; and when there is a sudden death we get called to the scene, especially when the deceased man hasn't seen a doctor lately – which I gather was the case?'

It was only the faintest suspicion of a question mark but the young woman responded.

'I know. Percival made an appointment twice for him, but he wouldn't keep it. He was quite unreasonable – they've all been worried –'

She broke off and then resumed in her former assured manner:

'If Mrs Fortescue returns to the house before you arrive, what do you want me to tell her?'

Practical as they make 'em, thought Inspector Neele.

Aloud he said:

'Just tell her that in a case of sudden death we have to make a few enquiries. Routine enquiries.'

He hung up.

CHAPTER 3

Neele pushed the telephone away and looked sharply at Miss Griffith.

'So they've been worried about him lately,' he said. 'Wanted him to see a doctor. You didn't tell me that.'

'I didn't think of it,' said Miss Griffith, and added: 'He never seemed to me really *ill* –'

'Not ill – but what?'

'Well, just odd. Unlike himself. Peculiar in his manner.'

'Worried about something?'

'Oh no, not *worried*. It's *we* who were worried –'

Inspector Neele waited patiently.

'It's difficult to say, really,' said Miss Griffith. 'He had moods, you know. Sometimes he was quite boisterous. Once or twice, frankly, I thought he had been drinking. . . . He boasted and told the most extraordinary stories which I'm sure couldn't possibly have been true. For most of the time I've been here he was always very close about his affairs – not giving anything away, you know. But lately he's been quite different, expansive, and positively – well – flinging money about. Most unlike his usual manner. Why, when the office boy had to go to his grandmother's funeral, Mr Fortescue called him in and gave him a five pound note and told him to put it on the second favourite and then roared with laughter. He wasn't – well, he just wasn't like himself. That's all I can say.'

'As though, perhaps, he had something on his mind?'

'Not in the usual meaning of the term. It was as though he were looking forward to something pleasurable – exciting –'

'Possibly a big deal that he was going to pull off?'

Miss Griffith agreed with more conviction.

'Yes – yes, that's much more what I mean. As though everyday things didn't matter any more. He was excited. And some very odd-looking people came to see him on business. People who'd never been here before. It worried Mr Percival dreadfully.'

'Oh it worried him, did it?'

'Yes. Mr Percival's always been very much in his father's confidence, you see. His father relied on him. But lately –'

'Lately they weren't getting along so well.'

'Well, Mr Fortescue was doing a lot of things that Mr Percival thought unwise. Mr Percival is always very careful and prudent. But suddenly his father didn't listen to him any more and Mr Percival was very upset.'

'And they had a real row about it all?'

Inspector Neele was still probing.

'I don't know about a *row*. . . . Of course, I realize now Mr Fortescue can't have been himself – shouting like that.'

'Shouted, did he? What did he say?'

'He came right out in the typists' room –'

'So that you all heard?'

'Well – yes.'

'And he called Percival names – abused him – swore at him. . . . What did he say Percival had done?'

'It was more that he hadn't done anything . . . he called him a miserable pettifogging little clerk. He said he had no large outlook, no conception of doing business in a big way. He said "I shall get Lance home again. He's worth ten of you – *and* he's married well. Lance has got guts even if he did risk a criminal prosecution once –"' Oh dear, I oughtn't to have said that!' Miss Griffith, carried away as others before her had been under Inspector Neele's expert handling, was suddenly overcome with confusion.

'Don't worry,' said Inspector Neele comfortingly. 'What's past is past.'

'Oh yes, it was a long time ago. Mr Lance was just young and high spirited and didn't really realize what he was doing.'

Inspector Neele had heard that view before and didn't agree with it. But he passed on to fresh questions.

'Tell me a little more about the staff here.'

Miss Griffith, hurrying to get away from her indiscretion, poured out information about the various personalities in the firm. Inspector Neele thanked her and then said he would like to see Miss Grosvenor again.

Detective-Constable Waite sharpened his pencil. He remarked wistfully that this was a Ritzy joint. His glance wandered appreciatively over the huge chairs, the big desk and the indirect lighting.

'All these people have got Ritzy names, too,' he said. 'Grosvenor

– that's something to do with a Duke. And Fortescue – that's a classy name, too.'

Inspector Neele smiled.

'His father's name wasn't Fortescue. Fontescu – and he came from somewhere in Central Europe. I suppose this man thought Fortescue sounded better.'

Detective-Constable Waite looked at his superior officer with awe.

'So you know all about him?'

'I just looked up a few things before coming along on the call.'

'Not got a record, had he?'

'Oh no. Mr Fortescue was much too clever for that. He's had certain connections with the Black Market and put through one or two deals that are questionable to say the least of it, but they've always been just within the law.'

'I see,' said Waite. 'Not a nice man.'

'A twister,' said Neele. 'But we've got nothing on him. The Inland Revenue have been after him for a long time but he's been too clever for them. Quite a financial genius, the late Mr Fortescue.'

'The sort of man,' said Constable Waite, 'who might have enemies?'

He spoke hopefully.

'Oh yes – certainly enemies. But he was poisoned at home remember. Or so it would seem. You know, Waite, I see a kind of pattern emerging. An old-fashioned familiar kind of pattern. The good boy, Percival. The bad boy, Lance – attractive to women. The wife who's younger than her husband and who's vague about which course she's going to play golf on. It's all very very familiar. But there's one thing that sticks out in a most incongruous way.'

Constable Waite asked 'What's that?' just as the door opened and Miss Grosvenor, her poise restored, and once more her glamorous self, enquired haughtily:

'You wished to see me?'

'I wanted to ask you a few questions about your employer – your late employer perhaps I should say.'

'Poor soul,' said Miss Grosvenor unconvincingly.

'I want to know if you have noticed any difference in him lately.'

'Well, yes. I did, as a matter of fact.'

'In what way?'

'I couldn't really say. . . . He seemed to talk a lot of nonsense. I couldn't really believe half of what he said. And then he lost his temper very easily – especially with Mr Percival. Not with me, because of course I *never* argue. I just say, "Yes, Mr Fortescue," whatever peculiar thing he says – said, I mean.'

'Did he – ever – well – make any passes at you?'

Miss Grosvenor replied rather regretfully:

'Well, no, I couldn't exactly say *that*.'

'There's just one other thing, Miss Grosvenor. Was Mr Fortescue in the habit of carrying grain about in his pocket?'

Miss Grosvenor displayed a lively surprise.

'Grain? In his pocket? Do you mean to feed pigeons or something?'

'It could have been for that purpose.'

'Oh I'm sure he didn't. Mr Fortescue? Feed pigeons? Oh no.'

'Could he have had barley – or rye – in his pocket today for any special reason? A sample, perhaps? Some deal in grain?'

'Oh no. He was expecting the Asiatic Oil people this afternoon. And the President of the Atticus Building Society. . . . No one else.'

'Oh well –' Neele dismissed the subject and Miss Grosvenor with a wave of the hand.

'Lovely legs she's got,' said Constable Waite with a sigh, 'And super nylons –'

'Legs are no help to me,' said Inspector Neele. 'I'm left with what I had before. A pocketful of rye – and no explanation of it.'

CHAPTER 4

Mary Dove paused on her way downstairs and looked out through the big window on the stairs. A car had just driven up from which two men were alighting. The taller of the two stood for a moment with his back to the house surveying his surroundings. Mary Dove appraised the two men thoughtfully. Inspector Neele and presumably a subordinate.

She turned from the window and looked at herself in the full-length mirror that hung on the wall where the staircase turned. . . . She saw a small demure figure with immaculate white collar and cuffs on a beige grey dress. Her dark hair was parted in the middle and drawn back in two shining waves to a knot in the back of the neck. . . . The lipstick she used was a pale rose colour.

On the whole Mary Dove was satisfied with her appearance. A very faint smile on her lips, she went on down the stairs.

Inspector Neele, surveying the house, was saying to himself:

Call it a lodge, indeed! Yewtree Lodge! The affectation of these rich people! The house was what he, Inspector Neele, would call a mansion. He knew what a lodge was. He'd been brought up in one! The lodge at the gates of Hartington Park, that vast unwieldy Palladian house with its twenty-nine bedrooms which had now been taken over by the National Trust. The lodge had been small and attractive from the outside, and had been damp, uncomfortable and devoid of anything but the most primitive form of sanitation within. Fortunately these facts had been accepted as quite proper and fitting by Inspector Neele's parents. They had no rent to pay and nothing whatever to do except open and shut the gates when required, and there were always plenty of rabbits and an occasional pheasant or so for the pot. Mrs Neele had never discovered the pleasures of electric irons, slow combustion stoves, airing cupboards, hot and cold water from taps, and the switching on of light by a mere flick of a finger. In winter the Neeles had an oil lamp and in summer they went to bed when it got dark. They were a healthy family and a happy one, all thoroughly behind the times.

So when Inspector Neele heard the word Lodge, it was his childhood memories that stirred. But this place, this pretentiously named Yewtree Lodge was just the kind of mansion that rich people built themselves and then called 'their little place in the country'. It wasn't in the country either, according to Inspector Neele's idea of the country. The house was a large solid red brick structure, sprawling lengthwise rather than upward, with rather too many gables, and a vast number of leaded paned windows. The gardens were highly artificial – all laid out in rose beds and pergolas and pools, and living up to the name of the house with large numbers of clipped yew hedges.

Plenty of yew here for anybody with a desire to obtain the raw material of taxine. Over on the right, behind the rose pergola, there was a bit of actual Nature left – a vast yew tree of the kind one associates with churchyards, its branches held up by stakes – like a kind of Moses of the forest world. That tree, the Inspector thought, had been there long before the rash of newly built red brick houses had begun to spread over the countryside. It had been there before the golf courses had been laid out and the fashionable architects had walked round with their rich clients pointing out the advantages of the various sites. And since it was a valuable antique, the tree had been kept and incorporated in the new set up and had, perhaps, given its name to the new desirable residence. Yewtree Lodge. And possibly the berries from that very tree –

Inspector Neele cut off these unprofitable speculations. Must get on with the job. He rang the bell.

It was opened promptly by a middle-aged man who fitted in quite accurately with the mental image Inspector Neele had formed of him over the phone. A man with a rather spurious air of smartness, a shifty eye and a rather unsteady hand.

Inspector Neele announced himself and his subordinate and had the pleasure of seeing an instant look of alarm come into the butler's eye. . . . Neele did not attach too much importance to that. It might easily have nothing to do with the death of Rex Fortescue. It was quite possibly a purely automatic reaction.

'Has Mrs Fortescue returned yet?'

'No, sir.'

'Nor Mr Percival Fortescue? Nor Miss Fortescue?'

'No, sir.'

'Then I would like to see Miss Dove, please.'

The man turned his head slightly.

'Here's Miss Dove now – coming downstairs.'

Inspector Neele took in Miss Dove as she came composedly down the wide staircase. This time the mental picture did not correspond with the reality. Unconsciously the word housekeeper had conjured up a vague impression of someone large and authoritative dressed in black with somewhere concealed about her a jingle of keys.

The Inspector was quite unprepared for the small trim figure descending towards him. The soft dove-coloured tones of her dress, the white collar and cuffs, the neat waves of hair, the faint Mona Lisa smile. It all seemed, somehow, just a little unreal, as though this young woman of under thirty was playing a part: not, he thought, the part of a housekeeper, but the part of Mary Dove. Her appearance was directed towards living up to her name.

She greeted him composedly.

'Inspector Neele?'

'Yes. This is Sergeant Hay. Mr Fortescue, as I told you through the phone, died in St Jude's Hospital at 12.43. It seems likely that his death was the result of something he ate at breakfast this morning. I should be glad therefore if Sergeant Hay could be taken to the kitchen where he can make enquiries as to the food served.'

Her eyes met his for a moment, thoughtfully, then she nodded.

'Of course,' she said. She turned to the uneasily hovering butler. 'Crump, will you take Sergeant Hay out and show him whatever he wants to see.'

The two men departed together. Mary Dove said to Neele:

'Will you come in here?'

She opened the door of a room and preceded him into it. It was a characterless apartment, clearly labelled 'Smoking Room,' with panelling, rich upholstery, large stuffed chairs, and a suitable set of sporting prints on the walls.

'Please sit down.'

He sat and Mary Dove sat opposite him. She chose, he noticed, to face the light. An unusual preference for a woman. Still more unusual if a woman had anything to hide. But perhaps Mary Dove had nothing to hide.

'It is very unfortunate,' she said, 'that none of the family is available. Mrs Fortescue may return at any minute. And so may Mrs Val. I have sent wires to Mr Percival Fortescue at various places.'

'Thank you, Miss Dove.'

'You say that Mr Fortescue's death was caused by something he may have eaten for breakfast? Food poisoning, you mean?'

'Possibly.' He watched her.

She said composedly, 'It seems unlikely. For breakfast this morning there were bacon and scrambled eggs, coffee, toast and marmalade. There was also a cold ham on the sideboard, but that had been cut yesterday, and no one felt any ill effects. No fish of any kind was served, no sausages – nothing like that.'

'I see you know exactly what was served.'

'Naturally. I order the meals. For dinner last night –'

'No.' Inspector Neele interrupted her. 'It would not be a question of dinner last night.'

'I thought the onset of food poisoning could sometimes be delayed as much as twenty-four hours.'

'Not in this case. . . . Will you tell me exactly what Mr Fortescue ate and drank before leaving the house this morning?'

'He had early tea brought to his room at eight o'clock. Breakfast was at a quarter past nine. Mr Fortescue, as I have told you, had scrambled eggs, bacon, coffee, toast and marmalade.'

'Any cereal?'

'No, he didn't like cereals.'

'The sugar for the coffee – is it lump sugar or granulated?'

'Lump. But Mr Fortescue did not take sugar in his coffee.'

'Was he in the habit of taking any medicines in the morning? Salts? A tonic? Some digestive remedy?'

'No, nothing of that kind.'

'Did you have breakfast with him also?'

'No. I do not take meals with the family.'

'Who was at breakfast?'

'Mrs Fortescue. Miss Fortescue. Mrs Val Fortescue. Mr Percival Fortescue, of course, was away.'

'And Mrs and Miss Fortescue ate the same things for breakfast?'

'Mrs Fortescue has only coffee, orange juice and toast, Mrs Val and Miss Fortescue always eat a hearty breakfast. Besides eating scrambled eggs and cold ham, they would probably have a cereal as well. Mrs Val drinks tea, not coffee.'

Inspector Neele reflected for a moment. The opportunities seemed at least to be narrowing down. Three people and three people only had had breakfast with the deceased, his wife, his daughter and his daughter-in-law. Any one of them might have seized an opportunity to add taxine to his cup of coffee. The bitterness of the coffee would have masked the bitter taste of the taxine. There was the early morning tea, of course, but Bernsdorff had intimated that the taste would be noticeable in tea. But perhaps, first thing in the morning, before the senses were alert . . . He looked up to find Mary Dove watching him.

'Your questions about tonic and medicines seem to me rather odd, Inspector,' she said. 'It seems to imply that either there was something wrong with a medicine, or that something had been added to it. Surely neither of those processes could be described as food poisoning.'

Neele eyed her steadily.

'I did not say – definitely – that Mr Fortescue died of food poisoning.'

'But some kind of poisoning. In fact – just poisoning.'

She repeated softly 'Poisoning. . . .'

She appeared neither startled nor dismayed, merely interested. Her attitude was of one sampling a new experience.

In fact she said as much, remarking after a moment's reflection: 'I have never had anything to do with a poisoning case before.'

'It's not very pleasant,' Neele informed her dryly.

'No – I suppose not. . . .'

She thought about it for a moment and then looked up at him with a sudden smile.

'I didn't do it,' she said. 'But I suppose everybody will tell you that!'

'Have you any idea who did do it, Miss Dove?'

She shrugged her shoulders.

'Frankly, he was an odious man. Anybody might have done it.'

'But people aren't poisoned just for being "odious", Miss Dove. There usually has to be a pretty solid motive.'

'Yes, of course.'

She was thoughtful.

'Do you care to tell me something about the household here?'

She looked up at him. He was a little startled to find her eyes cool and amused.

'This isn't exactly a statement you're asking me to make, is it? No, it couldn't be, because your Sergeant is busy upsetting the domestic staff. I shouldn't like to have what I say read out in court – but all the same I should rather like to say it – unofficially. Off the record, so to speak?'

'Go ahead then, Miss Dove. I've no witness, as you've already observed.'

She leaned back, swinging one slim foot and narrowing her eyes.

'Let me start by saying that I've no feeling of loyalty to my employers. I work for them because it's a job that pays well and I insist that it should pay well.'

'I was a little surprised to find you doing this type of job. It struck me that with your brains and education –'

'I ought to be confined in an office? Or compiling files in a Ministry? My dear Inspector Neele, this is the perfect racket. People will pay anything – *anything* – to be spared domestic worries. To find and engage a staff is a thoroughly tedious job. Writing to agencies, putting in advertisements, interviewing people, making arrangements for interviews, and finally keeping the whole thing running smoothly – it takes a certain capacity which most of these people haven't got.'

'And suppose your staff when you've assembled it, runs out on you? I've heard of such things.'

Mary smiled.

'If necessary, I can make the beds, dust the rooms, cook a meal *and* serve it without anyone noticing the difference. Of course I don't advertise that fact. It might give rise to ideas. But I can always be sure of tiding over any little gap. But there aren't often gaps. I work only for the extremely rich who will pay anything to be comfortable. I pay top prices and so I get the best of what's going.'

'Such as the butler?'

She threw him an amused, appreciative glance.

'There's always that trouble with a couple. Crump stays because of Mrs Crump, who is one of the best cooks I've ever come across. She's a jewel and one would put up with a good deal to keep her. Our Mr Fortescue likes his food – liked, I should say. In this household nobody has any scruples and they have plenty of money. Butter, eggs, cream, Mrs Crump can command what she likes. As for Crump, he just makes the grade. His silver's all right, and his waiting at table is not too bad. I keep the key of the wine cellar and a sharp eye on the whisky and gin, and supervise his valeting.'

Inspector Neele raised his eyebrows.

'The admirable Miss Crichton.'

'I find one must *know* how to do everything oneself. Then – one need never do it. But you wanted to know my impressions of the family.'

'If you don't mind.'

'They are really all quite odious. The late Mr Fortescue was the kind of crook who is always careful to play safe. He boasted a great deal of his various smart dealings. He was rude and overbearing in manner and was a definite bully. Mrs Fortescue, Adele – was his second wife and about thirty years younger than he was. He came across her at Brighton. She was a manicurist on the look-out for big money. She is very good looking – a real sexy piece, if you know what I mean.'

Inspector Neele was shocked but managed not to show it. A girl like Mary Dove ought not to say such things, he felt.

The young lady was continuing composedly:

'Adele married him for his money, of course, and his son, Percival, and his daughter, Elaine, were simply livid about it. They're as nasty as they can be to her, but very wisely she doesn't care or even notice. She knows she's got the old man where she wants him. Oh dear, the wrong tense again. I haven't really grasped yet that he's dead. . . .'

'Let's hear about the son.'

'Dear Percival? Val as his wife calls him. Percival is a mealy-mouthed hypocrite. He's prim and sly and cunning. He's terrified of his father and has always let himself be bullied, but he's quite clever at getting his own way. Unlike his father he's mean about money. Economy is one of his passions. That's why he's been so long about finding a house of his own. Having a suite of rooms here saved his pocket.'

'And his wife?'

'Jennifer's meek and seems very stupid. But I'm not so sure. She was a hospital nurse before her marriage – nursed Percival through pneumonia to a romantic conclusion. The old man was dis-. appointed by the marriage. He was a snob and wanted Percival to make what he called a "good marriage". He despised poor Mrs Val and snubbed her. She dislikes – disliked him a good deal, I think. Her principal interests are shopping and the cinema; her principal grievance is that her husband keeps her short of money.'

'What about the daughter?'

'Elaine? I'm rather sorry for Elaine. She's not a bad sort. One of those great schoolgirls who never grows up. She plays games quite well, and runs Guides and Brownies and all that sort of thing. There was some sort of affair not long ago with a disgruntled young schoolmaster, but Father discovered the young man had communistic ideas and came down on the romance like a ton of bricks.'

'She hadn't got the spirit to stand up to him?'

'*She* had. It was the young man who ratted. A question of money yet again, I fancy. Elaine is not particularly attractive, poor dear.'

'And the other son?'

'I've never seen him. He's attractive, by all accounts, and a thoroughly bad lot. Some little matter of a forged cheque in the past. He lives in East Africa.'

'And was estranged from his father.'

'Yes, Mr Fortescue couldn't cut him off with a shilling because he'd already made him a junior partner in the firm, but he held no communication with him for years, and in fact if Lance was ever mentioned, he used to say "Don't talk to me of that rascal. He's no son of mine." All the same –'

'Yes, Miss Dove?'

Mary said slowly: 'All the same, I shouldn't be surprised if old Fortescue hadn't been planning to get him back here.'

'What makes you think that?'

'Because, about a month ago, old Fortescue had a terrific row with Percival – he found out something that Percival had been doing behind his back – I don't know what it was – and he was absolutely furious. Percival suddenly stopped being the white-headed boy. He's been quite different lately, too.'

'Mr Fortescue was quite different?'

'No. I meant Percival. He's gone about looking worried to death.'

'Now what about servants? You've already described the Crumps. Who else is there?'

'Gladys Martin is the parlourmaid or waitress, as they like to call themselves nowadays. She does the downstairs rooms, lays the table, clears away and helps Crump wait at table. Quite a decent sort of girl but very nearly half-witted. The adenoidal type.'

Neele nodded.

'The housemaid is Ellen Curtis. Elderly, very crabbed, and very cross, but has been in good service and is a first-class housemaid. The rest is outside help – odd women who come in.'

'And those are the only people living here?'

'There's old Miss Ramsbottom.'

'Who is she?'

'Mr Fortescue's sister-in-law – his first wife's sister. His wife was a good deal older than he was and her sister again was a good deal older than her – which makes her well over seventy. She has a room of her own on the second floor – does her own cooking and all that, with just a woman coming in to clean. She's rather eccentric and she never liked her brother-in-law, but she came here while her sister was alive and stayed on when she died. Mr Fortescue never bothered about her much. She's quite a character, though, is Aunt Effie.'

'And that is all.'

'That's all.'

'So we come to you, Miss Dove.'

'You want particulars? I'm an orphan. I took a secretarial course at the St Alfred's Secretarial College. I took a job as shorthand typist, left it and took another, decided I was in the wrong racket, and started on my present career. I have been with three different employers. After about a year or eighteen months I get tired of a particular place and move on. I have been at Yewtree Lodge just over a year. I will type out the names and addresses of my various employers and give them, with a copy of my references to Sergeant – Hay, is it? Will that be satisfactory?'

'Perfectly, Miss Dove.' Neele was silent for a moment, enjoying a mental image of Miss Dove tampering with Mr Fortescue's breakfast. His mind went back farther, and he saw her methodically gathering yew berries in a little basket. With a sigh he returned to the present and reality. 'Now, I would like to see the girl – er Gladys – and then the housemaid, Ellen.' He added as he rose, 'By the way, Miss Dove, can you give me any idea why Mr Fortescue would be carrying loose grain in his pocket?'

'Grain?' She stared at him with what appeared to be genuine surprise.

'Yes – grain. Does that suggest something to you, Miss Dove?'

'Nothing at all.'

'Who looked after his clothes?'

'Crump.'

'I see. Did Mr Fortescue and Mrs Fortescue occupy the same bedroom?'

'Yes. He had a dressing-room and bath, of course, and so did she. . . .' Mary glanced down at her wristwatch. 'I really think that she ought to be back very soon now.'

The Inspector had risen. He said in a pleasant voice:

'Do you know one thing, Miss Dove? It strikes me as very odd that even though there are three golf courses in the immediate neighbourhood, it has yet not been possible to find Mrs Fortescue on one of them before now?'

'It would not be so odd, Inspector, if she did not actually happen to be playing golf at all.'

Mary's voice was dry. The Inspector said sharply:

'I was distinctly informed that she was playing golf.'

'She took her golf clubs and announced her intention of doing so. She was driving her own car, of course.'

He looked at her steadily, perceiving the inference.

'Who was she playing with? Do you know?'

'I think it possible that it might be Mr Vivian Dubois.'

Neele contented himself by saying: 'I see.'

'I'll send Gladys in to you. She'll probably be scared to death.' Mary paused for a moment by the door, then she said:

'I should hardly advise you to go too much by all I've told you. I'm a malicious creature.'

She went out. Inspector Neele looked at the closed door and wondered. Whether actuated by malice or not, what she had told him could not fail to be suggestive. If Rex Fortescue had been deliberately poisoned, and it seemed almost certain that that was the case, then the set-up at Yewtree Lodge seemed highly promising. Motives appeared to be lying thick on the ground.

CHAPTER 5

The girl who entered the room with obvious unwillingness was an unattractive, frightened looking girl, who managed to look faintly sluttish in spite of being tall and smartly dressed in a claret-coloured uniform.

She said at once, fixing imploring eyes upon him.

'I didn't do anything. I didn't really. I don't know anything about it.'

'That's all right,' said Neele heartily. His voice had changed slightly. It sounded more cheerful and a good deal commoner in intonation. He wanted to put the frightened rabbit Gladys at her ease.

'Sit down here,' he went on. 'I just want to know about breakfast this morning.'

'I didn't do anything at all.'

'Well, you laid the breakfast, didn't you?'

'Yes, I did that.' Even that admission came unwillingly. She looked both guilty and terrified, but Inspector Neele was used to witnesses who looked like that. He went on cheerfully, trying to put her at her ease, asking questions: who had come down first? And who next?

Elaine Fortescue had been the first down to breakfast. She'd come in just as Crump was bringing in the coffee pot. Mrs Fortescue was down next, and then Mrs Val, and the master last. They waited on themselves. The tea and coffee and the hot dishes were all on hot plates on the sideboard.

He learnt little of importance from her that he did not know already. The food and drink was as Mary Dove had described it. The master and Mrs Fortescue and Miss Elaine took coffee and Mrs Val took tea. Everything had been quite as usual.

Neele questioned her about herself and here she answered more readily. She'd been in private service first and after that in various cafés. Then she thought she'd like to go back to private service and had come to Yewtree Lodge last September. She'd been there two months.

'And you like it?'

'Well, it's all right, I suppose.' She added: 'It's not so hard on your feet – but you don't get so much freedom. . . .'

'Tell me about Mr Fortescue's clothes – his suits. Who looked after them? Brushed them and all that?'

Gladys looked faintly resentful.

'Mr Crump's supposed to. But half the time he makes me do it.'

'Who brushed and pressed the suit Mr Fortescue had on today?'

'I don't remember which one he wore. He's got ever so many.'

'Have you ever found grain in the pocket of one of his suits?'

'Grain?' She looked puzzled.

'Rye, to be exact.'

'Rye? That's bread, isn't it? A sort of black bread – got a nasty taste, I always think.'

'That's bread made from rye. Rye is the grain itself. There was some found in the pocket of your master's coat.'

'In his coat pocket?'

'Yes. Do you know how it got there?'

'I couldn't say I'm sure. I never saw any.'

He could get no more from her. For a moment or two he wondered if she knew more about the matter than she was willing to admit. She certainly seemed embarrassed and on the defensive – but on the whole he put it down to a natural fear of the police.

When he finally dismissed her, she asked:

'It's really true, is it? He's dead?'

'Yes, he's dead.'

'Very sudden, wasn't it? They said when they rang up from the office that he'd had a kind of fit.'

'Yes – it was a kind of fit.'

Gladys said: 'A girl I used to know had fits. Come on any time, they did. Used to scare me.'

For the moment this reminiscence seemed to overcome her suspicions.

Inspector Neele made his way to the kitchen.

His reception was immediate and alarming. A woman of vast proportions, with a red face and armed with a rolling-pin stepped towards him in a menacing fashion.

'Police, indeed,' she said. 'Coming here and saying things like that! Nothing of the kind, I'd have you know. Anything I've sent in to the dining-room has been just what it should be. Coming here and saying I poisoned the master. I'll have the law on you, police or no police. No bad food's ever been served in this house.'

It was some time before Inspector Neele could appease the irate artist. Sergeant Hay looked in grinning from the pantry and Inspector Neele gathered that he had already run the gauntlet of Mrs Crump's wrath.

The scene was terminated by the ringing of the telephone.

Neele went out into the hall to find Mary Dove taking the call. She was writing down a message on a pad. Turning her head over her shoulder she said: 'It's a telegram.'

The call concluded, she replaced the receiver and handed the pad on which she had been writing to the Inspector. The place of origin was Paris and the message ran as follows:

FORTESCUE YEWTREE LODGE BAYDON HEATH SURREY. SORRY YOUR LETTER DELAYED. WILL BE WITH YOU TOMORROW ABOUT TEATIME. SHALL EXPECT ROAST VEAL FOR DINNER. LANCE.

Inspector Neele raised his eyebrows.

'So the Prodigal Son had been summoned home,' he said.

CHAPTER 6

At the moment when Rex Fortescue had been drinking his last cup of tea, Lance Fortescue and his wife had been sitting under the trees on the Champs Elysées watching the people walking past.

'It's all very well to say "describe him," Pat. I'm a rotten hand at descriptions. What do you want to know? The Guvnor's a bit of an old crook, you know. But you won't mind that? You must be used to that more or less.'

'Oh yes,' said Pat. 'Yes – as you say – I'm acclimatized.'

She tried to keep a certain forlornness out of her voice. Perhaps, she reflected, the whole world was really crooked – or was it just that she herself had been unfortunate?

She was a tall, long-legged girl, not beautiful but with a charm that was made up of vitality and a warm-hearted personality. She moved well, and had lovely gleaming chestnut brown hair. Perhaps from a long association with horses, she had acquired the look of a thoroughbred filly.

Crookedness in the racing world she knew about – now, it seemed, she was to encounter crookedness in the financial world.

Though for all that, it seemed that her father-in-law whom she had not yet met, was, as far as the law was concerned, a pillar of rectitude. All these people who went about boasting of 'smart work' were the same – technically they always managed to be within the law. Yet it seemed to her that her Lance, whom she loved, and who had admittedly strayed outside the ringed fence in earlier days, had an honesty that these successful practitioners of the crooked lacked.

'I don't mean,' said Lance, 'that he's a swindler – not anything like that. But he knows how to put over a fast one.'

'Sometimes,' said Pat, 'I feel I hate people who put over fast ones.' She added: 'You're fond of him.' It was a statement, not a question.

Lance considered it for a moment, and then said in a surprised kind of voice:

'Do you know, darling, I believe I am.'

Pat laughed. He turned his head to look at her. His eyes narrowed. What a darling she was! He loved her. The whole thing was worth it for her sake.

'In a way, you know,' he said, 'it's Hell going back. City life. Home on the 5.18. It's not my kind of life. I'm far more at home among the down and outs. But one's got to settle down some time, I suppose. And with you to hold my hand the process may even be quite a pleasant one. And since the old boy has come round, one ought to take advantage of it. I must say I was surprised when I got his letter. . . . Percival, of all people, blotting his copybook. Percival, the good little boy. Mind you, Percy was always sly. Yes, he was always sly.'

'I don't think,' said Patricia Fortescue, 'that I'm going to like your brother Percival.'

'Don't let me put you against him. Percy and I never got on – that's all there is to it. I blued my pocket money, he saved his. I had disreputable but entertaining friends, Percy made what's called "worthwhile contacts". Poles apart we were, he and I. I always thought him a poor fish, and he – sometimes, you know, I think he almost hated me. I don't know why exactly. . . .'

'I think I can see why.'

'Can you, darling? You're so brainy. You know I've always wondered – it's a fantastic thing to say – but –'

'Well? Say it.'

'I've wondered if it wasn't Percival who was behind that cheque business – you know, when the old man kicked me out – and was he mad that he'd given me a share in the firm and so he couldn't disinherit me! Because the queer thing was that I never forged that cheque – though of course nobody would believe that after that time I swiped funds out of the till and put it on a horse. I was dead sure I could put it back, and anyway it was my own cash in a manner of speaking. But that cheque business – no. I don't know why I've got the ridiculous idea that Percival did that – but I have, somehow.'

'But it wouldn't have done *him* any good? It was paid into your account.'

'I know. So it doesn't make sense, does it?'

Pat turned sharply towards him.

'You mean – he did it to get you chucked out of the firm?'

'I wondered. Oh well – it's a rotten thing to say. Forget it. I wonder what old Percy will say when he sees the Prodigal returned. Those pale, boiled gooseberry eyes of his will pop right out of his head!'

'Does he know you are coming?'

'I shouldn't be surprised if he didn't know a damned thing! The old man's got rather a funny sense of humour, you know.'

'But what has your brother *done* to upset your father so much?'

'That's what *I*'d like to know. Something must have made the old man livid. Writing off to me the way he did.'

'When was it you got his first letter?'

'Must be four – no five months ago. A cagey letter, but a distinct holding out of the olive branch. "Your elder brother has proved himself unsatisfactory in many ways." "You seem to have sown your wild oats and settled down." "I can promise you that it will be well worth your while financially." "Shall welcome you and your wife." You know, darling, I think my marrying you had a lot to do with it. The old boy was impressed that I'd married into a class above me.'

Pat laughed.

'What? Into the aristocratic riff-raff?'

He grinned. 'That's right. But riff-raff didn't register and aristocracy did. You should see Percival's wife. She's the kind who says "Pass the preserves, please" and talks about a postage stamp.'

Pat did not laugh. She was considering the women of the family into which she had married. It was a point of view which Lance had not taken into account.

'And your sister?' she asked.

'Elaine? Oh she's all right. She was pretty young when I left home.

Sort of an earnest girl – but probably she's grown out of that. Very intense over things.'

It did not sound very reassuring. Pat said:

'She never wrote to you – after you went away?'

'I didn't leave an address. But she wouldn't have, anyway. We're not a devoted family.'

'No.'

He shot a quick look at her.

'Got the wind up? About my family? You needn't. We're not going to live with them, or anything like that. We'll have our own little place somewhere. Horses, dogs, anything you like.'

'But there will still be the 5.18.'

'For me, yes. To and fro to the city, all togged up. But don't worry, sweet – there are rural pockets, even round London. And lately I've felt the sap of financial affairs rising in me. After all, it's in my blood – from both sides of the family.'

'You hardly remember your mother, do you?'

'She always seemed to me incredibly old. She was old, of course. Nearly fifty when Elaine was born. She wore lots of clinking things and lay on a sofa and used to read me stories about knights and ladies which bored me stiff. Tennyson's "Idylls of the King". I suppose I was fond of her. . . . She was very – colourless, you know. I realize that, looking back.'

'You don't seem to have been particularly fond of anybody,' said Pat disapprovingly.

Lance grasped and squeezed her arm.

'I'm fond of you,' he said.

CHAPTER 7

Inspector Neele was still holding the telegraph message in his hand when he heard a car drive up to the front door and stop with a careless scrunching of brakes.

Mary Dove said, 'That will be Mrs Fortescue now.'

Inspector Neele moved forwards to the front door. Out of the tail of his eye, he saw Mary Dove melt unobtrusively into the background and disappear. Clearly she intended to take no part in the forthcoming scene. A remarkable display of tact and discretion –

and also a rather remarkable lack of curiosity. Most women, Inspector Neele decided, would have remained. . . .

As he reached the front door he was aware of the butler, Crump, coming forward from the back of the hall. So he had heard the car.

The car was a Rolls Bentley sports model coupé. Two people got out of it and came towards the house. As they reached the door, it opened. Surprised, Adele Fortescue stared at Inspector Neele.

He realized at once that she was a very beautiful woman, and he realized too, the force of Mary Dove's comment which had so shocked him at the time. Adele Fortescue *was* a sexy piece. In figure and type she resembled the blonde Miss Grosvenor, but whereas Miss Grosvenor was all glamour without and all respectability within, Adele Fortescue was glamour all through. Her appeal was obvious, not subtle. It said simply to every man 'Here am I. I'm a woman.' She spoke and moved and breathed sex – and yet, within it all, her eyes had a shrewd appraising quality. Adele Fortescue, he thought, liked men – but she would always like money even better.

His eyes went on to the figure behind her who carried her golf clubs. He knew the type very well. It was the type that specialized in the young wives of rich and elderly men. Mr Vivian Dubois, if this was he, had that rather forced masculinity which is, in reality, nothing of the kind. He was the type of man who 'understands' women.

'Mrs Fortescue?'

'Yes.' It was a wide blue-eyed gaze. 'But I don't know –'

'I am Inspector Neele. I'm afraid I have bad news for you.'

'Do you mean – a burglary – something of that kind?'

'No, nothing of that kind. It is about your husband. He was taken seriously ill this morning.'

'Rex? Ill?'

'We have been trying to get in touch with you since half-past eleven this morning.'

'Where is he? Here? Or in hospital?'

'He was taken to St Jude's Hospital. I'm afraid you must prepare yourself for a shock.'

'You don't mean – he isn't – *dead*.'

She lurched forward a little and clutched his arm. Gravely, feeling like someone playing a part in a stage performance, the Inspector supported her into the hall. Crump was hovering eagerly.

'Brandy she'll be needing,' he said.

The deep voice of Mr Dubois said:

'That's right, Crump. Get the brandy.' To the Inspector he said: 'In here.'

He opened a door on the left. The procession filed in. The Inspector and Adele Fortescue, Vivian Dubois, and Crump with a decanter and two glasses.

Adele Fortescue sank on to an easy chair, her eyes covered with her hand. She accepted the glass that the Inspector offered and took a tiny sip, then pushed it away.

'I don't want it,' she said. 'I'm all right. But tell me, what was it? A stroke, I suppose? Poor Rex.'

'It wasn't a stroke, Mrs Fortescue.'

'Did you say you were an Inspector?' It was Mr Dubois who made the enquiry.

Neele turned to him. 'That's right,' he said pleasantly. 'Inspector Neele of the CID.'

He saw the alarm grow in the dark eyes. Mr Dubois did not like the appearance of an Inspector of the CID. He didn't like it at all.

'What's up?' he said. 'Something wrong – eh?'

Quite unconsciously he backed away a little towards the door. Inspector Neele noted the movement.

'I'm afraid,' he said to Mrs Fortescue, 'that there will have to be an inquest.'

'An inquest? Do you mean – what *do* you mean?'

'I'm afraid this is all very distressing for you, Mrs Fortescue.' The words came smoothly. 'It seemed advisable to find out as soon as possible exactly what Mr Fortescue had to eat or drink before leaving for the office this morning.'

'Do you mean he might have been *poisoned*?'

'Well, yes, it would seem so.'

'I can't believe it. Oh – you mean *food* poisoning.'

Her voice dropped half an octave on the last words. His face wooden, his voice still smooth, Inspector Neele said:

'Madam? What did you think I meant?'

She ignored that question, hurrying on.

'But we've been all right – all of us.'

'You can speak for all the members of the family?'

'Well – no – of course – I can't really.'

Dubois said with a great show of consulting his watch:

'I'll have to push off, Adele. Dreadfully sorry. You'll be all right, won't you? I mean, there are the maids, and the little Dove and all that –'

'Oh Vivian, don't. Don't go.'

It was quite a wail, and it affected Mr Dubois adversely. His retreat quickened.

'Awfully sorry, old girl. Important engagement. I'm putting up at the Dormy House, by the way, Inspector. If you – er – want me for anything.'

Inspector Neele nodded. He had no wish to detain Mr Dubois. But he recognized Mr Dubois's departure for what it was. Mr Dubois was running away from trouble.

Adele Fortescue said, in an attempt to carry off the situation:

'It's such a shock, to come back and find the *police* in the house.'

'I'm sure it must be. But you see, it was necessary to act promptly in order to obtain the necessary specimens of foodstuffs, coffee, tea, etc.'

'Tea and coffee? But they're not poisonous? I expect it's the awful bacon we sometimes get. It's quite uneatable sometimes.'

'We shall find out, Mrs Fortescue. Don't worry. You'd be surprised at some of the things that can happen. We once had a case of digitalis poisoning. It turned out that foxglove leaves had been picked in mistake for horseradish.'

'You think something like that could happen here?'

'We shall know better after the autopsy, Mrs Fortescue.'

'The autop – oh I see.' She shivered.

The Inspector went on: 'You've got a lot of yew round the house, haven't you, madam. There's no possibility, I suppose, of the berries or leaves having got – mixed up in anything?'

He was watching her closely. She stared at him.

'Yew berries? Are they poisonous?'

The wonder seemed a little too wide-eyed and innocent.

'Children have been known to eat them with unfortunate results.'

Adele clasped her hands to her head.

'I can't bear to talk about it any more. Must I? I want to go and lie down. I can't stand any more. Mr Percival Fortescue will arrange everything – I can't – I can't – it isn't fair to ask me.'

'We are getting in touch with Mr Percival Fortescue as soon as possible. Unfortunately he is away in the North of England.'

'Oh yes, I forgot.'

'There's just one other thing, Mrs Fortescue. There was a small quantity of grain in your husband's pocket. Could you give me some explanation of that?'

She shook her head. She appeared quite bewildered.

'Would anyone have slipped it in there as a joke?'

'I don't see why it would be a joke.'

Inspector Neele did not see either. He said:

'I won't trouble you any further at present, Mrs Fortescue. Shall I send one of the maids to you? Or Miss Dove?'

'What?' The word came abstractedly. He wondered what she had been thinking about.

She fumbled with her bag and pulled out a handkerchief. Her voice trembled.

'It's so awful,' she said unsteadily. 'I'm only just beginning to take it in. I've really been *numbed* up to now. Poor Rex. Poor dear Rex.'

She sobbed in a manner that was almost convincing.

Inspector Neele watched her respectfully for a moment or two.

'It's been very sudden, I know,' he said. 'I'll send someone to you.'

He went towards the door, opened it and passed through. He paused for a moment before looking back into the room.

Adele Fortescue still held the handkerchief to her eyes. The ends of it hung down but did not quite obscure her mouth. On her lips was a very faint smile.

CHAPTER 8

'I've got what I could, sir.' So Sergeant Hay reporting. 'The marmalade, bit of the ham. Samples of tea, coffee and sugar, for what they're worth. Actual brews have been thrown out by now, of course, but there's one point. There was a good lot of coffee left over and they had it in the servants' hall at elevenses – that's important, I should say.'

'Yes, that's important. Shows that if he took it in his coffee, it must have been slipped into the actual cup.'

'By one of those present. Exactly. I've enquired, cautious like, about this yew stuff – berries or leaves – there's been none of it seen about the house. Nobody seems to know anything about the cereal in his pocket, either. . . . It just seems daft to them. Seems daft to me, too. He doesn't seem to have been one of those food faddists who'll eat any mortal thing so long as it isn't cooked. My sister's husband's like that. Raw carrots, raw peas, raw turnips. But even he doesn't eat raw grain. Why, I should say it would swell up in your inside something awful.'

The telephone rang and on a nod from the Inspector, Sergeant Hay sprinted off to answer it. Following him, Neele found that it was headquarters on the line. Contact had been made with Mr Percival Fortescue, who was returning to London immediately.

As the Inspector replaced the telephone, a car drew up at the front door. Crump went to the door and opened it. The woman who stood there had her arms full of parcels. Crump took them from her.

'Thanks, Crump. Pay the taxi, will you? I'll have tea now. Is Mrs Fortescue or Miss Elaine in?'

The butler hesitated, looking back over his shoulder.

'We've had bad news, m'am,' he said. 'About the master.'

'About Mr Fortescue?'

Neele came forward. Crump said: 'This is Mrs Percival, sir.'

'What is it? What's happened? An accident?'

The Inspector looked her over as he replied. Mrs Percival Fortescue was a plump woman with a discontented mouth. Her age he judged to be about thirty. Her questions came with a kind of eagerness. The thought flashed across his mind that she must be very bored.

'I'm sorry to have to tell you that Mr Fortescue was taken to St Jude's Hospital this morning seriously ill and has since died.'

'Died? You mean he's dead?' The news was clearly even more sensational than she had hoped for. 'Dear me – this is a surprise. My husband's away. You'll have to get in touch with him. He's in the North somewhere. I dare say they'll know at the office. He'll have to see to everything. Things always happen at the most awkward moment, don't they?'

She paused for a moment, turning things over in her mind.

'It all depends, I suppose,' she said, 'where they'll have the funeral. Down here, I suppose. Or will it be in London?'

'That will be for the family to say.'

'Of course. I only just wondered.' For the first time she took direct cognizance of the man who was speaking to her.

'Are you from the office?' she asked. 'You're not a doctor, are you?'

'I'm a police officer. Mr Fortescue's death was very sudden and –'

She interrupted him.

'Do you mean he was *murdered*?'

It was the first time that word had been spoken. Neele surveyed her eager questioning face carefully.

'Now why should you think that, madam?'

'Well, people are sometimes. You said sudden. And you're police. Have you seen her about it? What did she say?'

'I don't quite understand to whom you are referring?'

'Adele, of course. I always told Val his father was crazy to go marrying a woman years younger than himself. There's no fool like an old fool. Besotted about that awful creature, he was. And now look what comes of it. . . . A nice mess we're all in. Pictures in the paper and reporters coming round.'

She paused, obviously visualizing the future in a series of crude highly-coloured pictures. He thought that the prospect was still not wholly unpleasing. She turned back to him.

'What was it? Arsenic?'

In a repressive voice Inspector Neele said:

'The cause of death has yet to be ascertained. There will be an autopsy and an inquest.'

'But you know already, don't you? Or you wouldn't come down here.'

There was a sudden shrewdness in her plump rather foolish face.

'You've been asking about what he ate and drank, I suppose? Dinner last night. Breakfast this morning. And all the drinks, of course.'

He could see her mind ranging vividly over all the possibilities. He said, with caution:

'It seems possible that Mr Fortescue's illness resulted from something he ate at breakfast.'

'Breakfast?' She seemed surprised. 'That's difficult. I don't see how . . .'

She paused and shook her head.

'I don't see how she could have done it, then . . . unless she slipped something into the coffee – when Elaine and I weren't looking. . . .'

A quiet voice spoke softly beside them:

'Your tea is all ready in the library, Mrs Val.'

Mrs Val jumped.

'Oh thank you, Miss Dove. Yes, I could do with a cup of tea. Really, I feel quite bowled over. What about you, Mr – Inspector –'

'Thank you, not just now.'

The plump figure hesitated and then went slowly away.

As she disappeared through a doorway, Mary Dove murmured softly:

'I don't think she's ever heard of the term slander.'

Inspector Neele did not reply.

Mary Dove went on:

'Is there anything I can do for you?'

'Where can I find the housemaid, Ellen?'

'I will take you to her. She's just gone upstairs.'

II

Ellen proved to be grim but unafraid. Her sour old face looked triumphantly at the Inspector.

'It's a shocking business, sir. And I never thought I'd live to find myself in a house where that sort of thing has been going on. But in a way I can't say that it surprises me. I ought to have given my notice in long ago and that's a fact. I don't like the language that's used in this house, and I don't like the amount of drink that's taken, and I don't approve of the goings-on there've been. I've nothing against Mrs Crump, but Crump and that girl Gladys just don't know what proper service is. But it's the goings-on that I mind about most.'

'What goings-on do you mean exactly?'

'You'll soon hear about them if you don't know already. It's common talk all over the place. They've been seen here there and everywhere. All this pretending to play golf – or tennis – And I've seen things – with my own eyes – in this house. The library door was open and there they were, kissing and canoodling.'

The venom of the spinster was deadly. Neele really felt it unnecessary to say 'Whom do you mean?' but he said it nevertheless.

'Who should I mean? The mistress – and that man. No shame about it, they hadn't. But if you ask me, the master had got wise to it. Put someone on to watch them, he had. Divorce, that's what it would have come to. Instead, it's come to *this*.'

'When you say this, you mean –'

'You've been asking questions, sir, about what the master ate and drank and who gave it to him. They're in it together, sir, that's what I'd say. He got the stuff from somewhere and she gave it to the master, that was the way of it, I've no doubt.'

'Have you ever seen any yew berries in the house – or thrown away anywhere?'

The small eyes glinted curiously.

'Yew? Nasty poisonous stuff. Never you touch those berries, my mother said to me when I was a child. Was *that* what was used, sir?'

'We don't know yet what was used.'

'I've never seen her fiddling about with yew.' Ellen sounded disappointed. 'No, I can't say I've seen anything of that kind.'

Neele questioned her about the grain found in Fortescue's pocket but here again he drew a blank.

'No, sir. I know nothing about that.'

He went on to further questions, but with no gainful result. Finally he asked if he could see Miss Ramsbottom.

Ellen looked doubtful.

'I could ask her, but it's not everyone she'll see. She's a very old lady, you know, and she's a bit odd.'

The Inspector pressed his demand, and rather unwillingly Ellen led him along a passage and up a short flight of stairs to what he thought had probably been designed as a nursery suite.

He glanced out of a passage window as he followed her and saw Sergeant Hay standing by the yew tree talking to a man who was evidently a gardener.

Ellen tapped on a door, and when she received an answer, opened it and said:

'There's a police gentleman here who would like to speak to you, miss.'

The answer was apparently in the affirmative for she drew back and motioned Neele to go in.

The room he entered was almost fantastically over-furnished. The Inspector felt rather as though he had taken a step backward into not merely Edwardian but Victorian times. At a table drawn up to a gas fire an old lady was sitting laying out a patience. She wore a maroon-coloured dress and her sparse grey hair was slicked down each side of her face.

Without looking up or discontinuing her game she said impatiently:

'Well, come in, come in. Sit down if you like.'

The invitation was not easy to accept as every chair appeared to be covered with tracts or publications of a religious nature.

As he moved them slightly aside on the sofa Miss Ramsbottom asked sharply:

'Interested in mission work?'

'Well, I'm afraid I'm not very, ma'am.'

'Wrong. You should be. That's where the Christian spirit is nowadays. Darkest Africa. Had a young clergyman here last week. Black as your hat. But a true Christian.'

Inspector Neele found it a little difficult to know what to say.

The old lady further disconcerted him by snapping:

'I haven't got a wireless.'

'I beg your pardon?'

'Oh I thought perhaps you came about a wireless licence. Or one of these silly forms. Well, man, what is it?'

'I'm sorry to have to tell you, Miss Ramsbottom, that your brother-in-law, Mr Fortescue, was taken suddenly ill and died this morning.'

Miss Ramsbottom continued with her patience without any sign of perturbation, merely remarking in a conversational way:

'Struck down at last in his arrogance and sinful pride. Well, it had to come.'

'I hope it's not a shock to you?'

It obviously wasn't but the Inspector wanted to hear what she would say.

Miss Ramsbottom gave him a sharp glance over the top of her spectacles and said:

'If you mean I am not distressed, that is quite right. Rex Fortescue was always a sinful man and I never liked him.'

'His death was very sudden –'

'As befits the ungodly,' said the old lady with satisfaction.

'It seems possible that he may have been poisoned –'

The Inspector paused to observe the effect he had made.

He did not seem to have made any. Miss Ramsbottom merely murmured 'Red seven on black eight. Now I can move up the king.'

Struck apparently by the Inspector's silence, she stopped with a card poised in her hand and said sharply:

'Well, what did you expect me to say? I didn't poison him if that's what you want to know.'

'Have you any idea who might have done so?'

'That's a very improper question,' said the old lady sharply. 'Living in this house are two of my dead sister's children. I decline to believe that anybody with Ramsbottom blood in them could be guilty of murder. Because it's murder you're meaning, isn't it?'

'I didn't say so, madam.'

'Of course it's murder. Plenty of people have wanted to murder

Rex in their time. A very unscrupulous man. And old sins have long shadows, as the saying goes.'

'Have you anyone in particular in mind?'

Miss Ramsbottom swept up the cards and rose to her feet. She was a tall woman.

'I think you'd better go now,' she said.

She spoke without anger but with a kind of cold finality.

'If you want my opinion,' she went on, 'it was probably one of the servants. That butler looks to me a bit of a rascal, and that parlourmaid is definitely subnormal. Good evening.'

Inspector Neele found himself meekly walking out. Certainly a remarkable old lady. Nothing to be got out of her.

He came down the stairs into the square hall to find himself suddenly face to face with a tall dark girl. She was wearing a damp mackintosh and she stared into his face with a curious blankness.

'I've just come back,' she said. 'And they told me – about Father – that he's dead.'

'I'm afraid that's true.'

She pushed out a hand behind her as though blindly seeking for support. She touched an oak chest and slowly, stiffly, she sat down on it.

'Oh no,' she said. 'No . . .'

Slowly two tears rolled down her cheeks.

'It's awful,' she said. 'I didn't think that I even liked him. . . . I thought I hated him. . . . But that can't be so, or I wouldn't mind. I do mind.'

She sat there, staring in front of her and again tears forced themselves from her eyes and down her cheeks.

Presently she spoke again, rather breathlessly.

'The awful thing is that it makes everything come right. I mean, Gerald and I can get married now. I can do everything that I want to do. But I hate it happening this way. I don't want Father to be dead. . . . Oh I don't. Oh Daddy – Daddy. . . .'

For the first time since he had come to Yewtree Lodge, Inspector Neele was startled by what seemed to be genuine grief for the dead man.

CHAPTER 9

'Sounds like the wife to me,' said the Assistant Commissioner. He had been listening attentively to Inspector Neele's report.

It had been an admirable précis of the case. Short, but with no relevant detail left out.

'Yes,' said the AC. 'It looks like the wife. What do you think yourself, Neele, eh?'

Inspector Neele said that it looked like the wife to him too. He reflected cynically that it usually was the wife – or the husband as the case might be.

'She had the opportunity all right. And motive?' The AC paused. 'There *is* motive?'

'Oh, I think so, sir. This Mr Dubois, you know.'

'Think he was in it, too?'

'No, I shouldn't say that, sir.' Inspector Neele weighed the idea. 'A bit too fond of his own skin for that. He may have guessed what was in her mind, but I shouldn't imagine that he instigated it.'

'No, too careful.'

'Much too careful.'

'Well, we mustn't jump to conclusions, but it seems a good working hypothesis. What about the other two who had opportunity?'

'That's the daughter and the daughter-in-law. The daughter was mixed up with a young man whom her father didn't want her to marry. And he definitely wasn't marrying her unless she had the money. That gives *her* a motive. As to the daughter-in-law, I wouldn't like to say. Don't know enough about her yet. But any of the three of them *could* have poisoned him, and I don't see how anyone else could have done so. The parlourmaid, the butler, the cook, they all handled the breakfast or brought it in, but I don't see how any of them could have been sure of Fortescue himself getting the taxine and nobody else. That is, if it *was* taxine.'

The AC said, 'It was taxine all right. I've just got the preliminary report.'

'That settles that, then,' said Inspector Neele. 'We can go ahead.'

'Servants seem all right?'

'The butler and the parlourmaid both seem nervous. There's nothing uncommon about that. Often happens. The cook's fighting mad and the housemaid was grimly pleased. In fact all quite natural and normal.'

'There's nobody else whom you consider suspicious in any way?'

'No, I don't think so, sir.' Involuntarily, Inspector Neele's mind went back to Mary Dove and her enigmatic smile. There had surely been a faint yet definite look of antagonism. Aloud he said, 'Now that we know it's taxine, there ought to be some evidence to be got as to how it was obtained or prepared.'

'Just so. Well, go ahead, Neele. By the way, Mr Percival Fortescue is here now. I've had a word or two with him and he's waiting to see you. We've located the other son, too. He's in Paris at the Bristol, leaving today. You'll have him met at the airport, I suppose?'

'Yes, sir. That was my idea. . . .'

'Well, you'd better see Percival Fortescue now.' The AC chuckled. 'Percy Prim, that's what he is.'

Mr Percival Fortescue was a neat fair man of thirty odd, with pale hair and eyelashes and a slightly pedantic way of speech.

'This has been a terrible shock to me, Inspector Neele, as you can well imagine.'

'It must have been, Mr Fortescue,' said Inspector Neele.

'I can only say that my father was perfectly well when I left home the day before yesterday. This food poisoning, or whatever it was, must have been very sudden?'

'It was very sudden, yes. But it wasn't food poisoning, Mr Fortescue.'

Percival stared and frowned.

'No? So that's why –' he broke off.

'Your father,' said Inspector Neele, 'was poisoned by the administration of taxine.'

'Taxine? I've never heard of it.'

'Very few people have, I should imagine. It is a poison that takes effect very suddenly and drastically.'

The frown deepened.

'Are you telling me, Inspector, that my father was deliberately poisoned by someone?'

'It would seem so, yes, sir.'

'That's terrible!'

'Yes indeed, Mr Fortescue.'

Percival murmured: 'I understand now their attitude in the

hospital – their referring me here.' He broke off. After a pause he went on, 'The funeral?' He spoke interrogatively.

'The inquest is fixed for tomorrow after the post-mortem. The proceedings at the inquest will be purely formal and the inquest will be adjourned.'

'I understand. That is usually the case?'

'Yes, sir. Nowadays.'

'May I ask have you formed any ideas, any suspicions of who could – Really, I –' again he broke off.

'It's rather early days for that, Mr Fortescue,' murmured Neele.

'Yes, I suppose so.'

'All the same it would be helpful to us, Mr Fortescue, if you could give us some idea of your father's testamentary dispositions. Or perhaps you could put me in touch with his solicitor.'

'His solicitors are Billingsley, Horsethorpe & Walters of Bedford Square. As far as his Will goes I think I can more or less tell you its main dispositions.'

'If you will be kind enough to do so, Mr Fortescue. It's a routine that has to be gone through, I'm afraid.'

'My father made a new Will on the occasion of his marriage two years ago,' said Percival precisely. 'My father left the sum of £100,000 to his wife absolutely and £50,000 to my sister, Elaine. I am his residuary legatee. I am already, of course, a partner in the firm.'

'There was no bequest to your brother, Lancelot Fortescue?'

'No, there is an estrangement of long standing between my father and my brother.'

Neele threw a sharp glance at him – but Percival seemed quite sure of his statement.

'So as the Will stands,' said Inspector Neele, 'the three people who stand to gain are Mrs Fortescue, Miss Elaine Fortescue and yourself?'

'I don't think I shall be much of a gainer.' Percival sighed. 'There are death duties, you know, Inspector. And of late my father has been – well, all I can say is, highly injudicious in some of his financial dealings.'

'You and your father have not seen eye to eye lately about the conduct of the business?' Inspector Neele threw out the question in a genial manner.

'I put my point of view to him, but alas –' Percival shrugged his shoulders.

'Put it rather forcibly, didn't you?' Neele enquired. 'In fact, not to put too fine a point on it there was quite a row about it, wasn't there?'

'I should hardly say that, Inspector.' A red flush of annoyance mounted to Percival's forehead.

'Perhaps the dispute you had was about some other matter then, Mr Fortescue.'

'There was no dispute, Inspector.'

'Quite sure of that, Mr Fortescue? Well, no matter. Did I understand that your father and brother are still estranged?'

'That is so.'

'Then perhaps you can tell me what this means?'

Neele handed him the telephone message Mary Dove had jotted down.

Percival read it and uttered an exclamation of surprise and annoyance. He seemed both incredulous and angry.

'I can't understand it, I really can't. I can hardly believe it.'

'It seems to be true, though, Mr Fortescue. Your brother is arriving from Paris today.'

'But it's extraordinary, quite extraordinary. No, I really *can't* understand it.'

'Your father said nothing to you about it?'

'He certainly did *not*. How outrageous of him. To go behind my back and send for Lance.'

'You've no idea, I suppose, *why* he did such a thing?'

'Of course I haven't. It's all on a par with his behaviour lately – Crazy! Unaccountable. It's got to be stopped – I –'

Percival came to an abrupt stop. The colour ebbed away again from his pale face.

'I'd forgotten –' he said. 'For the moment I'd forgotten that my father was dead –'

Inspector Neele shook his head sympathetically.

Percival Fortescue prepared to take his departure – as he picked up his hat he said:

'Call upon me if there is anything I can do. But I suppose –' he paused – 'you will be coming down to Yewtree Lodge?'

'Yes, Mr Fortescue – I've got a man in charge there now.'

Percival shuddered in a fastidious way.

'It will all be most unpleasant. To think such a thing should happen to us –'

He sighed and moved towards the door.

'I shall be at the office most of the day. There is a lot to be seen to here. But I shall get down to Yewtree Lodge this evening.'

'Quite so, sir.'

Percival Fortescue went out.

'Percy Prim,' murmured Neele.

Sergeant Hay who was sitting unobtrusively by the wall looked up and said 'Sir?' interrogatively.

Then as Neele did not reply, he asked, 'What do you make of it all, sir?'

'I don't know,' said Neele. He quoted softly, '"They're all very unpleasant people."'

Sergeant Hay looked somewhat puzzled.

'Alice in Wonderland,' said Neele. 'Don't you know your Alice, Hay?'

'It's a classic, isn't it, sir?' said Hay. 'Third Programme stuff. I don't listen to the Third Programme.'

CHAPTER 10

It was about five minutes after leaving Le Bourget that Lance Fortescue opened his copy of the continental *Daily Mail*. A minute or two later he uttered a startled exclamation. Pat, in the seat beside him, turned her head enquiringly.

'It's the old man,' said Lance. 'He's dead.'

'Dead! Your father?'

'Yes, he seems to have been taken suddenly ill at the office, was taken to St Jude's Hospital and died there soon after arrival.'

'Darling, I'm so sorry. What was it, a stroke?'

'I suppose so. Sounds like it.'

'Did he ever have a stroke before?'

'No. Not that I know of.'

'I thought people never died from a first one.'

'Poor old boy,' said Lance. 'I never thought I was particularly fond of him, but somehow, now that he's dead . . .'

'Of course you were fond of him.'

'We haven't all got your nice nature, Pat. Oh well, it looks as though my luck's out again, doesn't it.'

'Yes. It's odd that it should happen just now. Just when you were on the point of coming home.'

He turned his head sharply towards her.

'Odd? What do you mean by odd, Pat?'

She looked at him with slight surprise.

'Well, a sort of coincidence.'

'You mean that whatever I set out to do goes wrong?'

'No, darling, I didn't mean that. But there is such a thing as a run of bad luck.'

'Yes, I suppose there is.'

Pat said again: 'I'm so sorry.'

When they arrived at Heathrow and were waiting to disembark from the plane, an official of the air company called out in a clear voice:

'Is Mr Lancelot Fortescue aboard?'

'Here,' said Lance.

'Would you just step this way, Mr Fortescue.'

Lance and Pat followed him out of the plane, preceding the other passengers. As they passed a couple in the last seat, they heard the man whisper to his wife:

'Well-known smugglers, I expect. Caught in the act.'

II

'It's fantastic,' said Lance. 'Quite fantastic.' He stared across the table at Detective-Inspector Neele.

Inspector Neele nodded his head sympathetically.

'Taxine – yewberries – the whole thing seems like some kind of melodrama. I dare say this sort of thing seems ordinary enough to you, Inspector. All in the day's work. But poisoning, in our family, seems wildly far-fetched.'

'You've no idea then at all,' asked Inspector Neele,' who might have poisoned your father?'

'Good lord, no. I expect the old man's made a lot of enemies in business, lots of people who'd like to skin him alive, do him down financially – all that sort of thing. But poisoning? Anyway I wouldn't be in the know. I've been abroad for a good many years and have known very little of what's going on at home.'

'That's really what I wanted to ask you about, Mr Fortescue. I understand from your brother that there was an estrangement between you and your father which had lasted for many years. Would you like to tell me the circumstances that led to your coming home at this time?'

'Certainly, Inspector. I heard from my father, let me see it must be about – yes, six months ago now. It was soon after my marriage. My father wrote and hinted that he would like to let bygones be bygones. He suggested that I should come home and enter the firm. He was rather vague in his terms and I wasn't really sure that I wanted to do what he asked. Anyway, the upshot was that I came over to England last – yes, last August, just about three months ago. I went down to see him at Yewtree Lodge and he made me, I must say, a very advantageous offer. I told him that I'd have to think about it and I'd have to consult my wife. He quite understood that. I flew back to East Africa, talked it over with Pat. The upshot was that I decided to accept the old boy's offer. I had to wind up my affairs there, but I agreed to do so before the end of last month. I told him I would wire to him the date of my actual arrival in England.'

Inspector Neele coughed.

'Your arrival back seems to have caused your brother some surprise.'

Lance gave a sudden grin. His rather attractive face lit up with the spirit of pure mischief.

'Don't believe old Percy knew a thing about it,' he said. 'He was away on his holiday in Norway at the time. If you ask me, the old man picked that particular time on purpose. He was going behind Percy's back. In fact I've a very shrewd suspicion that my father's offer to me was actuated by the fact that he had a blazing row with poor old Percy – or Val as he prefers to be called. Val, I think, had been more or less trying to run the old man. Well, the old man would never stand for anything of that kind. What the exact row was about I don't know, but he was furious. And I think he thought it a jolly good idea to get me there and thereby spike poor old Val's guns. For one thing he never liked Percy's wife much and he was rather pleased, in a snobbish kind of way, with my marriage. It would be just his idea of a good joke to get me home and suddenly confront Percy with the accomplished fact.'

'How long were you at Yewtree Lodge on this occasion?'

'Oh, not more than an hour or two. He didn't ask me to stay the night. The whole idea, I'm sure, was a kind of secret offensive behind Percy's back. I don't think he even wanted the servants to report upon it. As I say, things were left that I'd think it over, talk about it to Pat and then write him my decision, which I did. I wrote giving him the approximate date of my arrival, and I finally sent him a telegram yesterday from Paris.'

Inspector Neele nodded.

'A telegram which surprised your brother very much.'

'I bet it did. However, as usual, Percy wins. I've arrived too late.'

'Yes,' said Inspector Neele thoughtfully, 'you've arrived too late.' He went on briskly, 'On the occasion of your visit last August, did you meet any other members of the family?'

'My stepmother was there at tea.'

'You had not met her previously?'

'No.' He grinned suddenly. 'The old boy certainly knew how to pick them. She must be thirty years younger than him at least.'

'You will excuse my asking, but did you resent your father's remarriage, or did your brother do so?'

Lance looked surprised.

'I certainly didn't, and I shouldn't think Percy did either. After all, our own mother died when we were about – oh, ten, twelve years old. What I'm really surprised at is that the old man didn't marry again before.'

Inspector Neele murmured:

'It may be considered taking rather a risk to marry a woman very much younger than yourself.'

'Did my dear brother say that to you? It sounds rather like him. Percy is a great master of the art of insinuation. Is that the set-up, Inspector? Is my stepmother suspected of poisoning my father?'

Inspector Neele's face became blank.

'It's early days to have any definite ideas about anything, Mr Fortescue,' he said pleasantly. 'Now, may I ask you what your plans are?'

'Plans?' Lance considered. 'I shall have to make new plans, I suppose. Where is the family? All down at Yewtree Lodge?'

'Yes.'

'I'd better go down there straight away.' He turned to his wife. 'You'd better go to an hotel, Pat.'

She protested quickly. 'No, no, Lance, I'll come with you.'

'No, darling.'

'But I want to.'

'Really, I'd rather you didn't. Go and stay at the – oh it's so long since I stayed in London – Barnes's. Barnes's Hotel used to be a nice, quiet sort of place. That's still going, I suppose?'

'Oh, yes, Mr Fortescue.'

'Right, Pat, I'll settle you in there if they've got a room, then I'll go on down to Yewtree Lodge.'

'But why can't I come with you, Lance?'

Lance's face took suddenly a rather grim line.

'Frankly, Pat, I'm not sure of my welcome. It was Father who invited me there, but Father's dead. I don't know who the place belongs to now. Percy, I suppose, or perhaps Adele. Anyway, I'd like to see what reception I get before I bring you there. Besides —'

'Besides what?'

'I don't want to take you to a house where there's a poisoner at large.'

'Oh, what nonsense.'

Lance said firmly:

'Where you're concerned, Pat, I'm taking no risks.'

CHAPTER 11

Mr Dubois was annoyed. He tore Adele Fortescue's letter angrily across and threw it into the waste-paper basket. Then, with a sudden caution, he fished out the various pieces, struck a match and watched them burn to ashes. He muttered under his breath:

'Why have women got to be such damned fools? Surely common prudence . . .' But then, Mr Dubois reflected gloomily, women never had any prudence. Though he had profited by this lack many a time, it annoyed him now. He himself had taken every precaution. If Mrs Fortescue rang up they had instructions to say that he was out. Already Adele Fortescue had rung him up three times, and now she had written. On the whole, writing was far worse. He reflected for a moment or two, then he went to the telephone.

'Can I speak to Mrs Fortescue, please? Yes, Mr Dubois.' A minute or two later he heard her voice.

'Vivian, at last!'

'Yes, yes, Adele, but be careful. Where are you speaking from?'

'From the library.'

'Sure nobody's listening in, in the hall?'

'Why should they?'

'Well, you never know. Are the police still about the house?'

'No, they've gone for the moment, anyhow. Oh, Vivian dear, it's been *awful*.'

'Yes, yes, it must have I'm sure. But look here, Adele, we've got to be careful.'

'Oh, of course, darling.'

'Don't call me darling through the phone. It isn't safe.'

'Aren't you being a little bit panicky, Vivian? After all, everybody says darling nowadays.'

'Yes, yes, that's true enough. But listen. *Don't telephone to me and don't write.*'

'But Vivian —'

'It's just for the present, you understand. *We must be careful.*'

'Oh. All right.' Her voice sounded offended.

'Adele, listen. My letters to you. You did burn them, didn't you?'

There was a momentary hesitation before Adele Fortescue said:

'Of course. I told you I was going to do so.'

'That's all right, then. Well I'll ring off now. Don't phone and don't write. You'll hear from me in good time.'

He put the receiver back in its hook. He stroked his cheek thoughtfully. He didn't like that moment's hesitation. Had Adele burnt his letters? Women were all the same. They promised to burn things and then didn't.

Letters, Mr Dubois thought to himself. Women always wanted you to write them letters. He himself tried to be careful but sometimes one could not get out of it. What had he said exactly in the few letters he had written to Adele Fortescue? 'It was the usual sort of gup,' he thought, gloomily. But were there any special words – special phrases that the police could twist to make them say what they wanted them to say? He remembered the Edith Thompson case. His letters were innocent enough, he thought, but he could not be sure. His uneasiness grew. Even if Adele had not already burnt his letters, would she have the sense to burn them now? Or had the police already got hold of them? Where did she keep them, he wondered. Probably in that sitting-room of hers upstairs. That gimcrack little desk, probably. Sham antique Louis XIV. She had said something to him once about there being a secret drawer in it. Secret drawer! That would not fool the police long. But there were no police about the house now. She had said so. They had been there that morning, and now they had all gone away.

Up to now they had probably been busy looking for possible sources of poison in the food. They would not, he hoped, have got round to a room by room search of the house. Perhaps they would have to ask permission or get a search warrant to do that. It was possible that if he acted now, at once –

He visualized the house clearly in his mind's eye. It would be getting towards dusk. Tea would be brought in, either into the library or into the drawing-room. Everyone would be assembled downstairs and the servants would be having tea in the servants' hall. There would be no one upstairs on the first floor. Easy to walk up through the garden, skirting the yew hedges that provided such admirable cover. Then there was the little door at the side on to the terrace. That was never locked until just before bedtime. One could slip through there and, choosing one's moment, slip upstairs.

Vivian Dubois considered very carefully what it behoved him to do next. If Fortescue's death had been put down to a seizure or to a stroke as surely it ought to have been, the position would be very different. As it was – Dubois murmured under his breath, 'Better be safe than sorry.'

II

Mary Dove came slowly down the big staircase. She paused a moment at the window on the half landing, from which she had seen Inspector Neele arrive on the preceding day. Now, as she looked out in the fading light, she noticed a man's figure just disappearing round the yew hedge. She wondered if it was Lancelot Fortescue, the prodigal son. He had, perhaps, dismissed his car at the gate and was wandering round the garden recollecting old times there before tackling a possibly hostile family. Mary Dove felt rather sympathetic towards Lance. A faint smile on her lips, she went on downstairs. In the hall she encountered Gladys, who jumped nervously at the sight of her.

'Was that the telephone I heard just now?' Mary asked. 'Who was it?'

'Oh, that was a wrong number. Thought we were the laundry.' Gladys sounded breathless and rather hurried. 'And before that, it was Mr Dubois. He wanted to speak to the mistress.'

'I see.'

Mary went on across the hall. Turning her head, she said: 'It's tea-time, I think. Haven't you brought it in yet?'

Gladys said: 'I don't think it's half-past four yet, is it, miss?'

'It's twenty minutes to five. Bring it in now, will you?'

Mary Dove went on into the library where Adele Fortescue, sitting on the sofa, was staring at the fire, picking with her fingers at a small lace handkerchief. Adele said fretfully:

'Where's tea?'

Mary Dove said: 'It's just coming in.'

A log had fallen out of the fireplace and Mary Dove knelt down at the grate and replaced it with the tongs, adding another piece of wood and a little coal.

Gladys went out into the kitchen where Mrs Crump raised a red and wrathful face from the kitchen table where she was mixing pastry in a large bowl.

'The library bell's been ringing and ringing. Time you took in the tea, my girl.'

'All right, all right, Mrs Crump.'

'What I'll say to Crump tonight,' muttered Mrs Crump. 'I'll tell him off.'

Gladys went on into the pantry. She had not cut any sandwiches. Well, she jolly well wasn't going to cut sandwiches. They'd got plenty to eat without that, hadn't they? Two cakes, biscuits and scones and honey. Fresh black market farm butter. Plenty without her bothering to cut tomato or foie gras sandwiches. She'd got other things to think about. Fair temper Mrs Crump was in, all because Mr Crump had gone out this afternoon. Well, it was his day out, wasn't it? Quite right of him, Gladys thought. Mrs Crump called out from the kitchen:

'The kettle's boiling its head off. Aren't you ever going to make that tea?'

'Coming.'

She jerked some tea without measuring it into the big silver pot, carried it into the kitchen and poured the boiling water on it. She added the teapot and the kettle to the big silver tray and carried the whole thing through to the library where she set it on the small table near the sofa. She went back hurriedly for the other tray with the eatables on it. She carried the latter as far as the hall when the sudden jarring noise of the grandfather clock preparing itself to strike made her jump.

In the library, Adele Fortescue said querulously to Mary Dove:

'Where *is* everybody this afternoon?'

'I really don't know, Mrs Fortescue. Miss Fortescue came in some time ago. I think Mrs Percival's writing letters in her room.'

Adele said pettishly, 'Writing letters, writing letters. That woman never stops writing letters. She's like all people of her class. She takes an absolute delight in death and misfortune. Ghoulish, that's what I call it. Absolutely ghoulish.'

Mary murmured tactfully, 'I'll tell her that tea is ready.'

Going towards the door she drew back a little in the doorway as Elaine Fortescue came into the room. Elaine said:

'It's cold,' and dropped down by the fireplace, rubbing her hands before the blaze.

Mary stood for a moment in the hall. A large tray with cakes on it was standing on one of the hall chests. Since it was getting dark in the hall, Mary switched on the light. As she did so she thought she heard Jennifer Fortescue walking along the passage upstairs. Nobody, however, came down the stairs and Mary went up the staircase and along the corridor.

Percival Fortescue and his wife occupied a self-contained suite in one wing of the house. Mary tapped on the sitting-room door. Mrs Percival liked you to tap on doors, a fact which always roused Crump's scorn of her. Her voice said briskly:

'Come in.'

Mary opened the door and murmured:

'Tea is just coming in, Mrs Percival.'

She was rather surprised to see Jennifer Fortescue with her outdoor clothes on. She was just divesting herself of a long camel-hair coat.

'I didn't know you'd been out,' said Mary.

Mrs Percival sounded slightly out of breath.

'Oh, I was just in the garden, that's all. Just getting a little air. Really, though, it was too cold. I shall be glad to get down to the fire. The central heating here isn't as good as it might be. Somebody must speak to the gardeners about it, Miss Dove.'

'I'll do so,' Mary promised.

Jennifer Fortescue dropped her coat on a chair and followed Mary out of the room. She went down the stairs ahead of Mary, who drew back a little to give her precedence. In the hall, rather to Mary's surprise, she noticed the tray of eatables was still there. She was about to go out to the pantry and call to Gladys when Adele Fortescue appeared in the door of the library, saying in an irritable voice:

'Aren't we ever going to have anything to eat for tea?'

Quickly Mary picked up the tray and took it into the library, disposing the various things on low tables near the fireplace. She was carrying the empty tray out to the hall again when the front-door bell rang. Setting down the tray, Mary went to the door herself. If this was the prodigal son at last she was rather curious to see him. 'How unlike the rest of the Fortescues,' Mary thought, as she opened the door and looked up into the dark lean face and the faint quizzical twist of the mouth. She said quietly:

'Mr Lancelot Fortescue?'

'Himself.'

Mary peered beyond him.

'Your luggage?'

'I've paid off the taxi. This is all I've got.'

He picked up a medium-sized zip bag. Some faint feeling of surprise in her mind, Mary said:

'Oh, you did come in a taxi. I thought perhaps you'd walked up. And your wife?'

His face set in a rather grim line, Lance said:

'My wife won't be coming. At least, not just yet.'

'I see. Come this way, will you, Mr Fortescue. Everyone is in the library, having tea.'

She took him to the library door and left him there. She thought to herself that Lancelot Fortescue was a very attractive person. A second thought followed the first. Probably a great many other women thought so, too.

III

'Lance!'

Elaine came hurrying forward towards him. She flung her arms round his neck and hugged him with a schoolgirl abandon that Lance found quite surprising.

'Hallo. Here I am.'

He disengaged himself gently.

'This is Jennifer?'

Jennifer Fortescue looked at him with eager curiosity.

'I'm afraid Val's been detained in town,' she said. 'There's so much to see to, you know. All the arrangements to make and everything. Of course it all comes on Val. He has to see to *every-thing*. You can really have no idea what we're all going through.'

'It must be terrible for you,' said Lance gravely.

He turned to the woman on the sofa, who was sitting with a piece of scone and honey in her hand, quietly appraising him.

'Of course,' cried Jennifer, 'you don't know Adele, do you?'

Lance murmured, 'Oh yes, I do,' as he took Adele Fortescue's hand in his. As he looked down at her, her eyelids fluttered. She set down the scone she was eating with her left hand and just touched the arrangement of her hair. It was a feminine gesture. It marked her recognition of the entry to the room of a personable man. She said in her thick, soft voice:

'Sit down here on the sofa beside me, Lance.' She poured out a cup of tea for him. 'I'm so glad you've come,' she went on. 'We badly need another man in the house.'

Lance said:

'You must let me do everything I can to help.'

'You know – but perhaps you don't know – we've had the police here. They think – they think –' she broke off and cried out passionately: 'Oh, it's awful! Awful!'

'I know.' Lance was grave and sympathetic. 'As a matter of fact they met me at London Airport.'

'The police met you?'

'Yes.'

'What did they say?'

'Well,' Lance was deprecating. 'They told me what had happened.'

'He was poisoned,' said Adele, 'that's what they think, what they say. Not food poisoning. Real poisoning, by someone. I believe, I really do believe they think it's one of *us*.'

Lance gave her a sudden quick smile.

'That's their pigeon,' he said consolingly. 'It's no good our worrying. What a scrumptious tea! It's a long time since I've seen a good English tea.'

The others fell in with his mood soon enough. Adele said suddenly.

'But your wife – haven't you got a wife, Lance?'

'I've got a wife, yes. She's in London.'

'But aren't you – hadn't you better bring her down here?'

'Plenty of time to make plans,' said Lance. 'Pat – oh, Pat's quite all right where she is.'

Elaine said sharply:

'You don't mean – you don't think –'

Lance said quickly:

'What a wonderful looking chocolate cake. I must have some.'

Cutting himself a slice, he asked:

'Is Aunt Effie alive still?'

'Oh, yes, Lance. She won't come down and have meals with us or anything, but she's quite well. Only she's getting very peculiar.'

'She always was peculiar,' said Lance. 'I must go up and see her after tea.'

Jennifer Fortescue murmured:

'At her age one does really feel that she ought to be in some kind of a home. I mean somewhere where she would be properly looked after.'

'Heaven help any old ladies' home that got Aunt Effie in its midst,' said Lance. He added, 'Who's the demure piece of goods who let me in?'

Adele looked surprised.

'Didn't Crump let you in? The butler? Oh no, I forgot. It's his day out today. But surely Gladys –'

Lance gave a description. 'Blue eyes, hair parted in the middle, soft voice, butter wouldn't melt in the mouth. What goes on behind it all, I wouldn't like to say.'

'That,' said Jennifer, 'would be Mary Dove.'

Elaine said:

'She sort of runs things for us.'

'Does she, now?'

Adele said:

'She's really very useful.'

'Yes,' said Lance thoughtfully, 'I should think she might be.'

'But what is so nice is,' said Jennifer, 'that she knows her place. She never presumes, if you know what I mean.'

'Clever Mary Dove,' said Lance, and helped himself to another piece of chocolate cake.

CHAPTER 12

'So you've turned up again like a bad penny,' said Miss Ramsbottom.

Lance grinned at her. 'Just as you say, Aunt Effie.'

'Humph!' Miss Ramsbottom sniffed disapprovingly. 'You've

chosen a nice time to do it. Your father got himself murdered yesterday, the house is full of police poking about everywhere, grubbing in the dustbins, even. I've seen them out of the window.' She paused, sniffed again, and asked, 'Got your wife with you?'

'No. I left Pat in London.'

'That shows some sense. I shouldn't bring her *here* if I were you. You never know what might happen.'

'To her? To Pat?'

'To anybody,' said Miss Ramsbottom.

Lance Fortescue looked at her thoughtfully.

'Got any ideas about it all, Aunt Effie?' he asked.

Miss Ramsbottom did not reply directly. 'I had an Inspector here yesterday asking me questions. He didn't get much change out of me. But he wasn't such a fool as he looked, not by a long way.' She added with some indignation, 'What your grandfather would feel if he knew we had the police in the house – it's enough to make him turn in his grave. A strict Plymouth Brother he was all his life. The fuss there was when he found out I'd been attending Church of England services in the evening! And I'm sure *that* was harmless enough compared to murder.'

Normally Lance would have smiled at this, but his long, dark face remained serious. He said:

'D'you know, I'm quite in the dark after having been away so long. What's been going on here of late?'

Miss Ramsbottom raised her eyes to heaven.

'Godless doings,' she said firmly.

'Yes, yes, Aunt Effie, you would say that anyway. But what gives the police the idea that Dad was killed here, in this house?'

'Adultery is one thing and murder is another,' said Miss Ramsbottom. 'I shouldn't like to think it of her, I shouldn't indeed.'

Lance looked alert. 'Adele?' he asked.

'My lips are sealed,' said Miss Ramsbottom.

'Come on, old dear,' said Lance. 'It's a lovely phrase, but it doesn't mean a thing. Adele had a boy-friend? Adele and the boy-friend fed him henbane in the morning tea. Is that the set-up?'

'I'll trouble you not to joke about it.'

'I wasn't really joking, you know.'

'I'll tell you one thing,' said Miss Ramsbottom suddenly. 'I believe that girl knows something about it.'

'Which girl?' Lance looked surprised.

'The one that sniffs,' said Miss Ramsbottom. 'The one that ought to have brought me up my tea this afternoon, but didn't. Gone out without leave, so they say. I shouldn't wonder if she had gone to the police. Who let you in?'

'Someone called Mary Dove, I understand. Very meek and mild – but not really. Is she the one who's gone to the police?'

'*She* wouldn't go to the police,' said Miss Ramsbottom. 'No – I mean that silly little parlourmaid. She's been twitching and jumping like a rabbit all day. "What's the matter with you?" I said. "Have you got a guilty conscience?" She said "*I* never did anything – I wouldn't do a thing like that." "I hope you wouldn't," I said to her, "but there's something worrying you now, isn't there?" Then she began to sniff and said she didn't want to get anybody into trouble, she was sure it must all be a mistake. I said to her, I said, "Now, my girl, you speak the truth and shame the devil." That's what I said. "You go to the police," I said, "and tell them anything you know, because no good ever came," I said, "of hushing up the truth, however unpleasant it is." Then she talked a lot of nonsense about she couldn't go to the police, they'd never believe her and what on earth should she say? She ended up by saying anyway she didn't know anything at all.'

'You don't think,' Lance hesitated, 'that she was just making herself important?'

'No, I don't. I think she was scared. I think she saw something or heard something that's given her some idea about the whole thing. It may be important, or it mayn't be of the least consequence.'

'You don't think she herself could've had a grudge against Father and –' Lance hesitated.

Miss Ramsbottom was shaking her head decidedly.

'She's not the kind of girl your father would have taken the least notice of. No man ever will take much notice of her, poor girl. Ah, well, it's all the better for her soul, that, I dare say.'

Lance took no interest in Gladys's soul. He asked:

'You think she may have run along to the police station?'

Aunt Effie nodded vigorously.

'Yes. I think she mayn't like to've said anything to them in this house in case somebody overheard her.'

Lance asked, 'Do you think she may have seen someone tampering with the food?'

Aunt Effie threw him a sharp glance.

'It's possible, isn't it?' she said.

'Yes, I suppose so.' Then he added apologetically. 'The whole thing still seems so wildly improbable. Like a detective story.'

'Percival's wife is a hospital nurse,' said Miss Ramsbottom.

The remark seemed so unconnected with what had gone before that Lance looked at her in a puzzled fashion.

'Hospital nurses are used to handling drugs,' said Miss Ramsbottom.

Lance looked doubtful.

'This stuff – taxine – is it ever used in medicine?'

'They get it from yewberries, I gather. Children eat yewberries sometimes,' said Miss Ramsbottom. 'Makes them very ill, too. I remember a case when I was a child. It made a great impression on me. I never forgot it. Things you remember come in useful sometimes.'

Lance raised his head sharply and stared at her.

'Natural affection is one thing,' said Miss Ramsbottom, 'and I hope I've got as much of it as anyone. But I won't stand for wickedness. Wickedness has to be destroyed.'

II

'Went off without a word to me,' said Mrs Crump, raising her red, wrathful face from the pastry she was now rolling out on the board. 'Slipped out without a word to anybody. Sly, that's what it is. Sly! Afraid she'd be stopped, and I *would* have stopped her if I'd caught her! The idea! There's the master dead, Mr Lance coming home that hasn't been home for years and I said to Crump, I said, "Day out or no day out, I know my duty. There's not going to be cold supper tonight as is usual on a Thursday, but a proper dinner. A gentleman coming home from abroad with his wife, what was formerly married in the aristocracy, things must be properly done." You know me, miss, you know I take a pride in my work.'

Mary Dove, the recipient of these confidences, nodded her head gently.

'And what does Crump say?' Mrs Crump's voice rose angrily. '"It's my day off and I'm goin' off," that's what he says. "And a fig for the aristocracy," he says. No pride in his work, Crump hasn't. So off he goes and I tell Gladys she'll have to manage alone tonight. She just says, "All right, Mrs Crump," then, when my back's turned out *she* sneaks. It wasn't *her* day out, anyway. Friday's *her* day.

How we're going to manage now, I don't know! Thank goodness, Mr Lance hasn't brought his wife here with him today.'

'We shall manage, Mrs Crump,' Mary's voice was both soothing and authoritative, 'if we just simplify the menu a little.' She outlined a few suggestions. Mrs Crump nodded unwilling acquiescence. 'I shall be able to serve that quite easily,' Mary concluded.

'You mean you'll wait at table yourself, Miss?' Mrs Crump sounded doubtful.

'If Gladys doesn't come back in time.'

'*She* won't come back,' said Mrs Crump. 'Gallivanting off, wasting her money somewhere in the shops. She's got a young man, you know, miss, though you wouldn't think it to look at her. Albert his name is. Going to get married next spring, so she tells me. Don't know what the married state's like, these girls don't. What I've been through with Crump.' She sighed, then said in an ordinary voice, 'What about tea, miss. Who's going to clear it away and wash it up?'

'I'll do that,' said Mary. 'I'll go and do it now.'

The lights had not been turned on in the library though Adele Fortescue was still sitting on the sofa behind the tea tray.

'Shall I switch the lights on, Mrs Fortescue?' Mary asked. Adele did not answer.

Mary switched on the lights and went across to the window where she pulled the curtains across. It was only then that she turned her head and saw the face of the woman who had sagged back against the cushions. A half eaten scone spread with honey was beside her and her teacup was still half full. Death had come to Adele Fortescue suddenly and swiftly.

III

'Well?' demanded Inspector Neele impatiently.

The doctor said promptly:

'Cyanide – potassium cyanide probably – in the tea.'

'Cyanide,' muttered Neele.

The doctor looked at him with slight curiosity.

'You're taking this hard – any special reason –'

'She was cast as a murderess,' said Neele.

'And she turns out to be a victim. Hm. You'll have to think again, won't you?'

Neele nodded. His face was bitter and his jaw was grimly set.

Poisoned! Right under his nose. Taxine in Rex Fortescue's break-fast coffee, cyanide in Adele Fortescue's tea. Still an intimate family affair. Or so it seemed.

Adele Fortescue, Jennifer Fortescue, Elaine Fortescue and the newly arrived Lance Fortescue had had tea together in the library. Lance had gone up to see Miss Ramsbottom, Jennifer had gone to her own sitting-room to write letters, Elaine had been the last to leave the library. According to her Adele had then been in perfect health and had just been pouring herself out a last cup of tea.

A last cup of tea! Yes, it *had* indeed been her last cup of tea.

And after that a blank twenty minutes, perhaps, until Mary Dove had come into the room and discovered the body.

And during that twenty minutes –

Inspector Neele swore to himself and went out into the kitchen.

Sitting in a chair by the kitchen table, the vast figure of Mrs Crump, her belligerence pricked like a balloon, hardly stirred as he came in.

'Where's that girl? Has she come back yet?'

'Gladys? No – she's not back – Won't be, I suspect, until eleven o'clock.'

'She made the tea, you say, and took it in.'

'I didn't touch it, sir, as God's my witness. And what's more I don't believe Gladys did anything she shouldn't. She wouldn't do a thing like that – not Gladys. She's a good enough girl, sir – a bit foolish like, that's all – not wicked.'

No, Neele did not think that Gladys was wicked. He did not think that Gladys was a poisoner. And in any case the cyanide had not been in the teapot.

'But what made her go off suddenly – like this? It wasn't her day, out, you say.'

'No, sir, tomorrow's her day out.'

'Does Crump –'

Mrs Crump's belligerence suddenly revived. Her voice rose wrathfully.

'Don't you go fastening anything on Crump. Crump's out of it. He went off at three o'clock – and thankful I am now that he did. He's as much out of it as Mr Percival himself.'

Percival Fortescue had only just returned from London – to be greeted by the astounding news of this second tragedy.

'I wasn't accusing Crump,' said Neele mildly. 'I just wondered if he knew anything about Gladys's plans.'

'She had her best nylons on,' said Mrs Crump. 'She was up to something. Don't tell me! Didn't cut any sandwiches for tea, either. Oh yes, she was up to something. *I'll* give her a piece of my mind when she comes back.'

When she comes back –

A faint uneasiness possessed Neele. To shake it off he went upstairs to Adele Fortescue's bedroom. A lavish apartment – all rose brocade hangings and a vast gilt bed. On one side of the room was a door into a mirror-lined bathroom with a sunk orchid pink porcelain bath. Beyond the bathroom, reached by a communicating door, was Rex Fortescue's dressing room. Neele went back into Adele's bedroom, and through the door on the farther side of the room into her sitting-room.

The room was furnished in Empire style with a rose pile carpet. Neele only gave it a cursory glance for that particular room had had his close attention on the preceding day – with special attention paid to the small elegant desk.

Now, however, he stiffened to sudden attention. On the centre of the rose pile carpet was a small piece of caked mud.

Neele went over to it and picked it up. The mud was still damp.

He looked round – there were no footprints visible – only this one isolated fragment of wet earth.

IV

Inspector Neele looked round the bedroom that belonged to Gladys Martin. It was past eleven o'clock – Crump had come in half an hour ago – but there was still no sign of Gladys. Inspector Neele looked round him. Whatever Gladys's training had been, her own natural instincts were slovenly. The bed, Inspector Neele judged, was seldom made, the windows seldom opened. Gladys's personal habits, however, were not his immediate concern. Instead, he went carefully through her possessions.

They consisted for the most part of cheap and rather pathetic finery. There was little that was durable or of good quality. The elderly Ellen, whom he had called upon to assist him, had not been helpful. She didn't know what clothes Gladys had or hadn't. She couldn't say what, if anything, was missing. He turned from the clothes and the underclothes to the contents of the chest of drawers. There Gladys kept her treasures. There were picture postcards and newspaper cuttings, knitting patterns, hints on beauty culture, dressmaking and fashion advice.

Inspector Neele sorted them neatly into various categories. The picture postcards consisted mainly of views of various places where he presumed Gladys had spent her holidays. Amongst them were three picture postcards signed 'Bert'. Bert, he took to be the 'young man' referred to by Mrs Crump. The first postcard said – in an illiterate hand 'All the best. Missing you a lot. Yours ever, Bert.' The second said, 'Lots of nice looking girls here but not one that's a patch on you. Be seeing you soon. Don't forget our date. And remember after that – it's thumbs up and living happy ever after.' The third said merely, 'Don't forget. I'm trusting you. Love, B.'

Next, Neele looked through the newspaper cuttings and sorted them into three piles. There were the dressmaking and beauty hints, there were items about cinema stars to which Gladys had appeared greatly addicted and she had also, it appeared, been attracted by the latest marvels of science. There were cuttings about flying saucers, about secret weapons, about truth drugs used by Russians, and claims for fantastic drugs discovered by American doctors. All the witchcraft, so Neele thought, of our twentieth century. But in all the contents of the room there was nothing to give him a clue to her disappearance. She had kept no diary, not that he had expected that. It was a remote possibility. There was no unfinished letter, no record at all of anything she might have seen in the house which could have had a bearing on Rex Fortescue's death. Whatever Gladys had seen, whatever Gladys had known, there was no record of it. It would still have to be guesswork why the second tea tray had been left in the hall, and Gladys herself had so suddenly vanished.

Sighing, Neele left the room, shutting the door behind him.

As he prepared to descend the small winding stairs he heard a noise of running feet coming along the landing below.

The agitated face of Sergeant Hay looked up at him from the bottom of the stairs. Sergeant Hay was panting a little. 'Sir,' he said urgently. 'Sir! We've found her –'

'Found her?'

'It was the housemaid, sir – Ellen – remembered as she hadn't brought the clothes in from where they were hanging on the line – just round the corner from the back door. So she went out with a torch to take them in and she almost fell over the body – the girl's body – strangled, she was, with a stocking round her throat – been dead for hours, I'd say. And, sir, it's a wicked kind of joke – there was a *clothes peg clipped on her nose –*'

CHAPTER 13

An elderly lady travelling by train had brought three morning papers, and each of them as she finished it, folded it and laid it aside, showed the same headline. It was no longer a question now of a small paragraph hidden away in the corner of the papers. There were headlines with flaring announcements of Triple Tragedy at Yewtree Lodge.

The old lady sat very upright, looking out of the window of the train, her lips pursed together, an expression of distress and disapproval on her pink and white wrinkled face. Miss Marple had left St Mary Mead by the early train, changing at the junction and going on to London where she took a Circle train to another London terminus and thence on to Baydon Heath.

At the station she signalled a taxi and asked to be taken to Yewtree Lodge. So charming, so innocent, such a fluffy and pink and white old lady was Miss Marple that she gained admittance to what was now practically a fortress in a state of siege far more easily than could have been believed possible. Though an army of reporters and photographers were being kept at bay by the police, Miss Marple was allowed to drive in without question, so impossible would it have been to believe that she was anyone but an elderly relative of the family.

Miss Marple paid off the taxi in a careful assortment of small change, and rang the front-door bell. Crump opened it and Miss Marple summed him up with an experienced glance. 'A shifty eye,' she said to herself. 'Scared to death, too.'

Crump saw a tall, elderly lady wearing an old-fashioned tweed coat and skirt, a couple of scarves and a small felt hat with a bird's wing. The old lady carried a capacious handbag and an aged but good quality suitcase reposed by her feet. Crump recognized a lady when he saw one and said:

'Yes, madam?' in his best and most respectful voice.

'Could I see the mistress of the house, please?' said Miss Marple.

Crump drew back to let her in. He picked up the suitcase and put it carefully down in the hall.

'Well, madam,' he said rather dubiously, 'I don't know who exactly –'

Miss Marple helped him out.

'I have come,' she said, 'to speak about the poor girl who was killed. Gladys Martin.'

'Oh, I see, madam. Well in that case –' he broke off, and looked towards the library door from which a tall young woman had just emerged. 'This is Mrs Lance Fortescue, madam,' he said.

Pat came forward and she and Miss Marple looked at each other. Miss Marple was aware of a faint feeling of surpirse. She had not expected to see someone like Patricia Fortescue in this particular house. Its interior was much as she had pictured it, but Pat did not somehow match with that interior.

'It's about Gladys, madam,' said Crump helpfully.

Pat said rather hesitatingly:

'Will you come in here? We shall be quite alone.'

She led the way into the library and Miss Marple followed her.

'There wasn't anyone specially you wanted to see, was there?' said Pat, 'because perhaps I shan't be much good. You see my husband and I only came back from Africa a few days ago. We don't really know anything much about the household. But I can fetch my sister-in-law or my brother-in-law's wife.'

Miss Marple looked at the girl and liked her. She liked her gravity and her simplicity. For some strange reason she felt sorry for her. A background of shabby chintz and horses and dogs, Miss Marple felt vaguely, would have been much more suitable than this richly furnished interior décor. At the pony show and gymkhanas held locally round St Mary Mead, Miss Marple had met many Pats and knew them well. She felt at home with this rather unhappy looking girl.

'It's very simple, really,' said Miss Marple, taking off her gloves carefully and smoothing out the fingers of them. 'I read in the paper, you see, about Gladys Martin having been killed. And of course I know all about her. She comes from my part of the country. I trained her, in fact, for domestic service. And since this terrible thing has happened to her, I felt – well, I felt that I ought to come and see if there was anything I could do about it.'

'Yes,' said Pat. 'Of course. I see.'

And she did see. Miss Marple's action appeared to her natural and inevitable.

'I think it's a very good thing you have come,' said Pat. 'Nobody seems to know very much about her. I mean relations and all that.'

'No,' said Miss Marple, 'of course not. She hadn't got any relations. She came to me from the orphanage. St Faith's. A very well run place though sadly short of funds. We do our best for the girls there, try to give them a good training and all that. Gladys came to me when she was seventeen and I taught her how to wait at table and keep the silver and everything like that. Of course she didn't stay long. They never do. As soon as she got a little experience, she went and took a job in a café. The girls nearly always want to do that. They think it's freer, you know, and a gayer life. Perhaps it may be. I really don't know.'

'I never even saw her,' said Pat. 'Was she a pretty girl?'

'Oh, no,' said Miss Marple, 'not at all. Adenoids, and a good many spots. She was rather pathetically stupid, too. I don't suppose,' went on Miss Marple thoughtfully, 'that she ever made many friends anywhere. She was very keen on men, poor girl. But men didn't take much notice of her and other girls rather made use of her.'

'It sounds rather cruel,' said Pat.

'Yes, my dear,' said Miss Marple, 'life is cruel, I'm afraid. One doesn't really know what to do with the Gladyses. They enjoy going to the pictures and all that, but they're always thinking of impossible things that can't possibly happen to them. Perhaps that's happiness of a kind. But they get disappointed. I think Gladys was disappointed in café and restaurant life. Nothing very glamorous or interesting happened to her and it was just hard on the feet. Probably that's why she came back into private service. Do you know how long she'd been here?'

Pat shook her head.

'Not very long, I should think. Only a month or two.' Pat paused and then went on, 'It seems so horrible and futile that she should have been caught up in this thing. I suppose she'd seen something or noticed something.'

'It was the clothes peg that really worried me,' said Miss Marple in her gentle voice.

'The clothes peg?'

'Yes. I read about it in the papers. I suppose it is true? That when she was found there was a clothes peg clipped on to her nose.'

Pat nodded. The colour rose to Miss Marple's pink cheeks.

'That's what made me so very angry, if you can understand, my dear. It was such a cruel, contemptuous gesture. It gave me a kind of picture of the murderer. To do a thing like that! It's very wicked, you know, to affront human dignity. Particularly if you've already killed.'

Pat said slowly:

'I think I see what you mean.' She got up. 'I think you'd better come and see Inspector Neele. He's in charge of the case and he's here now. You'll like him, I think. He's a very human person.' She gave a sudden, quick shiver. 'The whole thing is such a horrible nightmare. Pointless. Mad. Without rhyme or reason in it.'

'I wouldn't say that, you know,' said Miss Marple. 'No, I wouldn't say that.'

Inspector Neele was looking tired and haggard. Three deaths and the press of the whole country whooping down the trail. A case that seemed to be shaping in well-known fashion had gone suddenly haywire. Adele Fortescue, that appropriate suspect, was now the second victim of an incomprehensible murder case. At the close of that fatal day the Assistant Commissioner had sent for Neele and the two men had talked far into the night.

In spite of his dismay, or rather behind it, Inspector Neele had felt a faint inward satisfaction. That pattern of the wife and the lover. It had been too slick, too easy. He had always mistrusted it. And now that mistrust of his was justified.

'The whole thing takes on an entirely different aspect,' the AC had said, striding up and down his room and frowning. 'It looks to me, Neele, as though we'd got someone mentally unhinged to deal with. First the husband, then the wife. But the very circumstances of the case seem to show that it's an inside job. It's all there, in the family. Someone who sat down to breakfast with Fortescue put taxine in his coffee or on his food, someone who had tea with the family that day put potassium cyanide in Adele Fortescue's cup of tea. Someone trusted, unnoticed, one of the family. Which of 'em, Neele?'

Neele said dryly:

'Percival wasn't there, so that lets him out again. That lets him out again,' Inspector Neele repeated.

The AC looked at him sharply. Something in the repetition had attracted his attention.

'What's the idea, Neele? Out with it, man.'

Inspector Neele looked stolid.

'Nothing, sir. Not so much as an idea. All I say is it was very convenient for him.'

'A bit too convenient, eh?' The AC reflected and shook his head. 'You think he might have managed it somehow? Can't see how, Neele. No, I can't see how.'

He added, 'And he's a cautious type, too.'

'But quite intelligent, sir.'

'You don't fancy the women. Is that it? Yet the women are indicated. Elaine Fortescue and Percival's wife. They were at breakfast and they were at tea that day. Either of them could have done it. No signs of anything abnormal about them? Well, it doesn't always show. There might be something in their past medical record.'

Inspector Neele did not answer. He was thinking of Mary Dove. He had no definite reason for suspecting her, but that was the way his thoughts lay. There was something unexplained about her, unsatisfactory. A faint, amused antagonism. That had been her attitude after the death of Rex Fortescue. What was her attitude now? Her behaviour and manner were, as always, exemplary. There was no longer, he thought, amusement. Perhaps not even antagonism, but he wondered whether, once or twice, he had not seen a trace of fear. He had been to blame, culpably to blame, in the matter of Gladys Martin. That guilty confusion of hers he had put down to no more than a natural nervousness of the police. He had come across that guilty nervousness so often. In this case it had been something more. Gladys had seen or heard something which had aroused her suspicions. It was probably, he thought, some quite small thing, something so vague and indefinite that she had hardly liked to speak about it. And now, poor little rabbit, she would never speak.

Inspector Neele looked with some interest at the mild, earnest face of the old lady who confronted him now at Yewtree Lodge. He had been in two minds at first how to treat her, but he quickly made up his mind. Miss Marple would be useful to him. She was upright, of unimpeachable rectitude and she had, like most old ladies, time on her hands and an old maid's nose for scenting bits of gossip. She'd get things out of servants and out of the women of the Fortescue family perhaps, that he and his policemen would never get. Talk, conjecture, reminiscences, repetitions of things said and done, out of it all she would pick the salient facts. So Inspector Neele was gracious.

'It's uncommonly good of you to have come here, Miss Marple,' he said.

'It was my duty, Inspector Neele. The girl had lived in my house. I feel, in a sense, responsible for her. She was a very silly girl, you know.'

Inspector Neele looked at her appreciatively.

'Yes,' he said, 'just so.'

She had gone, he felt, to the heart of the matter.

'She wouldn't know,' said Miss Marple, 'what she ought to do. If, I mean, something came up. Oh, dear, I'm expressing myself very badly.'

Inspector Neele said that he understood.

'She hadn't got good judgement as to what was important or not, that's what you mean, isn't it?'

'Oh yes, exactly, Inspector.'

'When you say that she was silly —' Inspector Neele broke off.

Miss Marple took up the theme.

'She was the credulous type. She was the sort of girl who would have given her savings to a swindler, if she'd had any savings. Of course, she never did have any savings because she always spent her money on most unsuitable clothes.'

'What about men?' asked the Inspector.

'She wanted a young man badly,' said Miss Marple. 'In fact that's really, I think, why she left St Mary Mead. The competition there is very keen. So few men. She did have hopes of the young man who delivered the fish. Young Fred had a pleasant word for all the girls, but of course he didn't mean anything by it. That upset poor Gladys quite a lot. Still, I gather she did get herself a young man in the end?'

Inspector Neele nodded.

'It seems so. Albert Evans, I gather, his name was. She seems to have met him at some holiday camp. He didn't give her a ring or anything so maybe she made it all up. He was a mining engineer, so she told the cook.'

'That seems *most* unlikely,' said Miss Marple, 'but I dare say it's what he *told* her. As I say, she'd believe anything. You don't connect *him* with this business at all?'

Inspector Neele shook his head.

'No. I don't think there are any complications of that kind. He never seems to have visited her. He sent her a postcard from time to time, usually from a seaport — probably 4th Engineer on a boat on the Baltic run.'

'Well,' said Miss Marple, 'I'm glad she had her little romance. Since her life has been cut short in this way –' She tightened her lips. 'You know, Inspector, it makes me very, very angry.' And she added, as she had said to Pat Fortescue, 'Especially the clothes peg. That, Inspector, was really wicked.'

Inspector Neele looked at her with interest.

'I know just what you mean, Miss Marple,' he said.

Miss Marple coughed apologetically.

'I wonder – I suppose it would be great presumption on my part – if only I could assist you in my very humble and, I'm afraid, very *feminine* way. This is a wicked murderer, Inspector Neele, and the wicked should not go unpunished.'

'That's an unfashionable belief nowadays, Miss Marple,' Inspector Neele said rather grimly. 'Not that I don't agree with you.'

'There is an hotel near the station, or there's the Golf Hotel,' said Miss Marple tentatively, 'and I believe there's a Miss Ramsbottom in this house who is interested in foreign missions.'

Inspector Neele looked at Miss Marple appraisingly.

'Yes,' he said. 'You've got something there, maybe. I can't say that I've had great success with the lady.'

'It's really very kind of you, Inspector Neele,' said Miss Marple. 'I'm so glad you don't think I'm just a sensation hunter.'

Inspector Neele gave a sudden, rather unexpected smile. He was thinking to himself that Miss Marple was very unlike the popular idea of an avenging fury. And yet, he thought that was perhaps exactly what she was.

'Newspapers,' said Miss Marple, 'are often so sensational in their accounts. But hardly, I fear, as accurate as one might wish.' She looked enquiringly at Inspector Neele. 'If one could be sure of having just the sober facts.'

'They're not particularly sober,' said Neele. 'Shorn of undue sensation, they're as follows. Mr Fortescue died in his office as a result of taxine poisoning. Taxine is obtained from the berries and leaves of yew trees.'

'Very convenient,' Miss Marple said.

'Possibly,' said Inspector Neele, 'but we've no evidence as to that. As yet, that is.' He stressed the point because it was here that he thought Miss Marple might be useful. If any brew or concoction of yewberries had been made in the house, Miss Marple was quite likely to come upon traces of it. She was the sort of old pussy who would make homemade liqueurs, cordials and herb teas herself. She would know methods of making and methods of disposal.

'And Mrs Fortescue?'

'Mrs Fortescue had tea with the family in the library. The last person to leave the room and the tea table was Miss Elaine Fortescue, her step-daughter. She states that as she left the room Mrs Fortescue was pouring herself out another cup of tea. Some twenty minutes or half-hour later Miss Dove, who acts as housekeeper, went in to remove the tea-tray. Mrs Fortescue was still sitting on the sofa, dead. Beside her was a teacup a quarter full and in the dregs of it was potassium cyanide.'

'Which is almost immediate in its action, I believe,' said Miss Marple.

'Exactly.'

'Such dangerous stuff,' murmured Miss Marple. 'One has it to take wasps' nests but I'm always very, very careful.'

'You're quite right,' said Inspector Neele. 'There was a packet of it in the gardener's shed here.'

'Again very convenient,' said Miss Marple. She added, 'Was Mrs Fortescue eating anything?'

'Oh, yes. They'd had quite a sumptuous tea.'

'Cake, I suppose? Bread and butter? Scones, perhaps? Jam? Honey?'

'Yes, there was honey and scones, chocolate cake and swiss roll and various other plates of things.' He looked at her curiously. 'The potassium cyanide was in the tea, Miss Marple.'

'Oh, yes, yes. I quite understand that. I was just getting the whole picture, so to speak. Rather significant, don't you think?'

He looked at her in a slightly puzzled fashion. Her cheeks were pink, her eyes were bright.

'And the third death, Inspector Neele?'

'Well, the facts there seem clear enough, too. The girl, Gladys, took in the tea-tray, then she brought the next tray into the hall, but left it there. She'd been rather absent-minded all the day, apparently. After that no one saw her. The cook, Mrs Crump, jumped to the conclusion that the girl had gone out for the evening without telling anybody. She based her belief, I think, on the fact that the girl was wearing a good pair of nylon stockings and her best shoes. There, however, she was proved quite wrong. The girl had obviously remembered suddenly that she had not taken in some clothes that were drying outside on the clothes line. She ran out to fetch them in, had taken down half of them apparently, when somebody took her unawares by slipping a stocking round her neck and – well, that was that.'

'Someone from outside?' said Miss Marple.

'Perhaps,' said Inspector Neele. 'But perhaps someone from inside. Someone who'd been waiting his or her opportunity to get the girl alone. The girl was upset, nervous, when we first questioned her, but I'm afraid we didn't quite appreciate the importance of that.'

'Oh, but how could you,' cried Miss Marple, 'because people so often do look guilty and embarrassed when they are questioned by the police.'

'That's just it. But this time, Miss Marple, it was rather more than that. I think the girl Gladys had seen someone performing some action that seemed to her needed explanation. It can't, I think, have been anything very definite. Otherwise she *would* have spoken out. But I think she did betray the fact to the person in question. That person realized that Gladys was a danger.'

'And so Gladys was strangled and a clothes peg clipped on her nose,' murmured Miss Marple to herself.

'Yes, that's a nasty touch. A nasty, sneering sort of touch. Just a nasty bit of unnecessary bravado.'

Miss Marple shook her head.

'Hardly *unnecessary*. It does all make a pattern, doesn't it?'

Inspector Neele looked at her curiously.

'I don't quite follow you, Miss Marple. What do you mean by a pattern?'

Miss Marple immediately became flustered.

'Well, I mean it does seem – I mean, regarded as a sequence, if you understand – well, one can't get away from facts, can one?'

'I don't think I quite understand.'

'Well, I mean – first we have Mr Fortescue. *Rex* Fortescue. Killed in his office in the city. And then we have Mrs Fortescue, sitting here in the library and having tea. There were scones and *honey*. And then poor Gladys with the clothes peg on her nose. Just to *point* the whole thing. That very charming Mrs Lance Fortescue said to me that there didn't seem to be any rhyme or reason in it, but I couldn't agree with her, because it's the rhyme that strikes one, isn't it?'

Inspector Neele said slowly: 'I don't think –'

Miss Marple went on quickly:

'I expect you're about thirty-five or thirty-six, aren't you, Inspector Neele? I think there was rather a reaction just then, when you were a little boy, I mean, against nursery rhymes. But if one has been brought up on Mother Goose – I mean it is really highly significant, isn't it? What I wondered was,' Miss Marple paused, then appearing to take her courage in her hands went on bravely: 'Of course it is great impertinence I know, on my part, saying this sort of thing to you.'

'Please say anything you like, Miss Marple.'

'Well, that's very kind of you. I shall. Though, as I say, I do it with the utmost diffidence because I know I am very old and rather muddle-headed, and I dare say my idea is of no value at all. But what I mean to say is have you gone into the question of blackbirds?'

CHAPTER 14

For about ten seconds Inspector Neele stared at Miss Marple with the utmost bewilderment. His first idea was that the old lady had gone off her head.

'Blackbirds?' he repeated.

Miss Marple nodded her head vigorously.

'Yes,' she said, and forthwith recited:

'"Sing a song of sixpence, a pocket full of rye,
Four and twenty blackbirds baked in a pie.
When the pie was opened the birds began to sing.
Wasn't that a dainty dish to set before the king?
The king was in his counting house, counting out his money,
The queen was in the parlour eating bread and honey,
The maid was in the garden hanging out the clothes,
When there came a little dickey bird and nipped off her nose."'

'Good Lord,' Inspector Neele said.

'I mean, it does fit,' said Miss Marple. 'It *was* rye in his pocket, wasn't it? One newspaper said so. The others just said cereal which might mean anything. Farmer's Glory or Cornflakes – or even maize – but it *was* rye?'

Inspector Neele nodded.

'There you are,' said Miss Marple, triumphantly. '*Rex* Fortescue.

Rex means *King*. In his *Counting House*. And Mrs Fortescue the Queen in the parlour, eating bread and honey. And so, of course, the murderer had to put that clothes peg on poor Gladys's nose.'

Inspector Neele said:

'You mean the whole set-up is crazy?'

'Well, one mustn't jump to conclusions – but it is certainly very *odd*. But you really must make enquiries about blackbirds. Because there must *be* blackbirds!'

It was at this point that Sergeant Hay came into the room saying urgently, 'Sir.'

He broke off at the sight of Miss Marple. Inspector Neele, recovering himself, said:

'Thank you, Miss Marple. I'll look into the matter. Since you are interested in the girl, perhaps you would care to look over the things from her room. Sergeant Hay will show you them presently.'

Miss Marple, accepting her dismissal, twittered her way out.

'Blackbirds!' murmured Inspector Neele to himself.

Sergeant Hay stared.

'Yes, Hay, what is it?'

'Sir,' said Sergeant Hay, urgently, again. 'Look at this.'

He produced an article wrapped in a somewhat grubby handker-chief.

'Found it in the shrubbery,' said Sergeant Hay. 'Could have been chucked there from one of the back windows.'

He tipped the object down on the desk in front of the Inspector who leaned forward and inspected it with rising excitement. The exhibit was a nearly full pot of marmalade.

The Inspector stared at it without speech. His face assumed a peculiarly wooden and stupid appearance. In actual fact this meant that Inspector Neele's mind was racing once more round an imaginary track. A moving picture was enacting itself before the eyes of his mind. He saw a new pot of marmalade, he saw hands carefully removing its cover, he saw a small quantity of marmalade removed, mixed with a preparation of taxine and replaced in the pot, the top smoothed over and the lid carefully replaced. He broke off at this point to ask Sergeant Hay:

'They don't take marmalade out of the pot and put into fancy pots?'

'No, sir. Got into the way of serving it in its own pot during the war when things were scarce, and it's gone on like that ever since.'

Neele murmured:

'That made it easier, of course.'

'What's more,' said Sergeant Hay, 'Mr Fortescue was the only one that took marmalade for breakfast (and Mr Percival when he was at home). The others had jam or honey.'

Neele nodded.

'Yes,' he said. 'That made it very simple, didn't it?'

After a slight gap the moving picture went on in his mind. It was the breakfast table now. Rex Fortescue stretching out his hand for the marmalade pot, taking out a spoonful of marmalade and spreading it on his toast and butter. Easier, far easier that way than the risk and difficulty of insinuating it into his coffee cup. A foolproof method of administering the poison! And afterwards? Another gap and a picture that was not quite so clear. The replacing of that pot of marmalade by another with eactly the same amount taken from it. And then an open window. A hand and an arm flinging out that pot into the shrubbery. Whose hand and arm?

Inspector Neele said in a businesslike voice:

'Well, we'll have of course to get this analysed. See if there are any traces of taxine. We can't jump to conclusions.'

'No, sir. There may be fingerprints too.'

'Probably not the ones we want,' said Inspector Neele gloomily. 'There'll be Gladys's, of course, and Crump's and Fortescue's own. Then probably Mrs Crump's, the grocer's assistant and a few others! If anyone put taxine in here they'd take care not to go playing about with their own fingers all over the pot. Anyway, as I say, we mustn't jump to conclusions. How do they order marmalade and where is it kept?'

The industrious Sergeant Hay had his answer pat for all these questions.

'Marmalade and jams come in in batches of six at a time. A new pot would be taken into the pantry when the old one was getting low.'

'That means,' said Neele, 'that it could have been tampered with several days before it was actually brought on to the breakfast table. And anyone who was in the house or had access to the house could have tampered with it.'

The term 'access to the house' puzzled Sergeant Hay slightly. He did not see in what way his superior's mind was working.

But Neele was postulating what seemed to him a logical assumption.

If the marmalade had been tampered with *beforehand* – then surely that ruled out *those persons who were actually at the breakfast table on the fatal morning.*

Which opened up some interesting new possibilities.

He planned in his mind interviews with various people – this time with rather a different angle of approach.

He'd keep an open mind. . . .

He'd even consider seriously that old Miss Whatshername's suggestions about the nursery rhyme. Because there was no doubt that that nursery rhyme fitted in a rather startling way. It fitted with a point that had worried him from the beginning. The pocketful of rye.

'Blackbirds?' murmured Inspector Neele to himself.

Sergeant Hay stared.

'It's not blackberry jelly, sir,' he said. 'It's *marmalade*.'

II

Inspector Neele went in search of Mary Dove.

He found her in one of the bedrooms on the first floor superintending Ellen, who was denuding the bed of what seemed to be clean sheets. A little pile of clean towels lay on a chair.

Inspector Neele looked puzzled.

'Somebody coming to stay?' he asked.

Mary Dove smiled at him. In contrast to Ellen, who looked grim and truculent, Mary was her usual imperturbable self.

'Actually,' she said, 'the opposite is the case.'

Neele looked enquiringly at her.

'This is the guest room we had prepared for Mr Gerald Wright.'

'Gerald Wright? Who is he?'

'He's a friend of Miss Elaine Fortescue's.' Mary's voice was carefully devoid of inflection.

'He was coming here – when?'

'I believe he arrived at the Golf Hotel the day after Mr Fortescue's death.'

'The day *after*.'

'So Miss Fortescue said.' Mary's voice was still impersonal: 'She told me she wanted him to come and stay in the house – so I had a room prepared. Now – after these other two – tragedies – it seems more suitable that he should remain at the hotel.'

'The Golf Hotel?'

'Yes.'

'Quite,' said Inspector Neele.

Ellen gathered up the sheets and towels and went out of the room.

Mary Dove looked enquiringly at Neele.

'You wanted to see me about something?'

Neele said pleasantly:

'It's becoming important to get exact times very clearly stated. Members of the family all seem a little vague about time – perhaps understandably. You, on the other hand, Miss Dove, I have found extremely accurate in your statements as to times.'

'Again understandably!'

'Yes – perhaps – I must certainly congratulate you on the way you have kept this house going in spite of the – well panic – these last deaths must have caused.' He paused and then asked curiously: 'How did you do it?'

He had realized, astutely, that the one chink in the armour of Mary Dove's inscrutability was her pleasure in her own efficiency. She unbent slightly now as she answered.

'The Crumps wanted to leave at once, of course.'

'We couldn't have allowed that.'

'I know. But I also told them that Mr Percival Fortescue would be more likely to be – well – generous – to those who had spared him inconvenience.'

'And Ellen?'

'Ellen does not wish to leave.'

'Ellen does not wish to leave,' Neele repeated. 'She has good nerves.'

'She enjoys disasters,' said Mary Dove. 'Like Mrs Percival, she finds in disaster a kind of pleasurable drama.'

'Interesting. Do you think Mrs Percival has – enjoyed the tragedies?'

'No – of course not. That is going too far. I would merely say that it has enabled her to – well – stand up to them –'

'And how have you yourself been affected, Miss Dove?'

Mary Dove shrugged her shoulders.

'It has not been a pleasant experience,' she said dryly.

Inspector Neele felt again a longing to break down this cool young woman's defences – to find out what was really going on behind the careful and efficient understatement of her whole attitude.

He merely said brusquely:

'Now – to recapitulate times and places: the last time you saw Gladys Martin was in the hall before tea, and that was at twenty minutes to five?'

'Yes – I told her to bring in tea.'

'You yourself were coming from where?'

'From upstairs – I thought I had heard the telephone a few minutes before.'

'Gladys, presumably, had answered the telephone?'

'Yes. It was a wrong number. Someone who wanted the Baydon Heath Laundry.'

'And that was the last time you saw her?'

'She brought the tea-tray into the library about ten minutes or so later.'

'After that Miss Elaine Fortescue came in?'

'Yes, about three or four minutes later. Then I went up to tell Mrs Percival tea was ready.'

'Did you usually do that?'

'Oh no – people came in to tea when they pleased – but Mrs Fortescue asked where everybody was. I thought I heard Mrs Percival coming – but that was a mistake –'

Neele interrupted. Here was something new.

'You mean you heard someone upstairs moving about?'

'Yes – at the head of the stairs, I thought. But no one came down so I went up. Mrs Percival was in her bedroom. She had just come in. She had been out for a walk –'

'Out for a walk – I see. The time being then –'

'Oh – nearly five o'clock, I think –'

'And Mr Lancelot Fortescue arrived – when?'

'A few minutes after I came downstairs again – I thought he had arrived earlier – but –'

Inspector Neele interrupted:

'Why did you think he had arrived earlier?'

'Because I thought I had caught sight of him through the landing window.'

'In the garden, you mean?'

'Yes – I caught a glimpse of someone through the yew hedge – and I thought it would probably be him.'

'This was when you were coming down after telling Mrs Percival Fortescue tea was ready?'

Mary corrected him.

'No – not then – it was earlier – when I came down the first time.'

Inspector Neele stared.

'Are you sure about that, Miss Dove?'

'Yes, I'm perfectly sure. That's why I was surprised to see him – when he actually did ring the bell.'

Inspector Neele shook his head. He kept his inner excitement out of his voice as he said:

'It couldn't have been Lancelot Fortescue you saw in the garden. His train – which was due at 4.28, was nine minutes later. He arrived at Baydon Heath Station at 4.37. He had to wait a few minutes for a taxi – that train is always very full. It was actually nearly a quarter to five (five minutes *after* you had seen the man in the garden) when he left the station and it is a ten-minute drive. He paid off the taxi at the gate here at about five minutes to five at the earliest. No – it wasn't Lancelot Fortescue you saw.'

'I'm sure I did see someone.'

'Yes, you saw someone. It was getting dark. You couldn't have seen the man clearly?'

'Oh no – I couldn't see his face or anything like that – just his build – tall and slender. We were expecing Lancelot Fortescue – so I jumped to the conclusion that that's who it was.'

'He was going – which way?'

'Along behind the yew hedge towards the east side of the house.'

'There is a side door there. Is it kept locked?'

'Not until the house is locked up for the night.'

'Anyone could have come in by that side door without being observed by any of the household?'

Mary Dove considered.

'I think so. Yes.' She added quickly: 'You mean – the person I heard later upstairs could have come in that way? Could have been hiding – upstairs?'

'Something of the kind.'

'But who –?'

'That remains to be seen. Thank you, Miss Dove.'

As she turned to go away Inspector Neele said in a casual voice: 'By the way, you can't tell me anything about *blackbirds*, I suppose?'

For the first time, so it seemed, Mary Dove was taken aback. She turned back sharply.

'I – what did you say?'

'I was just asking you about blackbirds.'

'Do you mean –'

'Blackbirds,' said Inspector Neele.

He had on his most stupid expression.

'You mean that silly business last summer? But surely that can't . . .' She broke off.

Inspector Neele said pleasantly:

'There's been a bit of talk about it, but I was sure I'd get a clear account from you.'

Mary Dove was her calm, practical self again.

'It must, I think, have been some silly, spiteful joke,' she said. 'Four dead blackbirds were on Mr Fortescue's desk in his study here. It was summer and the windows were open, and we rather thought it must have been the gardener's boy, though he insisted he'd never done anything of the kind. But they were actually blackbirds the gardener had shot which had been hanging up by the fruit bushes.'

'And somebody had cut them down and put them on Mr Fortescue's desk?'

'Yes.'

'Any sort of reason behind it – any association with blackbirds?'

Mary shook her head.

'I don't think so.'

'How did Mr Fortescue take it? Was he annoyed?'

'Naturally he was annoyed.'

'But not upset in any way?'

'I really can't remember.'

'I see,' said Inspector Neele.

He said no more. Mary Dove once more turned away, but this time, he thought, she went rather unwillingly as though she would have liked to know more of what was in his mind. Ungratefully, all that Inspector Neele felt was annoyance with Miss Marple. She had suggested to him that there would be blackbirds and sure enough, there the blackbirds were! Not four and twenty of them, that was true. What might be called a token consignment.

That had been as long ago as last summer and where it fitted in Inspector Neele could not imagine. He was not going to let this blackbird bogey divert him from the logical and sober investigation of murder by a sane murderer for a sane reason, but he would be forced from now on to keep the crazier possibilities of the case in mind.

CHAPTER 15

'I'm sorry, Miss Fortescue, to bother you again, but I want to be quite, quite clear about this. As far as we know you were the last person – or rather the last person but one – to see Mrs Fortescue alive. It was about twenty-past five when you left the library?'

'About then,' said Elaine, 'I can't say exactly.' She added defensively. 'One doesn't look at clocks the whole time.'

'No, of course not. During the time that you were alone with Mrs Fortescue after the others had left, what did you talk about?'

'Does it matter what we talked about?'

'Probably not,' said Inspector Neele, 'but it might give me some clue as to what was in Mrs Fortescue's mind.'

'You mean – you think she might have done it herself?'

Inspector Neele noticed the brightening on her face. It would certainly be a very convenient solution as far as the family was concerned. Inspector Neele did not think it was true for a moment. Adele Fortescue was not to his mind a suicidal type. Even if she had poisoned her husband and was convinced the crime was about to be brought home to her, she would not, he thought, have ever thought of killing herself. She would have been sure optimistically that even if she were tried for murder she would be sure to be acquitted. He was not, however, averse to Elaine Fortescue's entertaining the hypothesis. He said, therefore, quite truthfully:

'There's a possibility of it at least, Miss Fortescue. Now perhaps you'll tell me just what your conversation was about?'

'Well, it was really about my affairs.' Elaine hesitated.

'Your affairs being . . . ?' he paused questioningly with a genial expression.

'I – a friend of mine had just arrived in the neighbourhood, and I was asking Adele if she would have any objection to – to my asking him to stay here at the house.'

'Ah. And who is this friend?'

'It's a Mr Gerald Wright. He's a schoolmaster. He – he's staying at the Golf Hotel.'

'A very close friend, perhaps?'

Inspector Neele gave an avuncular beam which added at least fifteen years to his age.

'We may expect an interesting announcement shortly, perhaps?'

He felt almost compunction as he saw the awkward gesture of the girl's hand and the flush on her face. She was in love with the fellow all right.

'We – we're not actually engaged and of course we couldn't have it announced just now, but – well, yes I think we do – I mean we are going to get married.'

'Congratulations,' said Inspector Neele pleasantly. 'Mr Wright is staying at the Golf Hotel, you say? How long has he been there?'

'I wired him when Father died.'

'And he came at once. *I* see,' said Inspector Neele.

He used this favourite phrase of his in a friendly and reassuring way.

'What did Mr Fortescue say when you asked her about his coming here?'

'Oh, she said, all right, I could have anybody I pleased.'

'She was nice about it then?'

'Not exactly nice. I mean, she said –'

'Yes, what else did she say?'

Again Elaine flushed.

'Oh, something stupid about my being able to do a lot better for myself now. It was the sort of thing Adele would say.'

'Ah, well,' said Inspector Neele soothingly, 'relations say these sort of things.'

'Yes, yes, they do. But people often find it difficult to – to appreciate Gerald properly. He's an intellectual, you see, and he's got a lot of unconventional and progressive ideas that people don't like.'

'That's why he didn't get on with your father?'

Elaine flushed hotly.

'Father was very prejudiced and unjust. He hurt Gerald's feelings. In fact, Gerald was so upset by my father's attitude that he went off and I didn't hear from him for weeks.'

And probably wouldn't have heard from him now if your father hadn't died and left you a packet of money, Inspector Neele thought. Aloud he said:

'Was there any more conversation between you and Mrs Fortescue?'

'No. No, I don't think so.'

'And that was about twenty-five-past five and Mrs Fortescue was found dead at five minutes to six. You didn't return to the room during that half-hour?'

'No.'

'What were you doing?'

'I – I went out for a short walk.'

'To the Golf Hotel?'

'I – well, yes, but Gerald wasn't in.'

Inspector Neele said, 'I see' again, but this time with a rather dismissive effect. Elaine Fortescue got up and said:

'Is that all?'

'That's all, thank you, Miss Fortescue.'

As she got up to go, Neele said casually:

'You can't tell me anything about blackbirds, can you?'

She stared at him.

'Blackbirds? You mean the ones in the pie?'

They *would* be in the pie, the Inspector thought to himself. He merely said, 'When was this?'

'Oh! Three or four months ago – and there were some on Father's desk, too. He was furious –'

'Furious, was he? Did he ask a lot of questions?'

'Yes – of course – but we couldn't find out who put them there.'

'Have you any idea why he was so angry?'

'Well – it was rather a horrid thing to do, wasn't it?'

Neele looked thoughtfully at her – but he did not see any signs of evasion in her face. He said:

'Oh, just one more thing, Miss Fortescue. Do you know if your stepmother made a will at any time?'

Elaine shook her head.

'I've no idea – I – suppose so. People usually do, don't they?'

'They should do – but it doesn't always follow. Have you made a will yourself, Miss Fortescue?'

'No – no – I haven't – up to now I haven't had anything to leave – now, of course –'

He saw the realization of the changed position come into her eyes.

'Yes,' he said. 'Fifty thousand pounds is quite a responsibility – it changes a lot of things, Miss Fortescue.'

II

For some minutes after Elaine Fortescue left the room, Inspector Neele sat staring in front of him thoughtfully. He had, indeed, new food for thought. Mary Dove's statement that she had seen a man in the garden at approximately 4.35 opened up certain new possibilities. That is, of course, if Mary Dove was speaking the truth. It was never Inspector Neele's habit to assume that *anyone* was speaking the truth. But, examine her statement as he might, he could see no real reason why she should have lied. He was inclined to think that Mary Dove was speaking the truth when she spoke of having seen a man in the garden. It was quite clear that that man could not have been Lancelot Fortescue, although her reason for assuming that it was he was quite natural under the circumstances. It had not been Lancelot Fortescue, but it had been a man about the height and build of Lancelot Fortescue, and if there had been a man in the garden at that particular time, moreover a man moving furtively, as it seemed, to judge from the way he had crept behind the yew hedges, then that certainly opened up a line of thought.

Added to this statement of hers, there had been the further statement that she had heard someone moving about upstairs. That, in its turn, tied up with something else. The small piece of mud he had found on the floor of Adele Fortescue's boudoir. Inspector Neele's mind dwelt on the small dainty desk in that room. Pretty little sham antique with a rather obvious secret drawer in it. There had been three letters in that drawer, letters written by Vivian Dubois to Adele Fortescue. A great many love letters of one kind or another had passed through Inspector Neele's hands in the course of his career. He was acquainted with passionate letters, foolish letters, sentimental letters and nagging letters. There had also been cautious letters. Inspector Neele was inclined to classify these three as of the latter kind. Even if read in the divorce court, they could pass as inspired by a merely platonic friendship. Though in this case: 'Platonic friendship my foot!' thought the Inspector inelegantly. Neele, when he had found the letters, had sent them up at once to the Yard since at that time the main question was whether the Public Prosecutor's office thought that there was sufficient evidence to proceed with the case against Adele Fortescue or Adele Fortescue and Vivian Dubois together. Everything had pointed towards Rex Fortescue having been poisoned by his wife with or without her lover's connivance. These letters, though cautious, made it fairly clear that Vivian Dubois was her lover, but there had not been in the wording, so far as Inspector Neele could see, any signs of incitement to crime. There might have been incitement of a spoken kind, but Vivian Dubois would be far too cautious to put anything of that kind down on paper.

Inspector Neele surmised accurately that Vivian Dubois had asked Adele Fortescue to destroy his letters and that Adele Fortescue had told him she had done so.

Well, now they had two more deaths on their hands. And that meant, or should mean, that Adele Fortescue had not killed her husband.

Unless, that is – Inspector Neele considered a new hypothesis – Adele Fortescue had wanted to marry Vivian Dubois and Vivian Dubois had wanted, not Adele Fortescue, but Adele Fortescue's hundred thousand pounds which would come to her on the death of her husband. He had assumed, perhaps, that Rex Fortescue's death would be put down to natural causes. Some kind of seizure or stroke. After all, everybody seemed to be worried over Rex Fortescue's health during the last year. (Parenthetically, Inspector Neele said to himself that he must look into that question. He had a subconscious feeling that it might be important in some way.) To continue, Rex Fortescue's death had not gone according to plan. It had been diagnosed without loss of time as poisoning, and the correct poison named.

Supposing that Adele Fortescue and Vivian Dubois had been guilty, what state would they be in then? Vivian Dubois would have been scared and Adele Fortescue would have lost her head. She might have done or said foolish things. She might have rung up Dubois on the telephone, talking indiscreetly in a way that he would have realized might have been overheard in Yewtree Lodge. What would Vivian Dubois have done next?

It was early as yet to try and answer that question, but Inspector Neele proposed very shortly to make enquiries at the Golf Hotel as to whether Dubois had been in or out of the hotel between the hours of 4.15 and 6 o'clock. Vivian Dubois was tall and dark like Lance Fortescue. He might have slipped through the garden to the side door, made his way upstairs and then what? Looked for the letters and found them gone? Waited there, perhaps, till the coast was clear, then come down into the library when tea was over and Adele Fortescue was alone?

But all this was going too fast –

Neele had questioned Mary Dove and Elaine Fortescue; he must see now what Percival Fortescue's wife had to say.

CHAPTER 16

Inspector Neele found Mrs Percival in her own sitting-room upstairs, writing letters. She got up rather nervously when he came in.

'Is there anything – what – are there –'

'Please sit down, Mrs Fortescue. There are only just a few more questions I would like to ask you.'

'Oh, yes. Yes, of course, Inspector. It's all so dreadful, isn't it? So very dreadful.'

She sat down rather nervously in an armchair. Inspector Neele sat down in the small, straight chair near her. He studied her rather more carefully than he had done heretofore. In some ways a mediocre type of woman, he thought – and thought also that she was not very happy. Restless, unsatisfied, limited in mental outlook, yet he thought she might have been efficient and skilled in her own profession of hospital nurse. Though she had achieved leisure by her marriage with a well-to-do man, leisure had not satisfied her. She bought clothes, read novels and ate sweets, but he remembered her avid excitement on the night of Rex Fortescue's death, and he saw in it not so much a ghoulish satisfaction but rather a revelation of the arid deserts of boredom which encompassed her life. Her eyelids fluttered and fell before his searching glance. They gave her the appearance of being both nervous and guilty, but he could not be sure that that was really the case.

'I'm afraid,' he said soothingly, 'we have to ask people questions again and again. It must be very tiresome for you all. I do appreciate that, but so much hangs, you understand, on the exact *timing* of events. You came down to tea rather late, I understand? In fact, Miss Dove came up and fetched you.'

'Yes. Yes, she did. She came and said tea was in. I had no idea it was so late. I'd been writing letters.'

Inspector Neele just glanced over at the writing-desk.

'I see,' he said. 'Somehow, or other, I thought you'd been out for a walk.'

'Did she say so? Yes – now I believe you're right. I had been writing letters; then it was so stuffy and my head ached so I went out and – er – went for a walk. Only round the garden.'

'I see. You didn't meet anyone?'

'Meet anyone?' She stared at him. 'What do you mean?'

'I just wondered if you'd seen anybody or anybody had seen you during this walk of yours.'

'I saw the gardener in the distance, that's all.' She was looking at him suspiciously.

'Then you came in, came up here to your room and you were just taking your things off when Miss Dove came to tell you that tea was ready?'

'Yes. Yes, and so I came down.'

'And who was there?'

'Adele and Elaine, and a minute or two later Lance arrived. My brother-in-law, you know. The one who's come back from Kenya.'

'And then you all had tea?'

'Yes, we had tea. Then Lance went up to see Aunt Effie and I came up here to finish my letters. I left Elaine there with Adele.'

He nodded reassuringly.

'Yes. Miss Fortescue seems to have been with Mrs Fortescue for quite five or ten minutes after you left. Your husband hadn't come home yet?'

'Oh no. Percy – Val – didn't get home until about half-past six or seven. He'd been kept up in town.'

'He came back by train?'

'Yes. He took a taxi from the station.'

'Was it unusual for him to come back by train?

'He does sometimes. Not very often. I think he'd been to places in the city where it's rather difficult to park the car. It was easier for him to take a train home from Cannon Street.'

'I see,' said Inspector Neele. He went on, 'I asked your husband if Mrs Fortescue had made a will before she died. He said he thought not. I suppose you don't happen to have any idea?'

To his surprise Jennifer Fortescue nodded vigorously.

'Oh, yes,' she said. 'Adele made a will. She told me so.'

'Indeed! When was this?'

'Oh, it wasn't very long ago. About a month ago, I think.'

'That's very interesting,' said Inspector Neele.

Mrs Percival leant forward eagerly. Her face now was all animation. She clearly enjoyed exhibiting her superior knowledge.

'Val didn't know about it,' she said. 'Nobody knew. It just happened that I found out about it. I was in the street. I had just come out of the stationer's, then I saw Adele coming out of the solicitor's office. Ansell and Worrall's you know. In the High Street.'

'Ah,' said Neele, 'the local solicitors?'

'Yes. And I said to Adele "Whatever have you been doing there?" I said. And she laughed and said "Wouldn't you like to know?" And then as we walked along together she said "I'll tell you, Jennifer. I've been making my will." "Well," I said, "why are you doing that, Adele, you're not ill or anything, are you?" And she said no, of course she wasn't ill. She'd never felt better. But everyone ought to make a will. She said she wasn't going to those stuck-up family solicitors in London, Mr Billingsley. She said the old sneak would go round and tell the family. "No," she said, "My will's my own business, Jennifer, and I'll make it my own way and nobody's going to know about it." "Well, Adele," I said, "*I* shan't tell anybody." She said. "It doesn't matter if you do. You won't know what's in it." But I didn't tell anyone. No, not even Percy. I do think women ought to stick together, don't you, Inspector Neele?'

'I'm sure that's a very nice feeling on your part, Mrs Fortescue,' said Inspector Neele, diplomatically.

'I'm sure I'm never ill-natured,' said Jennifer. 'I didn't particularly care for Adele, if you know what I mean. I always thought she was the kind of woman who would stick at nothing in order to get what she wanted. Now she's dead, perhaps I misjudged her, poor soul.'

'Well, thank you very much, Mrs Fortescue, for being so helpful to me.'

'You're welcome, I'm sure. I'm only too glad to do anything I can. It's all so very terrible, isn't it? Who is the old lady who's arrived this morning?'

'She's a Miss Marple. She very kindly came here to give us what information she could about the girl Gladys. It seems Gladys Martin was once in service with her.'

'Really? How interesting.'

'There's one other thing, Mrs Percival. Do you know anything about blackbirds?'

Jennifer Fortescue started violently. She dropped her handbag on the floor and bent to pick it up.

'Blackbirds, Inspector? Blackbirds? What kind of blackbirds?'

Her voice was rather breathless. Smiling a little, Inspector Neele said:

'Just blackbirds. Alive or dead or even, shall we say, symbolical?'

Jennifer Fortescue said sharply:

'I don't know what you mean. I don't know what you're talking about.'

'You don't know anything about blackbirds, then, Mrs Fortescue?'

She said slowly:

'I suppose you mean the ones last summer in the pie. All very silly.'

'There were some left on Mr Fortescue's desk in his study, too, weren't there?'

'It was all a very silly practical joke. I don't know who's been talking to you about it. Mr Fortescue, my father-in-law, was very much annoyed by it.'

'Just annoyed? Nothing more?'

'Oh. I see what you mean. Yes, I suppose – yes, it's true. He asked us if there were any strangers about the place.'

'Strangers!' Inspector Neele raised his eyebrows.

'Well, that's what he said,' said Mrs Percival defensively.

'Strangers,' repeated Inspector Neele thoughtfully. Then he asked, 'Did he seem afraid in any way?'

'Afraid? I don't know what you mean.'

'Nervous. About strangers, I mean.'

'Yes. Yes, he did, rather. Of course I don't remember very well. It was several months ago, you know. I don't think it was anything except a silly practical joke. Crump perhaps. I really do think that Crump is a very unbalanced man, and I'm perfectly certain that he drinks. He's really very insolent in his manner sometimes. I've sometimes wondered if he could have had a grudge against Mr Fortescue. Do you think that's possible, Inspector?'

'Anything's possible,' said Inspector Neele and went away.

II

Percival Fortescue was in London, but Inspector Neele found Lancelot sitting with his wife in the library. They were playing chess together.

'I don't want to interrupt you,' said Neele, apologetically.

'We're only killing time, Inspector, aren't we, Pat?'

Pat nodded.

'I expect you'll think it's rather a foolish question I'm asking you,' said Neele. 'Do you know anything about blackbirds, Mr Fortescue?'

'Blackbirds?' Lance looked amused. 'What kind of blackbirds? Do you mean genuine birds, or the slave trade?'

Inspector Neele said with a sudden, disarming smile:

'I'm not sure what I mean, Mr Fortescue. It's just that a mention of blackbirds has turned up.'

'Good Lord.' Lancelot looked suddenly alert, 'Not the old Blackbird Mine, I suppose?'

Inspector Neele said sharply:

'The Blackbird Mine? What was that?'

Lance frowned in a puzzled fashion.

'The trouble is, Inspector, that I can't really remember much myself. I just have an idea about some shady transaction in my papa's past. Something on the West Coast of Africa. Aunt Effie, I believe, once threw it in his teeth, but I can't remember anything definite about it.'

'Aunt Effie? That will be Miss Ramsbottom, won't it?'

'Yes.'

'I'll go and ask her about it,' said Inspector Neele. He added ruefully, 'She's rather a formidable old lady, Mr Fortescue. Always makes me feel quite nervous.'

Lance laughed.

'Yes. Aunt Effie is certainly a character, but she may be helpful to you, Inspector, if you get on the right side of her. Especially if you're delving into the past. She's got an excellent memory, she takes a positive pleasure in remembering anything that's detrimental in any way.' He added thoughtfully, 'There's something else. I went up to see her, you know, soon after I got back here. Immediately after tea that day, as a matter of fact. And she was talking about Gladys. The maid who got killed. Not that we knew she was dead then, of course. But Aunt Effie was saying she was quite convinced that Gladys knew something that she hadn't told the police.'

'That seems fairly certain,' said Inspector Neele. 'She'll never tell it now, poor girl.'

'No. It seems Aunt Effie had given her good advice as to spilling anything she knew. Pity the girl didn't take it.'

Inspector Neele nodded. Bracing himself for the encounter he penetrated to Miss Ramsbottom's fortress. Rather to his surprise, he found Miss Marple there. The two ladies appeared to be discussing foreign missions.

'I'll go away, Inspector.' Miss Marple rose hurriedly to her feet.

'No need, madam,' said Inspector Neele.

'I've asked Miss Marple to come and stay in the house,' said Miss Ramsbottom. 'No sense in spending money in that ridiculous Golf Hotel. A wicked nest of profiteers, that is. Drinking and card playing all the evening. She'd better come and stay in a decent Christian household. There's a room next door to mine. Dr Mary Peters, the missionary, had it last.'

'It's very, very kind of you,' said Miss Marple, 'but I really think I mustn't intrude in a house of mourning.'

'Mourning? Fiddlesticks,' said Miss Ramsbottom. 'Who'll weep for Rex in this house? Or Adele either? Or is it the police you're worried about? Any objections, Inspector?'

'None from me, madam.'

'There you are,' said Miss Ramsbottom.

'It's very kind of you,' said Miss Marple gratefully. 'I'll go and telephone to the hotel to cancel my booking.' She left the room and Miss Ramsbottom said sharply to the Inspector:

'Well, and what do *you* want?'

'I wondered if you could tell me anything about the Blackbird Mine, ma'am.'

Miss Ramsbottom uttered a sudden, shrill cackle of laughter.

'Ha. You've got on to *that*, have you! Took the hint I gave you the other day. Well, what do you want to know about it?'

'Anything you can tell me, madam.'

'I can't tell you much. It's a long time ago now – oh, twenty to twenty-five years maybe. Some concession or other in East Africa. My brother-in-law went into it with a man called MacKenzie. They went out there to investigate the mine together and MacKenzie died out there of fever. Rex came home and said the claim or the concession or whatever you call it was worthless. That's all *I* know.'

'I think you know a little more than that, ma'am,' said Neele persuasively.

'Anything else is hearsay. You don't like hearsay in the law, so I've been told.'

'We're not in court yet, ma'am.'

'Well, *I* can't tell you anything. The MacKenzies kicked up a fuss. That's all I know. They insisted that Rex had swindled MacKenzie. I daresay he did. He was a clever, unscrupulous fellow, but I've no doubt whatever he did it was all legal. They couldn't prove anything. Mrs MacKenzie was an unbalanced sort of woman. She came here and made a lot of threats of revenge. Said Rex had murdered her husband. Silly, melodramatic fuss! I think she was a bit off her head – in fact, I believe she went into an asylum not long after. Came here dragging along a couple of young children who looked scared to death. Said she'd bring up her children to have revenge. Something like that. Tomfoolery, all of it. Well, that's all I can tell you. And mind you, the Blackbird Mine wasn't the only swindle that Rex put over in his lifetime. You'll find a good many more if you look for them. What put you on to the Blackbird? Did you come across some trail leading to the MacKenzies?'

'You don't know what became of the family, ma'am?'

'No idea,' said Miss Ramsbottom. 'Mind you, I don't think Rex would have actually murdered MacKenzie, but he might have left him to die. The same thing before the Lord, but not the same thing before the law. If he did, retributions's caught up with him. The mills of God grind slowly, but they grind exceeding small – you'd better go away now, I can't tell you any more and it's no good your asking.'

'Thank you very much for what you have told me,' said Inspector Neele.

'Send that Marple woman back,' Miss Ramsbottom called after him. 'She's frivolous, like all Church of England people, but she knows how to run a charity in a sensible way.'

Inspector Neele made a couple of telephone calls, the first to Ansell and Worrall and the second to the Golf Hotel, then he summoned Sergeant Hay and told him that he was leaving the house for a short period.

'I've a call to pay at a solicitor's office – after that, you can get me at the Golf Hotel if anything urgent turns up.'

'Yes, sir.'

'And find out anything you can about blackbirds,' added Neele over his shoulder.

'Blackbirds, sir?' Sergeant Hay repeated, thoroughly mystified.

'That's what I said – not blackberry jelly – blackbirds.'

'Very good, sir,' said Sergeant Hay bewilderedly.

CHAPTER 17

Inspector Neele found Mr Ansell the type of solicitor who was more easily intimidated than intimidating. A member of a small and not very prosperous firm, he was anxious not to stand upon his rights but instead to assist the police in every way possible.

Yes, he said, he had made a will for the late Mrs Adele Fortescue. She had called at his office about five weeks previously. It had seemed to him rather a peculiar business but naturally he had not said anything. Peculiar things did happen in a solicitor's business, and of course the Inspector would understand that discretion, etc., etc. The Inspector nodded to show he understood. He had already discovered Mr Ansell had not transacted any legal business previously for Mrs Fortescue or for any of the Fortescue family.

'Naturally,' said Mr Ansell, 'she didn't want to go to her husband's firm of lawyers about this.'

Shorn of verbiage, the facts were simple. Adele Fortescue had made a will leaving everything of which she died possessed to Vivian Dubois.

'But I gathered,' said Mr Ansell, looking at Neele in an interrogating manner, 'that she hadn't actually much to leave.'

Inspector Neele nodded. At the time Adele Fortescue made her will that was true enough. But since then Rex Fortescue had died, and Adele Fortescue had inherited £100,000 and presumably that £100,000 (less death duties) now belonged to Vivian Edward Dubois.

II

At the Golf Hotel, Inspector Neele found Vivian Dubois nervously awaiting his arrival. Dubois had been on the point of leaving, indeed his bags were packed, when he had received over the telephone a civil request from Inspector Neele to remain. Inspector Neele had been very pleasant about it, quite apologetic. But behind the conventional words the request had been an order. Vivian Dubois had demurred, but not too much.

246

He said now:

'I do hope you realize, Inspector Neele, that it is very inconvenient for me to have to stay on. I really have urgent business that needs attending to.'

'I didn't know you were in business, Mr Dubois,' said Inspector Neele, genially.

'I'm afraid none of us can be as leisured as we would like to appear to be nowadays.'

'Mrs Fortescue's death must have been a great shock to you, Mr Dubois. You were great friends, were you not?'

'Yes,' said Dubois, 'she was a charming woman. We played golf quite often together.'

'I expect you'll miss her very much.'

'Yes, indeed.' Dubois sighed. 'The whole thing is really quite, quite terrible.'

'You actually telephoned her, I believe, on the afternoon of her death?'

'Did I? I really cannot remember now.'

'About four o'clock, I understand.'

'Yes, I believe I did.'

'Don't you remember what your conversation was about, Mr Dubois?'

'It wasn't of any significance. I think I asked her how she was feeling and if there was any further news about her husband's death – a more or less conventional enquiry.'

'*I* see,' said Inspector Neele. He added, 'And then you went out for a walk?'

'Er – yes – yes, I – I did, I think. At least, not a walk, I played a few holes of golf.'

Inspector Neele said gently:

'I think not, Mr Dubois. . . . Not that particular day. . . . The porter here noticed you walking down the road towards Yewtree Lodge.'

Dubois's eyes met his, then shied away again nervously.

'I'm afraid I can't remember, Inspector.'

'Perhaps you actually went to call upon Mrs Fortescue?'

Dubois said sharply:

'No. No, I didn't do that. I never went near the house.'

'Where did you go, then?'

'Oh, I – went on down the road, down as far as the Three Pigeons and then I turned around and came back by the links.'

'You're quite sure you didn't go to Yewtree Lodge?'

'Quite sure, Inspector.'

The Inspector shook his head.

'Come, now, Mr Dubois,' he said, 'it's much better to be frank with us, you know. You may have had some quite innocent reason for going there.'

'I tell you I never went to see Mrs Fortescue that day.'

The Inspector stood up.

'You know, Mr Dubois,' he said pleasantly, 'I think we'll have to ask you for a statement and you'll be well advised and quite within your rights in having a solicitor present when you are making that statement.'

The colour fled from Mr Dubois's face, leaving it a sickly greenish colour.

'You're threatening me,' he said. 'You're threatening me.'

'No, no, nothing of the kind.' Inspector Neele spoke in a shocked voice. 'We're not allowed to do anything of that sort. Quite the contrary. I'm actually pointing out to you that you have certain rights.'

'I had nothing to do with it at all, I tell you! Nothing to do with it.'

'Come now, Mr Dubois, you were at Yewtree Lodge round about half-past four on that day. Somebody looked out of the window, you know, and saw you.'

'I was only in the garden. I didn't go into the house.'

'Didn't you?' said Inspector Neele. 'Are you sure? Didn't you go in by the side door, and up the stairs to Mrs Fortescue's sitting-room on the first floor? You were looking for something, weren't you, in the desk there?'

'*You've* got them, I suppose,' said Dubois sullenly. 'That fool Adele kept them, then – she swore she burnt them – But they don't mean what you think they mean.'

'You're not denying, are you, Mr Dubois, that you were a very *close* friend of Mrs Fortescue's?'

'No, of course I'm not. How can I when you've got the letters? All I say is, there's no need to go reading any sinister meaning into them. Don't think for a moment that we – that she – ever thought of getting rid of Rex Fortescue. Good God, I'm not *that* kind of man!'

'But perhaps she was that kind of woman?'

'Nonsense,' cried Vivian Dubois, 'wasn't she killed too?'

'Oh yes, yes.'

'Well, isn't it natural to believe that the same person who killed her husband killed her?'

'It might be. It certainly might be. But there are other solutions. For instance – (this is quite a hypothetical case, Mr Dubois) it's possible that Mrs Fortescue got rid of her husband, and that after his death she became somewhat of a danger to someone else. Someone who had, perhaps, not helped her in what she had done but who had at least encouraged her and provided, shall we say, the *motive* for the deed. She might be, you know, a danger to that particular person.'

Dubois stammered:

'You c-c-can't build up a case against me. You can't.'

'She made a will, you know,' said Inspector Neele. 'She left all her money to you. Everything she possessed.'

'I don't want the money. I don't want a penny of it.'

'Of course, it isn't very much really,' said Inspector Neele. 'There's jewellery and some furs, but I imagine very little actual cash.'

Dubois stared at him, his jaw dropping.

'But I thought her husband –'

He stopped dead.

'Did you, Mr Dubois?' said Inspector Neele, and there was steel now in his voice. 'That's very interesting. I wondered if you knew the terms of Rex Fortescue's will –'

III

Inspector Neele's second interview at the Golf Hotel was with Mr Gerald Wright. Mr Gerald Wright was a thin, intellectual and very superior young man. He was, Inspector Neele noted, not unlike Vivian Dubois in build.

'What can I do for you, Inspector Neele?' he asked.

'I thought you might be able to help us with a little information, Mr Wright.'

'Information? Really? It seems very unlikely.'

'It's in connection with the recent events at Yewtree Lodge. You've heard of them, of course?'

Inspector Neele put a little irony into the question. Mr Wright smiled patronizingly.

'Heard of them,' he said, 'is hardly the right word. The newspapers appear to be full of nothing else. How incredibly blood-thirsty our public press is! What an age we live in! On one side the manufacture of atom bombs, on the other our r ewspapers delight in reporting brutal murders! But you said you had some questions to ask. Really, I cannot see what they can be. I know nothing about this Yewtree Lodge affair. I was actually in the Isle of Man when Mr Rex Fortescue was killed.'

'You arrived here very shortly afterwards, didn't you, Mr Wright? You had a telegram, I believe, from Miss Elaine Fortescue?'

'Our police know everything, do they not? Yes, Elaine sent for me. I came, of course, at once.'

'And you are, I understand, shortly to be married?'

'Quite right, Inspector Neele. You have no objections, I hope.'

'It is entirely Miss Fortescue's business. I understand the attachment between you dates from some time back? Six or seven months ago, in fact?'

'Quite correct.'

'You and Miss Fortescue became engaged to be married. Mr Fortescue refused to give his consent, informed you that if his daughter married against his wishes he did not propose to give her an income of any kind. Whereupon, I understand, you broke off the engagement and departed.'

Gerald Wright smiled rather pityingly.

'A very crude way of putting things, Inspector Neele. Actually, I was victimized for my political opinions. Rex Fortescue was the worst type of capitalist. Naturally I could not sacrifice my political beliefs and convictions for money.'

'But you have no objections to marrying a wife who has just inherited £50,000?'

Gerald Wright gave a thin satisfied smile.

'Not at all, Inspector Neele. The money will be used for the benefit of the community. But surely you did not come here to discuss with me either my financial circumstances – or my political convictions?'

'No, Mr Wright. I wanted to talk to you about a simple question of fact. As you are aware, Mrs Adele Fortescue died as a result of cyanide poisoning on the afternoon of November the 5th.

'Since you were in the neighbourhood of Yewtree Lodge on that afternoon I thought it possible that you might have seen or heard something that had a bearing on the case.'

'And what leads you to believe that I was, as you call it, in the neighbourhood of Yewtree Lodge at the time?'

'You left this hotel at a quarter past four on that particular afternoon, Mr Wright. On leaving the hotel you walked down the road in the direction of Yewtree Lodge. It seems natural to suppose that you were going there?'

'I thought of it,' said Gerald Wright, 'but I considered that it would be a rather pointless thing to do. I already had an arrangement to meet Miss Fortescue – Elaine – at the hotel at six o'clock. I went for a walk along a lane that branches off from the main road and returned to the Golf Hotel just before six o'clock. Elaine did not keep her appointment. Quite naturally, under the circumstances.'

'Anybody see you on this walk of yours, Mr Wright?'

'A few cars passed me, I think, on the road. I did not see anyone I knew, if that's what you mean. The lane was little more than a cart-track and too muddy for cars.'

'So between the time you left the hotel at a quarter past four until six o'clock when you arrived back again, I've only your word for it as to where you were?'

Gerald Wright continued to smile in a superior fashion.

'Very distressing for us both, Inspector, but there it is.'

Inspector Neele said softly:

'Then if someone said they looked out of a landing window and saw you in the garden of Yewtree Lodge at about 4.35 –' he paused and left the sentence unfinished.

Gerald Wright raised his eyebrows and shook his head.

'Visibility must have been very bad by then,' he said. 'I think it would be difficult for anyone to be sure.'

'Are you acquainted with Mr Vivian Dubois, who is also staying here?'

'Dubois. Dubois? No, I don't think so. Is that the tall, dark man with a pretty taste in suede shoes?'

'Yes. He also was out for a walk that afternoon, and he also left the hotel and walked past Yewtree Lodge. You did not notice him in the road by any chance?'

'No. No. I can't say I did.'

Gerald Wright looked for the first time faintly worried. Inspector Neele said thoughtfully:

'It wasn't really a very nice afternoon for walking, especially after dark in a muddy lane. Curious how energetic everyone seems to have felt.'

IV

On Inspector Neele's return to the house he was greeted by Sergeant Hay with an air of satisfaction.

'I've found out about the blackbirds for you, sir,' he said.

'You have, have you?'

'Yes, sir, in a pie they were. Cold pie was left out for Sunday night's supper. Somebody got at that pie in the larder or somewhere. They'd taken off the crust and they'd taken out the veal and 'am what was inside it, and what d'you think they put in instead? Some stinkin' blackbirds they got out of the gardener's shed. Nasty sort of trick to play, wasn't it?'

'"*Wasn't that a dainty dish to set before the king?*"' said Inspector Neele.

He left Sergeant Hay staring after him.

CHAPTER 18

'Just wait a minute,' said Miss Ramsbottom. 'This Patience is going to come out.'

She transferred a king and his various impedimenta into an empty space, put a red seven on a black eight, built up the four, five and six of spades on her foundation heap, made a few more rapid transfers of cards and then leaned back with a sigh of satisfaction.

'That's the Double Jester,' she said. 'It doesn't often come out.'

She leaned back in a satisfied fashion, then raised her eyes at the girl standing by the fireplace.

'So you're Lance's wife,' she said.

Pat, who had been summoned upstairs to Miss Ramsbottom's presence, nodded her head.

'Yes,' she said.

'You're a tall girl,' said Miss Ramsbottom, 'and you look healthy.'

'I'm very healthy.'

Miss Ramsbottom nodded in a satisfied manner.

'Percival's wife is pasty,' she said. 'Eats too many sweets and doesn't take enough exercise. Well, sit down, child, sit down. Where did you meet my nephew?'

'I met him out in Kenya when I was staying there with some friends.'

'You've been married before, I understand.'

'Yes. Twice.'

Miss Ramsbottom gave a profound sniff.

'Divorce, I suppose.'

'No,' said Pat. Her voice trembled a little. 'They both – died. My first husband was a fighter pilot. He was killed in the war.'

'And your second husband? Let me see – somebody told me. Shot himself, didn't he?'

Pat nodded.

'Your fault?'

'No,' said Pat. 'It wasn't my fault.'

'Racing man, wasn't he?'

'Yes.'

'I've never been on a race-course in my life,' said Miss Ramsbottom. 'Betting and card playing – all devices of the devil!'

Pat did not reply.

'I wouldn't go inside a theatre or a cinema,' said Miss Ramsbottom. 'Ah, well, it's a wicked world nowadays. A lot of wickedness was going on in this house, but the Lord struck them down.'

Pat still found it difficult to say anything. She wondered if Lance's Aunt Effie was really quite all there. She was, however, a trifle disconcerted by the old lady's shrewd glance at her.

'How much,' demanded Aunt Effie, 'do you know about the family you've married into?'

'I suppose,' said Pat, 'as much as one ever knows of the family one marries into.'

'H'm, something in that, something in that. Well, I'll tell you this. My sister was a fool, my brother-in-law was a rogue, Percival is a sneak, and your Lance was always the bad boy of the family.'

'I think that's all nonsense,' said Pat robustly.

'Maybe you're right,' said Miss Ramsbottom, unexpectedly. 'You can't just stick labels on people. But don't underestimate Percival. There's a tendency to believe that those who are labelled good are also stupid. Percival isn't the least bit stupid. He's quite clever in a sanctimonious kind of way. I've never cared for him. Mind you, I don't *trust* Lance and I don't *approve* of him, but I can't help being fond of him. . . . He's a reckless sort of fellow – always has been. You've got to look after him and see he doesn't go too far.

Tell him not to underestimate Percival, my dear. Tell him not to believe everything that Percival says. They're all liars in this house.' The old lady added with satisfaction, 'Fire and brimstone shall be their portion.'

II

Inspector Neele was finishing a telephone conversation with Scotland Yard.

The Assistant Commissioner at the other end said:

'We ought to be able to get that information for you – by circularizing the various private sanatoriums. Of course she *may* be dead.'

'Probably is. It's a long time ago.'

Old sins cast long shadows. Miss Ramsbottom had said that – said it with significance, too – as though she was giving him a hint.

'It's a fantastic theory,' said the AC.

'Don't I know it, sir. But I don't feel we can ignore it altogether. Too much fits in –'

'Yes – yes – rye – blackbirds – the man's Christian name –'

Neele said:

'I'm concentrating on the other lines too – Dubois is a possibility – so is Wright – the girl Gladys could have caught sight of either of them outside the side door – she could have left the tea-tray in the hall and gone out to see who it was and what they were doing – whoever it was could have strangled her then and there and then carried her body round to the clothes line and put the peg on her nose –'

'A crazy thing to do in all conscience! A nasty one too.'

'Yes, sir. That's what upset the old lady – Miss Marple, I mean. Nice old lady – and very shrewd. She's moved into the house – to be near old Miss Ramsbottom – and I've no doubt she'll get to hear anything that's going.'

'What's your next move, Neele?'

'I've an appointment with the London solicitors. I want to find out a little more about Rex Fortescue's affairs. And though it's old history, I want to hear a little more about the Blackbird Mine.'

III

Mr Billingsley, of Billingsley, Horsethorpe & Walters, was an urbane man whose discretion was concealed habitually by a mis-leadingly forthcoming manner. It was the second interview that Inspector Neele had had with him, and on this occasion Mr Billingsley's discretion was less noticeable than it had been on the former one. The triple tragedy at Yewtree Lodge had shaken Mr Billingsley out of his professional reserve. He was now only too anxious to put all the facts he could before the police.

'Most extraordinary business, this whole thing,' he said. 'A most extraordinary business. I don't remember anything like it in all my professional career.'

'Frankly, Mr Billingsley,' said Inspector Neele, 'we need all the help we can get.'

'You can count on me, my dear sir. I shall be only too happy to assist you in every way I can.'

'First let me ask you how well you knew the late Mr Fortescue, and how well do you know the affairs of his firm?'

'I knew Rex Fortescue fairly well. That is to say I've known him for a period of, well, sixteen years I should say. Mind you, we are not the only firm of solicitors he employed, not by a long way.'

Inspector Neele nodded. He knew that. Billingsley, Horsethorpe & Walters were what one might describe as Rex Fortescue's reputable solicitors. For his less reputable dealings he had employed several different and slightly less scrupulous firms.

'Now what do you want to know?' continued Mr Billingsley. 'I've told you about his will. Percival Fortescue is the residuary legatee.'

'I'm interested now,' said Inspector Neele, 'in the will of his widow. On Mr Fortescue's death she came into the sum of one hundred thousand pounds, I understand?'

Billingsley nodded his head.

'A considerable sum of money,' he said, 'and I may tell you in confidence, Inspector, that it is one the firm could ill have afforded to pay out.'

'The firm, then, is not prosperous?'

'Frankly,' said Mr Billingsley, 'and strictly between ourselves, it's drifting on to the rocks and has been for the last year and a half.'

'For any particular reason?'

'Why yes. I should say the reason was Rex Fortescue himself. For the last year Rex Fortescue's been acting like a madman. Selling good stock here, buying speculative stuff there, talking big about it all the time in the most extraordinary way. Wouldn't listen to advice. Percival – the son, you know – he came here urging me to use my influence with his father. *He'd* tried, apparently, and been swept aside. Well, I did what I could, but Fortescue wouldn't listen to reason. Really, he seems to have been a changed man.'

'But not, I gather, a depressed man,' said Inspector Neele.

'No, no. Quite the contrary. Flamboyant, bombastic.'

Inspector Neele nodded. An idea which had already taken form in his mind was strenghtened. He thought he was beginning to understand some of the causes of friction between Percival and his father. Mr Billingsley was continuing.

'But it's no good asking me about the wife's will. *I* didn't make any will for her.'

'No. I know that,' said Neele. 'I'm merely verifying that she had something to leave. In short, a hundred thousand pounds.'

Mr Billingsley was shaking his head violently.

'No, no, my dear sir. You're wrong there.'

'Do you mean the hundred thousand pounds was only left to her for her lifetime?'

'No – no – it was left to her outright. But there was a clause in the will governing that bequest. That is to say, Fortescue's wife did not inherit the sum unless she survived him for one month. That, I may say, is a clause fairly common nowadays. It has come into operation owing to the uncertainties of air travel. If two people are killed in an air accident, it becomes exceedingly difficult to say who was the survivor and a lot of very curious problems arise.'

Inspector Neele was staring at him.

'Then Adele Fortescue had not got a hundred thousand pounds to leave. What happens to that money?'

'It goes back into the firm. Or rather, I should say, it goes to the residuary legatee.'

'And the residuary legatee is Mr Percival Fortescue.'

'That's right,' said Billingsley, 'it goes to Percival Fortescue. And with the state the firm's affairs are in,' he added unguardedly, 'I should say that he'll need it!'

IV

'The things you policemen want to know,' said Inspector Neele's doctor friend.

'Come on, Bob, spill it.'

'Well, as we're alone together you can't quote me, fortunately! But I should say, you know, that your idea's dead right. GPI by the sound of it all. The family suspected it and wanted to get him to see a doctor. He wouldn't. It acts just in the way you describe. Loss of judgement, megalomania, violent fits of irritation and anger – boastfulness – delusions of grandeur – of being a great financial genius. Anyone suffering from that would soon put a solvent firm on the rocks – unless he could be restrained – and that's not so easy to do – especially if the man himself has an idea of what you're after. Yes – I should say it was a bit of luck for your friends that he died.'

'They're no friends of mine,' said Neele. He repeated what he had once said before:

'They're all very unpleasant people. . . .'

CHAPTER 19

In the drawing-room at Yewtree Lodge, the whole Fortescue family was assembled. Percival Fortescue, leaning against the mantelpiece, was addressing the meeting.

'It's all very well,' said Percival. 'But the whole position is most unsatisfactory. The police come and go and don't tell us anything. One supposes they're pursuing some line of research. In the meantime everything's at a standstill. One can't make plans, one can't arrange things for the future.'

'It's all so inconsiderate,' said Jennifer. 'And so stupid.'

'There still seems to be this ban against anyone leaving the house,' went on Percival. 'Still, I think among ourselves we might discuss future plans. What about you, Elaine? I gather you're going to marry – what's-his-name – Gerald Wright? Have you any idea when?'

'As soon as possible,' said Elaine.

Percival frowned.

'You mean, in about six months' time?'

'No, I don't. Why should we wait six months?'

'I think it would be more decent,' said Percival.

'Rubbish,' said Elaine. 'A month. That's the longest we'll wait.'

'Well, it's for you to say,' said Percival. 'And what are your plans when you are married, if you have any?'

'We're thinking of starting a school.'

Percival shook his head.

'That's a very risky speculation in these times. What with the shortage of domestic labour, the difficulty of getting an adequate teaching staff – really, Elaine, it sounds all right. But I should think twice about it if I were you.'

'We have thought. Gerald feels that the whole future of this country lies in right education.'

'I am seeing Mr Billingsley the day after tomorrow,' said Percival. 'We've got to go into various questions of finance. He was suggesting that you might like to make this money that's been left to you by Father into a trust for yourself and your children. It's a very sound thing to do nowadays.'

'I don't want to do that,' said Elaine. 'We shall need the money to start up our school. There's a very suitable house we've heard of for sale. It's in Cornwall. Beautiful grounds and quite a good house. It would have to be built on to a good deal – several wings added.'

'You mean – you mean you're going to take all your money out of the business? Really, Elaine, I *don't* think you're wise.'

'Much wiser to take it out than leave it in, I should say,' said Elaine. 'Businesses are going phut all over the place. You said yourself, Val, before Father died, that things were getting into a pretty bad state.'

'One says that sort of thing,' said Percival vaguely, 'but I must say, Elaine, to take out all your capital and sink it in the buying, equipping and running of a school is crazy. If it's not a success look what happens? You're left without a penny.'

'It *will* be a success,' said Elaine, doggedly.

'I'm with you.' Lance, lying sprawled out in a chair, spoke up encouragingly. 'Have a crack at it, Elaine. In my opinion it'll be a damned odd sort of school, but it's what you want to do – you and Gerald. If you do lose your money you'll at any rate have had the satisfaction of doing what you wanted to do.'

'Just what one might have expected you to say, Lance,' said Percival, acidly.

'I know, I know,' said Lance. 'I'm the spendthrift prodigal son.

But I still think I've had more fun out of life than you have, Percy, old boy.'

'It depends on what you call fun,' said Percival coldly. 'Which brings us to your own plans, Lance. I suppose you'll be off again back to Kenya – or Canada – or climbing Mount Everest or something fairly fantastic?'

'Now what makes you think that?' said Lance.

'Well, you've never had much use for a stay-at-home life in England, have you?'

'One changes as one gets older,' said Lance. 'One settles down. D'you know, Percy my boy, I'm quite looking forward to having a crack at being a sober businessman.'

'Do you mean . . .'

'I mean I'm coming into the firm with you, old boy.' Lance grinned. 'Oh, you're the senior partner, of course. You've got the lion's share. I'm only a very junior partner. But I *have* got a holding in it that gives me the right to be in on things, doesn't it?'

'Well – yes – of course, if you put it that way. But I can assure you, my dear boy, you'll be very, very bored.'

'I wonder now. I don't believe I shall be bored.'

Percival frowned.

'You don't seriously mean, Lance, that you're coming into the business?'

'Having a finger in the pie? Yes, that's exactly what I am doing.'

Percival shook his head.

'Things are in a very bad way, you know. You'll find that out. It's going to be about all we can do to pay out Elaine her share, if she insists on having it paid out.'

'There you are, Elaine,' said Lance. 'You see how wise you were to insist on grabbing your money while it's still there to grab.'

'Really, Lance,' Percival spoke angrily, 'these jokes of yours are in very bad taste.'

'I do think, Lance, you might be more careful what you say,' said Jennifer.

Sitting a little way away near the window, Pat studied them one by one. If this was what Lance had meant by twisting Percival's tail, she could see that he was achieving his object. Percival's neat impassivity was quite ruffled. He snapped again, angrily:

'Are you serious, Lance?'

'Dead serious.'

'It won't work, you know. You'll soon get fed up.'

'Not me. Think what a lovely change it'll be for me. A city office, typists coming and going. I shall have a blonde secretary like Miss Grosvenor – is it Grosvenor? I suppose you've snaffled her. But I shall get one just like her. "Yes, Mr Lancelot; no, Mr Lancelot. Your tea, Mr Lancelot."'

'Oh, don't play the fool,' snapped Percival.

'Why are you so angry, my dear brother? Don't you look forward to having me sharing your city cares?'

'You haven't the least conception of the mess everything's in.'

'No. You'll have to put me wise to all that.'

'First you've got to understand that for the last six months – no, more, a year, father's not been himself. He's done the most incredibly foolish things, financially. Sold out good stock, acquired various wild-cat holdings. Sometimes he's really thrown away money hand over fist. Just, one might say, for the fun of spending it.'

'In fact,' said Lance, 'it's just as well for the family that he had taxine in his tea.'

'That's a very ugly way of putting it, but in essence you're quite right. It's about the only thing that saved us from bankruptcy. But we shall have to be extremely conservative and go very cautiously for a bit.'

Lance shook his head.

'I don't agree with you. Caution never does anyone any good. You must take a few risks, strike out. You must go for something big.'

'I don't agree,' said Percy. 'Caution and economy. Those are our watchwords.'

'Not mine,' said Lance.

'You're only the junior partner, remember,' said Percival.

'All right, all right. But I've got a little say-so all the same.'

Percival walked up and down the room agitatedly.

'It's no good, Lance. I'm fond of you and all that –'

'Are you?' Lance interpolated. Percival did not appear to hear him.

'. . . but I really don't think we're going to pull together at all. Our outlooks are totally different.'

'That may be an advantage,' said Lance.

'The only sensible thing,' said Percival, 'is to dissolve the partnership.'

'You're going to buy me out – is that the idea?'

'My dear boy, it's the only sensible thing to do, with our ideas so different.'

'If you find it hard to pay Elaine out her legacy, how are you going to manage to pay me my share?'

'Well, I didn't mean in cash,' said Percival. 'We could – er – divide up the holdings.'

'With you keeping the gilt-edged and me taking the worst of the speculative off you, I suppose?'

'They seem to be what you prefer,' said Percival.

Lance grinned suddenly.

'You're right in a way, Percy, old boy. But I can't indulge my own taste entirely. I've got Pat here to think of.'

Both men looked towards her. Pat opened her mouth, then shut it again. Whatever game Lance was playing, it was best that she should not interfere. That Lance was driving at something special, she was quite sure, but she was still a little uncertain as to what his actual object was.

'Line 'em up, Percy,' said Lance, laughing. 'Bogus Diamond Mines, Inaccessible Rubies, the Oil Concessions where no oil is. Do you think I'm quite as big as a fool as I look?'

Percival said:

'Of course, some of these holdings are highly speculative, but remember, they *may* turn out immensely valuable.'

'Changed your tune, haven't you?' said Lance, grinning. 'Going to offer me father's latest wildcat acquisitions as well as the old Blackbird Mine and things of that kind. By the way, has the Inspector been asking you about this Blackbird Mine?'

Percival frowned.

'Yes, he did. I can't imagine what he wanted to know about it. I couldn't tell him much. You and I were children at the time. I just remember vaguely that father went out there and came back saying the whole thing was no good.'

'What was it – a gold mine?'

'I believe so. Father came back pretty certain that there was no gold there. And, mind you, he wasn't the sort of man to be mistaken.'

'Who got him into it? A man called MacKenzie, wasn't it?'

'Yes. MacKenzie died out there.'

'MacKenzie died out there,' said Lance thoughtfully. 'Wasn't there a terrific scene? I seem to remember ... Mrs MacKenzie, wasn't it? Came here. Ranted and stormed at father. Hurled down curses on his head. She accused him, if I remember rightly, of murdering her husband.'

'Really,' said Percival repressively. 'I can't recollect anything of the kind.'

'I remember it, though,' said Lance. 'I was a good bit younger than you, of course. Perhaps that's why it appealed to me. As a child it struck me as full of drama. Where was Blackbird? West Africa wasn't it?'

'Yes, I think so.'

'I must look up the concession sometime,' said Lance, 'when I'm at the office.'

'You can be quite sure,' said Percival, 'that father made no mistake. If he came back saying there was no gold, there was no gold.'

'You're probably right there,' said Lance. 'Poor Mrs MacKenzie. I wonder what happened to her and to those two kids she brought along. Funny – they must be grown up by now.'

CHAPTER 20

At the Pinewood Private Sanatorium, Inspector Neele, sitting in the visitors' parlour, was facing a grey-haired, elderly lady. Helen MacKenzie was sixty-three, though she looked younger. She had pale blue, rather vacant looking eyes, and a weak, indeterminate chin. She had a long upper lip which occasionally twitched. She held a large book in her lap and was looking down at it as Inspector Neele talked to her. In Inspector Neele's mind was the conversation he had just had with Doctor Crosbie, the head of the establishment.

'She's a voluntary patient, of course,' said Doctor Crosbie, 'not certified.'

'She's not dangerous, then?'

'Oh, no. Most of the time she's as sane to talk to to as you or me. It's one of her good periods now so that you'll be able to have a perfectly normal conversation with her.'

Bearing this in mind, Inspector Neele started his first conversational essay.

'It's very kind of you to see me, madam,' he said. 'My name is

Neele. I've come to see you about a Mr Fortescue who has recently died. A Mr Rex Fortescue. I expect you know the name.'

Mrs MacKenzie's eyes were fixed on her book. She said:

'I don't know what you're talking about.'

'Mr Fortescue, madam. Mr Rex Fortescue.'

'No,' said Mrs MacKenzie. 'No. Certainly not.'

Inspector Neele was slightly taken aback. He wondered whether this was what Doctor Crosbie called being completely normal.

'I think, Mrs MacKenzie, you knew him a good many years ago.'

'Not really,' said Mrs MacKenzie. 'It was yesterday.'

'I see,' said Inspector Neele, falling back upon his formula rather uncertainly. 'I believe,' he went on, 'that you paid him a visit many years ago at his residence, Yewtree Lodge.'

'A very ostentatious house,' said Mrs MacKenzie.

'Yes. Yes, you might call it that. He had been connected with your husband, I believe, over a certain mine in Africa. The Blackbird Mine, I believe it was called.'

'I have to read my book,' said Mrs MacKenzie. 'There's not much time and I have to read my book.'

'Yes, madam. Yes, I quite see that.' There was a pause, then Inspector Neele went on, 'Mr MacKenzie and Mr Fortescue went out together to Africa to survey the mine.'

'It was my husband's mine,' said Mrs MacKenzie. 'He found it and staked a claim to it. He wanted money to capitalize it. He went to Rex Fortescue. If I'd been wiser, if I'd known more, I wouldn't have let him do it.'

'No, I see that. As it was, they went out together to Africa, and there your husband died of fever.'

'I must read my book,' said Mrs MacKenzie.

'Do you think Mr Fortescue swindled your husband over the Blackbird Mine, Mrs MacKenzie?'

Without raising her eyes from the book, Mrs MacKenzie said:

'How stupid you are.'

'Yes, yes, I dare say. . . . But you see it's all a long time ago and making enquiries about a thing that is over a long time ago is rather difficult.'

'Who said it was over?'

'I see. You don't think it is over?'

'*No question is ever settled until it is settled right.* Kipling said that. Nobody reads Kipling nowadays, but he was a great man.'

'Do you think the question will be settled right one of these days?'

'Rex Fortescue is dead, isn't he? You said so.'

'He was poisoned,' said Inspector Neele.

Rather disconcertingly, Mrs MacKenzie laughed.

'What nonsense,' she said, 'he died of fever.'

'I'm talking about Mr Rex Fortescue.'

'So am I.' She looked up suddenly and her pale blue eyes fixed his. 'Come now,' she said, 'he died in his bed, didn't he? He died in his bed?'

'He died in St Jude's Hospital,' said Inspector Neele.

'Nobody knows where my husband died,' said Mrs MacKenzie. 'Nobody knows how he died or where he was buried. . . . All anyone knows is what Rex Fortescue *said*. And Rex Fortescue was a liar!'

'Do you think there may have been foul play?'

'Foul play, foul play, fowls lay eggs, don't they?'

'You think that Rex Fortescue was responsible for your husband's death?'

'I had an egg for breakfast this morning,' said Mrs MacKenzie. 'Quite fresh, too. Surprising, isn't it, when one thinks that it was thirty years ago?'

Neele drew a deep breath. It seemed unlikely that he was ever going to get anywhere at this rate, but he persevered.

'Somebody put dead blackbirds on Rex Fortescue's desk about a month or two before he died.'

'That's interesting. That's very, very interesting.'

'Have you any idea, madam, who might have done that?'

'Ideas aren't any help to one. One has to have action. I brought them up for that, you know, to take action.'

'You're talking about your children?'

She nodded her head rapidly.

'Yes. Donald and Ruby. They were nine and seven and left without a father. I told them. I told them every day. I made them swear it every night.'

Inspector Neele leant forward.

'What did you make them swear?'

'That they'd kill him, of course.'

'I see.'

Inspector Neele spoke as though it was the most reasonable remark in the world.

'Did they?'

'Donald went to Dunkirk. He never came back. They sent me a wire saying he was dead, "Deeply regret killed in action." Action, you see, the wrong kind of action.'

'I'm sorry to hear that, madam. What about your daughter?'

'I haven't got a daughter,' said Mrs MacKenzie.

'You spoke of her just now,' said Neele. 'Your daughter, Ruby.'

'Ruby. Yes, Ruby.' She leaned forward. 'Do you know what I've done to Ruby?'

'No, madam. What have you done to her?'

She whispered suddenly:

'Look here at the Book.'

He saw then that what she was holding in her lap was a Bible. It was a very old Bible and as she opened it, on the front page, Inspector Neele saw that various names had been written. It was obviously a family Bible in which the old-fashioned custom had been continued of entering each new birth. Mrs MacKenzie's thin forefinger pointed to the two last names. 'Donald MacKenzie' with the date of his birth, and 'Ruby MacKenzie' with the date of hers. But a thick line was drawn through Ruby MacKenzie's name.

'You see?' said Mrs MacKenzie. 'I struck her out of the Book. I cut her off for ever! The Recording Angel won't find her name there.'

'You cut her name out of the book? Now, why, madam?'

Mrs MacKenzie looked at him cunningly.

'You know why,' she said.

'But I don't. Really, madam, I don't.'

'She didn't keep faith. You know she didn't keep faith.'

'Where is your daughter now, madam?'

'I've told you. I have no daughter. There isn't such a person as Ruby MacKenzie any longer.'

'You mean she's dead?'

'Dead?' The woman laughed suddenly. 'It would be better for her if she were dead. Much better. Much, much better.' She sighed and turned restlessly in her seat. Then, her manner reverting to a kind of formal courtesy, she said, 'I'm so sorry, but really I'm afraid I can't talk to you any longer. You see, the time is getting very short, and I *must* read my book.'

To Inspector Neele's further remarks Mrs MacKenzie returned no reply. She merely made a faint gesture of annoyance and continued to read her Bible with her finger following the line of the verse she was reading.

Neele got up and left. He had another brief interview with the Superintendent.

'Do any of her relations come to see her?' he asked. 'A daughter, for instance?'

'I believe a daughter did come to see her in my predecessor's time, but her visit agitated the patient so much that he advised her not to come again. Since then everything is arranged through solicitors.'

'And you've no idea where this Ruby MacKenzie is now?'

The Superintendent shook his head.

'No idea whatsoever.'

'You've no idea whether she's married, for instance?'

'I don't know, all I can do is to give you the address of the solicitors who deal with us.'

Inspector Neele had already tracked down those solicitors. They were unable, or said they were unable, to tell him anything. A trust fund had been established for Mrs MacKenzie which they managed. These arrangements had been made some years previously and they had not seen Miss MacKenzie since.

Inspector Neele tried to get a description of Ruby MacKenzie but the results were not encouraging. So many relations came to visit patients that after a lapse of years they were bound to be remembered dimly, with the appearance of one mixed up with the appearance of another. The Matron who had been there for many years, seemed to remember that Miss MacKenzie was small and dark. The only other nurse who had been there for any length of time recalled that she was heavily built and fair.

'So there we are, sir,' said Inspector Neele as he reported to the Assistant Commissioner. 'There's a whole crazy set-up and it fits together. It *must* mean something.'

The AC nodded thoughtfully.

'The blackbirds in the pie tying up with the Blackbird Mine, rye in the dead man's pocket, bread and honey with Adele Fortescue's tea – (not that that is conclusive. After all, anyone might have had bread and honey for tea!). The third murder, that girl strangled with a clothes line and a clothes peg nipped on to her nose. Yes, crazy as the set-up is, it certainly can't be ignored.'

'Half a minute, sir,' said Inspector Neele.

'What is it?'

Neele was frowning.

'You know, what you've just said. It didn't ring true. It was wrong somewhere.' He shook his head and sighed. 'No. I can't place it.'

CHAPTER 21

Lance and Pat wandered round the well kept grounds surrounding Yewtree Lodge.

'I hope I'm not hurting your feelings, Lance,' Pat murmured, 'if I say this is quite the nastiest garden I've ever been in.'

'It won't hurt my feelings,' said Lance. 'Is it? Really I don't know. It seems to have three gardeners working on it very industriously.'

Pat said:

'Probably that's what's wrong with it. No expense spared, no signs of any individual taste. All the right rhododendrons and all the right bedding out done in the proper season, I expect.'

'Well, what would *you* put in an English garden, Pat, if you had one?'

'My garden,' said Pat, 'would have hollyhocks, larkspurs and Canterbury bells, no bedding out and none of these horrible yews.'

She glanced up at the dark yew hedges, disparagingly.

'Association of ideas,' said Lance easily.

'There's something awfully frightening about a poisoner,' said Pat. 'I mean it must be a horrid, brooding revengeful mind.'

'So that's how you see it? Funny! I just think of it as businesslike and cold-blooded.'

'I suppose one could look at it that way.' She resumed, with a slight shiver, 'All the same, to do *three* murders . . . Whoever did it *must* be mad.'

'Yes,' said Lance, in a low voice. 'I'm afraid so.' Then breaking out sharply, he said, 'For God's sake, Pat, do go away from here. Go back to London. Go down to Devonshire or up to the Lakes. Go to Stratford-on-Avon or go and look at the Norfolk Broads. The police wouldn't mind your going – you had nothing to do with all this. You were in Paris when the old man was killed and in London when the other two died. I tell you it worries me to death to have you here.'

Pat paused a moment before saying quietly:

'You know who it is, don't you?'

'No, I don't.'

'But you *think* you know. . . . That's why you're frightened for me . . . I wish you'd tell me.'

'I can't tell you. I don't know anything. But I wish to God you'd go away from here.'

'Darling,' said Pat, 'I'm not going. I'm staying here. For better, for worse. That's how I feel about it.' She added, with a sudden catch in her voice, 'Only with me it's always for worse.'

'What on earth do you mean, Pat?'

'I bring bad luck. That's what I mean. I bring bad luck to anybody I come in contact with.'

'My dear adorable nitwit, you haven't brought bad luck to me. Look how after I married you the old man sent for me to come home and make friends with him.'

'Yes, and what happened when you did come home? I tell you, I'm unlucky to people.'

'Look here, my sweet, you've got a thing about all this. It's superstition, pure and simple.'

'I can't help it. Some people do bring bad luck. I'm one of them.'

Lance took her by the shoulders and shook her violently. 'You're my Pat and to be married to you is the greatest luck in the world. So get that into your silly head.' Then, calming down, he said in a more sober voice, 'But, seriously, Pat, do be very careful. If there *is* someone unhinged round here, I don't want you to be the one who stops the bullet or drinks the henbane.'

'Or drinks the henbane as you say.'

'When I'm not around, stick to that old lady. What's-her-name Marple. Why do you think Aunt Effie asked her to stay here?'

'Goodness knows why Aunt Effie does anything. Lance, how long are *we* going to stay here?'

Lance shrugged his shoulders.

'Difficult to say.'

'I don't think,' said Pat, 'that we're really awfully welcome.' She hesitated as she spoke the words. 'The house belongs to your brother now, I suppose? He doesn't really want us here, does he?'

Lance chuckled suddenly.

'Not he, but he's got to stick us for the present at any rate.'

'And afterwards? What are we going to do, Lance? Are we going back to East Africa or what?'

'Is that what you'd like to do, Pat?'

She nodded vigorously.

'That's lucky,' said Lance, 'because it's what I'd like to do, too. I don't take much to this country nowadays.'

Pat's face brightened.

'How lovely. From what you said the other day, I was afraid you might want to stop here.'

A devilish glint appeared in Lance's eyes.

'You're to hold your tongue about our plans, Pat,' he said. 'I have it in my mind to twist dear brother Percival's tail a bit.'

'Oh, Lance, do be careful.'

'I'll be careful, my sweet, but I don't see why old Percy should get away with everything.'

II

With her head a little on one side looking like an amiable cockatoo, Miss Marple sat in the large drawing-room listening to Mrs Percival Fortescue. Miss Marple looked particularly incongruous in the drawing-room. Her light spare figure was alien to the vast brocaded sofa in which she sat with its many-hued cushions strewn round her. Miss Marple sat very upright because she had been taught to use a back-board as a girl, and not to loll. In a large armchair beside her, dressed in elaborate black, was Mrs Percival, talking away volubly at nineteen to the dozen. 'Exactly,' thought Miss Marple, 'like poor Mrs Emmett, the bank manager's wife.' She remembered how one day Mrs Emmett had come to call and talk about the selling arrangements for Poppy Day, and how after the preliminary business had been settled, Mrs Emmett had suddenly begun to talk and talk and talk. Mrs Emmett occupied rather a difficult position in St Mary Mead. She did not belong to the old guard of ladies in reduced circumstances who lived in neat houses round the church, and who knew intimately all the ramifications of the county families even though they might not be strictly county themselves. Mr Emmett, the bank manager, had undeniably married beneath him and the result was that his wife was in a position of great loneliness since she could not, of course, associate with the wives of the tradespeople. Snobbery here raised its hideous head and marooned Mrs Emmett on a permanent island of loneliness.

The necessity to talk grew upon Mrs Emmett, and on that particular day it had burst its bounds, and Miss Marple had received the full flood of the torrent. She had been sorry for Mrs

Emmett then, and today she was rather sorry for Mrs Percival Fortescue.

Mrs Percival had had a lot of grievances to bear and the relief of airing them to a more or less total stranger was enormous.

'Of course I never want to complain,' said Mrs Percival. 'I've never been of the complaining kind. What I always say is that one must put up with things. What can't be cured must be endured and I'm sure I've never said a word to *anyone*. It's really difficult to know who I *could* have spoken to. In some ways one is very isolated here – very isolated. It's very convenient, of course, and a great saving of expense to have our own set of rooms in this house. But of course it's not at all like having a place of your own. I'm sure you agree.'

Miss Marple said she agreed.

'Fortunately our new house is almost ready to move into. It is a question really of getting the painters and decorators out. These men are so slow. My husband, of course, has been quite satisfied living here. But then it's different for a man. That's what I always say – it's so different for a man. Don't you agree?'

Miss Marple agreed that it was very different for a man. She could say this without a qualm as it was what she really believed. 'The gentlemen' were, in Miss Marple's mind, in a totally different category from her own sex. They required two eggs plus bacon for breakfast, three good nourishing meals a day and were never to be contradicted or argued with before dinner. Mrs Percival went on:

'My husband, you see, is away all day in the city. When he comes home he's just tired and wants to sit down and read. But I, on the contrary, am alone here all day with no congenial company *at all*. I've been perfectly comfortable and all that. Excellent food. But what I do feel one needs is a really pleasant social circle. The people round here are really not my kind. Part of them are what I call a flashy, bridge-playing lot. Not *nice* bridge. I like a hand at bridge myself as well as anyone, but of course they're all very rich down here. They play for enormously high stakes, and there's a great deal of drinking. In fact, the sort of life that I call really fast society. Then, of course, there's a sprinkling of – well, you can only call them *old pussies* who love to potter round with a trowel and do gardening.'

Miss Marple looked slightly guilty since she was herself an inveterate gardener.

'I don't want to say anything against the dead,' resumed Mrs Percy rapidly, 'but there's no doubt about it, Mr Fortescue, my father-in-law, I mean, made a very foolish second marriage. My – well I can't call her my mother-in-law, she was the same age as I am. The real truth of it is she was man-mad. Absolutely man-mad. And the way she spent money! My father-in-law was an absolute fool about her. Didn't care what bills she ran up. It vexed Percy very much, very much indeed. Percy is always so careful about money matters. He hates waste. And then what with Mr Fortescue being so peculiar and so bad tempered, flashing out in these terrible rages, spending money like water backing wildcat schemes. Well – it wasn't at all nice.'

Miss Marple ventured upon making a remark.

'That must have worried your husband, too?'

'Oh, yes, it did. For the last year Percy's been very worried indeed. It's really made him quite different. His manner, you know, changed even towards me. Sometimes when I talked to him he used not to answer.' Mrs Percy sighed, then went on, 'Then Elaine, my sister-in-law, you know, she's a *very* odd sort of girl. Very out of doors and all that. Not exactly unfriendly, but not sympathetic, you know. She never wanted to go up to London and shop, or go to a matinée or anything of that kind. She wasn't even interested in clothes.' Mrs Percival sighed again and murmured, 'But of course I don't want to complain in any way.' A qualm of compunction came over her. She said, hurriedly: 'You must think it most odd, talking to you like this when you are a comparative stranger. But really, what with all the strain and shock – I think really it's the shock that matters most. Delayed shock. I feel so nervous, you know, that I really – well, I really must speak to *someone*. You remind me so much of a dear old lady, Miss Trefusis James. She fractured her femur when she was seventy-five. It was very long business nursing her and we became great friends. She gave me a fox fur cape when I left and I did think it was kind of her.'

'I know just how you feel,' said Miss Marple.

And this again was true. Mrs Percival's husband was obviously bored by her and paid very little attention to her, and the poor woman had managed to make no local friends. Running up to London and shopping, matinées and a luxurious house to live in did not make up for the lack of humanity in her relations with her husband's family.

'I hope it's not rude of me to say so,' said Miss Marple in a gentle old lady's voice, 'but I really feel that the late Mr Fortescue cannot have been a very nice man.'

'He wasn't,' said his daughter-in-law. 'Quite frankly my dear, between you and me, he was a detestable old man. I don't wonder – I really don't – that someone put him out of the way.'

'You've no idea at all who –' began Miss Marple and broke off. 'Oh dear, perhaps this is a question I should not ask – not even an idea who – who – well, who it might have been?'

'Oh, I think it was that horrible man, Crump,' said Mrs Percival. 'I've always disliked him very much. He's got a manner, not really rude, you know, but yet it *is* rude. Impertinent, that's more it.'

'Still, there would have to be a motive, I suppose.'

'I really don't know that that sort of person requires much motive. I dare say Mr Fortescue ticked him off about something, and I rather suspect that sometimes he drinks too much. But what I really think is that he's a bit unbalanced, you know. Like that footman, or butler, whoever it was, who went round the house shooting everybody. Of course, to be quite honest with you, I *did* suspect that it was *Adele* who poisoned Mr Fortescue. But now, of course, one can't suspect that since she's been poisoned herself. She may have accused Crump, you know. And then he lost his head and perhaps managed to put something in the sandwiches and Gladys saw him do it and so he killed her too – I think it's really dangerous having him in the house at all. Oh dear, I wish I could get away, but I suppose these horrible policemen won't let one do anything of the kind.' She leant forward impulsively and put a plump hand on Miss Marple's arm. 'Sometimes I feel I must get away – that if it doesn't all stop soon I shall – I shall actually *run away*.'

She leant back studying Miss Marple's face.

'But perhaps – that wouldn't be wise?'

'No – I don't think it would be very wise – the police could soon find you, you know.'

'Could they? Could they really? You think they're clever enough for that?'

'It is very foolish to underestimate the police. Inspector Neele strikes me as a particularly intelligent man.'

'Oh! I thought he was rather stupid.'

Miss Marple shook her head.

'I can't help feeling' – Jennifer Fortescue hesitated – 'that it's dangerous to stay here.'

'Dangerous for you, you mean?'

'Ye-es – well, yes –'

'Because of something you – know?'

Mrs Percival seemed to take breath.

'Oh no – of course I don't know anything. What should I know? It's just – just that I'm nervous. That man Crump –'

But it was not, Miss Marple thought, of Crump that Mrs Percival Fortescue was thinking – watching the clenching and unclenching of Jennifer's hands. Miss Marple thought that for some reason Jennifer Fortescue was very badly frightened indeed.

CHAPTER 22

It was growing dark. Miss Marple had taken her knitting over to the window in the library. Looking out of the glass pane she saw Pat Fortescue walking up and down the terrace outside. Miss Marple unlatched the window and called through it.

'Come in, my dear. Do come in. I'm sure it's much too cold and damp for you to be out there without a coat on.'

Pat obeyed the summons. She came in and shut the window and turned on two of the lamps.

'Yes,' she said, 'it's not a very nice afternoon.' She sat down on the sofa by Miss Marple. 'What are you knitting?'

'Oh, just a little matinée coat, dear. For a baby, you know. I always say young mothers can't have too many matineé coats for their babies. It's the second size. I always knit the second size. Babies so soon grow out of the first size.'

Pat stretched out long legs towards the fire.

'It's nice in here today,' she said. 'With the fire and the lamps and you knitting things for babies. It all seems cosy and homely and like England ought to be.'

'It's like England is,' said Miss Marple. 'There are not so many Yewtree Lodges, my dear.'

'I think that's a good thing,' said Pat. 'I don't believe this was ever a happy house. I don't believe anybody was ever happy in it, in spite of all the money they spent and the things they had.'

'No,' Miss Marple agreed. 'I shouldn't say it had been a happy house.'

'I suppose Adele may have been happy,' said Pat. 'I never met her, of course, so I don't know, but Jennifer is pretty miserable and Elaine's been eating her heart out over a young man whom she probably knows in her heart of hearts doesn't care for her. Oh, *how* I want to get away from here!' She looked at Miss Marple and smiled suddenly. 'D'you know,' she said, 'that Lance told me to stick as close to you as I could. He seemed to think I should be safe that way.'

'Your husband's no fool,' said Miss Marple.

'No. Lance isn't a fool. At least, he is in some ways. But I wish he'd tell me exactly what he's afraid of. One thing seems clear enough. Somebody in this house is mad, and madness is always frightening because you don't know how mad people's minds will work. You don't know what they'll do next.'

'My poor child,' said Miss Marple.

'Oh, I'm all right, really. I ought to be tough enough by now.'

Miss Marple said gently:

'You've had a good deal of unhappiness, haven't you, my dear?'

'Oh, I've had some very good times, too. I had a lovely childhood in Ireland, riding, hunting, and a great big, bare, draughty house with lots and lots of sun in it. If you've had a happy childhood, nobody can take that away from you, can they? It was afterwards – when I grew up – that things seemed always to go wrong. To begin with, I suppose, it was the war.'

'Your husband was a fighter pilot, wasn't he?'

'Yes. We'd only been married about a month when Don was shot down.' She stared ahead of her into the fire. 'I thought at first I wanted to die too. It seemed so unfair, so cruel. And yet – in the end – I almost began to see that it had been the best thing. Don was wonderful in the war. Brave and reckless and gay. He had all the qualities that are needed, wanted in a war. But I don't believe, somehow, peace would have suited him. He had a kind of – oh, how shall I put it? – arrogant insubordination. He wouldn't have fitted in or settled down. He'd have fought against things. He was – well, anti-social in a way. No, he wouldn't have fitted in.'

'It's wise of you to see that, my dear.' Miss Marple bent over her knitting, picked up a stitch, counted under her breath, 'Three plain, two purl, slip one, knit two together,' and then said, aloud: 'And your second husband, my dear?'

'Freddy? Freddy shot himself.'

'Oh dear. How very sad. What a tragedy.'

'We were very happy together,' said Pat. 'I began to realize, about two years after we were married, that Freddy wasn't – well, wasn't always straight. I began to find out the sort of things that were going on. But it didn't seem to matter, between us two, that is. Because, you see, Freddy loved me and I loved him. I tried not to know what was going on. That was cowardly of me, I suppose, but I couldn't have changed him, you know. You can't change people.'

'No,' said Miss Marple, 'you can't change people.'

'I'd taken him and loved him and married him for what he was, and I sort of felt that I just had to – put up with it. Then things went wrong and he couldn't face it, and he shot himself. After he died I went out to Kenya with some friends there. I couldn't stop on in England and go on meeting all – all the old crowd that knew about it all. And out in Kenya I met Lance.' Her face changed and softened. She went on looking into the fire, and Miss Marple looked at her. Presently Pat turned her head and said: 'Tell me, Miss Marple, what do you really thing of Percival?'

'Well, I've not seen very much of him. Just at breakfast usually. That's all. I don't think he very much likes my being here.'

Pat laughed suddenly.

'He's mean, you know. Terribly mean about money. Lance says he always was. Jennifer complains of it, too. Goes over the house-keeping accounts with Miss Dove. Complaining of every item. But Miss Dove manages to hold her own. She's really rather a wonderful person. Don't you think so?'

'Yes, indeed. She reminds me of Mrs Latimer in my own village, St Mary Mead. She ran the WVS, you know, and the Girl Guides, and indeed, she ran practically everything there. It wasn't for quite five years that we discovered that – oh, but I mustn't gossip. Nothing is more boring than people talking to you about places and people whom you've never seen and know nothing about. You must forgive me, my dear.'

'Is St Mary Mead a very nice village?'

'Well, I don't know what you would call a nice village, my dear. It's quite a *pretty* village. There are some nice people living in it and some extremely unpleasant people as well. Very curious things go on there just as in any other village. Human nature is much the same everywhere, is it not?'

'You go up and see Miss Ramsbottom a good deal, don't you?' said Pat. 'Now she *really* frightens me.'

'Frightens you? Why?'

'Because I think she's crazy. I think she's got religious mania. You don't think she could be – really – *mad*, do you?'

'In what way, mad?'

'Oh, you know what I mean, Miss Marple, well enough. She sits up there and never goes out and broods about sin. Well, she might have felt in the end that it was her mission in life to execute judgement.'

'Is that what your husband thinks?'

'I don't know what Lance thinks. He won't tell me. But I'm quite sure of one thing – that he believes that it's someone who's mad, and it's someone in the family. Well, Percival's sane enough, I should say. Jennifer's just stupid and rather pathetic. She's a bit nervy but that's all, and Elaine is one of those queer, tempestuous, tense girls. She's desperately in love with this young man of hers and she'll never admit to herself for a moment that he's marrying her for her money.'

'You think he is marrying her for money?'

'Yes, I do. Don't you think so?'

'I should say quite certainly,' said Miss Marple. 'Like young Ellis who married Marion Bates, the rich ironmonger's daughter. She was a very plain girl and absolutely besotted about him. However, it turned out quite well. People like young Ellis and this Gerald Wright are only really disagreeable when they've married a poor girl for love. They are so annoyed with themselves for doing it that they take it out on the girl. But if they marry a rich girl they continue to respect her.'

'I don't see,' went on Pat, frowning, 'how it can be anybody from outside. And so – and so that accounts for the atmosphere that is here. Everyone watching everybody else. Only something's got to happen soon –'

'There won't be any more deaths,' said Miss Marple. 'At least, I shouldn't think so.'

'You can't be sure of that.'

'Well, as a matter of fact, I am fairly sure. The murderer's accomplished his purpose, you see.'

'His?'

'Well, his or her. One says his for convenience.'

'You say his or her purpose. What sort of purpose?'

Miss Marple shook her head – she was not yet quite sure herself.

CHAPTER 23

Once again Miss Somers had just made tea in the typists' room, and once again the kettle had not been boiling when Miss Somers poured the water on to the tea. History repeats itself. Miss Griffith, accepting her cup, thought to herself, 'I really *must* speak to Mr Percival about Somers. I'm sure we can do better. But with all this terrible business going on, one doesn't like to bother him over office details.'

As so often before, Miss Griffith said sharply:

'Water not boiling *again*, Somers,' and Miss Somers, going pink, replied in her usual formula:

'Oh, dear, I was sure it was boiling *this* time.'

Further developments on the same line were interrupted by the entrance of Lance Fortescue. He looked round him somewhat vaguely, and Miss Griffith, jumping up, came forward to meet him.

'Mr Lance,' she exclaimed.

He swung round towards her and his face lit up in a smile.

'Hallo. Why, it's Miss Griffith.'

Miss Griffith was delighted. Eleven years since he had seen her and he knew her name. She said in a confused voice:

'Fancy your remembering.'

And Lance said easily, with all his charm to the fore:

'Of course I remember.'

A flicker of excitement was running round the typists' room. Miss Somers's troubles over the tea were forgotten. She was gaping at Lance with her mouth slightly open. Miss Bell gazed eagerly over the top of her typewriter and Miss Chase unobtrusively drew out her compact and powdered her nose. Lance Fortescue looked round him.

'So everything's still going on just the same here,' he said.

'Not many changes, Mr Lance. How brown you look and how well! I suppose you must have had a very interesting life abroad.'

'You could call it that,' said Lance, 'but perhaps I am now going to try and have an interesting life in London.'

'You're coming back here to the office?'

'Maybe.'

'Oh, but how delightful.'

'You'll find me very rusty,' said Lance. 'You'll have to show me all the ropes, Miss Griffith.'

Miss Griffith laughed delightedly.

'It will be very nice to have you back, Mr Lance. Very nice indeed.'

Lance threw her an appreciative glance.

'That's sweet of you,' he said, 'that's very sweet of you.'

'We never believed – none of us thought . . .' Miss Griffith broke off and flushed.

Lance patted her on the arm.

'You didn't believe the devil was as black as he was painted? Well, perhaps he wasn't. But that's all old history now. There's no good going back over it. The future's the thing.' He added, 'Is my brother here?'

'He's in the inner office, I think.'

Lance nodded easily and passed on. In the ante-room to the inner sanctum a hard-faced woman of middle age rose behind a desk and said forbiddingly:

'Your name and business, please?'

Lance looked at her doubtfully.

'Are you – Miss Grosvenor?' he asked.

Miss Grosvenor had been described to him as a glamorous blonde. She had indeed seemed so in the pictures that had appeared in the newspapers reporting the inquest on Rex Fortescue. This, surely, could not be Miss Grosvenor.

'Miss Grosvenor left last week. I am Mrs Hardcastle, Mr Percival Fortescue's personal secretary.'

'How like old Percy,' thought Lance. 'To get rid of a glamorous blonde and take on a Gorgon instead. I wonder why? Was it safety or was it because this one comes cheaper?' Aloud he said easily:

'I'm Lancelot Fortescue. You haven't met me yet.'

'Oh, I'm so sorry, Mr Lancelot,' Mrs Hardcastle apologized, 'this is the first time, I think, you've been to the office?'

'The first time but not the last,' said Lance, smiling.

He crossed the room and opened the door of what had been his father's private office. Somewhat to his surprise it was not Percival who was sitting behind the desk there, but Inspector Neele. Inspector Neele looked up from a large wad of papers which he was sorting, and nodded his head.

'Good morning, Mr Fortescue, you've come to take up your duties, I suppose.'

'So you've heard I decided to come into the firm?'

'Your brother told me so.'

'He did, did he? With enthusiasm?'

Inspector Neele endeavoured to conceal a smile.

'The enthusiasm was not marked,' he said gravely.

'Poor Percy,' commented Lance.

Inspector Neele looked at him curiously.

'Are you really going to become a City man?'

'You don't think it's likely, Inspector Neele?'

'It doesn't seem quite in character, Mr Fortescue.'

'Why not? I'm my father's son.'

'And your mother's.'

Lance shook his head.

'You haven't got anything there, Inspector. My mother was a Victorian romantic. Her favourite reading was the *Idylls of the King*, as indeed you may have deduced from our curious Christian names. She was an invalid and always, I should imagine, out of touch with reality. I'm not like that at all. I have no sentiment, very little sense of romance and I'm a realist first and last.'

'People aren't always what they think themselves to be,' Inspector Neele pointed out.

'No, I suppose that's true,' said Lance.

He sat down in a chair and stretched his long legs out in his own characteristic fashion. He was smiling to himself. Then he said unexpectedly:

'You're shrewder than my brother, Inspector.'

'In what way, Mr Fortescue?'

'I've put the wind up Percy all right. He thinks I'm all set for the City life. He thinks he's going to have my fingers fiddling about in his pie. He thinks I'll launch out and spend the firm's money and try and embroil him in wildcat schemes. It would be almost worth doing just for the fun of it! Almost, but not quite. I couldn't really stand an office life, Inspector. I like the open air and some possibilities of adventure. I'd stifle in a place like this.' He added quickly, 'This is off the record, mind. Don't give me away to Percy, will you?'

'I don't suppose the subject will arise, Mr Fortescue.'

'I must have my bit of fun with Percy,' said Lance. 'I want to make him sweat a bit. I've got to get a bit of my own back.'

'That's rather a curious phrase, Mr Fortescue,' said Neele. 'Your own back – for what?'

Lance shrugged his shoulders.

'Oh, it's old history now. Not worth going back over.'

'There was a little matter of a cheque, I understand, in the past. Would that be what you're referring to?'

'How much you know, Inspector!'

'There was no question of prosecution, I understand,' said Neele. 'Your father wouldn't have done that.'

'No. He just kicked me out, that's all.'

Inspector Neele eyed him speculatively, but it was not Lance Fortescue of whom he was thinking, but of Percival. The honest, industrious, parsimonious Percival. It seemed to him that wherever he got in the case he was always coming up against the enigma of Percival Fortescue, a man of whom everybody knew the outer aspects, but whose inner personality was much harder to gauge. One would have said from observing him, a somewhat colourless and insignificant character, a man who had been very much under his father's thumb. Percy Prim in fact, as the AC had once said. Neele was trying now, through Lance, to get at a closer appreciation of Percival's personality. He murmured in a tentative manner:

'Your brother seems always to have been very much – well, how shall I put it – under your father's thumb.'

'I wonder.' Lance seemed definitely to be considering the point. 'I wonder. Yes, that would be the effect, I think, given. But I'm not sure that it was really the truth. It's astonishing, you know, when I look back through life, to see how Percy always got his own way without seeming to do so, if you know what I mean.'

Yes, Inspector Neele thought, it was indeed astonishing. He sorted through the papers in front of him, fished out a letter and shoved it across the desk towards Lance.

'This is a letter you wrote last August, isn't it, Mr Fortescue?'

Lance took it, glanced at it and returned it.

'Yes,' he said, 'I wrote it after I got back to Kenya last summer. Dad kept it, did he? Where was it – here in the office?'

'No, Mr Fortescue, it was among your father's papers in Yewtree Lodge.'

The Inspector considered it speculatively as it lay on the desk in front of him. It was not a long letter.

'Dear Dad,

I've talked things over with Pat and I agree to your proposition. It will take me a little time to get things fixed up here, say about the end of October or beginning of November. I'll let you know nearer the time. I hope we'll pull together better than we used to do. Anyway, I'll do my best. I can't say more. Look after yourself.

Yours,   Lance.'

'Where did you address this letter, Mr Fortescue? To the office or Yewtree Lodge?'

Lance frowned in an effort of recollection.

'It's difficult. I can't remember. You see it's almost three months now. The office, I think. Yes, I'm almost sure. Here to the office.' He paused a moment before asking with frank curiosity, 'Why?'

'I wondered,' said Inspector Neele. 'Your father did not put it on the file here among his private papers. He took it back with him to Yewtree Lodge, and I found it in his desk there. I wondered why he should have done that.'

Lance laughed.

'To keep it out of Percy's way, I suppose.'

'Yes,' said Inspector Neele, 'it would seem so. Your brother, then, had access to your father's private papers here?'

'Well,' Lance hesitated and frowned, 'not exactly. I mean, I suppose he could have looked through them at any time if he liked, but he wouldn't be . . .'

Inspector Neele finished the sentence for him.

'Wouldn't be supposed to do so?'

Lance grinned broadly. 'That's right. Frankly, it would have been snooping. But Percy, I should imagine, always did snoop.'

Inspector Neele nodded. He also thought it probable that Percival Fortescue snooped. It would be in keeping with what the Inspector was beginning to learn of his character

'And talk of the devil,' murmured Lance, as at that moment the door opened and Percival Fortescue came in. About to speak to the Inspector he stopped, frowning, as he saw Lance.

'Hallo,' he said. 'You here? You didn't tell me you were coming here today.'

'I felt a kind of zeal for work coming over me,' said Lance, 'so here I am ready to make myself useful. What do you want me to do?'

Percival said testily:

'Nothing at present. Nothing at all. We shall have to come to some kind of arrangement as to what side of the business you're going to look after. We shall have to arrange for an office for you.'

Lance enquired with a grin:

'By the way, why did you get rid of glamorous Grosvenor, old boy, and replace her by Horsefaced Hetty out there?'

'Really, Lance,' Percival protested sharply.

'Definitely a change for the worse,' said Lance. 'I've been looking forward to the glamorous Grosvenor. Why did you sack her? Thought she knew a bit too much?'

'Of course not. What an idea!' Percy spoke angrily, a flush mounting his pale face. He turned to the Inspector. 'You mustn't pay any attention to my brother,' he said coldly. 'He has a rather peculiar sense of humour.' He added, 'I never had a very high opinion of Miss Grosvenor's intelligence. Mrs Hardcastle has excellent references and is most capable besides being very moderate in her terms.'

'Very moderate in her terms,' murmured Lance, casting his eyes towards the ceiling. 'You know, Percy, I don't really approve of skimping over the office personnel. By the way, considering how loyally the staff has stood by us during these last tragic weeks, don't you think we ought to raise their salaries all round?'

'Certainly not,' snapped Percival Fortescue. 'Quite uncalled for and unnecessary.'

Inspector Neele noticed the gleam of devilry in Lance's eyes. Percival, however, was far too much upset to notice it.

'You always had the most extraordinarily extravagant ideas,' he stuttered. 'In the state in which this firm has been left, economy is our only hope.'

Inspector Neele coughed apologetically.

'That's one of the things I wanted to talk to you about, Mr Fortescue,' he said to Percival.

'Yes, Inspector?' Percival switched his attention to Neele.

'I want to put certain suggestions before you, Mr Fortescue. I understand that for the past six months or longer, possibly a year, your father's general behaviour and conduct has been a source of increasing anxiety to you.'

'He wasn't well,' said Percival, with finality. 'He certainly wasn't at all well.'

'You tried to induce him to see a doctor but you failed. He refused categorically?'

'That is so.'

'May I ask you if you suspected that your father was suffering from what is familiarly referred to as GPI, General Paralysis of the Insane, a condition with signs of megalomania and irritability which terminates sooner or later in hopeless insanity?'

Percival looked surprised. 'It is remarkably astute of you, Inspector. That is exactly what I did fear. That is why I was so anxious for my father to submit to medical treatment.'

Neele went on:

'In the meantime, until you could persuade your father to do that, he was capable of causing a great deal of havoc to the business?'

'He certainly was,' Percival agreed.

'A very unfortunate state of affairs,' said the Inspector.

'Quite terrible. No one knows the anxiety I have been through.'

Neele said gently:

'From the business point of view, your father's death was an extremely fortunate circumstance.'

Percival said sharply:

'You can hardly think I would regard my father's death in that light.'

'It is not a question of how you regard it, Mr Fortescue. I'm speaking merely of a question of fact. Your father died before his finances were completely on the rocks.'

Percival said impatiently:

'Yes, yes. As a matter of actual fact, you are right.'

'It was a fortunate occurrence for your whole family, since they are dependent on this business.'

'Yes. But really, Inspector, I don't see what you're driving at . . .' Percival broke off.

'Oh, I'm not driving at anything, Mr Fortescue,' said Neele. 'I just like getting my facts straight. Now there's another thing. I understood you to say that you'd had no communication of any kind with your brother here since he left England many years ago.'

'Quite so,' said Percival.

'Yes, but it isn't quite so, is it, Mr Fortescue? I mean that last spring when you were so worried about your father's health, you actually wrote to your brother in Africa, told him of your anxiety about your father's behaviour. You wanted, I think, your brother to combine with you in getting your father medically examined and put under restraint, if necessary.'

'I – I – really, I don't see . . .' Percival was badly shaken.

'That is so, isn't it, Mr Fortescue?'

'Well, actually, I thought it only right. After all, Lancelot *was* a junior partner.'

Inspector Neele transferred his gaze to Lance. Lance was grinning.

'You received that letter?' Inspector Neele asked.

Lance Fortescue nodded.

'What did you reply to it?'

Lance's grin widened.

'I told Percy to go and boil his head and to let the old man alone. I said the old man probably knew what he was doing quite well.'

Inspector Neele's gaze went back again to Percival.

'Were those the terms of your brother's answer?'

'I – I – well, I suppose roughly, yes. Far more offensively couched, however.'

'I thought the Inspector had better have a bowdlerized version,' said Lance. He went on, 'Frankly, Inspector Neele, that is one of the reasons why, when I got a letter from my father, I came home to see for myself what I thought. In the short interview I had with my father, frankly I couldn't see anything much wrong with him. He was slightly excitable, that was all. He appeared to me perfectly capable of managing his own affairs. Anyway, after I got back to Africa and had talked things over with Pat, I decided that I'd come home and – what shall we say – see fair play.'

He shot a glance at Percival as he spoke.

'I object,' said Percival Fortescue. 'I object strongly to what you are suggesting. I was not intending to victimize my father, I was concerned for his health. I admit that I was also concerned . . .' he paused.

Lance filled the pause quickly.

'You were also concerned for your pocket, eh? For Percy's little pocket.' He got up and all of a sudden his manner changed. 'All right, Percy, I'm through. I was going to string you along a bit by pretending to work here. I wasn't going to let you have things all your own sweet way, but I'm damned if I'm going on with it. Frankly, it makes me sick to be in the same room with you. You've always been a dirty, mean little skunk all your life. Prying and snooping and lying and making trouble. I'll tell you another thing. I can't prove it, but I've always believed it was you who forged that cheque there was all the row about, that got me shot out of here. For one thing it was a damn bad forgery, a forgery that drew attention to itself in letters a foot high. My record was too bad for me to be able to protest effectively, but I often wondered that the old boy didn't realize that if I *had* forged his name I could have made a much better job of it than that.'

Lance swept on, his voice rising, 'Well, Percy, I'm not going on with this silly game. I'm sick of this country, and of the City. I'm sick of little men like you with their pinstripe trousers and their black coats and their mincing voices and their mean, shoddy financial deals. We'll share out as you suggested, and I'll get back with Pat to a different country – a country where there's room to breathe and move about. You can make your own division of securities. Keep the gilt-edged and the conservative ones, keep the safe two per cent and three per cent and three and a half per cent. Give me father's latest wildcat speculations as you call them. Most of them are probably duds. But I'll bet that one or two of them will pay better in the end than all your playing safe with three per cent Trustee Stocks will do. Father was a shrewd old devil. He took chances, plenty of them. Some of those chances paid five and six and seven hundred per cent. I'll back his judgement and his luck. As for you, you little worm ...' Lance advanced towards his brother, who retreated rapidly, round the end of the desk towards Inspector Neele. 'All right,' said Lance, 'I'm not going to touch you. You wanted me out of here, you're getting me out of here. You ought to be satisfied.' He added as he strode towards the door, 'You can throw in the old Blackbird Mine concession too, if you like. If we've got the murdering MacKenzies on our trail, I'll draw them off to Africa.' He added as he swung through the doorway, 'Revenge – after all these years – scarcely seems credible. But Inspector Neele seems to take it seriously, don't you Inspector?'

'Nonsense,' said Percival. 'Such a thing is impossible!'

'Ask him,' said Lance. 'Ask him why he's making all these enquiries into blackbirds and rye in father's pocket.'

Gently stroking his upper lip, Inspector Neele said:

'You remember the blackbirds last summer, Mr Fortescue. There *are* certain grounds for enquiry.'

'Nonsense,' said Percival again. 'Nobody's heard of the MacKenzies for years.'

'And yet,' said Lance, 'I'd almost dare to swear that there's a MacKenzie in our midst. I rather imagine the Inspector thinks so, too.'

II

Inspector Neele caught up Lancelot Fortescue as the latter emerged into the street below.

Lance grinned at him rather sheepishly.

'I didn't mean to do that,' he said. 'But I suddenly lost my temper. Oh! well – it would have come to the same before long. I'm meeting Pat at the Savoy – are you coming my way, Inspector?'

'No, I'm returning to Baydon Heath. But there's just something I'd like to ask you, Mr Fortescue.'

'Yes!'

'When you came into the inner office and saw me there – you were surprised. Why?'

'Because I didn't expect to see you, I suppose. I thought I'd find Percy there.'

'You weren't told that he'd gone out?'

Lance looked at him curiously.

'No. They said he was in his office.'

'I see – nobody knew he'd gone out. There's no second door out of the inner office – but there is a door leading straight into the corridor from the little ante-chamber – I suppose your brother went out that way – but I'm surprised Mrs Hardcastle didn't tell you so.'

Lance laughed.

'She'd probably been to collect her cup of tea.'

'Yes – yes – quite so.'

Lance looked at him.

'What's the idea, Inspector?'

'Just puzzling over a few little things, that's all, Mr Fortescue –'

CHAPTER 24

In the train on the way down to Baydon Heath, Inspector Neele had singularly little success doing *The Times* crossword. His mind was distracted by various possibilities. In the same way he read the news with only half his brain taking it in. He read of an earthquake in Japan, of the discovery of uranium deposits in Tanganyika, of the body of a merchant seaman washed up near Southampton, and of the imminent strike among the dockers. He read of the latest victims of the cosh and of a new drug that had achieved wonders in advanced cases of tuberculosis.

All these items made a queer kind of pattern in the back of his mind. Presently he returned to the crossword puzzle and was able to put down three clues in rapid succession.

When he reached Yewtree Lodge he had come to a certain decision. He said to Sergeant Hay:

'Where's that old lady? Is she still here?'

'Miss Marple? Oh, yes, she's here still. Great buddies with the old lady upstairs.'

'I see.' Neele paused for a moment and then said: 'Where is she now? I'd like to see her.'

Miss Marple arrived in a few minutes' time, looking rather flushed and breathing fast.

'You want to see me, Inspector Neele? I do hope I haven't kept you waiting. Sergeant Hay couldn't find me at first. I was in the kitchen, talking to Mrs Crump. I was congratulating her on her pastry and how light her hand is, and telling her how delicious the soufflé was last night. I always think, you know, it's better to approach a subject gradually, don't you? At least, I suppose it isn't so easy for you. You more or less have to come almost straight away to the questions you want to ask. But of course for an old lady like me who has all the time in the world, as you might say, it's really *expected* of her that there should be a great deal of unnecessary talk. And the way to a cook's heart, as they say, is through her pastry.'

'What you really wanted to talk to her about,' said Inspector Neele, 'was Gladys Martin?'

Miss Marple nodded.

'Yes. Gladys. You see, Mrs Crump could really tell me a lot about the girl. Not in connection with the murder. I don't mean that. But about her spirits lately and the odd things she said. I don't mean odd in the sense of peculiar. I mean just the odds and ends of conversation.'

'Did you find it helpful?' asked Inspector Neele.

'Yes,' said Miss Marple. 'I found it very helpful indeed. I really think, you know, that things are becoming very much clearer, don't you?'

'I do and I don't,' said Inspector Neele.

Sergeant Hay, he noticed, had left the room. He was glad of it because what he was about to do now was, to say the least of it, slightly unorthodox.

'Look here, Miss Marple,' he said, 'I want to talk to you seriously.'

'Yes, Inspector Neele?'

'In a way,' said Inspector Neele, 'you and I represent different points of view. I admit, Miss Marple, that I've heard something about you at the Yard.' He smiled, 'It seems you're fairly well known there.'

'I don't know how it is,' fluttered Miss Marple, 'but I so often seem to get mixed up in things that are really *no* concern of mine. Crimes I mean, and peculiar happenings.'

'You've got a reputation,' said Inspector Neele.

'Sir Henry Clithering, of course,' said Miss Marple, 'is a *very* old friend of mine.'

'As I said before,' Neele went on, 'you and I represent opposite points of view. One might almost call them sanity and insanity.'

Miss Marple put her head a little on one side.

'Now what exactly do you mean by that, I wonder, Inspector?'

'Well, Miss Marple, there's a sane way of looking at things. This murder benefits certain people. One person, I may say, in particular. The second murder benefits the same person. The third murder one might call a murder for safety.'

'But which do you call the third murder?' Miss Marple asked.

Her eyes, a very bright china blue, looked shrewdly at the Inspector. He nodded.

'Yes. You've got something there perhaps. You know, the other day when the AC was speaking to me of these murders, something that he said seemed to me to be wrong. That was it. I was thinking, of course, of the nursery rhyme. The king in his counting-house, the queen in the parlour and the maid hanging out the clothes.'

'Exactly,' said Miss Marple. 'A sequence in that order, but actually Gladys must have been murdered *before* Mrs Fortescue, mustn't she?'

'I think so,' said Neele. 'I take it it's quite certainly so. Her body wasn't discovered till late that night, and of course it was difficult then to say exactly how long she'd been dead. But I think myself that she must almost certainly have been murdered round about five o'clock, because otherwise . . .'

Miss Marple cut in. 'Because otherwise she would certainly have taken the second tray into the drawing-room?'

'Quite so. She took one tray in with the tea on it, she brought the second tray into the hall, and then *something happened*. She saw something or she heard something. The question is what that something was. It *might* have been Dubois coming down the stairs from Mrs Fortescue's room. It *might* have been Elaine Fortescue's young man, Gerald Wright, coming in at the side door. Whoever it was, lured her away from the tea-tray and out into the garden. And once that had happened I don't see any possibility of her death being long delayed. It was cold out and she was only wearing her thin uniform.'

'Of course you're quite right,' said Miss Marple. 'I mean it was never a case of "the maid was in the garden hanging up the clothes." She wouldn't be hanging up clothes at that time of the evening and she wouldn't go out to the clothes line without putting a coat on. That was all camouflage, like the clothes peg, to make the thing fit in with the rhyme.'

'Exactly,' said Inspector Neele, 'crazy. That's where I can't yet see eye to eye with you. I can't – I simply can't swallow this nursery rhyme business.'

'But it *fits*, Inspector. You must agree it fits.'

'It fits,' said Neele heavily, 'but all the same the sequence is wrong. I mean the rhyme definitely suggests that the maid was the third murder. But we know that the Queen was the third murder. Adele Fortescue was not killed until between twenty-five-past five and five minutes to six. By then Gladys must already have been dead.'

'And that's all wrong, isn't it?' said Miss Marple. 'All wrong for the nursery rhyme – that's very significant, isn't it?'

Inspector Neele shrugged his shoulders.

'It's probably splitting hairs. The deaths fulfil the conditions of the rhyme, and I suppose that's all that was needed. But I'm talking now as though I were on your side. I'm going to outline *my* side of the case now, Miss Marple. I'm washing out the blackbirds and the rye and all the rest of it. I'm going by sober facts and common sense and the reasons for which sane people do murders. First, the death of Rex Fortescue, and *who benefits by his death*. Well, it benefits quite a lot of people, but most of all it benefits his son, Percival. His son Percival wasn't at Yewtree Lodge that morning. He couldn't have put poison in his father's coffee or in anything that he ate for breakfast. Or that's what we thought at first.'

'Ah,' Miss Marple's eyes brightened. 'So there *was* a method, was there? I've been thinking about it, you know, a good deal, and I've had several ideas. But of course no evidence or proof.'

'There's no harm in my letting you know,' said Inspector Neele. 'Taxine was added to a new jar of marmalade. That jar of marmalade was placed on the breakfast table and the top layer of it was eaten by Mr Fortescue at breakfast. Later that jar of marmalade was thrown out into the bushes and a similar jar with a similar amount taken out of it was placed in the pantry. The jar in the bushes was found and I've just had the result of the analysis. It shows definite evidence of taxine.'

'So that was it,' murmured Miss Marple. 'So simple and easy to do.'

'Consolidated Investments,' Neele went on, 'was in a bad way. If the firm had had to pay out a hundred thousand pounds to Adele Fortescue under her husband's will, it would, I think, have crashed. If Mrs Fortescue had survived her husband for a month that money would have *had* to be paid out to her. *She* would have had no feeling for the firm or its difficulties. But she didn't survive her husband for a month. She died, and as a result of her death the gainer was the residuary legatee of Rex Fortescue's will. In other words, Percival Fortescue again.

'Always Percival Fortescue,' the Inspector continued bitterly. 'And though he *could* have tampered with the marmalade, he couldn't have poisoned his stepmother or strangled Gladys. According to his secretary he was in his city office at five o'clock that afternoon, and he didn't arrive back here until nearly seven.'

'That makes it *very* difficult, doesn't it?' said Miss Marple.

'It makes it impossible,' said Inspector Neele gloomily. 'In other words, Percival is *out*.' Abandoning restraint and prudence, he spoke with some bitterness, almost unaware of his listener. 'Wherever I go, wherever I turn, I always come up against the same person. Percival Fortescue! Yet it *can't* be Percival Fortescue.' Calming himself a little he said, 'Oh, there are other possibilities, other people who had a perfectly good motive.'

'Mr Dubois, of course,' said Miss Marple sharply. 'And that young Mr Wright. I do so agree with you, Inspector. Wherever there is a question of *gain*, one has to be *very suspicious*. The great thing to avoid is having in any way a trustful mind.'

In spite of himself, Neele smiled.

'Always think the worst, eh?' he asked.

It seemed a curious doctrine to be proceeding from this charming and fragile looking old lady.

'Oh yes,' said Miss Marple fervently. 'I always believe the worst. What is so sad is that one is usually justified in doing so.'

'All right,' said Neele, 'let's think the worst. Dubois could have done it, Gerald Wright could have done it, (that is to say if he'd been acting in collusion with Elaine Fortescue and she tampered with the marmalade), Mrs Percival could have done it, I suppose. She was on the spot. But none of the people I have mentioned tie up with the crazy angle. They don't tie up with blackbirds and pockets full of rye. That's *your* theory and it may be that you're right. If so, it boils down to one person, doesn't it? Mrs MacKenzie's in a mental home and has been for a good number of years. She hasn't been messing about with marmalade pots or putting cyanide in the drawing-room afternoon tea. Her son Donald was killed at Dunkirk. That leaves the daughter, Ruby MacKenzie. And if your theory is correct, if this whole series of murders arises out of the old Blackbird Mine business, then Ruby MacKenzie must be here in this house, and there's only one person that Ruby MacKenzie could be.'

'I think, you know,' said Miss Marple, 'that you're being a little too dogmatic.'

Inspector Neele paid no attention.

'Just one person,' he said grimly.

He got up and went out of the room.

II

Mary Dove was in her own sitting-room. It was a small, rather austerely furnished room, but comfortable. That is to say Miss Dove herself had made it comfortable. When Inspector Neele tapped at the door Mary Dove raised her head, which had been bent over a pile of tradesmen's books, and said in her clear voice:

'Come in.'

The Inspector entered.

'Do sit down, Inspector.' Miss Dove indicated a chair. 'Could you wait just one moment? The total of the fishmonger's account does not seem to be correct and I must check it.'

Inspector Neele sat in silence watching her as she totted up the column. How wonderfully calm and self-possessed the girl was, he thought. He was intrigued, as so often before, by the personality that underlay that self-assured manner. He tried to trace in her features any resemblance to those of the woman he had talked to at the Pinewood Sanatorium. The colouring was not unlike, but he could detect no real facial resemblance. Presently Mary Dove raised her head from her accounts and said:

'Yes, Inspector? What can I do for you?'

Inspector Neele said quietly:

'You know, Miss Dove, there are certain very peculiar features about this case.'

'Yes?'

'To begin with there is the odd circumstance of the rye found in Mr Fortescue's pocket.'

'That was very extraordinary,' Mary Dove agreed. 'You know I really cannot think of any explanation for that.'

'Then there is the curious circumstance of the blackbirds. Those four blackbirds on Mr Fortescue's desk last summer, and also the incident of the blackbirds being substituted for the veal and ham in the pie. You were here, I think, Miss Dove, at the time of both those occurrences?'

'Yes, I was. I remember now. It was most upsetting. It seemed such a very purposeless, spiteful thing to do, especially at the time.'

'Perhaps not entirely purposeless. What do you know, Miss Dove, about the Blackbird Mine?'

'I don't think I've ever heard of the Blackbird Mine.'

'Your name, you told me, is Mary Dove. Is that your real name, Miss Dove?'

Mary Dove raised her eyebrows. Inspector Neele was almost sure that a wary expression had come into her blue eyes.

'What an extraordinary question, Inspector. Are you suggesting that my name is *not* Mary Dove?'

'That is exactly what I am suggesting. I'm suggesting,' said Neele pleasantly, 'that your name is Ruby MacKenzie.'

She stared at him. For a moment her face was entirely blank with neither protest on it nor surprise. There was, Inspector Neele thought, a very definite effect of calculation. After a minute or two she said in a quiet, colourless voice:

'What do you expect me to say?'

'Please answer me. Is your name Ruby MacKenzie?'

'I have told you my name is Mary Dove.'

'Yes, but have you proof of that, Miss Dove?'

'What do you want to see? My birth certificate?'

'That might be helpful or it might not. You might, I mean, be in possession of the birth certificate of *a* Mary Dove. That Mary Dove might be a friend of yours or might be someone who had died.'

'Yes, there are a lot of possibilities, aren't there?' Amusement had crept back into Mary Dove's voice. 'It's really quite a dilemma for you, isn't it, Inspector?'

'They might possibly be able to recognize you at Pinewood Sanatorium,' said Neele.

'Pinewood Sanatorium!' Mary raised her eyebrows. 'What or where is Pinewood Sanatorium?'

'I think you know very well, Miss Dove.'

'I assure you I am quite in the dark.'

'And you deny categorically that you are Ruby MacKenzie?'

'I shouldn't really like to deny *anything*. I think, you know, Inspector, that it's up to you to prove I *am* this Ruby MacKenzie, whoever she is.' There was definite amusement now in her blue eyes, amusement and challenge. Looking him straight in the eyes, Mary Dove said, 'Yes, it's up to you, Inspector. Prove that I'm Ruby MacKenzie if you can.'

CHAPTER 25

'The old Tabby's looking for you, sir,' said Sergeant Hay in a conspiratorial whisper, as Inspector Neele descended the stairs. 'It appears as how she's got a lot more to say to you.'

'Hell and damnation,' said Inspector Neele.

'Yes, sir,' said Sergeant Hay, not a muscle of his face moving.

He was about to move away when Neele called him back.

'Go over those notes given us by Miss Dove, Hay, notes as to her former employment and situations. Check up on them – and, yes, there are just one or two other things that I would like to know. Put these enquiries in hand, will you?'

He jotted down a few lines on a sheet of paper and gave them to Sergeant Hay who said:

'I'll get on to it at once, sir.'

Hearing a murmur of voices in the library as he passed, Inspector Neele looked in. Whether Miss Marple had been looking for him or not, she was now fully engaged talking to Mrs Percival Fortescue while her knitting needles clicked busily. The middle of the sentence which Inspector Neele caught was:

'. . . I have really always thought it was a vocation you needed for nursing. It certainly is very noble work.'

Inspector Neele withdrew quietly. Miss Marple had noticed him, he thought, but she had taken no notice of his presence.

She went on in her gentle, soft voice:

'I had such a charming nurse looking after me when I once broke my wrist. She went on from me to nurse Mrs Sparrow's son, a very nice young naval officer. Quite a romance, really, because they became engaged. So romantic I thought it. They were married and were very happy and had two dear little children.' Miss Marple sighed sentimentally. 'It was pneumonia, you know. So much depends on nursing in pneumonia, does it not?'

'Oh, yes,' said Jennifer Fortescue, 'nursing is nearly everything in pneumonia, though of course nowadays M and B works wonders, and it's not the long, protracted battle it used to be.'

'I'm sure you must have been an excellent nurse, my dear,' said Miss Marple. 'That was the beginning of *your* romance, was it not? I mean, you came here to nurse Mr Percival Fortescue, did you not?'

'Yes,' said Jennifer. 'Yes, yes – that's how it did happen.'

Her voice was not encouraging, but Miss Marple seemed to take no notice.

'I understand. One should not listen to servants' gossip, of course, but I'm afraid an old lady like myself is always interested to hear about the people in the house. Now what was I saying? Oh, yes. There was another nurse at first, was there not, and she got sent away – something like that. Carelessness, I believe.'

'I don't think it was carelessness,' said Jennifer. 'I believe her father or something was desperately ill, and so I came to replace her.'

'I see,' said Miss Marple. 'And you fell in love and that was that. Yes, very nice indeed, very nice.'

'I'm not so sure about that,' said Jennifer Fortescue. 'I often wish' – her voice trembled – 'I often wish I was back in the wards again.'

'Yes, yes, I understand. You were keen on your profession.'

'I wasn't so much at the time, but now when I think of it – life's so monotonous, you know. Day after day with nothing to do, and Val so absorbed in business.'

Miss Marple shook her head.

'Gentlemen have to work so hard nowadays,' she said. 'There really doesn't seem any leisure, no matter how much money there is.'

'Yes, it makes it very lonely and dull for a wife sometimes. I often wish I'd never come here,' said Jennifer. 'Oh, well, I dare say it serves me right. I ought never to have done it.'

'Ought never to have done what, my dear?'

'I ought never to have married Val. Oh, well –' she sighed abruptly. 'Don't let's talk of it any more.'

Obligingly Miss Marple began to talk about the new skirts that were being worn in Paris.

II

'So kind of you not to interrupt just now,' said Miss Marple when, having tapped at the door of the study, Inspector Neele had told her to come in. 'There were just one or two little points, you know, that I wanted to verify.' She added reproachfully, 'We didn't really finish our talk just now.'

'I'm so sorry, Miss Marple.' Inspector Neele summoned up a charming smile. 'I'm afraid I was rather rude. I summoned you to a consultation and did all the talking myself.'

'Oh, that's quite all right,' said Miss Marple immediately, 'because, you see, I wasn't really quite ready then to put all *my* cards on the table. I mean I wouldn't like to make any accusation unless I was absolutely sure about it. Sure, that is, in *my own mind*. And I *am* sure, now.'

'You're sure about what, Miss Marple?'

'Well, certainly about who killed Mr Fortescue. What you told me about the marmalade, I mean, just clinches the matter. Showing *how*, I mean, as well as *who*, and well within the mental capacity.'

Inspector Neele blinked a little.

'I'm so sorry,' said Miss Marple, perceiving this reaction on his part, 'I'm afraid I find it difficult sometimes to make myself perfectly clear.'

'I'm not quite sure yet, Miss Marple, what we're talking about.'

'Well, perhaps,' said Miss Marple, 'we'd better begin all over again. I mean if you could spare the time. I would rather like to put my own point of view before you. You see, I've talked a good deal to people, to old Miss Ramsbottom and to Mrs Crump and to her husband. He, of course, is a liar, but that doesn't really matter because if you know liars are liars, it comes to the same thing. But I did want to get the telephone calls clear and the nylon stockings and all that.'

Inspector Neele blinked again and wondered what he had let himself in for and why he had ever thought that Miss Marple might be a desirable and clear-headed colleague. Still, he thought to himself, however muddle-headed she was, she might have picked up some useful bits of information. All Inspector Neele's successes in his profession had come from listening well. He was prepared to listen now.

'Please tell me all about it, Miss Marple,' he said, 'but start at the beginning, won't you.'

'Yes, of course,' said Miss Marple, 'and the beginning is Gladys. I mean I came here because of Gladys. And you very kindly let me look through all her things. And what with that and the nylon stockings and the telephone calls and one thing and another, it did come out perfectly clear. I mean about Mr Fortescue and the taxine.'

'You have a theory?' asked Inspector Neele, 'as to who put the taxine into Mr Fortescue's marmalade.'

'It isn't a theory,' said Miss Marple. 'I know.'

For the third time Inspector Neele blinked.

'It was Gladys, of course,' said Miss Marple.

CHAPTER 26

Inspector Neele stared at Miss Marple and slowly shook his head.

'Are you saying,' he said incredulously, 'that Gladys Martin deliberately murdered Rex Fortescue? I'm sorry, Miss Marple, but I simply don't believe it.'

'No, of course she didn't *mean* to murder him,' said Miss Marple, 'but she did it all the same! You said yourself that she was nervous and upset when you questioned her. And that she looked guilty.'

'Yes, but not guilty of *murder*.'

'Oh, no, I agree. As I say, she didn't *mean* to murder anybody, but she put the taxine in the marmalade. She didn't think it was poison, of course.'

'What *did* she think it was?' Inspector Neele's voice still sounded incredulous.

'I rather imagine she thought it was a truth drug,' said Miss Marple. 'It's very interesting, you know, and very instructive – the things these girls cut out of papers and keep. It's always been the same, you know, all through the ages. Recipes for beauty, for attracting the man you love. And witchcraft and charms and marvellous happenings. Nowadays they're mostly lumped together under the heading of Science. Nobody believes in magicians any more, nobody believes that anyone can come along and wave a wand and turn you into a frog. But if you read in the paper that by injecting certain glands scientists can alter your vital tissues and you'll develop froglike characteristics, well, everybody would believe that. And having read in the papers about truth drugs, of course Gladys would believe it absolutely when he told her that that's what it was.'

'When who told her?' asked Inspector Neele.

'Albert Evans,' said Miss Marple. 'Not of course that that is *really* his name. But anyway he met her last summer at a holiday camp, and he flattered her up and made love to her, and I should imagine told her some story of injustice or persecution, or something like that. Anyway, the point was that Rex Fortescue had to be made to confess what he had done and make restitution. I don't *know* this, of course, Inspector Neele, but I'm pretty sure about it. He got her to take a post here, and it's really very easy nowadays with the shortage of domestic staff, to obtain a post where you want one. Staffs are changing the whole time. Then they arranged a date together. You remember on that last postcard he said, "Remember our date." That was to be the great day they were working for. Gladys would put the drug that he gave her into the top of the marmalade, so that Mr Fortescue would eat it at breakfast and she would also put the rye in his pocket. I don't know what story he told her to account for the rye, but as I told you from the beginning, Inspector Neele, Gladys Martin was a *very* credulous girl. In fact, there's hardly anything she wouldn't believe if a personable young man put it to her the right way.'

'Go on,' said Inspector Neele in a dazed voice.

'The idea probably was,' continued Miss Marple, 'that Albert was going to call upon him at the office that day, and that by that time the truth drug would have worked, and that Mr Fortescue would have confessed everything and so on and so on. You can imagine the poor girl's feelings when she hears that Mr Fortescue is dead.'

'But, surely,' Inspector Neele objected, 'she would have told?'

Miss Marple asked sharply:

'What was the first thing she said to you when you questioned her?'

'She said "I didn't do it",' Inspector Neele said.

'Exactly,' said Miss Marple, triumphantly. 'Don't you see that's exactly what she *would* say? If she broke an ornament, you know, Gladys would always say, "I didn't do it, Miss Marple. I can't think *how* it happened." They can't help it, poor dears. They're very upset at what they've done and their great idea is to avoid blame. You don't think that a nervous young woman who had murdered someone when she didn't mean to murder him, is going to admit it, do you? That would have been *quite* out of character.'

'Yes,' Neele said, 'I suppose it would.'

He ran his mind back over his interview with Gladys. Nervous, upset, guilty, shifty-eyed, all those things. They might have had small significance, or a big one. He could not really blame himself for having failed to come to the right conclusion.

'Her first idea, as I say,' went on Miss Marple, 'would be to deny it all. Then in a confused way she would try to sort it all out in her mind. Perhaps Albert hadn't known how strong the stuff was, or he'd made a mistake and given her too much of it. She'd think of excuses for him and explanations. She'd hope he'd get in touch with her, which, of course, he did. By telephone.'

'Do you know that?' asked Neele sharply.

Miss Marple shook her head.

'No. I admit I'm assuming it. But there were unexplained calls that day. That is to say, people rang up and when Crump, or Mrs Crump answered, the phone was hung up. That's what he'd do, you know. Ring up and wait until Gladys answered the phone, and then he'd make an appointment with her to meet him.'

'I see,' said Neele. 'You mean she had an appointment to meet him on the day she died.'

Miss Marple nodded vigorously.

'Yes, that was indicated. Mrs Crump was right about one thing. The girl had on her best nylon stockings and her good shoes. She was going to meet someone. Only she wasn't going *out* to meet him. He was coming to Yewtree Lodge. That's why she was on the lookout that day and flustered and late with tea. Then, as she brought the second tray into the hall, I think she looked along the passage to the side door, and saw him there, beckoning to her. She put the tray down and went to meet him.'

'And then he strangled her,' said Neele.

Miss Marple pursed her lips together. 'It would only take a minute,' she said, 'but he couldn't risk her talking. She had to die, poor, silly, credulous girl. And then – he put a clothes peg on her nose!' Stern anger vibrated the old lady's voice. 'To make it fit in with the rhyme. The rye, the blackbirds, the counting-house, the bread and honey, and the clothes peg – the nearest he could get to a little dicky bird that nipped off her nose –'

'And I suppose at the end of it all he'll go to Broadmoor and we shan't be able to hang him because he's crazy!' said Neele slowly.

'I think you'll hang him all right,' said Miss Marple. 'And he's not crazy, Inspector, not for a moment!'

Inspector Neele looked hard at her.

'Now see here, Miss Marple, you've outlined a theory to me. Yes – yes – although you say you *know*, it's only a *theory*. You're saying that a man is responsible for these crimes, who called himself Albert Evans, who picked up the girl Gladys at a holiday camp and used her for his own purposes. This Albert Evans was someone who wanted revenge for the old Blackbird Mine business. You're suggesting, aren't you, that Mrs MacKenzie's son, Don MacKenzie, didn't die at Dunkirk. That he's still alive, that he's behind all this?'

But to Inspector Neele's surprise, Miss Marple was shaking her head violently.

'Oh no!' she said, 'Oh *no*! I'm not suggesting that *at all*. Don't you see, Inspector Neele, all this blackbird business is really a complete *fake*. It was *used*, that was all, used by somebody who heard about the blackbirds – the ones in the library and in the pie. The blackbirds were genuine enough. They were put there by someone who knew about the old business, who wanted revenge for it. But only the revenge of trying to frighten Mr Fortescue or to make him uncomfortable. I don't believe, you know, Inspector Neele, that children can really be brought up and taught to wait and brood and carry out revenge. Children, after all, have got a lot of *sense*. But anyone whose father had been swindled and perhaps left to die, might be willing to play a malicious trick on the person who was supposed to have done it. That's what happened, I think. And the killer used it.'

'The killer,' said Inspector Neele. 'Come now, Miss Marple, let's have your ideas about the killer. Who was he?'

'You won't be surprised,' said Miss Marple. 'Not really. Because you'll see, as soon as I tell you who he is, or rather who I think he is, for one must be accurate must one not? – you'll see that he's just the type of person who *would* commit these murders. He's sane, brilliant and quite unscrupulous. And he did it, of course, for money, probably for a good deal of money.'

'Percival Fortescue?' Inspector Neele spoke almost imploringly, but he knew as he spoke that he was wrong. The picture of the man that Miss Marple had built up for him had no resemblance to Percival Fortescue.

'Oh, no,' said Miss Marple. 'Not Percival. Lance.'

CHAPTER 27

'It's impossible,' said Inspector Neele.

He leaned back in his chair and watched Miss Marple with fascinated eyes. As Miss Marple had said, he was not surprised. His words were a denial, not of probability, but of possibility. Lance Fortescue fitted the description: Miss Marple had outlined it well enough. But Inspector Neele simply could not see how Lance could be the answer.

Miss Marple leaned forward in her chair and gently, persuasively, and rather in the manner of someone explaining the simple facts of arithmetic to a small child, outlined her theory.

'He's always been like that, you see. I mean, he's always been *bad*. Bad all through, although with it he's always been *attractive*. Especially attractive to *women*. He's got a brilliant mind and he'll take risks. He's always taken risks and because of his charm people have always believed the best and not the worst about him. He came home in the summer to see his father. I don't believe for a moment that his father wrote to him or sent for him – unless, of course, you've got actual evidence to that effect.' She paused enquiringly.

Neele shook his head. 'No,' he said, 'I've no evidence of his father sending for him. I've got a letter that Lance is supposed to have written to him after being here. But Lance could quite easily have slipped that among his father's papers in the study here the day he arrived.'

'Sharp of him,' said Miss Marple, nodding her head. 'Well, as I say, he probably flew over here and attempted a reconciliation with his father, but Mr Fortescue wouldn't have it. You see, Lance had recently got married and the small pittance he was living on and which he had doubtless been supplementing in various dishonest ways, was not enough for him any more. He was very much in love with Pat (who is a dear, sweet girl) and he wanted a respectable, settled life with her – nothing shifty. And that, from his point of view, meant having a lot of money. When he was at Yewtree Lodge he must have heard about these blackbirds. Perhaps his father mentioned them. Perhaps Adele did. He jumped to the conclusion that MacKenzie's daughter was established in the house and it occurred to him that she would make a very good scapegoat for murder. Because, you see, when he realized that he couldn't get his father to do what he wanted, he must have cold-bloodedly decided that murder it would have to be. He may have realized that his father wasn't – er, very well – and have feared that by the time his father died there would have been a complete crash.'

'He knew about his father's health all right,' said the Inspector.

'Ah – that explains a good deal. Perhaps the coincidence of his father's Christian name being *Rex* together with the blackbird incident suggested the idea of the nursery rhyme. Make a crazy business of the whole thing – and tie it up with that old revenge threat of the MacKenzies. Then, you see, he could dispose of Adele, too, and that hundred thousand pounds going out of the firm. But there would have to be a third character, the 'maid in the garden hanging up the clothes' – and I suppose that suggested the whole wicked plan to him. An innocent accomplice whom he could silence before she could talk. And that would give him what he wanted – a genuine alibi for the first murder. The rest was easy. He arrived here from the station just before five o'clock, which was the time when Gladys brought the second tray into the hall. He came to the side door, saw her and beckoned to her. Strangling her and carrying her body round the house to where the clothes lines were would only have taken three or four minutes. Then he rang the front-door bell, was admitted to the house, and joined the family for tea. After tea he went up to see Miss Ramsbottom. When he came down, he slipped into the drawing-room, found Adele alone there drinking a last cup of tea and sat down by her on the sofa, and while he was talking to her, he managed to slip the cyanide into her tea. It wouldn't be difficult, you know. A little piece of white stuff, like sugar. He might have stretched out his hand to the sugar basin and taken a lump and apparently dropped it into her cup. He'd laugh and say "Look, I've dropped more sugar into your tea." She'd say she didn't mind, stir it and drink it. It would be as easy and audacious as that. Yes, he's an audacious fellow.'

Inspector Neele said slowly:

'It's actually possible – yes. But I cannot see – really, Miss Marple, I cannot see – what he stood to gain by it. Granted that unless old Fortescue died the business would soon be on the rocks, is Lance's share big enough to cause him to plan three murders? I don't think so. I really don't think so.'

'That *is* a little difficult,' admitted Miss Marple. 'Yes, I agree with you. That does present difficulties. I suppose . . .' She hesitated, looking at the Inspector. 'I suppose – I am so very ignorant in financial matters – but I suppose it is really true that the Blackbird Mine *is* worthless?'

Neele reflected. Various scraps fitted together in his mind. Lance's willingness to take the various speculative or worthless shares off Percival's hands. His parting words today in London that Percival had better get rid of the Blackbird and its hoodoo. A gold mine. A worthless gold mine. But perhaps the mine had *not* been worthless. And yet, somehow, that seemed unlikely. Old Rex Fortescue was hardly likely to have made a mistake on that point, although of course there might have been soundings recently. Where *was* the mine? West Africa, Lance had said. Yes but somebody else – was it Miss Ramsbottom? – had said it was in *East* Africa. Had Lance been deliberately misleading when he said West instead of East? Miss Ramsbottom was old and forgetful, and yet *she* might have been right and not Lance. East Africa. Lance had just come from East Africa. Had he perhaps some recent knowledge?

Suddenly with a click another piece fitted into the Inspector's puzzle. Sitting in the train, reading *The Times*. *Uranium deposits found in Tanganyika*. Supposing that the uranium deposits were on the site of the old Blackbird? That would explain everything. Lance had come to have knowledge of that, being on the spot, and with uranium deposits there, there was a fortune to be grasped. An enormous fortune! He sighed. He looked at Miss Marple.

'How do you think?' he asked reproachfully, 'that I'm ever going to be able to prove all this?'

Miss Marple nodded at him encouragingly, as an aunt might have encouraged a bright nephew who was going in for a scholarship exam.

'You'll prove it,' she said. 'You're a very, *very* clever man,

Inspector Neele. I've seen that from the first. Now you know who it is you ought to be able to get the evidence. At that holiday camp, for instance, they'll recognize his photograph. He'll find it hard to explain why he stayed there for a week calling himself Albert Evans.'

Yes, Inspector Neele thought, Lance Fortescue was brilliant and unscrupulous – but he was foolhardy, too. The risks he took were just a little too great.

Neele thought to himself, 'I'll get him!' Then, doubt sweeping over him, he looked at Miss Marple.

'It's all pure assumption, you know,' he said.

'Yes – but you are sure, aren't you?'

'I suppose so. After all, I've known his kind before.'

The old lady nodded.

'Yes – that matters so much – that's really why *I'm* sure.'

Neele looked at her playfully.

'Because of your knowledge of criminals.'

'Oh no – of course not. Because of Pat – a dear girl – and the kind that always marries a bad lot – that's really what drew my attention to him at the start –'

'I may be sure – in my own mind,' said the Inspector – 'but there's a lot that needs explaining – the Ruby MacKenzie business for instance. I could swear that –'

Miss Marple interrupted:

'And you're quite right. But you've been thinking of the wrong person. Go and talk to Mrs Percy.'

II

'Mrs Fortescue,' said Inspector Neele, 'do you mind telling me your name before you were married.'

'Oh!' Jennifer gasped. She looked frightened.

'You needn't be nervous madam,' said Inspector Neele, 'but it's much better to come out with the truth. I'm right, I think, in saying that your name before you were married was Ruby MacKenzie?'

'My – well, oh well – oh dear – well, why shouldn't it be?' said Mrs Percival Fortescue.

'No reason at all,' said Inspector Neele gently, and added, 'I was talking to your mother a few days ago at Pinewood Sanatorium.'

'She's very angry with me,' said Jennifer. 'I never go and see her now because it only upsets her. Poor Mumsy, she was so devoted to Dad, you know.'

'And she brought you up to have very melodramatic ideas of revenge?'

'Yes,' said Jennifer. 'She kept making us swear on the Bible that we'd never forget and that we'd kill him one day. Of course, once I'd gone into hospital and started my training, I began to realize that her mental balance wasn't what it should be.'

'You yourself must have felt revengeful though, Mrs Fortescue?'

'Well, of course I did. Rex Fortescue practically murdered my father! I don't mean he actually shot him, or knifed him or anything like that. But I'm quite certain that he *did* leave Father to die. That's the same thing, isn't it?'

'It's the same thing morally – yes.'

'So I did want to pay him back,' said Jennifer. 'When a friend of mine came to nurse his son I got her to leave and to propose my replacing her. I don't know exactly what I meant to do . . . I didn't, really I didn't, Inspector, I never meant to *kill* Mr Fortescue. I had some idea, I think, of nursing his son so badly that the son would die. But of course if you *are* a nurse by profession you can't do that sort of thing. Actually I had quite a job pulling Val through. And then he got fond of me and asked me to marry him and I thought, "Well, really that's a far more sensible revenge than anything else." I mean, to marry Mr Fortescue's eldest son and get the money he swindled Father out of back that way. I think it was a far more sensible way.'

'Yes, indeed,' said Inspector Neele, 'far more sensible.' He added, 'It was you, I suppose, who put the blackbirds on the desk and in the pie?'

Mrs Percival flushed.

'Yes. I suppose it was silly of me really. . . . But Mr Fortescue had been talking about suckers one day and boasting of how he'd swindled people – got the best of them. Oh, in quite a *legal* way. And I thought I'd just like to give him – well, a kind of fright. And it *did* give him a fright! He was awfully upset.' She added anxiously, 'But I didn't do anything *else*! I didn't really, Inspector. You don't – you don't honestly think I would *murder* anyone, do you?'

Inspector Neele smiled.

'No,' he said, 'I don't.' He added, 'By the way, have you given Miss Dove any money lately?'

Jennifer's jaw dropped.

'How did you know?'

'We know a lot of things,' said Inspector Neele and added to himself: 'And guess a good many, too.'

Jennifer continued, speaking rapidly.

'She came to me and said that you'd accused her of being Ruby MacKenzie. She said if I'd get hold of five hundred pounds she'd let you go on thinking so. She said if you knew that I was Ruby MacKenzie, I'd be suspected of murdering Mr Fortescue and my stepmother. I had an awful job getting the money, because of course I couldn't tell Percival. He doesn't know about me. I had to sell my diamond engagement ring and a very beautiful necklace Mr Fortescue gave me.'

'Don't worry, Mrs Percival,' said Inspector Neele, 'I think we can get your money back for you.'

III

It was on the following day that Inspector Neele had another interview with Miss Mary Dove.

'I wonder, Miss Dove,' he said, 'if you'd give me a cheque for five hundred pounds payable to Mrs Percival Fortescue.'

He had the pleasure of seeing Mary Dove lose countenance for once.

'The silly fool told you, I suppose,' she said.

'Yes. Blackmail, Miss Dove, is rather a serious charge.'

'It wasn't exactly blackmail, Inspector. I think you'd find it hard to make out a case of blackmail against me. I was just doing Mrs Percival a special service to oblige her.'

'Well, if you'll give me that cheque, Miss Dove, we'll leave it like that.'

Mary Dove got her chequebook and took out her fountain pen.

'It's very annoying,' she said with a sigh. 'I'm particularly hard up at the moment.'

'You'll be looking for another job soon, I suppose?'

'Yes. This one hasn't turned out quite according to plan. It's all been very unfortunate from my point of view.'

Inspector Neele agreed.

'Yes, it put you in rather a difficult position, didn't it? I mean, it was quite likely that at any moment we might have to look into your antecedents.'

Mary Dove, cool once more, allowed her eyebrows to rise.

'Really, Inspector, my past is quite blameless, I assure you.'

'Yes, it is,' Inspector Neele agreed, cheerfully. 'We've nothing against you at all, Miss Dove. It's a curious coincidence, though, that in the last three places which you have filled so admirably, there have happened to be robberies about three months after you left. The thieves have seemed remarkably well informed as to where mink coats, jewels, etc., were kept. Curious coincidence, isn't it?'

'Coincidences do happen, Inspector.'

'Oh, yes,' said Neele. 'They happen. But they mustn't happen too often, Miss Dove. I dare say,' he added, 'that we may meet again in the future.'

'I hope' – said Mary Dove – 'I don't mean to be rude, Inspector Neele – but I hope we don't.'

CHAPTER 28

Miss Marple smoothed over the top of her suitcase, tucked in an end of woolly shawl and shut the lid down. She looked round her bedroom. No, she had left nothing behind. Crump came in to fetch down her luggage. Miss Marple went into the next room to say goodbye to Miss Ramsbottom.

'I'm afraid,' said Miss Marple, 'that I've made a very poor return for your hospitality. I hope you will be able to forgive me some day.'

'Hah,' said Miss Ramsbottom.

She was as usual playing patience.

'Black knave, red queen,' she observed, then she darted a shrewd, sideways glance at Miss Marple. 'You found out what you wanted to, I suppose,' she said.

'Yes.'

'And I suppose you've told that police inspector all about it? Will he be able to prove a case?'

'I'm almost sure he will,' said Miss Marple. 'It may take a little time.'

'I'm not asking you any questions,' said Miss Ramsbottom. 'You're a shrewd woman. I knew that as soon as I saw you. I don't blame you for what you've done. Wickedness is wickedness and has got to be punished. There's a bad streak in this family. It didn't come from our side, I'm thankful to say. Elvira, my sister, was a fool. Nothing worse.

'Black knave,' repeated Miss Ramsbottom, fingering the card. 'Handsome, but a black heart. Yes, I was afraid of it. Ah, well, you can't always help loving a sinner. The boy always had a way with him. Even got round me. . . . Told a lie about the time he left me that day. I didn't contradict him, but I wondered. . . . I've wondered ever since. But he was Elvira's boy – I couldn't bring myself to say anything. Ah, well, you're a righteous woman, Jane Marple, and right must prevail. I'm sorry for his wife, though.'

'So am I,' said Miss Marple.

In the hall Pat Fortescue was waiting to say goodbye.

'I wish you weren't going,' she said. 'I shall miss you.'

'It's time for me to go,' said Miss Marple. 'I've finished what I came here to do. It hasn't been – altogether pleasant. But it's important, you know, that wickedness shouldn't triumph.'

Pat looked puzzled.

'I don't understand.'

'No, my dear. But perhaps you will, some day. If I might venture to advise, if anything ever – goes wrong in your life – I think the happiest thing for you would be to go back to where you were happy as a child. Go back to Ireland, my dear. Horses and dogs. All that.'

Pat nodded.

'Sometimes I wish I'd done just that when Freddy died. But if I had' – her voice changed and softened – 'I'd never have met Lance.'

Miss Marple sighed.

'We're not staying here, you know,' said Pat. 'We're going back to East Africa as soon as everything's cleared up. I'm so glad.'

'God bless you, dear child,' said Miss Marple. 'One needs a great deal of courage to get through life. I think you have it.'

She patted the girl's hand and, releasing it, went through the front door to the waiting taxi.

II

Miss Marple reached home late that evening.

Kitty – the latest graduate from St Faith's Home – let her in and greeted her with a beaming face.

'I've got a herring for your supper, miss. I'm so glad to see you home – you'll find everything very nice in the house. Regular spring cleaning I've had.'

'That's very nice, Kitty – I'm glad to be home.'

Six spider webs on the cornice, Miss Marple noted. These girls never raised their heads! She was none the less too kind to say so.

'Your letters is on the hall table, miss. And there's one as went to Daisymead by mistake. Always doing that, aren't they? Does look a bit alike, Dane and Daisy, and the writing's so bad I don't wonder this time. They've been away there and the house shut up, they only got back and sent it round today. Said as how they hoped it wasn't important.'

Miss Marple picked up her correspondence. The letter to which Kitty had referred was on top of the others. A faint chord of remembrance stirred in Miss Marple's mind at the sight of the blotted scrawled handwriting. She tore it open.

DEAR MADAM,

I hope as you'll forgive me writing this but I really don't know what to do indeed I don't and I never meant no harm. Dear madam, you'll have seen the newspapers it was murder they say but it wasn't me that did it, not really, because I would never do anything wicked like that and I know as how he wouldn't either. Albert, I mean. I'm telling this badly, but you see we met last summer and was going to be married only Bert hadn't got his rights, he'd been done out of them, swindled by this Mr Fortescue who's dead. And Mr Fortescue he just denied everything and of course everybody believed him and not Bert because he was rich and Bert was poor. But Bert had a friend who works in a place where they make these new drugs and there's what they call a truth drug you've read about it perhaps in the paper and it makes people speak the truth whether they want to or not. Bert was going to see Mr Fortescue in his office on Nov. 5th and taking a lawyer with him and I was to be sure to give him the drug at breakfast that morning and then it would work just right for when they came and he'd admit as all what Bert said was quite true. Well, madam, I put it in the marmalade but now he's dead and I think as how it must have been too strong but it wasn't Bert's fault because Bert would never do a thing like that but I can't tell the police because maybe they'd think Bert did it on purpose which I know he didn't. Oh, madam, I don't know what to do or what to say and the police are here in the house and it's awful and they ask you questions and look at you so stern and I don't know what to do and I haven't heard from Bert. Oh, madam, I don't like to ask it of you but if you could only come here and help me they'd listen to you and you were always so kind to me, and I didn't mean anything wrong and Bert didn't either. If you could only help us. Yours respectfully,

GLADYS MARTIN.

PS – I'm enclosing a snap of Bert and me. One of the boys took it at the camp and give it me. Bert doesn't know I've got it – he hates being snapped. But you can see, madam, what a nice boy he is.

Miss Marple, her lips pursed together, stared down at the photograph. The pair pictured there were looking at each other. Miss Marple's eyes went from Glady's pathetic adoring face, the mouth slightly open, to the other face – the dark handsome smiling face of Lance Fortescue.

The last words of the pathetic letter echoed in her mind:

You can see what a nice boy he is.

The tears rose in Miss Marple's eyes. Succeeding pity, there came anger – anger against a heartless killer.

And then, displacing both these emotions, there came a surge of triumph – the triumph some specialist might feel who has successfully reconstructed an extinct animal from a fragment of jawbone and a couple of teeth.

A MURDER IS ANNOUNCED

1 A MURDER IS ANNOUNCED

Between 7.30 and 8.30 every morning except Sundays, Johnnie Butt made the round of the village of Chipping Cleghorn on his bicycle, whistling vociferously through his teeth, and alighting at each house or cottage to shove through the letter box such morning papers as had been ordered by the occupants of the house in question from Mr Totman, stationer, of the High Street. Thus, at Colonel and Mrs Easterbrook's he delivered *The Times* and the *Daily Graphic*; at Mrs Swettenham's he left *The Times* and the *Daily Worker*; at Miss Hinchliffe and Miss Murgatroyd's he left the *Daily Telegraph* and the *News Chronicle*; at Miss Blacklock's he left the *Telegraph*, *The Times* and the *Daily Mail*.

At all these houses, and indeed at practically every house in Chipping Cleghorn, he delivered every Friday a copy of the *North Benham News and Chipping Cleghorn Gazette*, known locally simply as 'the *Gazette*'.

Thus, on Friday mornings, after a hurried glance at the headlines in the daily paper (*International situation critical! UNO meets today! Bloodhounds seek blonde typist's killer! Three collieries idle. Twenty-three die of food poisoning in Seaside Hotel, etc.*) most of the inhabitants of Chipping Cleghorn eagerly opened the *Gazette* and plunged into the local news. After a cursory glance at Correspondence (in which the passionate hates and feuds of rural life found full play) nine out of ten subscribers then turned to the PERSONAL column. Here were grouped together higgledy piggledy articles For Sale or Wanted, frenzied appeals for Domestic Help, innumerable insertions regarding dogs, announcements concerning poultry and garden equipment; and various other items of an interesting nature to those living in the small community of Chipping Cleghorn.

This particular Friday, October 29th – was no exception to the rule –

II

Mrs Swettenham, pushing back the pretty little grey curls from her forehead, opened *The Times*, looked with a lacklustre eye at the left-hand centre page, decided that, as usual, if there *was* any exciting news *The Times* had succeeded in camouflaging it in an impeccable manner; took a look at Births, Marriages and Deaths, particularly the latter; then, her duty done, she put aside *The Times* and eagerly seized the *Chipping Cleghorn Gazette*.

When her son Edmund entered the room a moment later, she was already deep in the Personal Column.

'Good morning, dear,' said Mrs Swettenham. 'The Smedleys are selling their Daimler. 1935 – that's rather a long time ago, isn't it?'

Her son grunted, poured himself out a cup of coffee, helped himself to a couple of kippers, sat down at the table and opened the *Daily Worker* which he propped up against the toastrack.

'*Bull mastiff puppies*,' read out Mrs Swettenham. 'I really don't know how people manage to feed big dogs nowadays – I really *don't* . . . H'm, Selina Lawrence is advertising for a cook again. I could tell her it's just a waste of time advertising in these days. She hasn't put her address, only a box number – that's *quite* fatal – I could have told her so – servants simply insist on knowing where they are going. They like a good address . . . *False teeth* – I can't think why false teeth are so popular. *Best prices paid . . . Beautiful bulbs. Our special selection.* They sound rather cheap . . . Here's a girl wants an "*Interesting post – Would travel.*" I dare say! Who wouldn't . . . *Dachshunds* . . . I've never really cared for dachshunds myself – I don't mean because they're *German*, because we've got over all that – I just don't care for them, that's all – Yes, Mrs Finch?'

The door had opened to admit the head and torso of a grim-looking female in an aged velvet beret.

'Good morning, Mum,' said Mrs Finch. 'Can I clear?'

'Not yet. We haven't finished,' said Mrs Swettenham. 'Not quite finished,' she added ingratiatingly.

Casting a look at Edmund and his paper, Mrs Finch sniffed, and withdrew.

'I've only just begun,' said Edmund, just as his mother remarked:

'I do wish you wouldn't read that horrid paper, Edmund. Mrs Finch doesn't like it *at all*.'

'I don't see what my political views have to do with Mrs Finch.'

'And it isn't,' pursued Mrs Swettenham, 'as though you *were* a worker. You don't do any work at all.'

'That's not in the least true,' said Edmund indignantly. 'I'm writing a book.'

'I meant *real* work,' said Mrs Swettenham. 'And Mrs Finch does matter. If she takes a dislike to us and won't come, who else could we get?'

'Advertise in the *Gazette*,' said Edmund, grinning.

'I've just told you that's no use. Oh dear me, nowadays unless one has an old Nannie in the family, who will go into the kitchen and do everything, one is simply *sunk*.'

'Well, why haven't we an old Nannie? How remiss of you not to have provided me with one? What were you thinking about?'

'You had an *ayah*, dear.'

'No foresight,' murmured Edmund.

Mrs Swettenham was once more deep in the Personal Column.

'*Second-hand Motor Mower for sale.* Now I wonder . . . Goodness, what a price! . . . More Dachshunds . . . "*Do write or communicate desperate Woggles.*" What silly nicknames people have . . . *Cocker Spaniels* . . . Do you remember darling Susie, Edmund? She really was *human*. Understood every word you said to her . . . *Sheraton sideboard for Sale. Genuine family antique. Mrs Lucas, Dayas Hall* . . . What a liar that woman is! Sheraton indeed . . . !'

Mrs Swettenham sniffed and then continued her reading.

'*All a mistake, darling. Undying love. Friday as usual – J.* . . . I suppose they've had a lovers' quarrel – or do you think it's a code for burglars? . . . *More* Dachshunds! Really, I do think people have gone a little crazy about breeding Dachshunds. I mean, there *are* other dogs. Your Uncle Simon used to breed Manchester Terriers. Such graceful little things. I do like dogs with *legs* . . . *Lady going abroad will sell her navy two piece suit* . . . no measurements or price given. . . . *A marriage is announced* – no, a *murder* . . . *What?* . . . *Well*, I never! Edmund, *Edmund*, listen to this . . . *A murder is announced and will take place on Friday, October 29th at Little Paddocks at 6.30 p.m. Friends please accept this, the only intimation.* What an extraordinary thing? *Edmund!*'

'What's that?' Edmund looked up from his newspaper.

'Friday, October 29th . . . Why, that's *today*.'

'Let me see.' Her son took the paper from her.

'But what does it mean?' Mrs Swettenham asked with lively curiosity.

Edmund Swettenham rubbed his nose doubtfully.

'Some sort of party, I suppose. The Murder Game – that kind of thing.'

'Oh,' said Mrs Swettenham doubtfully. 'It seems a very odd way of doing it. Just sticking it in the advertisements like that. Not at all like Letitia Blacklock who always seems to me such a sensible woman.'

'Probably got up by the bright young things she has in the house.'

'It's very short notice. Today. Do you think we're just supposed to go?'

'It says "Friends, please accept this, the only intimation?"' her son pointed out.

'Well, I think these new fangled ways of giving invitations are very tiresome,' said Mrs Swettenham decidedly.

'All right, Mother, you needn't go.'

'No,' agreed Mrs Swettenham.

There was a pause.

'Do you really *want* that last piece of toast, Edmund?'

'I should have thought my being properly nourished mattered more than letting that old hag clear the table.'

'Sh, dear, she'll *hear* you . . . Edmund, what happens at a Murder Game?'

'I don't know, exactly . . . They pin pieces of paper upon you, or something . . . No, I think you draw them out of a hat. And somebody's the victim and somebody else is a detective – and then they turn the lights out and somebody taps you on the shoulder and then you scream and lie down and sham dead.'

'It sounds quite exciting.'

'Probably a beastly bore. I'm not going.'

'Nonsense, Edmund,' said Mrs Swettenham resolutely. '*I'm* going and *you're* coming with me. That's *settled*!'

III

'Archie,' said Mrs Easterbrook to her husband, 'listen to *this*.'

Colonel Easterbrook paid no attention, because he was already snorting with impatience over an article in *The Times*.

'Trouble with these fellows is,' he said, 'that none of them knows the first thing about India! Not the first thing!'

'I know, dear, I know.'

'If they did, they wouldn't write such piffle.'

'Yes, I know. Archie, do listen. *A murder is announced and will take place on Friday, October 29th* (that's today) *at Little Paddocks at 6.30 p.m. Friends please accept this, the only intimation.*'

She paused triumphantly. Colonel Easterbrook looked at her indulgently but without much interest.

'Murder Game,' he said.

'Oh.'

'That's all it is. Mind you,' he unbent a little, 'it can be very good fun if it's well done. But it needs good organizing by someone who knows the ropes. You draw lots. One person's the murderer, nobody knows who. Lights out. Murderer chooses his victim. The victim has to count twenty before he screams. Then the person who's chosen to be the detective takes charge. Questions everybody. Where they were, what they were doing, tries to trip the real fellow up. Yes, it's a good game — if the detective — er — knows something about police work.'

'Like you, Archie. You had all those interesting cases to try in your district.'

Colonel Easterbrook smiled indulgently and gave his moustache a complacent twirl.

'Yes, Laura,' he said. 'I dare say I could give them a hint or two.'

And he straightened his shoulders.

'Miss Blacklock ought to have asked you to help her in setting the thing up.'

The Colonel snorted.

'Oh, well, she's got that young cub staying with her. Expect this is his idea. Nephew or something. Funny idea, though, sticking it in the paper.'

'It was in the Personal Column. We might never have seen it. I suppose it *is* an invitation, Archie?'

'Funny kind of invitation. I can tell you one thing. They can count *me* out.'

'Oh, Archie,' Mrs Easterbrook's voice rose in a shrill wail.

'Short notice. For all they know I might be busy.'

'But you're not, are you, darling?' Mrs Easterbrook lowered her voice persuasively. 'And I do think, Archie, that you really *ought* to go — just to help poor Miss Blacklock out. I'm sure she's counting on you to make the thing a success. I mean, you know so much about police work and procedure. The whole thing will fall flat if you don't go and help to make it a success. After all, one must be *neighbourly*.'

Mrs Easterbrook put her synthetic blonde head on one side and opened her blue eyes very wide.

'Of course, if you put it like that, Laura . . .' Colonel Easterbrook twirled his grey moustache again, importantly, and looked with indulgence on his fluffy little wife. Mrs Easterbrook was at least thirty years younger than her husband.

'If you put it like *that*, Laura,' he said.

'I really do think it's your *duty*, Archie,' said Mrs Easterbrook solemnly.

IV

The *Chipping Cleghorn Gazette* had also been delivered at Boulders, the picturesque three cottages knocked into one inhabited by Miss Hinchliffe and Miss Murgatroyd.

'Hinch?'

'What is it, Murgatroyd.'

'Where are you?'

'Henhouse.'

'Oh.'

Paddling gingerly through the long wet grass, Miss Amy Murgatroyd approached her friend. The latter, attired in corduroy slacks and battledress tunic was conscientiously stirring in handfuls of balancer meal to a repellently steaming basin full of cooked potato peelings and cabbage stumps.

She turned her head with its short man-like crop and weather-beaten countenance towards her friend.

Miss Murgatroyd, who was fat and amiable, wore a checked tweed skirt and a shapeless pullover of brilliant royal blue. Her curly bird's nest of grey hair was in a good deal of disorder and she was slightly out of breath.

'In the *Gazette*,' she panted. 'Just listen – what can it *mean*? *A murder is announced . . . and will take place on Friday, October 29th at Little Paddocks at 6.30 p.m. Friends please accept this, the only intimation.*'

She paused, breathless, as she finished reading, and awaited some authoritative pronouncement.

'Daft,' said Miss Hinchliffe.

'Yes, but what do you think it *means*?'

'Means a drink, anyway,' said Miss Hinchliffe.

'You think it's a sort of invitation?'

'We'll find out what it means when we get there,' said Miss Hinchliffe. 'Bad sherry, I expect. You'd better get off the grass, Murgatroyd. You've got your bedroom slippers on still. They're soaked.'

'Oh, dear.' Miss Murgatroyd looked down ruefully at her feet. 'How many eggs today?'

'Seven. That damned hen's still broody. I must get her into the coop.'

'It's a funny way of putting it, don't you think?' Amy Murgatroyd asked, reverting to the notice in the *Gazette*. Her voice was slightly wistful.

But her friend was made of sterner and more single-minded stuff. She was intent on dealing with recalcitrant poultry and no announcement in a paper, however enigmatic, could deflect her.

She squelched heavily through the mud and pounced upon a speckled hen. There was a loud and indignant squawking.

'Give me ducks every time,' said Miss Hinchliffe. '*Far* less trouble . . .'

V

'Oo, scrumptious!' said Mrs Harmon across the breakfast table to her husband, the Rev. Julian Harmon, 'there's going to be a murder at Miss Blacklock's.'

'A murder?' said her husband, slightly surprised. 'When?'

'This afternoon . . . at least, this evening. 6.30. Oh, bad luck, darling, you've got your preparations for confirmation then. It *is* a shame. And you do so love murders!'

'I don't really know what you're talking about, Bunch?'

Mrs Harmon, the roundness of whose form and face had early led to the soubriquet of 'Bunch' being substituted for her baptismal name of Diana, handed the *Gazette* across the table.

'There. All among the second-hand pianos, and the old teeth.'

'What a very extraordinary announcement.'

'Isn't it?' said Bunch happily. 'You wouldn't think that Miss Blacklock cared about murders and games and things, would you? I suppose it's the young Simmonses put her up to it – though I should have thought Julia Simmons would find murders rather crude. Still, there it is, and I do think, darling, it's a *shame* you can't be there. Anyway, I'll go and tell you all about it, though it's rather wasted on me, because I don't really like games that happen in the dark. They frighten me, and I *do* hope I shan't have to be the one who's murdered. If someone suddenly puts a hand on my shoulder and whispers, "You're dead," I know my heart will give such a big bump that perhaps it really *might* kill me! Do you think that's likely?'

'No, Bunch. I think you're going to live to be an old, old woman – with me.'

'And die on the same day and be buried in the same grave. That would be lovely.'

Bunch beamed from ear to ear at this agreeable prospect.

'You seem very happy, Bunch?' said her husband, smiling.

'Who'd *not* be happy if they were me?' demanded Bunch, rather confusedly. 'With you and Susan and Edward, and all of you fond of me and not caring if I'm stupid . . . And the sun shining! And this lovely big house to live in!'

The Rev. Julian Harmon looked round the big bare dining room and assented doubtfully.

'Some people would think it was the last straw to have to live in this great rambling draughty place.'

'Well, I like big rooms. All the nice smells from outside can get in and stay there. And you can be untidy and leave things about and they don't clutter you.'

'No labour saving devices or central heating? It means a lot of work for you, Bunch.'

'Oh, Julian, it doesn't. I get up at half-past six and light the boiler and rush around like a steam engine, and by eight it's all done. And I keep it nice, don't I? With beeswax and polish and big jars of autumn leaves. It's not really harder to keep a big house clean than a small one. You go round with mops and things much quicker, because your behind isn't always bumping into things like it is in a small room. And I like sleeping in a big cold room – it's so cosy to snuggle down with just the tip of your nose telling you what it's like up above. And whatever size of house you live in, you peel the same amount of potatoes and wash up the same amount of plates and all that. Think how nice it is for Edward and Susan to have a big empty room to play in where they can have railways and dolls' tea parties all over the floor and never have to put them away? And then it's nice to have extra bits of the house that you can let people have to live in. Jimmy Symes and Johnnie Finch – they'd have had to live with their in-laws otherwise. And you know, Julian, it isn't nice living with your in-laws. You're devoted to Mother, but you wouldn't really have liked to start our married life living with her and Father. And I shouldn't have liked it, either. I'd have gone on feeling like a little girl.'

Julian smiled at her.

'You're rather like a little girl still, Bunch.'

Julian Harmon himself had clearly been a model designed by Nature for the age of sixty. He was still about twenty-five years short of achieving Nature's purpose.

'I know I'm stupid –'

'You're not stupid, Bunch. You're very clever.'

'No, I'm not. I'm not a bit intellectual. Though I do try . . . And I really love it when you talk to me about books and history and things. I think perhaps it wasn't an awfully good idea to read aloud Gibbon to me in the evenings, because if it's been a cold wind out, and it's nice and hot by the fire, there's something about Gibbon that does, rather, make you go to sleep.'

Julian laughed.

'But I do love listening to you, Julian. Tell me the story again about the old vicar who preached about Ahasuerus.'

'You know that by heart, Bunch.'

'Just tell it me again. *Please.*'

Her husband complied.

'It was old Scrymgour. Somebody looked into his church one day. He was leaning out of the pulpit and preaching fervently to a couple of old charwomen. He was shaking his finger at them and saying, "Aha! I know what you are thinking. *You* think that the Great Ahasuerus of the First Lesson was Artaxerxes the Second. But he *wasn't!*" And then with enormous triumph, "He was Artaxerxes the *Third.*"'

It had never struck Julian Harmon as a particularly funny story himself, but it never failed to amuse Bunch.

Her clear laugh floated out.

'The old pet!' she exclaimed. 'I think you'll be exactly like that some day, Julian.'

Julian looked rather uneasy.

'I know,' he said with humility. 'I do feel very strongly that I can't always get the proper simple approach.'

'I shouldn't worry,' said Bunch, rising and beginning to pile the breakfast plates on a tray. 'Mrs Butt told me yesterday that Butt, who never went to church and used to be practically the local atheist, comes every Sunday now on purpose to hear you preach.'

She went on, with a very fair imitation of Mrs Butt's super-refined voice:

'"And Butt was saying only the other day, Madam, to Mr Timkins from Little Worsdale, that we'd got real *culture* here in Chipping Cleghorn. *Not* like Mr Goss, at Little Worsdale, who talks to the congregation as though they were children who hadn't had any education. Real culture, Butt said, that's what *we've* got. Our Vicar's a highly educated gentleman – Oxford, not Milchester, and he gives us the full benefit of his education. All about the Romans and the Greeks he knows, and the Babylonians and the Assyrians, too. And even the Vicarage cat, Butt says, is called after an Assyrian king!" So there's glory for you,' finished Bunch triumphantly. 'Goodness, I must get on with things or I shall never get done. Come along, Tiglath Pileser, you shall have the herring bones.'

Opening the door and holding it dexterously ajar with her foot, she shot through with the loaded tray, singing in a loud and not particularly tuneful voice, her own version of a sporting song.

> '*It's a fine murdering day,* (sang Bunch)
> *And as balmy as May*
> *And the sleuths from the village are gone,*'

A rattle of crockery being dumped in the sink drowned the next lines, but as the Rev. Julian Harmon left the house, he heard the final triumphant assertion:

> '*And we'll all go a'murdering today!*'

2   BREAKFAST AT LITTLE PADDOCKS

At Little Paddocks also, breakfast was in progress.

Miss Blacklock, a woman of sixty odd, the owner of the house, sat at the head of the table. She wore country tweeds – and with them, rather incongruously, a choker necklace of large false pearls.

She was reading Lane Norcott in the *Daily Mail*. Julia Simmons was languidly glancing through the *Telegraph*. Patrick Simmons was checking up on the crossword in *The Times*. Miss Dora Bunner was giving her attention wholeheartedly to the local weekly paper.

Miss Blacklock gave a subdued chuckle, Patrick muttered: '*Adherent* – not *adhesive* – that's where I went wrong.'

Suddenly a loud cluck, like a startled hen, came from Miss Bunner.

'Letty – *Letty* – have you seen this? Whatever *can* it mean?'

'What's the matter, Dora?'

'The most extraordinary advertisement. It says Little Paddocks quite distinctly. But whatever can it *mean*?'

'If you'd let me see, Dora dear –'

Miss Bunner obediently surrendered the paper into Miss Black-lock's outstretched hand, pointing to the item with a tremulous forefinger.

'Just look, Letty.'

Miss Blacklock looked. Her eyebrows went up. She threw a quick scrutinizing glance round the table. Then she read the advertisement out loud.

'*A murder is announced and will take place on Friday, October 29th at Little Paddocks at 6.30 p.m. Friends please accept this, the only intimation.*'

Then she said sharply. 'Patrick, is this your idea?'

Her eyes rested searchingly on the handsome devil-may-care face of the young man at the other end of the table.

Patrick Simmons' disclaimer came quickly.

'No, indeed, Aunt Letty. Whatever put that idea into your head? Why should I know anything about it?'

'I wouldn't put it past you,' said Miss Blacklock grimly. 'I thought it might be your idea of a joke.'

'A joke? Nothing of the kind.'

'And you, Julia?'

Julia, looking bored, said: 'Of course not.'

Miss Bunner murmured: 'Do you think Mrs Haymes –' and looked at an empty place where someone had breakfasted earlier.

'Oh, I don't think our Phillipa would try and be funny,' said Patrick. 'She's a serious girl, she is.'

'But what's the idea, anyway?' said Julia, yawning. 'What does it mean?'

Miss Blacklock said slowly, 'I suppose – it's some silly sort of hoax.'

'But why?' Dora Bunner exclaimed. 'What's the point of it? It seems a very stupid sort of joke. And in very bad taste.'

Her flabby cheeks quivered indignantly, and her short-sighted eyes sparkled with indignation.

Miss Blacklock smiled at her.

'Don't work yourself up over it, Bunny,' she said. 'It's just somebody's idea of humour, but I wish I knew whose.'

'It says today,' pointed out Miss Bunner. 'Today at 6.30 p.m. What do you think is going to happen?'

'*Death!*' said Patrick in sepulchral tones. 'Delicious Death.'

'Be quiet, Patrick,' said Miss Blacklock as Miss Bunner gave a little yelp.

'I only meant the special cake that Mitzi makes,' said Patrick apologetically. 'You know we *always* call it Delicious Death.'

Miss Blacklock smiled a little absentmindedly.

Miss Bunner persisted: 'But Letty, what do you really think –'

Her friend cut across the words with reassuring cheerfulness.

'I know one thing that will happen at 6.30,' she said dryly. 'We'll have half the village up here, agog with curiosity. I'd better make sure we've got some sherry in the house.'

II

'You *are* worried, aren't you, Lotty?'

Miss Blacklock started. She had been sitting at her writing table, absentmindedly drawing little fishes on the blotting paper. She looked up into the anxious face of her old friend.

She was not quite sure what to say to Dora Bunner. Bunny, she knew, mustn't be worried or upset. She was silent for a moment or two, thinking.

She and Dora Bunner had been at school together. Dora then had been a pretty fair-haired, blue-eyed rather stupid girl. Her being stupid hadn't mattered, because her gaiety and high spirits and her prettiness had made her an agreeable companion. She ought, her friend thought, to have married some nice Army officer, or a country solicitor. She had so many good qualities – affection, devotion, loyalty. But life had been unkind to Dora Bunner. She had had to earn her living. She had been painstaking but never competent at anything she undertook.

The two friends had lost sight of each other. But six months ago a letter had come to Miss Blacklock, a rambling, pathetic letter. Dora's health had given way. She was living in one room, trying to subsist on her old age pension. She endeavoured to do needlework, but her fingers were stiff with rheumatism. She mentioned their schooldays – since then life had driven them apart – but could – possibly – her old friend help?

Miss Blacklock had responded impulsively. Poor Dora, poor pretty silly fluffy Dora. She had swooped down upon Dora, had carried her off, had installed her at Little Paddocks with the comforting fiction that 'the housework is getting too much for me. I need someone to help me run the house.' It was not for long – the doctor had told her that – but sometimes she found poor old Dora a sad trial. She muddled everything, upset the temperamental foreign 'help,' miscounted the laundry, lost bills and letters – and sometimes reduced the competent Miss Blacklock to an agony of exasperation. Poor old muddle-headed Dora, so loyal, so anxious to help, so pleased and proud to think she was of assistance – and, alas, so completely unreliable.

She said sharply:

'Don't, Dora. You know I asked you –'

'Oh,' Miss Bunner looked guilty. 'I know. I forgot. But – but you *are*, aren't you?'

'Worried? No. At least,' she added truthfully, 'not exactly. You mean about that silly notice in the *Gazette*?'

'Yes – even if it's a joke, it seems to me it's a – a spiteful sort of joke.'

'Spiteful?'

'Yes. It seems to me there's *spite* there somewhere. I mean – it's not a *nice* kind of joke.'

Miss Blacklock looked at her friend. The mild eyes, the long obstinate mouth, the slightly upturned nose. Poor Dora, so maddening, so muddleheaded, so devoted and such a problem. A dear fussy old idiot and yet, in a queer way, with an instinctive sense of values.

'I think you're right, Dora,' said Miss Blacklock. 'It's not a nice joke.'

'I don't like it at all,' said Dora Bunner with unsuspected vigour.

'It frightens me.' She added, suddenly: 'And it frightens *you*, Letitia.'

'Nonsense,' said Miss Blacklock with spirit.

'It's *dangerous*. I'm sure it is. Like those people who send you bombs done up in parcels.'

'My dear, it's just some silly idiot trying to be funny.'

'But it *isn't* funny.'

It wasn't really very funny . . . Miss Blacklock's face betrayed her thoughts, and Dora cried triumphantly, 'You see. You think so, too!'

'But Dora, my dear –'

She broke off. Through the door there surged a tempestuous young woman with a well developed bosom heaving under a tight jersey. She had on a dirndl skirt of a bright colour and had greasy dark plaits wound round and round her head. Her eyes were dark and flashing.

She said gustily:

'I can speak to you, yes, please, no?'

Miss Blacklock sighed.

'Of course, Mitzi, what is it?'

Sometimes she thought it would be preferable to do the entire work of the house as well as the cooking rather than be bothered with the eternal nerve storms of her refugee 'lady help.'

'I tell you at once – it is in order, I hope? I give you my notices and I *go* – I go at *once!*'

'For what reason? Has somebody upset you?'

'Yes, I am upset,' said Mitzi dramatically. 'I do not wish to die! Already in Europe I escape. My family they all die – they are all killed – my mother, my little brother, my so sweet little niece – all, all they are killed. But me I run away – I hide. I get to England. I work. I do work that never – never would I do in my own country – I –'

'I know all that,' said Miss Blacklock crisply. It was, indeed, a constant refrain on Mitzi's lips. 'But why do you want to leave *now*?'

'Because again they come to kill me!'

'Who do?'

'My enemies. The Nazis! Or perhaps this time it is the Bolsheviks. They find out I am here. They come to kill me. I have read it – yes – it is in the newspaper!'

'Oh, you mean in the *Gazette*?'

'*Here*, it is written here.' Mitzi produced the *Gazette* from where she had been holding it behind her back. 'See – here it says a *murder*. At Little Paddocks. That is here, is it not? This evening at 6.30. Ah! I do not wait to be murdered – *no*.'

'But why should this apply to *you*? It's – we think it is a joke.'

'A *joke*? It is not a joke to murder someone?'

'No, of course not. But my dear child, if anyone wanted to murder you, they wouldn't advertise the fact in the paper, would they?'

'You do not think they would?' Mitzi seemed a little shaken. 'You think, perhaps, they do not mean to murder anyone at all? Perhaps it is *you* they mean to murder, Miss Blacklock.'

'I certainly can't believe anyone wants to murder me,' said Miss Blacklock lightly. 'And really, Mitzi, I don't see why anyone should want to murder you. After all, why should they?'

'Because they are bad peoples . . . Very bad peoples. I tell you, my mother, my little brother, my so sweet niece . . .'

'Yes, yes.' Miss Blacklock stemmed the flow, adroitly. 'But I cannot really believe *anyone* wants to murder you, Mitzi. Of course, if you want to go off like this at a moment's notice, I cannot possibly stop you. But I think you will be very silly if you do.'

She added firmly, as Mitzi looked doubtful:

'We'll have that beef the butcher sent stewed for lunch. It looks very tough.'

'I make you a goulash, a special goulash.'

'If you prefer to call it that, certainly. And perhaps you could use up that rather hard bit of cheese in making some cheese straws. I think some people may come in this evening for drinks.'

'This evening? What do you mean, this evening?'

'At half-past six.'

'But that is the time in the paper. Who should come then? *Why* should they come?'

'They're coming to the funeral,' said Miss Blacklock with a twinkle. 'That'll do now, Mitzi. I'm busy. Shut the door after you,' she added firmly.

'And that's settled *her* for the moment,' she said as the door closed behind a puzzled-looking Mitzi.

'You are so efficient, Letty,' said Miss Bunner admiringly.

3   AT 6.30 PM

'Well, here we are, all set,' said Miss Blacklock. She looked round the double drawing-room with an appraising eye. The rose-patterned chintzes – the two bowls of bronze chrysanthemums, the small vase of violets and the silver cigarette box on a table by the wall, the tray of drinks on the centre table.

Little Paddocks was a medium-sized house built in the early Victorian style. It had a long shallow veranda and green shuttered windows. The long, narrow drawing-room which lost a good deal of light owing to the veranda roof had originally had double doors at one end leading into a small room with a bay window. A former generation had removed the double doors and replaced them with portières of velvet. Miss Blacklock had dispensed with the portières so that the two rooms had become definitely one. There was a fireplace each end, but neither fire was lit although a gentle warmth pervaded the room.

'You've had the central heating lit,' said Patrick.

Miss Blacklock nodded.

'It's been so misty and damp lately. The whole house felt clammy. I got Evans to light it before he went.'

'The precious precious coke?' said Patrick mockingly.

'As you say, the precious coke. But otherwise there would have been the even more precious coal. You know the Fuel Office won't even let us have the little bit that's due to us each week – not unless we can say definitely that we haven't got any other means of cooking.'

'I suppose there was once heaps of coke and coal for everybody?' said Julia with the interest of one hearing about an unknown country.

'Yes, and cheap, too.'

'And anyone could go and buy as much as they wanted, without filling in anything, and there wasn't any shortage? There was lots of it there?'

'All kinds and qualities – and *not* all stones and slates like what we get nowadays.'

'It must have been a wonderful world,' said Julia, with awe in her voice.

Miss Blacklock smiled. 'Looking back on it, *I* certainly think so. But then I'm an old woman. It's natural for me to prefer my own times. But you young things oughtn't to think so.'

'I needn't have had a job then,' said Julia. 'I could just have stayed at home and done the flowers, and written notes. . . . Why did one write notes and who were they to?'

'All the people that you now ring up on the telephone,' said Miss Blacklock with a twinkle. 'I don't believe you even know *how* to write, Julia.'

'Not in the style of that delicious "Complete Letter Writer" I found the other day. Heavenly! It told you the correct way of refusing a proposal of marriage from a widower.'

'I doubt if you would have enjoyed staying at home as much as you think,' said Miss Blacklock. 'There were duties, you know.' Her voice was dry. 'However, I don't really know much about it. Bunny and I,' she smiled affectionately at Dora Bunner, 'went into the labour market early.'

'Oh, we did, we did *indeed*,' agreed Miss Bunner. 'Those naughty, naughty children. I'll never forget them. Of course, Letty was clever. She was a business woman, secretary to a big financier.'

The door opened and Phillipa Haymes came in. She was tall and fair and placid looking. She looked round the room in surprise.

'Hallo,' she said. 'Is it a party? Nobody told me.'

'Of course,' cried Patrick. 'Our Phillipa doesn't know. The only woman in Chipping Cleghorn who doesn't, I bet.'

Phillipa looked at him enquiringly.

'Here you behold,' said Patrick dramatically, waving a hand, 'the scene of a murder!'

Phillipa Haymes looked faintly puzzled.

'Here,' Patrick indicated the two big bowls of chrysanthemums, 'are the funeral wreaths and these dishes of cheese straws and olives represent the funeral baked meats.'

Phillipa looked enquiringly at Miss Blacklock.

'Is it a joke?' she asked. 'I'm always terribly stupid at seeing jokes.'

'It's a very nasty joke,' said Dora Bunner with energy. 'I don't like it at all.'

'Show her the advertisement,' said Miss Blacklock. 'I *must* go and shut up the ducks. It's dark. They'll be in by now.'

'Let me do it,' said Phillipa.

'Certainly not, my dear. You've finished your day's work.'

'I'll do it, Aunt Letty,' offered Patrick.

'No, you won't,' said Miss Blacklock with energy. 'Last time you didn't latch the door properly.'

'I'll do it, Letty dear,' cried Miss Bunner. 'Indeed, I should love to. I'll just slip on my galoshes – and now where did I put my cardigan?'

But Miss Blacklock, with a smile, had already left the room.

'It's no good, Bunny,' said Patrick. 'Aunt Letty's so efficient that she can never bear anybody else to do things for her. She really much prefers to do everything herself.'

'She loves it,' said Julia.

'I didn't notice you making any offers of assistance,' said her brother.

Julia smiled lazily.

'You've just said Aunt Letty likes to do things herself,' she pointed out. 'Besides,' she held out a well-shaped leg in a sheer stocking. 'I've got my best stockings on.'

'Death in silk stockings!' declaimed Patrick.

'Not silk – nylons, you idiot.'

'That's not nearly such a good title.'

'Won't somebody please tell me,' cried Phillipa, plaintively, 'why there is all this insistence on death?'

Everybody tried to tell her at once – nobody could find the *Gazette* to show her because Mitzi had taken it into the kitchen.

Miss Blacklock returned a few minutes later.

'There,' she said briskly, '*that's* done.' She glanced at the clock. 'Twenty-past six. Somebody ought to be here soon – unless I'm entirely wrong in my estimate of my neighbours.'

'I don't see why anybody should come,' said Phillipa, looking bewildered.

'Don't you, dear? . . . I dare say you wouldn't. But most people are rather more inquisitive than you are.'

'Phillipa's attitude to life is that she just isn't interested,' said Julia, rather nastily.

Phillipa did not reply.

Miss Blacklock was glancing round the room. Mitzi had put the sherry and three dishes containing olives, cheese straws and some little fancy pastries on the table in the middle of the room.

'You might move that tray – or the whole table if you like – round the corner into the bay window in the other room, Patrick, if you don't mind. After all, I am *not* giving a party! *I* haven't asked anyone. And I don't intend to make it obvious that I expect people to turn up.'

'You wish, Aunt Letty, to disguise your intelligent anticipation?'

'Very nicely put, Patrick. Thank you, my dear boy.'

'Now we can all give a lovely performance of a quiet evening at home,' said Julia, 'and be quite surprised when somebody drops in.'

Miss Blacklock had picked up the sherry bottle. She stood holding it uncertainly in her hand.

Patrick reassured her.

'There's quite half a bottle there. It ought to be enough.'

'Oh, yes – yes . . .' She hesitated. Then, with a slight flush, she said:

'Patrick, would you mind . . . there's a new bottle in the cupboard in the pantry. . . . Bring it and a corkscrew. I – we – might as well have a new bottle. This – this has been opened some time.'

Patrick went on his errand without a word. He returned with the new bottle and drew the cork. He looked up curiously at Miss Blacklock as he placed it on the tray.

'Taking things seriously, aren't you, darling?' he asked gently.

'Oh,' cried Dora Bunner, shocked. 'Surely, Letty, you can't imagine –'

'Hush,' said Miss Blacklock quickly. 'That's the bell. You see, my intelligent anticipation is being justified.'

II

Mitzi opened the door of the drawing-room and admitted Colonel and Mrs Easterbrook. She had her own methods of announcing people.

'Here is Colonel and Mrs Easterbrook to see you,' she said conversationally.

Colonel Easterbrook was very bluff and breezy to cover some slight embarrassment.

'Hope you don't mind us dropping in,' he said. (A subdued gurgle came from Julia.) 'Happened to be passing this way – eh what? Quite a mild evening. Notice you've got your central heating on. We haven't started ours yet.'

'Aren't your chrysanthemums *lovely?*' gushed Mrs Easterbrook. '*Such* beauties!'

'They're rather scraggy, really,' said Julia.

Mrs Easterbrook greeted Phillipa Haymes with a little extra cordiality to show that she *quite* understood that Phillipa was not really an agricultural labourer.

'How is Mrs Lucas's garden getting on?' she asked. 'Do you think it will ever be straight again? Completely neglected all through the war – and then only that dreadful old man Ashe who simply did nothing but sweep up a few leaves and put in a few cabbage plants.'

'It's yielding to treatment,' said Phillipa. 'But it will take a little time.'

Mitzi opened the door again and said:

'Here are the ladies from Boulders.'

''Evening,' said Miss Hinchliffe, striding over and taking Miss Blacklock's hand in her formidable grip. 'I said to Murgatroyd: "Let's just drop in at Little Paddocks!" I wanted to ask you how your ducks are laying.'

'The evenings do draw in so quickly now, don't they?' said Miss Murgatroyd to Patrick in a rather fluttery way. 'What lovely chrysanthemums!'

'Scraggy!' said Julia.

'Why can't you be co-operative?' murmured Patrick to her in a reproachful aside.

'You've got your central heating on,' said Miss Hinchliffe. She said it accusingly. 'Very early.'

'The house gets so damp this time of year,' said Miss Blacklock.

Patrick signalled with his eyebrows: 'Sherry yet?' and Miss Blacklock signalled back: 'Not yet.'

She said to Colonel Easterbrook:

'Are you getting any bulbs from Holland this year?'

The door again opened and Mrs Swettenham came in rather guiltily, followed by a scowling and uncomfortable Edmund.

'Here we are!' said Mrs Swettenham gaily, gazing round her with frank curiosity. Then, feeling suddenly uncomfortable, she went on: 'I just thought I'd pop in and ask you if by any chance you wanted a kitten, Miss Blacklock? Our cat is just –'

'About to be brought to bed of the progeny of a ginger tom,' said Edmund. 'The result will, I think, be frightful. Don't say you haven't been warned!'

'She's a very good mouser,' said Mrs Swettenham hastily. And added: 'What *lovely* chrysanthemums!'

'You've got your central heating on, haven't you?' asked Edmund, with an air of originality.

'Aren't people just like gramophone records?' murmured Julia.

'I don't like the news,' said Colonel Easterbrook to Patrick, buttonholing him fiercely. 'I don't like it at all. If you ask me, war's inevitable – absolutely inevitable.'

'I never pay any attention to news,' said Patrick.

Once more the door opened and Mrs Harmon came in.

Her battered felt hat was stuck on the back of her head in a vague attempt to be fashionable and she had put on a rather limp frilly blouse instead of her usual pullover.

'Hallo, Miss Blacklock,' she exclaimed, beaming all over her round face. 'I'm not too late, am I? When does the murder begin?'

III

There was an audible series of gasps. Julia gave an approving little giggle, Patrick crinkled up his face and Miss Blacklock smiled at her latest guest.

'Julian is just frantic with rage that he can't be here,' said Mrs Harmon. 'He *adores* murders. That's really why he preached such a good sermon last Sunday – I suppose I oughtn't to say it was a good sermon as he's my husband – but it really was good, didn't you think? – so much better than his usual sermons. But as I was saying it was all because of *Death Does the Hat Trick*. Have you read it? The girl at Boots' kept it for me specially. It's simply *baffling*. You keep thinking you know – and then the whole thing switches round – and there are a lovely lot of murders, four or five of them. Well, I left it in the study when Julian was shutting himself up there to do his sermon, and he just picked it up and simply *could not* put it down! And consequently he had to write his sermon in a frightful hurry and had to just put down what he wanted to say very simply – without any scholarly twists and bits and learned references – and naturally it was heaps better. Oh, dear, I'm talking too much. But do tell me, when is the murder going to begin?'

Miss Blacklock looked at the clock on the mantelpiece.

'If it's going to begin,' she said cheerfully, 'it ought to begin soon.

It's just a minute to the half hour. In the meantime, have a glass of sherry.'

Patrick moved with alacrity through the archway. Miss Blacklock went to the table by the archway where the cigarette box was.

'I'd love some sherry,' said Mrs Harmon. 'But what do you mean by *if*?'

'Well,' said Miss Blacklock. 'I'm as much in the dark as you are. I don't know what –'

She stopped and turned her head as the little clock on the mantelpiece began to chime. It had a sweet silvery bell-like tone. Everybody was silent and nobody moved. They all stared at the clock.

It chimed a quarter – and then the half. As the last note died away all the lights went out.

IV

Delighted gasps and feminine squeaks of appreciation were heard in the darkness. 'It's beginning,' cried Mrs Harmon in an ecstasy. Dora Bunner's voice cried out plaintively, 'Oh, I don't like it!' Other voices said, 'How terribly terribly frightening!' 'It gives me the creeps.' 'Archie, where are you?' 'What do I have to *do*?' 'Oh, dear – did I step on your foot? I'm so sorry.'

Then, with a crash the door swung open. A powerful flashlight played rapidly round the room. A man's hoarse nasal voice, reminiscent to all of pleasant afternoons at the cinema directed the company crisply to:

'Stick 'em up!

'Stick 'em up, I tell you!' the voice barked.

Delightedly, hands were raised willingly above heads.

'Isn't it wonderful?' breathed a female voice. 'I'm *so* thrilled.'

And then, unexpectedly, a revolver spoke. It spoke twice. The ping of two bullets shattered the complacency of the room. Suddenly the game was no longer a game. Somebody screamed. . . .

The figure in the doorway whirled suddenly round, it seemed to hesitate, a third shot rang out, it crumpled and then it crashed to the ground. The flashlight dropped and went out.

There was darkness once again. And gently, with a little Victorian protesting moan, the drawing-room door, as was its habit when not propped open, swung gently to and latched with a click.

V

Inside the drawing-room there was a pandemonium. Various voices spoke at once. 'Lights.' 'Can't you find the switch?' 'Who's got a lighter?' 'Oh, I don't like it, I don't *like* it.' 'But those shots were *real*!' 'It was a *real* revolver he had.' 'Was it a burglar?' 'Oh, Archie, I want to get out of here.' 'Please, has somebody got a lighter?'

And then, almost at the same moment, two lighters clicked and burned with small steady flames.

Everybody blinked and peered at each other. Startled face looked into startled face. Against the wall by the archway Miss Blacklock stood with her hand up to her face. The light was too dim to show more than that something dark was trickling over her fingers.

Colonel Easterbrook cleared his throat and rose to the occasion. 'Try the switches, Swettenham,' he ordered.

Edmund, near the door, obediently jerked the switch up and down.

'Off at the main, or a fuse,' said the Colonel. 'Who's making that awful row?'

A female voice had been screaming steadily from somewhere beyond the closed door. It rose now in pitch and with it came the sound of fists hammering on a door.

Dora Bunner, who had been sobbing quietly, called out: 'It's Mitzi. Somebody's murdering Mitzi. . . .'

Patrick muttered: 'No such luck.'

Miss Blacklock said: 'We must get candles. Patrick, will you –'

The Colonel was already opening the door. He and Edmund, their lighters flickering, stepped into the hall. They almost stumbled over a recumbent figure there.

'Seems to have knocked him out,' said the Colonel. 'Where's that woman making that hellish noise?'

'In the dining-room,' said Edmund.

The dining-room was just across the hall. Someone was beating on the panels and howling and screaming.

'She's locked in,' said Edmund, stooping down. He turned the key and Mitzi came out like a bounding tiger.

The dining-room light was still on. Silhouetted against it Mitzi presented a picture of insane terror and continued to scream. A touch of comedy was introduced by the fact that she had been engaged in cleaning silver and was still holding a chamois leather and a large fish slice.

'Be quiet, Mitzi,' said Miss Blacklock.

'Stop it,' said Edmund, and as Mitzi showed no disposition to stop screaming, he leaned forward and gave her a sharp slap on the cheek. Mitzi gasped and hiccupped into silence.

'Get some candles,' said Miss Blacklock. 'In the kitchen cupboard. Patrick, you know where the fusebox is?'

'The passage behind the scullery? Right, I'll see what I can do.'

Miss Blacklock had moved forward into the light thrown from the dining room and Dora Bunner gave a sobbing gasp. Mitzi let out another full-blooded scream.

'The blood, the *blood*!' she gasped. 'You are shot – Miss Blacklock, you bleed to death.'

'Don't be so stupid,' snapped Miss Blacklock. 'I'm hardly hurt at all. It just grazed my ear.'

'But Aunt Letty,' said Julia, 'the blood.'

And indeed Miss Blacklock's white blouse and pearls and her hand were a horrifyingly gory sight.

'Ears always bleed,' said Miss Blacklock. 'I remember fainting in the hairdresser's when I was a child. The man had only just snipped my ear. There seemed to be a basin of blood at once. But we *must* have some light.'

'I get the candles,' said Mitzi.

Julia went with her and they returned with several candles stuck into saucers.

'Now let's have a look at our malefactor,' said the Colonel. 'Hold the candles down low, will you, Swettenham? As many as you can.'

'I'll come the other side,' said Phillipa.

With a steady hand she took a couple of saucers. Colonel Easterbrook knelt down.

The recumbent figure was draped in a roughly-made black cloak with a hood to it. There was a black mask over the face and he wore black cotton gloves. The hood had slipped back disclosing a ruffled fair head.

Colonel Easterbrook turned him over, felt the pulse, the heart . . . then drew away his fingers with an exclamation of distaste, looking down on them. They were sticky and red.

'Shot himself,' he said.

'Is he badly hurt?' asked Miss Blacklock.

'H'm. I'm afraid he's dead . . . May have been suicide – or he may have tripped himself up with that cloak thing and the revolver went off as he fell. If I could see better –'

At that moment, as though by magic, the lights came on again.

With a queer feeling of unreality those inhabitants of Chipping Cleghorn who stood in the hall of Little Paddocks realized that they stood in the presence of violent and sudden death. Colonel Easterbrook's hand was stained red. Blood was still trickling down Miss Blacklock's neck over her blouse and coat, and the grotesquely sprawled figure of the intruder lay at their feet. . . .

Patrick, coming from the dining-room, said, 'It seemed to be just one fuse gone . . .' He stopped.

Colonel Easterbrook tugged at the small black mask.

'Better see who the fellow is,' he said. 'Though I don't suppose it's anyone we know. . . .'

He detached the mask. Necks were craned forward. Mitzi hiccupped and gasped, but the others were very quiet.

'He's quite young,' said Mrs Harmon with a note of pity in her voice.

And suddenly Dora Bunner cried out excitedly:

'Letty, Letty, it's the young man from the Spa Hotel in Medenham Wells. The one who came out here and wanted you to give him money to get back to Switzerland and you refused. I suppose the whole thing was just a pretext – to spy out the house. . . . Oh, dear – he might easily have killed you. . . .'

Miss Blacklock, in command of the situation, said incisively:

'Phillipa, take Bunny into the dining-room and give her a half glass of brandy. Julia dear, just run up to the bathroom and bring me the sticking plaster out of the bathroom cupboard – it's so messy bleeding like a pig. Patrick, will you ring up the police at once?'

4   THE ROYAL SPA HOTEL

George Rydesdale, Chief Constable of Middleshire, was a quiet man. Of medium height, with shrewd eyes under rather bushy brows, he was in the habit of listening rather than talking. Then, in his unemotional voice, he would give a brief order – and the order was obeyed.

He was listening now to Detective-Inspector Dermot Craddock. Craddock was now officially in charge of the case. Rydesdale had recalled him last night from Liverpool where he had been sent to make certain enquiries in connection with another case. Rydesdale had a good opinion of Craddock. He not only had brains and imagination, he had also, which Rydesdale appreciated even more, the self-discipline to go slow, to check and examine each fact, and to keep an open mind until the very end of a case.

'Constable Legg took the call, sir,' Craddock was saying. 'He seems to have acted very well, with promptitude and presence of mind. And it can't have been easy. About a dozen people all trying to talk at once, including one of those Mittel Europas who go off at the deep end at the mere sight of a policeman. Made sure she was going to be locked up, and fairly screamed the place down.'

'Deceased has been identified?'

'Yes, sir. Rudi Scherz. Swiss nationality. Employed at the Royal Spa Hotel, Medenham Wells, as a receptionist. If you agree, sir, I thought I'd take the Royal Spa Hotel first, and go out to Chipping Cleghorn afterwards. Sergeant Fletcher is out there now. He'll see the bus people and then go on to the house.'

Rydesdale nodded approval.

The door opened, and the Chief Constable looked up.

'Come in, Henry,' he said. 'We've got something here that's a little out of the ordinary.'

Sir Henry Clithering, ex-Commissioner of Scotland Yard, came in with slightly raised eyebrows. He was a tall, distinguished-looking elderly man.

'It may appeal to even your blasé palate,' went on Rydesdale.

'I was never blasé,' said Sir Henry indignantly.

'The latest idea,' said Rydesdale, 'is to advertise one's murders beforehand. Show Sir Henry that advertisement, Craddock.'

'The *North Benham News and Chipping Cleghorn Gazette*,' said Sir Henry. 'Quite a mouthful.' He read the half-inch of print indicated by Craddock's finger. 'H'm, yes, somewhat unusual.'

'Any line on who inserted this advertisement?' asked Rydesdale.

'By the description, sir, it was handed in by Rudi Scherz himself – on Wednesday.'

'Nobody questioned it? The person who accepted it, didn't think it odd?'

'The adenoidal blonde who receives the advertisements is quite incapable of thinking, I should say, sir. She just counted the words and took the money.'

'What was the idea?' asked Sir Henry.

'Get a lot of the locals curious,' suggested Rydesdale. 'Get them all together at a particular place at a particular time, then hold them up and relieve them of their spare cash and valuables. As an idea, it's not without originality.'

'What sort of a place is Chipping Cleghorn?' asked Sir Henry.

'A large sprawling picturesque village. Butcher, baker, grocer, quite a good antique shop – two teashops. Self-consciously a beauty spot. Caters for the motoring tourist. Also highly residential. Cottages formerly lived in by agricultural labourers now converted and lived in by elderly spinsters and retired couples. A certain amount of building done round about in Victorian times.'

'I know,' said Sir Henry. 'Nice old Pussies and retired Colonels. Yes, if they noticed that advertisement they'd all come sniffing round at 6.30 to see what was up. Lord, I wish I had my own particular old Pussy here. Wouldn't she like to get her nice ladylike teeth into this. Right up her street it would be.'

'Who's your own particular Pussy, Henry? An aunt?'

'No,' Sir Henry sighed. 'She's no relation.' He said reverently: 'She's just the finest detective God ever made. Natural genius cultivated in a suitable soil.'

He turned upon Craddock.

'Don't you despise the old Pussies in this village of yours, my boy,' he said. 'In case this turns out to be a high powered mystery, which I don't suppose for a moment it will, remember that an elderly unmarried woman who knits and gardens is streets ahead of any detective sergeant. She can tell you what might have happened and what ought to have happened and even what actually *did* happen! And she can tell you *why* it happened!'

'I'll bear that in mind, sir,' said Detective-Inspector Craddock in his most formal manner, and nobody would have guessed that Dermot Eric Craddock was actually Sir Henry's godson and was on easy and intimate terms with his godfather.

Rydesdale gave a quick outline of the case to his friend.

'They'd all turn up at 6.30, I grant you that,' he said. 'But would that Swiss fellow know they would? And another thing, would they be likely to have much loot on them to be worth the taking?'

'A couple of old-fashioned brooches, a string of seed pearls – a little loose change, perhaps a note or two – not more,' said Sir Henry, thoughtfully. 'Did this Miss Blacklock keep much money in the house?'

'She says not, sir. Five pounds odd, I understand.'

'Mere chicken feed,' said Rydesdale.

'What you're getting at,' said Sir Henry, 'is that this fellow liked to playact – it wasn't the loot, it was the fun of playing and acting the hold-up. Cinema stuff? Eh? It's quite possible. How did he manage to shoot himself?'

Rydesdale drew a paper towards him.

'Preliminary medical report. The revolver was discharged at close range – singeing . . . h'm . . . nothing to show whether accident or suicide. Could have been done deliberately, or he could have tripped and fallen and the revolver which he was holding close to him could have gone off. . . . Probably the latter.' He looked at Craddock. 'You'll have to question the witnesses very carefully and make them say exactly what they saw.'

Detective-Inspector Craddock said sadly: 'They'll all have seen something different.'

'It's always interested me,' said Sir Henry, 'what people do see at a moment of intense excitement and nervous strain. What they do see and, even more interesting, what they don't see.'

'Where's the report on the revolver?'

'Foreign make _ (fairly common on the Continent) – Scherz did not hold a permit for it – and did not declare it on coming into England.'

'Bad lad,' said Sir Henry.

'Unsatisfactory character all round. Well, Craddock, go and see what you can find out about him at the Royal Spa Hotel.'

II

At the Royal Spa Hotel, Inspector Craddock was taken straight to the Manager's office.

The Manager, Mr Rowlandson, a tall florid man with a hearty manner, greeted Inspector Craddock with expansive geniality.

'Glad to help you in any way we can, Inspector,' he said. 'Really a most surprising business. I'd never have credited it – never. Scherz seemed a very ordinary, pleasant young chap – not at all my idea of a hold-up man.'

'How long has he been with you, Mr Rowlandson?'

'I was looking that up just before you came. A little over three months. Quite good credentials, the usual permits, etc.'

'And you found him satisfactory?'

Without seeming to do so, Craddock marked the infinitesimal pause before Rowlandson replied.

'Quite satisfactory.'

Craddock made use of a technique he had found efficacious before now.

'No, no, Mr Rowlandson,' he said, gently shaking his head. 'That's not really quite the case, is it?'

'We-ll –' The Manager seemed slightly taken aback.

'Come now, there was something wrong. What was it?'

'That's just it. I don't know.'

'But you *thought* there was something wrong?'

'Well – yes – I did. . . . But I've nothing really to go upon. I shouldn't like my conjectures to be written down and quoted against me.'

Craddock smiled pleasantly.

'I know just what you mean. You needn't worry. But I've got to get some idea of what this fellow, Scherz, was like. You suspected him of – what?'

Rowlandson said, rather reluctantly:

'Well, there was trouble, once or twice, about the bills. Items charged that oughtn't to have been there.'

'You mean you suspected that he charged up certain items which didn't appear in the hotel records, and that he pocketed the difference when the bill was paid?'

'Something like that. . . . Put it at the best, there was gross carelessness on his part. Once or twice quite a big sum was involved. Frankly, I got our accountant to go over his books suspecting that he was – well, a wrong 'un, but though there were various mistakes and a good deal of slipshod method, the actual cash was quite correct. So I came to the conclusion that I must be mistaken.'

'Supposing you hadn't been wrong? Supposing Scherz had been helping himself to various small sums here and there, he could have covered himself, I suppose, by making good the money?'

'Yes, if he *had* the money. But people who help themselves to "small sums," as you put it – are usually hard up for those sums and spend them offhand.'

'So, if he wanted money to replace missing sums, he would have had to get money – by a hold-up or other means?'

'Yes. I wonder if this is his first attempt. . . .'

'Might be. It was certainly a very amateurish one. Is there anyone else he could have got money from? Any women in his life?'

'One of the waitresses in the Grill. Her name's Myrna Harris.'
'I'd better have a talk with her.'

III

Myrna Harris was a pretty girl with a glorious head of red hair and a pert nose.

She was alarmed and wary, and deeply conscious of the indignity of being interviewed by the police.

'I don't know a thing about it, sir. Not a thing,' she protested. 'If I'd known what he was like I'd never have gone out with Rudi at all. Naturally, seeing as he worked in Reception here, I thought he was all right. Naturally I did. What I say is the hotel ought to be more careful when they employ people – especially foreigners. Because you never know where you are with foreigners. I suppose he might have been in with one of these gangs you read about?'

'We think,' said Craddock, 'that he was working quite on his own.'

'Fancy – and him so quiet and respectable. You'd never think. Though there have been things missed – now I come to think of it. A diamond brooch – and a little gold locket, I believe. But I never dreamed that it could have been Rudi.'

'I'm sure you didn't,' said Craddock. 'Anyone might have been taken in. You knew him fairly well?'

'I don't know that I'd say *well*.'

'But you were friendly?'

'Oh, we were friendly – that's all, just friendly. Nothing serious at all. I'm always on my guard with foreigners, anyway. They've often got a way with them, but you never know, do you? Some of those Poles during the war! And even some of the Americans! Never let on they're married men until it's too late. Rudi talked big and all that – but I always took it with a grain of salt.'

Craddock seized on the phrase.

'Talked big, did he? That's very interesting, Miss Harris. I can see you're going to be a lot of help to us. In what way did he talk big?'

'Well, about how rich his people were in Switzerland – and how important. But that didn't go with his being as short of money as he was. He always said that because of the money regulation he couldn't get money from Switzerland over here. That might be, I suppose, but his things weren't expensive. His clothes, I mean. They weren't really class. I think, too, that a lot of the stories he used to tell me were so much hot air. About climbing in the Alps, and saving people's lives on the edge of a glacier. Why, he turned quite giddy just going along the edge of Boulter's Gorge. Alps, indeed!'

'You went out with him a good deal?'

'Yes – well – yes, I did. He had awfully good manners and he knew how to – to look after a girl. The best seats at the pictures, always. And even flowers he'd buy me, sometimes. And he was just a lovely dancer – lovely.'

'Did he mention this Miss Blacklock to you at all?'

'She comes in and lunches here sometimes, doesn't she? And she's stayed here once. No I don't think Rudi ever mentioned her. I didn't know he knew her.'

'Did he mention Chipping Cleghorn?'

He thought a faintly wary look came into Myrna Harris's eyes but he couldn't be sure.

'I don't think so. . . . I think he did once ask about buses – what time they went – but I can't remember if that was Chipping Cleghorn or somewhere else. It wasn't just lately.'

He couldn't get more out of her. Rudi Scherz had seemed just as usual. She hadn't seen him the evening before. She'd no idea – no idea *at all* – she stressed the point, that Rudi Scherz was a crook.

And probably, Craddock thought, that was quite true.

5   MISS BLACKLOCK
AND MISS BUNNER

Little Paddocks was very much as Detective-Inspector Craddock had imagined it to be. He noted ducks and chickens and what had been until lately an attractive herbaceous border, in which a few late Michaelmas daisies showed a last dying splash of purple beauty. The lawn and the paths showed signs of neglect.

Summing up, Detective-Inspector Craddock thought: 'Probably not much money to spend on gardeners – fond of flowers and a good eye for planning and massing a border. House needs painting. Most houses do, nowadays. Pleasant little property.'

As Craddock's car stopped before the front door, Sergeant

Fletcher came round the side of the house. Sergeant Fletcher looked like a guardsman, with an erect military bearing, and was able to impart several different meanings to the one monosyllable: 'Sir.'

'So there you are, Fletcher.'

'Sir,' said Sergeant Fletcher.

'Anything to report?'

'We've finished going over the house, sir. Scherz doesn't seem to have left any fingerprints anywhere. He wore gloves, of course. No signs of any of the doors or windows being forced to effect an entrance. He seems to have come out from Medenham on the bus, arriving here at six o'clock. Side door of the house was locked at 5.30, I understand. Looks as though he must have walked in through the front door. Miss Blacklock states that that door isn't usually locked until the house is shut up for the night. The maid, on the other hand, states that the front door was locked all the afternoon – but she'd say anything. Very temperamental you'll find her. Mittel Europa refugee of some kind.'

'Difficult, is she?'

'Sir!' said Sergeant Fletcher, with intense feeling.

Craddock smiled.

Fletcher resumed his report.

'Lighting system is quite in order everywhere. We haven't spotted yet how he operated the lights. It was just the one circuit went. Drawing-room and hall. Of course, nowadays the wall brackets and lamps wouldn't all be on one fuse – but this is an old-fashioned installation and wiring. Don't see how he could have tampered with the fuse-box because it's out by the scullery and he'd have had to go through the kitchen, so the maid would have seen him.'

'Unless she was in it with him?'

'That's very possible. Both foreigners – and I wouldn't trust her a yard – not a yard.'

Craddock noticed two enormous frightened black eyes peering out of a window by the front door. The face, flattened against the pane, was hardly visible.

'That her there?'

'That's right, sir.'

The face disappeared.

Craddock rang the front-door bell.

After a long wait the door was opened by a good-looking young woman with chestnut hair and a bored expression.

'Detective-Inspector Craddock,' said Craddock.

The young woman gave him a cool stare out of very attractive hazel eyes and said:

'Come in. Miss Blacklock is expecting you.'

The hall, Craddock noted, was long and narrow and seemed almost incredibly full of doors.

The young woman threw open a door on the left, and said: 'Inspector Craddock, Aunt Letty. Mitzi wouldn't go to the door. She's shut herself up in the kitchen and she's making the most marvellous moaning noises. I shouldn't think we'd get *any* lunch.'

She added in an explanatory manner to Craddock: 'She doesn't like the police,' and withdrew, shutting the door behind her.

Craddock advanced to meet the owner of Little Paddocks.

He saw a tall active-looking woman of about sixty. Her grey hair had a slight natural wave and made a distinguished setting for an intelligent, resolute face. She had keen grey eyes and a square determined chin. There was a surgical dressing on her left ear. She wore no make-up and was plainly dressed in a well-cut tweed coat and skirt and pullover. Round the neck of the latter she wore, rather unexpectedly, a set of old-fashioned cameos – a Victorian touch which seemed to hint at a sentimental streak not otherwise apparent.

Close beside her, with an eager round face and untidy hair escaping from a hair net, was a woman of about the same age whom Craddock had no difficulty in recognizing as the 'Dora Bunner – companion' of Constable Legg's notes – to which the latter had added an off-the-record commentary of 'Scatty!'

Miss Blacklock spoke in a pleasant well-bred voice.

'Good morning, Inspector Craddock. This is my friend, Miss Bunner, who helps me run the house. Won't you sit down? You won't smoke, I suppose?'

'Not on duty, I'm afraid, Miss Blacklock.'

'What a shame!'

Craddock's eyes took in the room with a quick, practised glance. Typical Victorian double drawing-room. Two long windows in this room, built out bay window in the other ... chairs ... sofa ... centre table with a big bowl of chrysanthemums – another bowl in window – all fresh and pleasant without much originality. The only incongruous note was a small silver vase with dead violets in it on a table near the archway into the further room. Since he could not imagine Miss Blacklock tolerating dead flowers in a room, he imagined it to be the only indication that something out of the way had occurred to distract the routine of a well-run household.

He said:

'I take it, Miss Blacklock, that this is the room in which the – incident occurred?'

'Yes.'

'And you should have seen it last night,' Miss Bunner exclaimed. 'Such a *mess*. Two little tables knocked over, and the leg off one – people barging about in the dark – and someone put down a lighted cigarette and burnt one of the best bits of furniture. People – young people especially, are so careless about these things. . . . Luckily none of the china got broken –'

Miss Blacklock interrupted gently but firmly:

'Dora, all these things, vexatious as they may be, are only trifles. It will be best, I think, if we just answer Inspector Craddock's questions.'

'Thank you, Miss Blacklock. I shall come to what happened last night, presently. First of all I want you to tell me when you first saw the dead man – Rudi Scherz.'

'Rudi Scherz?' Miss Blacklock looked slightly surprised. 'Is that his name? Somehow, I thought . . . Oh, well, it doesn't matter. My first encounter with him was when I was in Medenham Spa for a day's shopping about – let me see, about three weeks ago. We – Miss Bunner and I – were having lunch at the Royal Spa Hotel. As we were just leaving after lunch, I heard my name spoken. It was this young man. He said: "It is Miss Blacklock, is it not?" And went on to say that perhaps I did not remember him, but that he was the son of the proprietor of the Hotel des Alpes at Montreux where my sister and I had stayed for nearly a year during the war.'

'The Hotel des Alpes, Montreux,' noted Craddock. 'And did you remember him, Miss Blacklock?'

'No, I didn't. Actually I had no recollection of ever having seen him before. These boys at hotel reception desks all look exactly alike. We had had a very pleasant time at Montreux and the proprietor there had been extremely obliging, so I tried to be as civil as possible and said I hoped he was enjoying being in England, and he said, yes, that his father had sent him over for six months to learn the hotel business. It all seemed quite natural.'

'And your next encounter?'

'About – yes, it must have been ten days ago, he suddenly turned up here. I was very surprised to see him. He apologized for troubling me, but said I was the only person he knew in England. He told me that he urgently needed money to return to Switzerland as his mother was dangerously ill.'

'But Letty didn't give it to him,' Miss Bunner put in breathlessly.

'It was a thoroughly fishy story,' said Miss Blacklock, with vigour. 'I made up my mind that he was definitely a wrong 'un. That story about wanting the money to return to Switzerland was *nonsense*. His father could easily have wired for arrangements to have been made in this country. These hotel people are all in with each other. I suspected that he'd been embezzling money or something of that kind.' She paused and said dryly: 'In case you think I'm hardhearted, I was secretary for many years to a big financier and one becomes wary about appeals for money. I know simply all the hard luck stories there are.

'The only thing that did surprise me,' she added thoughtfully, 'was that he gave in so easily. He went away at once without any more argument. It's as though he had never expected to get the money.'

'Do you think now, looking back on it, that his coming was really by way of a pretext to spy out the land?'

Miss Blacklock nodded her head vigorously.

'That's exactly what I do think – now. He made certain remarks as I let him out – about the rooms. He said, "You have a very nice dining-room" (which of course it isn't – it's a horrid dark little room) just as an excuse to look inside. And then he sprang forward and unfastened the front door, said, "Let me." I think now he wanted to have a look at the fastening. Actually, like most people round here, we never lock the front door until it gets dark. *Anyone* could walk in.'

'And the side door? There is a side door to the garden, I understand?'

'Yes. I went out through it to shut up the ducks not long before the people arrived.'

'Was it locked when you went out?'

Miss Blacklock frowned.

'I can't remember. . . . I think so. I certainly locked it when I came in.'

'That would be about quarter-past six?'

'Somewhere about then.'

'And the front door?'

'That's not usually locked until later.'

'Then Scherz could have walked in quite easily that way. Or he could have slipped in whilst you were out shutting up the ducks. He'd already spied out the lie of the land and had probably noted various places of concealment – cupboards, etc. Yes, that all seems quite clear.'

'I beg your pardon, it isn't at all clear,' said Miss Blacklock. 'Why on earth should anyone take all that elaborate trouble to come and burgle this house and stage that silly sort of hold-up?'

'Do you keep much money in the house, Miss Blacklock?'

'About five pounds in that desk there, and perhaps a pound or two in my purse.'

'Jewellery?'

'A couple of rings and brooches and the cameos I'm wearing. You must agree with me, Inspector, that the whole thing's absurd.'

'It wasn't burglary at all,' cried Miss Bunner. 'I've told you so, Letty, all along. It was *revenge*! Because you wouldn't give him that money! He deliberately shot at you – twice.'

'Ah,' said Craddock. 'We'll come now to last night. What happened exactly, Miss Blacklock? Tell me in your own words as nearly as you can remember.'

Miss Blacklock reflected a moment.

'The clock struck,' she said. 'The one on the mantelpiece. I remember saying that if anything were going to happen it would have to happen soon. And then the clock struck. We all listened to it without saying anything. It chimes, you know. It chimed the two quarters and then, quite suddenly, the lights went out.'

'What lights were on?'

'The wall brackets in here and the further room. The standard lamp and the two small reading lamps weren't on.'

'Was there a flash first, or a noise when the lights went out?'

'I don't think so.'

'I'm sure there *was* a flash,' said Dora Bunner. '*And* a crackling noise. Dangerous!'

'And then, Miss Blacklock?'

'The door opened –'

'Which door? There are two in the room.'

'Oh, this door in here. The one in the other room doesn't open. It's a dummy. The door opened and there he was – a masked man with a revolver. It just seemed too fantastic for words, but of course at the time I just thought it was a silly joke. He said something – I forget what –'

'Hands up or I shoot!' supplied Miss Bunner, dramatically.

'Something like that,' said Miss Blacklock, rather doubtfully.

'And you all put your hands up?'

'Oh, *yes*,' said Miss Bunner. 'We all did. I mean, it was *part* of it.'

'*I* didn't,' said Miss Blacklock, crisply. 'It seemed so utterly silly. And I was annoyed by the whole thing.'

'And then?'

'The flashlight was right in my eyes. It dazzled me. And then, quite incredibly, I heard a bullet whizz past me and hit the wall by my head. Somebody shrieked and then I felt a burning pain in my ear and heard the second report.'

'It was *terrifying*,' put in Miss Bunner.

'And what happened next, Miss Blacklock?'

'It's difficult to say – I was so staggered by the pain and the surprise. The – the figure turned away and seemed to stumble and then there was another shot and his torch went out and everybody began pushing and calling out. All banging into each other.'

'Where were you standing, Miss Blacklock?'

'She was over by the table. She'd got that vase of violets in her hand,' said Miss Bunner breathlessly.

'I was over here,' Miss Blacklock went over to the small table by the archway. 'Actually it was the cigarette-box I'd got in my hand.'

Inspector Craddock examined the wall behind her. The two bullet holes showed plainly. The bullets themselves had been extracted and had been sent for comparison with the revolver.

He said quietly:

'You had a very near escape, Miss Blacklock.'

'He *did* shoot at her,' said Miss Bunner. 'Deliberately *at* her! I saw him. He turned the flash round on everybody until he found her and then he held it right at her and just fired at *her*. He meant to kill *you*, Letty.'

'Dora dear, you've just got that into your head from mulling the whole thing over and over.'

'He shot at *you*,' repeated Dora stubbornly. 'He meant to shoot you and when he'd missed, he shot himself. I'm *certain* that's the way it was!'

'I don't think he meant to shoot himself for a minute,' said Miss Blacklock. 'He wasn't the kind of man who shoots himself.'

'You tell me, Miss Blacklock, that until the revolver was fired you thought the whole business was a joke?'

'Naturally. What else could I think it was?'

'Who do you think was the author of this joke?'

'You thought Patrick had done it at first,' Dora Bunner reminded her.

'Patrick?' asked the Inspector sharply.

'My young cousin, Patrick Simmons,' Miss Blacklock continued sharply, annoyed with her friend. 'It did occur to me when I saw this advertisement that it might be some attempt at humour on his part, but he denied it absolutely.'

'And then you were worried, Letty,' said Miss Bunner. 'You *were* worried, although you pretended not to be. And you were quite right to be worried. It said a murder is announced – and it *was* announced – *your* murder! And if the man hadn't missed, you *would* have been murdered. And then where should we all be?'

Dora Bunner was trembling as she spoke. Her face was puckered up and she looked as though she were going to cry.

Miss Blacklock patted her on the shoulder.

'It's all right, Dora dear – don't get excited. It's so bad for you. Everything's quite all right. We've had a nasty experience, but it's over now.' She added, 'You must pull yourself together for my sake, Dora. I rely on you, you know, to keep the house going. Isn't it the day for the laundry to come?'

'Oh, dear me, Letty, how *fortunate* you reminded me! I wonder if they'll return that missing pillowcase. I must make a note in the book about it. I'll go and see to it at once.'

'And take those violets away,' said Miss Blacklock. 'There's nothing I hate more than dead flowers.'

'What a pity. I picked them fresh yesterday. They haven't lasted at all – oh, dear, I must have forgotten to put any water in the vase. Fancy that! I'm always forgetting things. Now I must go and see about the laundry. They might be here any moment.'

She bustled away, looking quite happy again.

'She's not very strong,' said Miss Blacklock, 'and excitements are bad for her. Is there anything more you want to know, Inspector?'

'I just want to know exactly how many people make up your household here and something about them.'

'Yes, well in addition to myself and Dora Bunner, I have two young cousins living here at present, Patrick and Julia Simmons.'

'Cousins? Not a nephew and niece?'

'No. They call me Aunt Letty, but actually they are distant cousins. Their mother was my second cousin.'

'Have they always made their home with you?'

'Oh, dear no, only for the last two months. They lived in the South of France before the war. Patrick went into the Navy and Julia, I believe, was in one of the Ministries. She was at Llandudno. When the war was over their mother wrote and asked me if they could possibly come to me as paying guests – Julia is training as a dispenser in Milchester General Hospital, Patrick is studying for an engineering degree at Milchester University. Milchester, as you know, is only fifty minutes by bus, and I was very glad to have them here. This house is really too large for me. They pay a small sum for board and lodging and it all works out very well.' She added with a smile, 'I like having somebody young about the place.'

'Then there is a Mrs Haymes, I believe?'

'Yes. She works as an assistant gardener at Dayas Hall, Mrs Lucas's place. The cottage there is occupied by the old gardener and his wife and Mrs Lucas asked if I could billet her here. She's a very nice girl. Her husband was killed in Italy, and she has a boy of eight who is at a prep school and whom I have arranged to have here in the holidays.'

'And by way of domestic help?'

'A jobbing gardener comes in on Tuesdays and Fridays. A Mrs Huggins from the village comes up five mornings a week and I have a foreign refugee with a most unpronounceable name as a kind of lady cook help. You will find Mitzi rather difficult, I'm afraid. She has a kind of persecution mania.'

Craddock nodded. He was conscious in his own mind of yet another of Constable Legg's invaluable commentaries. Having appended the word 'Scatty' to Dora Bunner, and 'All right' to Letitia Blacklock, he had embellished Mitzi's record with the one word 'Liar'.

As though she had read his mind Miss Blacklock said:

'Please don't be too prejudiced against the poor thing because she's a liar. I do really believe that, like so many liars, there is a real substratum of truth behind her lies. I mean that though, to take an instance, her atrocity stories have grown and grown until every kind of unpleasant story that has ever appeared in print has happened to her or her relations personally, she did have a bad shock initially and did see one, at least, of her relations killed. I think a lot of these displaced persons feel, perhaps justly, that their claim to our notice and sympathy lies in their atrocity value and so they exaggerate and invent.'

She added: 'Quite frankly, Mitzi is a maddening person. She exasperates and infuriates us all, she is suspicious and sulky, is perpetually having "feelings" and thinking herself insulted. But in spite of it all, I really am sorry for her.' She smiled. 'And also, when she wants to, she can cook very nicely.'

'I'll try not to ruffle her more than I can help,' said Craddock soothingly. 'Was that Miss Julia Simmons who opened the door to me?'

'Yes. Would you like to see her now? Patrick has gone out. Phillipa Haymes you will find working at Dayas Hall.'

'Thank you, Miss Blacklock. I'd like to see Miss Simmons now if I may.'

6   JULIA, MITZI AND PATRICK

Julia, when she came into the room, and sat down in the chair vacated by Letitia Blacklock, had an air of composure that Craddock for some reason found annoying. She fixed a limpid gaze on him and waited for his questions.

Miss Blacklock had tactfully left the room.

'Please tell me about last night, Miss Simmons.'

'Last night?' murmured Julia with a blank stare. 'Oh, we all slept like logs. Reaction, I suppose.'

'I mean last night from six o'clock onwards.'

'Oh, I see. Well, a lot of tiresome people came –'

'They were?'

She gave him another limpid stare.

'Don't you know all this already?'

'I'm asking the questions, Miss Simmons,' said Craddock pleasantly.

'My mistake. I always find repetitions so dreary. Apparently you don't. . . . Well, there was Colonel and Mrs Easterbrook, Miss Hinchliffe and Miss Murgatroyd, Mrs Swettenham and Edmund Swettenham, and Mrs Harmon, the Vicar's wife. They arrived in that order, and if you want to know what they said – they all said the same things in turn. "I see you've got your central heating on" and "What *lovely* chrysanthemums!"'

Craddock bit his lip. The mimicry was good.

'The exception was Mrs Harmon. She's rather a pet. She came in with her hat falling off and her shoelaces untied and she asked straight out when the murder was going to happen? It embarrassed everybody because they'd all been pretending they'd dropped in by chance. Aunt Letty said in her dry way that it was due to happen quite soon. And then that clock chimed and just as it finished, the lights went out, the door was flung open and a masked figure said, "Stick 'em up, guys," or something like that. It was exactly like a bad film. Really quite ridiculous. And then he fired two shots at Aunt Letty and suddenly it wasn't ridiculous any more.'

'Where was everybody when this happened?'

'When the lights went out? Well, just standing about, you know. Mrs Harmon was sitting on the sofa – Hinch (that's Miss Hinchliffe) had taken up a manly stance in front of the fireplace.'

'You were all in this room, or the far room?'

'Mostly, I think, in this room. Patrick had gone into the other to get the sherry. I think Colonel Easterbrook went after him, but I don't really know. We were – well – as I said, just standing about.'

'Where were you yourself?'

'I think I was over by the window. Aunt Letty went to get the cigarettes.'

'On that table by the archway?'

'Yes – and then the lights went out and the bad film started.'

'The man had a powerful torch. What did he do with it?'

'Well, he shone it on us. Horribly dazzling. It just made you blink.'

'I want you to answer this very carefully, Miss Simmons. Did he hold the torch steady, or did he move it about?'

Julia considered. Her manner was now definitely less weary.

'He moved it,' she said slowly. 'Like a spotlight in a dance hall. It was full in my eyes and then it went on round the room and then the shots came. Two shots.'

'And then?'

'He whirled round – and Mitzi began to scream like a siren from somewhere and his torch went out and there was another shot. And then the door closed (it does, you know, slowly, with a whining noise – quite uncanny) and there we were all in the dark, not knowing what to do, and poor Bunny squealing like a rabbit and Mitzi going all out across the hall.'

'Would it be your opinion that the man shot himself deliberately, or do you think he stumbled and the revolver went off accidentally?'

'I haven't the faintest idea. The whole thing was so stagey. Actually I thought it was still some silly joke – until I saw the blood from Letty's ear. But even if you were actually going to fire a revolver to make the thing more real, you'd be careful to fire it well above someone's head, wouldn't you?'

'You would indeed. Do you think he could see clearly who he was firing at? I mean, was Miss Blacklock clearly outlined in the light of the torch?'

'I've no idea. I wasn't looking at her. I was looking at the man.'

'What I'm getting at is – do you think the man was deliberately aiming at her – at her in particular, I mean?'

Julia seemed a little startled by the idea.

'You mean deliberately picking on Aunt Letty? Oh, I shouldn't think so. . . . After all, if he wanted to take a pot shot at Aunt Letty, there would be heaps of more suitable opportunities. There would be no point in collecting all the friends and neighbours just to make it more difficult. He could have shot her from behind a hedge in the good old Irish fashion any day of the week, and probably got away with it.'

And that, thought Craddock, was a very complete reply to Dora Bunner's suggestion of a deliberate attack on Letitia Blacklock.

He said with a sigh, 'Thank you, Miss Simmons. I'd better go and see Mitzi now.'

'Mind her fingernails,' warned Julia. 'She's a tartar!'

II

Craddock, with Fletcher in attendance, found Mitzi in the kitchen. She was rolling pastry and looked up suspiciously as he entered.

Her black hair hung over her eyes; she looked sullen, and the purple jumper and brilliant green skirt she wore were not becoming to her pasty complexion.

'What do you come in my kitchen for, Mr Policeman? You are police, yes? Always, always there is persecution – ah! I should be used to it by now. They say it is different here in England, but no, it is just the same. You come to torture me, yes, to make me say things, but I shall say *nothing*. You will tear off my fingernails, and put lighted matches on my skin – oh, yes, and worse than that. But I will not speak, do you hear? I shall say nothing – nothing at all. And you will send me away to a concentration camp, and I shall not care.'

Craddock looked at her thoughtfully, selecting what was likely to be the best method of attack. Finally he sighed and said:

'OK then, get your hat and coat.'

'What is that you say?' Mitzi looked startled.

'Get your hat and coat and come along. I haven't got my nail-pulling apparatus and the rest of the bag of tricks with me. We keep all that down at the station. Got the handcuffs handy, Fletcher?'

'Sir!' said Sergeant Fletcher with appreciation.

'But I do not want to come,' screeched Mitzi, backing away from him.

'Then you'll answer civil questions civilly. If you like, you can have a solicitor present.'

'A lawyer? I do not like a lawyer. I do not want a lawyer.'

She put the rolling pin down, dusted her hands on a cloth and sat down.

'What do you want to know?' she asked sulkily.

'I want your account of what happened here last night.'

'You know very well what happened.'

'I want your account of it.'

'I tried to go away. Did she tell you that? When I saw that in the paper saying about murder. I wanted to go away. She would not let me. She is very hard – not at all sympathetic. She made me stay. But I knew – *I* knew what would happen. *I* knew I should be murdered.'

'Well, you weren't murdered, were you?'

'No,' admitted Mitzi grudgingly.

'Come now, tell me what happened.'

'I was nervous. Oh, I was nervous. All that evening. I hear things. People moving about. Once I think someone is in the hall moving stealthily – but it is only that Mrs Haymes coming in through the side door (so as not to dirty the front steps, *she* says. Much *she* cares!). She is a Nazi herself, that one, with her fair hair and her blue eyes, so superior and looking at me and thinking that I – I am only dirt –'

'Never mind Mrs Haymes.'

'Who does she think *she* is? Has she had expensive university education like I have? Has she a degree in Economics? No, she is just a paid labourer. She digs and mows grass and is paid so much every Saturday. Who is she to call herself a lady?'

'Never mind Mrs Haymes, I said. Go on.'

'I take the sherry and the glasses, and the little pastries that I have made so nice into the drawing room. Then the bell rings and I answer the door. Again and again I answer the door. It is degrading – but I do it. And then I go back into the pantry and I start to polish the silver, and I think it will be very handy, that, because if someone comes to kill me, I have there close at hand the big carving knife, all sharp.'

'Very foresighted of you.'

'And then, suddenly – I hear shots. I think: "It has come – it is happening." I run through the dining-room (the other door – it will not open) I stand a moment to listen and then there comes another shot and a big thud, out there in the hall, and I turn the door handle, but it is locked outside. I am shut in there like a rat in a trap. And I go mad with fear. I scream and I scream and I beat upon the door. And at last – at last – they turn the key and let me out. And then I bring candles, many many candles – and the lights go on, and I see blood – blood! Ach, Gott in Himmel, the blood! It is not the first time I have seen blood. My little brother – I see him killed before my eyes – I see blood in the street – people shot, dying – I –'

'Yes,' said Inspector Craddock. 'Thank you very much.'

'And now,' said Mitzi dramatically, 'you can arrest me and take me to prison!'

'Not today,' said Inspector Craddock.

III

As Craddock and Fletcher went through the hall to the front door it was flung open and a tall handsome young man almost collided with them.

'Sleuths, as I live,' cried the young man.

'Mr Patrick Simmons?'

'Quite right, Inspector. You're the Inspector, aren't you, and the other's the Sergeant?'

'You are quite right, Mr Simmons. Can I have a word with you, please?'

'I am innocent, Inspector. I swear I am innocent.'

'Now then, Mr Simmons, don't play the fool. I've a good many other people to see and I don't want to waste time. What's this room? Can we go in here?'

'It's the so-called study – but nobody studies.'

'I was told that you were studying?' said Craddock.

'I found I couldn't concentrate on mathematics, so I came home.'

In a businesslike manner Inspector Craddock demanded full name, age, details of war service.

'And now, Mr Simmons, will you describe what happened last night?'

'We killed the fatted calf, Inspector. That is, Mitzi set her hand to making savoury pastries, Aunt Letty opened a new bottle of sherry –'

Craddock interrupted.

'A new bottle? Was there an old one?'

'Yes. Half full. But Aunt Letty didn't seem to fancy it.'

'Was she nervous, then?'

'Oh, not really. She's extremely sensible. It was old Bunny, I think, who had put the wind up her – prophesying disaster all day.'

'Miss Bunner was definitely apprehensive, then?'

'Oh, yes, she enjoyed herself thoroughly.'

'She took the advertisement seriously?'

'It scared her into fits.'

'Miss Blacklock seems to have thought, when she first read that advertisement, that you had had something to do with it. Why was that?'

'Ah, sure, I get blamed for everything round here!'

'You *didn't* have anything to do with it, did you, Mr Simmons?'

'Me? Never in the world.'

'Had you ever seen or spoken to this Rudi Scherz?'

'Never seen him in my life.'

'It was the kind of joke you might have played, though?'

'Who's been telling you that? Just because I once made Bunny an apple-pie bed – and sent Mitzi a postcard saying the Gestapo was on her track –'

'Just give me your account of what happened.'

'I'd just gone into the small drawing-room to fetch the drinks when, Hey Presto, the lights went out. I turned round and there's a fellow standing in the doorway saying, "Stick your hands up," and everybody gasping and squealing, and just when I'm thinking – can I rush him? he starts firing a revolver and then crash down he goes and his torch goes out and we're in the dark again, and Colonel Easterbrook starts shouting orders in his barrack-room voice. "Lights," he says, and will my lighter go on? No, it won't as is the way of those cussed inventions.'

'Did it seem to you that the intruder was definitely aiming at Miss Blacklock?'

'Ah, how could I tell? I should say he just loosed off his revolver for the fun of the thing – and then found, maybe, he'd gone too far.'

'And shot himself?'

'It could be. When I saw the face of him, he looked like the kind of little pasty thief who might easily lose his nerve.'

'And you're sure you had never seen him before?'

'Never.'

'Thank you, Mr Simmons. I shall want to interview the other people who were here last night. Which would be the best order in which to take them?'

'Well, our Phillipa – Mrs Haymes – works at Dayas Hall. The gates of it are nearly opposite this gate. After that, the Swettenhams are the nearest. Anyone will tell you.'

7   AMONG THOSE PRESENT

Dayas Hall had certainly suffered during the war years. Couch grass grew enthusiastically over what had once been an asparagus bed, as evidenced by a few waving tufts of asparagus foliage. Groundsel, bindweed and other garden pests showed every sign of vigorous growth.

A portion of the kitchen garden bore evidence of having been reduced to discipline and here Craddock found a sour-looking old man leaning pensively on a spade.

'It's Mrs 'Aymes you want? I couldn't say where you'd find 'er. 'As 'er own ideas, she 'as, about what she'll do. Not one to take advice. I could show her – show 'er willing – but what's the good, won't listen these young ladies won't! Think they know everything because they've put on breeches and gone for a ride on a tractor. But it's *gardening* that's needed here. And that isn't learned in a day. *Gardening*, that's what this place needs.'

'It looks as though it does,' said Craddock.

The old man chose to take this remark as an aspersion.

'Now look here, mister, what do you suppose I can do with a place this size? Three men and a boy, that's what it used to 'ave. And that's what it wants. There's not many men could put in the word on it that I do. 'Ere sometimes I am till eight o'clock at night. Eight o'clock.'

'What do you work by? An oil lamp?'

'Naterally I don't mean this time o' year. Naterally. *Summer* evenings I'm talking about.'

'Oh,' said Craddock, 'I'd better go and look for Mrs Haymes.'

The rustic displayed some interest.

'What are you wanting 'er for? Police, aren't you? She been in trouble, or is it the do there was up to Little Paddocks? Masked men bursting in and holding up a roomful of people with a revolver. An' that sort of thing wouldn't 'ave 'appened afore the war. Deserters, that's what it is. Desperate men roaming the countryside. Why don't the military round 'em up?'

'I've no idea,' said Craddock. 'I suppose this hold-up caused a lot of talk?'

'That it did. What's us coming to? That's what Ned Barker said. Comes of going to the pictures so much, he said. But Tom Riley he says it comes of letting these furriners run about loose. And depend on it, he says, that girl as cooks up there for Miss Blacklock and 'as such a nasty temper – *she's* in it, he said. She's a communist or worse, he says, and we don't like that sort 'ere. And Marlene, who's behind the bar, you understand, she will 'ave it that there must be something very valuable up at Miss Blacklock's. Not that you'd think it, she says, for I'm sure Miss Blacklock goes about as plain as plain, except for them great rows of false pearls she wears. And then she says – Supposin' as them pearls is *real*, and Florrie (what's old Bellamy's daughter) *she* says, "Nonsense," she says – "*noovo ar* – that's what they are – costume jewellery," she says. Costume jewellery – that's a fine way of labelling a string of false pearls. Roman pearls, the gentry used to call 'em once – and Parisian diamonds – my wife was a lady's maid and I know. But what does it all mean – just glass! I suppose it's "costume jewellery" that young Miss Simmons wears – gold ivy leaves and dogs and such like. 'Tisn't often you see a real bit of gold nowadays – even wedding rings they make of this grey plattinghum stuff. Shabby, I call it – for all that it costs the earth.'

Old Ashe paused for breath and then continued:

'"Miss Blacklock don't keep much money in the 'ouse, that I do know," says Jim Huggins, speaking up. He should know, for it's his wife as goes up and does for 'em at Little Paddocks, and she's a woman as knows most of what's going on. Nosey, if you take me.'

'Did he say what Mrs Huggins' view was?'

'That Mitzi's mixed up in it, that's what she thinks. Awful temper she 'as, and the airs she gives herself! Called Mrs Huggins a working woman to her face the other morning.'

Craddock stood a moment, checking over in his orderly mind the substance of the old gardener's remarks. It gave him a good cross-section of rural opinion in Chipping Cleghorn, but he didn't think there was anything to help him in his task. He turned away and the old man called after him grudgingly:

'Maybe you'd find her in the apple orchard. She's younger than I am for getting the apples down.'

And sure enough in the apple orchard Craddock found Phillipa Haymes. His first view was a pair of nice legs encased in breeches sliding easily down the trunk of a tree. Then Phillipa, her face flushed, her fair hair ruffled by the branches, stood looking at him in a startled fashion.

'Make a good Rosalind,' Craddock thought automatically, for Detective-Inspector Craddock was a Shakespeare enthusiast and had played the part of the melancholy Jaques with great success in a performance of *As You Like It* for the police orphanage.

A moment later he amended his view. Phillipa Haymes was too wooden for Rosalind, her fairness and her impassivity were intensely English, but English of the twentieth rather than of the sixteenth century. Well-bred, unemotional English, without a sparkle of mischief.

'Good morning, Mrs Haymes. I'm sorry if I startled you. I'm Detective-Inspector Craddock of the Middleshire Police. I wanted to have a word with you.'

'About last night?'

'Yes.'

'Will it take long? Shall we —'

She looked about her rather doubtfully.

Craddock indicated a fallen tree trunk.

'Rather informal,' he said pleasantly, 'but I don't want to interrupt your work longer than necessary.'

'Thank you.'

'It's just for the record. You came in from work at what time last night?'

'At about half-past five. I'd stayed about twenty minutes later in order to finish some watering in the greenhouse.'

'You came in by which door?'

'The side door. One cuts across by the ducks and the henhouse from the drive. It saves you going round, and besides it avoids dirtying up the front porch. I'm in rather a mucky state sometimes.'

'You always come in that way?'

'Yes.'

'The door was unlocked?'

'Yes. During the summer it's usually wide open. This time of the year it's shut but not locked. We all go out and in a good deal that way. I locked it when I came in.'

'Do you always do that?'

'I've been doing it for the last week. You see, it gets dark at six. Miss Blacklock goes out to shut up the ducks and the hens sometime in the evening, but she very often goes out through the kitchen door.'

'And you are quite sure you did lock the side door this time?'

'I really am quite sure about that.'

'Quite so, Mrs Haymes. And what did you do when you came in?'

'Kicked off my muddy footwear and went upstairs and had a bath and changed. Then I came down and found that a kind of party was in progress. I hadn't known anything about this funny advertisement until then.'

'Now please describe just what occurred when the hold-up happened.'

'Well, the lights went out suddenly –'

'Where were you?'

'By the mantelpiece. I was searching for my lighter which I thought I had put down there. The lights went out – and everybody giggled. Then the door was flung open and this man shone a torch on us and flourished a revolver and told us to put our hands up.'

'Which you proceeded to do?'

'Well, I didn't, actually. I thought it was just fun, and I was tired and I didn't think I needed really to put them up.'

'In fact you were bored by the whole thing?'

'I was, rather. And then the revolver went off. The shots sounded deafening and I was really frightened. The torch went whirling round and dropped and went out, and then Mitzi started screaming. It was just like a pig being killed.'

'Did you find the torch very dazzling?'

'No, not particularly. It was quite a strong one, though. It lit up Miss Bunner for a moment and she looked quite like a turnip ghost – you know, all white and staring with her mouth open and her eyes starting out of her head.'

'The man moved the torch?'

'Oh, yes, he played it all round the room.'

'As though he were looking for someone?'

'Not particularly, I should say.'

'And after that, Mrs Haymes?'

Phillipa Haymes frowned.

'Oh, it was all a terrible muddle and confusion. Edmund Swettenham and Patrick Simmons switched on their lights and they went out into the hall and we followed, and someone opened the dining room door – the lights hadn't fused there – and Edmund Swettenham gave Mitzi a terrific slap on the cheek and brought her out of her screaming fit, and after that it wasn't so bad.'

'You saw the body of the dead man?'

'Yes.'

'Was he known to you? Had you ever seen him before?'

'Never.'

'Have you any opinion as to whether his death was accidental, or do you think he shot himself deliberately?'

'I haven't the faintest idea.'

'You didn't see him when he came to the house previously?'

'No. I believe it was in the middle of the morning and I shouldn't have been there. I'm out all day.'

'Thank you, Mrs Haymes. One thing more. You haven't any valuable jewellery? Rings, bracelets, anything of that kind?'

Phillipa shook her head.

'My engagement ring – a couple of brooches.'

'And as far as you know, there was nothing of particular value in the house?'

'No. I mean there is some quite nice silver – but nothing out of the ordinary.'

'Thank you, Mrs Haymes.'

II

As Craddock retraced his steps through the kitchen garden he came face to face with a large red-faced lady, carefully corseted.

'Good morning,' she said belligerently. 'What do you want here?'

'Mrs Lucas? I am Detective-Inspector Craddock.'

'Oh, that's who you are. I beg your pardon. I don't like strangers forcing their way into my garden wasting the gardeners' time. But I quite understand you have to do your duty.'

'Quite so.'

'May I ask if we are to expect a repetition of that outrage last night at Miss Blacklock's? Is it a gang?'

'We are satisfied, Mrs Lucas, that it was *not* the work of a gang.'

'There are far too many robberies nowadays. The police are getting slack.' Craddock did not reply. 'I suppose you've been talking to Phillipa Haymes?'

'I wanted her account as an eyewitness.'

'You couldn't have waited until one o'clock, I suppose? After all, it would be fairer to question her in *her* time, rather than in *mine* . . .'

'I'm anxious to get back to headquarters.'

'Not that one expects consideration nowadays. Or a decent day's work. On duty late, half an hour's pottering. A break for elevenses at ten o'clock. No work done at all the moment the rain starts. When you want the lawn mown there's always something wrong with the mower. And off duty five or ten minutes before the proper time.'

'I understood from Mrs Haymes that she left here at twenty minutes past five yesterday instead of five o'clock.'

'Oh, I dare say she did. Give her her due, Mrs Haymes is quite keen on her work, though there have been days when I have come out here and not been able to find her anywhere. She is a lady by birth, of course, and one feels it's one's duty to do something for these poor young war widows. Not that it isn't very inconvenient. Those long school holidays and the arrangement is that she has extra time off then. I told her that there are really excellent camps nowadays where children can be sent and where they have a delightful time and enjoy it far more than wandering about with their parents. They need practically not come home at all in the summer holidays.'

'But Mrs Haymes didn't take kindly to that idea?'

'She's as obstinate as a mule, that girl. Just the time of year when I want the tennis court mowed and marked nearly every day. Old Ashe gets the lines crooked. But *my* convenience is never considered!'

'I presume Mrs Haymes takes a smaller salary than is usual.'

'Naturally. What else could she expect?'

'Nothing, I'm sure,' said Craddock. 'Good morning, Mrs Lucas.'

III

'It was dreadful,' said Mrs Swettenham happily. 'Quite – quite – dreadful, and what I say is that they ought to be far more careful what advertisements they accept at the *Gazette* office. At the time, when I read it, I thought it was very odd. I said so, didn't I, Edmund?'

'Do you remember just what you were doing when the lights went out, Mrs Swettenham?' asked the Inspector.

'How that reminds me of my old Nannie! *Where was Moses when the light went out?* The answer, of course, was "In the Dark". Just like us yesterday evening. All standing about and wondering what was going to happen. And then, you know, the *thrill* when it suddenly went pitch black. And the door opening – just a dim figure standing there with a revolver and that blinding light and a menacing voice saying "Your money or your life!" Oh, I've never enjoyed anything so much. And then a minute later, of course, it was all *dreadful. Real* bullets, just *whistling* past our ears! It must have been just like the commandos in the war.'

'Whereabouts were you standing or sitting at the time, Mrs Swettenham?'

'Now let me see, where was I? Who was I talking to, Edmund?'

'I really haven't the least idea, Mother.'

'Was it Miss Hinchliffe I was asking about giving the hens cod liver oil in the cold weather? Or was it Mrs Harmon – no, she'd only just arrived. I think I was just saying to Colonel Easterbrook that I thought it was really very dangerous to have an atom research station in England. It ought to be on some lonely island in case the radio-activity gets loose.'

'You don't remember if you were sitting or standing?'

'Does it really matter, Inspector? I was somewhere over by the window or near the mantelpiece, because I know I was *quite* near the clock when it struck. Such a thrilling moment! Waiting to see if anything might be going to happen.'

'You describe the light from the torch as blinding. Was it turned full on to you?'

'It was right in my eyes. I couldn't see a thing.'

'Did the man hold it still, or did he move it about, from person to person?'

'Oh, I don't really know. Which did he do, Edmund?'

'It moved rather slowly over us all, so as to see what we were all doing, I suppose, in case we should try and rush him.'

'And where exactly in the room were *you*, Mr Swettenham?'

'I'd been talking to Julia Simmons. We were both standing up in the middle of the room – the long room.'

'Was everyone in that room, or was there anyone in the far room?'

'Phillipa Haymes had moved in there, I think. She was over by that far mantelpiece. I think she was looking for something.'

'Have you any idea as to whether the third shot was suicide or an accident?'

'I've no idea at all. The man seemed to swerve round very suddenly and then crumple up and fall – but it was all very confused. You must realize that you couldn't really see anything. And then that refugee girl started yelling the place down.'

'I understand it was you who unlocked the dining-room door and let her out?'

'Yes.'

'The door was definitely locked on the outside?'

Edmund looked at him curiously.

'Certainly it was. Why, you don't imagine –'

'I just like to get my facts quite clear. Thank you, Mr Swettenham.'

IV

Inspector Craddock was forced to spend quite a long time with Colonel and Mrs Easterbrook. He had to listen to a long disquisition on the psychological aspect of the case.

'The psychological approach – that's the only thing nowadays,' the Colonel told him. 'You've got to understand your criminal. Now the whole setup here is quite plain to a man who's had the wide experience that I have. Why does this fellow put that advert in? Psychology. He wants to advertise himself – to focus attention on · himself. He's been passed over, perhaps despised as a foreigner by the other employees at the Spa Hotel. A girl has turned him down, perhaps. He wants to rivet her attention on him. Who is the idol of the cinema nowadays – the gangster – the tough guy? Very well, he will be a tough guy. Robbery with violence. A mask? A revolver? But he wants an audience – he must have an audience. So he arranges for an audience. And then, at the supreme moment, his part runs away with him – he's more than a burglar. He's a killer. He shoots – blindly –'

Inspector Craddock caught gladly at a word:

'You say "blindly," Colonel Easterbrook. You didn't think that he was firing deliberately at one particular object – at Miss Blacklock, that is to say?'

'No, no. He just loosed off, as I say, blindly. And that's what brought him to himself. The bullet hit someone – actually it was only a graze, but he didn't know that. He comes to himself with a bang. All this – this make-believe he's been indulging in – is *real*. He's shot at someone – perhaps killed someone. . . . It's all up with him. And so in blind panic he turns the revolver on himself.'

Colonel Easterbrook paused, cleared his throat appreciatively and said in a satisfied voice, 'Plain as a pike-staff, that's what it is, plain as a pikestaff.'

'It really is wonderful,' said Mrs Easterbrook, 'the way you know exactly what happened, Archie.'

Her voice was warm with admiration.

Inspector Craddock thought it was wonderful, too, but he was not quite so warmly appreciative.

'Exactly where were you in the room, Colonel Easterbrook, when the actual shooting business took place?'

'I was standing with my wife – near a centre table with some flowers on it.'

'I caught hold of your arm, didn't I, Archie, when it happened? I was simply scared to death. I just had to hold on to you.'

'Poor little kitten,' said the Colonel playfully.

V

The Inspector ran Miss Hinchliffe to earth by a pigsty.

'Nice creatures, pigs,' said Miss Hinchliffe, scratching a wrinkled pink back. 'Coming on well, isn't he? Good bacon round about Christmas time. Well, what do you want to see me about? I told your people last night I hadn't the least idea who the man was.

Never seen him anywhere in the neighbourhood snooping about or anything of that sort. Our Mrs Mopp says he came from one of the big hotels in Medenham Wells. Why didn't he hold up someone there if he wanted to? Get a much better haul.'

That was undeniable – Craddock proceeded with his enquiries.

'Where were you exactly when the incident took place?'

'Incident! Reminds me of my ARP days. Saw some incidents then, I can tell you. Where was I when the shooting started? That what you want to know?'

'Yes.'

'Leaning up against the mantelpiece hoping to God someone would offer me a drink soon,' replied Miss Hinchliffe promptly.

'Do you think that the shots were fired blindly, or aimed carefully at one particular person?'

'You mean aimed at Letty Blacklock? How the devil should I know? Damned hard to sort out what your impressions really were or what really happened after it's all over. All I know is the lights went out, and that torch went whirling round dazzling us all, and then the shots were fired and I thought to myself, "If that damned young fool Patrick Simmons is playing his jokes with a loaded revolver somebody will get hurt."'

'You thought it was Patrick Simmons?'

'Well, it seemed likely. Edmund Swettenham is intellectual and writes books and doesn't care for horseplay, and old Colonel Easterbrook wouldn't think that sort of thing funny. But Patrick's a wild boy. However, I apologize to him for the idea.'

'Did your friend think it might be Patrick Simmons?'

'Murgatroyd? You'd better talk to her yourself. Not that you'll get any sense out of her. She's down the orchard. I'll yell for her if you like.'

Miss Hinchliffe raised her stentorian voice in a powerful bellow:

'Hi-youp, Murgatroyd . . .'

'Coming . . .' floated back a thin cry.

'Hurry up – Polieece,' bellowed Miss Hinchliffe.

Miss Murgatroyd arrived at a brisk trot very much out of breath. Her skirt was down at the hem and her hair was escaping from an inadequate hair net. Her round, good-natured face beamed.

'Is it Scotland Yard?' she asked breathlessly. 'I'd no idea. Or I wouldn't have left the house.'

'We haven't called in Scotland Yard yet, Miss Murgatroyd. I'm Inspector Craddock from Milchester.'

'Well, that's very nice, I'm sure,' said Miss Murgatroyd vaguely. 'Have you found any clues?'

'Where were you at the time of the crime, that's what he wants to know, Murgatroyd?' said Miss Hinchliffe. She winked at Craddock.

'Oh, dear,' gasped Miss Murgatroyd. 'Of course. I ought to have been prepared. *Alibis*, of course. Now, let me see, I was just with everybody else.'

'You weren't with me,' said Miss Hinchliffe.

'Oh, dear, Hinch, wasn't I? No, of course, I'd been admiring the chrysanthemums. Very poor specimens, really. And then it all happened – only I didn't really know it had happened – I mean I didn't know that anything like that had happened. I didn't imagine for a moment that it was a real revolver – and all so awkward in the dark, and that dreadful screaming. I got it all wrong, you know. I thought *she* was being murdered – I mean the refugee girl. I thought she was having her throat cut across the hall somewhere. I didn't know it was *him* – I mean, I didn't even know there was a man. It was really just a voice, you know, saying, "Put them up, please."'

'"Stick 'em up!"' Miss Hinchliffe corrected. 'And no suggestion of "please" about it.'

'It's so terrible to think that until that girl started screaming I was actually enjoying myself. Only being in the dark was very awkward and I got a knock on my corn. Agony, it was. Is there anything more you want to know, Inspector?'

'No,' said Inspector Craddock, eyeing Miss Murgatroyd speculatively. 'I don't really think there is.'

Her friend gave a short bark of laughter.

'He's got you taped, Murgatroyd.'

'I'm sure, Hinch,' said Miss Murgatroyd, 'that I'm only too willing to say anything I can.'

'He doesn't want that,' said Miss Hinchliffe.

She looked at the Inspector. 'If you're doing this geographically I suppose you'll go to the Vicarage next. You might get something there. Mrs Harmon looks as vague as they make them – but I sometimes think she's got brains. Anyway, she's got something.'

As they watched the Inspector and Sergeant Fletcher stalk away, Amy Murgatroyd said breathlessly:

'Oh, Hinch, was I very awful? I do get so flustered!'

'Not at all.' Miss Hinchliffe smiled. 'On the whole, I should say you did very well.'

VI

Inspector Craddock looked round the big shabby room with a sense of pleasure. It reminded him a little of his own Cumberland home. Faded chintz, big shabby chairs, flowers and books strewn about, and a spaniel in a basket. Mrs Harmon, too, with her distraught air, and her general disarray and her eager face he found sympathetic.

But she said at once, frankly, 'I shan't be any help to you. Because I shut my eyes. I hate being dazzled. And then there were shots and I screwed them up tighter than ever. And I did wish, oh, I did wish, that it had been a *quiet* murder. I don't like bangs.'

'So you didn't see anything.' The Inspector smiled at her. 'But you heard –?'

'Oh, my goodness yes, there was plenty to *hear*. Doors opening and shutting, and people saying silly things and gasping and old Mitzi screaming like a steam engine – and poor Bunny squealing like a trapped rabbit. And everyone pushing and falling over everyone else. However, when there really didn't seem to be any more bangs coming, I opened my eyes. Everyone was out in the hall then, with candles. And then the lights came on and suddenly it was all as usual – I don't mean really as usual, but we were ourselves again, not just – people in the dark. People in the dark are quite different, aren't they?'

'I think I know what you mean, Mrs Harmon.'

Mrs Harmon smiled at him.

'And there he was,' she said. 'A rather weaselly-looking foreigner – all pink and surprised looking – lying there dead – with a revolver beside him. It didn't – oh, it didn't seem to make *sense*, somehow.'

It did not make sense to the Inspector, either. . . .

The whole business worried him.

8   ENTER MISS MARPLE

Craddock laid the typed transcript of the various interviews before the Chief Constable. The latter had just finished reading the wire received from the Swiss Police.

'So he had a police record all right,' said Rydesdale. 'H'm – very much as one thought.'

'Yes, sir.'

'Jewellery . . . h'm, yes . . . falsified entries . . . yes . . . cheque . . . Definitely a dishonest fellow.'

'Yes, sir – in a small way.'

'Quite so. And small things lead to large things.'

'I wonder, sir.'

The Chief Constable looked up.

'Worried, Craddock?'

'Yes, sir.'

'Why? It's a straightforward story. Or isn't it? Let's see what all these people you've been talking to have to say.'

He drew the report towards him and read it through rapidly.

'The usual thing – plenty of inconsistencies and contradictions. Different people's accounts of a few moments of stress never agree. But the main picture seems clear enough.'

'I know, sir – but it's an unsatisfactory picture. If you know what I mean – it's the wrong picture.'

'Well, let's take the facts. Rudi Scherz took the 5.20 bus from Medenham to Chipping Cleghorn arriving there at six o'clock. Evidence of conductor and two passengers. From the bus stop he walked away in the direction of Little Paddocks. He got into the house with no particular difficulty – probably through the front door. He held up the company with a revolver, he fired two shots, one of which slightly wounded Miss Blacklock, he then killed himself with a third shot, whether accidentally or deliberately there is not sufficient evidence to show. The reasons *why* he did all this are profoundly unsatisfactory, I agree. But *why* isn't really a question we are called upon to answer. A Coroner's jury may bring it in suicide – or accidental death. Whichever verdict it is, it's the same as far as we're concerned. We can write finis.'

'You mean we can always fall back upon Colonel Easterbrook's psychology,' said Craddock gloomily.

Rydesdale smiled.

'After all, the Colonel's probably had a good deal of experience,' he said. 'I'm pretty sick of the psychological jargon that's used so glibly about everything nowadays – but we can't really rule it out.'

'I still feel the picture's all wrong, sir.'

'Any reason to believe that somebody in the setup at Chipping Cleghorn is lying to you?'

Craddock hesitated.

'I think the foreign girl knows more than she lets on. But that may be just prejudice on my part.'

'You think she might possibly have been in it with this fellow? Let him into the house? Put him up to it?'

'Something of the kind. I wouldn't put it past her. But that surely indicates that there really was something valuable, money or jewellery, in the house, and that doesn't seem to have been the case. Miss Blacklock negatived it quite decidedly. So did the others. That leaves us with the proposition that there was something valuable in the house that nobody knew about –'

'Quite a best seller plot.'

'I agree it's ridiculous, sir. The only other point is Miss Bunner's certainty that it was a definite attempt by Scherz to murder Miss Blacklock.'

'Well, from what you say – and from her statement, this Miss Bunner –'

'Oh, I agree, sir,' Craddock put in quickly, 'she's an utterly unreliable witness. Highly suggestible. Anyone could put a thing into her head – but the interesting thing is that this is quite her own theory – no one *has* suggested it to her. Everybody else negatives it. For once she's *not* swimming with the tide. It definitely *is* her own impression.'

'And why should Rudi Scherz want to kill Miss Blacklock?'

'There you are, sir. I don't know. Miss Blacklock doesn't know – unless she's a much better liar than I think she is. Nobody knows. So presumably it isn't true.'

He sighed.

'Cheer up, Craddock,' said the Chief Constable.

'I'm taking you off to lunch with Sir Henry and myself. The best that the Royal Spa Hotel in Medenham Wells can provide.'

'Thank you, sir.' Craddock looked slightly surprised.

'You see, we received a letter –' He broke off as Sir Henry Clithering entered the room. 'Ah, there you are, Henry.'

Sir Henry, informal this time, said, ''Morning, Dermot.'

'I've got something for you, Henry,' said the Chief Constable.

'What's that?'

'Authentic letter from an old Pussy. Staying at the Royal Spa Hotel. Something she thinks we might like to know in connection with this Chipping Cleghorn business.'

'The old Pussies,' said Sir Henry triumphantly. 'What did I tell you? They hear everything. They see everything. And, unlike the famous adage, they speak all evil. What's this particular one got hold of?'

Rydesdale consulted the letter.

'Writes just like my old grandmother,' he complained. 'Spiky. Like a spider in the ink bottle, and all underlined. A good deal about how she hopes it won't be taking up our valuable time, but might possibly be of some slight assistance, etc., etc. What's her name? Jane – something – Murple – no, Marple, Jane Marple.'

'Ye Gods and Little Fishes,' said Sir Henry, 'can it be? George, it's my own particular, one and only, four starred Pussy. The super Pussy of all old Pussies. And she has managed somehow to be at Medenham Wells, instead of peacefully at home in St Mary Mead, just at the right time to be mixed up in a murder. Once more a murder is announced – for the benefit and enjoyment of Miss Marple.'

'Well, Henry,' said Rydesdale sardonically. 'I'll be glad to see your paragon. Come on! We'll lunch at the Royal Spa and we'll interview the lady. Craddock, here, is looking highly sceptical.'

'Not at all, sir,' said Craddock politely.

He thought to himself that sometimes his godfather carried things a bit far.

II

Miss Jane Marple was very nearly, if not quite, as Craddock had pictured her. She was far more benignant than he had imagined and a good deal older. She seemed indeed very old. She had snow white hair and a pink crinkled face and very soft innocent blue eyes, and she was heavily enmeshed in fleecy wool. Wool round her shoulders in the form of a lacy cape and wool that she was knitting and which turned out to be a baby's shawl.

She was all incoherent delight and pleasure at seeing Sir Henry, and became quite flustered when introduced to the Chief Constable and Detective-Inspector Craddock.

'But really, Sir Henry, how fortunate . . . how very fortunate. So long since I have seen you. . . . Yes, my rheumatism. Very bad of late. Of course I couldn't have afforded this hotel (really fantastic what they charge nowadays) but Raymond – my nephew, Raymond West, you may remember him –?'

'Everyone knows *his* name.'

'Yes, the dear boy has been so successful with his clever books – he prides himself upon never writing about anything pleasant. The dear boy insisted on paying all my expenses. And his dear wife is making a name for herself too, as an artist. Mostly jugs of dying flowers and broken combs on windowsills. I never dare tell her, but I still admire Blair Leighton and Alma Tadema. Oh, but I'm chattering. And the Chief Constable himself – indeed I never expected – so afraid I shall be taking up his time –'

'Completely ga-ga,' thought the disgusted Detective Inspector Craddock.

'Come into the Manager's private room,' said Rydesdale. 'We can talk better there.'

When Miss Marple had been disentangled from her wool, and her spare knitting pins collected, she accompanied them, fluttering and protesting, to Mr Rowlandson's comfortable sitting room.

'Now, Miss Marple, let's hear what you have to tell us,' said the Chief Constable.

Miss Marple came to the point with unexpected brevity.

'It was a cheque,' she said. 'He altered it.'

'He?'

'The young man at the desk here, the one who is supposed to have staged that hold-up and shot himself.'

'He altered a cheque, you say?'

Miss Marple nodded.

'Yes. I have it here.' She extracted it from her bag and laid it on the table. 'It came this morning with my others from the Bank. You can see it was for seven pounds, and he altered it to seventeen. A stroke in front of the 7, and *teen* added after the word seven with a nice artistic little blot just blurring the whole word. Really very nicely done. A certain amount of *practice*, I should say. It's the same ink, because I wrote the cheque actually at the desk. I should think he'd done it quite often before, wouldn't you?'

'He picked the wrong person to do it to, this time,' remarked Sir Henry.

Miss Marple nodded agreement.

'Yes. I'm afraid he would never have gone very far in crime. I was quite the wrong person. Some busy young married woman, or some girl having a love affair – that's the kind who write cheques for all sorts of different sums and don't really look through their pass-books carefully. But an old woman who has to be careful of the pennies, and who has formed habits – that's quite the wrong person to choose. Seventeen pounds is a sum I *never* write a cheque for. Twenty pounds, a round sum, for the monthly wages and books. And as for my personal expenditure, I usually cash seven – it used to be five, but everything has gone up so.'

'And perhaps he reminded you of someone?' prompted Sir Henry, mischief in his eye.

Miss Marple smiled and shook her head at him.

'You are very naughty, Sir Henry. As a matter of fact he *did*. Fred Tyler, at the fish shop. Always slipped an extra 1 in the shillings column. Eating so much fish as we do nowadays, it made a long bill, and lots of people never added it up. Just ten shillings in his pocket every time, not much but enough to get himself a few neckties and take Jessie Spragge (the girl in the draper's) to the pictures. Cut a splash, that's what these young fellows want to do. Well, the very first week I was here, there was a mistake in my bill. I pointed it out to the young man and he apologized very nicely and looked very much upset, but I thought to myself then: "You've got a shifty eye, young man."'

'What I mean by a shifty eye,' continued Miss Marple, 'is the kind that looks very straight at you and never looks away or blinks.'

Craddock gave a sudden movement of appreciation. He thought to himself 'Jim Kelly to the life' remembering a notorious swindler he had helped to put behind bars not long ago.

'Rudi Scherz was a thoroughly unsatisfactory character,' said Rydesdale. 'He's got a police record in Switzerland, we find.'

'Made the place too hot for him, I suppose, and came over here with forged papers?' said Miss Marple.

'Exactly,' said Rydesdale.

'He was going about with the little red-haired waitress from the dining room,' said Miss Marple. 'Fortunately I don't think

her heart's affected at all. She just liked to have someone a bit
"different", and he used to give her flowers and chocolates which
the English boys don't do much. Has she told you all she knows?'
she asked, turning suddenly to Craddock. 'Or not quite all
yet?'

'I'm not absolutely sure,' said Craddock cautiously.

'I think there's a little to come,' said Miss Marple. 'She's looking
very worried. Brought me kippers instead of herrings this morning,
and forgot the milk jug. Usually she's an excellent waitress. Yes,
she's worried. Afraid she might have to give evidence or something
like that. But I expect' – her candid blue eyes swept over the manly
proportions and handsome face of Detective-Inspector Craddock
with truly feminine Victorian appreciation – 'that *you* will be able
to persuade her to tell you all she knows.'

Detective-Inspector Craddock blushed and Sir Henry chuckled.

'It might be important,' said Miss Marple. 'He may have told her
who it was.'

Rydesdale stared at her.

'Who what was?'

'I express myself so badly. Who it was who put him up to it, I
mean.'

'So you think someone put him up to it?'

Miss Marple's eyes widened in surprise.

'Oh, but surely – I mean . . . Here's a personable young man –
who filches a little bit here and a little bit there – alters a small
cheque, perhaps helps himself to a small piece of jewellery if it's left
lying around, or takes a little money from the till – all sorts of small
petty thefts. Keeps himself going in ready money so that he can dress
well, and take a girl about – all that sort of thing. And then suddenly
he goes off, with a revolver, and holds up a room full of people,
and shoots at someone. He'd *never* have done a thing like that – not
for a moment! He wasn't that kind of person. It doesn't make
sense.'

Craddock drew in his breath sharply. That was what Letitia
Blacklock had said. What the Vicar's wife had said. What he himself
felt with increasing force. *It didn't make sense.* And now Sir Henry's
old Pussy was saying it, too, with complete certainty in her fluting
old lady's voice.

'Perhaps you'll tell us, Miss Marple,' he said, and his voice was
suddenly aggressive, 'what did happen, then?'

She turned on him in surprise.

'But how should I know what happened? There was an account in the paper – but it says so little. One can make conjectures, of course, but one has no accurate information.'

'George,' said Sir Henry. 'Would it be very unorthodox if Miss Marple were allowed to read the notes of the interviews Craddock had with these people at Chipping Cleghorn?'

'It may be unorthodox,' said Rydesdale, 'but I've not got where I am by being orthodox. She can read them. I'd be curious to hear what she has to say.'

Miss Marple was all embarrassment.

'I'm afraid you've been listening to Sir Henry. Sir Henry is always too kind. He thinks too much of any little observations I may have made in the past. Really, I have no gifts – no gifts at all – except perhaps a certain knowledge of human nature. People, I find, are apt to be far too trustful. I'm afraid that I have a tendency always to believe the *worst*. Not a nice trait. But so often justified by subsequent events.'

'Read these,' said Rydesdale, thrusting the typewritten sheets upon her. 'They won't take you long. After all, these people are your kind – you must know a lot of people like them. You may be able to spot something that we haven't. The case is just going to be closed. Let's have an amateur's opinion on it before we shut up the files. I don't mind telling you that Craddock here isn't satisfied. He says, like you, that it doesn't make sense.'

There was silence whilst Miss Marple read. She put the typewritten sheets down at last.

'It's very interesting,' she said with a sigh. 'All the different things that people say – and think. The things they see – or think that they see. And all so complex, nearly all so trivial and if one thing isn't trivial, it's so hard to spot which one – like a needle in a haystack.'

Craddock felt a twinge of disappointment. Just for a moment or two, he had wondered if Sir Henry might be right about this funny old lady. She might have put her finger on something – old people were often very sharp. He'd never, for instance, been able to conceal anything from his own great aunt Emma. She had finally told him that his nose twitched when he was about to tell a lie.

But just a few fluffy generalities, that was all that Sir Henry's famous Miss Marple could produce. He felt annoyed with her and said rather curtly:

'The truth of the matter is that the facts are indisputable. Whatever conflicting details these people give, they all saw one thing. They saw a masked man with a revolver and a torch open the door and hold them up, and whether they think he said "Stick 'em up" or "Your money or your life," or whatever phrase is associated with a hold-up in their minds, they *saw* him.'

'But surely,' said Miss Marple gently. 'They couldn't – actually – have seen anything at all. . . .'

Craddock caught his breath. She'd got it! She was sharp, after all. He was testing her by that speech of his, but she hadn't fallen for it. It didn't actually make any difference to the facts, or to what happened, but she'd realized, as he'd realized, that those people who had seen a masked man holding them up couldn't really have *seen* him at all.

'If I understand rightly,' Miss Marple had a pink flush on her cheeks, her eyes were bright and pleased as a child's, 'there wasn't any light in the hall outside – and not on the landing upstairs either?'

'That's right,' said Craddock.

'And so, if a man stood in the doorway and flashed a powerful torch into the room, *nobody could see anything but the torch*, could they?'

'No, they couldn't. I tried it out.'

'And so when some of them say they saw a masked man, etc., they are really, though they don't realize it, recapitulating from what they saw *afterwards* – when the lights came on. So it really all fits in very well, doesn't it, on the assumption that Rudi Scherz was the – I think, "fall guy" is the expression I mean?'

Rydesdale stared at her in such surprise that she grew pinker still.

'I may have got the term wrong,' she murmured. 'I am not very clever about Americanisms – and I understand they change very quickly. I got it from one of Mr Dashiel Hammett's stories. (I understand from my nephew Raymond that he is considered at the top of the tree in what is called the "tough" style of literature.) A *"fall guy"*, if I understand it rightly, means someone who will be blamed for a crime really committed by someone else. This Rudi Scherz seems to me exactly the right type for that. Rather stupid really, you know, but full of cupidity and probably extremely credulous.'

Rydesdale said, smiling tolerantly:

'Are you suggesting that he was persuaded by someone to go out and take pot shots at a room full of people? Rather a tall order.'

'I think he was told that it was a *joke*,' said Miss Marple. 'He was paid for doing it, of course. Paid, that is, to put an advertisement in the newspaper, to go out and spy out the household premises, and then, on the night in question, he was to go there, assume a mask and a black cloak and throw open a door, brandishing a torch, and cry "Hands up!"'

'And fire off a revolver?'

'No, no,' said Miss Marple. 'He never had a revolver.'

'But everyone says –' began Rydesdale, and stopped.

'Exactly,' said Miss Marple. 'Nobody could possibly have *seen* a revolver even if he had one. And I don't think he had. I think that after he'd called "Hands up" somebody came up quietly behind him in the darkness and fired those two shots over his shoulder. It frightened him to death. He swung round and as he did so, that other person shot him and then let the revolver drop beside him. . . .'

The three men looked at her. Sir Henry said softly:

'It's a possible theory.'

'But who is Mr X who came up in the darkness?' asked the Chief Constable.

Miss Marple coughed.

'You'll have to find out from Miss Blacklock who wanted to kill her.'

Good for old Dora Bunner, thought Craddock. Instinct against intelligence every time.

'So you think it was a deliberate attempt on Miss Blacklock's life?' asked Rydesdale.

'It certainly has that appearance,' said Miss Marple. 'Though there are one or two difficulties. But what I was really wondering about was whether there mightn't be a short cut. I've no doubt that whoever arranged this with Rudi Scherz took pains to tell him to keep his mouth shut about it, and perhaps he did keep his mouth shut, but if he talked to anybody it would probably be to that girl, Myrna Harris. And he may – he just may – have dropped some hint as to the kind of person who'd suggested the whole thing.'

'I'll see her now,' said Craddock, rising.

Miss Marple nodded.

'Yes, do, Inspector Craddock. I'll feel happier when you have. Because once she's told you anything she knows she'll be much safer.'

'Safer? . . . Yes, I see.'

He left the room. The Chief Constable said doubtfully, but tactfully:

'Well, Miss Marple, you've certainly given us something to think about.'

III

'I'm sorry about it, I am really,' said Myrna Harris. 'It's ever so nice of you not to be ratty about it. But you see Mum's the sort of person who fusses like anything. And it did look as though I'd – what's the phrase – been an accessory before the fact' (the words ran glibly off her tongue). 'I mean, I was afraid you'd never take my word for it that I only thought it was just a bit of fun.'

Inspector Craddock repeated the reassuring phrases with which he had broken down Myrna's resistance.

'I will. I'll tell you *all* about it. But you will keep me out of it if you can because of Mum? It all started with Rudi breaking a date with me. We were going to the pictures that evening and then he said he wouldn't be able to come and I was a bit stand-offish with him about it – because after all, it had been his idea and I don't fancy being stood up by a foreigner. And he said it wasn't his fault, and I said that was a likely story, and then he said he'd got a bit of a lark on that night – and that he wasn't going to be out of pocket by it and how would I fancy a wristwatch? So I said, what do you mean by a lark? And he said not to tell anyone, but there was to be a party somewhere and he was to stage a sham hold-up. Then he showed me the advertisement he'd put in and I had to laugh. He was a bit scornful about it all. Said it was kid's stuff really – but that was just like the English. They never really grew up – and of course, I said what did he mean by talking like that about Us – and we had a bit of an argument, but we made it up. Only you can understand, can't you, sir, that when I read all about it, and it hadn't been a joke at all and Rudi had shot someone and then shot himself – why, I didn't know *what* to do. I thought if I said I knew about it beforehand, it would look as though I were in on the whole thing. But it really did seem like a joke when he told me about it. I'd have sworn he meant it that way. I didn't even know he'd got a revolver. He never said anything about taking a revolver with him.'

Craddock comforted her and then asked the most important question.

'Who did he say it was who had arranged this party?'

But there he drew a blank.

'He never said who it was that was getting him to do it. I suppose nobody was, really. It was all his own doing.'

'He didn't mention a name? Did he say he – or she?'

'He didn't say anything except that it was going to be a scream. "I shall laugh to see all their faces." That's what he said.'

He hadn't had long to laugh, Craddock thought.

IV

'It's only a theory,' said Rydesdale as they drove back to Medenham. 'Nothing to support it, nothing at all. Put it down as old maid's vapourings and let it go, eh?'

'I'd rather not do that, sir.'

'It's all very improbable. A mysterious X appearing suddenly in the darkness behind our Swiss friend. Where did he come from? Who was he? Where had he been?'

'He could have come in through the side door,' said Craddock, 'just as Scherz came. Or,' he added slowly, 'he could have come from the kitchen.'

'*She* could have come from the kitchen, you mean?'

'Yes, sir, it's a possibility. I've not been satisfied about that girl all along. She strikes me as a nasty bit of goods. All that screaming and hysterics – it could have been put on. She could have worked on this young fellow, let him in at the right moment, rigged the whole thing, shot him, bolted back into the dining-room, caught up her bit of silver and her chamois and started her screaming act.'

'Against that we have the fact that – er – what's his name – oh, yes, Edmund Swettenham, definitely says the key was turned on the outside of the door, and that he turned it to release her. Any other door into that part of the house?'

'Yes, there's a door to the back stairs and kitchen just under the stairs, but it seems the handle came off three weeks ago and nobody's come to put it on yet. In the meantime you can't open the door. I'm bound to say that story seems correct. The spindle and the two handles were on a shelf outside the door in the hall and they were thickly coated with dust, but of course a professional would have ways of opening that door all right.'

'Better look up the girl's record. See if her papers are in order. But it seems to me the whole thing is very theoretical.'

Again the Chief Constable looked enquiringly at his subordinate. Craddock replied quietly:

'I know, sir, and of course if you think the case ought to be closed, it must be. But I'd appreciate it if I could work on it for just a little longer.'

Rather to his surprise the Chief Constable said quietly and approvingly:

'Good lad.'

'There's the revolver to work on. If this theory is correct, it wasn't Scherz's revolver and certainly nobody so far has been able to say that Scherz ever had a revolver.'

'It's a German make.'

'I know, sir. But this country's absolutely full of continental makes of guns. All the Americans brought them back and so did our chaps. You can't go by that.'

'True enough. Any other lines of enquiry?'

'There's got to be a motive. If there's anything in this theory at all, it means that last Friday's business wasn't a mere joke and wasn't an ordinary hold-up, it was a cold-blooded attempt at murder. *Somebody tried to murder Miss Blacklock.* Now *why*? It seems to me that if anyone knows the answer to that it must be Miss Blacklock herself.'

'I understand she rather poured cold water on that idea?'

'She poured cold water on the idea that *Rudi Scherz* wanted to murder her. And she was quite right. And there's another thing, sir.'

'Yes?'

'Somebody might try again.'

'That would certainly prove the truth of the theory,' said the Chief Constable dryly. 'By the way, look after Miss Marple, won't you?'

'Miss Marple? Why?'

'I gather she is taking up residence at the Vicarage in Chipping Cleghorn and coming into Medenham Wells twice a week for her treatments. It seems that Mrs What'shername is the daughter of an old friend of Miss Marple's. Good sporting instincts, that old bean. Oh, well, I suppose she hasn't much excitement in her life and sniffing round after possible murderers gives her a kick.'

'I wish she wasn't coming,' said Craddock seriously.

'Going to get under your feet?'

'Not that, sir, but she's a nice old thing. I shouldn't like anything to happen to her . . . always supposing, I mean, that there's anything *in* this theory.'

9   CONCERNING A DOOR

'I'm sorry to bother you again, Miss Blacklock –'

'Oh, it doesn't matter. I suppose, as the inquest was adjourned for a week, you're hoping to get more evidence?'

Detective-Inspector Craddock nodded.

'To begin with, Miss Blacklock, Rudi Scherz was not the son of the proprietor of the Hotel des Alpes at Montreux. He seems to have started his career as an orderly in a hospital at Berne. A good many of the patients missed small pieces of jewellery. Under another name he was a waiter at one of the small winter sports places. His speciality there was making out duplicate bills in the restaurant with items on one that didn't appear on the other. The difference, of course, went into his pocket. After that he was in a department store in Zürich. Their losses from shoplifting were rather above the average whilst he was with them. It seems likely that the shoplifting wasn't entirely due to customers.'

'He was a picker up of unconsidered trifles, in fact?' said Miss Blacklock dryly. 'Then I was right in thinking that I had not seen him before?'

'You were quite right – no doubt you were pointed out to him at the Royal Spa Hotel and he pretended to recognize you. The Swiss police had begun to make his own country rather too hot for him, and he came over here with a very nice set of forged papers and took a job at the Royal Spa.'

'Quite a good hunting ground,' said Miss Blacklock dryly. 'It's extremely expensive and very well-off people stay there. Some of them are careless about their bills, I expect.'

'Yes,' said Craddock. 'There were prospects of a satisfactory harvest.'

Miss Blacklock was frowning.

'I see all that,' she said. 'But why come to Chipping Cleghorn?

What does he think we've got here that could possibly be better than the rich Royal Spa Hotel?'

'You stick to your statement that there's nothing of especial value in the house?'

'Of course there isn't. *I* should know. I can assure you, Inspector, we've not got an unrecognized Rembrandt or anything like that.'

'Then it looks, doesn't it, as though your friend, Miss Bunner was right? He came here to attack *you*.'

('There, Letty, what did I tell you!'

'Oh, nonsense, Bunny')

'But is it nonsense?' said Craddock. 'I think, you know, that it's true.'

Miss Blacklock stared very hard at him.

'Now, let's get this straight. You really believe that this young man came out here – having previously arranged by means of an advertisement that half the village would turn up agog at that particular time –'

'But he mayn't have meant *that* to happen,' interrupted Miss Bunner eagerly. 'It may have been just a horrid sort of warning – to *you*, Letty – that's how I read it at the time – "*A murder is announced*" – I felt in my bones that it was sinister – if it had all gone as planned he would have shot you and got away – and how would anyone have ever known who it was?'

'That's true enough,' said Miss Blacklock. 'But –'

'I knew that advertisement wasn't a joke, Letty. I said so. And look at Mitzi – *she* was frightened, too!'

'Ah,' said Craddock, 'Mitzi. I'd like to know rather more about that young woman.'

'Her permit and papers are quite in order.'

'I don't doubt that,' said Craddock dryly. 'Scherz's papers appeared to be quite correct, too.'

'But why should this Rudi Scherz want to murder me? That's what you don't attempt to explain, Inspector Craddock.'

'There may have been someone behind Scherz,' said Craddock slowly. 'Have you thought of that?'

He used the words metaphorically though it flashed across his mind that if Miss Marple's theory was correct, the words would also be true in a literal sense. In any case they made little impression on Miss Blacklock, who still looked sceptical.

'The point remains the same,' she said. 'Why on earth should anyone want to murder *me*?'

'It's the answer to that that I want *you* to give me, Miss Blacklock.'

'Well, I can't! That's flat. I've no enemies. As far as I'm aware I've always lived on perfectly good terms with my neighbours. I don't know any guilty secrets about anyone. The whole idea is ridiculous! And if what you're hinting is that Mitzi has something to do with this, that's absurd, too. As Miss Bunner has just told you she was frightened to death when she saw that advertisement in the *Gazette*. She actually wanted to pack up and leave the house then and there.'

'That may have been a clever move on her part. She may have known you'd press her to stay.'

'Of course, if you've made up your mind about it, you'll find an answer to everything. But I can assure you that if Mitzi had taken an unreasoning dislike to me, she might conceivably poison my food, but I'm sure she wouldn't go in for all this elaborate rigmarole.'

'The whole idea's absurd. I believe you police have got an anti-foreigner complex. Mitzi may be a liar but she's *not* a cold-blooded murderer. Go and bully her if you must. But when she's departed in a whirl of indignation, or shut herself up howling in her room, I've a good mind to make *you* cook the dinner. Mrs Harmon is bringing some old lady who is staying with her to tea this afternoon and I wanted Mitzi to make some little cakes – but I suppose you'll upset her completely. Can't you *possibly* go and suspect somebody else?'

II

Craddock went out to the kitchen. He asked Mitzi questions that he had asked her before and received the same answers.

Yes, she had locked the front door soon after four o'clock. No, she did not always do so, but that afternoon she had been nervous because of 'that dreadful advertisement'. It was no good locking the side door because Miss Blacklock and Miss Bunner went out that way to shut up the ducks and feed the chickens and Mrs Haymes usually came in that way from work.

'Mrs Haymes says she locked the door when she came in at 5.30.'

'Ah, and you believe her – oh, yes, you believe her. . . .'

'Do you think we shouldn't believe her?'

'What does it matter what I think? You will not believe *me*.'

'Supposing you give us a chance. You think Mrs Haymes didn't
lock that door?'

'I thinking she was very careful not to lock it.'

'What do you mean by that?' asked Craddock.

'That young man, he does not work alone. No, he knows *where*
to come, he knows that *when* he comes a door will be left open for
him – oh, very conveniently open!'

'What are you trying to say?'

'What is the use of what I say? You will not listen. You say I am a
poor refugee girl who tells lies. You say that a fair-haired English
lady, oh, no, *she* does not tell lies – she is so British – so honest. So
you believe her and not me. But I could tell you. Oh, yes, I could tell
you!'

She banged down a saucepan on the stove.

Craddock was in two minds whether to take notice of what might
be only a stream of spite.

'We note everything we are told,' he said.

'I shall not tell you anything at all. Why should I? You are all
alike. You persecute and despise poor refugees. If I say to you that
when, a week before, that young man come to ask Miss Blacklock
for money and she sends him away, as you say, with a flea in the ear
– if I tell you that after that I hear him talking with Mrs Haymes –
yes, out there in the summerhouse – all you say is that I make it up!'

And so you probably are making it up, thought Craddock. But he
said aloud:

'You couldn't hear what was said out in the summerhouse.'

'There you are wrong,' screamed Mitzi triumphantly. 'I go out to
get nettles – it makes very nice vegetables, nettles. They do not think
so, but I cook it and not tell them. And I hear them talking in there.
He say to her "But where can I hide?" And she say "I will show you"
– and then she say, "At a quarter-past six," and I think, "Ach so!
That is how you behave, my fine lady! After you come back from
work, you go out to meet a man. You bring him into the house."
Miss Blacklock, I think, she will not like that. She will turn you out. I
will watch, I think, and listen and then I will tell Miss Blacklock. But
I understand now I was wrong. It was not love she planned with
him, it was to rob and to murder. But you will say I make all this up.
Wicked Mitzi, you will say. I will take her to prison.'

Craddock wondered. She might be making it up. But possibly she
might not. He asked cautiously:

'You are sure it was this Rudi Scherz she was talking to?'

'Of course I am sure. He just leave and I see him go from the drive across to the summerhouse. And presently,' said Mitzi defiantly, 'I go out to see if there are any nice young green nettles.'

Would there, the Inspector wondered, be any nice young green nettles in October? But he appreciated that Mitzi had had to produce a hurried reason for what had undoubtedly been nothing more than plain snooping.

'You didn't hear any more than what you have told me?'

Mitzi looked aggrieved.

'That Miss Bunner, the one with the long nose, she call and call me. Mitzi! Mitzi! So I have to go. Oh, she is irritating. Always interfering. Says she will teach me to cook. *Her* cooking! It tastes, yes, everything she does, of water, water, *water*!'

'Why didn't you tell me this the other day?' asked Craddock sternly.

'Because I did not remember – I did not think. . . . Only afterwards do I say to myself, it was planned then – planned with *her*.'

'You are quite sure it was Mrs Haymes?'

'Oh, yes, I am sure. Oh, yes, I am very sure. She is a thief, that Mrs Haymes. A thief and the associate of thieves. What she gets for working in the garden, it is not enough for such a fine lady, no. She has to rob Miss Blacklock who has been kind to her. Oh, she is bad, bad, bad, that one!'

'Supposing,' said the Inspector, watching her closely, 'that someone was to say that *you* had been seen talking to Rudi Scherz?'

The suggestion had less effect than he had hoped for. Mitzi merely snorted and tossed her head.

'If anyone say they see me talking to him, that is lies, lies, lies, lies,' she said contemptuously. 'To tell lies about anyone, that is easy, but in England you have to prove them true. Miss Blacklock tell me that, and it is true, is it not? I do not speak with murderers and thieves. And no English policeman shall say I do. And how can I do cooking for lunch if you are here, talk, talk, talk? Go out of my kitchens, please. I want now to make a very careful sauce.'

Craddock went obediently. He was a little shaken in his suspicions of Mitzi. Her story about Phillipa Haymes had been told with great conviction. Mitzi might be a liar (he thought she was), but he fancied that there might be some substratum of truth in this particular tale. He resolved to speak to Phillipa on the subject. She had seemed to him when he questioned her a quiet, well-bred young woman. He had had no suspicion of her.

Crossing the hall, in his abstraction, he tried to open the wrong door. Miss Bunner, descending the staircase, hastily put him right.

'Not that door,' she said. 'It doesn't open. The next one to the left. Very confusing, isn't it. So many doors.'

'There are a good many,' said Craddock, looking up and down the narrow hall.

Miss Bunner amiably enumerated them for him.

'First the door to the cloakroom, and then the cloaks cupboard door and then the dining room – that's on that side. And on this side, the dummy door that you were trying to get through and then there's the drawing room door proper, and then the china cupboard door and the door of the little flower room, and at the end this side door. Most confusing. Especially these two being so near together. I've often tried the wrong one by mistake. We used to have the hall table against it, as a matter of fact, but then we moved it along against the wall there.'

Craddock had noted, almost mechanically, a thin line horizontally across the panels of the door he had been trying to open. He realized now it was the mark where the table had been. Something stirred vaguely in his mind as he asked, 'Moved? How long ago?'

In questioning Dora Bunner there was fortunately no need to give a reason for any question. Any query on any subject seemed perfectly natural to the garrulous Miss Bunner who delighted in the giving of information, however trivial.

'Now let me see, really quite recently – ten days or a fortnight ago.'

'Why was it moved?'

'I really can't remember. Something to do with the flowers. I think Phillipa did a big vase – she arranges flowers quite beautifully – all autumn colouring and twigs and branches, and it was so big it caught your hair as you went past, and so Phillipa said, "Why not move the table along and anyway the flowers would look much better against the bare wall than against the panels of the door." Only we had to take down "Wellington at Waterloo." Not a print I'm really very fond of. We put it under the stairs.'

'It's not really a dummy, then?' Craddock asked, looking at the door.

'Oh, no, it's a *real* door, if that's what you mean. It's the door of the small drawing-room, but when the rooms were thrown into one, one didn't need two doors, so that one was fastened up.'

'Fastened up?' Craddock tried it again, gently. 'You mean it's nailed up? Or just locked?'

'Oh, locked, I think, and bolted too.'

He saw the bolt at the top and tried it. The bolt slid back easily – too easily. . . .

'When was it last open?' he asked Miss Bunner.

'Oh, years and years ago, I imagine. It's never been opened since I've been here, I know that.'

'You don't know where the key is?'

'There are a lot of keys in the hall drawer. It's probably among those.'

Craddock followed her and looked at a rusty assortment of old keys pushed far back in the drawer. He scanned them and selected one that looked different from the rest and went back to the door. The key fitted and turned easily. He pushed and the door slid open noiselessly.

'Oh, do be careful,' cried Miss Bunner. 'There may be something resting against it inside. We never open it.'

'Don't you?' said the Inspector.

His face now was grim. He said with emphasis:

'This door's been opened quite recently, Miss Bunner. The lock's been oiled and the hinges.'

She stared at him, her foolish face agape.

'But who could have done that?' she asked.

'That's what I mean to find out,' said Craddock grimly. He thought – 'X from outside? No – X was here – in this house – X was in the drawing-room that night. . . .'

10   PIP AND EMMA

Miss Blacklock listened to him this time with more attention. She was an intelligent woman, as he had known, and she grasped the implications of what he had to tell her.

'Yes,' she said quietly. 'That does alter things. . . . No one had any right to meddle with that door. Nobody *has* meddled with it to my knowledge.'

'You see what it means,' the Inspector urged. 'When the lights went out, *anybody in this room the other night* could have slipped out of that door, come up behind Rudi Scherz and fired at you.'

'Without being seen or heard or noticed?'

'Without being seen or heard or noticed. Remember when the lights went out people moved, exclaimed, and bumped into each other. And after that all that could be seen was the blinding light of the electric torch.'

Miss Blacklock said slowly, 'And you believe that one of those people – one of my nice commomplace neighbours – slipped out and tried to murder me? *Me? But why?* For goodness' sake, why?'

'I've a feeling that you *must* know the answer to that question, Miss Blacklock.'

'But I don't, Inspector. I can assure you, I don't.'

'Well, let's make a start. Who gets your money if you were to die?'

Miss Blacklock said rather reluctantly:

'Patrick and Julia. I've left the furniture in this house and a small annuity to Bunny. Really, I've not much to leave. I had holdings in German and Italian securities which became worthless, and what with taxation, and the lower percentages that are now paid on invested capital, I can assure you I'm not worth murdering – I put most of my money into an annuity about a year ago.'

'Still, you *have* some income, Miss Blacklock, and your nephew and niece would come into it.'

'And so Patrick and Julia would plan to murder me? I simply don't believe it. They're not desperately hard up or anything like that.'

'Do you know that for a fact?'

'No. I suppose I only know it from what they've told me. . . . But I really refuse to suspect them. *Some*day I *might* be worth murdering, but not now.'

'What do you mean by someday you might be worth murdering, Miss Blacklock?' Inspector Craddock pounced on the statement.

'Simply that one day – possibly quite soon – I *may* be a very rich woman.'

'That sounds interesting. Will you explain?'

'Certainly. You may not know it, but for more than twenty years I was secretary to and closely associated with Randall Goedler.'

Craddock was interested. Randall Goedler had been a big name in the world of finance. His daring speculations and the rather theatrical publicity with which he surrounded himself had made him a personality not quickly forgotten. He had died, if Craddock remembered rightly, in 1937 or 1938.

'He's rather before your time, I expect,' said Miss Blacklock. 'But you've probably heard of him.'

'Oh, yes. He was a millionaire, wasn't he?'

'Oh, several times over – though his finances fluctuated. He always risked most of what he made on some new *coup*.'

She spoke with a certain animation, her eyes brightened by memory.

'Anyway he died a very rich man. He had no children. He left his fortune in trust for his wife during her lifetime and after her death to me absolutely.'

A vague memory stirred in the Inspector's mind.

IMMENSE FORTUNE TO COME TO FAITHFUL SECRETARY – something of that kind.

'For the last twelve years or so,' said Miss Blacklock with a slight twinkle, '*I've* had an excellent motive for murdering Mrs Goedler – but that doesn't help you, does it?'

'Did – excuse me for asking this – did Mrs Goedler resent her husband's disposition of his fortune?'

Miss Blacklock was now looking frankly amused.

'You needn't be so very discreet. What you really mean is, was I Randall Goedler's mistress? No, I wasn't. I don't think Randall ever gave me a sentimental thought, and I certainly didn't give him one. He was in love with Belle (his wife), and remained in love with her until he died. I think in all probability it was gratitude on his part that prompted his making his will. You see, Inspector, in the very early days, when Randall was still on an insecure footing, he came very near to disaster. It was a question of just a few thousands of actual cash. It was a big *coup*, and a very exciting one; daring, as all his schemes were; but he just hadn't got that little bit of cash to tide him over. I came to the rescue. I had a little money of my own. I believed in Randall. I sold every penny I had out and gave it to him. It did the trick. A week later he was an immensely wealthy man.

'After that, he treated me more or less as a junior partner. Oh! they were exciting days.' She sighed. 'I enjoyed it all thoroughly. Then my father died, and my only sister was left a hopeless invalid. I had to give it all up and go and look after her. Randall died a couple of years later. I had made quite a lot of money during our association and I didn't really expect him to leave me anything, but I was very touched, yes, and very proud to find that if Belle predeceased me (and she was one of those delicate creatures whom everyone always says won't live long) I was to inherit his entire fortune. I think really the poor man didn't know who to leave it to. Belle's a dear, and she was delighted about it. She's really a very sweet person. She lives up in Scotland. I haven't seen her for years – we just write at Christmas. You see, I went with my sister to a sanatorium in Switzerland just before the war. She died of consumption out there.'

She was silent for a moment or two, then said:

'I only came back to England just over a year ago.'

'You said you might be a rich woman very soon. . . . How soon?'

'I heard from the nurse attendant who looks after Belle Goedler that Belle is sinking rapidly. It may be – only a few weeks.'

She added sadly:

'The money won't mean much to me now. I've got quite enough for my rather simple needs. Once I should have enjoyed playing the markets again – but now. . . . Oh, well, one grows old. Still, you do see, Inspector, don't you, that if Patrick and Julia wanted to kill me for a financial reason they'd be crazy not to wait for another few weeks.'

'Yes, Miss Blacklock, but what happens if you should predecease Mrs Goedler? Who does the money go to then?'

'D'you know, I've never really thought. Pip and Emma, I suppose. . . .'

Craddock stared and Miss Blacklock smiled.

'Does that sound rather crazy? I believe, if I predecease Belle, the money would go to the legal offspring – or whatever the term is – of Randall's only sister, Sonia. Randall had quarrelled with his sister. She married a man whom he considered a crook and worse.'

'And was he a crook?'

'Oh, definitely, I should say. But I believe a very attractive person to women. He was a Greek or a Roumanian or something – what was his name now – Stamfordis, Dmitri Stamfordis.'

'Randall Goedler cut his sister out of his will when she married this man?'

'Oh, Sonia was a very wealthy woman in her own right. Randall had already settled packets of money on her, as far as possible in a way so that her husband couldn't touch it. But I believe that when the lawyers urged him to put in someone in case I predeceased Belle, he reluctantly put down Sonia's offspring, simply because he couldn't think of anyone else and he wasn't the sort of man to leave money to charities.'

'And there were children of the marriage?'

'Well, there are Pip and Emma.' She laughed. 'I know it sounds ridiculous. All I know is that Sonia wrote once to Belle after her marriage, telling her to tell Randall that she was extremely happy and that she had just had twins and was calling them Pip and Emma. As far as I know she never wrote again. But Belle, of course, may be able to tell you more.'

Miss Blacklock had been amused by her own recital. The Inspector did not look amused.

'It comes to this,' he said. 'If you had been killed the other night, there are presumably at least two people in the world who would have come into a very large fortune. You are wrong, Miss Black-lock, when you say that there is no one who has a motive for desiring your death. There are two people, at least, who are vitally interested. How old would this brother and sister be?'

Miss Blacklock frowned.

'Let me see ... 1922 ... no – it's difficult to remember ... I suppose about twenty-five or twenty-six.' Her face had sobered. 'But you surely don't think –'

'I think somebody shot at you with the intent to kill you. I think it possible that that same person or persons might try again. I would like you, if you will, to be very *very* careful, Miss Blacklock. One murder has been arranged and did not come off. I think it possible that another murder may be arranged very soon.'

II

Phillipa Haymes straightened her back and pushed back a tendril of hair from her damp forehead. She was cleaning a flower border.

'Yes, Inspector?'

She looked at him enquiringly. In return he gave her a rather closer scrutiny than he had done before. Yes, a good-looking girl, a very English type with her pale ash-blonde hair and her rather long face. An obstinate chin and mouth. Something of repression – of tautness about her. The eyes were blue, very steady in their glance, and told you nothing at all. The sort of girl, he thought, who would keep a secret well.

'I'm sorry always to bother you when you're at work, Mrs Haymes,' he said, 'but I didn't want to wait until you came back for lunch. Besides, I thought it might be easier to talk to you here, away from Little Paddocks.'

'Yes, Inspector?'

No emotion and little interest in the voice. But was there a note of wariness – or did he imagine it?

'A certain statement has been made to me this morning. This statement concerns you.'

Phillipa raised her eyebrows very slightly.

'You told me, Mrs Haymes, that this man, Rudi Scherz, was quite unknown to you?'

'Yes.'

'That when you saw him there, dead, it was the first time you had set eyes on him. Is that so?'

'Certainly. I had never seen him before.'

'You did not, for instance, have a conversation with him in the summerhouse of Little Paddocks?'

'In the *summer*house?'

He was almost sure he caught a note of fear in her voice.

'Yes, Mrs Haymes.'

'*Who* says so?'

'I am told that you had a conversation with this man, Rudi Scherz, and that he asked you where he could hide and you replied that you would show him, and that a time, a quarter-past six, was definitely mentioned. It would be a quarter-past six, roughly, when Scherz would get here from the bus stop on the evening of the hold-up.'

There was a moment's silence. Then Phillipa gave a short scornful laugh. She looked amused.

'I don't know who told you that,' she said. 'At least I can guess. It's a very silly, clumsy story – spiteful, of course. For some reason Mitzi dislikes me even more than she dislikes the rest of us.'

'You deny it?'

'Of course it's not true. . . . I never met or saw Rudi Scherz in my life, and I was nowhere near the house that morning. I was over here, working.'

Inspector Craddock said very gently:

'Which morning?'

There was a momentary pause. Her eyelids flickered.

'Every morning. I'm here every morning. I don't get away until one o'clock.'

She added scornfully:

'It's no good listening to what Mitzi tells you. She tells lies all the time.'

'And that's that,' said Craddock when he was walking away with Sergeant Fletcher. 'Two young women whose stories flatly contradict each other. Which one am I to believe?'

'Everyone seems to agree that this foreign girl tells whoppers,' said Fletcher. 'It's been my experience in dealing with aliens that lying comes more easy than truth telling. Seems to be clear she's got a spite against this Mrs Haymes.'

'So, if you were me, you'd believe Mrs Haymes?'

'Unless you've got reason to think otherwise, sir.'

And Craddock hadn't, not really – only the remembrance of a pair of over-steady blue eyes and the glib enunciation of the words *that morning*. For to the best of his recollection he hadn't said whether the interview in the summerhouse had taken place in the morning or the afternoon.

Still, Miss Blacklock, or if not Miss Blacklock, certainly Miss Bunner, might have mentioned the visit of the young foreigner who had come to cadge his fare back to Switzerland. And Phillipa Haymes might have therefore assumed that the conversation was supposed to have taken place on that particular morning.

But Craddock still thought that there had been a note of fear in her voice as she asked:

'In the *summer*house?'

He decided to keep an open mind on the subject.

III

It was very pleasant in the Vicarage garden. One of those sudden spells of autumn warmth had descended upon England. Inspector Craddock could never remember if it was St Martin's or St Luke's Summer, but he knew that it was very pleasant – and also very enervating. He sat in a deck chair provided for him by an energetic Bunch, just on her way to a Mother's Meeting, and, well protected with shawls and a large rug round her knees, Miss Marple sat knitting beside him. The sunshine, the peace, the steady click of Miss Marple's knitting needles, all combined to produce a soporific feeling in the Inspector. And yet, at the same time, there was a nightmarish feeling at the back of his mind. It was like a familiar dream where an undertone of menace grows and finally turns Ease into Terror. . . .

He said abruptly, 'You oughtn't to be here.'

Miss Marple's needles stopped clicking for a moment. Her placid china blue eyes regarded him thoughtfully.

She said, 'I know what you mean. You're a very conscientious boy. But it's perfectly all right. Bunch's father (he was vicar of our parish, a very fine scholar) and her mother (who is a most remarkable woman – real spiritual power) are very old friends of mine. It's the most natural thing in the world that when I'm at Medenham I should come on here to stay with Bunch for a little.'

'Oh, perhaps,' said Craddock. 'But – but don't snoop around. . . . I've a feeling – I have really – that it isn't *safe*.'

Miss Marple smiled a little.

'But I'm afraid,' she said, 'that we old women always do snoop. It would be very odd and much more noticeable if I didn't. Questions about mutual friends in different parts of the world and whether they remember so and so, and do they remember who it was that Lady Somebody's daughter married? All that helps, doesn't it?'

'Helps?' said the Inspector, rather stupidly.

'Helps to find out if people are who they say they are,' said Miss Marple.

She went on:

'Because that's what's worrying you, isn't it? And that's really the particular way the world has changed since the war. Take this place, Chipping Cleghorn, for instance. It's very much like St Mary Mead where I live. Fifteen years ago one *knew* who everybody was. The Bantrys in the big house – and the Hartnells and the Price Ridleys and the Weatherbys. . . . They were people whose fathers and mothers and grandfathers and grandmothers, or whose aunts and uncles, had lived there before them. If somebody new came to live there, they brought letters of introduction, or they'd been in the same regiment or served on the same ship as someone there already. If anybody new – really new – really a stranger – came, well, they stuck out – everybody wondered about them and didn't rest till they found out.'

She nodded her head gently:

'But it's not like that any more. Every village and small country place is full of people who've just come and settled there without any ties to bring them. The big houses have been sold, and the

cottages have been converted and changed. And people just come –
and all you know about them is what they say of themselves.
They've come, you see, from all over the world. People from India
and Hong Kong and China, and people who used to live in France
and Italy in little cheap places and odd islands. And people who've
made a little money and can afford to retire. But nobody *knows* any
more who anyone is. You can have Benares brassware in your house
and talk about *tiffin* and *chota Hazri* – and you can have pictures of
Taormina and talk about the English church and the library – like
Miss Hinchliffe and Miss Murgatroyd. You can come from the
South of France, or have spent your life in the East. People take you
at your own valuation. They don't wait to call until they've had a
letter from a friend saying that the So-and-So's are delightful people
and she's known them all their lives.'

And that, thought Craddock, was exactly what *was* oppressing
him. He didn't *know*. They were just faces and personalities and
they were backed up by ration books and identity cards – nice neat
identity cards with numbers on them, without photographs or
fingerprints. Anybody who took the trouble could have a suitable
identity card – and partly because of that, the subtler links that had
held together English social rural life had fallen apart. In a town
nobody expected to know his neighbour. In the country now
nobody knew his neighbour either, though possibly he still thought
he did. . . .

Because of the oiled door, Craddock knew that there had been
somebody in Letitia Blacklock's drawing-room who was not the
pleasant friendly country neighbour he or she pretended to be. . . .

And because of that he was afraid for Miss Marple who was frail
and old and who noticed things. . . .

He said: 'We can, to a certain extent, check up on these
people. . . .' But he knew that that wasn't so easy. India and China
and Hong Kong and the South of France . . . It wasn't as easy as it
would have been fifteen years ago. There were people, as he knew
only too well, who were going about the country with borrowed
identities – borrowed from people who had met sudden death by
'incidents' in the cities. There were organizations who bought up
identities, who faked identity and ration cards – there were a
hundred small rackets springing into being. You *could* check up –
but it would take time – and time was what he hadn't got, because
Randall Goedler's widow was very near death.

It was then that, worried and tired, lulled by the sunshine, he told Miss Marple about Randall Goedler and about Pip and Emma.

'Just a couple of names,' he said. 'Nicknames at that! They mayn't exist. They may be respectable citizens living in Europe somewhere. On the other hand one, or both, of them may be here in Chipping Cleghorn.'

Twenty-five years old approximately – Who filled that description? He said, thinking aloud:

'That nephew and niece of hers – or cousins or whatever they are . . . I wonder when she saw them last –'

Miss Marple said gently: 'I'll find out for you, shall I?'

'Now, please, Miss Marple, don't –'

'It will be quite simple, Inspector, you really need not worry. And it won't be noticeable if I do it, because, you see, it won't be official. If there is anything wrong you don't want to put them on their guard.'

Pip and Emma, thought Craddock, Pip and Emma? He was getting obsessed by Pip and Emma. That attractive dare-devil young man, the good-looking girl with the cool stare. . . .

He said: 'I may find out more about them in the next forty-eight hours. I'm going up to Scotland. Mrs Goedler, if she's able to talk, may know a good deal more about them.'

'I think that's a very wise move.' Miss Marple hesitated. 'I hope,' she murmured, 'that you have warned Miss Blacklock to be careful?'

'I've warned her, yes. And I shall leave a man here to keep an unobtrusive eye on things.'

He avoided Miss Marple's eye which said plainly enough that a policeman keeping an eye on things would be little good if the danger was in the family circle. . . .

'And remember,' said Craddock, looking squarely at her. 'I've warned *you*.'

'I assure you, Inspector,' said Miss Marple, 'that I can take care of myself.'

11   MISS MARPLE COMES TO TEA

If Letitia Blacklock seemed slightly absent-minded when Mrs Harmon came to tea and brought a guest who was staying with her, Miss Marple, the guest in question, was hardly likely to notice the fact since it was the first time she had met her.

The old lady was very charming in her gentle gossipy fashion. She revealed herself almost at once to be one of those old ladies who have a constant preoccupation with burglars.

'They can get in anywhere, my dear,' she assured her hostess, 'absolutely *anywhere* nowadays. So many new American methods. I myself pin my faith to a very old-fashioned device. *A cabin hook and eye.* They can pick locks and draw back bolts but a brass hook and eye defeats them. Have you ever tried that?'

'I'm afraid we're not very good at bolts and bars,' said Miss Blacklock cheerfully. 'There's really nothing much to burgle.'

'A chain on the front door,' Miss Marple advised. 'Then the maid need only open it a crack and see who is there and they can't force their way in.'

'I expect Mitzi, our Mittel European, would love that.'

'The hold-up you had must have been very, very frightening,' said Miss Marple. 'Bunch has been telling me all about it.'

'I was scared stiff,' said Bunch.

'It was an alarming experience,' admitted Miss Blacklock.

'It really seems like Providence that the man tripped himself up and shot himself. These burglars are so *violent* nowadays. How did he get in?'

'Well, I'm afraid we don't lock our doors much.'

'Oh, Letty,' exclaimed Miss Bunner. 'I forgot to tell you the Inspector was most peculiar this morning. He insisted on opening the second door – you know – the one that's never been opened – the one over there. He hunted for the key and everything and said the door had been oiled. But I can't see why because –'

Too late she got Miss Blacklock's signal to be quiet, and paused open-mouthed.

'Oh, Lotty, I'm so – sorry – I mean, oh, I *do* beg your pardon, Letty – oh, dear, how stupid I am.'

'It doesn't matter,' said Miss Blacklock, but she was annoyed. 'Only I don't think Inspector Craddock wants that talked about. I didn't know you had been there when he was experimenting, Dora. You do understand, don't you, Mrs Harmon?'

'Oh, yes,' said Bunch. 'We won't breathe a word, will we, Aunt Jane. But I wonder *why* he –'

She relapsed into thought. Miss Bunner fidgeted and looked miserable, bursting out at last: 'I always say the wrong thing – Oh, dear, I'm nothing but a trial to you, Letty.'

Miss Blacklock said quickly, 'You're my great comfort, Dora. And anyway in a small place like Chipping Cleghorn, there aren't really any secrets.'

'Now that is very true,' said Miss Marple. 'I'm afraid, you know, that things do get round in the most extraordinary way. Servants, of course, and yet it can't only be that, because one has so few servants nowadays. Still, there are the daily women and perhaps they are worse, because they go to everybody in turn and pass the news round.'

'Oh!' said Bunch Harmon suddenly. 'I've got it! Of course, if that door could open too, someone might have gone out of here in the dark and done the hold-up – only of course they didn't – because it was the man from the Royal Spa Hotel. Or wasn't it? . . . No, I don't see after all . . .' she frowned.

'Did it all happen in this room then?' asked Miss Marple, adding apologetically: 'I'm afraid you must think me sadly *curious*, Miss Blacklock – but it really is so very exciting – just like something one reads about in the paper – and actually to have happened to someone one knows . . . I'm just longing to hear all about it and to picture it all, if you know what I mean –'

Immediately Miss Marple received a confused and voluble account from Bunch and Miss Bunner – with occasional emendations and corrections from Miss Blacklock.

In the middle of it Patrick came in and good-naturedly entered into the spirit of the recital – going so far as to enact himself the part of Rudi Scherz.

'And Aunt Letty was there – in the corner by the archway . . . Go and stand there, Aunt Letty.'

Miss Blacklock obeyed, and then Miss Marple was shown the actual bullet holes.

'What a marvellous – what a providential escape,' she gasped.

'I was just going to offer my guests cigarettes –' Miss Blacklock indicated the big silver box on the table.

'People are so careless when they smoke,' said Miss Bunner disapprovingly. 'Nobody really respects good furniture as they used to do. Look at the horrid burn somebody made on this beautiful table by putting a cigarette down on it. *Disgraceful.*'

Miss Blacklock sighed.

'Sometimes, I'm afraid, one thinks too much of one's possessions.'

'But it's such a lovely table, Letty.'

Miss Bunner loved her friend's possessions with as much fervour as though they had been her own. Bunch Harmon had always thought it was a very endearing trait in her. She showed no sign of envy.

'It is a lovely table,' said Miss Marple politely. 'And what a very pretty china lamp on it.'

Again it was Miss Bunner who accepted the compliment as though she and not Miss Blacklock was the owner of the lamp.

'Isn't it delightful? Dresden. There is a pair of them. The other's in the spare room, I think.'

'You know where everything in this house is, Dora – or you think you do,' said Miss Blacklock, good-humouredly. 'You care far more about my things than I do.'

Miss Bunner flushed.

'I *do* like nice things,' she said. Her voice was half defiant – half wistful.

'I must confess,' said Miss Marple, 'that my own few possessions are very dear to me, too – so many *memories*, you know. It's the same with photographs. People nowadays have so few photographs about. Now I like to keep all the pictures of my nephews and nieces as babies – and then as children – and so on.'

'You've got a horrible one of me, aged three,' said Bunch. 'Holding a fox terrier and squinting.'

'I expect your aunt has many photographs of you,' said Miss Marple, turning to Patrick.

'Oh, we're only distant cousins,' said Patrick.

'I believe Elinor did send me one of you as a baby, Pat,' said Miss Blacklock. 'But I'm afraid I didn't keep it. I'd really forgotten how many children she'd had or what their names were until she wrote me about you two being over here.'

'Another sign of the times,' said Miss Marple. 'Nowadays one so often doesn't know one's younger relations *at all*. In the old days, with all the big family reunions, that would have been impossible.'

'I last saw Pat and Julia's mother at a wedding thirty years ago,' said Miss Blacklock. 'She was a very pretty girl.'

'That's why she has such handsome children,' said Patrick with a grin.

'You've got a marvellous old album,' said Julia. 'Do you remember, Aunt Letty, we looked through it the other day. The hats!'

'And how smart we thought ourselves,' said Miss Blacklock with a sigh.

'Never mind, Aunt Letty,' said Patrick, 'Julia will come across a snapshot of herself in about thirty years' time – and won't she think she looks a guy!'

'Did you do that on purpose?' said Bunch, as she and Miss Marple were walking home. 'Talk about photographs I mean?'

'Well, my dear, it *is* interesting to know that Miss Blacklock didn't know either of her two young relatives by sight. . . . Yes – I think Inspector Craddock will be interested to hear that.'

12   MORNING ACTIVITIES
IN CHIPPING CLEGHORN

Edmund Swettenham sat down rather precariously on a garden roller.

'Good morning, Phillipa,' he said.

'Hallo.'

'Are you very busy?'

'Moderately.'

'What are you doing?'

'Can't you see?'

'No. I'm not a gardener. You seem to be playing with earth in some fashion.'

'I'm pricking out winter lettuce.'

'Pricking out? What a curious term! Like pinking. Do you know what pinking is? I only learnt the other day. I always thought it was a term for professional duelling.'

'Do you want anything particular?' asked Phillipa coldly.

'Yes. I want to see you.'

Phillipa gave him a quick glance.

'I wish you wouldn't come here like this. Mrs Lucas won't like it.'

'Doesn't she allow you to have followers?'

'Don't be absurd.'

'Followers. That's another nice word. It describes my attitude perfectly. Respectful – at a distance – but firmly pursuing.'

'Please go away, Edmund. You've no business to come here.'

'You're wrong,' said Edmund triumphantly. 'I *have* business here. Mrs Lucas rang up my mama this morning and said she had a good many vegetable marrows.'

'Masses of them.'

'And would we like to exchange a pot of honey for a vegetable marrow or so.'

'That's not a fair exchange at all! Vegetable marrows are quite unsaleable at the moment – everybody has such a lot.'

'Naturally. That's why Mrs Lucas rang up. Last time, if I remember rightly, the exchange suggested was some skim milk – *skim* milk, mark you – in exchange for some lettuces. It was then very early in the season for lettuces. They were about a shilling each.'

Phillipa did not speak.

Edmund tugged at his pocket and extracted a pot of honey.

'So here,' he said, 'is my alibi. Used in a loose and quite indefensible meaning of the term. If Mrs Lucas pops her bust round the door of the potting shed, I'm here in quest of vegetable marrows. There is absolutely no question of dalliance.'

'I see.'

'Do you ever read Tennyson?' enquired Edmund conversationally.

'Not very often.'

'You should. Tennyson is shortly going to make a comeback in a big way. When you turn on your wireless in the evening it will be the *Idylls of the King* you will hear and not interminable Trollope. I always thought the Trollope pose was the most unbearable affectation. Perhaps a little of Trollope, but not to drown in him. But speaking of Tennyson, have you read "Maud"?'

'Once, long ago.'

'It's got some points about it.' He quoted softly: '"Faultily faultless, icily regular, splendidly null." That's you, Phillipa.'

'Hardly a compliment!'

'No, it wasn't meant to be. I gather Maud got under the poor fellow's skin just like you've got under mine.'

'Don't be absurd, Edmund.'

'Oh, hell, Phillipa, why are you like you are? What goes on behind your splendidly regular features? What do you think? What do you *feel*? Are you happy, or miserable, or frightened, or what? There must be *something*.'

Phillipa said quietly.

'What I feel is my own business.'

'It's mine, too. I want to make you talk. I want to know what goes on in that quiet head of yours. I've a *right* to know. I have really. I didn't want to fall in love with you. I wanted to sit quietly and write my book. Such a nice book, all about how miserable the world is. It's frightfully easy to be clever about how miserable everybody is. And it's all a habit, really. Yes, I've suddenly become convinced of that. After reading a life of Burne Jones.'

Phillipa had stopped pricking out. She was staring at him with a puzzled frown.

'What has Burne Jones got to do with it?'

'Everything. When you've read all about the Pre-Raphaelites you realize just what fashion is. They were all terrifically hearty and slangy and jolly, and laughed and joked, and everything was fine and wonderful. That was fashion, too. They weren't any happier or heartier than we are. And we're not any more miserable than they were. It's all fashion, I tell you. After the last war, we went in for sex. Now it's all frustration. None of it matters. Why are we talking about all this? I started out to talk about *us*. Only I got cold feet and shied off. Because you won't help me.'

'What do you want me to do?'

'*Talk!* Tell me things. Is it your husband? Do you adore him and he's dead and so you've shut up like a clam? Is that it? All right, you adored him, and he's dead. Well, other girls' husbands are dead – lots of them – and some of the girls loved their husbands. They tell you so in bars, and cry a bit when they're drunk enough, and then want to go to bed with you so that they'll feel better. It's one way of getting over it, I suppose. You've got to get over it, Phillipa. You're young – and you're extremely lovely – and I love you like Hell. Talk about your damned husband, tell me about him.'

'There's nothing to tell. We met and got married.'

'You must have been very young.'

'Too young.'

'Then you weren't happy with him? Go *on*, Phillipa.'

'There's nothing to go on about. We were married. We were as happy as most people are, I suppose. Harry was born. Ronald went overseas. He – he was killed in Italy.'

'And now there's Harry?'

'And now there's Harry.'

'I like Harry. He's a really nice kid. He likes me. We get on. What about it, Phillipa? Shall we get married? You can go on gardening and I can go on writing my book and in the holidays we'll leave off working and enjoy ourselves. We can manage, with tact, not to have to live with Mother. She can fork out a bit to support her adored son. I sponge, I write tripey books, I have defective eyesight and I talk too much. That's the worst. Will you try it?'

Phillipa looked at him. She saw a tall rather solemn young man with an anxious face and large spectacles. His sandy head was rumpled and he was regarding her with a reassuring friendliness.

'No,' said Phillipa.

'Definitely no?'

'Definitely no.'

'Why?'

'You don't know anything about me.'

'Is that all?'

'No, you don't know anything about anything.'

Edmund considered.

'Perhaps not,' he admitted. 'But who does? Phillipa, my adored one –' He broke off.

A shrill and prolonged yapping was rapidly approaching.

> '*Pekes in the high hall garden,* (said Edmund)
> *When twilight was falling* (only it's eleven a.m.)
> *Phil, Phil, Phil, Phil,*
> *They were crying and calling*

'Your name doesn't lend itself to the rhythm, does it? Sounds like an "Ode to a Fountain Pen". Have you got another name?'

'Joan. *Please* go away. That's Mrs Lucas.'

'*Joan, Joan, Joan, Joan.* Better, but still not good. *When greasy Joan the pot doth keel* – that's not a nice picture of married life, either.'

'Mrs Lucas is –'

'Oh, *hell!*' said Edmund. 'Get me a blasted vegetable marrow.'

II

Sergeant Fletcher had the house at Little Paddocks to himself.

It was Mitzi's day off. She always went by the eleven o'clock bus into Medenham Wells. By arrangement with Miss Blacklock, Sergeant Fletcher had the run of the house. She and Dora Bunner had gone down to the village.

Fletcher worked fast. Someone in the house had oiled and prepared that door, and whoever had done it, had done it in order to be able to leave the drawing-room unnoticed as soon as the lights went out. That ruled out Mitzi who wouldn't have needed to use the door.

Who was left? The neighbours, Fletcher thought, might also be ruled out. He didn't see how they could have found an opportunity to oil and prepare the door. That left Patrick and Julia Simmons, Phillipa Haymes, and possibly Dora Bunner. The young Simmonses were in Milchester. Phillipa Haymes was at work. Sergeant Fletcher was free to search out any secrets he could. But the house was disappointingly innocent. Fletcher, who was an expert on electricity could find nothing suggestive in the wiring or appurtenances of the electric fixtures to show how the lights had been fused. Making a rapid survey of the household bedrooms he found an irritating normality. In Phillipa Haymes' room were photographs of a small boy with serious eyes, an earlier photo of the same child, a pile of schoolboy letters, a theatre programme or two. In Julia's room there was a drawer full of snapshots of the South of France. Bathing photos, a villa set amidst mimosa. Patrick's held some souvenirs of Naval days. Dora Bunner's held few personal possessions and they seemed innocent enough.

And yet, thought Fletcher, someone in the house must have oiled that door.

His thoughts broke off at a sound below stairs. He went quickly to the top of the staircase and looked down.

Mrs Swettenham was crossing the hall. She had a basket on her arm. She looked into the drawing-room, crossed the hall and went into the dining-room. She came out again without the basket.

Some faint sound that Fletcher made, a board that creaked unexpectedly under his feet, made her turn her head. She called up:

'Is that you, Miss Blacklock?'

'No, Mrs Swettenham, it's me,' said Fletcher.

Mrs Swettenham gave a faint scream.

'Oh! how you startled me. I thought it might be another burglar.'

Fletcher came down the stairs.

'This house doesn't seem very well protected against burglars,' he said. 'Can anybody always walk in and out just as they like?'

'I just brought up some of my quinces,' explained Mrs Swettenham. 'Miss Blacklock wants to make quince jelly and she hasn't got a quince tree here. I left them in the dining-room.'

Then she smiled.

'Oh, I see, you mean how did I get in? Well, I just came in through the side door. We all walk in and out of each other's houses, Sergeant. Nobody dreams of locking a door until it's dark. I mean it would be so awkward, wouldn't it, if you brought things and couldn't get in to leave them? It's not like the old days when you rang a bell and a servant always came to answer it.' Mrs Swettenham sighed. 'In India, I remember,' she said mournfully, 'we had eighteen servants – eighteen. Not counting the *ayah*. Just as a matter of course. And at home, when I was a girl, we always had three – although Mother always felt it was terribly poverty-stricken not to be able to afford a kitchen-maid. I must say that I find life very odd nowadays, Sergeant, though I know one mustn't complain. So much worse for the miners always getting psittiscosis (or is that parrot disease?) and having to come out of the mines and try to be gardeners though they don't know weeds from spinach.'

She added, as she tripped towards the door, 'I mustn't keep you. I expect you're very busy. Nothing else is going to happen, is it?'

'Why should it, Mrs Swettenham?'

'I just wondered, seeing you here. I thought it might be a *gang*. You'll tell Miss Blacklock about the quinces, won't you?'

Mrs Swettenham departed. Fletcher felt like a man who has received an unexpected jolt. He had been assuming – erroneously, he now perceived – that it must have been someone in the house who had done the oiling of the door. He saw now that he was wrong. An outsider had only to wait until Mitzi had departed by bus and Letitia Blacklock and Dora Bunner were both out of the house. Such an opportunity must have been simplicity itself. That meant that he couldn't rule out anybody who had been in the drawing-room that night.

III

'Murgatroyd.'

'Yes, Hinch?'

'I've been doing a bit of thinking.'

'Have you, Hinch?'

'Yes, the great brain has been working. You know, Murgatroyd, the whole setup the other evening was decidedly fishy.'

'Fishy?'

'Yes. Tuck your hair up, Murgatroyd, and take this trowel. Pretend it's a revolver.'

'Oh,' said Miss Murgatroyd, nervously.

'All right. It won't bite you. Now come along to the kitchen door. You're going to be the burglar. You stand *here*. Now you're going into the kitchen to hold up a lot of nitwits. Take the torch. Switch it on.'

'But it's broad daylight!'

'Use your imagination, Murgatroyd. Switch it on.'

Miss Murgatroyd did so, rather clumsily, shifting the trowel under one arm while she did so.

'Now then,' said Miss Hinchliffe, 'off you go. Remember the time you played Hermia in *A Midsummer Night's Dream* at the Women's Institute? Act. Give it all you've got. "Stick 'em up!" Those are your lines – and don't ruin them by saying "Please".'

Obediently, Miss Murgatroyd raised her torch, flourished the trowel and advanced on the kitchen door.

Transferring the torch to her right hand she swiftly turned the handle and stepped forward, resuming the torch in her left hand.

'Stick 'em up!' she fluted, adding vexedly: 'Dear me, this is very difficult, Hinch.'

'Why?'

'The door. It's a swing door, it keeps coming back and I've got both hands full.'

'Exactly,' boomed Miss Hinchliffe. 'And the drawing-room door at Little Paddocks always swings to. It isn't a swing door like this, but it won't stay open. That's why Letty Blacklock bought that absolutely delectable heavy glass doorstop from Elliot's in the High

Street. I don't mind saying I've never forgiven her for getting in ahead of me there. I was beating the old brute down from eight guineas to six pound ten, and then Blacklock comes along and buys the damned thing. I'd never seen as attractive a doorstop, you don't often get those glass bubbles in that big size.'

'Perhaps the burglar put the doorstop against the door to keep it open,' suggested Miss Murgatroyd.

'Use your common sense, Murgatroyd. What does he do? Throw the door open, say "excuse me a moment," stoop and put the stop into position and then resume business by saying "Hands up?" Try holding the door with your shoulder.'

'It's still very awkward,' complained Miss Murgatroyd.

'Exactly,' said Miss Hinchliffe. 'A revolver, a torch and a door to hold open – a bit too much, isn't it? So what's the answer?'

Miss Murgatroyd did not attempt to supply an answer. She looked enquiringly and admiringly at her masterful friend and waited to be enlightened.

'We know he'd got a revolver, because he fired it,' said Miss Hinchliffe. 'And we know he had a torch because we all saw it – that is unless we're all the victims of mass hypnotism like explanations of the Indian rope trick (what a bore that old Easterbrook is with his Indian stories) so the question is, did someone hold that door open for him?'

'But who could have done that?'

'Well, *you* could have for one, Murgatroyd. As far as I remember, you were standing directly behind it when the lights went out.' Miss Hinchliffe laughed heartily. 'Highly suspicious character, aren't you, Murgatroyd? But who'd think it to look at you. Here, give me that trowel – thank heavens it isn't really a revolver. You'd have shot yourself by now!'

IV

'It's a most extraordinary thing,' muttered Colonel Easterbrook. 'Most extraordinary. Laura.'

'Yes, darling?'

'Come into my dressing room a moment.'

'What is it, darling?'

Mrs Easterbrook appeared through the open door.

'Remember my showing you that revolver of mine?'

'Oh, yes, Archie, a nasty horrid black thing.'

'Yes. Hun souvenir. Was in this drawer, wasn't it?'

'Yes, it was.'

'Well, it's not there now.'

'Archie, how *extraordinary!*'

'You haven't moved it or anything?'

'Oh, no, I'd never dare to touch the horrid thing.'

'Think old mother what'sername did?'

'Oh, I shouldn't think so, for a minute. Mrs Butt would never do a thing like that. Shall I ask her?'

'No – no, better not. Don't want to start a lot of talk. Tell me, do you remember when it was I showed it to you?'

'Oh, about a week ago. You were grumbling about your collars and the laundry and you opened this drawer wide and there it was at the back and I asked you what it was.'

'Yes, that's right. About a week ago. You don't remember the date?'

Mrs Easterbrook considered, eyelids down over her eyes, a shrewd brain working.

'Of course,' she said. 'It was Saturday. The day we were to have gone in to the pictures, but we didn't.'

'H'm – sure it wasn't before that? Wednesday? Thursday or even the week before that again?'

'No, dear,' said Mrs Easterbrook. 'I remember *quite* distinctly. It was Saturday the 30th. It just seems a long time because of all the trouble there's been. And I can tell you *how* I remember. It's because it was the day after the hold-up at Miss Blacklock's. Because when I saw your revolver it reminded me of the shooting the night before.'

'Ah,' said Colonel Easterbrook, 'then that's a great load off my mind.'

'Oh, Archie, why?'

'Just because if that revolver had disappeared before the shooting – well, it might possibly have been my revolver that was pinched by that Swiss fellow.'

'But how would he have known you had one?'

'These gangs have a most extraordinary communication service. They get to know everything about a place and who lives there.'

'What a lot you do know, Archie.'

'Ha. Yes. Seen a thing or two in my time. Still as you definitely remember seeing my revolver *after* the hold-up – well, that settles it. The revolver that Swiss fellow used can't have been mine, can it?'

'Of course it can't.'

'A great relief. I should have had to go to the police about it. And they ask a lot of awkward questions. Bound to. As a matter of fact I never took out a licence for it. Somehow, after a war, one forgets these peacetime regulations. I looked on it as a war souvenir, not as a firearm.'

'Yes, I see. Of course.'

'But all the same – where on earth can the damned thing be?'

'Perhaps Mrs Butt took it. She's always seemed quite honest, but perhaps she felt nervous after the hold-up and thought she'd like to – to have a revolver in the house. Of course, she'll never admit doing that. I shan't even ask her. She might get offended. And what should we do then? This is such a big house – I simply couldn't –'

'Quite so,' said Colonel Easterbrook. 'Better not say anything.'

13   MORNING ACTIVITIES IN CHIPPING CLEGHORN (continued)

Miss Marple came out of the vicarage gate and walked down the little lane that led into the main street.

She walked fairly briskly with the aid of the Rev. Julian Harmon's stout ashplant stick.

She passed the Red Cow and the butcher's and stopped for a brief moment to look into the window of Mr Elliot's antique shop. This was cunningly situated next door to the Bluebird Tearooms and Café so that rich motorists, after stopping for a nice cup of tea and somewhat euphemistically named 'Home Made Cakes' of a bright saffron colour, could be tempted by Mr Elliot's judiciously planned shop window.

In this antique bow frame, Mr Elliot catered for all tastes. Two pieces of Waterford glass reposed on an impeccable wine cooler. A walnut bureau, made up of various bits and pieces proclaimed itself a Genuine Bargain and on a table, in the window itself, were a nice assortment of cheap doorknockers and quaint pixies, a few chipped bits of Dresden, a couple of sad-looking bead necklaces, a mug with 'A Present from Tunbridge Wells' on it, and some titbits of Victorian silver.

Miss Marple gave the window her rapt attention, and Mr Elliot, an elderly obese spider, peeped out of his web to appraise the possibilities of this new fly.

But just as he decided that the charms of the Present from Tunbridge Wells were about to be too much for the lady who was staying at the vicarage (for of course Mr Elliot, like everybody else, knew exactly who she was), Miss Marple saw out of the corner of her eye Miss Dora Bunner entering the Bluebird Café, and immediately decided that what she needed to counteract the cold wind was a nice cup of morning coffee.

Four or five ladies were already engaged in sweetening their morning shopping by a pause for refreshment. Miss Marple, blinking a little in the gloom of the interior of the Bluebird, and hovering artistically, was greeted by the voice of Dora Bunner at her elbow.

'Oh, good morning, Miss Marple. Do sit down here. I'm all alone.'

'Thank you.'

Miss Marple subsided gratefully on to the rather angular little blue-painted arm-chair which the Bluebird affected.

'Such a sharp wind,' she complained. 'And I can't walk very fast because of my rheumatic leg.'

'Oh, I know. I had sciatica one year – and really, most of the time I was in *agony*.'

The two ladies talked rheumatism, sciatica and neuritis for some moments with avidity. A sulky-looking girl in a pink overall with a flight of bluebirds down the front of it took their order for coffee and cakes with a yawn and an air of weary patience.

'The cakes,' Miss Bunner said in a conspiratorial whisper, 'are really *quite* good here.'

'I was so interested in that very pretty girl I met as we were coming away from Miss Blacklock's the other day,' said Miss Marple. 'I think she said she does gardening. Or is she on the land? Hynes – was that her name?'

'Oh, yes, Phillipa Haymes. Our "Lodger," as we call her.' Miss Bunner laughed at her own humour. 'Such a nice quiet girl. A *lady*, if you know what I mean.'

'I wonder now. I knew a Colonel Haymes – in the Indian cavalry. Her father perhaps?'

'She's *Mrs* Haymes. A widow. Her husband was killed in Sicily or Italy. Of course, it might be *his* father.'

'I wondered, perhaps, if there might be a little romance on the way?' Miss Marple suggested roguishly. 'With that tall young man?'

'With Patrick, do you mean? Oh, I don't –'

'No, I meant a young man with spectacles. I've seen him about.'

'Oh, of course, Edmund Swettenham. Sh! That's his mother, Mrs Swettenham, over in the corner. I don't know, I'm sure. You think he admires her? He's such an odd young man – says the most disturbing things sometimes. He's supposed to be *clever*, you know,' said Miss Bunner with frank disapproval.

'Cleverness isn't everything,' said Miss Marple, shaking her head. 'Ah, here is our coffee.'

The sulky girl deposited it with a clatter. Miss Marple and Miss Bunner pressed cakes on each other.

'I was so interested to hear you were at school with Miss Blacklock. Yours is indeed an old friendship.'

'Yes, indeed.' Miss Bunner sighed. 'Very few people would be as loyal to their old friends as dear Miss Blacklock is. Oh, dear, those days seem a long time ago. Such a pretty girl and enjoyed life so much. It all seemed so *sad*.'

Miss Marple, though with no idea of what had seemed so sad, sighed and shook her head.

'Life is indeed hard,' she murmured.

'*And sad affliction bravely borne*,' murmured Miss Bunner, her eyes suffusing with tears. 'I always think of that verse. True patience; true resignation. Such courage and patience *ought* to be rewarded, that is what I say. What I feel is that *nothing* is too good for dear Miss Blacklock, and whatever good things come to her, she truly *deserves* them.'

'Money,' said Miss Marple, 'can do a lot to ease one's path in life.'

She felt herself safe in this observation since she judged that it must be Miss Blacklock's prospects of future affluence to which her friend referred.

The remark, however, started Miss Bunner on another train of thought.

'Money!' she exclaimed with bitterness. 'I don't believe, you know, that until one has really experienced it, one can know what money, or rather the lack of it, *means*.'

Miss Marple nodded her white head sympathetically.

Miss Bunner went on rapidly, working herself up, and speaking with a flushed face:

'I've heard people say so often "I'd rather have flowers on the table than a meal without them." But how many meals have those people ever missed? They don't know what it is – nobody knows who hasn't been through it – to be really *hungry*. Bread, you know, and a jar of meat paste, and a scrape of margarine. Day after day, and how one longs for a good plate of meat and two vegetables. And the *shabbiness*. Darning one's clothes and hoping it won't show. And applying for jobs and always being told you're too old. And then perhaps getting a job and after all one isn't strong enough. One faints. And you're back again. It's the *rent* – always the *rent* – that's *got* to be paid – otherwise you're out in the street. And in these days it leaves so little over. One's old age pension doesn't go far – indeed it doesn't.'

'I know,' said Miss Marple gently. She looked with compassion at Miss Bunner's twitching face.

'I wrote to Letty. I just happened to see her name in the paper. It was a luncheon in aid of Milchester Hospital. There it was in black and white, Miss Letitia Blacklock. It brought the past back to me. I hadn't heard of her for years and years. She'd been secretary, you know, to that very rich man, Goedler. She was always a clever girl – the kind that gets on in the world. Not so much looks – as *character*. I thought – well, I thought – perhaps she'll remember me – and she's one of the people I *could* ask for a little help. I mean someone you've known as a girl – been at school with – well, they do *know* about you – they know you're not just a – begging letter-writer –'

Tears came into Dora Bunner's eyes.

'And then Lotty came and took me away – said she needed someone to help her. Of course, I was very surprised – *very* surprised – but then newspapers do get things wrong. How kind she was – and how *sympathetic*. And remembering all the old days so well . . . I'd do anything for her – I really would. And I try *very* hard, but I'm afraid sometimes I muddle things – my head's not what it was. I make mistakes. And I forget and say foolish things. She's very patient. What's so nice about her is that she always pretends that I *am* useful to her. That's real kindness, isn't it?'

Miss Marple said gently: 'Yes, that's real kindness.'

'I used to worry, you know, even after I came to Little Paddocks – about what would become of me if – if anything were to happen to Miss Blacklock. After all, there are so many accidents – these motors dashing about – one never knows, does one? But naturally I never *said* anything – but she must have guessed. Suddenly, one day she told me that she'd left me a small annuity in her will – and – what

I value far more – all her beautiful furniture. I was quite *overcome* . . . But she said nobody else would value it as I should – and that is quite true – I can't bear to see some lovely piece of china smashed – or wet glasses put down on a table and leaving a mark. I do really look after her things. Some people – some people especially, are so terribly careless – and sometimes worse than careless!

'I'm not really as stupid as I look,' Miss Bunner continued with simplicity. 'I can see, you know, when Letty's being imposed upon. Some people – I won't name names – but they take *advantage*. Dear Miss Blacklock is, perhaps, just a shade too *trusting*.'

Miss Marple shook her head.

'*That's* a mistake.'

'Yes, it is. You and I, Miss Marple, know the world. Dear Miss Blacklock –' She shook her head.

Miss Marple thought that as the secretary of a big financier Miss Blacklock might be presumed to know the world too. But probably what Dora Bunner meant was that Letty Blacklock had always been comfortably off, and that the comfortably off do not know the deeper abysses of human nature.

'That Patrick!' said Miss Bunner with a suddenness and an asperity that made Miss Marple jump. 'Twice, at least, to my knowledge, he's got money out of her. Pretending he's hard up. Run into debt. All that sort of thing. She's far too generous. All she said to me when I remonstrated with her was: "The boy's young, Dora. Youth is the time to have your fling."'

'Well, that's true enough,' said Miss Marple. 'Such a handsome young man, too.'

'Handsome is as handsome does,' said Dora Bunner. 'Much too fond of poking fun at people. And a lot of going on with girls, I expect. I'm just a figure of fun to him – that's all. He doesn't seem to realize that people have their feelings.'

'Young people *are* rather careless that way,' said Miss Marple.

Miss Bunner leaned forward suddenly with a mysterious air.

'You won't breathe a word, will you, my dear?' she demanded. 'But I can't help feeling that he *was* mixed up in this dreadful business. I think he knew that young man – or else Julia did. I daren't hint at such a thing to dear Miss Blacklock – at least I did, and she just snapped my head off. And, of course, it's *awkward* – because he's her nephew – or at any rate her *cousin* – and if the Swiss young man shot himself Patrick might be held morally responsible, mightn't he? If he'd put him up to it, I mean. I'm really terribly confused about the whole thing. Everyone making such a fuss about that other door into the drawing room. That's another thing that worries me – the detective saying it had been oiled. Because you see, I saw –'

She came to an abrupt stop.

Miss Marple paused to select a phrase.

'Most difficult for you,' she said sympathetically. 'Naturally you wouldn't want anything to get round to the police.'

'That's just it,' Dora Bunner cried. 'I lie awake at nights and worry . . . because, you see, I came upon Patrick in the shrubbery the other day. I was looking for eggs – one hen lays out – and there he was holding a feather and a cup – an oily cup. And he jumped most guiltily when he saw me and he said: "I was just wondering what this was doing here." Well, of course, he's a quick thinker. I should say he thought that up quickly when I startled him. And how did he come to find a thing like that in the shrubbery unless he was looking for it, knowing perfectly well it was there? Of course, I didn't *say* anything.'

'No, no, of course not.'

'But I gave him a *look*, if you know what I mean.'

Dora Bunner stretched out her hand and bit abstractedly into a lurid salmon coloured cake.

'And then another day I happened to overhear him having a very curious conversation with Julia. They seemed to be having a kind of quarrel. He was saying: "If I thought you had anything to do with a thing like that!" and Julia (she's always so calm, you know) said: "Well, little brother, what would you do about it?" And then, *most* unfortunately, I trod on that board that always squeaks, and they saw me. So I said, quite gaily: "You two having a quarrel?" and Patrick said, "I'm warning Julia not to go in for these black market deals." Oh, it was all very slick, but I don't believe they were talking about anything of the sort! And if you ask me, I believe Patrick had tampered with that lamp in the drawing room – to make the lights go out, because I remember distinctly that it was the shepherdess – *not* the shepherd. And the next day –'

She stopped and her face grew pink. Miss Marple turned her head to see Miss Blacklock, standing behind them – she must just have come in.

'Coffee and gossip, Bunny?' said Miss Blacklock with quite a shade of reproach in her voice. 'Good morning, Miss Marple. Cold, isn't it?'

'We were just talking,' said Miss Bunner, hurriedly. 'So many rules and regulations nowadays. One really doesn't know where one is.'

The doors flew open with a clang and Bunch Harmon came into the Bluebird with a rush.

'Hallo,' she said, 'am I too late for coffee?'

'No, dear,' said Miss Marple. 'Sit down and have a cup.'

'We must get home,' said Miss Blacklock. 'Done your shopping, Bunny?'

Her tone was indulgent once more, but her eyes still held a slight reproach.

'Yes – yes, thank you, Letty. I must just pop into the chemists' in passing and get some aspirin and some corn-plasters.'

As the doors of the Bluebird swung to behind them, Bunch asked:

'What were you talking about?'

Miss Marple did not reply at once. She waited whilst Bunch gave the order, then she said:

'Family solidarity is a very strong thing. Very strong. Do you remember some famous case – I really can't remember what it was. They said the husband poisoned his wife. In a glass of wine. Then, at the trial, the daughter said she'd drunk half her mother's glass – so that knocked the case against her father to pieces. They do say – but that may be just rumour – that she never spoke to her father or lived with him again. Of course, a father is one thing – and a nephew or a distant cousin is another. But still there it is – no one wants a member of their own family hanged, do they?'

'No,' said Bunch, considering. 'I shouldn't think they would.'

Miss Marple leaned back in her chair. She murmured under her breath, 'People are really very alike, everywhere.'

'Who am I like?'

'Well, really, dear, you are very much like yourself. I don't know that you remind me of anyone in particular. Except perhaps –'

'Here it comes,' said Bunch.

'I was just thinking of a parlourmaid of mine, dear.'

'A parlourmaid? I should make a terrible parlourmaid.'

'Yes, dear, so did she. She was no good at all at waiting at table. Put everything on the table crooked, mixed up the kitchen knives with the dining room ones, and her cap (this was a long time ago, dear) her cap was *never* straight.'

Bunch adjusted her hat automatically.

'Anything else?' she demanded anxiously.

'I kept her because she was so pleasant to have about the house – and because she used to make me laugh. I liked the way she said things straight out. Came to me one day, "Of course, I don't know, ma'am," she says, "but Florrie, the way she sits down, it's just like a married woman." And sure enough poor Florrie was in trouble – the gentlemanly assistant at the hairdresser's. Fortunately it was in good time, and I was able to have a little talk with him, and they had a very nice wedding and settled down quite happily. She was a good girl, Florrie, but inclined to be taken in by a gentlemanly appearance.'

'She didn't do a murder, did she?' asked Bunch. 'The parlour-maid, I mean.'

'No, indeed,' said Miss Marple. 'She married a Baptist Minister and they had a family of five.'

'Just like me,' said Bunch. 'Though I've only got as far as Edward and Susan up to date.'

She added, after a minute or two:

'Who are you thinking about now, Aunt Jane?'

'Quite a lot of people, dear, quite a lot of people,' said Miss Marple, vaguely.

'In St Mary Mead?'

'Mostly . . . I was really thinking about Nurse Ellerton – really an excellent kindly woman. Took care of an old lady, seemed really fond of her. Then the old lady died. And another came and *she* died. Morphia. It all came out. Done in the kindest way, and the shocking thing was that the woman herself really couldn't see that she'd done anything wrong. They hadn't long to live in any case, she said, and one of them had cancer and quite a lot of pain.'

'You mean – it was a mercy killing?'

'No, *no*. They signed their money away to her. She liked money, you know. . . .

'And then there was that young man on the liner – Mrs Pusey at the paper shop, *her* nephew. Brought home stuff he'd stolen and got her to dispose of it. Said it was things that he'd bought abroad. She was quite taken in. And then when the police came round and started asking questions, he tried to bash her on the head, so that she shouldn't be able to give him away. . . . Not a nice young man – but very good-looking. Had two girls in love with him. He spent a lot of money on one of them.'

'The nastiest one, I suppose,' said Bunch.

'Yes, dear. And there was Mrs Cray at the wool shop. Devoted to her son, spoilt him, of course. He got in with a very queer lot. Do you remember Joan Croft, Bunch?'

'N-no, I don't think so.'

'I thought you might have seen her when you were with me on a visit. Used to stalk about smoking a cigar or a pipe. We had a bank hold-up once, and Joan Croft was in the bank at the time. She knocked the man down and took his revolver away from him. She was congratulated on her courage by the Bench.'

Bunch listened attentively. She seemed to be learning by heart.

'And –' she prompted.

'That girl at St Jean des Collines that summer. Such a quiet girl – not so much quiet as silent. Everybody liked her, but they never got to know her much better. . . . We heard afterwards that her husband was a *forger*. It made her feel cut off from people. It made her, in the end, a little queer. Brooding does, you know.'

'Any Anglo-Indian Colonels in your reminiscences, darling?'

'Naturally, dear. There was Major Vaughan at The Larches and Colonel Wright at Simla Lodge. Nothing wrong with either of them. But I do remember Mr Hodgson, the bank manager, went on a cruise and married a woman young enough to be his daughter. No idea of where she came from – except what she told him of course.'

'And that wasn't true?'

'No, dear, it definitely wasn't.'

'Not bad,' said Bunch nodding, and ticking people off on her fingers. 'We've had devoted Dora, and handsome Patrick, and Mrs Swettenham and Edmund, and Phillipa Haymes, and Colonel Easterbrook and Mrs Easterbrook – and if you ask me, I should say you're absolutely right about *her*. But there wouldn't be any reason for her murdering Letty Blacklock.'

'Miss Blacklock, of course, might know something about her that she didn't want known.'

'Oh, darling, that old Tanqueray stuff? Surely that's dead as the hills.'

'It might not be. You see, Bunch, you are not the kind that minds much about what people think of you.'

'I see what you mean,' said Bunch suddenly. 'If you'd been up against it, and then, rather like a shivering stray cat, you'd found a home and a bowl of cream and a warm stroking hand and you were called Pretty Pussy and somebody thought the world of you . . . You'd do a lot to keep that . . . Well, I must say, you've presented me with a very complete gallery of people.'

'You didn't get them all right, you know,' said Miss Marple, mildly.

'Didn't I? Where did I slip up? Julia? *Julia, pretty Juliar is peculiar.*'

'Three and sixpence,' said the sulky waitress, materializing out of the gloom.

'And,' she added, her bosom heaving beneath the bluebirds, 'I'd like to know, Mrs Harmon, why you call me peculiar. I had an aunt who joined the Peculiar People, but I've always been good Church of England myself, as the late Rev. Hopkinson can tell you.'

'I'm terribly sorry,' said Bunch. 'I was just quoting a song. I didn't mean you at all. I didn't know your name was Julia.'

'Quite a coincidence,' said the sulky waitress, cheering up. 'No offence, I'm sure, but hearing my name, as I thought – well, naturally if you think someone's talking about you, it's only human nature to listen. Thank you.'

She departed with her tip.

'Aunt Jane,' said Bunch, 'don't look so upset. What is it?'

'But surely,' murmured Miss Marple. 'That couldn't be so. There's no *reason* –'

'Aunt Jane!'

Miss Marple sighed and then smiled brightly.

'It's nothing, dear,' she said.

'Did you think you knew who did the murder?' asked Bunch. 'Who was it?'

'I don't know at all,' said Miss Marple. 'I got an idea for a moment – but it's gone. I wish I did know. Time's so short. So terribly short.'

'What do you mean short?'

'That old lady up in Scotland may die any moment.'

Bunch said, staring:

'Then you really do believe in Pip and Emma. You think it was them – and that they'll try again?'

'Of course they'll try again,' said Miss Marple, almost absent-mindedly. 'If they tried once, they'll try again. If you've made up your mind to murder someone, you don't stop because the first time it didn't come off. Especially if you're fairly sure you're not suspected.'

'But if it's Pip and Emma,' said Bunch, 'there are only two people it *could* be. It *must* be Patrick and Julia. They're brother and sister and they're the only ones who are the right age.'

'My dear, it isn't nearly as simple as that. There are all sorts of ramifications and combinations. There's Pip's wife if he's married, or Emma's husband. There's their mother – she's an interested party even if she doesn't inherit direct. If Letty Blacklock hasn't seen her for thirty years, she'd probably not recognize her now. One elderly woman is very like another. You remember Mrs Wotherspoon drew her own and Mrs Bartlett's old age pension although Mrs Bartlett had been dead for years. Anyway, Miss Blacklock's shortsighted. Haven't you noticed how she peers at people? And then there's the father. Apparently he was a real bad lot.'

'Yes, but he's a foreigner.'

'By birth. But there's no reason to believe he speaks broken English and gesticulates with his hands. I dare say he could play the part of – of an Anglo-Indian Colonel as well as anybody else.'

'Is *that* what you think?'

'No, I don't. I don't indeed, dear. I just think that there's a great deal of money at stake, a great deal of money. And I'm afraid I know only too well the really terrible things that people will do to lay their hands on a lot of money.'

'I suppose they will,' said Bunch. 'It doesn't really do them any good, does it? Not in the end?'

'No – but they don't usually know that.'

'I can understand it.' Bunch smiled suddenly, her sweet rather crooked smile. 'One feels it would be different for oneself. . . . Even I feel that.' She considered: 'You pretend to yourself that you'd do a lot of good with all that money. Schemes . . . Homes for Unwanted Children . . . Tired Mothers . . . A lovely rest abroad somewhere for elderly women who have worked too hard. . . .'

Her face grew sombre. Her eyes were suddenly dark and tragic.

'I know what you're thinking,' she said to Miss Marple. 'You're thinking that I'd be the worst kind. Becuase I'd kid myself. If you just wanted the money for selfish reasons you'd at any rate *see* what you were like. But once you began to pretend about doing good with it, you'd be able to persuade yourself, perhaps, that it wouldn't very much matter killing someone. . . .'

Then her eyes cleared.

'But I shouldn't,' she said. 'I shouldn't really kill anyone. Not even if they were old, or ill, or doing a lot of harm in the world. Not even if they were blackmailers or – or absolute *beasts*.' She fished a fly carefully out of the dregs of the coffee and arranged it on the table to dry. 'Because people like living, don't they? So do flies. Even if you're old and in pain and you can just crawl out in the sun. Julian says those people like living even more than young strong people do. It's harder, he says, for them to die, the struggle's greater. I like living myself – not just being happy and enjoying myself and having a good time. I mean *living* – waking up and feeling, all over me, that I'm *there* – ticking over.'

She blew on the fly gently; it waved its legs, and flew rather drunkenly away.

'Cheer up, darling Aunt Jane,' said Bunch. '*I*'d never kill anybody.'

14   EXCURSION INTO THE PAST

After a night in the train, Inspector Craddock alighted at a small station in the Highlands.

It struck him for a moment as strange that the wealthy Mrs Goedler – an invalid – with a choice of a London house in a fashionable square, an estate in Hampshire, and a villa in the South of France, should have selected this remote Scottish home as her residence. Surely she was cut off here from many friends and distractions. It must be a lonely life – or was she too ill to notice or care about her surroundings?

A car was waiting to meet him. A big old-fashioned Daimler with an elderly chauffeur driving it. It was a sunny morning and the inspector enjoyed the twenty mile drive, though he marvelled anew at this preference for isolation. A tentative remark to the chauffeur brought partial enlightenment.

'It's her own home as a girl. Ay, she's the last of the family. And she and Mr Goedler were always happier here than anywhere, though it wasn't often he could get away from London. But when he did they enjoyed themselves like a couple of bairns.'

When the grey walls of the old keep came in sight, Craddock felt that time was slipping backwards. An elderly butler received him, and after a wash and a shave, he was shown into a room with a huge fire burning in the grate, and breakfast was served to him.

After breakfast, a tall middle-aged woman in nurse's dress, with a pleasant and competent manner, came in and introduced herself as Sister McClelland.

'I have my patient all ready for you, Mr Craddock. She is, indeed, looking forward to seeing you.'

'I'll do my best not to excite her,' Craddock promised.

'I had better warn you of what will happen. You will find Mrs Goedler apparently quite normal. She will talk and enjoy talking and then – quite suddenly – her powers will fail. Come away at once, then, and send for me. She is, you see, kept almost entirely under the influence of morphia. She drowses most of the time. In preparation for your visit, I have given her a strong stimulant. As soon as the effect of the stimulant wears off, she will relapse into semi-consciousness.'

'I quite understand, Miss McClelland. Would it be in order for you to tell me exactly what the state of Mrs Goedler's health is?'

'Well, Mr Craddock, she is a dying woman. Her life cannot be prolonged for more than a few weeks. To say that she should have been dead years ago would strike you as odd, yet it is the truth. What has kept Mrs Goedler alive is her intense enjoyment and love of being alive. That sounds, perhaps, an odd thing to say of someone who has lived the life of an invalid for many years and has not left her home here for fifteen years, but it is true. Mrs Goedler has never been a strong woman – but she has retained to an astonishing degree the will to live.' She added with a smile, 'She is a very charming woman, too, as you will find.'

Craddock was shown into a large bedroom where a fire was burning and where an old lady lay in a large canopied bed. Though she was only about seven or eight years older than Letitia Blacklock, her fragility made her seem older than her years.

Her white hair was carefully arranged, a froth of pale blue wool enveloped her neck and shoulders. There were lines of pain on the face, but lines of sweetness, too. And there was, strangely enough, what Craddock could only describe as a roguish twinkle in her faded blue eyes.

'Well, this is interesting,' she said. 'It's not often I receive a visit from the police. I hear Letitia Blacklock wasn't much hurt by this attempt on her? How is my dear Blackie?'

'She's very well, Mrs Goedler. She sent you her love.'

'It's a long time since I've seen her. . . . For many years now, it's been just a card at Christmas. I asked her to come up here when she came back to England after Charlotte's death, but she said it would be painful after so long and perhaps she was right. . . . Blackie always had a lot of sense. I had an old school friend to see me about a year ago, and Lor!' – she smiled – 'we bored each other to death. After we'd finished all the "Do you remembers?" there wasn't anything to say. *Most* embarrassing.'

Craddock was content to let her talk before pressing his questions. He wanted, as it were, to get back into the past, to get the feel of the Goedler-Blacklock ménage.

'I suppose,' said Belle shrewdly, 'that you want to ask about the money? Randall left it all to go to Blackie after my death. Really, of course, Randall never dreamed that I'd outlive him. He was a big strong man, never a day's illness, and I was always a mass of aches and pains and complaints and doctors coming and pulling long faces over me.'

'I don't think complaints would be the right word, Mrs Goedler.' The old lady chuckled.

'I didn't mean it in the complaining sense. I've never been *too* sorry for myself. But it was always taken for granted that I, being the weakly one, would go first. It didn't work out that way. No – it didn't work out that way. . . .'

'Why, exactly, did your husband leave his money the way he did?'

'You mean, why did he leave it to Blackie? Not for the reason you've probably been thinking.' The roguish twinkle was very apparent. 'What minds you policemen have! Randall was never in the least in love with her and she wasn't with him. Letitia, you know, has really got a man's mind. She hasn't any feminine feelings or weaknesses. I don't believe she was ever in love with any man. She was never particularly pretty and she didn't care for clothes. She used a little make-up in deference to prevailing custom, but not to make herself look prettier.' There was pity in the old voice as she went on: 'She never knew any of the fun of being a woman.'

Craddock looked at the frail little figure in the big bed with interest. Belle Goedler, he realized, *had* enjoyed – still enjoyed – being a woman. She twinkled at him.

'I've always thought,' she said, 'it must be terribly dull to be a man.'

Then she said thoughtfully:

'I think Randall looked on Blackie very much as a kind of younger brother. He relied on her judgement which was always excellent. She kept him out of trouble more than once, you know.'

'She told me that she came to his rescue once with money?'

'That, yes, but I meant more than that. One can speak the truth after all these years. Randall couldn't really distinguish between what was crooked and what wasn't. His conscience wasn't sensitive. The poor dear really didn't know what was just smart – and what was dishonest. Blackie kept him straight. That's one thing about Letitia Blacklock, she's absolutely dead straight. She would never do anything that was dishonest. She's a very fine character, you know. I've always admired her. They had a terrible girlhood, those girls. The father was an old country doctor – terrifically pig-headed and narrow-minded – the complete family tyrant. Letitia broke away, came to London, and trained herself as a chartered accountant. The other sister was an invalid, there was a deformity of kinds and she never saw people or went out. That's why when the old man died, Letitia gave up everything to go home and look after her sister. Randall was wild with her – but it made no difference. If Letitia thought a thing was her duty she'd do it. And you couldn't move her.'

'How long was that before your husband died?'

'A couple of years, I think. Randall made his will before she left the firm, and he didn't alter it. He said to me: "We've no one of our own." (Our little boy died, you know, when he was two years old.) "After you and I are gone, Blackie had better have the money. She'll play the markets and make 'em sit up."'

'You see,' Belle went on, 'Randall enjoyed the whole money-making game so much – it wasn't just the money – it was the adventure, the risks, the excitement of it all. And Blackie liked it too. She had the same adventurous spirit and the same judgement. Poor darling, she'd never had any of the usual fun – being in love, and leading men on and teasing them – and having a home and children and all the real fun of life.'

Craddock thought it was odd, the real pity and indulgent contempt felt by this woman, a woman whose life had been hampered by illness, whose only child had died, whose husband had died, leaving her to a lonely widowhood, and who had been a hopeless invalid for years.

She nodded her head at him.

'I know what you're thinking. But I've *had* all the things that make life worthwhile – they may have been taken from me – but I have had them. I was pretty and gay as a girl, I married the man I loved, and he never stopped loving me . . . My child died, but I had him for two precious years . . . I've had a lot of physical pain – but if you have pain, you know how to enjoy the exquisite pleasure of the times when pain stops. And everyone's been kind to me, always. . . . I'm a lucky woman, really.'

Craddock seized upon an opening in her former remarks.

'You said just now, Mrs Goedler, that your husband left his fortune to Miss Blacklock because he had no one else to leave it to. But that's not strictly true, is it? He had a sister.'

'Oh, Sonia. But they quarrelled years ago and made a clean break of it.'

'He disapproved of her marriage?'

'Yes, she married a man called – now what was his name –?'

'Stamfordis.'

'That's it. Dmitri Stamfordis. Randall always said he was a crook. The two men didn't like each other from the first. But Sonia was wildly in love with him and quite determined to marry him. And I really never saw why she shouldn't. Men have such odd ideas about these things. Sonia wasn't a mere girl – she was twenty-five, and she knew exactly what she was doing. He was a crook, I dare say – I mean really a crook. I believe he had a criminal record – and Randall always suspected the name he was passing under here wasn't his own. Sonia knew all that. The point was, which of course Randall couldn't appreciate, that Dmitri was really a wildly attractive person to women. And he was just as much in love with Sonia as she was with him. Randall insisted that he was just marrying her for her money – but that wasn't true. Sonia was very handsome, you know. And she had plenty of spirit. If the marriage had turned out badly, if Dmitri had been unkind to her or unfaithful to her, she would just have cut her losses and walked out on him. She was a rich woman and could do as she chose with her life.'

'The quarrel was never made up?'

'No. Randall and Sonia never had got on very well. She resented his trying to prevent the marriage. She said, "Very well. You're quite impossible! This is the last you hear of me!"'

'But it was not the last you heard of her?'

Belle smiled.

'No, I got a letter from her about eighteen months afterwards. She wrote from Budapest, I remember, but she didn't give an address. She told me to tell Randall that she was extremely happy and that she'd just had twins.'

'And she told you their names?'

Again Belle smiled. 'She said they were born just after midday –

and she intended to call them Pip and Emma. That may have been just a joke, of course.'

'Didn't you hear from her again?'

'No. She said she and her husband and the babies were going to America on a short stay. I never heard any more. . . .'

'You don't happen, I suppose, to have kept that letter?'

'No, I'm afraid not. . . . I read it to Randall and he just grunted: "She'll regret marrying that fellow one of these days." That's all he ever said about it. We really forgot about her. She went right out of our lives. . . .'

'Nevertheless Mr Goedler left his estate to her children in the event of Miss Blacklock predeceasing you?'

'Oh, that was my doing. I said to him, when he told me about the will: "And suppose Blackie dies before I do?" He was quite surprised. I said, "Oh, I know Blackie is as strong as a horse and I'm a delicate creature – but there's such a thing as accidents, you know, and there's such a thing as creaking gates . . ." And he said, "There's no one – absolutely no one." I said, "There's Sonia." And he said at once, "And let that fellow get hold of my money? No – indeed!" I said, "Well, her children then. Pip and Emma, and there may be lots more by now" – and so he grumbled, but he did put it in.'

'And from that day to this,' Craddock said slowly, 'you've heard nothing of your sister-in-law or her children?'

'Nothing – they may be dead – they may be – anywhere.'

They may be in Chipping Cleghorn, thought Craddock.

As though she read his thoughts, a look of alarm came into Belle Goedler's eyes. She said, 'Don't let them hurt Blackie. Blackie's *good* – really good – you mustn't let harm come to –'

Her voice trailed off suddenly. Craddock saw the sudden grey shadows round her mouth and eyes.

'You're tired,' he said. 'I'll go.'

She nodded.

'Send Mac to me,' she whispered. 'Yes, tired . . .' She made a feeble motion of her hand. 'Look after Blackie . . . Nothing must happen to Blackie . . . look after her. . . .'

'I'll do my very best, Mrs Goedler.' He rose and went to the door.

Her voice, a thin thread of sound, followed him . . .

'Not long now – until I'm dead – dangerous for her – Take care . . .'

Sister McClelland passed him as he went out. He said, uneasily:

'I hope I haven't done her harm.'

'Oh, I don't think so, Mr Craddock. I told you she would tire quite suddenly.'

Later, he asked the nurse:

'The only thing I hadn't time to ask Mrs Goedler was whether she had any old photographs? If so, I wonder –'

She interrupted him.

'I'm afraid there's nothing of that kind. All her personal papers and things were stored with their furniture from the London house at the beginning of the war. Mrs Goedler was desperately ill at the time. Then the storage depository was blitzed. Mrs Goedler was very upset at losing so many personal souvenirs and family papers. I'm afraid there's nothing of that kind.'

So that was that, Craddock thought.

Yet he felt his journey had not been in vain. Pip and Emma, those twin wraiths, were not quite wraiths.

Craddock thought, 'Here's a brother and sister brought up somewhere in Europe. Sonia Goedler was a rich woman at the time of her marriage, but money in Europe hasn't remained money. Queer things have happened to money during these war years. And so there are two young people, the son and daughter of a man who had a criminal record. Suppose they came to England, more or less penniless. What would they do? Find out about any rich relatives. Their uncle, a man of vast fortune, is dead. Possibly the first thing they'd do would be to look up that uncle's will. See if by any chance money had been left to them or to their mother. So they go to Somerset House and learn the contents of his will, and then, perhaps, they learn of the existence of Miss Letitia Blacklock. Then they make enquiries about Randall Goedler's widow. She's an invalid, living up in Scotland, and they find out she hasn't long to live. *If this Letitia Blacklock dies before her*, they will come into a vast fortune. What then?'

Craddock thought, 'They wouldn't go to Scotland. They'd find out where Letitia Blacklock is living now. And they'd go there – but not as themselves . . . They'd go together – or separately? Emma . . . I wonder? . . . Pip and Emma . . . I'll eat my hat if Pip, or Emma, or both of them, aren't in Chipping Cleghorn now. . . .'

15   DELICIOUS DEATH

In the kitchen at Little Paddocks, Miss Blacklock was giving instructions to Mitzi.

'Sardine sandwiches as well as the tomato ones. And some of those little scones you make so nicely. And I'd like you to make that special cake of yours.'

'Is it a party then, that you want all these things?'

'It's Miss Bunner's birthday, and some people will be coming to tea.'

'At her age one does not have birthdays. It is better to forget.'

'Well, she doesn't want to forget. Several people are bringing her presents – and it will be nice to make a little party of it.'

'That is what you say last time – and see what happened!'

Miss Blacklock controlled her temper.

'Well, it won't happen this time.'

'How do you know what may happen in this house? All day long I shiver and at night I lock my door and I look in the wardrobe to see no one is hidden there.'

'That ought to keep you nice and safe,' said Miss Blacklock, coldly.

'The cake that you want me to make, it is the –' Mitzi uttered a sound that to Miss Blacklock's English ear sounded like Schwitzebzr or alternatively like cats spitting at each other.

'That's the one. The rich one.'

'Yes. It is rich. For it have I *nothing*! Impossible to make such a cake. I need for it chocolate and much butter, and sugar and raisins.'

'You can use this tin of butter that was sent us from America. And some of the raisins we were keeping for Christmas, and here is a slab of chocolate and a pound of sugar.'

Mitzi's face suddenly burst into radiant smiles.

'So, I make him for you good – good,' she cried, in an ecstasy. 'It will be rich, rich, of a melting richness! And on top I will put the icing – chocolate icing – I make him so nice – and write on it *Good Wishes*. These English people with their cakes that tastes of sand, never *never*, will they have tasted such a cake. Delicious, they will say – delicious –'

Her face clouded again.

'Mr Patrick. He called it Delicious Death. My cake! I will not have my cake called that!'

'It was a compliment really,' said Miss Blacklock. 'He meant it was worth dying to eat such a cake.'

Mitzi looked at her doubtfully.

'Well, I do not like that word – *death*. They are not dying because they eat my cake, no, they feel much much better. . . .'

'I'm sure we all shall.'

Miss Blacklock turned away and left the kitchen with a sigh of relief at the successful ending of the interview. With Mitzi one never knew.

She ran into Dora Bunner outside.

'Oh, Letty, shall I run in and tell Mitzi just how to cut the sandwiches?'

'No,' said Miss Blacklock, steering her friend firmly into the hall. 'She's in a good mood now and I don't want her disturbed.'

'But I could just show her –'

'Please don't show her *anything*, Dora. These central Europeans don't *like* being shown. They hate it.'

Dora looked at her doubtfully. Then she suddenly broke into smiles.

'Edmund Swettenham just rang up. He wished me many happy returns of the day and said he was bringing me a pot of honey as a present this afternoon. Isn't it kind? I can't imagine how he knew it was my birthday.'

'Everybody seems to know. You must have been talking about it, Dora.'

'Well, I did just happen to mention that today I should be fifty-nine –'

'You're sixty-four,' said Miss Blacklock with a twinkle.

'And Miss Hinchliffe said, "You don't look it. What age do you think *I* am?" Which was rather awkward because Miss Hinchliffe always looks so peculiar that she might be any age. She said she was bringing me some eggs, by the way. I said our hens hadn't been laying very well, lately.'

'We're not doing so badly out of your birthday,' said Miss Blacklock. 'Honey, eggs – a magnificent box of chocolates from Julia –'

'I don't know where she gets such things.'

'Better not ask. Her methods are probably strictly illegal.'

'And your lovely brooch.' Miss Bunner looked down proudly at her bosom on which was pinned a small diamond leaf.

'Do you like it? I'm glad. I never cared for jewellery.'

'I love it.'

'Good. Let's go and feed the ducks.'

II

'Ha,' cried Patrick dramatically, as the party took their places round the dining room table. 'What do I see before me? *Delicious Death*.'

'Hush,' said Miss Blacklock. 'Don't let Mitzi hear you. She objects to your name for her cake very much.'

'Nevertheless, Delicious Death it is! Is it Bunny's birthday cake?'

'Yes, it is,' said Miss Bunner. 'I really am having the most wonderful birthday.'

Her cheeks were flushed with excitement and had been ever since Colonel Easterbrook had handed her a small box of sweets and declaimed with a bow, 'Sweets to the Sweet!'

Julia had turned her head away hurriedly, and had been frowned at by Miss Blacklock.

Full justice was done to the good things on the tea table and they rose from their seats after a round of crackers.

'I feel slightly sick,' said Julia. 'It's that cake. I remember I felt just the same last time.'

'It's worth it,' said Patrick.

'These foreigners certainly understand confectionery,' said Miss Hinchliffe. 'What they can't make is a plain boiled pudding.'

Everybody was respectfully silent, though it seemed to be hovering on Patrick's lips to ask if anyone really *wanted* a plain boiled pudding.

'Got a new gardener?' asked Miss Hinchliffe of Miss Blacklock as they returned to the drawing room.

'No, why?'

'Saw a man snooping round the henhouse. Quite a decent-looking army type.'

'Oh, *that*,' said Julia. 'That's our detective.'

Mrs Easterbrook dropped her handbag.

'Detective?' she exclaimed. 'But – but – why?'

'I don't know,' said Julia. 'He prowls about and keeps an eye on the house. He's protecting Aunt Letty, I suppose.'

'Absolute nonsense,' said Miss Blacklock. 'I can protect myself, thank you.'

'But surely it's all over now,' cried Mrs Easterbrook. 'Though I meant to ask you, why did they adjourn the inquest?'

'Police aren't satisfied,' said her husband. 'That's what that means.'

'But aren't satisfied of what?'

Colonel Easterbrook shook his head with the air of a man who could say a good deal more if he chose. Edmund, who disliked the Colonel, said, 'The truth of it is, we're all under suspicion.'

'But suspicion of *what*?' repeated Mrs Easterbrook.

'Never mind, kitten,' said her husband.

'Loitering with intent,' said Edmund. 'The intent being to commit murder upon the first opportunity.'

'Oh, don't, please don't, Mr Swettenham.' Dora Bunner began to cry. 'I'm sure nobody here could possibly want to kill dear, dear Letty.'

There was a moment of horrible embarrassment. Edmund turned scarlet, murmured, 'Just a joke.' Phillipa suggested in a high clear voice that they might listen to the six o'clock news and the suggestion was received with enthusiastic assent.

Patrick murmured to Julia: 'We need Mrs Harmon here. She'd be sure to say in that high clear voice of hers, "But I suppose somebody *is* still waiting for a good chance to murder you, Miss Blacklock?"'

'I'm glad she and that old Miss Marple couldn't come,' said Julia. 'That old woman is the prying kind. And a mind like a sink, I should think. Real Victorian type.'

Listening to the news led easily into a pleasant discussion on the horrors of atomic warfare. Colonel Easterbrook said that the real menace to civilization was undoubtedly Russia, and Edmund said that he had several charming Russian friends – which annoucement was coldly received.

The party broke up with renewed thanks to the hostess.

'Enjoy yourself, Bunny?' asked Miss Blacklock, as the last guest was sped.

'Oh, I did. But I've got a terrible headache. It's the excitement, I think.'

'It's the cake,' said Patrick. 'I feel a bit liverish myself. And you've been nibbling chocolates all the morning.'

'I'll go and lie down, I think,' said Miss Bunner. 'I'll take a couple of aspirins and try and have a nice sleep.'

'That would be a very good plan,' said Miss Blacklock.

Miss Bunner departed upstairs.

'Shall I shut up the ducks for you, Aunt Letty?'

Miss Blacklock looked at Patrick severely.

'If you'll be sure to latch that door properly.'

'I will. I swear I will.'

'Have a glass of sherry, Aunt Letty,' said Julia. 'As my old nurse used to say, "It will settle your stomach." A revolting phrase – but curiously apposite at this moment.'

'Well, I dare say it might be a good thing. The truth is one isn't used to rich things. Oh, Bunny, how you made me jump. What is it?'

'I can't find my aspirin,' said Miss Bunner disconsolately.

'Well, take some of mine, dear, they're by my bed.'

'There's a bottle on my dressing table,' said Phillipa.

'Thank you – thank you very much. If I can't find mine – but I know I've got it *somewhere*. A new bottle. Now where could I have put it?'

'There's heaps in the bathroom,' said Julia impatiently. 'This house is chock full of aspirin.'

'It vexes me to be so careless and mislay things,' replied Miss Bunner, retreating up the stairs again.

'Poor old Bunny,' said Julia, holding up her glass. 'Do you think we ought to have given her some sherry?'

'Better not, I think,' said Miss Blacklock. 'She had a lot of excitement today, and it isn't really good for her. I'm afraid she'll be the worse for it tomorrow. Still, I really do think she has enjoyed herself!'

'She's loved it,' said Phillipa.

'Let's give Mitzi a glass of sherry,' suggested Julia.

'Hi, Pat,' she called as she heard him entering the side door, 'fetch Mitzi.'

So Mitzi was brought in and Julia poured her out a glass of sherry.

'Here's to the best cook in the world,' said Patrick.

Mitzi was gratified – but felt nevertheless that a protest was due.

'That is not so. I am not really a cook. In my country I do intellectual work.'

'Then you're wasted,' said Patrick. 'What's intellectual work compared to a *chef d'oeuvre* like Delicious Death?'

'Oo – I say to you I do not like –'

'Never mind what you like, my girl,' said Patrick. 'That's my name for it and here's to it. Let's all drink to Delicious Death and to hell with the after effects.'

III

'Phillipa, my dear, I want to talk to you.'

'Yes, Miss Blacklock?'

Phillipa Haymes looked up in slight surprise.

'You're not worrying about sanything, are you?'

'Worrying?'

'I've noticed that you've looked worried lately. There isn't anything wrong, is there?'

'Oh no, Miss Blacklock. What should there be?'

'Well – I wondered. I thought, perhaps, that you and Patrick –?'

'Patrick?' Phillipa looked really surprised.

'It's not so, then. Please forgive me if I've been impertinent. But you've been thrown together a lot – and although Patrick is my cousin, I don't think he's the type to make a satisfactory husband. Not for some time to come, at all events.'

Phillipa's face had frozen into a hard immobility.

'I shan't marry again,' she said.

'Oh, yes, you will someday, my child. You're young. But we needn't discuss that. There's no other trouble. You're not worried about – money, for instance?'

'No, I'm quite all right.'

'I know you get anxious sometimes about your boy's education. That's why I want to tell you something. I drove into Milchester this afternoon to see Mr Beddingfield, my lawyer. Things haven't been very settled lately and I thought I would like to make a new will – in view of certain eventualities. Apart from Bunny's legacy, everything goes to you, Phillipa.'

'What?' Phillipa spun round. Her eyes stared. She looked dismayed, almost frightened.

'But I don't want it – really I don't . . . Oh, I'd rather not . . . And anyway, why? Why to *me*?'

'Perhaps,' said Miss Blacklock in a peculiar voice, 'because there's no one else.'

'But there's Patrick and Julia.'

'Yes, there's Patrick and Julia.' The odd note in Miss Blacklock's voice was still there.

'They are your relations.'

'Very distant ones. They have no claim on me.'

'But I – I haven't either – I don't know what you think . . . Oh, I don't want it.'

Her gaze held more hostility than gratitude. There was something almost like fear in her manner.

'I know what I'm doing, Phillipa. I've become fond of you – and there's the boy . . . You won't get very much if I should die now – but in a few weeks' time it might be different.'

Her eyes met Phillipa's steadily.

'But you're not going to die!' Phillipa protested.

'Not if I can avoid it by taking due precautions.'

'Precautions?'

'Yes. Think it over . . . And don't worry any more.'

She left the room abruptly. Phillipa heard her speaking to Julia in the hall.

Julia entered the drawing room a few moments later.

There was a slightly steely glitter in her eyes.

'Played your cards rather well, haven't you, Phillipa? I see you're one of those quiet ones . . . a dark horse.'

'So you heard –'

'Yes, I heard. I rather think I was meant to hear.'

'What do you mean?'

'Our Letty's no fool . . . Well, anyway, you're all right, Phillipa. Sitting pretty, aren't you?'

'Oh, Julia – I didn't mean – I never meant –'

'Didn't you? Of course you did. You're fairly up against things, aren't you? Hard up for money. But just remember this – if anyone bumps off Aunt Letty now, *you*'ll be suspect No. 1.'

'But I shan't be. It would be idiotic if I killed her now when – if I waited –'

'So you *do* know about old Mrs Whatshername dying up in Scotland? I wondered . . . Phillipa, I'm beginning to believe you're a very dark horse indeed.'

'I don't want to do you and Patrick out of anything.'

'Don't you, my dear? I'm sorry – but I don't believe you.'

16 INSPECTOR CRADDOCK RETURNS

Inspector Craddock had had a bad night on his journey home. His dreams had been less dreams than nightmares. Again and again he was racing through the grey corridors of an old-world castle in a desperate attempt to get somewhere, or to prevent something, in time. Finally he dreamt that he awoke. An enormous relief surged over him. Then the door of his compartment slid slowly open, and Letitia Blacklock looked in at him with blood running down her face, and said reproachfully: 'Why didn't you save me? You could have if you'd tried.'

This time he really awoke.

Altogether, the inspector was thankful finally to reach Milchester. He went straight away to make his report to Rydesdale who listened carefully.

'It doesn't take us much further,' he said. 'But it confirms what Miss Blacklock told you. Pip and Emma – h'm, I wonder.'

'Patrick and Julia Simmons are the right age, sir. If we could establish that Miss Blacklock hadn't seen them since they were children –'

With a very faint chuckle, Rydesdale said: 'Our ally, Miss Marple, has established that for us. Actually Miss Blacklock had never seen either of them at all until two months ago.'

'Then, surely, sir –'

'It's not so easy as all that, Craddock. We've been checking up. On what we've got, Patrick and Julia seem definitely to be out of it. His Naval record is genuine – quite a good record bar a tendency to "insubordination". We've checked with Cannes, and an indignant Mrs Simmons says of course her son and daughter are at Chipping Cleghorn with her cousin Letitia Blacklock. So that's that!'

'And Mrs Simmons *is* Mrs Simmons?'

'She's been Mrs Simmons for a very long time, that's all I can say,' said Rydesdale dryly.

'That seems clear enough. Only – those two fitted. Right age. Not known to Miss Blacklock, personally. If we wanted Pip and Emma – well, there they were.'

The Chief Constable nodded thoughtfully, then he pushed across a paper to Craddock.

'Here's a little something we've dug up on Mrs Easterbrook.'

The Inspector read with lifted eyebrows.

'Very interesting,' he remarked. 'Hoodwinked that old ass pretty well, hasn't she? It doesn't tie in with this business though, as far as I can see.'

'Apparently not.'

'And here's an item that concerns Mrs Haymes.'

Again Craddock's eyebrows rose.

'I think I'll have another talk with the lady,' he said.

'You think this information might be relevant?'

'I think it might be. It would be a long shot, of course. . . .'

The two men were silent for a moment or two.

'How has Fletcher got on, sir?'

'Fletcher has been exceedingly active. He's made a routine search of the house by agreement with Miss Blacklock – but he didn't find anything significant. Then he's been checking up on who could have had the opportunity of oiling that door. Checking who was up at the house on the days that that foreign girl was out. A little more complicated than we thought, because it appears she goes for a walk most afternoons. Usually down to the village where she has a cup of coffee at the Bluebird. So that when Miss Blacklock and Miss Bunner are out – which is most afternoons – they go blackberrying – the coast is clear.'

'And the doors are always left unlocked?'

'They used to be. I don't suppose they are now.'

'What are Fletcher's results? Who's known to have been in the house when it was left empty?'

'Practically the whole lot of them.'

Rydesdale consulted a page in front of him.

'Miss Murgatroyd was there with a hen to sit on some eggs. (Sounds complicated but that's what she says.) Very flustered about it all and contradicts herself, but Fletcher thinks that's temperamental and not a sign of guilt.'

'Might be,' Craddock admitted. 'She flaps.'

'Then Mrs Swettenham came up to fetch some horse meat that Miss Blacklock had left for her on the kitchen table, because Miss Blacklock had been in to Milchester in the car that day and always gets Mrs Swettenham's horse meat for her. That makes sense to you?'

Craddock considered.

'Why didn't Miss Blacklock leave the horse meat when she passed Mrs Swettenham's house on her way back from Milchester?'

'I don't know, but she didn't. Mrs Swettenham says she (Miss B.) always leaves it on the kitchen table, and she (Mrs S.) likes to fetch it when Mitzi isn't there because Mitzi is sometimes so rude.'

'Hangs together quite well. And the next?'

'Miss Hinchliffe. Says she wasn't there at all lately. But she was. Because Mitzi saw her coming out of the side door one day and so did a Mrs Butt (she's one of the locals). Miss H. then admitted she might have been there but had forgotten. Can't remember what she went for. Says she probably just dropped in.'

'That's rather odd.'

'So was her manner, apparently. Then there's Mrs Easterbrook. She was exercising the dear dogs out that way and she just popped in to see if Miss Blacklock would lend her a knitting pattern but Miss Blacklock wasn't in. She says she waited a little.'

'Just so. Might be snooping round. Or might be oiling a door. And the Colonel?'

'Went there one day with a book on India that Miss Blacklock has expressed a desire to read.'

'Had she?'

'Her account is that she tried to get out of having to read it, but it was no use.'

'And that's fair enough,' sighed Craddock. 'If anyone is really determined to lend you a book, you never can get out of it!'

'We don't know if Edmund Swettenham was up there. He's extremely vague. Said he did drop in occasionally on errands for his mother, but thinks not lately.'

'In fact, it's all inconclusive.'

'Yes.'

Rydesdale said, with a slight grin:

'Miss Marple has also been active. Fletcher reports that she had morning coffee at the Bluebird. She's been to sherry at Boulders, and to tea at Little Paddocks. She's admired Mrs Swettenham's garden – and dropped in to see Colonel Easterbrook's Indian curios.'

'She may be able to tell us if Colonel Easterbrook's a pukka colonel or not.'

'She'd know, I agree – he seems all right. We'd have to check with the Far Eastern authorities to get certain identification.'

'And in the meantime' – Craddock broke off – 'do you think Miss Blacklock would consent to go away?'

'Go away from Chipping Cleghorn?'

'Yes. Take the faithful Bunner with her, perhaps, and leave for an unknown destination. Why shouldn't she go up to Scotland and stay with Belle Goedler? It's a pretty unget-at-able place.'

'Stop there and wait for her to die? I don't think she'd do that. I don't think any nice-natured woman would like that suggestion.'

'If it's a matter of saving her life –'

'Come now, Craddock, it isn't quite so easy to bump someone off as you seem to think.'

'Isn't it, sir?'

'Well – in one way – it's easy enough I agree. Plenty of methods. Weed killer. A bash on the head when she's out shutting up the poultry, a pot shot from behind a hedge. All quite simple. But to bump someone off and not be suspected of bumping them off – that's not quite so easy. And they must realize by now that they're all under observation. The original carefully planned scheme failed. Our unknown murderer has got to think up something else.'

'I know that, sir. But there's the time element to consider. Mrs Goedler's a dying woman – she might pop off any minute. That means that our murderer can't afford to wait.'

'True.'

'And another thing, sir. He – or she – must know that we're checking up on everybody.'

'And that takes time,' said Rydesdale with a sigh. 'It means checking with the East, with India. Yes, it's a long tedious business.'

'So that's another reason for – hurry. I'm sure, sir, that the danger is very real. It's a very large sum that's at stake. If Belle Goedler dies –'

He broke off as a constable entered.

'Constable Legg on the line from Chipping Cleghorn, sir.'

'Put him through here.'

Inspector Craddock, watching the Chief Constable, saw his features harden and stiffen.

'Very good,' barked Rydesdale. 'Detective-Inspector Craddock will be coming out immediately.'

He put the receiver down.

'Is it –' Craddock broke off.

Rydesdale shook his head.

'No,' he said. 'It's Dora Bunner. She wanted some aspirin.

Apparently she took some from a bottle beside Letitia Blacklock's bed. There were only a few tablets left in the bottle. She took two and left one. The doctor's got that one and is sending it to be analysed. He says it's definitely *not* aspirin.'

'She's dead?'

'Yes, found dead in her bed this morning. Died in her sleep, doctor says. He doesn't think it was natural though her health was in a bad state. Narcotic poisoning, that's his guess. Autopsy's fixed for tonight.'

'Aspirin tablets by Letitia Blacklock's bed. The clever clever devil. Patrick told me Miss Blacklock threw away a half bottle of sherry – opened a new one. I don't suppose she'd have thought of doing that with an open bottle of aspirin. Who had been in the house this time – within the last day or two? The tablets can't have been there long.'

Rydesdale looked at him.

'All our lot were there yesterday,' he said. 'Birthday party for Miss Bunner. Any of them could have nipped upstairs and done a neat little substitution. Or of course anyone living in the house could have done it any time.'

17 THE ALBUM

Standing by the Vicarage gate, well wrapped up, Miss Marple took the note from Bunch's hand.

'Tell Miss Blacklock,' said Bunch, 'that Julian is terribly sorry he can't come up himself. He's got a parishioner dying out at Locke Hamlet. He'll come up after lunch if Miss Blacklock would like to see him. The note's about the arrangements for the funeral. He suggests Wednesday if the inquest's on Tuesday. Poor old Bunny. It's so typical of her, somehow, to get hold of poisoned aspirin meant for someone else. Goodbye, darling. I hope the walk won't be too much for you. But I've simply got to get that child to hospital at once.'

Miss Marple said the walk wouldn't be too much for her, and Bunch rushed off.

Whilst waiting for Miss Blacklock, Miss Marple looked round the drawing-room, and wondered just exactly what Dora Bunner had meant that morning in the Bluebird by saying that she believed Patrick had 'tampered with the lamp' to 'make the lights go out.' What lamp? And how had he 'tampered' with it?

She must, Miss Marple decided, have meant the small lamp that stood on the table by the archway. She had said something about a shepherdess or a shepherd – and this was actually a delicate piece of Dresden china, a shepherd in a blue coat and pink breeches holding what had originally been a candlestick and had now been adapted to electricity. The shade was of plain vellum and a little too big so that it almost masked the figure. What else was it that Dora Bunner had said? 'I remember distinctly that it was the shepherdess. And the next day –' Certainly it was a shepherd now.

Miss Marple remembered that when she and Bunch had come to tea, Dora Bunner had said something about the lamp being one of a *pair*. Of course – a shepherd and a shepherdess. And it had been the shepherdess on the day of the hold-up – and the next morning it had been the *other* lamp – the lamp that was here now, the shepherd. The lamps had been changed over during the night. And Dora Bunner had had reason to believe (or had believed without reason) that it was Patrick who had changed them.

Why? Because, if the original lamp were examined, it would show just how Patrick had managed to 'make the lights go out.' How had he managed? Miss Marple looked earnestly at the lamp in front of her. The flex ran along the table over the edge and was plugged into the wall. There was a small pear-shaped switch halfway along the flex. None of it suggested anything to Miss Marple because she knew very little about electricity.

Where was the shepherdess lamp? she wondered. In the 'spare room' or thrown away, or – where was it Dora Bunner had come upon Patrick Simmons with a feather and an oily cup? In the shrubbery? Miss Marple made up her mind to put all these points to Inspector Craddock.

At the very beginning Miss Blacklock leapt to the conclusion that her nephew Patrick had been behind the insertion of that advertisement. That kind of instinctive belief was often justified, or so Miss Marple believed. Because, if you knew people fairly well, you knew the kind of things they thought of . . .

Patrick Simmons . . .

A handsome young man. An engaging young man. A young man whom women liked, both young women and old women. The kind of man, perhaps, that Randall Goedler's sister had married. Could

Patrick Simmons be 'Pip'? But he'd been in the Navy during the war. The police could soon check up on that.

Only – sometimes – the most amazing impersonations *did* happen.

You could get away with a great deal if you had enough audacity. . . .

The door opened and Miss Blacklock came in. She looked, Miss Marple thought, many years older. All the life and energy had gone out of her.

'I'm very sorry, disturbing you like this,' said Miss Marple. 'But the Vicar had a dying parishioner and Bunch had to rush a sick child to hospital. The Vicar wrote you a note.'

She held it out and Miss Blacklock took it and opened it.

'Do sit down, Miss Marple,' she said. 'It's very kind of you to have brought this.'

She read the note through.

'The Vicar's a very understanding man,' she said quietly. 'He doesn't offer one fatuous consolation . . . Tell him that these arrangements will do very well. Her – her favourite hymn was *Lead Kindly Light*.'

Her voice broke suddenly.

Miss Marple said gently:

'I am only a stranger, but I am so very very sorry.'

And suddenly, uncontrollably, Letitia Blacklock wept. It was a piteous overmastering grief, with a kind of hopelessness about it. Miss Marple sat quite still.

Miss Blacklock sat up at last. Her face was swollen and blotched with tears.

'I'm sorry,' she said. 'It – it just came over me. What I've lost. She – she was the only link with the past, you see. The only one who – who *remembered*. Now that she's gone I'm quite alone.'

'I know what you mean,' said Miss Marple. 'One *is* alone when the last one who *remembers* is gone. I have nephews and nieces and kind friends – but there's no one who knew me as a young girl – no one who belongs to the old days. I've been alone for quite a long time now.'

Both women sat silent for some moments.

'You understand very well,' said Letitia Blacklock. She rose and went over to her desk. 'I must write a few words to the Vicar.' She held the pen rather awkwardly and wrote slowly.

'Arthritic,' she explained. 'Sometimes I can hardly write at all.'

She sealed up the envelope and addressed it.

'If you wouldn't mind taking it, it would be very kind.'

Hearing a man's voice in the hall she said quickly:

'That's Inspector Craddock.'

She went to the mirror over the fireplace and applied a small powder puff to her face.

Craddock came in with a grim, angry face.

He looked at Miss Marple with disapprobation.

'Oh,' he said. 'So *you're* here.'

Miss Blacklock turned from the mantelpiece.

'Miss Marple kindly came up with a note from the Vicar.'

Miss Marple said in a flurried manner:

'I am going at once – at once. Please don't let me hamper you in *any* way.'

'Were you at the tea party here yesterday afternoon?'

Miss Marple said, nervously:

'No – no, I wasn't. Bunch drove me over to call on some friends.'

'Then there's nothing you can tell me.' Craddock held the door open in a pointed manner, and Miss Marple scuttled out in a somewhat abashed fashion.

'Nosey Parkers, these old women,' said Craddock.

'I think you're being unfair to her,' said Miss Blacklock. 'She really did come with a note from the Vicar.'

'I bet she did.'

'I don't think it was idle curiosity.'

'Well, perhaps you're right, Miss Blacklock, but my own diagnosis would be a severe attack of Nosey Parkeritis. . . .'

'She's a very harmless old creature,' said Miss Blacklock.

'Dangerous as a rattlesnake if you only knew,' the Inspector thought grimly. But he had no intention of taking anyone into his confidence unnecessarily. Now that he knew definitely there was a killer at large, he felt that the less said the better. He didn't want the next person bumped off to be Jane Marple.

Somewhere – a killer . . . Where?

'I won't waste time offering sympathy, Miss Blacklock,' he said. 'As a matter of fact I feel pretty bad about Miss Bunner's death. We ought to have been able to prevent it.'

'I don't see what you could have done.'

'No – well, it wouldn't have been easy. But now we've got to work fast. Who's doing this, Miss Blacklock? Who's had two shots at killing you, and will probably, if we don't work fast enough, soon have another?'

Letitia Blacklock shivered. 'I don't know, Inspector – I don't know at *all*!'

'I've checked up with Mrs Goedler. She's given me all the help she can. It wasn't very much. There are just a few people who would definitely profit by your death. First Pip and Emma. Patrick and Julia Simmons are the right age, but their background seems clear enough. Anyway, we can't concentrate on these two alone. Tell me, Miss Blacklock, would you recognize Sonia Goedler if you saw her?'

'Recognize Sonia? Why, of course –' she stopped suddenly. 'No,' she said slowly, 'I don't know that I would. It's a long time. Thirty years . . . She'd be an elderly woman now.'

'What was she like when you remember her?'

'Sonia?' Miss Blacklock considered for some moments. 'She was rather small, dark . . .'

'Any special peculiarities? Mannerisms?'

'No – no, I don't think so. She was gay – very gay.'

'She mayn't be so gay now,' said the Inspector. 'Have you got a photograph of her?'

'Of Sonia? Let me see – not a proper photograph. I've got some old snapshots – in an album somewhere – at least I think there's one of her.'

'Ah. Can I have a look at it?'

'Yes, of course. Now where did I put the album?'

'Tell me, Miss Blacklock, do you consider it remotely possible that Mrs Swettenham might be Sonia Goedler?'

'*Mrs Swettenham?*' Miss Blacklock looked at him in lively astonishment. 'But her husband was in the Government Service – in India first, I think, and then in Hong Kong.'

'What you mean is, that that's the story she's told you. You don't, as we say in the courts, know it of your own knowledge, do you?'

'No,' said Miss Blacklock slowly. 'When you put it like that, I don't . . . But Mrs Swettenham? Oh, it's absurd!'

'Did Sonia Goedler ever do any acting? Amateur theatricals?'

'Oh, yes. She was good.'

'There you are! Another thing, Mrs Swettenham wears a wig. At least,' the Inspector corrected himself, 'Mrs Harmon says she does.'

'Yes – yes, I suppose it might be a wig. All those little grey curls.

But I still think it's absurd. She's really very nice and exceedingly funny sometimes.'

'Then there's Miss Hinchliffe and Miss Murgatroyd. Could either of them be Sonia Goedler?'

'Miss Hinchliffe is too tall. She's as tall as a man.'

'Miss Murgatroyd then?'

'Oh, but – oh, no, I'm sure Miss Murgatroyd couldn't be Sonia.'

'You don't see very well, do you, Miss Blacklock?'

'I'm short-sighted, is that what you mean?'

'Yes. What I'd like to see is a snapshot of this Sonia Goedler, even if it's a long time ago and not a good likeness. We're trained, you know, to pick out resemblances, in a way no amateur can ever do.'

'I'll try and find it for you.'

'Now?'

'What, at once?'

'I'd prefer it.'

'Very well. Now, let me see. I saw that album when we were tidying a lot of books out of the cupboard. Julia was helping me. She laughed, I remember, at the clothes we used to wear in those days . . . The books we put in the shelf in the drawing room. Where did we put the albums and the big bound volumes of the Art Journal? What a wretched memory I have! Perhaps Julia will remember. She's at home today.'

'I'll find her.'

The Inspector departed on his quest. He did not find Julia in any of the downstairs rooms. Mitzi, asked where Miss Simmons was, said crossly that it was not her affair.

'Me! I stay in my kitchen and concern myself with the lunch. And nothing do I eat that I have not cooked myself. Nothing, do you hear?'

The Inspector called up the stairs 'Miss Simmons,' and getting no response, went up.

He met Julia face to face just as he turned the corner of the landing. She had just emerged from a door that showed behind it a small twisty staircase.

'I was up in the attic,' she explained. 'What is it?'

Inspector Craddock explained.

'Those old photograph albums? Yes, I remember them quite well. We put them in the big cupboard in the study, I think. I'll find them for you.'

She led the way downstairs and pushed open the study door. Near the window there was a large cupboard. Julia pulled it open and disclosed a heterogeneous mass of objects.

'Junk,' said Julia. 'All junk. But elderly people simply will *not* throw things away.'

The Inspector knelt down and took a couple of old-fashioned albums from the bottom shelf.

'Are these they?'

'Yes.'

Miss Blacklock came in and joined them.

'Oh, *so that's* where we put them. I couldn't remember.'

Craddock had the books on the table and was turning the pages.

Women in large cartwheel hats, women with dresses tapering down to their feet so that they could hardly walk. The photos had captions neatly printed underneath them, but the ink was old and faded.

'It would be in this one,' said Miss Blacklock. 'On about the second or third page. The other book is after Sonia had married and gone away.' She turned a page. 'It ought to be here.' She stopped.

There were several empty spaces on the page. Craddock bent down and deciphered the faded writing. 'Sonia . . . Self . . . R.G.' A little farther along, 'Sonia and Belle on beach.' And again on the opposite page, 'Picnic at Skeyne.' He turned over another page, 'Charlotte, Self, Sonia. R.G.'

Craddock stood up. His lips were grim.

'*Somebody has removed these photographs* – not long ago, I should say.'

'There weren't any blank spaces when we looked at them the other day. Were there, Julia?'

'I didn't look very closely – only at some of the dresses. But no . . . you're right, Aunt Letty, there *weren't* any blank spaces.'

Craddock looked grimmer still.

'Somebody,' he said, 'has removed every photo of Sonia Goedler from this album.'

18   THE LETTERS

'Sorry to worry you again, Mrs Haymes.'

'It doesn't matter,' said Phillipa coldly.

'Shall we go into this room here?'

'The study? Yes, if you like, Inspector. It's very cold. There's no fire.'

'It doesn't matter. It's not for long. And we're not so likely to be overheard here.'

'Does that matter?'

'Not to me, Mrs Haymes. It might to you.'

'What do you mean?'

'I think you told me, Mrs Haymes, that your husband was killed fighting in Italy?'

'Well?'

'Wouldn't it have been simpler to have told me the truth – that he was a deserter from his regiment.'

He saw her face grow white, and her hands close and unclose themselves.

She said bitterly:

'Do you have to rake up *everything*?'

Craddock said dryly:

'We expect people to tell us the truth about themselves.'

She was silent. Then she said:

'Well?'

'What do you mean by "Well?", Mrs Haymes?'

'I mean, what are you going to do about it? Tell everybody? Is that necessary – or fair – or kind?'

'Does nobody know?'

'Nobody here. Harry' – her voice changed – 'my son, he doesn't know. I don't want him to know. I don't want him to know – ever.'

'Then let me tell you that you're taking a very big risk, Mrs Haymes. When the boy is old enough to understand, tell him the truth. If he finds out by himself some day – it won't be good for him. If you go on stuffing him up with tales of his father dying like a hero –'

'I don't do that. I'm not completely dishonest. I just don't talk about it. His father was – killed in the war. After all, that's what it amounts to – for us.'

'But your husband is still alive?'

'Perhaps. How should I know?'

'When did you see him last, Mrs Haymes?'

Phillipa said quickly:

'I haven't seen him for years.'

'Are you quite sure that's true? You didn't, for instance, see him about a fortnight ago?'

'What are you suggesting?'

'It never seemed to me very likely that you met Rudi Scherz in the summerhouse here. But Mitzi's story was very emphatic. I suggest, Mrs Haymes, that the man you came back from work to meet that morning was your husband.'

'I didn't meet anybody in the summerhouse.'

'He was hard up for money, perhaps, and you supplied him with some?'

'I've not seen him, I tell you. I didn't meet anybody in the summerhouse.'

'Deserters are often rather desperate men. They often take part in robberies, you know. Hold-ups. Things of that kind. *And they have foreign revolvers very often that they've brought back from abroad.*'

'I don't know where my husband is. I haven't seen him for years.'

'Is that your last word, Mrs Haymes?'

'I've nothing else to say.'

II

Craddock came away from his interview with Phillipa Haymes feeling angry and baffled.

'Obstinate as a mule,' he said to himself angrily.

He was fairly sure that Phillipa was lying, but he hadn't succeeded in breaking down her obstinate denials.

He wished he knew a little more about ex-Captain Haymes. His information was meagre. An unsatisfactory army record, but nothing to suggest that Haymes was likely to turn criminal.

And anyway Haymes didn't fit in with the oiled door.

Someone in the house had done that, or someone with easy access to it.

He stood looking up the staircase, and suddenly he wondered what Julia had been doing up in the attic. An attic, he thought, was an unlikely place for the fastidious Julia to visit.

What had she been doing up there?

He ran lightly up to the first floor. There was no one about. He opened the door out of which Julia had come and went up the narrow stairs to the attic.

There were trunks there, old suitcases, various broken articles of furniture, a chair with a leg off, a broken china lamp, part of an old dinner service.

He turned to the trunks and opened the lid of one.

Clothes. Old-fashioned, quite good quality women's clothes. Clothes belonging, he supposed, to Miss Blacklock, or to her sister who had died.

He opened another trunk.

Curtains.

He passed to a small attaché case. It had papers in it and letters. Very old letters, yellowed with time.

He looked at the outside of the case which had the initials C.L.B. on it. He deduced correctly that it had belonged to Letitia's sister Charlotte. He unfolded one of the letters. It began *Dearest Charlotte. Yesterday Belle felt well enough to go for a picnic. R.G. also took a day off. The Asvogel flotation has gone splendidly, R.G. is terribly pleased about it. The Preference shares are at a premium.*

He skipped the rest and looked at the signature:

Your loving sister, Letitia.

He picked up another.

Darling Charlotte. I wish you would sometimes make up your mind to see people. You do exaggerate, you know. It isn't nearly as bad as you think. And people really don't mind things like that. It's not the disfigurement you think it is.

He nodded his head. He remembered Belle Goedler saying that Charlotte Blacklock had a disfigurement or deformity of some kind. Letitia had, in the end, resigned her job, to go and look after her sister. These letters all breathed the anxious spirit of her affection and love for an invalid. She had written her sister, apparently, long accounts of everyday happenings, of any little detail that she thought might interest the sick girl. And Charlotte had kept these letters. Occasionally odd snapshots had been enclosed.

Excitement suddenly flooded Craddock's mind. Here, it might be, he would find a clue. In these letters there would be written down things that Letitia Blacklock herself had long forgotten. Here was a faithful picture of the past and somewhere amongst it, there might be a clue that would help him to identify the unknown. Photographs, too. There might, just possibly, be a photograph of Sonia Goedler here that the person who had taken the other photos out of the album did not know about.

Inspector Craddock packed the letters up again, carefully, closed the case, and started down the stairs.

Letitia Blacklock, standing on the landing below, looked at him in amazement.

'Was that you up in the attic? I heard footsteps. I couldn't imagine who –'

'Miss Blacklock, I have found some letters here, written by you to your sister Charlotte many years ago. Will you allow me to take them away and read them?'

She flushed angrily.

'Must you do a thing like that? Why? What good can they be to you?'

'They might give me a picture of Sonia Goedler, of her character – there may be some allusion – some incident – that will help.'

'They are private letters, Inspector.'

'I know.'

'I suppose you will take them anyway . . . You have the power to do so, I suppose, or you can easily get it. Take them – take them! But you'll find very little about Sonia. She married and went away only a year or two after I began to work for Randall Goedler.'

Craddock said obstinately:

'There may be *something*.' He added, 'We've got to try everything. I assure you the danger is very real.'

She said, biting her lips:

'I know. Bunny is dead – from taking an aspirin tablet that was meant for me. It may be Patrick, or Julia, or Phillipa, or Mitzi next – somebody young with their life in front of them. Somebody who drinks a glass of wine that is poured out for me, or eats a chocolate that is sent to me. Oh! take the letters – take them away. And afterwards burn them. They don't mean anything to anyone but me and Charlotte. It's all over – gone – past. Nobody remembers now . . .'

Her hand went up to the choker of false pearls she was wearing.

Craddock thought how incongruous it looked with her tweed coat and skirt.

She said again:

'Take the letters.'

III

It was the following afternoon that the Inspector called at the Vicarage.

It was a dark gusty day.

Miss Marple had her chair pulled close to the fire and was knitting. Bunch was on hands and knees, crawling about the floor, cutting out material to a pattern.

She sat back and pushed a mop of hair out of her eyes, looking up expectantly at Craddock.

'I don't know if it's a breach of confidence,' said the Inspector, addressing himself to Miss Marple, 'but I'd like you to look at this letter.'

He explained the circumstances of his discovery in the attic.

'It's rather a touching collection of letters,' he said. 'Miss Blacklock poured out everything in the hopes of sustaining her sister's interest in life and keeping her health good. There's a very clear picture of an old father in the background – old Dr Blacklock. A real old pig-headed bully, absolutely set in his ways, and convinced that everything he thought and said was right. Probably killed thousands of patients through obstinacy. He wouldn't stand for any new ideas or methods.'

'I don't really know that I blame him there,' said Miss Marple. 'I always feel that the young doctors are only too anxious to experiment. After they've whipped out all our teeth, and administered quantities of very peculiar glands, and removed bits of our insides, they then confess that nothing can be done for us. I really prefer the old-fashioned remedy of big black bottles of medicine. After all, one can always pour those down the sink.'

She took the letter that Craddock handed her.

He said: 'I want you to read it because I think that that generation is more easily understood by you than by me. I don't know really quite how these people's minds worked.'

Miss Marple unfolded the fragile paper.

Dearest Charlotte,

I've not written for two days because we've been having the most terrible domestic complications. Randall's sister Sonia (you remember her? She came to take you out in the car that day? How I wish you would go out *more*), Sonia has declared her intention of marrying one, Dmitri Stamfordis. I have only seen him once. Very attractive – not to be trusted, I should say. R.G. raves against him and says he is a crook and a swindler. Belle, bless her, just smiles and lies on her sofa. Sonia, who though she looks so impassive has really a terrific temper, is simply wild with R.G. I really thought yesterday she was going to murder him!

I've done my best. I've talked to Sonia and I've talked to R.G. and I've got them both into a more reasonable frame of mind and then they come together and it all starts over again! You've no idea how *tiring* it is. R.G. has been making enquiries – and it does really seem as though this Stamfordis man was thoroughly undesirable.

In the meantime business is being neglected. I carry on at the office and in a way it's rather fun because R.G. gives me a free hand. He said to me yesterday: 'Thank Heaven, there's one sane person in the world. You're never likely to fall in love with a crook, Blackie, are you?' I said I didn't think I was likely to fall in love with anybody. R.G. said: 'Let's start a few new hares in the City.' He's really rather a mischievous devil sometimes and he sails terribly near the wind. 'You're quite determined to keep me on the straight and narrow path aren't you, Blackie?' he said the other day. And I shall too! I can't understand how people can't *see* when a thing's dishonest – but R.G. really and truly *doesn't*. He only knows what is actually against the law.

Belle only laughs at all this. She thinks the fuss about Sonia is all nonsense. 'Sonia has her own money,' she said. 'Why shouldn't she marry this man if she wants to?' I said it might turn out to be a terrible mistake and Belle said, 'It's never a mistake to marry a man you want to marry – even if you regret it.' And then she said, 'I suppose Sonia doesn't want to break with Randall because of money. Sonia's very fond of money.'

No more now. How is father? I won't say Give him my love. But you can if you think it's better to do so. Have you seen more people? You really must not be *morbid*, darling.

Sonia asks to be remembered to you. She has just come in and is closing and unclosing her hands like an angry cat sharpening its claws. I think she and R.G. have had another row. Of course Sonia can be *very* irritating. She stares you down with that cool stare of hers.

Lots of love, darling, and buck up. This iodine treatment may make a lot of difference. I've been enquiring about it and it really does seem to have good results.

Your loving sister,

Letitia

Miss Marple folded the letter and handed it back. She looked abstracted.

'Well, what do you think about her?' Craddock urged. 'What picture do you get of her?'

'Of Sonia? It's difficult, you know, to see anyone through another person's mind . . . Determined to get her own way – that, definitely, I think. And wanting the best of two worlds . . .'

'*Closing and unclosing her hands like an angry cat,*' murmured Craddock. 'You know, that reminds me of someone . . .'

He frowned.

'Making enquiries . . .' murmured Miss Marple.

'If we could get hold of the result of those enquiries,' said Craddock.

'Does that letter remind you of anything in St Mary Mead?' asked Bunch rather indistinctly since her mouth was full of pins.

'I really can't say it does, dear . . . Dr Blacklock is, perhaps, a little like Mr Curtiss the Wesleyan Minister. He wouldn't let his child wear a plate on her teeth. Said it was the Lord's Will if her teeth stuck out. "After all," I said to him, "you do trim your beard and cut your hair. It might be the Lord's Will that your hair should grow out." He said that was quite different. So like a man. But that doesn't help us with our present problem.'

'We've never traced that revolver, you know. It wasn't Rudi Scherz. If I knew who had had a revolver in Chipping Cleghorn –'

'Colonel Easterbrook has one,' said Bunch. 'He keeps it in his collar drawer.'

'How do you know, Mrs Harmon?'

'Mrs Butt told me. She's my daily. Or rather, my twice weekly. Being a military gentleman, she said, he'd naturally have a revolver and very handy it would be if burglars were to come along.'

'When did she tell you this?'

'Ages ago. About six months ago, I should think.'

'Colonel Easterbrook?' murmured Craddock.

'It's like those pointer things at fairs, isn't it?' said Bunch, still speaking through a mouthful of pins. 'Go round and round and stop at something different every time.'

'You're telling me!' said Craddock and groaned.

'Colonel Easterbrook was up at Little Paddocks to leave a book there one day. He could have oiled that door then. He was quite straightforward about being there though. Not like Miss Hinchliffe.'

Miss Marple coughed gently. 'You must make allowances for the times we live in, Inspector,' she said.

Craddock looked at her, uncomprehendingly.

'After all,' said Miss Marple, 'you *are* the police, aren't you? People can't say everything they'd like to say to the police, can they?'

'I don't see why not,' said Craddock. 'Unless they've got some criminal matter to conceal.'

'She means butter,' said Bunch, crawling actively round a table leg to anchor a floating bit of paper. 'Butter and corn for hens, and sometimes cream – and sometimes, even, a side of bacon.'

'Show him that note from Miss Blacklock,' said Miss Marple. 'It's some time ago now, but it reads like a first class mystery story.'

'What have I done with it? Is this the one you mean, Aunt Jane?'

Miss Marple took it and looked at it.

'Yes,' she said with satisfaction. 'That's the one.'

She handed it to the Inspector.

'*I have made inquiries – Thursday is the day*,' Miss Blacklock had written. '*Any time after three. If there is any for me leave it in the usual place.*'

Bunch spat out her pins and laughed. Miss Marple was watching the Inspector's face.

The Vicar's wife took it upon herself to explain.

'Thursday is the day one of the farms round here makes butter. They let anybody they like have a bit. It's usually Miss Hinchliffe who collects it. She's very much in with all the farmers – because of her pigs, I think. But it's all a bit hush-hush, you know, a kind of local scheme of barter. One person gets butter, and sends along cucumbers, or something like that – and a little something when a pig's killed. And now and then an animal has an accident and has to be destroyed. Oh, you know the sort of thing. Only one can't, very well, say it right out to the police. Because I suppose quite a lot of this barter is illegal – only nobody really knows because it's all so complicated. But I expect Hinch had slipped into Little Paddocks with a pound of butter or something and had put it in the *usual place*. That's a flour bin under the dresser, by the way. It doesn't have flour in it.'

Craddock sighed.

'I'm glad I came here to you ladies,' he said.

'There used to be clothing coupons, too,' said Bunch. 'Not usually bought – that wasn't considered honest. No money passes. But people like Mrs Butt or Mrs Finch or Mrs Huggins like a nice woollen dress or a winter coat that hasn't seen too much wear, and they pay for it with coupons instead of money.'

'You'd better not tell me any more,' said Craddock. 'It's all against the law.'

'Then there oughtn't to be such silly laws,' said Bunch, filling her mouth up with pins again. '*I* don't do it, of course, because Julian doesn't like me to, so I don't. But I know what's going on, of course.'

A kind of despair was coming over the Inspector.

'It all sounds so pleasant and ordinary,' he said. 'Funny and petty and simple. And yet one woman and a man have been killed, and another woman may be killed before I can get anything definite to go on. I've left off worrying about Pip and Emma for the moment. I'm concentrating on Sonia. I wish I knew what she looked like. There was a snapshot or two in with these letters, but none of the snaps could have been of her.'

'How do you know it couldn't have been her? Do you know what she looked like?'

'She was small and dark, Miss Blacklock said.'

'Really,' said Miss Marple, 'that's *very* interesting.'

'There was one snap that reminded me vaguely of someone. A tall fair girl with her hair all done up on top of her head. I don't know who she could have been. Anyway, it can't have been Sonia. Do you think Mrs Swettenham could have been dark when she was a girl?'

'Not very dark,' said Bunch. 'She's got blue eyes.'

'I hoped there might be a photo of Dmitri Stamfordis – but I suppose that was too much to hope for . . . Well' – he took up the letter – 'I'm sorry this doesn't suggest anything to you, Miss Marple.'

'Oh! but it does,' said Miss Marple. 'It suggests a good deal. Just read it through again, Inspector – especially where it says that Randall Goedler was making enquiries about Dmitri Stamfordis.'

Craddock stared at her.

The telephone rang.

Bunch got up from the floor and went out into the hall where, in accordance with the best Victorian traditions, the telephone had originally been placed and where it still was.

She re-entered the room to say to Craddock:

'It's for you.'

Slightly surprised, the Inspector went out to the instrument – carefully shutting the door of the living room behind him.

'Craddock? Rydesdale here.'

'Yes, sir.'

'I've been looking through your report. In the interview you had with Phillipa Haymes I see she states positively that she hasn't seen her husband since his desertion from the army?'

'That's right, sir – she was most emphatic. But in my opinion she wasn't speaking the truth.'

'I agree with you. Do you remember a case about ten days ago – man run over by a lorry – taken to Milchester General with concussion and a fractured pelvis?'

'The fellow who snatched a child practically from under the wheels of a lorry, and got run down himself?'

'That's the one. No papers of any kind on him and nobody came forward to identify him. Looked as though he might be on the run. He died last night without regaining consciousness. But he's been identified – deserter from the Army – Ronald Haymes, ex-Captain in the South Loamshires.'

'Phillipa Haymes' husband?'

'Yes. He'd got an old Chipping Cleghorn bus ticket on him, by the way – and quite a reasonable amount of money.'

'So he did get money from his wife? I always thought he was the man Mitzi overheard talking to her in the summerhouse. She denied it flatly, of course. But surely, sir, that lorry accident was before –'

Rydesdale took the words out of his mouth.

'Yes, he was taken to Milchester General on the 28th. The hold-up at Little Paddocks was on the 29th. That lets him out of any possible connection with it. But his wife, of course, knew nothing about the accident. She may have been thinking all along that he *was* concerned in it. She'd hold her tongue – naturally – after all he *was* her husband.'

'It was a fairly gallant bit of work, wasn't it, sir?' said Craddock slowly.

'Rescuing that child from the lorry? Yes. Plucky. Don't suppose it was cowardice that made Haymes desert. Well, all that's past history. For a man who'd blotted his copybook, it was a good death.'

'I'm glad for her sake,' said the Inspector. 'And for that boy of theirs.'

'Yes, he needn't be too ashamed of his father. And the young woman will be able to marry again now.'

Craddock said slowly:

'I was thinking of that, sir. . . . It opens up – possibilities.'

'You'd better break the news to her as you're on the spot.'

'I will, sir. I'll push along there now. Or perhaps I'd better wait until she's back at Little Paddocks. It may be rather a shock – and there's someone else I rather want to have a word with first.'

19   RECONSTRUCTION OF THE CRIME

'I'll put on a lamp by you before I go,' said Bunch. 'It's so dark in here. There's going to be a storm, I think.'

She lifted the small reading lamp to the other side of the table where it would throw light on Miss Marple's knitting as she sat in a wide high-backed chair.

As the flex pulled across the table, Tiglath Pileser the cat leapt upon it and bit and clawed it violently.

'No, Tiglath Pileser, you mustn't . . . He really is awful. Look, he's nearly bitten it through – it's all frayed. Don't you understand, you idiotic puss, that you may get a nasty electric shock if you do that?'

'Thank you, dear,' said Miss Marple, and put out a hand to turn on the lamp.

'It doesn't turn on there. You have to press that silly little switch half way along the flex. Wait a minute. I'll take these flowers out of the way.'

She lifted a bowl of Christmas roses across the table. Tiglath Pileser, his tail switching, put out a mischievous paw and clawed Bunch's arm. She spilled some of the water out of the vase. It fell on the frayed area of flex and on Tiglath Pileser himself, who leapt to the floor with an indignant hiss.

Miss Marple pressed the small pear-shaped switch. Where the water had soaked the frayed flex there was a flash and a crackle.

'Oh, dear,' said Bunch. 'It's fused. Now I suppose all the lights in here are off.' She tried them. 'Yes, they are. So stupid being all on the same thingummibob. And it's made a burn on the table, too. Naughty Tiglath Pileser – it's all his fault. Aunt Jane – what's the matter? Did it startle you?'

'It's nothing, dear. Just something I saw quite suddenly which I ought to have seen before . . .'

'I'll go and fix the fuse and get the lamp from Julian's study.'

'No, dear, don't bother. You'll miss your bus. I don't want any more light. I just want to sit quietly and – think about something. Hurry dear, or you won't catch your bus.'

When Bunch had gone, Miss Marple sat quite still for about two minutes. The air of the room was heavy and menacing with the gathering storm outside.

Miss Marple drew a sheet of paper towards her.

She wrote first: *Lamp?* and underlined it heavily.

After a moment or two, she wrote another word.

Her pencil travelled down the paper, making brief cryptic notes. . . .

II

In the rather dark living-room of Boulders with its low ceiling and latticed window panes, Miss Hinchliffe and Miss Murgatroyd were having an argument.

'The trouble with you, Murgatroyd,' said Miss Hinchliffe, 'is that you won't *try*.'

'But I tell you, Hinch, I can't remember a thing.'

'No look here, Amy Murgatroyd, we're going to do some constructive thinking. So far we haven't shone on the detective angle. I was quite wrong over that door business. You didn't hold the door open for the murderer after all. You're cleared, Murgatroyd!'

Miss Murgatroyd gave a rather watery smile.

'It's just our luck to have the only silent cleaning woman in Chipping Cleghorn,' continued Miss Hinchliffe. 'Usually I'm thankful for it, but this time it means we've got off to a bad start.

Everybody else in the place knows about that second door in the drawing room being used – and we only heard about it yesterday –'

'I still don't quite understand how –'

'It's perfectly simple. Our original premises were quite right. You can't hold open a door, wave a torch and shoot with a revolver all at the same time. We kept in the revolver and the torch and cut out the door. Well, we were wrong. It was the revolver we ought to have cut out.'

'But he *did* have a revolver,' said Miss Murgatroyd. 'I saw it. It was there on the floor beside him.'

'When he was dead, yes. It's all quite clear. *He* didn't fire that revolver –'

'Then who did?'

'That's what we're going to find out. But whoever did it, the same person put a couple of poisoned aspirin tablets by Letty Blacklock's bed – and thereby bumped off poor Dora Bunner. And that couldn't have been Rudi Scherz, because he's as dead as a doornail. It was someone who was in the room that night of the hold-up and probably someone who was at the birthday party, too. And the only person *that* lets out is Mrs Harmon.'

'You think someone put those aspirins there the day of the birthday party?'

'Why not?'

'But how could they?'

'Well, we all went to the loo, didn't we?' said Miss Hinchliffe coarsely. 'And I washed my hands in the bathroom because of that sticky cake. And little Sweetie Easterbrook powdered her grubby little face in Blacklock's bedroom, didn't she?'

'Hinch! Do you think *she* –'

'I don't know yet. Rather obvious, if she did. I don't think if you were going to plant some tablets, that you'd want to be seen in the bedroom at all. Oh, yes, there were plenty of opportunities.'

'The men didn't go upstairs.'

'There are back stairs. After all, if a man leaves the room, you don't follow him to see if he really is going where you think he is going. It wouldn't be delicate! Anyway, don't *argue*, Murgatroyd. I want to get back to the original attempt on Letty Blacklock. Now, to begin with, get the facts firmly into your head, because it's all going to depend upon you.'

Miss Murgatroyd looked alarmed.

'Oh, dear, Hinch, you know what a muddle I get into!'

'It's not a question of your brains, or the grey fluff that passes for brains with you. It's a question of *eyes*. It's a question of what you *saw*.'

'But I didn't see *anything*.'

'The trouble with you is, Murgatroyd, as I said just now, that you won't *try*. Now pay attention. This is what happened. Whoever it is that's got it in for Letty Blacklock was there in that room that evening. He (I say *he* because it's easier, but there's no reason why it should be a man more than a woman except, of course, that men are dirty dogs), well, he has previously oiled that second door that leads out of the drawing-room and which is supposed to be nailed up or something. Don't ask me *when* he did it, because that confuses things. Actually, by choosing my time, I could walk into any house in Chipping Cleghorn and do anything I liked there for half an hour or so with no one being the wiser. It's just a question of working out where the daily women are and when the occupiers are out and exactly where they've gone and how long they'll be. Just good staff work. Now, to continue. He's oiled that second door. It will open without a sound. Here's the setup: Lights go out, door A (the regular door) opens with a flourish. Business with torch and hold-up lines. In the meantime, while we're all goggling, X (that's the best term to use) slips quietly out by door B into the dark hall, comes up behind that Swiss idiot, takes a couple of shots at Letty Blacklock and then shoots the Swiss. Drops the revolver, where lazy thinkers like you will assume it's evidence that the Swiss did the shooting, and nips back into the room again by the time that someone gets a lighter going. Got it?'

'Yes – ye-es, but who was it?'

'Well, if *you* don't know, Murgatroyd, nobody does!'

'*Me?*' Miss Murgatroyd fairly twittered in alarm. 'But I don't know anything *at all*. I don't *really*, Hinch!'

'Use that fluff of yours you call a brain. To begin with, where was everybody when the lights went out?'

'I don't know.'

'Yes, you do. You're maddening, Murgatroyd. You know where *you* were, don't you? You were behind the door.'

'Yes – yes, I was. It knocked against my corn when it flew open.'

'Why don't you go to a proper chiropodist instead of messing about yourself with your feet. You'll give yourself blood poisoning one of these days. Come on, now – *you're* behind the door. *I'm* standing against the mantelpiece with my tongue hanging out for a drink. Letty Blacklock is by the table near the archway, getting the cigarettes. Patrick Simmons has gone through the archway into the small room where Letty Blacklock has had the drinks put. Agreed?'

'Yes, yes, I remember all that.'

'Good, now somebody else followed Patrick into that room or was just starting to follow him. One of the men. The annoying thing is that I can't remember whether it was Easterbrook or Edmund Swettenham. Do you remember?'

'No, I don't.'

'You wouldn't! And there was someone else who went through to the small room; Phillipa Haymes. I remember that distinctly because I remember noticing what a nice flat back she has, and I thought to myself "that girl would look well on a horse." I was watching her and thinking just that. She went over to the mantelpiece in the other room. I don't know what it was she wanted there, because at that moment the lights went out.

'So that's the position. In the far drawing-room are Patrick Simmons, Phillipa Haymes, and *either* Colonel Easterbrook or Edmund Swettenham – we don't know which. Now, Murgatroyd, pay attention. The most probable thing is that it was *one of those three* who did it. If anyone wanted to get out of that far door, they'd naturally take care to put themselves in a convenient place when the lights went out. So, as I say, in all probability, it's one of those three. And in that case, Murgatroyd, there's not a thing you can do about it!'

Miss Murgatroyd brightened perceptibly.

'On the other hand,' continued Miss Hinchliffe, 'there's the possibility that it *wasn't* one of those three. And that's where you come in, Murgatroyd.'

'But how should *I* know anything about it?'

'As I said before, if you don't nobody does.'

'But I don't! I really *don't*! I couldn't see anything *at all*!'

'Oh, yes, you could. You're the only person who *could* see. You were standing behind the door. You couldn't look *at* the torch – because the door was between you and it. You were facing the other way, the same way as the torch was pointing. The rest of us were just dazzled. But *you* weren't dazzled.'

'No – no, perhaps not, but I didn't *see* anything, the torch went round and round –'

'Showing you *what*? It rested on *faces*, didn't it? And on tables? And on chairs?'

'Yes – yes, it did . . . Miss Bunner, her mouth wide open and her eyes popping out of her head, staring and blinking.'

'That's the stuff!' Miss Hinchliffe gave a sigh of relief. 'The difficulty there is in making you use that grey fluff of yours! Now then, keep it up.'

'But I didn't see any more, I didn't, really.'

'You mean you saw an empty room? Nobody standing about? Nobody sitting down?'

'No, of course not *that*. Miss Bunner with her mouth open and Mrs Harmon was sitting on the arm of a chair. She had her eyes tight shut and her knuckles all doubled up to her face –like a child.'

'Good, that's Mrs Harmon and Miss Bunner. Don't you see yet what I'm getting at? The difficulty is that I don't want to put ideas into your head. But when we've eliminated who you *did* see – we can get on to the important point which is, was there anyone you *didn't* see. Got it? Besides the tables and the chairs and the chrysanthemums and the rest of it, there were certain people: Julia Simmons, Mrs Swettenham, Mrs Easterbrook – *either* Colonel Easterbrook or Edmund Swettenham – Dora Bunner and Bunch Harmon. All right, you saw Bunch Harmon and Dora Bunner. Cross them off. Now *think*, Murgatroyd, *think*, was there one of those people who definitely *wasn't* there?'

Miss Murgatroyd jumped slightly as a branch knocked against the open window. She shut her eyes. She murmured to herself . . .

'The flowers . . . on the table . . . the big armchair . . . the torch didn't come round as far as you, Hinch – Mrs Harmon, yes . . .'

The telephone rang sharply. Miss Hinchliffe went to it.

'Hallo, yes? The station?'

The obedient Miss Murgatroyd, her eyes closed, was reliving the night of the 29th. The torch, sweeping slowly round . . . a group of people . . . the windows . . . the sofa . . . Dora Bunner . . . the wall . . . the table with lamp . . . the archway . . . the sudden spat of the revolver . . .

'. . . but that's *extraordinary*!' said Miss Murgatroyd.

'What?' Miss Hinchliffe was barking angrily into the telephone. 'Been there since this morning? What time? Damn and blast you, and you only ring me up *now*? I'll set the SPCA after you. An oversight? Is *that* all you've got to say?'

She banged down the receiver.

'It's that dog,' she said. 'The red setter. Been at the station since this morning – since this morning at eight o'clock! Without a drop of water! And the idiots only ring me up now. I'm going to get her right away.'

She plunged out of the room, Miss Murgatroyd squeaking shrilly in her wake.

'But listen, Hinch, a most extraordinary thing . . . I don't understand it . . .'

Miss Hinchliffe had dashed out of the door and across to the shed which served as a garage.

'We'll go on with it when I come back,' she called. 'I can't wait for you to come with me. You've got your bedroom slippers on as usual.'

She pressed the starter of the car and backed out of the garage with a jerk. Miss Murgatroyd skipped nimbly sideways.

'But listen, Hinch, I *must* tell you –'

'When I come back . . .'

The car jerked and shot forwards. Miss Murgatroyd's voice came faintly after it on a high excited note.

'But, Hinch, *she wasn't there* . . .'

III

Overhead, the clouds had been gathering thick and blue. As Miss Murgatroyd stood looking after the retreating car, the first big drops began to fall.

In an agitated fashion, Miss Murgatroyd plunged across to a line of string on which she had, some hours previously, hung out a couple of jumpers and a pair of woollen combinations to dry.

She was murmuring under her breath:

'Really *most* extraordinary . . . Oh, dear, I shall never get these down in time . . . And they were nearly dry. . . .'

She struggled with a recalcitrant clothes peg, then turned her head as she heard someone approaching.

Then she smiled a pleased welcome.

'Hallo – do go inside, you'll get wet.'

'Let me help you.'

'Oh, if you don't mind . . . so annoying if they all get soaked again. I really ought to let down the line, but I think I can just reach.'

'Here's your scarf. Shall I put it round your neck?'

'Oh, thank you . . . Yes, perhaps . . . If I could just reach this peg . . .'

The woollen scarf was slipped round her neck and then, suddenly, pulled tight . . .

Miss Murgatroyd's mouth opened, but no sound came except a small choking gurgle.

And the scarf was pulled tighter still . . .

IV

On her way back from the station, Miss Hinchliffe stopped the car to pick up Miss Marple who was hurrying along the street.

'Hallo,' she shouted. 'You'll get very wet. Come and have tea with us. I saw Bunch waiting for the bus. You'll be all alone at the Vicarage. Come and join us. Murgatroyd and I are doing a bit of reconstruction of the crime. I rather think we're just getting somewhere. Mind the dog. She's rather nervous.'

'What a beauty?'

'Yes, lovely bitch, isn't she? Those fools kept her at the station since this morning without letting me know. I told them off, the lazy b – s. Oh! excuse my language. I was brought up by grooms at home in Ireland.'

The little car turned with a jerk into the small backyard of Boulders.

A crowd of eager ducks and fowls encircled the two ladies as they descended.

'Curse Murgatroyd,' said Miss Hinchliffe, 'she hasn't given 'em their corn.'

'Is it difficult to get corn?' Miss Marple enquired.

Miss Hinchliffe winked.

'I'm in with most of the farmers,' she said.

Shooing away the hens, she escorted Miss Marple towards the cottage.

'Hope you're not too wet?'

'No, this is a very good mackintosh.'

'I'll light the fire if Murgatroyd hasn't lit it. Hiyah, Murgatroyd? Where is the woman? Murgatroyd! Where's that dog? *She's* disappeared now.'

A slow dismal howl came from outside.

'Curse the silly bitch.' Miss Hinchliffe tramped to the door and called:

'Hyoup, Cutie – Cutie. Damn' silly name but that's what they called her apparently. We must find her another name. Hiyah, Cutie.'

The red setter was sniffing at something lying below the taut string where a row of garments swirled in the wind.

'Murgatroyd's not even had the sense to bring the washing in. Where *is* she?'

Again the red setter nosed at what seemed to be a pile of clothes, and raised her nose high in the air and howled again.

'What's the *matter* with the dog?'

Miss Hinchliffe strode across the grass.

And quickly, apprehensively, Miss Marple ran after her. They stood there, side by side, the rain beating down on them and the other woman's arm went round the younger one's shoulders.

She felt the muscles go stiff and taut as Miss Hinchliffe stood looking down on the thing lying there, with the blue congested face and the protruding tongue.

'I'll kill whoever did this,' said Miss Hinchliffe in a low quiet voice, 'If I once get my hands on her . . .'

Miss Marple said questioningly:

'*Her?*'

Miss Hinchliffe turned a ravaged face towards her.

'Yes. I know who it is – near enough . . . That is, it's one of three possibles.'

She stood for another moment, looking down at her dead friend, and then turned towards the house. Her voice was dry and hard.

'We must ring up the police,' she said. 'And while we're waiting for them, I'll tell you. My fault, in a way, that Murgatroyd's lying out there. I made a game of it . . . Murder isn't a game. . . .'

'No,' said Miss Marple. 'Murder isn't a game.'

'You know something about it, don't you?' said Miss Hinchliffe as she lifted the receiver and dialled.

She made a brief report and hung up.

'They'll be here in a few minutes . . . Yes, I heard that you'd been mixed up in this sort of business before . . . I think it was Edmund Swettenham told me so . . . Do you want to hear what we were doing, Murgatroyd and I?'

Succinctly she described the conversation held before her departure for the station.

'She called after me, you know, just as I was leaving . . . That's how I know it's a woman and not a man . . . If I'd waited – if only I'd *listened*! God dammit, the dog could have stopped where she was for another quarter of an hour.'

'Don't blame yourself, my dear. That does no good. One can't foresee.'

'No, one can't ... Something tapped against the window, I remember. Perhaps *she* was outside there, then – yes, of course, she must have been ... coming to the house ... and there were Murgatroyd and I shouting at each other. Top of our voices ... She heard ... She heard it all ...'

'You haven't told me yet what your friend said.'

'Just one sentence! "*She wasn't there.*"'

She paused. 'You see? There were three women we hadn't eliminated. Mrs Swettenham, Mrs Easterbrook, Julia Simmons. And one of those three – *wasn't there* ... She wasn't there in the drawing-room because she had slipped out through the other door and was out in the hall.'

'Yes,' said Miss Marple, 'I see.'

'It's *one* of those three women. I don't know which. But I'll find out!'

'Excuse me,' said Miss Marple. 'But did she – did Miss Murgatroyd, I mean, say it exactly as you said it?'

'How d'you mean – as I said it?'

'Oh, dear, how can I explain? You said it like this. *She-wasn't-there*. An equal emphasis on every word. You see, there are three ways you could say it. You could say, "*She* wasn't there." Very personal. Or again. "She *wasn't* there." Confirming some suspicion already held. Or else you could say (and this is nearer to the way you said it just now), "She wasn't *there* ..." quite blankly – with the emphasis, if there was emphasis – on the "*there*."'

'I don't know,' Miss Hinchliffe shook her head. 'I can't remember ... How the hell can I remember? I think, yes, surely she'd say "*She* wasn't there"? That would be the natural way, I should think. But I simply don't know. Does it make any difference?'

'Yes,' said Miss Marple, thoughtfully. 'I think so. It's a very *slight* indication, of course, but I think it *is* an indication. Yes, I should think it makes a lot of difference ...'

20   MISS MARPLE IS MISSING

The postman, rather to his disgust, had lately been given orders to make an afternoon delivery of letters in Chipping Cleghorn as well as a morning one.

On this particular afternoon he left three letters at Little Paddocks at exactly ten minutes to five.

One was addressed to Phillipa Haymes in a schoolboy's hand; the other two were for Miss Blacklock. She opened them as she and Phillipa sat down at the tea table. The torrential rain had enabled Phillipa to leave Dayas Hall early today, since once she had shut up the greenhouses there was nothing more to do.

Miss Blacklock tore open her first letter which was a bill for repairing the kitchen boiler. She snorted angrily.

'Dymond's prices are *preposterous* – quite preposterous. Still, I suppose all the other people are just as bad.'

She opened the second letter which was in a handwriting quite unknown to her.

Dear Cousin Letty (*it said*),
   I hope it will be all right for me to come to you on Tuesday? I wrote to Patrick two days ago but he hasn't answered. So I presume it's all right. Mother is coming to England next month and hopes to see you then.
   My train arrives at Chipping Cleghorn at 6.15 if that's convenient?
                                             Yours affectionately,
                                                      Julia Simmons

Miss Blacklock read the letter once with astonishment pure and simple, and then again with a certain grimness. She looked up at Phillipa who was smiling over her son's letter.

'Are Julia and Patrick back, do you know?'

Phillipa looked up.

'Yes, they came in just after I did. They went upstairs to change. They were wet.'

'Perhaps you'd not mind going and calling them.'

'Of course, I will.'

'Wait a moment – I'd like you to read this.'

She handed Phillipa the letter she had received.

Phillipa read it and frowned. 'I don't understand . . .'

'Nor do I, quite . . . I think it's about time I did. Call Patrick and Julia, Phillipa.'

Phillipa called from the bottom of the stairs:

'Patrick! Julia! Miss Blacklock wants you.'

Patrick came running down the stairs and entered the room.

'Don't go, Phillipa,' said Miss Blacklock.

'Hallo, Aunt Letty,' said Patrick cheerfully. 'Want me?'

'Yes, I do. Perhaps you'll give me an explanation of *this*?'

Patrick's face showed an almost comical dismay as he read.

'I meant to telegraph her! What an ass I am!'

'This letter, I presume, is from your sister Julia?'

'Yes – yes, it is.'

Miss Blacklock said grimly:

'*Then who, may I ask, is the young woman whom you brought here as Julia Simmons,* and whom I was given to understand was your sister and my cousin?'

'Well – you see – Aunt Letty – the fact of the matter is – I can explain it all – I know I oughtn't to have done it – but it really seemed more of a lark than anything else. If you'll just let me explain –'

'I am waiting for you to explain. *Who is this young woman?*'

'Well, I met her at a cocktail party soon after I got demobbed. We got talking and I said I was coming here and then – well, we thought it might be rather a good wheeze if I brought her along . . . You see, Julia, the real Julia was mad to go on the stage and Mother had seven fits at the idea – however, Julia got a chance to join a jolly good repertory company up in Perth or somewhere and she thought she'd give it a try – but she thought she'd keep Mum calm by letting Mum think that she was here with me studying to be a dispenser like a good little girl.'

'I still want to know who this other young woman *is*.'

Patrick turned with relief as Julia, cool and aloof, came into the room.

'The balloon's gone up,' he said.

Julia raised her eyebrows. Then, still cool, she came forward and sat down.

'OK,' she said. 'That's that. I suppose you're very angry?' She studied Miss Blacklock's face with almost dispassionate interest. 'I should be if I were you.'

'*Who are you?*'

Julia sighed.

'I think the moment's come when I make a clean breast of things. Here we go. I'm one half of the Pip and Emma combination. To be exact, my christened name is Emma Jocelyn Stamfordis – only Father soon dropped the Stamfordis. I think he called himself De Courcy next.

'My father and mother, let me tell you, split up about three years after Pip and I were born. Each of them went their own way. And they split us up. I was Father's part of the loot. He was a bad parent on the whole, though quite a charming one. I had various desert spells of being educated in convents – when Father hadn't any money, or was preparing to engage in some particularly nefarious deal. He used to pay the first term with every sign of affluence and then depart and leave me on the nuns' hands for a year or two. In the intervals, he and I had some very good times together, moving in cosmopolitan society. However, the war separated us completely. I've no idea of what's happened to him. I had a few adventures myself. I was with the French Resistance for a time. Quite exciting. To cut a long story short, I landed up in London and began to think about my future. I knew that Mother's brother with whom she'd had a frightful row, had died a very rich man. I looked up his will to see if there was anything for me. There wasn't – not directly, that is to say. I made a few enquiries about his widow – it seemed she was quite gaga and kept under drugs and was dying by inches. Frankly, it looked as though *you* were my best bet. You were going to come into a hell of a lot of money and from all I could find out, you didn't seem to have anyone much to spend it on. I'll be quite frank. It occurred to me that if I could get to know you in a friendly kind of way, and if you took a fancy to me – well, after all, conditions have changed a bit, haven't they, since Uncle Randall died? I mean any money we ever had has been swept away in the cataclysm of Europe. I thought you might pity a poor orphan girl, all alone in the world, and make her, perhaps a small allowance.'

'Oh, you did, did you?' said Miss Blacklock grimly.

'Yes. Of course, I hadn't seen you then . . . I visualized a kind of sob stuff approach . . . Then, by a marvellous stroke of luck, I met Patrick here – and he turned out to be your nephew or your cousin, or something. Well, that struck me as a marvellous chance. I went bullheaded for Patrick and he fell for me in a most gratifying way. The real Julia was all wet about this acting stuff and I soon persuaded her it was her duty to Art to go and fix herself up in some uncomfortable lodgings in Perth and train to be the new Sarah Bernhardt.

'You mustn't blame Patrick too much. He felt awfully sorry for me, all alone in the world – and he soon thought it would be a really marvellous idea for me to come here as his sister and do my stuff.'

'And he also approved of your continuing to tell a tissue of lies to the police?'

'Have a heart, Letty. Don't you see that when that ridiculous hold-up business happened – or rather after it happened – I began to feel I was in a bit of a spot. Let's face it, I've got a perfectly good motive for putting you out of the way. You've only got my word for it now that I wasn't the one who tried to do it. You can't expect me deliberately to go and incriminate myself. Even Patrick got nasty ideas about me from time to time, and if even *he* could think things like that, what on earth would the police think? That Detective-Inspector struck me as a man of singularly sceptical mind. No, I figured out the only thing for me to do was to sit tight as Julia and just fade away when term came to an end.

'How was I to know that fool Julia, the real Julia, would go and have a row with the producer, and fling the whole thing up in a fit of temperament? She writes to Patrick and asks if she can come here, and instead of wiring her "Keep away" he goes and forgets to do anything at all!' She cast an angry glance at Patrick. 'Of all the utter *idiots*!'

She sighed.

'You don't know the straits I've been put to in Milchester! Of course, I haven't been to the hospital at all. But I had to go *somewhere*. Hours and hours I've spent in the pictures seeing the most frightful films over and over again.'

'*Pip and Emma*,' murmured Miss Blacklock. 'I never believed, somehow, in spite of what the Inspector said, that they were *real* –'

She looked searchingly at Julia.

'You're Emma,' she said. 'Where's Pip?'

Julia's eyes, limpid and innocent, met hers.

'I don't know,' she said. 'I haven't the least idea.'

'I think you're lying, Julia. When did you see him last?'

Was there a momentary hesitation before Julia spoke?

She said clearly and deliberately:

'I haven't seen him since we were both three years old – when my mother took him away. I haven't seen either him or my mother. I don't know where they are.'

'And that's all you have to say?'

Julia sighed.

'I could say I was sorry. But it wouldn't really be true; because actually I'd do the same thing again – though not if I'd known about this murder business, of course.'

'Julia,' said Miss Blacklock, '(I call you that because I'm used to it). You were with the French Resistance, you say?'

'Yes. for eighteen months.'

'Then I suppose you learned to shoot?'

Again those cool blue eyes met hers.

'I can shoot all right. I'm a first class shot. I didn't shoot at you, Letitia Blacklock, though you've only got my word for that. But I can tell you this, that if *I* had shot at you, I wouldn't have been likely to miss.'

II

The sound of a car driving up to the door broke through the tenseness of the moment.

'Who can that be?' asked Miss Blacklock.

Mitzi put a tousled head in. She was showing the whites of her eyes.

'It is the police come again,' she said. 'This, it is persecution! Why will they not leave us alone? I will not bear it. I will write to the Prime Minister. I will write to your King.'

Craddock's hand put her firmly and not too kindly aside. He came in with such a grim set to his lips that they all looked at him apprehensively. This was a new Inspector Craddock.

He said sternly:

'Miss Murgatroyd has been murdered. She was strangled – not more than an hour ago.' His eye singled out Julia. 'You – Miss Simmons – where have you been all day?'

Julia said warily:

'In Milchester. I've just got in.'

'And you?' The eye went on to Patrick.

'Yes.'

'Did you both come back here together?'

'Yes – yes, we did,' said Patrick.

'No,' said Julia. 'It's no good, Patrick. That's the kind of lie that will be found out at once. The bus people know us well. I came back on the earlier bus, Inspector – the one that gets here at four o'clock.'

'And what did you do then?'

'I went for a walk.'

'In the direction of Boulders?'

'No, I went across the fields.'

He stared at her. Julia, her face pale, her lips tense, stared back.

Before anyone could speak, the telephone rang.

Miss Blacklock, with an enquiring glance at Craddock, picked up the receiver.

'Yes. Who? Oh, Bunch. What? No. No, she hasn't. I've no idea . . . Yes, he's here now.'

She lowered the instrument and said:

'Mrs Harmon would like to speak to you, Inspector. Miss Marple has not come back to the Vicarage and Mrs Harmon is worried about her.'

Craddock took two strides forward and gripped the telephone.

'Craddock speaking.'

'I'm worried, Inspector.' Bunch's voice came through with a childish tremor in it. 'Aunt Jane's out somewhere – and I don't know where. And they say that Miss Murgatroyd's been killed. Is it true?'

'Yes, it's true, Mrs Harmon. Miss Marple was there with Miss Hinchliffe when they found the body.'

'Oh, so *that's* where she is.' Bunch sounded relieved.

'No – no, I'm afraid she isn't. Not now. She left there about – let me see – half an hour ago. She hasn't got home?'

'No – she hasn't. It's only ten minutes' walk. Where can she be?'

'Perhaps she's called in on one of your neighbours?'

'I've rung them up – *all of them*. She's not there. I'm frightened, Inspector.'

'So am I,' thought Craddock.

He said quickly:

'I'll come round to you – at once.'

'Oh, *do* – there's a piece of paper. She was writing on it before she went out. I don't know if it means anything . . . It just seems gibberish to me.'

Craddock replaced the receiver.

Miss Blacklock said anxiously:

'Has something happened to Miss Marple? Oh, I hope not.'

'I hope not, too.' His mouth was grim.

'She's so old – and frail.'

'I know.'

Miss Blacklock, standing with her hand pulling at the choker of pearls round her neck, said in a hoarse voice:

'It's getting worse and worse. Whoever's doing these things must be mad, Inspector – quite mad . . .'

'I wonder.'

The choker of pearls round Miss Blacklock's neck broke under the clutch of her nervous fingers. The smooth white globules rolled all over the room.

Letitia cried out in an anguished tone.

'My pearls – my *pearls* –' The agony in her voice was so acute that they all looked at her in astonishment. She turned, her hand to her throat, and rushed sobbing out of the room.

Phillipa began picking up the pearls.

'I've never seen her so upset over anything,' she said. 'Of course – she always wears them. Do you think, perhaps, that someone special gave them to her? Randall Goedler, perhaps.'

'It's possible,' said the Inspector slowly.

'They're not – they couldn't be – *real* by any chance?' Phillipa asked from where, on her knees, she was still collecting the white shining globes.

Taking one in his hand, Craddock was just about to reply contemptuously, 'Real? Of course not!' when he suddenly stifled the words.

After all, *could* the pearls be real?

They were so large, so even, so white that their falseness seemed palpable, but Craddock remembered suddenly a police case where a string of real pearls had been bought for a few shillings in a pawnbroker's shop.

Letitia Blacklock had assured him that there was no jewellery of value in the house. If these pearls were, by any chance, genuine, they must be worth a fabulous sum. And if Randall Goedler had given them to her – then they might be worth any sum you cared to name.

They looked false – they *must* be false, but – if they were real?

Why not? She might herself be unaware of their value. Or she might choose to protect her treasure by treating it as though it were a cheap ornament worth a couple of guineas at most. What would

they be worth if real? A fabulous sum . . . Worth doing murder for –
if anybody knew about them.

With a start, the Inspector wrenched himself away from his
speculations. Miss Marple was missing. He must go to the Vicarage.

III

He found Bunch and her husband waiting for him, their faces
anxious and drawn.

'She hasn't come back,' said Bunch.

'Did she say she was coming back here when she left Boulders?'
asked Julian.

'She didn't actually say so,' said Craddock slowly, throwing his
mind back to the last time he had seen Jane Marple.

He remembered the grimness of her lips and the severe frosty light
in those usually gentle blue eyes.

Grimness, an inexorable determination . . . to do what? To go
where?

'She was talking to Sergeant Fletcher when I last saw her,' he said.
'Just by the gate. And then she went through it and out. I took it she
was going straight home to the Vicarage. I would have sent her in
the car – but there was so much to attend to, and she slipped away
very quietly. Fletcher may know something! Where's Fletcher?'

But Sergeant Fletcher, it seemed, as Craddock learned when he
rang up Boulders, was neither to be found there nor had he left any
message where he had gone. There was some idea that he had
returned to Milchester for some reason.

The Inspector rang up headquarters in Milchester, but no news of
Fletcher was to be found there.

Then Craddock turned to Bunch as he remembered what she had
told him over the telephone.

'Where's that paper? You said she'd been writing something on a
bit of paper.'

Bunch brought it to him. He spread it out on the table and looked
down on it. Bunch leant over his shoulder and spelled it out as he
read. The writing was shaky and not easy to read:

Lamp.

Then came the word *'Violets.'*

Then after a space:

Where is bottle of aspirin?

The next item in this curious list was more difficult to make out. '*Delicious Death*,' Bunch read. 'That's Mitzi's cake.'

'*Making enquiries*,' read Craddock.

'Enquiries? What about, I wonder? What's this? *Severe affliction bravely borne* . . . What on earth –!'

'*Iodine*,' read the Inspector. '*Pearls*. Ah, pearls.'

'And then *Lotty* – no, *Letty*. Her *e*'s look like *o*'s. And then *Berne*. And what's this? *Old Age Pension* . . .'

They looked at each other in bewilderment.

Craddock recapitulated swiftly:

'Lamp. Violets. Where is bottle of aspirin? Delicious Death. Making enquiries. Severe affliction bravely borne. Iodine. Pearls. Letty. Berne. Old Age Pension.'

Bunch asked: 'Does it mean anything? Anything at all? I can't see any connection.'

Craddock said slowly: 'I've just a glimmer – but I don't see. It's odd that she should have put down that about pearls.'

'What about pearls? What does it mean?'

'Does Miss Blacklock always wear that three tier choker of pearls?'

'Yes, she does. We laugh about it sometimes. They're so dreadfully false looking, aren't they? But I suppose she thinks it's fashionable.'

'There might be another reason,' said Craddock slowly.

'You don't mean that they're *real*. Oh! they *couldn't* be!'

'How often have you had an opportunity of seeing real pearls of that size, Mrs Harmon?'

'But they're so glassy.'

Craddock shrugged his shoulders.

'Anyway, they don't matter now. It's Miss Marple that matters. We've got to find her.'

They'd got to find her before it was too late – but perhaps it was already too late? Those pencilled words showed that she was on the track . . . But that was dangerous – horribly dangerous. And where the hell was Fletcher?

Craddock strode out of the Vicarage to where he'd left his car. Search – that was all he could do – search.

A voice spoke to him out of the dripping laurels.

'Sir!' said Sergeant Fletcher urgently. '*Sir* . . .'

21   THREE WOMEN

Dinner was over at Little Paddocks. It had been a silent and uncomfortable meal.

Patrick, uneasily aware of having fallen from grace, only made spasmodic attempts at conversation – and such as he did make were not well received. Phillipa Haymes was sunk in abstraction. Miss Blacklock herself had abandoned the effort to behave with her normal cheerfulness. She had changed for dinner and had come down wearing her necklace of cameos but for the first time fear showed from her darkly circled eyes, and betrayed itself by her twitching hands.

Julia alone, had maintained her air of cynical detachment throughout the evening.

'I'm sorry, Letty,' she said, 'that I can't pack my bag and go. But I presume the police wouldn't allow it. I don't suppose I'll darken your roof – or whatever the expression is – for long. I should imagine that Inspector Craddock will be round with a warrant and the handcuffs any moment. In fact, I can't imagine why something of the kind hasn't happened already.'

'He's looking for the old lady – for Miss Marple,' said Miss Blacklock.

'Do you think she's been murdered, too?' Patrick asked with scientific curiosity. 'But why? What could she know?'

'I don't know,' said Miss Blacklock dully. 'Perhaps Miss Murgatroyd told her something.'

'If she's been murdered too,' said Patrick, 'there seems to be logically only one person who could have done it.'

'Who?'

'Hinchliffe, of course,' said Patrick triumphantly. 'That's where she was last seen alive – at Boulders. My solution would be that she never left Boulders.'

'My head aches,' said Miss Blacklock in a dull voice. She pressed her fingers to her forehead. 'Why should Hinch murder Miss Marple? It doesn't make sense.'

'It would if Hinch had really murdered Murgatroyd,' said Patrick triumphantly.

Phillipa came out of her apathy to say:

'Hinch wouldn't murder Murgatroyd.'

Patrick was in an argumentative mood.

'She might have if Murgatroyd had blundered on something to show that she – Hinch – was the criminal.'

'Anyway, Hinch was at the station when Murgatroyd was killed.'

'She could have murdered Murgatroyd before she left.'

Startling them all, Letitia Blacklock suddenly screamed out:

'Murder, murder, *murder* –! Can't you talk of *anything* else? I'm frightened, don't you understand? I'm frightened. I wasn't before. I thought I could take care of myself . . . But what can you do against a murderer who's waiting – and watching – and biding his time! Oh, God!'

She dropped her head forward on her hands. A moment later she looked up and apologized stiffly.

'I'm sorry. I – I lost control.'

'That's all right, Aunt Letty,' said Patrick affectionately. 'I'll look after you.'

'You?' was all Letitia Blacklock said, but the disillusionment behind the word was almost an accusation.

That had been shortly before dinner, and Mitzi had then created a diversion by coming and declaring that she was not going to cook the dinner.

'I do not do anything more in this house. I go to my room. I lock myself in. I stay there until it is daylight. I am afraid – people are being killed – that Miss Murgatroyd with her stupid English face – who would want to kill *her*? Only a maniac! Then it is a maniac that is about! And a maniac does not care *who* he kills. But me, I do not want to be killed! There are shadows in that kitchen – and I hear noises – I think there is someone out in the yard and then I think I see a shadow by the larder door and then it is footsteps I hear. So I go now to my room and I lock the door and perhaps even I put the chest of drawers against it. And in the morning I tell that cruel hard policeman that I go away from here. And if he will not let me I say: "I scream and I scream and I scream until you have to let me go!"'

Everybody, with a vivid recollection of what Mitzi could do in the screaming line, shuddered at the threat.

'So I go to my room,' said Mitzi, repeating the statement once more to make her intentions quite clear. With a symbolic action she cast off the cretonne apron she had been wearing. 'Good night, Miss

Blacklock. Perhaps in the morning, you may not be alive. So in case that is so, I say goodbye.'

She departed abruptly and the door, with its usual gentle little whine, closed softly after her.

Julia got up.

'I'll see to dinner,' she said in a matter-of-fact way. 'Rather a good arrangement – less embarrassing for you all than having me sit down at table with you. Patrick (since he's constituted himself your protector, Aunt Letty) had better taste every dish first. I don't want to be accused of poisoning you on top of everything else.'

So Julia had cooked and served a really excellent meal.

Phillipa had come out to the kitchen with an offer of assistance but Julia had said firmly that she didn't want any help.

'Julia, there's something I want to say –'

'This is no time for girlish confidences,' said Julia firmly. 'Go on back in the dining-room, Phillipa.'

Now dinner was over and they were in the drawing-room with coffee on the small table by the fire – and nobody seemed to have anything to say. They were waiting – that was all.

At 8.30 Inspector Craddock rang up.

'I shall be with you in about a quarter of an hour's time,' he announced. 'I'm bringing Colonel and Mrs Easterbrook and Mrs Swettenham and her son with me.'

'But really, Inspector . . . I can't cope with people tonight –'

Miss Blacklock's voice sounded as though she were at the end of her tether.

'I know how you feel, Miss Blacklock. I'm sorry. But this is urgent.'

'Have you – found Miss Marple?'

'No,' said the Inspector and rang off.

Julia took the coffee tray out to the kitchen where, to her surprise, she found Mitzi contemplating the piled up dishes and plates by the sink.

Mitzi burst into a torrent of words.

'See what you do in my so nice kitchen! That frying pan – only, *only* for omelettes do I use it! And you, what have you used it for?'

'Frying onions.'

'Ruined – *ruined*. It will have now to be *washed* and never – *never* – do I wash my omelette pan. I rub it carefully over with a greasy newspaper, that is all. And this saucepan here that you have used – that one, I use him only for milk –'

'Well, I don't know what pans you use for what,' said Julia crossly. 'You chose to go to bed and why on earth you've chosen to get up again, I can't imagine. Go away again and leave me to wash up in peace.'

'No, I will not let you use my kitchen.'

'Oh, Mitzi, you *are* impossible!'

Julia stalked angrily out of the kitchen and at that moment the door bell rang.

'I do not go to the door,' Mitzi called from the kitchen. Julia muttered an impolite continental expression under her breath and stalked to the front door.

It was Miss Hinchliffe.

''Evening,' she said in her gruff voice. 'Sorry to barge in. Inspector's rung up, I expect?'

'He didn't tell us you were coming,' said Julia, leading the way to the drawing room.

'He said I needn't come unless I liked,' said Miss Hinchliffe. 'But I do like.'

Nobody offered Miss Hinchliffe sympathy or mentioned Miss Murgatroyd's death. The ravaged face of the tall vigorous woman told its own tale, and would have made any expression of sympathy an impertinence.

'Turn all the lights on,' said Miss Blacklock. 'And put more coal on the fire. I'm cold – horribly cold. Come and sit here by the fire, Miss Hinchliffe. The Inspector said he would be here in a quarter of an hour. It must be nearly that now.'

'Mitzi's come down again,' said Julia.

'Has she? Sometimes I think that girl's mad – quite mad. But then perhaps we're all mad.'

'I've no patience with this saying that all people who commit crimes are mad,' barked Miss Hinchliffe. 'Horribly and intelligently sane – that's what I think a criminal is!'

The sound of a car was heard outside and presently Craddock came in with Colonel and Mrs Easterbrook and Edmund and Mrs Swettenham.

They were all curiously subdued.

Colonel Easterbrook said in a voice that was like an echo of his usual tones:

'Ha! A good fire.'

Mrs Easterbrook wouldn't take off her fur coat and sat down close to her husband. Her face, usually pretty and rather vapid, was like a little pinched weasel face. Edmund was in one of his furious moods and scowled at everybody. Mrs Swettenham made what was evidently a great effort, and which resulted in a kind of parody of herself.

'It's awful – isn't it?' she said conversationally. 'Everything, I mean. And really the less one says, the better. Because one doesn't know *who next* – like the Plague. Dear Miss Blacklock, don't you think you ought to have a little brandy? Just half a wineglass even? I always think there's nothing like brandy – such a wonderful stimulant. I – it seems so terrible of us – forcing our way in here like this, but Inspector Craddock *made* us come. And it seems so terrible – she hasn't been found, you know. That poor old thing from the Vicarage, I mean. Bunch Harmon is nearly frantic. Nobody knows *where* she went instead of going home. She didn't come to us. I've not even seen her today. And I should know if she *had* come to the house because I was in the drawing-room – at the back, you know, and Edmund was in his study writing – and that's at the front – so if she'd come either way we *should* have seen. And, oh, I do hope and pray that nothing has happened to that dear sweet old thing – all her faculties still and *everything*.'

'Mother,' said Edmund in a voice of acute suffering, 'can't you shut up?'

'I'm sure, dear, I don't want to say a *word*,' said Mrs Swettenham, and sat down on the sofa by Julia.

Inspector Craddock stood near the door. Facing him, almost in a row, were the three women. Julia and Mrs Swettenham on the sofa. Mrs Easterbrook on the arm of her husband's chair. He had not brought about this arrangement, but it suited him very well.

Miss Blacklock and Miss Hinchliffe were crouching over the fire. Edmund stood near them. Phillipa was far back in the shadows.

Craddock began without preamble.

'You all know that Miss Murgatroyd's been killed,' he began. 'We've reason to believe that the person who killed her was a woman. And for certain other reasons we can narrow it down still more. I'm about to ask certain ladies here to account for what they were doing between the hours of four and four-twenty this afternoon. I have already had an account of her movements from – from the young lady who has been calling herself Miss Simmons. I will ask her to repeat that statement. At the same time, Miss Simmons, I must caution you that you need not answer if you think your answers may incriminate you, and anything you say will be taken down by Constable Edwards and may be used as evidence in court.'

'You have to say that, don't you?' said Julia. She was rather pale, but still composed. 'I repeat that between four and four-thirty I was walking along the field leading down to the brook by Compton Farm. I came back to the road by that field with three poplars in it. I didn't meet anyone as far as I can remember. I did not go near Boulders.'

'Mrs Swettenham?'

Edmund said, 'Are you cautioning all of us?'

The Inspector turned to him.

'No. At the moment only Miss Simmons. I have no reason to believe that any other statement made will be incriminating, but anyone, of course, is entitled to have a solicitor present and to refuse to answer questions unless he *is* present.'

'Oh, but that would be very silly and a complete waste of time,' cried Mrs Swettenham. 'I'm sure I can tell you at once exactly what I was doing. That's what you want, isn't it? Shall I begin now?'

'Yes, please, Mrs Swettenham.'

'Now, let me see.' Mrs Swettenham closed her eyes, opened them again. 'Of course I had nothing *at all* to do with killing Miss Murgatroyd. I'm sure *everybody* here knows *that*. But I'm a woman of the world, I know quite well that the police have to ask all the most unnecessary questions and write the answers down very carefully, because it's all for what they call "the record". That's it, isn't it?' Mrs Swettenham flashed the question at the diligent Constable Edwards and added graciously, 'I'm not going too fast for you, I hope?'

Constable Edwards, a good shorthand writer, but with little social *savoir-faire*, turned red to the ears and replied:

'It's quite all right, madam. Well, perhaps a *little* slower would be better.'

Mrs Swettenham resumed her discourse with emphatic pauses where she considered a comma or a full stop might be appropriate.

'Well, of course it's difficult to say – exactly – because I've not got, really, a very good sense of time. And ever since the war quite half our clocks haven't gone at all, and the ones that do go are often either fast or slow or stop because we haven't wound them up.' Mrs Swettenham paused to let this picture of confused time sink in and then went on earnestly, 'What I *think* I was doing at four o'clock was turning the heel of my sock (and for some extraordinary reason

I was going round the wrong way – in purl, you know, not plain) but if I *wasn't* doing that, I must have been outside snipping off the dead chrysanthemums – no, that was earlier – before the rain.'

'The rain,' said the inspector, 'started at 4.10 exactly.'

'Did it now? That helps a lot. Of course, I was upstairs putting a washbasin in the passage where the rain always comes through. And it was coming through so fast that I guessed at once that the gutter was stopped up again. So I came down and got my mackintosh and rubber boots. I called Edmund, but he didn't answer, so I thought perhaps he'd got to a very important place in his novel and I wouldn't disturb him, and I've done it quite often myself before. With the broom handle, you know, tied on to that long thing you push up windows with.'

'You mean,' said Craddock, noting bewilderment on his subordinate's face, 'that you were cleaning out the gutter?'

'Yes, it was all choked up with leaves. It took a long time and I got rather wet, but I got it clear at last. And then I went in and got changed and washed – so *smelly*, dead leaves – and then I went into the kitchen and put the kettle on. It was 6.15 by the kitchen clock.'

Constable Edwards blinked.

'Which means,' finished Mrs Swettenham triumphantly, 'that it was exactly twenty minutes to five.'

'Or near enough,' she added.

'Did anybody see what you were doing whilst you were out cleaning the gutter?'

'No, indeed,' said Mrs Swettenham, 'I'd soon have roped them in to help if they had! It's a most difficult thing to do single-handed.'

'So, by your own statement, you were outside, in a mackintosh and boots, at the time when the rain was coming down, and according to you, you were employed during that time in cleaning out a gutter but you have no one who can substantiate that statement?'

'You can look at the gutter,' said Mrs Swettenham. 'It's beautifully clear.'

'Did you hear your mother call to you, Mr Swettenham?'

'No,' said Edmund. 'I was fast asleep.'

'Edmund,' said his mother reproachfully, 'I thought you were *writing*.'

Inspector Craddock turned to Mrs Easterbrook.

'Now, Mrs Easterbrook?'

'I was sitting with Archie in his study,' said Mrs Easterbrook fixing wide innocent eyes on him. 'We were listening to the wireless together, weren't we, Archie?'

There was a pause. Colonel Easterbrook was very red in the face. He took his wife's hand in his.

'You don't understand these things, kitten,' he said. 'I – well, I must say, Inspector, you've rather sprung this business on us. My wife, you know, has been terribly upset by all this. She's nervous and highly strung and doesn't appreciate the importance of – of taking due consideration before she makes a statement.'

'Archie,' cried Mrs Easterbrook reproachfully, 'are you going to say you weren't with me?'

'Well, I wasn't, was I, my dear? I mean one's got to stick to the facts. Very important in this sort of enquiry. I was talking to Lampson, the farmer at Croft End, about some chicken netting. That was about a quarter to four. I didn't get home until after the rain had stopped. Just before tea. A quarter to five. Laura was toasting the scones.'

'And had *you* been out also, Mrs Easterbrook?'

The pretty face looked more like a weasel's than ever. Her eyes had a trapped look.

'No – no, I just sat listening to the wireless. I didn't go out. Not then. I'd been out earlier. About – about half-past three. Just for a little walk. Not far.'

She looked as though she expected more questions, but Craddock said quietly:

'That's all, Mrs Easterbrook.'

He went on: 'These statements will be typed out. You can read them and sign them if they are substantially correct.'

Mrs Easterbrook looked at him with sudden venom.

'Why don't you ask the others where they were? That Haymes woman? And Edmund Swettenham? How do you know he *was* asleep indoors? Nobody saw him.'

Inspector Craddock said quietly:

'Miss Murgatroyd, before she died, made a certain statement. On the night of the hold-up here, *someone* was absent from this room. Someone who was supposed to have been in the room all the time. Miss Murgatroyd told her friend the names of the people she *did* see. By a process of elimination, she made the discovery that there was someone she did *not* see.'

'Nobody could see anything,' said Julia.

'Murgatroyd could,' said Miss Hinchliffe, speaking suddenly

in her deep voice. 'She was over there behind the door, where Inspector Craddock is now. She was the only person who could see anything of what was happening.'

'*Aha! That is what you think, is it!*' demanded Mitzi.

She made one of her dramatic entrances, flinging open the door and almost knocking Craddock sideways. She was in a frenzy of excitement.

'Ah, you do not ask Mitzi to come in here with the others, do you, you stiff policeman? I am only Mitzi! Mitzi in the kitchen! Let her stay in the kitchen where she belongs! But I tell you that Mitzi, as well as anyone else, and perhaps better, yes, better, can see things. Yes, I see things. I see something the night of the burglary. I see something and I do not quite believe it, and I hold my tongue till now. I think to myself I will not tell what it is I have seen, not yet. I will wait.'

'And when everything had calmed down, you meant to ask for a little money from a certain person, eh?' said Craddock.

Mitzi turned on him like an angry cat.

'And why not? Why look down your nose? Why should I not be paid for it if I have been so generous as to keep silence? Especially if some day there will be money – much *much* money. Oh! I have heard things – I know what goes on. I know this Pippemmer – this secret society of which *she*' – she flung a dramatic finger towards Julia – 'is an agent. Yes, I would have waited and asked for money – but now I am afraid. I would rather be *safe*. For soon, perhaps, someone will kill *me*. So I will tell what I know.'

'All right then,' said the Inspector sceptically. 'What *do* you know?'

'I tell you.' Mitzi spoke solemnly. 'On that night I am *not* in the pantry cleaning silver as I say – I am already in the dining-room when I hear the gun go off. I look through the keyhole. The hall it is black, but the gun go off again and the torch it falls – and it swings round as it falls – and I see *her*. I see *her* there close to him, with the gun in her hand. I see Miss Blacklock.'

'Me?' Miss Blacklock sat up in astonishment. 'You must be mad!'

'But that's impossible,' cried Edmund. 'Mitzi couldn't have seen Miss Blacklock –'

Craddock cut in and his voice had the corrosive quality of a deadly acid.

'*Couldn't she, Mr Swettenham? And why not?* Because it *wasn't*

Miss Blacklock who was standing there with the gun? It was *you*, wasn't it?'

'I? – of course not – what the *hell*!'

'*You* took Colonel Easterbrook's revolver. *You* fixed up the business with Rudi Scherz – as a good joke. You had followed Patrick Simmons into the far room and when the lights went out, you slipped out through the carefully oiled door. You shot at Miss Blacklock and then you killed Rudi Scherz. A few seconds later you were back in the drawing-room clicking your lighter.'

For a moment Edmund seemed at a loss for words, then he spluttered out:

'The whole idea is *monstrous*. Why *me*? What earthly motive had *I* got?'

'If Miss Blacklock dies before Mrs Goedler, two people inherit, remember. The two we know of as Pip and Emma. Julia Simmons has turned out to be Emma –'

'And you think I'm Pip?' Edmund laughed. 'Fantastic – absolutely *fantastic*! I'm about the right age – nothing else. And I can prove to you, you damned fool, that I *am* Edmund Swettenham. Birth certificate, schools, university – everything.'

'He isn't Pip.' The voice came from the shadows in the corner. Phillipa Haymes came forward, her face pale. '*I'm Pip*, Inspector.'

'*You*, Mrs Haymes?'

'Yes. Everybody seems to have assumed that Pip was a boy – Julia knew, of course, that her twin was another girl – I don't know why she didn't say so this afternoon –'

'Family solidarity,' said Julia. 'I suddenly realized who you were. I'd had no idea till that moment.'

'I'd had the same idea as Julia did,' said Phillipa, her voice trembling a little. 'After I – lost my husband and the war was over, I wondered what I was going to do. My mother died many years ago. I found out about my Goedler relations. Mrs Goedler was dying and at her death the money would go to a Miss Blacklock. I found out where Miss Blacklock lived and I – I came here. I took a job with Mrs Lucas. I hoped that, since this Miss Blacklock was an elderly woman without relatives, she might, perhaps, be willing to help. Not me, because I could work, but help with Harry's education. After all, it *was* Goedler money and she'd no one particular of her own to spend it on.

'And then,' Phillipa spoke faster, it was as though, now her long reserve had broken down, she couldn't get the words out fast enough, 'that hold-up happened and I began to be frightened. Because it seemed to me that the only possible person with a motive for killing Miss Blacklock was *me*. I hadn't the least idea who Julia was – we aren't identical twins and we're not much alike to look at. No, it seemed as though I was the only one bound to be suspected.'

She stopped and pushed her fair hair back from her face, and Craddock suddenly realized that the faded snapshot in the box of letters must have been a photograph of Phillipa's mother. The likeness was undeniable. He knew too why that mention of closing and unclosing hands had seemed familiar – Phillipa was doing it now.

'Miss Blacklock has been good to me. Very *very* good to me – I didn't try to kill her. I never thought of killing her. But all the same, I'm Pip.' She added, 'You see, you needn't suspect Edmund any more.'

'Needn't I?' said Craddock. Again there was that acid biting tone in his voice. 'Edmund Swettenham's a young man who's fond of money. A young man, perhaps, who would like to marry a rich wife. But she wouldn't be a rich wife *unless Miss Blacklock died before Mrs Goedler*. And since it seemed almost certain that Mrs Goedler would die before Miss Blacklock, well – he had to do something about it – *didn't you, Mr Swettenham?*'

'It's a damned lie!' Edmund shouted.

And then, suddenly, a sound rose on the air. It came from the kitchen – a long unearthly shriek of terror.

'That isn't Mitzi!' cried Julia.

'No,' said Inspector Craddock, 'it's someone who's murdered three people . . .'

22   THE TRUTH

When the Inspector turned on Edmund Swettenham, Mitzi had crept quietly out of the room and back to the kitchen. She was running water into the sink when Miss Blacklock entered.

Mitzi gave her a shamefaced sideways look.

'What a liar you are, Mitzi,' said Miss Blacklock pleasantly. 'Here – that isn't the way to wash up. The silver first, and fill the sink right up. You can't wash up in about two inches of water.'

Mitzi turned the taps on obediently.

'You are not angry at what I say, Miss Blacklock?' she asked.

'If I were to be angry at all the lies you tell, I should never be out of a temper,' said Miss Blacklock.

'I will go and say to the Inspector that I make it all up, shall I?' asked Mitzi.

'He knows that already,' said Miss Blacklock, pleasantly.

Mitzi turned off the taps and as she did so two hands came up behind her head and with one swift movement forced it down into the water-filled sink.

'Only *I* know that you're telling the truth for once,' said Miss Blacklock viciously.

Mitzi thrashed and struggled but Miss Blacklock was strong and her hands held the girl's head firmly under water.

Then, from somewhere quite close behind her, Dora Bunner's voice rose piteously on the air:

'*Oh Lotty – Lotty – don't do it . . . Lotty.*'

Miss Blacklock screamed. Her hands flew up in the air, and Mitzi, released, came up choking and spluttering.

Miss Blacklock screamed again and again. For there was no one, except Mitzi, there in the kitchen with her . . .

'*Dora, Dora, forgive me. I had to . . . I had to –*'

She rushed distractedly towards the scullery door – and the bulk of Sergeant Fletcher barred her way, just as Miss Marple stepped, flushed and triumphant, out of the broom cupboard.

'I could always mimic people's voices,' said Miss Marple.

'You'll have to come with me, madam,' said Sergeant Fletcher. 'I was a witness of your attempt to drown this girl. And there will be other charges. I must warn you, Letitia Blacklock –'

'Charlotte Blacklock,' corrected Miss Marple. 'That's who she is, you know. Under that choker of pearls she always wears you'll find the scar of the operation.'

'Operation?'

'Operation for goitre.'

Miss Blacklock, quite calm now, looked at Miss Marple.

'So you know all about it?' she said.

'Yes, I've known for some time.'

Charlotte Blacklock sat down by the table and began to cry.

'You shouldn't have done that,' she said. 'Not made Dora's voice come. I loved Dora. I really loved Dora.'

Inspector Craddock and the others had crowded in the doorway.

Constable Edwards, who added a knowledge of first aid and artificial respiration to his other accomplishments, was busy with Mitzi. As soon as Mitzi could speak she was lyrical with self-praise.

'I do that good, do I not? I am clever! And I am brave! Oh, I am brave! Very very nearly was *I* murdered, too. But I am so brave I risk *everything*.'

With a rush Miss Hinchliffe thrust aside the others and leapt upon the weeping figure of Charlotte Blacklock by the table.

It took all Sergeant Fletcher's strength to hold her off.

'Now then –' he said. 'Now then – no, no, Miss Hinchliffe –'

Between clenched teeth Miss Hinchliffe was muttering:

'Let me get at her. Just let me get at her. It was she who killed Amy Murgatroyd.'

Charlotte Blacklock looked up and sniffed.

'I didn't want to kill her. I didn't want to kill anybody – I had to – but it's Dora I mind about – after Dora was dead, I was all alone – ever since she died – I've been alone – oh, Dora – Dora –'

And once again she dropped her head on her hands and wept.

23   EVENING AT THE VICARAGE

Miss Marple sat in the tall armchair. Bunch was on the floor in front of the fire with her arms round her knees.

The Reverend Julian Harmon was leaning forward and was for once looking more like a schoolboy than a man foreshadowing his own maturity. And Inspector Craddock was smoking his pipe and drinking a whisky and soda and was clearly very much off duty. An outer circle was composed of Julia, Patrick, Edmund and Phillipa.

'I think it's your story, Miss Marple,' said Craddock.

'Oh no, my dear boy. I only just helped a little, here and there. *You* were in charge of the whole thing, and conducted it all, and you know so much that I don't.'

'Well, tell it together,' said Bunch impatiently. 'Bit each. Only let Aunt Jane start because I like the muddly way her mind works. When did you first think that the whole thing was a put up job by the Blacklock?'

'Well, my dear Bunch, it's hard to say. Of course, right at the very beginning, it did seem as though the ideal person – or rather the *obvious* person, I should say – to have arranged the hold-up *was* Miss Blacklock herself. She was the only person who was known to have been in contact with Rudi Scherz, and how much easier to arrange something like that when it's your own house. The central heating, for instance. No fires – because that would have meant light in the room. But the only person who could have arranged *not* to have a fire was the mistress of the house herself.

'Not that I thought of all that at the time – it just seemed to me that it was a pity it *couldn't* be as simple as that! Oh, no, I was taken in like everyone else, I thought that someone really did want to kill Letitia Blacklock.'

'I think I'd like to get clear first on what really happened,' said Bunch. 'Did this Swiss boy recognize her?'

'Yes. He'd worked in –'

She hesitated and looked at Craddock.

'In Dr Adolf Koch's clinic in Berne,' said Craddock. 'Koch was a world famous specialist on operations for goitre. Charlotte Blacklock went there to have her goitre removed and Rudi Scherz was one of the orderlies. When he came to England he recognized in the hotel a lady who had been a patient and on the spur of the moment he spoke to her. I dare say he mightn't have done that if he'd paused to think, because he left the place under a cloud, but that was sometime after Charlotte had been there, so she wouldn't know anything about it.'

'So he never said anything to her about Montreux and his father being a hotel proprietor?'

'Oh, no, she made that up to account for his having spoken to her.'

'It must have been a great shock to her,' said Miss Marple, thoughtfully. 'She felt reasonably safe – and then – the almost impossible mischance of somebody turning up who had known her – not as one of the two Miss Blacklocks – she was prepared for *that* – but definitely as *Charlotte* Blacklock, a patient who'd been operated on for goitre.

'But you wanted to go through it all from the beginning. Well, the beginning, I think – if Inspector Craddock agrees with me – was when Charlotte Blacklock, a pretty, light-hearted, affectionate girl, developed that enlargement of the thyroid gland that's called a goitre. It ruined her life, because she was a very sensitive girl. A girl, too, who had always set a lot of stress on her personal appearance.

And girls just at that age in their teens, are particularly sensitive about themselves. If she'd had a mother, or a reasonable father, I don't think she would have got into the morbid state she undoubtedly did get into. She had no one, you see, to take her out of herself, and force her to see people and lead a normal life and not think too much about her infirmity. And, of course, in a different household, she might have been sent for an operation many years earlier.

'But Dr Blacklock, I think, was an old-fashioned, narrow-minded, tyrannical and obstinate man. He didn't believe in these operations. Charlotte must take it from him that nothing could be done – apart from dosage with iodine and other drugs. Charlotte *did* take it from him, and I think her sister also placed more faith in Dr Blacklock's powers as a physician than he deserved.

'Charlotte was devoted to her father in a rather weak and soppy way. She thought, definitely, that her father knew best. But she shut herself up more and more as the goitre became larger and more unsightly, and refused to see people. She was actually a kindly, affectionate creature.'

'That's an odd description of a murderess,' said Edmund.

'I don't know that it is,' said Miss Marple. 'Weak and kindly people are often very treacherous. And if they've got a grudge against life it saps the little moral strength that they may possess.

'Letitia Blacklock, of course, had quite a different personality. Inspector Craddock told me that Belle Goedler described her as really *good* – and I think Letitia *was* good. She was a woman of great integrity who found – as she put it herself – a great difficulty in understanding how people couldn't see what was dishonest. Letitia Blacklock, however tempted, would never have contemplated any kind of fraud for a moment.

'Letitia was devoted to her sister. She wrote her long accounts of everything that happened in an effort to keep her sister in touch with life. She was worried by the morbid state Charlotte was getting into.

'Finally Dr Blacklock died. Letita, without hesitation, threw up her position with Randall Goedler and devoted herself to Charlotte. She took her to Switzerland to consult authorities there on the possibility of operating. It had been left very late – but as we know the operation was successful. The deformity was gone – and the scar this operation had left was easily hidden by a choker of pearls or beads.

'The war had broken out. A return to England was difficult and the two sisters stayed in Switzerland doing various Red Cross and other work. That's right, isn't it, Inspector?'

'Yes, Miss Marple.'

'They got occasional news from England – amongst other things, I expect, they heard that Belle Goedler could not live long. I'm sure it would be only human nature for them both to have planned and talked together of the days ahead when a big fortune would be theirs to spend. One has got to realize, I think, that this prospect meant much more to *Charlotte* than it did to Letitia. For the first time in her life, Charlotte could go about feeling herself a normal woman, a woman at whom no one looked with either repulsion or pity. She was free at last to enjoy life – and she had a whole lifetime, as it were, to crowd into her remaining years. To travel, to have a house and beautiful grounds – to have clothes and jewels, and go to plays and concerts, to gratify every whim – it was all a kind of fairytale come true to Charlotte.

'And then Letitia, the strong healthy Letitia, got flu which turned to pneumonia and died within the space of a week! Not only had Charlotte lost her sister, but the whole dream existence she had planned for herself was cancelled. I think, you know, that she may have felt almost resentful towards Letitia. Why need Letitia have died, just then, when they had just had a letter saying Belle Goedler could not last long? Just one more month, perhaps, and the money would have been Letitia's – and hers when Letitia died . . .

'Now this is where I think the difference between the two came in. Charlotte didn't really feel that what she suddenly thought of doing was wrong – not really wrong. The money was meant to come to Letitia – it *would* have come to Letitia in the course of a few months – and she regarded herself and Letitia as one.

'Perhaps the idea didn't occur to her until the doctor or someone asked her her sister's Christian name – and then she realized how to nearly everyone they had appeared as the two Miss Blacklocks – elderly, well-bred Englishwomen, dressed much the same, with a strong family resemblance – (and, as I pointed out to Bunch, one elderly woman is *so* like another). Why shouldn't it be Charlotte who had died and *Letitia* who was alive?

'It was an impulse, perhaps, more than a plan. Letitia was buried under Charlotte's name. "Charlotte" was dead, "Letitia" came to England. All the natural initiative and energy, dormant for so many years, were now in the ascendant. As Charlotte she had played second fiddle. She now assumed the airs of command, the feeling of command that had been Letitia's. They were not really so unlike in mentality – though there was, I think, a big difference *morally*.

'Charlotte had, of course, to take one or two obvious precautions. She bought a house in a part of England quite unknown to her. The only people she had to avoid were a few people in her own native town in Cumberland (where in any case she'd lived as a recluse) and, of course, Belle Goedler who had known Letitia so well that any impersonation would have been out of the question. Handwriting difficulties were got over by the arthritic condition of her hands. It was really very easy because so few people had ever really known Charlotte.'

'But supposing she'd met people who'd known Letitia?' asked Bunch. 'There must have been plenty of those.'

'They wouldn't matter in the same way. Someone might say: "I came across Letitia Blacklock the other day. She's changed so much I really wouldn't have known her." But there still wouldn't be any suspicion in their minds that she wasn't Letitia. People *do* change in the course of ten years. *Her* failure to recognize *them* could always be put down to her short-sightedness: and you must remember that she knew every detail of Letitia's life in London – the people she met – the places she went. She'd got Letitia's letters to refer to, and she could quickly have disarmed any suspicion by mention of some incident, or an enquiry after a mutual friend. No, it was recognition as *Charlotte* that was the only thing she had to fear.

'She settled down at Little Paddocks, got to know her neighbours and, when she got a letter asking dear Letitia to be kind, she accepted with pleasure the visit of two young cousins she had never seen. Their acceptance of her as Aunt Letty increased her security.

'The whole thing was going splendidly. And then – she made her big mistake. It was a mistake that arose solely from her kindness of heart and her naturally affectionate nature. She got a letter from an old school friend who had fallen on evil days, and she hurried to the rescue. Perhaps it may have been partly because she was, in spite of everything, lonely. Her secret kept her in a way apart from people. And she had been genuinely fond of Dora Bunner and remembered her as a symbol of her own gay carefree days at school. Anyway, on an impulse, she answered Dora's letter in person. And very surprised Dora must have been! She'd written to *Letitia* and the sister who turned up in answer to her letter was *Charlotte*. There was never any question of pretending to be Letitia to Dora. Dora was one of the few old friends who had been admitted to see Charlotte in her lonely and unhappy days.

'And because she knew that Dora would look at the matter in exactly the same way as she did herself, she told Dora what she had done. Dora approved wholeheartedly. In her confused muddle-headed mind it seemed only right that dear Lotty should not be done out of her inheritance by Letty's untimely death. Lotty *deserved* a reward for all the patient suffering she had borne so bravely. It would have been most unfair if all that money should have gone to someone nobody had ever heard of.

'She quite understood that nothing must be allowed to get out. It was like an extra pound of butter. You couldn't talk about it but there was nothing wrong about having it. So Dora came to Little Paddocks – and very soon Charlotte began to understand that she had made a terrible mistake. It was not merely the fact that Dora Bunner, with her muddles and her mistakes and her bungling, was quite maddening to live with. Charlotte could have put up with that – because she really cared for Dora, and anyway knew from the doctor that Dora hadn't got a very long time to live. But Dora very soon became a real danger. Though Charlotte and Letitia had called each other by their full names, Dora was the kind of person who always uses abbreviations. To her the sisters had always been Letty and Lotty. And though she schooled her tongue resolutely to call her friend Letty – the old name often slipped out. Memories of the past, too, were rather apt to come to her tongue – and Charlotte had constantly to be on the watch to check these forgetful allusions. It began to get on her nerves.

'Still, nobody was likely to pay much attention to Dora's inconsistencies. The real blow to Charlotte's security came, as I say, when she was recognized and spoken to by Rudi Scherz at the Royal Spa Hotel.

'I think that the money Rudi Scherz used to replace his earlier defalcations at the hotel may have come from Charlotte Blacklock. Inspector Craddock doesn't believe – and I don't either – that Rudi Scherz applied to her for money with any idea of blackmail in his head.'

'He hadn't the faintest idea he knew anything to blackmail her about,' said Inspector Craddock. 'He knew that he was quite a personable young man – and he was aware by experience that personable young men sometimes can get money out of elderly ladies if they tell a hard luck story convincingly enough.

'But she may have seen it differently. She may have thought that it was a form of insidious blackmail, that perhaps he suspected something – and that later, if there was publicity in the papers as there might be after Belle Goedler's death, he would realize that in her he had found a gold mine.

'And she was committed to the fraud now. She'd established herself as Letitia Blacklock. With the bank. With Mrs Goedler. The only snag was this rather dubious Swiss hotel clerk, an unreliable character, and possibly a blackmailer. If only he were out of the way – she'd be safe.

'Perhaps she made it all up as a kind of fantasy first. She'd been starved of emotion and drama in her life. She pleased herself by working out the details. How would she go about getting rid of him?

'She made her plan. And at last she decided to act on it. She told her story of a sham hold-up at a party to Rudi Scherz, explained that she wanted a stranger to act the part of the "gangster" and offered him a generous sum for his co-operation.

'And the fact that he agreed without any suspicion is what makes me quite certain that Scherz had no idea that he had any kind of hold over her. To him she was just a rather foolish old woman, very ready to part with money.

'She gave him the advertisement to insert, arranged for him to pay a visit to Little Paddocks to study the geography of the house, and showed him the spot where she would meet him and let him into the house on the night in question. Dora Bunner, of course, knew nothing about all this.

'The day came –' He paused.

Miss Marple took up the tale in her gentle voice.

'She must have spent a very miserable day. You see, it still wasn't too late to draw back ... Dora Bunner told us that Letty was frightened that day and she must have been frightened. Frightened of what she was going to do, frightened of the plan going wrong – but not frightened enough to draw back.

'It had been fun, perhaps, getting the revolver out of Colonel Easterbrook's collar drawer. Taking along eggs, or jam – slipping upstairs in the empty house. It had been fun getting the second door in the drawing room oiled, so that it would open and shut noiselessly. Fun suggesting the moving of the table outside the door so that Phillipa's flower arrangements would show to better advantage. It may have all seemed like a game. But what was going to happen next definitely wasn't a game any longer. Oh, yes, she was frightened . . . Dora Bunner was right about that.'

'All the same, she went though with it,' said Craddock. 'And it all went according to plan. She went out just after six to "shut up the ducks", and she let Scherz in then and gave him the mask and cloak and gloves and the torch. Then, at 6.30, when the clock begins to chime, she's ready by that table near the archway with her hand on the cigarette box. It's all so natural. Patrick, acting as host, has gone for the drinks. She, the hostess, is fetching the cigarettes. She's judged, quite correctly, that when the clock begins to chime, everyone will look at the clock. They did. Only one person, the devoted Dora, kept her eyes fixed on her friend. And she told us, in her very first statement, exactly what Miss Blacklock did. She said that Miss Blacklock had picked up the vase of violets.

'She'd previously frayed the cord of the lamp so that the wires were nearly bare. The whole thing only took a second. The cigarette box, the vase and the little switch were all close together. She picked up the violets, spilt the water on the frayed place, and switched on the lamp. Water's a good conductor of electricity. The wires fused.'

'Just like the other afternoon at the Vicarage,' said Bunch. 'That's what startled you so, wasn't it, Aunt Jane?'

'Yes, my dear. I've been puzzling about those lights. I'd realized that there were two lamps, a pair, and that one had been changed for the other – probably during the night.'

'That's right,' said Craddock. 'When Fletcher examined that lamp the next morning it was, like all the others, perfectly in order, no frayed flex or fused wires.'

'I'd understood what Dora Bunner meant by saying it had been the shepherdess the night before,' said Miss Marple, 'but I fell into the error of thinking, as she thought, that *Patrick* had been responsible. The interesting thing about Dora Bunner was that she was quite unreliable in repeating things she had heard – she always used her imagination to exaggerate or distort them, and she was usually wrong in what she *thought* – but she was quite accurate about the things she *saw*. She saw Letitia pick up the violets –'

'And she saw what she described as a flash and a crackle,' put in Craddock.

'And of course, when dear Bunch spilt the water from the Christmas roses on to the lamp wire – I realized at once that only Miss Blacklock herself could have fused the lights because only she was near that table.'

'I could kick myself,' said Craddock. 'Dora Bunner even prattled about a burn on the table where someone had "put their cigarette down" – but nobody had even lit a cigarette . . . And the violets were dead because there was no water in the vase – a slip on Letitia's part – she ought to have filled it up again. But I suppose she thought nobody would notice and as a matter of fact Miss Bunner was quite ready to believe that she herself had put no water in the vase to begin with.'

He went on:

'She was highly suggestible, of course. And Miss Blacklock took advantage of that more than once. Bunny's suspicions of Patrick were I think, induced by her.'

'Why pick on me?' demanded Patrick in an aggrieved tone.

'It was not, I think, a serious suggestion – but it would keep Bunny distracted from any suspicion that Miss Blacklock might be stage managing the business. Well, we know what happened next. As soon as the lights went and everyone was exclaiming, she slipped out through the previously oiled door and up behind Rudi Scherz who was flashing his torch round the room and playing his part with gusto. I don't suppose he realized for a moment she was there behind him with her gardening gloves pulled on and the revolver in her hand. She waits till the torch reaches the spot she must aim for – the wall near which she is supposed to be standing. Then she fires rapidly twice and as he swings round startled, she holds the revolver close to his body and fires again. She lets the revolver fall by his body, throws her gloves carelessly on the hall table, then back through the other door and across to where she had been standing when the lights went out. She nicked her ear – I don't quite know how –'

'Nail scissors, I expect,' said Miss Marples. 'Just a snip on the lobe of the ear lets out a lot of blood. That was very good psychology, of course. The actual blood running down over her white blouse made it seem certain that she *had* been shot at, and that it had been a near miss.'

'It ought to have gone off quite all right,' said Craddock. 'Dora Bunner's insistence that Scherz had definitely aimed at Miss Blacklock had its uses. Without meaning it, Dora Bunner conveyed the impression that she'd actually seen her friend wounded. It might have been brought in Suicide or Accidental Death. And the case would have been closed. That it was kept open is due to Miss Marple here.'

'Oh, no, no.' Miss Marple shook her head energetically. 'Any little efforts on my part were quite incidental. It was you who weren't satisfied, Mr Craddock. It was *you* who wouldn't let the case be closed.'

'I wasn't happy about it,' said Craddock. 'I knew it was all wrong somewhere. But I didn't see *where* it was wrong, till you showed me. And after that Miss Blacklock had a real piece of bad luck. I discovered that that second door had been tampered with. Until that moment, whatever we agreed *might* have happened – we'd nothing to go upon but a pretty theory. But that oiled door was *evidence*. And I hit upon it by pure chance – by catching hold of a handle by mistake.'

'I think you were *led* to it, Inspector,' said Miss Marple. 'But then I'm old-fashioned.'

'So the hunt was up again,' said Craddock. 'But this time with a difference. We were looking now for someone with a motive to kill Letitia Blacklock.'

'And there *was* someone with a motive, and Miss Blacklock knew it,' said Miss Marple. 'I think she recognized Phillipa almost at once. Because Sonia Goedler seems to have been one of the very few people who had been admitted to Charlotte's privacy. And when one is old (you wouldn't know this yet, Mr Craddock) one has a much better memory for a face you've seen when you were young than you have for anyone you've only met a year or two ago. Phillipa must have been just about the same age as her mother was when Charlotte remembered her, and she was very like her mother. The odd thing is that I think Charlotte was very pleased to recognize Phillipa. She became very fond of Phillipa and I think, unconsciously, it helped to stifle any qualms of conscience she may have had. She told herself that when she inherited the money, she was going to look after Phillipa. She would treat her as a daughter. Phillipa and Harry should live with her. She felt quite happy and beneficent about it. But once the Inspector began asking questions and finding out about "Pip and Emma" Charlotte became very uneasy. She didn't want to make a scapegoat of Phillipa. Her whole idea had been to make the business look like a hold-up by a young criminal and his accidental death. But now, with the discovery of the oiled door, the whole viewpoint was changed. And, except for Phillipa, there wasn't (as far as *she* knew, for she had absolutely no idea of Julia's identity) anyone with the least possible motive for wishing to kill her. She did her best to shield Phillipa's identity. She was quick-witted enough to tell you when you asked her, that Sonia was small and dark and she took the old snapshots out of the album, so that you shouldn't notice any resemblance, at the same time as she removed snapshots of Letitia herself.'

'And to think I suspected Mrs Swettenham of being Sonia Goedler,' said Craddock disgustedly.

'My poor Mama,' murmured Edmund. 'A woman of blameless life – or so I have always believed.'

'But of course,' Miss Marple went on. 'It was Dora Bunner who was the real danger. Every day Dora got more forgetful and more talkative. I remember the way Miss Blacklock looked at her the day we went to tea there. Do you know why? Dora had just called her Lotty again. It seemed to us a mere harmless slip of the tongue. But it frightened Charlotte. And so it went on. Poor Dora could not stop herself talking. That day we had coffee together in the Bluebird, I had the oddest impression that Dora was talking about *two* people, not one – and so, of course, she was. At one moment she spoke of her friend as not pretty but having so much character – but almost at the same moment she described her as a pretty light-hearted girl. She'd talk of Letty as so clever and so successful – and then say what a sad life she'd had, and then there was that quotation about stern affliction bravely borne – which really didn't seem to fit Letitia's life at all. Charlotte must, I think, have overheard a good deal that morning she came into the café. She certainly must have heard Dora mention about the lamp having been changed – about its being the shepherd and not the shepherdess. And she realized then what a very real danger to her security poor devoted Dora Bunner was.

'I'm afraid that that conversation with me in the café really sealed Dora's fate – if you'll excuse such a melodramatic expression. But I think it would have come to the same in the end . . . Because life couldn't be safe for Charlotte while Dora Bunner was alive. She loved Dora – she didn't want to kill Dora – but she couldn't see any other way. And, I expect (like Nurse Ellerton that I was telling you about, Bunch) she persuaded herself that it was really almost a *kindness*. Poor Bunny – not long to live anyway and perhaps a painful end. The queer thing is that she did her best to make Bunny's last day a happy day. The birthday party – and the special cake . . .'

'Delicious Death,' said Phillipa with a shudder.

'Yes – yes, it was rather like that . . . she tried to give her friend a delicious death . . . The party, and all the things she liked to eat, and trying to stop people saying things to upset her. And then the tablets, whatever they were, in the aspirin bottle by her own bed so that Bunny, when she couldn't find the new bottle of aspirin she'd just bought, would go there to get some. And it would look, as it did look, that the tablets had been meant for *Letitia* . . .

'And so Bunny died in her sleep, quite happily, and Charlotte felt safe again. But she missed Dora Bunner – she missed her affection and her loyalty, she missed being able to talk to her about the old days . . . She cried bitterly the day I came up with that note from Julian – and her grief was quite genuine. She'd killed her own dear friend . . .'

'That's horrible,' said Bunch. 'Horrible.'

'But it's very human,' said Julian Harmon. 'One forgets how human murderers are.'

'I know,' said Miss Marple. 'Human. And often very much to be pitied. But very dangerous, too. Especially a weak kindly murderer like Charlotte Blacklock. Because, once a weak person gets *really* frightened, they get savage with terror and they've no self-control at all.'

'Murgatroyd?' said Julian.

'Yes, poor Miss Murgatroyd. Charlotte must have come up to the cottage and heard them rehearsing the murder. The window was open and she listened. It had never occurred to her until that moment that there was anyone else who could be a danger to her. Miss Hinchliffe was urging her friend to remember what she'd seen and until that moment Charlotte hadn't realized that anyone could have seen anything at all. She'd assumed that everybody would automatically be looking at Rudi Scherz. She must have held her breath outside the window and listened. Was it going to be all right? And then, just as Miss Hinchliffe rushed off to the station Miss Murgatroyd got to a point which showed that she had stumbled on the truth. She called after Miss Hinchliffe: "She wasn't *there* . . ."'

'I asked Miss Hinchliffe, you know, if that was the way she said it . . . Because if she'd said "*She* wasn't there" it wouldn't have meant the same thing.'

'Now that's too subtle a point for me,' said Craddock.

Miss Marple turned her eager pink and white face to him.

'Just think what's going on in Miss Murgatroyd's mind . . . One does see things, you know, and not know one sees them. In a railway accident once, I remember noticing a large blister of paint at the side of the carriage. I could have *drawn* it for you afterward. And once, when there was a fly-bomb in London – splinters of glass everywhere – and the shock – but what I remember best is a woman standing in front of me who had a big hole halfway up the leg of her stockings and the stockings didn't match. So when Miss Murgatroyd stopped thinking and just tried to remember what she *saw*, she remembered a good deal.

'She started, I think, near the mantelpiece, where the torch must have hit first – then it went along the two windows and there were people in between the windows and her. Mrs Harmon with her knuckles screwed into her eyes for instance. She went on in her mind following the torch past Miss Bunner with her mouth open and her eyes staring – past a blank wall and a table with a lamp and a cigarette box. And then came the shots – and quite suddenly she remembered a most incredible thing. She'd seen the wall where, later, there were the two bullet holes, the wall where Letitia Blacklock had been standing when she was shot, and at the moment when the revolver went off and Letty was shot, *Letty hadn't been there* . . .

'You see what I mean now? She'd been thinking of the three women Miss Hinchliffe had told her to think about. If one of them hadn't been there, it would have been the *personality* she'd have fastened upon. She'd have said – in effect – "*That's* the one! *She* wasn't there!" But it was a *place* that was in her mind – a place where someone should have been – but the place wasn't filled – there wasn't anybody there. The place was there – but the person wasn't. And she couldn't take it in all at once. "How extraordinary, Hinch," she said. "She wasn't *there*." . . . So that could only mean Letitia Blacklock . . .'

'But you knew before that, didn't you?' said Bunch. 'When the lamp fused. When you wrote down those things on the paper.'

'Yes, my dear. It all came together then, you see – all the various isolated bits – and made a coherent pattern.'

Bunch quoted softly:

'*Lamp?* Yes. *Violets?* Yes. *Bottle of Aspirin.* You meant that Bunny had been going to buy a new bottle that day, and so she ought not to have needed to take Letitia's?'

'Not unless her own bottle had been taken or hidden. It had to appear as though Letitia Blacklock was the one meant to be killed.'

'Yes, I see. And then "Delicious Death." The cake – but more than the cake. The whole party setup. A happy day for Bunny before she died. Treating her rather like a dog you were going to destroy. That's what I find the most horrible thing of all – the sort of – of spurious kindness.'

'She *was* quite a kindly woman. What she said at the last in the kitchen was quite true. "I didn't want to kill anybody." What she wanted was a great deal of money that didn't belong to her! And before that desire – (and it had become a kind of obsession – the money was to pay her back for all the suffering life had inflicted on her) – everything else went to the wall. People with a grudge against the world are always dangerous. They seem to think life owes them something. I've known many an invalid who has suffered far worse and been cut off from life much more than Charlotte Blacklock – and they've managed to lead happy contented lives. It's what's in *yourself* that makes you happy or unhappy. But, oh dear, I'm afraid I'm straying away from what we were talking about. Where were we?'

'Going over your list,' said Bunch. 'What did you mean by "Making enquiries?" Enquiries about what?'

Miss Marple shook her head playfully at Inspector Craddock.

'You ought to have seen that, Inspector Craddock. You showed me that letter from Letitia Blacklock to her sister. It had the word "enquiries" in it twice – each time spelt with an *e*. But in the note I asked Bunch to show you, Miss Blacklock had written "inquiries" with an *i*. People don't often alter their spelling as they get older. It seemed to me very significant.'

'Yes,' Craddock agreed. 'I ought to have spotted that.'

Bunch was continuing. '*Severe affliction bravely borne*. That's what Bunny said to you in the café and of course Letitia hadn't had any affliction. *Iodine*. That put you on the track of goitre?'

'Yes, dear. Switzerland, you know, and Miss Blacklock giving the impression that her sister had died of consumption. But I remembered then that the greatest authorities on goitre and the most skilful surgeons operating on it are Swiss. And it linked up with those really rather preposterous pearls that Letitia Blacklock always wore. Not really her *style* – but just right for concealing the scar.'

'I understand now her agitation the night the string broke,' said Craddock. 'It seemed at the time quite disproportionate.'

'And after that, it *was* Lotty you wrote not Letty as we thought,' said Bunch.

'Yes, I remembered that the sister's name was Charlotte, and that

Dora Bunner had called Miss Blacklock Lotty once or twice – and that each time she did so, she had been very upset afterwards.'

'And what about Berne and Old Age Pension?'

'Rudi Scherz had been an orderly in a hospital in Berne.'

'And Old Age Pension.'

'Oh, my dear Bunch, I mentioned that to you in the Bluebird though I didn't really see the application then. How Mrs Wotherspoon drew Mrs Bartlett's Old Age Pension as well as her own – though Mrs Bartlett had been dead for years – simply because one old woman is so like another old woman – yes, it all made a pattern and I felt so worked up I went out to cool my head a little and think what could be done about proving all this. Then Miss Hinchliffe picked me up and we found Miss Murgatroyd . . .'

Miss Marple's voice dropped. It was no longer excited and pleased. It was quiet and remorseless.

'I knew then something had *got* to be done. Quickly! But there still wasn't any *proof*. I thought out a possible plan and I talked to Sergeant Fletcher.'

'And I have had Fletcher on the carpet for it!' said Craddock. 'He'd no business to go agreeing to your plans without reporting first to me.'

'He didn't like it, but I talked him into it,' said Miss Marple. 'We went up to Little Paddocks and I got hold of Mitzi.'

Julia drew a deep breath and said, 'I can't imagine how you ever got her to do it.'

'I worked on her, my dear,' said Miss Marple. 'She thinks far too much about herself anyway, and it will be good for her to have done something for others. I flattered her up, of course, and said I was sure if she'd been in her own country she'd have been in the Resistance movement, and she said, "Yes, indeed." And I said I could see she had got just the temperament for that sort of work. She was brave, didn't mind taking risks, and could act a part. I told her stories of deeds done by girls in the Resistance movements, some of them true, and some of them, I'm afraid, invented. She got tremendously worked up!'

'Marvellous,' said Patrick.

'And then I got her to agree to do her part. I rehearsed her till she was word perfect. Then I told her to go upstairs to her room and not come down until Inspector Craddock came. The worst of these excitable people is that they're apt to go off half-cocked and start the whole thing before the time.'

'She did it very well,' said Julia.

'I don't quite see the point,' said Bunch. 'Of course, I wasn't there –' she added apologetically.

'The point was a little complicated – and rather touch and go. The idea was that Mitzi whilst admitting, as though casually, that blackmail *had* been in her mind, was now so worked up and terrified that she was willing to come out with the truth. She'd seen, through the keyhole of the dining-room, Miss Blacklock in the hall with a revolver behind Rudi Scherz. She'd seen, that is, *what had actually taken place*. Now the only danger was that Charlotte Blacklock might have realized that, as the key was in the keyhole, Mitzi couldn't possibly have seen anything at all. But I banked on the fact that you don't think of things like that when you've just had a bad shock. All she could take in was that Mitzi had seen her.'

Craddock took over the story.

'But – and this was essential – I pretended to receive this with scepticism, and I made an immediate attack as though unmasking my batteries at last, upon someone who had not been previously suspected. I accused Edmund –'

'And very nicely *I* played *my* part,' said Edmund. 'Hot denial. All according to plan. What wasn't according to plan, Phillipa, my love, was you throwing in your little chirp and coming out into the open as "Pip." Neither the Inspector nor I had any idea you were Pip. *I* was going to be Pip! It threw us off our stride for the moment, but the Inspector made a masterly comeback and made some perfectly filthy insinuations about my wanting a rich wife which will probably stick in your subconscious and make irreparable trouble between us one day.'

'I don't see why that was necessary?'

'Don't you? It meant that, *from Charlotte Blacklock's point of view*, the only person who suspected or knew the truth, was *Mitzi*. The suspicions of the police were elsewhere. They had treated Mitzi for the moment as a liar. But if Mitzi were to persist, they might listen to her and take her seriously. So Mitzi had got to be silenced.'

'Mitzi went straight out of the room and back to the kitchen – just like I had told her,' said Miss Marple. 'Miss Blacklock came out after her almost immediately. Mitzi was apparently alone in the kitchen. Sergeant Fletcher was behind the scullery door. And I was in the broom cupboard in the kitchen. Luckily I'm very thin.'

Bunch looked at Miss Marple.

'What did you expect to happen, Aunt Jane?'

'One of two things. Either Charlotte would offer Mitzi money to hold her tongue – and Sergeant Fletcher would be a witness to that offer, or else – or else I thought she'd try to kill Mitzi.'

'But she couldn't hope to get away with *that*? She'd have been suspected at once.'

'Oh, my dear, she was past reasoning. She was just a snapping terrified cornered rat. Think what had happened that day. The scene between Miss Hinchliffe and Miss Murgatroyd. Miss Hinchliffe driving off to the station. As soon as she comes back Miss Murgatroyd will explain that Letitia Blacklock wasn't in the room that night. There's just a few minutes in which to make sure Miss Murgatroyd can't tell anything. No time to make a plan or set a stage. Just crude murder. She greets the poor woman and strangles her. Then a quick rush home, to change, to be sitting by the fire when the others come in, as though she'd never been out.

'And then came the revelation of Julia's identity. She breaks her pearls and is terrified they may notice her scar. Later, the Inspector telephones that he's bringing everyone there. No time to think, to rest. Up to her neck in murder now, no mercy killing – or undesirable young man to be put out of the way. Crude plain murder. Is she safe? Yes, so far. And then comes Mitzi – yet *another* danger. Kill Mitzi, stop her tongue! She's beside herself with fear. Not human any longer. Just a dangerous animal.'

'But why were you in the broom cupboard, Aunt Jane?' asked Bunch. 'Couldn't you have left it to Sergeant Fletcher?'

'It was safer with two of us, my dear. And besides, I knew I could mimic Dora Bunner's voice. If anything could break Charlotte Blacklock down – that would.'

'And it did . . . !'

'Yes . . . she went to pieces.'

There was a long silence as memory laid hold of them and then, speaking with determined lightness, to ease the strain, Julia said:

'It's made a wonderful difference to Mitzi. She told me yesterday that she was taking a post near Southampton. And she said (Julia produced a very good imitation of Mitzi's accent):

'"I go there and if they say to me you have to register with the police – you are an alien, I say to them, 'Yes, I will register! The police, they know me well. I assist the police! Without me the police never would they have made the arrest of a very dangerous criminal. I risked my life because I am brave – brave like a lion – I do not care about risks.' 'Mitzi,' they say to me, 'you are a *heroine*, you are superb.' 'Ach! it is nothing, I say.'"'

Julia stopped.

'And a great deal more,' she added.

'I think,' said Edmund thoughtfully, 'that soon Mitzi will have assisted the police in not one but hundreds of cases!'

'She's softened towards me,' said Phillipa. 'She actually presented me with the recipe for Delicious Death as a kind of wedding present. She added that I was on no account to divulge the secret to Julia, because Julia had ruined her omelette pan.'

'Mrs Lucas,' said Edmund, 'is all over Phillipa now that since Belle Goedler's death, Phillipa and Julia have inherited the Goedler millions. She sent us some silver asparagus tongs as a wedding present. I shall have enormous pleasure in *not* asking her to the wedding!'

'And so they lived happily ever after,' said Patrick. 'Edmund and Phillipa – and Julia and Patrick?' he added, tentatively.

'Not with me, you won't live happily ever after,' said Julia. 'The remarks that Inspector Craddock improvised to address to Edmund apply far more aptly to you. You *are* the sort of soft young man who would like a rich wife. Nothing doing!'

'There's gratitude for you,' said Patrick. 'After all I did for that girl.'

'Nearly landed me in prison on a murder charge – that's what your forgetfulness nearly did for me,' said Julia. 'I shall never forget that evening when your sister's letter came. I really thought I was for it. I couldn't see any way out.

'As it is,' she added musingly, 'I think I shall go on the stage.'

'What? You, too?' groaned Patrick.

'Yes. I might go to Perth. See if I can get your Julia's place in the rep there. Then, when I've learnt my job, I shall go into theatre management – and put on Edmund's plays, perhaps.'

'I thought you wrote novels,' said Julian Harmon.

'Well, so did I,' said Edmund. 'I began writing a novel. Rather good it was. Pages about an unshaven man getting out of bed and what he smelt like, and the grey streets, and a horrible old woman with dropsy and a vicious young tart who dribbled down her chin – and they all talked interminably about the state of the world and wondered what they were alive for. And suddenly I began to wonder too . . . And then a rather comic idea occurred to me . . . and I jotted it down – and then I worked up rather a good little scene . . .

All very obvious stuff. But somehow, I got interested . . . And before I knew what I was doing I'd finished a roaring farce in three acts.'

'What's it called?' asked Patrick. '*What the butler saw?*'

'Well, it easily might be . . . As a matter of fact I've called it *Elephants Do Forget*. What's more, it's been accepted and it's going to be produced!'

'Elephants Do Forget,' murmured Bunch. 'I thought they didn't?'

The Rev. Julian Harmon gave a guilty start.

'My goodness. I've been so interested. My *sermon*!'

'Detective stories again,' said Bunch. 'Real life ones this time.'

'You might preach on Thou Shall Do No Murder,' suggested Patrick.

'No,' said Julian Harmon quietly. 'I shan't take that as my text.'

'No,' said Bunch. 'You're quite right, Julian. I know a much nicer text, a happy text.' She quoted in a fresh voice, 'For lo the Spring is here and the Voice of the Turtle is heard in the Land – I haven't got it quite right – but you know the one I mean. Though why a *turtle* I can't think. I shouldn't think turtles have got nice voices at all.'

'The word turtle,' explained the Rev. Julian Harmon, 'is not very happily translated. It doesn't mean a reptile but the turtle dove. The Hebrew word in the original is –'

Bunch interrupted him by giving him a hug and saying:

'I know one thing – *You* think that the Ahasuerus of the Bible is Artaxerxes the Second, but between you and me it was Artaxerxes the Third.'

As always, Julian Harmon wondered why his wife should think that story so particularly funny . . .

'Tiglath Pileser wants to go and help you,' said Bunch. 'He ought to be a very proud cat. *He* showed us how the lights fused.'

EPILOGUE

'We ought to order some papers,' said Edmund to Phillipa upon the day of their return to Chipping Cleghorn after the honeymoon. 'Let's go along to Totman's.'

Mr Totman, a heavy-breathing, slow-moving man, received them with affability.

'Glad to see you back, sir. *And* madam.'

'We want to order some papers.'

'Certainly, sir. And your mother is keeping well, I hope? Quite settled down at Bournemouth?'

'She loves it,' said Edmund, who had not the faintest idea whether this was so or not, but like most sons, preferred to believe that all was well with those loved, but frequently irritating beings, parents.

'Yes, sir. Very agreeable place. Went there for my holiday last year. Mrs Totman enjoyed it very much.'

'I'm glad. About papers, we'd like –'

'And I hear you have a play on in London, sir. Very amusing, so they tell me.'

'Yes, it's doing very well.'

'Called *Elephants Do Forget*, so I hear. You'll excuse me, sir, asking you, but I always thought that they *didn't* – forget, I mean.'

'Yes – yes, exactly – I've begun to think it was a mistake calling it that. So many people have said just what you say.'

'A kind of natural history fact, I've always understood.'

'Yes – yes. Like earwigs making good mothers.'

'Do they indeed, sir? Now, that's a fact I *didn't* know.'

'About the papers –'

'*The Times*, sir, I think it was?' Mr Totman paused with pencil uplifted.

'The *Daily Worker*,' said Edmund firmly. 'And the *Daily Telegraph*,' said Phillipa. 'And the *New Statesman*,' said Edmund. 'The *Radio Times*,' said Phillipa. 'The *Spectator*,' said Edmund. 'The *Gardener's Chronicle*,' said Phillipa.

They both paused to take breath.

'Thank you, sir,' said Mr Totman. '*And* the *Gazette*, I suppose?'

'No,' said Edmund.

'No,' said Phillipa.

'Excuse me, you *do* want the *Gazette*?'

'No.'

'No.'

'You mean' – Mr Totman liked to get things perfectly clear – 'You *don't* want the *Gazette*!'

'No, we don't.'

'Certainly not.'

'You don't want the *North Benham News and the Chipping Cleghorn Gazette*?'

'No.'

'You don't want me to send it along to you every week?'

'*No.*' Edmund added: 'Is that quite clear now?'

'Oh, yes, sir – yes.'

Edmund and Phillipa went out, and Mr Totman padded into his back parlour.

'Got a pencil, Mother?' he said. 'My pen's run out.'

'Here you are,' said Mrs Totman, seizing the order book. 'I'll do it. What do they want?'

'*Daily Worker, Daily Telegraph, Radio Times, New Statesman, Spectator* – let me see – *Gardener's Chronicle.*'

'*Gardener's Chronicle,*' repeated Mrs Totman, writing busily. 'And the *Gazette.*'

'They don't want the *Gazette.*'

'What?'

'They don't want the *Gazette*. They said so.'

'Nonsense,' said Mrs Totman. 'You don't hear properly. Of course they want the *Gazette*! Everybody has the *Gazette*. How else would they know what's going on round here?'

THE MOVING
FINGER

CHAPTER 1

When at last I was taken out of the plaster, and the doctors had pulled me about to their hearts' content, and nurses had wheedled me into cautiously using my limbs, and I had been nauseated by their practically using baby talk to me, Marcus Kent told me I was to go and live in the country.

'Good air, quiet life, nothing to do – that's the prescription for you. That sister of yours will look after you. Eat, sleep and imitate the vegetable kingdom as far as possible.'

I didn't ask him if I'd ever be able to fly again. There are questions that you don't ask because you're afraid of the answers to them. In the same way during the last five months I'd never asked if I was going to be condemned to lie on my back all my life. I was afraid of a bright hypocritical reassurance from Sister. 'Come now, *what* a question to ask! We don't let our patients go talking in *that* way!'

So I hadn't asked – and it had been all right. I wasn't to be a helpless cripple. I could move my legs, stand on them, finally walk a few steps – and if I did feel rather like an adventurous baby learning to toddle, with wobbly knees and cotton wool soles to my feet – well, that was only weakness and disuse and would pass.

Marcus Kent, who is the right kind of doctor, answered what I hadn't said.

'You're going to recover completely,' he said. 'We weren't sure until last Tuesday when you had that final overhaul, but I can tell you so authoritatively now. But – it's going to be a long business. A long and, if I may say so, a wearisome business. When it's a question of healing nerves and muscles, the brain must help the body. Any impatience, and fretting, will throw you back. And whatever you do, don't "will yourself to get well quickly." Anything of that kind and you'll find yourself back in a nursing home. You've got to take life slowly and easily, the *tempo* is marked *Legato*. Not only has your body got to recover, but your nerves have been weakened by the necessity of keeping you under drugs for so long.

'That's why I say, go down to the country, take a house, get interested in local politics, in local scandal, in village gossip. Take an inquisitive and violent interest in your neighbours. If I may make a suggestion, go to a part of the world where you haven't got any friends scattered about.'

I nodded. 'I had already,' I said, 'thought of that.'

I could think of nothing more insufferable than members of one's own gang dropping in full of sympathy and their own affairs.

'But Jerry, you're looking marvellous – isn't he? Absolutely. Darling, I must tell you – What do you think Buster has done now?'

No, none of that for me. Dogs are wise. They crawl away into a quiet corner and lick their wounds and do not rejoin the world until they are whole once more.

So it came about that Joanna and I, sorting wildly through house-agents' glowing eulogies of properties all over the British Isles, selected Little Furze, Lymstock, as one of the 'possibles' to be viewed, mainly because we had never been to Lymstock, and knew no one in that neighbourhood.

And when Joanna saw Little Furze she decided at once that it was just the house we wanted.

It lay about half a mile out of Lymstock on the road leading up to the moors. It was a prim low white house, with a sloping Victorian veranda painted a faded green. It had a pleasant view over a slope of heather-covered land with the church spire of Lymstock down below to the left.

It had belonged to a family of maiden ladies, the Misses Barton, of whom only one was left, the youngest, Miss Emily.

Miss Emily Barton was a charming little old lady who matched her house in an incredible way. In a soft apologetic voice she explained to Joanna that she had never let her house before, indeed would never have thought of doing so, 'but you see, my dear, things are so different nowadays – *taxation*, of course, and then my stocks and shares, so *safe*, as I always imagined, and indeed the bank manager *himself* recommended some of them, but they seem to be paying *nothing* at all these days – *foreign*, of course! And really it makes it all so *difficult*. One does not (I'm sure you will understand me, my dear, and not take offence, you look so kind) *like* the idea of letting one's house to strangers – but something must be done, and really, having seen you, I shall be quite *glad* to think of you being here – it needs, you know, *young life*. And I must confess I did shrink from the idea of having *Men* here!'

At this point, Joanna had to break the news of me. Miss Emily rallied well.

'Oh dear, I see. How sad! A flying accident? So brave, these young men. Still, your brother will be practically an invalid –'

The thought seemed to soothe the gentle little lady. Presumably I should not be indulging in those grosser masculine activities which Emily Barton feared. She enquired diffidently if I smoked.

'Like a chimney,' said Joanna. 'But then,' she pointed out, 'so do I.'

'Of course, of course. So stupid of me. I'm afraid, you know, I haven't moved with the times. My sisters were all older than myself, and my dear mother lived to be ninety-seven – just fancy! – and was most particular. Yes, yes, everyone smokes now. The only thing is, there are no ashtrays in the house.'

Joanna said that we would bring lots of ashtrays, and she added with a smile, 'We won't put down cigarette ends on your nice furniture, that I do promise you. Nothing makes me so mad myself as to see people do that.'

So it was settled and we took Little Furze for a period of six months, with an option of another three, and Emily Barton explained to Joanna that she herself was going to be very comfortable because she was going into rooms kept by an old parlourmaid, 'my faithful Florence,' who had married 'after being with us for fifteen years. *Such* a nice girl, and her husband is in the building trade. They have a nice house in the High Street and two beautiful rooms on the top floor where I shall be *most* comfortable, and Florence so pleased to have me.'

So everything seemed to be most satisfactory, and the agreement was signed and in due course Joanna and I arrived and settled in, and Miss Emily Barton's maid Partridge having consented to remain, we were well looked after with the assistance of a 'girl' who came in every morning and who seemed to be half-witted but amiable.

Partridge, a gaunt, dour female of middle age, cooked admirably, and though disapproving of late dinner (it having been Miss Emily's custom to dine lightly off a boiled egg) nevertheless accommodated herself to our ways and went so far as to admit that she could see I needed my strength building up.

When we had settled in and been at Little Furze a week Miss Emily Barton came solemnly and left cards. Her example was followed by Mrs Symmington, the lawyer's wife, Miss Griffith, the doctor's sister, Mrs Dane Calthrop, the vicar's wife, and Mr Pye of Prior's End.

Joanna was much impressed.

'I didn't know,' she said in an awestruck voice, 'that people really *called* – with *cards*.'

'That is because, my child,' I said, 'you know nothing about the country.'

'Nonsense. I've stayed away for heaps of weekends with people.'

'That is not at all the same thing,' I said.

I am five years older than Joanna. I can remember as a child the big white shabby untidy house we had with the fields running down to the river. I can remember creeping under the nets of raspberry canes unseen by the gardener, and the smell of white dust in the stable yard and an orange cat crossing it, and the sound of horse hoofs kicking something in the stables.

But when I was seven and Joanna two, we went to live in London with an aunt, and thereafter our Christmas and Easter holidays were spent there with pantomimes and theatres and cinemas and excursions to Kensington Gardens with boats, and later to skating rinks. In August we were taken to an hotel by the seaside somewhere.

Reflecting on this, I said thoughtfully to Joanna, and with a feeling of compunction as I realized what a selfish, self-centred invalid I had become:

'This is going to be pretty frightful for you, I'm afraid. You'll miss everything so.'

For Joanna is very pretty and very gay, and she likes dancing and cocktails, and love affairs and rushing about in high-powered cars.

Joanna laughed and said she didn't mind at all.

'As a matter of fact, I'm glad to get away from it all. I really was fed up with the whole crowd, and although you won't be sympathetic, I was really very cut up about Paul. It will take me a long time to get over it.'

I was sceptical over this. Joanna's love affairs always run the same course. She has a mad infatuation for some completely spineless young man who is a misunderstood genius. She listens to his endless complaints and works like anything to get him recognition. Then, when he is ungrateful, she is deeply wounded and says her heart is broken – until the next gloomy young man comes along, which is usually about three weeks later!

So I did not take Joanna's broken heart very seriously. But I did see that living in the country was like a new game to my attractive sister.

'At any rate,' she said, 'I look all right, don't I?'

I studied her critically and was not able to agree.

Joanna was dressed (by Mirotin) for *le Sport*. That is to say she was wearing a skirt of outrageous and preposterous checks. It was skin-tight, and on her upper half she had a ridiculous little short-sleeved jersey with a Tyrolean effect. She had sheer silk stockings and some irreproachable but brand new brogues.

'No,' I said, 'you're all wrong. You ought to be wearing a very old tweed skirt, preferably of dirty green or faded brown. You'd wear a nice cashmere jumper matching it, and perhaps a cardigan coat, and you'd have a felt hat and thick stockings and old shoes. Then, and only then, you'd sink into the background of Lymstock High Street, and not stand out as you do at present.' I added: 'Your face is all wrong, too.'

'What's wrong with that? I've got on my Country Tan Make-up No. 2.'

'Exactly,' I said. 'If you lived in Lymstock, you would have on just a little powder to take the shine off the nose, and possibly a *soupçon* of lipstick – not very well applied – and you would almost certainly be wearing all your eyebrows instead of only a quarter of them.'

Joanna gurgled and seemed much amused.

'Do you think they'll think I'm awful?' she said.

'No,' I said. 'Just queer.'

Joanna had resumed her study of the cards left by our callers. Only the vicar's wife had been so fortunate, or possibly unfortunate, as to catch Joanna at home.

Joanna murmured:

'It's rather like Happy Families, isn't it? Mrs Legal the lawyer's wife, Miss Dose the doctor's daughter, etc.' She added with enthusiasm: 'I do think this is a nice place, Jerry! So sweet and funny and old-world. You just can't think of anything nasty happening here, can you?'

And although I knew what she said was really nonsense, I agreed with her. In a place like Lymstock nothing nasty could happen. It is odd to think that it was just a week later that we got the first letter.

II

I see that I have begun badly. I have given no description of Lymstock and without understanding what Lymstock is like, it is impossible to understand my story.

To begin with, Lymstock has its roots in the past. Somewhere about the time of the Norman Conquest, Lymstock was a place of importance. That importance was chiefly ecclesiastical. Lymstock had a priory, and it had a long succession of ambitious and powerful priors. Lords and barons in the surrounding countryside made themselves right with Heaven by leaving certain of their lands to the priory. Lymstock Priory waxed rich and important and was a power in the land for many centuries. In due course, however, Henry the Eighth caused it to share the fate of its contemporaries. From then on a castle dominated the town. It was still important. It had rights and privileges and wealth.

And then, somewhere in seventeen hundred and something, the tide of progress swept Lymstock into a backwater. The castle crumbled. Neither railways nor main roads came near Lymstock. It turned into a little provincial market town, unimportant and forgotten, with a sweep of moorland rising behind it, and placid farms and fields ringing it round.

A market was held there once a week, on which day one was apt to encounter cattle in the lanes and roads. It had a small race meeting twice a year which only the most obscure horses attended. It had a charming High Street with dignified houses set flat back, looking slightly incongruous with their ground-floor windows displaying buns or vegetables or fruit. It had a long straggling draper's shop, a large and portentous ironmonger's, a pretentious post office, and a row of straggly indeterminate shops, two rival butchers and an International Stores. It had a doctor, a firm of solicitors, Messrs Galbraith, Galbraith and Symmington, a beautiful and unexpectedly large church dating from fourteen hundred and twenty, with some Saxon remains incorporated in it, a new and hideous school, and two pubs.

Such was Lymstock, and urged on by Emily Barton, anybody who was anybody came to call upon us, and in due course Joanna, having bought a pair of gloves and assumed a velvet beret rather the worse for wear, sallied forth to return them.

To us, it was all quite novel and entertaining. We were not there for life. It was, for us, an interlude. I prepared to obey my doctor's instructions and get interested in my neighbours.

Joanna and I found it all great fun.

I remembered, I suppose, Marcus Kent's instructions to enjoy the local scandals. I certainly didn't suspect how those scandals were going to be introduced to my notice.

The odd part of it was that the letter, when it came, amused us more than anything else.

It arrived, I remember, at breakfast. I turned it over, in the idle way one does when time goes slowly and every event must be spun out to its full extent. It was, I saw, a local letter with a typewritten address.

I opened it before the two with London postmarks, since one of them was a bill and the other from a rather tiresome cousin.

Inside, printed words and letters had been cut out and gummed to a sheet of paper. For a minute or two I stared at the words without taking them in. Then I gasped.

Joanna, who was frowning over some bills, looked up.

'Hallo,' she said, 'what is it? You look quite startled.'

The letter, using terms of the coarsest character, expressed the writer's opinion that Joanna and I were not brother and sister.

'It's a particularly foul anonymous letter,' I said.

I was still suffering from shock. Somehow one didn't expect that kind of thing in the placid backwater of Lymstock.

Joanna at once displayed lively interest.

'*No?* What does it say?'

In novels, I have noticed, anonymous letters of a foul and disgusting character are never shown, if possible, to women. It is implied that women must at all cost be shielded from the shock it might give their delicate nervous systems.

I am sorry to say it never occurred to me not to show the letter to Joanna. I handed it to her at once.

She vindicated my belief in her toughness by displaying no emotion but that of amusement.

'What an awful bit of dirt! I've always heard about anonymous letters, but I've never seen one before. Are they always like this?'

'I can't tell you,' I said. 'It's my first experience, too.'

Joanna began to giggle.

'You must have been right about my make-up, Jerry. I suppose they think I just *must* be an abandoned female!'

'That,' I said, 'coupled with the fact that our father was a tall, dark lantern-jawed man and our mother a fair-haired blue-eyed little creature, and that I take after him and you take after her.'

Joanna nodded thoughtfully

'Yes, we're not a bit alike. Nobody would take us for brother and sister.'

'Somebody certainly hasn't,' I said with feeling.

Joanna said she thought it was frightfully funny.

She dangled the letter thoughtfully by one corner and asked what we were to do with it.

'The correct procedure, I believe,' I said, 'is to drop it into the fire with a sharp exclamation of disgust.'

I suited the action to the word, and Joanna applauded.

'You did that beautifully,' she added. 'You ought to have been on the stage. It's lucky we still have fires, isn't it?'

'The waste-paper basket would have been much less dramatic,' I agreed. 'I could, of course, have set light to it with a match and slowly watched it burn – or watched it slowly burn.'

'Things never burn when you want them to,' said Joanna. 'They go out. You'd probably have had to strike match after match.'

She got up and went towards the window. Then, standing there, she turned her head sharply.

'I wonder,' she said, 'who wrote it?'

'We're never likely to know,' I said.

'No – I suppose not.' She was silent a moment, and then said: 'I don't know when I come to think of it that it is so funny after all. You know, I thought they – they *liked* us down here.'

'So they do,' I said. 'This is just some half-crazy brain on the borderline.'

'I suppose so. Ugh – Nasty!'

As she went out into the sunshine I thought to myself as I smoked my after-breakfast cigarette that she was quite right. It was nasty. Someone resented our coming here – someone resented Joanna's bright young sophisticated beauty – someone wanted to *hurt*. To take it with a laugh was perhaps the best way – but deep down it wasn't funny. . . .

Dr Griffith came that morning. I had fixed up for him to give me a weekly overhaul. I liked Owen Griffith. He was dark, ungainly, with awkward ways of moving and deft, very gentle hands. He had a jerky way of talking and was rather shy.

He reported progress to be encouraging. Then he added:

'You're feeling all right, aren't you? Is it my fancy, or are you a bit under the weather this morning?'

'Not really,' I said. 'A particularly scurrilous anonymous letter arrived with the morning coffee, and it's left rather a nasty taste in the mouth.'

He dropped his bag on the floor. His thin dark face was excited.

'Do you mean to say that *you've* had one of them?'

I was interested.

'They've been going about, then?'

'Yes. For some time.'

'Oh,' I said, 'I see. I was under the impression that our presence as strangers was resented here.'

'No, no, it's nothing to do with that. It's just –' He paused and then asked, 'What did it say? At least –' he turned suddenly red and embarrassed – 'perhaps I oughtn't to ask?'

'I'll tell you with pleasure,' I said. 'It just said that the fancy tart I'd brought down with me wasn't my sister – not 'alf! And that, I may say, is a Bowdlerized version.'

His dark face flushed angrily.

'How damnable! Your sister didn't – she's not upset, I hope?'

'Joanna,' I said, 'looks a little like the angel off the top of the Christmas tree, but she's eminently modern and quite tough. She found it highly entertaining. Such things haven't come her way before.'

'I should hope not, indeed,' said Griffith warmly.

'And anyway,' I said firmly. 'That's the best way to take it, I think. As something utterly ridiculous.'

'Yes,' said Owen Griffith. 'Only –'

He stopped, and I chimed in quickly:

'Quite so,' I said. 'Only is the word!'

'The trouble is,' he said, 'that this sort of thing, once it starts, grows.'

'So I should imagine.'

'It's pathological, of course.'

I nodded. 'Any idea who's behind it?' I asked.

'No, I wish I had. You see, the anonymous letter pest arises from one of two causes. Either it's *particular* – directed at one particular person or set of people, that is to say it's *motivated*, it's someone who's got a definite grudge (or thinks they have) and who chooses a particularly nasty and underhand way of working it off. It's mean and disgusting but it's not necessarily crazy, and it's usually fairly easy to trace the writer – a discharged servant, a jealous woman – and so on. But if it's *general*, and not particular, then it's more serious. The letters are sent indiscriminately and serve the purpose of working off some frustration in the writer's mind. As I say, it's definitely pathological. And the craze grows. In the end, of course, you track down the person in question – it's often someone extremely unlikely, and that's that. There was a bad outburst of the kind over the other side of the county last year – turned out to be the head of the millinery department in a big draper's establishment. Quiet, refined woman – had been there for years. I remember something of the same kind in my last practice up north – but that turned out to be purely personal spite. Still, as I say, I've seen something of this kind of thing, and, quite frankly, it frightens me!'

'Has it been going on long?' I asked.

'I don't think so. Hard to say, of course, because people who get these letters don't go round advertising the fact. They put them in the fire.'

He paused.

'I've had one myself. Symmington, the solicitor, he's had one. And one or two of my poorer patients have told me about them.'

'All much the same sort of thing?'

'Oh yes. A definite harping on the sex theme. That's always a feature.' He grinned. 'Symmington was accused of illicit relations with his lady clerk – poor old Miss Ginch, who's forty at least, with pince-nez and teeth like a rabbit. Symmington took it straight to the police. My letters accused me of violating professional decorum with my lady patients, stressing the details. They're all quite childish and absurd, but horribly venomous.' His face changed, grew grave. 'But all the same, I'm *afraid*. These things can be dangerous, you know.'

'I suppose they can.'

'You see,' he said, 'crude, childish spite though it is, sooner or later one of these letters will hit the mark. And then, God knows what may happen! I'm afraid, too, of the effect upon the slow, suspicious uneducated mind. If they see a thing written, they believe it's true. All sorts of complications may arise.'

'It was an illiterate sort of letter,' I said thoughtfully, 'written by somebody practically illiterate, I should say.'

'Was it?' said Owen, and went away.

Thinking it over afterwards, I found that 'Was it?' rather disturbing.

CHAPTER 2

I am not going to pretend that the arrival of our anonymous letter did not leave a nasty taste in the mouth. It did. At the same time, it soon passed out of my mind. I did not, you see, at that point, take it seriously. I think I remember saying to myself that these things probably happen fairly often in out-of-the-way villages. Some hysterical woman with a taste for dramatizing herself was probably at the bottom of it. Anyway, if the letters were as childish and silly as the one we had got, they couldn't do much harm.

The next *incident*, if I may put it so, occurred about a week later, when Partridge, her lips set tightly together, informed me that Beatrice, the daily help, would not be coming today.

'I gather, sir,' said Partridge, 'that the girl has been Upset.'

I was not very sure what Partridge was implying, but I diagnosed (wrongly) some stomachic trouble to which Partridge was too delicate to allude more directly. I said I was sorry and hoped she would soon be better.

'The girl is perfectly well, sir,' said Partridge. 'She is Upset in her Feelings.'

'Oh,' I said rather doubtfully.

'Owing,' went on Partridge, 'to a letter she has received. Making, I understand, Insinuations.'

The grimness of Partridge's eye, coupled with the obvious capital I of Insinuations, made me apprehensive that the insinuations were concerned with me. Since I would hardly have recognized Beatrice by sight if I had met her in the town, so unaware of her had I been – I felt a not unnatural annoyance. An invalid hobbling about on two sticks is hardly cast for the role of deceiver of village girls. I said irritably:

'What nonsense!'

'My very words, sir, to the girl's mother,' said Partridge. '"Goings On in this house," I said to her, "there never have been and never will be while I am in charge. As to Beatrice," I said, "girls are different nowadays, and as to Goings On elsewhere I can say nothing." But the truth is, sir, that Beatrice's friend from the garage as she walks out with got one of them nasty letters too, and he isn't acting reasonable at all.'

'I have never heard anything so preposterous in my life,' I said angrily.

'It's my opinion, sir,' said Partridge, 'that we're well rid of the girl. What I say is, she wouldn't take on so if there wasn't *something* she didn't want found out. No smoke without fire, that's what I say.'

I had no idea how horribly tired I was going to get of that particular phrase.

II

That morning, by way of adventure, I was to walk down to the village. (Joanna and I always called it the village, although technically we were incorrect, and Lymstock would have been annoyed to hear us.)

The sun was shining, the air was cool and crisp with the sweetness of spring in it. I assembled my sticks and started off, firmly refusing to permit Joanna to accompany me.

'No,' I said, 'I will not have a guardian angel teetering along beside me and uttering encouraging chirrups. A man travels fastest who travels alone, remember. I have much business to transact. I shall go to Galbraith, Galbraith and Symmington, and sign that transfer of shares, I shall call in at the baker's and complain about the currant loaf, and I shall return that book we borrowed. I have to go to the bank, too. Let me away, woman, the morning is all too short.'

It was arranged that Joanna should pick me up with the car and drive me back up the hill in time for lunch.

'That ought to give you time to pass the time of day with everyone in Lymstock.'

'I have no doubt,' I said, 'that I shall have seen anybody who is anybody by then.'

For morning in the High Street was a kind of rendezvous for shoppers, when news was exchanged.

I did not, after all, walk down to the town unaccompanied. I had gone about two hundred yards, when I heard a bicycle bell behind me, then a scrunching of brakes, and then Megan Hunter more or less fell off her machine at my feet.

'Hallo,' she said breathlessly as she rose and dusted herself off.

I rather liked Megan and always felt oddly sorry for her.

She was Symmington the lawyer's stepdaughter, Mrs Symmington's daughter by a first marriage. Nobody talked much about Mr (or Captain) Hunter, and I gathered that he was considered best forgotten. He was reported to have treated Mrs Symmington very badly. She had divorced him a year or two after the marriage. She was a woman with means of her own and had settled down with her little daughter in Lymstock 'to forget,' and had eventually married the only eligible bachelor in the place, Richard Symmington. There were two boys of the second marriage to whom their parents were devoted, and I fancied that Megan sometimes felt odd man out in the establishment. She certainly did not resemble her mother, who was a small anæmic woman, fadedly pretty, who talked in a thin melancholy voice of servant difficulties and her health.

Megan was a tall awkward girl, and although she was actually twenty, she looked more like a schoolgirlish sixteen. She had a shock of untidy brown hair, hazel green eyes, a thin bony face, and an unexpected charming one-sided smile. Her clothes were drab and unattractive and she usually had on lisle thread stockings with holes in them.

She looked, I decided this morning, much more like a horse than a human being. In fact she would have been a very nice horse with a little grooming.

She spoke, as usual, in a kind of breathless rush.

'I've been up to the farm – you know, Lasher's – to see if they'd got any duck's eggs. They've got an awfully nice lot of little pigs. Sweet! Do you like pigs? I do. I even like the smell.'

'Well-kept pigs shouldn't smell,' I said.

'Shouldn't they? They all do round here. Are you walking down to the town? I saw you were alone, so I thought I'd stop and walk with you, only I stopped rather suddenly.'

'You've torn your stocking,' I said.

Megan looked rather ruefully at her right leg.

'So I have. But it's got two holes already, so it doesn't matter very much, does it?'

'Don't you ever mend your stockings, Megan?'

'Rather. When Mummy catches me. But she doesn't notice awfully what I do – so it's lucky in a way, isn't it?'

'You don't seem to realize you're grown up,' I said.

'You mean I ought to be more like your sister? All dolled up?'

I rather resented this description of Joanna.

'She looks clean and tidy and pleasing to the eye,' I said.

'She's awfully pretty,' said Megan. 'She isn't a bit like you, is she? Why not?'

'Brothers and sisters aren't always alike.'

'No. Of course I'm not very like Brian or Colin. And Brian and Colin aren't like each other.' She paused and said, 'It's very rum, isn't it?'

'What is?'

Megan replied briefly: 'Families.'

I said thoughtfully, 'I suppose they are.'

I wondered just what was passing in her mind. We walked on in silence for a moment or two, then Megan said in a rather shy voice:

'You fly, don't you?'

'Yes.'

'That's how you got hurt?'

'Yes, I crashed.'

Megan said:

'Nobody down here flies.'

'No,' I said. 'I suppose not. Would you like to fly, Megan?'

'Me?' Megan seemed surprised. 'Goodness, no. I should be sick. I'm sick in a train even.'

She paused, and then asked with that directness which only a child usually displays:

'Will you get all right and be able to fly again, or will you always be a bit of a crock?'

'My doctor says I shall be quite all right.'

'Yes, but is he the kind of man who tells lies?'

'I don't think so,' I replied. 'In fact, I'm quite sure of it. I trust him.'

'That's all right then. But a lot of people do tell lies.'

I accepted this undeniable statement of fact in silence.

Megan said in a detached judicial kind of way:

'I'm glad. I was afraid you looked bad tempered because you were crocked up for life – but if it's just natural, it's different.'

'I'm not bad tempered,' I said coldly.

'Well, irritable, then.'

'I'm irritable because I'm in a hurry to get fit again – and these things can't be hurried.'

'Then why fuss?'

I began to laugh.

'My dear girl, aren't you ever in a hurry for things to happen?'

Megan considered the question. She said:

'No. Why should I be? There's nothing to be in a hurry about. Nothing ever happens.'

I was struck by something forlorn in the words. I said gently: 'What do you do with yourself down here?'

She shrugged her shoulders.

'What is there to do?'

'Haven't you got any hobbies? Do you play games? Have you got friends round about?'

'I'm stupid at games. And I don't like them much. There aren't many girls round here, and the ones there are I don't like. They think I'm awful.'

'Nonsense. Why should they?'

Megan shook her head.

'Didn't you go to school at all?'

'Yes, I came back a year ago.'

'Did you enjoy school?'

'It wasn't bad. They taught you things in an awfully silly way, though.'

'How do you mean?'

'Well – just bits and pieces. Chopping and changing from one thing to the other. It was a cheap school, you know, and the teachers weren't very good. They could never answer questions properly.'

'Very few teachers can,' I said.

'Why not? They ought to.'

I agreed.

'Of course I'm pretty stupid,' said Megan. 'And such a lot of things seem to me such rot. History, for instance. Why, it's quite different out of different books!'

'That is its real interest,' I said.

'And grammar,' went on Megan. 'And silly compositions. And all the blathering stuff Shelley wrote, twittering on about skylarks, and Wordsworth going all potty over some silly daffodils. And Shakespeare.'

'What's wrong with Shakespeare?' I enquired with interest.

'Twisting himself up to say things in such a difficult way that you can't get at what he means. Still, I like *some* Shakespeare.'

'He would be gratified to know that, I'm sure,' I said.

Megan suspected no sarcasm. She said, her face lighting up:

'I like Goneril and Regan, for instance.'

'Why those two?'

'Oh, I don't know. They're *satisfactory*, somehow. Why do you think they were like that?'

'Like what?'

'Like they were. I mean *something* must have made them like that?'

For the first time I wondered. I had always accepted Lear's elder daughters as two nasty bits of goods and had let it go at that. But Megan's demand for a first cause interested me.

'I'll think about it,' I said.

'Oh, it doesn't really matter. I just wondered. Anyway, it's only English Literature, isn't it?'

'Quite, quite. Wasn't there any subject you enjoyed?'

'Only Maths.'

'Maths?' I said, rather surprised.

Megan's face had lit up.

'I loved Maths. But it wasn't awfully well taught. I'd like to be taught Maths really well. It's heavenly. I think there's something heavenly about numbers, anyway, don't you?'

'I've never felt it,' I said truthfully.

We were now entering the High Street. Megan said sharply:

'Here's Miss Griffith. Hateful woman.'

'Don't you like her?'

'I loathe her. She's always at me to join her foul Guides. I hate Guides. Why dress yourself up and go about in clumps, and put badges on yourself for something you haven't really learnt to do properly. I think it's all rot.'

On the whole, I rather agreed with Megan. But Miss Griffith had descended on us before I could voice my assent.

The doctor's sister, who rejoiced in the singularly inappropriate name of Aimée, had all the positive assurance that her brother lacked. She was a handsome woman in a masculine weather-beaten way, with a deep hearty voice.

'Hallo, you two,' she bayed at us. 'Gorgeous morning, isn't it? Megan, you're just the person I wanted to see. I want some help addressing envelopes for the Conservative Association.'

Megan muttered something elusive, propped up her bicycle against the kerb and dived in a purposeful way into the International Stores.

'Extraordinary child,' said Miss Griffith, looking after her. 'Bone lazy. Spends her time mooning about. Must be a great trial to poor Mrs Symmington. I know her mother's tried more than once to get her to take up something – shorthand-typing, you know, or cookery, or keeping Angora rabbits. She needs an *interest* in life.'

I thought that was probably true, but felt that in Megan's place I should have withstood firmly any of Aimée Griffith's suggestions for the simple reason that her aggressive personality would have put my back up.

'I don't believe in idleness,' went on Miss Griffith. 'And certainly not for young people. It's not as though Megan was pretty or attractive or anything like that. Sometimes I think the girl's half-witted. A great disappointment to her mother. The father, you know,' she lowered her voice slightly, 'was definitely a wrong 'un. Afraid the child takes after him. Painful for her mother. Oh, well, it takes all sorts to make a world, that's what I say.'

'Fortunately,' I responded.

Aimée Griffith gave a 'jolly' laugh.

'Yes, it wouldn't do if we were all made to one pattern. But I don't like to see anyone not getting all they can out of life. I enjoy life myself and I want everyone to enjoy it too. People say to me you must be bored to death living down there in the country all the year round. Not a bit of it, I say. I'm always busy, always happy! There's always something going on in the country. My time's taken up, what with my Guides, and the Institute and various committees – to say nothing of looking after Owen.'

At this minute, Miss Griffith saw an acquaintance on the other side of the street, and uttering a bay of recognition she leapt across the road, leaving me free to pursue my course to the bank.

I always found Miss Griffith rather overwhelming, though I admired her energy and vitality, and it was pleasant to see the beaming contentment with her lot in life which she always displayed, and which was a pleasant contrast to the subdued complaining murmurs of so many women.

My business at the bank transacted satisfactorily, I went on to the offices of Messrs Galbraith, Galbraith and Symmington. I don't know if there were any Galbraiths extant. I never saw any. I was shown into Richard Symmington's inner office which had the agreeable mustiness of a long-established legal firm.

Vast numbers of deed boxes, labelled Lady Hope, Sir Everard Carr, William Yatesby-Hoares, Esq., Deceased, etc., gave the required atmosphere of decorous county families and legitimate long-established business.

Studying Mr Symmington as he bent over the documents I had

brought, it occurred to me that if Mrs Symmington had encountered disaster in her first marriage, she had certainly played it safe in her second. Richard Symmington was the acme of calm respectability, the sort of man who would never give his wife a moment's anxiety. A long neck with a pronounced Adam's apple, a slightly cadaverous face and a long thin nose. A kindly man, no doubt, a good husband and father, but not one to set the pulses madly racing.

Presently Mr Symmington began to speak. He spoke clearly and slowly, delivering himself of much good sense and shrewd acumen. We settled the matter in hand and I rose to go, remarking as I did so:

'I walked down the hill with your stepdaughter.'

For a moment Mr Symmington looked as though he did not know who his stepdaughter was, then he smiled.

'Oh yes, of course, Megan. She – er – has been back from school some time. We're thinking about finding her something to do – yes, to do. But of course she's very young still. And backward for her age, so they say. Yes, so they tell me.'

I went out. In the outer office was a very old man on a stool writing slowly and laboriously, a small cheeky looking boy and a middle-aged woman with frizzy hair and pince-nez who was typing with some speed and dash.

If this was Miss Ginch I agreed with Owen Griffith that tender passages between her and her employer were exceedingly unlikely.

I went into the baker's and said my piece about the currant loaf. It was received with the exclamations and incredulity proper to the occasion, and a new currant loaf was thrust upon me in replacement – 'fresh from the oven this minute' – as its indecent heat pressed against my chest proclaimed to be no less than truth.

I came out of the shop and looked up and down the street hoping to see Joanna with the car. The walk had tired me a good deal and it was awkward getting along with my sticks and the currant loaf.

But there was no sign of Joanna as yet.

Suddenly my eyes were held in glad and incredulous surprise.

Along the pavement towards me there came floating a goddess. There is really no other word for it.

The perfect features, the crisply curling golden hair, the tall exquisitely shaped body! And she walked like a goddess, without effort, seeming to swim nearer and nearer. A glorious, an incredible, a breath-taking girl!

In my intense excitement something had to go. What went was the currant loaf. It slipped from my clutches. I made a dive after it and lost my stick, which clattered to the pavement, and I slipped and nearly fell myself.

It was the strong arm of the goddess that caught and held me. I began to stammer:

'Th-thanks awfully, I'm f-f-frightfully sorry.'

She had retrieved the currant loaf and handed it to me together with the stick. And then she smiled kindly and said cheerfully:

'Don't mention it. No trouble, I assure you,' and the magic died completely before the flat competent voice.

A nice healthy-looking well set-up girl, no more.

I fell to reflecting what would have happened if the Gods had given Helen of Troy exactly those flat accents. How strange that a girl could trouble your inmost soul so long as she kept her mouth shut, and that the moment she spoke the glamour could vanish as though it had never been.

I had known the reverse happen, though. I had seen a little sad monkey-faced woman whom no one would turn to look at twice. Then she had opened her mouth and suddenly enchantment had lived and bloomed and Cleopatra had cast her spell anew.

Joanna had drawn up at the kerb beside me without my noticing her arrival. She asked if there was anything the matter.

'Nothing,' I said, pulling myself together. 'I was reflecting on Helen of Troy and others.'

'What a funny place to do it,' said Joanna. 'You looked *most* odd, standing there clasping currant bread to your breast with your mouth wide open.'

'I've had a shock,' I said. 'I have been transplanted to Ilium and back again.'

'Do you know who that is?' I added, indicating a retreating back that was swimming gracefully away.

Peering after the girl Joanna said that it was the Symmingtons' nursery governess.

'Is that what struck you all of a heap?' she asked. 'She's good-looking, but a bit of a wet fish.'

'I know,' I said. 'Just a nice kind girl. And I'd been thinking her Aphrodite.'

Joanna opened the door of the car and I got in.

'It's funny, isn't it?' she said. 'Some people have lots of looks and absolutely no SA. That girl has. It seems such a pity.'

I said that if she was a nursery governess it was probably just as well.

CHAPTER 3

That afternoon we went to tea with Mr Pye.

Mr Pye was an extremely ladylike plump little man, devoted to his *petit point* chairs, his Dresden shepherdesses and his collection of bric-à-brac. He lived at Prior's Lodge in the grounds of which were the ruins of the old Priory.

Prior's Lodge was certainly a very exquisite house and under Mr Pye's loving care it showed to its best advantage. Every piece of furniture was polished and set in the exact place most suited to it. The curtains and cushions were of exquisite tone and colour, and of the most expensive silks.

It was hardly a man's house, and it did strike me that to live there would be rather like taking up one's abode in a period room at a museum. Mr Pye's principal enjoyment in life was taking people round his house. Even those completely insensitive to their surroundings could not escape. Even if you were so hardened as to consider the essentials of living a radio, a cocktail bar, a bath and a bed surrounded by the necessary walls, Mr Pye did not despair of leading you to better things.

His small plump hands quivered with sensibility as he described his treasures, and his voice rose to a falsetto squeak as he narrated the exciting circumstances under which he had brought his Italian bedstead home from Verona.

Joanna and I being both fond of antiquities and of period furniture, met with approval.

'It is really a pleasure, a great pleasure, to have such an acquisition to our little community. The dear good people down here, you know, so painfully bucolic – not to say *provincial*. They don't know anything. Vandals – absolute vandals! And the inside of their houses – it would make you weep, dear lady, I assure you it would make you weep. Perhaps it has done so?'

Joanna said that she hadn't gone quite as far as that.

'But you see what I mean? They mix things so terribly! I've seen with my own eyes a most delightful little Sheraton piece – delicate, perfect – a collector's piece, absolutely – and next to it a Victorian occasional table, or quite possibly a fumed oak revolving bookcase – yes, even that – *fumed oak*.'

He shuddered – and murmured plaintively:

'Why are people so blind? You agree – I'm sure you agree, that beauty is the only thing worth living for.'

Hypnotized by his earnestness, Joanna said, yes, yes, that was so.

'Then why,' demanded Mr Pye, 'do people surround themselves with ugliness?'

Joanna said it was very odd.

'Odd? It's *criminal*! That's what I call it – criminal! And the excuses they give! They say something is *comfortable*. Or that it is *quaint*. Quaint! Such a horrible word.

'The house you have taken,' went on Mr Pye, 'Miss Emily Barton's house. Now that is charming, and she has some quite nice pieces. Quite nice. One or two of them are really first class. And she has taste, too – although I'm not quite so sure of that as I was. Sometimes, I am afraid, I think it's really sentiment. She likes to keep things as they were – but not for *le bon motif* – not because of the resultant harmony – but because it is the way her mother had them.'

He transferred his attention to me, and his voice changed. It altered from that of the rapt artist to that of the born gossip.

'You didn't know the family at all? No, quite so – yes, through house agents. But, my dears, you *ought* to have known that family! When I came here the old mother was still alive. An incredible person – quite incredible! A *monster*, if you know what I mean. Positively a monster. The old-fashioned Victorian monster, devouring her young. Yes, that's what it amounted to. She was monumental, you know, must have weighed seventeen stone, and all the five daughters revolved round her. "The girls"! That's how she always spoke of them. The girls! And the eldest was well over sixty then. "Those stupid girls!" she used to call them sometimes. Black slaves, that's all they were, fetching and carrying and agreeing with her. Ten o'clock they had to go to bed and they weren't allowed a fire in their bedroom, and as for asking their own friends to the house, that would have been unheard of. She despised them, you know, for not getting married, and yet so arranged their lives that it was practically impossible for them to meet anybody. I believe Emmy, or perhaps it was Agnes, did have some kind of affair with a curate. But his family wasn't good enough and Mama soon put a stop to *that*!'

'It sounds like a novel,' said Joanna.

'Oh, my dear, it was. And then the dreadful old woman died, but of course it was far too late *then*. They just went on living there and talking in hushed voices about what poor Mama would have wished. Even re-papering her bedroom they felt to be quite sacrilegious. Still they did enjoy themselves in the parish in a quiet way. . . . But none of them had much stamina, and they just died off one by one. Influenza took off Edith, and Minnie had an operation and didn't recover and poor Mabel had a stroke – Emily looked after her in the most devoted manner. Really that poor woman has done nothing but nursing for the last ten years. A charming creature, don't you think. Like a piece of Dresden. So sad for her having financial anxieties – but of course all investments have depreciated.'

'We feel rather awful being in her house,' said Joanna.

'No, no, my dear young lady. You mustn't feel that way. Her dear good Florence is devoted to her and she told me herself how happy she was to have got such nice tenants.' Here Mr Pye made a little bow. 'She told me she thought she had been most fortunate.'

'The house,' I said, 'has a very soothing atmosphere.'

Mr Pye darted a quick glance at me.

'Really? You feel that? Now, that's very interesting. I wondered, you know. Yes, I wondered.'

'What do you mean, Mr Pye?' asked Joanna.

Mr Pye spread out his plump hands.

'Nothing, nothing. One wondered, that is all. I do believe in atmosphere, you know. People's thoughts and feelings. They give their impression to the walls and the furniture.'

I did not speak for a moment or two. I was looking round me and wondering how I would describe the atmosphere of Prior's Lodge. It seemed to me that the curious thing was that it hadn't any atmosphere! That was really very remarkable.

I reflected on this point so long that I heard nothing of the conversation going on between Joanna and her host. I was recalled to myself, however, by hearing Joanna uttering farewell preliminaries. I came out of my dream and added my quota.

We all went out into the hall. As we came towards the front door a letter came through the box and fell on the mat.

'Afternoon post,' murmured Mr Pye as he picked it up. 'Now, my dear young people, you will come again, won't you? Such a pleasure to meet some broader minds, if you understand me. Someone with an appreciation of Art. Really you know, these dear good people down here, if you mention the Ballet, it conveys to them pirouetting toes, and *tulle* skirts and old gentlemen with opera glasses in the Naughty Nineties. It does indeed. Fifty years behind the times – that's what I put them down as. A wonderful country, England. It has, you know, *pockets*. Lymstock is one of them. Interesting from a collector's point of view – I always feel I have voluntarily put myself under a glass shade when I am here. The peaceful backwater where nothing ever happens.'

Shaking hands with us twice over, he helped me with exaggerated care into the car. Joanna took the wheel, she negotiated with some care the circular sweep round a plot of unblemished grass, then with a straight drive ahead, she raised a hand to wave goodbye to our host where he stood on the steps of the house. I leaned forward to do the same.

But our gesture of farewell went unheeded. Mr Pye had opened his mail.

He was standing staring down at the open sheet in his hand.

Joanna has described him once as a plump pink cherub. He was still plump, but he was not looking like a cherub now. His face was a dark congested purple, contorted with rage and surprise.

And at that moment I realized that there had been something familiar about the look of that envelope. I had not realized it at the time – indeed it had been one of those things that you note unconsciously without knowing that you do note them.

'Goodness,' said Joanna. 'What's bitten the poor pet?'

'I rather fancy,' I said, 'that it's the Hidden Hand again.'

She turned an astonished face towards me and the car swerved.

'Careful, wench,' I said.

Joanna refixed her attention on the road. She was frowning.

'You mean a letter like the one you got?'

'That's my guess.'

'What is this place?' asked Joanna. 'It looks the most innocent sleepy harmless little bit of England you can imagine –'

'Where to quote Mr Pye, nothing ever happens,' I cut in. 'He chose the wrong minute to say that. Something has happened.'

'But who writes these things, Jerry?'

I shrugged my shoulders.

'My dear girl, how should I know? Some local nitwit with a screw loose, I suppose.'

'But why? It seems so idiotic.'

'You must read Freud and Jung and that lot to find out. Or ask our Dr Owen.'

Joanna tossed her head.

'Dr Owen doesn't like me.'

'He's hardly seen you.'

'He's seen quite enough, apparently, to make him cross over if he sees me coming along the High Street.'

'A most unusual reaction,' I said sympathetically. 'And one you're not used to.'

Joanna was frowning again.

'No, but seriously, Jerry, why *do* people write anonymous letters?'

'As I say, they've got a screw loose. It satisfies some urge, I suppose. If you've been snubbed, or ignored, or frustrated, and your life's pretty drab and empty, I suppose you get a sense of power from stabbing in the dark at people who are happy and enjoying themselves.'

Joanna shivered. 'Not nice.'

'No, not nice. I should imagine the people in these country places tend to be inbred – and so you would get a fair amount of odd characters.'

'Somebody, I suppose, quite uneducated and inarticulate? With better education –'

Joanna did not finish her sentence, and I said nothing. I have never been able to accept the easy belief that education is a panacea for every ill.

As we drove through the town before climbing up the hill road, I looked curiously at the few figures abroad in the High Street. Was one of those sturdy country-women going about with a load of spite and malice behind her placid brow, planning perhaps even now a further outpouring of vindictive spleen?

But I still did not take the thing seriously.

II

Two days later we went to a bridge party at the Symmingtons'.

It was a Saturday afternoon – the Symmingtons always had their bridge parties on a Saturday, because the office was shut then.

There were two tables. The players were the Symmingtons, ourselves, Miss Griffith, Mr Pye, Miss Barton and a Colonel

Appleton whom we had not yet met and who lived at Combeacre, a village some seven miles distant. He was a perfect specimen of the Blimp type, about sixty years of age, liked playing what he called a 'plucky game' (which usually resulted in enormous sums above the line being scored by his opponents) and was so intrigued by Joanna that he practically never took his eyes off her the whole afternoon.

I was forced to admit that my sister was probably the most attractive thing that had been seen in Lymstock for many a long day.

When we arrived, Elsie Holland, the children's governess, was hunting for some extra bridge scorers in an ornate writing desk. She glided across the floor with them in the same celestial way I had first noticed, but the spell could not be cast a second time. Exasperating that it should be so – a waste of a perfectly lovely form and face. But I noticed now only too clearly the exceptionally large white teeth like tombstones, and the way she showed her gums when she laughed. She was, unfortunately, one of your prattling girls.

'Are these the ones, Mrs Symmington? It's ever so stupid of me not to remember where we put them away last time. It's my fault, too, I'm afraid. I had them in my hand and then Brian called out his engine had got caught, and I ran out and what with one thing and another I must have just stuffed them in somewhere stupid. These aren't the right ones, I see now, they're a bit yellow at the edges. Shall I tell Agnes tea at five? I'm taking the kiddies to Long Barrow so there won't be any noise.'

A nice kind bright girl. I caught Joanna's eyes. She was laughing. I stared at her coldly. Joanna always knows what is passing in my mind, curse her.

We settled down to bridge.

I was soon to know to a nicety the bridge status of everyone in Lymstock. Mrs Symmington was an exceedingly good bridge player and was quite a devotee of the game. Like many definitely unintellectual women, she was not stupid and had a considerable natural shrewdness. Her husband was a good sound player, slightly overcautious. Mr Pye can best be described as brilliant. He had an uncanny flair for psychic bidding. Joanna and I, since the party was in our honour, played at a table with Mrs Symmington and Mr Pye. It was Symmington's task to pour oil on troubled waters and by the exercise of tact to reconcile the three other players at his table. Colonel Appleton, as I have said, was wont to play 'a plucky game.' Little Miss Barton was without exception the worst bridge player I have ever come across and always enjoyed herself enormously. She did manage to follow suit, but had the wildest ideas as to the strength of her hand, never knew the score, repeatedly led out of the wrong hand and was quite unable to count trumps and often forgot what they were. Aimée Griffith's play can be summed up in her own words. 'I like a good game of bridge with no nonsense – and I don't play any of these rubbish conventions. I say what I mean. And no post-mortems! After all, it's only a game!' It will be seen, therefore, that their host had not too easy a task.

Play proceeded fairly harmoniously, however, with occasional forgetfulness on the part of Colonel Appleton as he stared across at Joanna.

Tea was laid in the dining-room, round a big table. As we were finishing, two hot and excited little boys rushed in and were introduced, Mrs Symmington beaming with maternal pride, as was their father.

Then, just as we were finishing, a shadow darkened my plate, and I turned my head to see Megan standing in the french window.

'Oh,' said her mother. 'Here's Megan.'

Her voice held a faintly surprised note, as though she had forgotten that Megan existed.

The girl came in and shook hands, awkwardly and without any grace.

'I'm afraid I forgot about your tea, dear,' said Mrs Symmington. 'Miss Holland and the boys took theirs out with them, so there's no nursery tea today. I forgot you weren't with them.'

Megan nodded.

'That's all right. I'll go to the kitchen.'

She slouched out of the room. She was untidily dressed as usual and there were potatoes in both heels.

Mrs Symmington said with a little apologetic laugh:

'My poor Megan. She's just at that awkward age, you know. Girls are always shy and awkward when they've just left school before they're properly grown up.'

I saw Joanna's fair head jerk backwards in what I knew to be a warlike gesture.

'But Megan's twenty, isn't she?' she said.

'Oh, yes, yes. She is. But of course she's very young for her age. Quite a child still. It's so nice, I think, when girls don't grow up too quickly.' She laughed again. 'I expect all mothers want their children to remain babies.'

'I can't think why,' said Joanna. 'After all, it would be a bit awkward if one had a child who remained mentally six while his body grew up.'

'Oh, you mustn't take things so literally, Miss Burton,' said Mrs Symmington.

It occurred to me at that moment that I did not much care for Mrs Symmington. That anæmic, slighted, faded prettiness concealed, I thought, a selfish and grasping nature. She said, and I disliked her a little more still:

'My poor Megan. She's rather a difficult child, I'm afraid. I've been trying to find something for her to do – I believe there are several things one can learn by correspondence. Designing and dressmaking – or she might try and learn shorthand and typing.'

The red glint was still in Joanna's eye. She said as we sat down again at the bridge table.

'I suppose she'll be going to parties and all that sort of thing. Are you going to give a dance for her?'

'A dance?' Mrs Symmington seemed surprised and amused. 'Oh, no, we don't do things like that down here.'

'I see. Just tennis parties and things like that.'

'Our tennis court has not been played on for years. Neither Richard nor I play. I suppose, later, when the boys grow up – Oh, Megan will find plenty to do. She's quite happy just pottering about, you know. Let me see, did I deal? Two No Trumps.'

As we drove home, Joanna said with a vicious pressure on the accelerator pedal that made the car leap forward:

'I feel awfully sorry for that girl.'

'Megan?'

'Yes. Her mother doesn't like her.'

'Oh, come now, Joanna, it's not as bad as that.'

'Yes, it is. Lots of mothers don't like their children. Megan, I should imagine, is an awkward sort of creature to have about the house. She disturbs the pattern – the Symmington pattern. It's a complete unit without her – and that's a most unhappy feeling for a sensitive creature to have – and she *is* sensitive.'

'Yes,' I said, 'I think she is.'

I was silent for a moment.

Joanna suddenly laughed mischievously.

'Bad luck for you about the governess.'

'I don't know what you mean,' I said with dignity.

'Nonsense. Masculine chagrin was written on your face every time you looked at her. I agree with you. It is a waste.'

'I don't know what you're talking about.'

'But I'm delighted, all the same. It's the first sign of reviving life. I was quite worried about you at the nursing home. You never even looked at that remarkably pretty nurse you had. An attractive minx, too – absolutely God's gift to a sick man.'

'Your conversation, Joanna, I find definitely low.'

My sister continued without paying the least attention to my remarks.

'So I was much relieved to see you'd still got an eye for a nice bit of skirt. She *is* a good looker. Funny that the SA should have been left out so completely. It is odd, you know, Jerry. What *is* the thing that some women have and others haven't? What is it that makes one woman, even if she only says "Foul weather" so attractive that every man within range wants to come over and talk about the weather with her? I suppose Providence makes a mistake every now and then when sending out the parcel. One Aphrodite face and form, one temperament ditto. And something goes astray and the Aphrodite temperament goes to some little plain-faced creature, and then all the other women go simply mad and say, "I can't think what the men see in her. She isn't even good-looking!"'

'Have you quite finished, Joanna?'

'Well, you do agree, don't you?'

I grinned. 'I'll admit to disappointment.'

'And I don't see who else there is here for you. You'll have to fall back upon Aimée Griffith.'

'God forbid,' I said.

'She's quite good-looking, you know.'

'Too much of an Amazon for me.'

'She seems to enjoy her life all right,' said Joanna. 'Absolutely disgustingly hearty, isn't she? I shouldn't be at all surprised if she had a cold bath every morning.'

'And what are you going to do for yourself?' I asked.

'Me?'

'Yes. You'll need a little distraction down here if I know you.'

'Who's being low now? Besides, you forget Paul.' Joanna heaved a not very convincing sigh.

'I shan't forget him nearly as quickly as you will. In about ten days you'll be saying, "Paul? Paul Who? I never knew a Paul."'

'You think I'm completely fickle,' said Joanna.

'When people like Paul are in question, I'm only too glad that you should be.'

'You never did like him. But he really was a bit of a genius.'

'Possibly, though I doubt it. Anyway, from all I've heard, geniuses are people to be heartily disliked. One thing, you won't find any geniuses down here.'

Joanna considered for a moment, her head on one side.

'I'm afraid not,' she said regretfully.

'You'll have to fall back upon Owen Griffith,' I said. He's the only unattached male in the place. Unless you count old Colonel Appleton. He was looking at you like a hungry bloodhound most of the afternoon.'

Joanna laughed.

'He was, wasn't he? It was quite embarrassing.'

'Don't pretend. You're never embarrassed.'

Joanna drove in silence through the gate and round to the garage. She said then:

'There may be something in that idea of yours.'

'What idea?'

Joanna replied:

'I don't see why any man should deliberately cross the street to avoid me. It's rude, apart from anything else.'

'I see,' I said. 'You're going to hunt the man down in cold blood.'

'Well, I don't like being avoided.'

I got slowly and carefully out of the car, and balanced my sticks. Then I offered my sister a piece of advice.

'Let me tell you this, girl. Owen Griffith isn't any of your tame whining artistic young men. Unless you're careful you'll stir up a hornet's nest about your ears. That man could be dangerous.'

'Oo, do you think so?' demanded Joanna with every symptom of pleasure at the prospect.

'Leave the poor devil alone,' I said sternly.

'How dare he cross the street when he saw me coming?'

'All you women are alike. You harp on one theme. You'll have Sister Aimée gunning for you, too, if I'm not mistaken.'

'She dislikes me already,' said Joanna. She spoke meditatively, but with a certain satisfaction.

'We have come down here,' I said sternly, 'for peace and quiet, and I mean to see we get it.'

But peace and quiet were the last things we were to have.

CHAPTER 4

It was, I think, about a week later, that Partridge informed me that Mrs Baker would like to speak to me for a minute or two if I would be so kind.

The name Mrs Baker conveyed nothing at all to me.

'Who is Mrs Baker?' I said, bewildered – 'Can't she see Miss Joanna?'

But it appeared that I was the person with whom an interview was desired. It further transpired that Mrs Baker was the mother of the girl Beatrice.

I had forgotten Beatrice. For a fortnight now, I had been conscious of a middle-aged woman with wisps of grey hair, usually on her knees retreating crablike from bathroom and stairs and passages when I appeared, and I knew, I suppose, that she was our new Daily Woman. Otherwise the Beatrice complication had faded from my mind.

I could not very well refuse to see Beatrice's mother, especially as I learned that Joanna was out, but I was, I must confess, a little nervous at the prospect. I sincerely hoped that I was not going to be accused of having trifled with Beatrice's affections. I cursed the mischievous activities of anonymous letter-writers to myself at the same time as, aloud, I commanded that Beatrice's mother should be brought to my presence.

Mrs Baker was a big broad weather-beaten woman with a rapid flow of speech. I was relieved to notice no signs of anger or accusation.

'I hope, sir,' she said, beginning at once when the door had closed behind Partridge, 'that you'll excuse the liberty I've taken in coming to see you. But I thought, sir, as you was the proper person to come to, and I should be thankful if you could see your way to telling me what I ought to do in the circumstances, because in my opinion, sir, something ought to be done, and I've never been one to let the grass grow under my feet, and what I say is, no use moaning and groaning, but "Up and doing" as vicar said in his sermon only the week before last.'

I felt slightly bewildered and as though I had missed something essential in the conversation.

'Certainly,' I said. 'Won't you – er – sit down, Mrs Baker? I'm sure I shall be glad to – er help you in any way I can –'

I paused expectantly.

'Thank you, sir.' Mrs Baker sat down on the edge of a chair. 'It's very good of you, I'm sure. And glad I am that I came to you, I said to Beatrice, I said, and her howling and crying on her bed, Mr Burton will know what to do, I said, being a London gentleman. And something must be done, what with young men being so hot-headed and not listening to reason the way they are, and not listening to a word a girl says, and anyway, if it was *me*, I says to Beatrice I'd give him as good as I got, and what about that girl down at the mill?'

I felt more than ever bewildered.

'I'm sorry,' I said. 'But I don't quite understand. What has happened?'

'It's the letters, sir. Wicked letters – indecent, too, using such words and all. Worse than I've ever seen in the Bible, even.'

Passing over an interesting side-line here, I said desperately:

'Has your daughter been having more letters?'

'Not her, sir. She had just the one. That one as was the occasion of her leaving here.'

'There was absolutely no reason –' I began, but Mrs Baker firmly and respectfully interrupted me:

'There is no need to tell me, sir, that what was wrote was all wicked lies. I had Miss Partridge's word for that – and indeed I would have known it for myself. You aren't that type of gentleman, sir, that I well know, and you an invalid and all. Wicked untruthful lies it was, but all the same I says to Beatrice as she'd better leave because you know what talk is, sir. No smoke without fire, that's what people say. And a girl can't be too careful. And besides the girl herself felt bashful like after what had been written, so I says, "Quite right," to Beatrice when she said she wasn't coming up here again, though I'm sure we both regretted the inconvenience being such –'

Unable to find her way out of this sentence, Mrs Baker took a deep breath and began again.

'And that, I hoped, would be the end of any nasty talk. But now George, down at the garage, him what Beatrice is going with, he's got one of them. Saying awful things about our Beatrice, and how she's going on with Fred Ledbetter's Tom – and I can assure you, sir, the girl has been no more than civil to him and passing the time of day so to speak.'

My head was now reeling under this new complication of Mr Ledbetter's Tom.

'Let me get this straight,' I said. 'Beatrice's – er – young man has had an anonymous letter making accusations about her and another young man?'

'That's right, sir, and not nicely put at all – horrible words used, and it drove young George mad with rage, it did, and he came round and told Beatrice he wasn't going to put up with that sort of thing from her, and he wasn't going to have her go behind his back with other chaps – and she says it's all a lie – and he says no smoke without fire, he says, and rushes off being hot-like in his temper, and Beatrice she took on ever so, poor girl, and I said I'll put my hat on and come straight up to you, sir.'

Mrs Baker paused and looked at me expectantly, like a dog waiting for reward after doing a particularly clever trick.

'But why come to me?' I demanded.

'I understood, sir, that you'd had one of these nasty letters yourself, and I thought, sir, that being a London gentleman, you'd know what to do about them.'

'If I were you,' I said, 'I should go to the police. This sort of thing ought to be stopped.'

Mrs Baker looked deeply shocked.

'Oh, no, sir, I couldn't go to the police.'

'Why not?'

'I've never been mixed up with the police, sir. None of us ever have.'

'Probably not. But the police are the only people who can deal with this sort of thing. It's their business.'

'Go to Bert Rundle?'

Bert Rundle was the constable, I knew.

'There's a sergeant, or an inspector, surely, at the police station.'

'Me, go into the police station?'

Mrs Baker's voice expressed reproach and incredulity. I began to feel annoyed.

'That's the only advice I can give you.'

Mrs Baker was silent, obviously quite unconvinced. She said wistfully and earnestly:

'These letters ought to be stopped, sir, they did ought to be stopped. There'll be mischief done sooner or later.'

'It seems to me there is mischief done now,' I said.

'I meant *violence*, sir. These young fellows, they get violent in their feelings – and so do the older ones.'

I asked:

'Are a good many of these letters going about?'

Mrs Baker nodded.

'It's getting worse and worse, sir. Mr and Mrs Beadle at the Blue Boar – very happy they've always been – and now these letters come and it sets him thinking things – things that aren't so, sir.'

I leaned forward:

'Mrs Baker,' I said, 'have you any idea, any idea at all, who is writing these abominable letters?'

To my great surprise she nodded her head.

'We've got our idea, sir. Yes, we've all got a very fair idea.'

'Who is it?'

I had fancied she might be reluctant to mention a name, but she replied promptly:

' 'Tis Mrs Cleat – that's what we all think, sir. 'Tis Mrs Cleat for sure.'

I had heard so many names this morning that I was quite bewildered. I asked:

'Who is Mrs Cleat?'

Mrs Cleat, I discovered, was the wife of an elderly jobbing gardener. She lived in a cottage on the road leading down to the Mill. My further questions only brought unsatisfactory answers. Questioned as to why Mrs Cleat should write these letters, Mrs Baker would only say vaguely that ' 'Twould be like her.'

In the end, I let her go, reiterating once more my advice to go to the police, advice which I could see Mrs Baker was not going to act upon. I was left with the impression that I had disappointed her.

I thought over what she had said. Vague as the evidence was, I decided that if the village was all agreed that Mrs Cleat was the culprit, then it was probably true. I decided to go and consult Griffith about the whole thing. Presumably he would know this Cleat woman. If he thought advisable, he or I might suggest to the police that she was at the bottom of this growing annoyance.

I timed my arrival for about the moment I fancied Griffith would have finished his 'Surgery.' When the last patient had left, I went into the surgery.

'Hallo, it's you, Burton.'

'Yes. I want to talk to you.'

I outlined my conversation with Mrs Baker, and passed on to him the conviction that this Mrs Cleat was responsible. Rather to my disappointment, Griffith shook his head.

'It's not so simple as that,' he said.

'You don't think this Cleat woman is at the bottom of it?'

'She may be. But I should think it most unlikely.'

'Then why do they all think it is her?'

He smiled.

'Oh,' he said, 'you don't understand. Mrs Cleat is the local witch.'

'Good gracious!' I exclaimed.

'Yes, sounds rather strange nowadays, nevertheless that's what it amounts to. The feeling lingers you know, that there are certain people, certain families, for instance, whom it isn't wise to offend. Mrs Cleat came from a family of "wise women". And I'm afraid she's taken pains to cultivate the legend. She's a queer woman with a bitter and sardonic sense of humour. It's been easy enough for her, if a child cuts its finger, or had a bad fall, or sickened with mumps, to nod her head and say, "Yes, he stole my apples last week" or "He pulled my cat's tail." Soon enough mothers pulled their children away, and other women brought honey or a cake they'd baked to give to Mrs Cleat so as to keep on the right side of her so that she shouldn't "ill wish" them. It's superstitious and silly, but it happens. So naturally, now, they think she's at the bottom of this.'

'But she isn't?'

'Oh, no. She isn't the type. It's – it's not so simple as that.'

'Have you any idea?' I looked at him curiously.

He shook his head, but his eyes were absent.

'No,' he said. 'I don't know at all. But I don't like it, Burton – some harm is going to come of this.'

II

When I got back to the house I found Megan sitting on the veranda steps, her chin resting on her knees.

She greeted me with her usual lack of ceremony.

'Hallo,' she said. 'Do you think I could come to lunch?'

'Certainly,' I said.

'If it's chops, or anything difficult like that and they won't go round, just tell me,' shouted Megan as I went round to apprise Partridge of the fact that there would be three to lunch.

I fancy that Partridge sniffed. She certainly managed to convey without saying a word of any kind, that she didn't think much of that Miss Megan.

I went back to the veranda.

'Is it quite all right?' asked Megan anxiously.

'Quite all right,' I said. 'Irish stew.'

'Oh well, that's rather like dogs' dinner anyway, isn't it? I mean it's mostly potato and flavour.'

'Quite,' I said.

I took out my cigarette case and offered it to Megan. She flushed.

'How nice of you.'

'Won't you have one?'

'No, I don't think I will, but it was very nice of you to offer it to me – just as though I was a real person.'

'Aren't you a real person?' I said, amused.

Megan shook her head, then, changing the subject, she stretched out a long dusty leg for my inspection.

'I've darned my stockings,' she announced proudly.

I am not an authority on darning, but it did occur to me that the strange puckered blot of violently contrasting wool was perhaps not quite a success.

'It's much more uncomfortable than the hole,' said Megan.

'It looks as though it might be,' I agreed.

'Does your sister darn well?'

I tried to think if I had ever observed any of Joanna's handiwork in this direction.

'I don't know,' I had to confess.

'Well, what does she do when she gets a hole in her stocking?'

'I rather think,' I said reluctantly, 'that she throws them away and buys another pair.'

'Very sensible,' said Megan. 'But I can't do that. I get an allowance now – forty pounds a year. You can't do much on that.'

I agreed.

'If only I wore black stockings, I could ink my legs,' said Megan sadly. 'That's what I always did at school. Miss Batworthy, the mistress who looked after our mending was like her name – blind as a bat. It was awfully useful.'

'It must have been,' I said.

We were silent while I smoked my pipe. It was quite a companionable silence.

Megan broke it by saying suddenly and violently:

'I suppose you think I'm awful, like everyone else?'

I was so startled that my pipe fell out of my mouth. It was a meerschaum, just colouring nicely, and it broke. I said angrily to Megan:

'Now, see what you've done.'

That most unaccountable of children, instead of being upset, merely grinned broadly.

'I do like you,' she said.

It was a most warming remark. It is the remark that one fancies, perhaps erroneously, that one's dog would say if he could talk. It occurred to me that Megan, for all she looked like a horse had the disposition of a dog. She was certainly not quite human.

'What did you say before the catastrophe?' I asked, carefully picking up the fragments of my cherished pipe.

'I said I supposed you thought me awful,' said Megan, but not at all in the same tone she had said it before.

'Why should I?'

Megan said gravely:

'Because I am.'

I said sharply:

'Don't be stupid.'

Megan shook her head.

'That's just it. I'm not really stupid. People think I am. They don't know that inside I know just what they're like, and that all the time I'm hating them.'

'*Hating* them?'

'Yes,' said Megan.

Her eyes, those melancholy, unchildlike eyes stared straight into mine, without blinking. It was a long mournful gaze.

'You would hate people if you were like me,' she said. 'If you weren't wanted.'

'Don't you think you're being rather morbid?' I asked.

'Yes,' said Megan. 'That's what people always say when you're saying the truth. And it is true. I'm not wanted and I can quite see why. Mummie doesn't like me a bit. I remind her, I think, of my father, who was cruel to her and pretty dreadful from all I can hear. Only mothers can't say they don't want their children and just go away. Or eat them. Cats eat the kittens they don't like. Awfully sensible, I think. No waste or mess. But human mothers have to keep their children, and look after them. It hasn't been so bad while I could be sent away to school – but you see what Mummie would really like is to be just herself and my stepfather and the boys.'

I said slowly:

'I still think you're morbid, Megan, but accepting some of what you say as true, why don't you go away and have a life of your own?'

She gave me an unchildlike smile.

'You mean take up a career. Earn my living?'

'Yes.'

'What at?'

'You could train for something, I suppose. Shorthand typing – book-keeping.'

'I don't believe I could. I am stupid about doing things. And besides –'

'Well?'

She had turned her face away, now she turned it slowly back again. It was crimson and there were tears in her eyes. She spoke now with all the childishness back in her voice.

'Why should I go away? And be made to go away? They don't want me, but I'll *stay*. I'll stay and make everyone sorry. I'll make them all sorry. Hateful pigs! I hate everyone here in Lymstock. They all think I'm stupid and ugly. I'll show them. I'll show them. I'll –'

It was a childish, oddly pathetic rage.

I heard a step on the gravel round the corner of the house.

'Get up,' I said savagely. 'Go into the house through the drawing-room. Go up to the first floor to the bathroom. End of the passage. Wash your face. Quick.'

She sprang awkwardly to her feet and darted through the window as Joanna came round the corner of the house.

'Gosh, I'm hot,' she called out. She sat down beside me and fanned her face with the Tyrolean scarf that had been round her head. 'Still I think I'm educating these damned brogues now. I've walked miles. I've learnt one thing, you shouldn't have these fancy holes in your brogues. The gorse prickles go through. Do you know, Jerry, I think we ought to have a dog.'

'So do I,' I said. 'By the way, Megan is coming to lunch.'

'Is she? Good.'

'You like her?' I asked.

'I think she's a changeling,' said Joanna. 'Something left on a doorstep, you know, while the fairies take the right one away. It's very interesting to meet a changeling. Oof, I must go up and wash.'

'You can't yet,' I said, 'Megan is washing.'

'Oh, she's been foot-slogging too, has she?'

Joanna took out her mirror and looked at her face long and earnestly. 'I don't think I like this lipstick,' she announced presently.

Megan came out through the window. She was composed, moderately clean, and showed no signs of the recent storm. She looked doubtfully at Joanna.

'Hallo,' said Joanna, still preoccupied by her face. 'I'm so glad you've come to lunch. Good gracious, I've got a freckle on my nose. I must do something about it. Freckles are so earnest and Scottish.'

Partridge came out and said coldly that luncheon was served.

'Come on,' said Joanna, getting up. 'I'm starving.'

She put her arm through Megan's and they went into the house together.

CHAPTER 5

I see that there has been one omission in my story. So far I have made little or no mention of Mrs Dane Calthrop, or indeed of the Rev. Caleb Dane Calthrop.

And yet both the vicar and his wife were distinct personalities. Dane Calthrop himself was perhaps a being more remote from everyday life than anyone I have ever met. His existence was in his books and in his study, and in his intimate knowledge of early church history. Mrs Dane Calthrop, on the other hand, was quite terrifyingly on the spot. I have perhaps purposely put off mentioning her, because I was from the first a little afraid of her. She was a woman of character and of almost Olympian knowledge. She was not in the least the typical vicar's wife – but that, as I set it down, makes me ask myself, what do I know of vicars' wives?

The only one I remember well was a quiet nondescript creature, devoted to a big strong husband with a magnetic way of preaching; she had so little general conversation that it was a puzzle to know how to sustain a conversation with her.

Otherwise I was depending on the fictional presentment of vicars' wives, caricatures of females poking their noses everywhere, and uttering platitudes. Probably no such type exists.

Mrs Dane Calthrop never poked her nose in anywhere, yet she had an uncanny power of knowing things and I soon discovered that almost everyone in the village was slightly afraid of her. She gave no advice and never interfered, yet she represented, to any uneasy conscience, the Deity personified.

I have never seen a woman more indifferent to her material surroundings. On hot days she would stride about clad in Harris tweed, and in rain or even sleet, I have seen her absent-mindedly race down the village street in a cotton dress of printed poppies. She had a long thin well-bred face like a greyhound, and a most devastating sincerity of speech.

She stopped me in the High Street the day after Megan had come to lunch. I had the usual feeling of surprise, because Mrs Dane Calthrop's progress resembled coursing more than walking, and her eyes were always fixed on the distant horizon so that you felt sure her real objective was about a mile and a half away.

'Oh,' she said, 'Mr Burton!'

She said it rather triumphantly, as someone might who had solved a particularly clever puzzle.

I admitted that I was Mr Burton and Mrs Dane Calthrop stopped focusing on the horizon and seemed to be trying to focus on me instead.

'Now what,' she said, 'did I want to see you about?'

I could not help her there. She stood frowning, deeply perplexed.

'Something rather nasty,' she said.

'I'm sorry about that,' I said, startled.

'Ah,' cried Mrs Dane Calthrop. 'I hate my love with an A. That's it. Anonymous letters! What's this story you've brought down here about anonymous letters?'

'I didn't bring it,' I said. 'It was here already.'

'Nobody got any until you came, though,' said Mrs Dane Calthrop accusingly.

'But they did, Mrs Dane Calthrop. The trouble had already started.'

'Oh dear,' said Mrs Dane Calthrop. 'I don't like that.'

She stood there, her eyes absent and far away again. She said:

'I can't help feeling it's all *wrong*. We're not like that here. Envy, of course, and malice, and all the mean spiteful little sins – but I didn't think there was anyone who would do that – No, I really didn't. And it distresses me, you see, because *I* ought to know.'

Her fine eyes came back from the horizon and met mine. They were worried, and seemed to hold the honest bewilderment of a child.

'How should you know?' I said.

'I usually do. I've always felt that's my function. Caleb preaches good sound doctrine and administers the sacraments. That's a priest's duty, but if you admit marriage at all for a priest, then I think his wife's duty is to know what people are feeling and thinking, even if she can't do anything about it. And I haven't the least idea whose mind is –'

She broke off, adding absently:

'They are such silly letters, too.'

'Have you – er – had any yourself?'

I was a little diffident of asking, but Mrs Dane Calthrop replied perfectly naturally, her eyes opening a little wider:

'Oh yes, two – no, three. I forget exactly what they said. Something very silly about Caleb and the school-mistress, I think. Quite absurd, because Caleb has absolutely no taste for fornication. He never has had. So lucky, being a clergyman.'

'Quite,' I said, 'Oh, quite.'

'Caleb would have been a saint,' said Mrs Dane Calthrop, 'if he hadn't been just a little too intellectual.'

I did not feel qualified to answer this criticism, and anyway Mrs Dane Calthrop went on, leaping back from her husband to the letters in rather a puzzling way.

'There are so many things the letters might say, but don't. That's what is so curious.'

'I should hardly have thought they erred on the side of restraint,' I said bitterly.

'But they don't seem to *know* anything. None of the real things.'

'You mean?'

Those fine vague eyes met mine.

'Well, of course. There's plenty of adultery here – and everything else. Any amount of shameful secrets. Why doesn't the writer use those?' She paused and then asked abruptly, 'What did they say in your letter?'

'They suggested that my sister wasn't my sister.'

'And she is?'

Mrs Dane Calthrop asked the question with unembarrassed friendly interest.

'Certainly Joanna is my sister.'

Mrs Dane Calthrop nodded her head.

'That just shows you what I mean. I dare say there are other things –'

Her clear uninterested eyes looked at me thoughtfully, and I suddenly understood why Lymstock was afraid of Mrs Dane Calthrop.

In everybody's life there are hidden chapters which they hope may never be known. I felt that Mrs Dane Calthrop knew them.

For once in my life, I was positively delighted when Aimée Griffith's hearty voice boomed out:

'Hallo, Maud. Glad I've just caught you. I want to suggest an alteration of date for the Sale of Work. Morning, Mr Burton.'

She went on:

'I must just pop into the grocer's and leave my order, then I'll come along to the Institute if that suits you?'

'Yes, yes, that will do quite well,' said Mrs Dane Calthrop.

Aimée Griffith went into the International Stores.

Mrs Dane Calthrop said: 'Poor thing.'

I was puzzled. Surely she could not be pitying Aimée?

She went on, however:

'You know, Mr Burton, I'm rather afraid –'

'About this letter business?'

'Yes, you see it means – it must mean –' She paused lost in thought, her eyes screwed up. Then she said slowly, as one who solves a problem, 'Blind hatred . . . yes, blind hatred. But even a blind man might stab to the heart by pure chance. . . . And what would happen then, Mr Burton?'

We were to know that before another day had passed.

II

It was Partridge who brought the news of the tragedy. Partridge enjoys calamity. Her nose always twitches ecstatically when she has to break bad news of any kind.

She came into Joanna's room with her nose working overtime, her eyes bright, and her mouth pulled down into an exaggerated gloom. 'There's terrible news, this morning, miss,' she observed as she drew up the blinds.

It takes a minute or two for Joanna, with her London habits, to become fully conscious in the morning. She said, 'Er ah,' and rolled over without real interest.

Partridge placed her early tea beside her and began again.

'Terrible it is. Shocking! I couldn't hardly believe it when I heard.'

'What's terrible?' said Joanna, struggling into wakefulness.

'Poor Mrs Symmington.' She paused dramatically. 'Dead.'

'Dead?' Joanna sat up in bed, now wide awake.

'Yes, miss, yesterday afternoon, and what's worse, took her own life.'

'Oh no, Partridge?'

Joanna was really shocked – Mrs Symmington was not, somehow, the sort of person you associated with tragedies.

'Yes, miss, it's the truth. Did it deliberate. Not but what she was drove to it, poor soul.'

'Drove to it?' Joanna had an inkling of the truth then. 'Not –?'

Her eyes questioned Partridge and Partridge nodded.

'That's right, miss. One of them nasty letters!'

'What did it say?'

But that, to Partridge's regret, she had not succeeded in learning.

'They're beastly things,' said Joanna. 'But I don't see why they should make one want to kill oneself.'

Partridge sniffed and then said with meaning:

'Not unless they were *true*, miss.'

'Oh,' said Joanna.

She drank her tea after Partridge had left the room, then she threw on a dressing-gown and came in to me to tell me the news.

I thought of what Owen Griffith had said. Sooner or later the shot in the dark went home. It had done with Mrs Symmington. She, apparently the most unlikely of women, had had a secret. . . . It was true, I reflected, that for all her shrewdness she was not a woman of much stamina. She was the anæmic clinging type that crumples easily.

Joanna nudged me and asked me what I was thinking about.

I repeated to her what Owen had said.

'Of course,' said Joanna waspishly, 'he would know all about it. That man thinks he knows everything.'

'He's clever,' I said.

'He's conceited,' said Joanna. She added, 'Abominably conceited!'

After a minute or two she said:

'How awful for her husband – and for the girl. What do you think Megan will feel about it?'

I hadn't the slightest idea and said so. It was curious that one could never gauge what Megan would think or feel.

Joanna nodded and said:

'No, one never does know with changelings.'

After a minute or two she said:

'Do you think – would you like – I wonder if she'd like to come and stay with us for a day or two? It's rather a shock for a girl that age.'

'We might go along and suggest it,' I agreed.

'The children are all right,' said Joanna. 'They've got that governess woman. But I expect she's just the sort of creature who would drive someone like Megan mad.'

I thought that was very possible. I could imagine Elsie Holland uttering platitude after platitude and suggesting innumerable cups of tea. A kindly creature, but not, I thought, the person for a sensitive girl.

I had thought myself of bringing Megan away, and I was glad that Joanna had thought of it spontaneously without prompting from me.

We went down to the Symmingtons' house after breakfast.

We were a little nervous, both of us. Our arrival might look like sheer ghoulish curiosity. Luckily we met Owen Griffith just coming out through the gate. He looked worried and preoccupied.

He greeted me, however, with some warmth.

'Oh, hallo, Burton. I'm glad to see you. What I was afraid would happen sooner or later has happened. A damnable business!'

'Good morning, Dr Griffith,' said Joanna, using the voice she keeps for one of our deafer aunts.

Griffith started and flushed.

'Oh – oh, good morning, Miss Burton.'

'I thought perhaps,' said Joanna, 'that you didn't see me.'

Owen Griffith got redder still. His shyness enveloped him like a mantle.

'I'm – I'm so sorry – preoccupied – I didn't.'

Joanna went on mercilessly: 'After all, I *am* life size.'

'Merely kit-kat,' I said in a stern aside to her. Then I went on:

'My sister and I, Griffith, wondered whether it would be a good thing if the girl came and stopped with us for a day or two? What do you think? I don't want to butt in – but it must be rather grim for the poor child. What would Symmington feel about it, do you think?'

Griffith turned the idea over in his mind for a moment or two.

'I think it would be an excellent thing,' he said at last. 'She's a queer nervy sort of girl, and it would be good for her to get away from the whole thing. Miss Holland is doing wonders – she's an excellent head on her shoulders, but she really has quite enough to do with the two children and Symmington himself. He's quite broken up – bewildered.'

'It was –' I hesitated – 'suicide?'

Griffith nodded.

'Oh yes. No question of accident. She wrote, "I can't go on" on a scrap of paper. The letter must have come by yesterday afternoon's post. The envelope was down on the floor by her chair and the letter itself was screwed up into a ball and thrown into the fireplace.'

'What did –'

I stopped, rather horrified at myself.

'I beg your pardon,' I said.

Griffith gave a quick unhappy smile.

'You needn't mind asking. The letter will have to be read at the inquest. No getting out of it, more's the pity. It was the usual kind of thing – couched in the same foul style. The specific accusation was that the second boy, Colin, was not Symmington's child.'

'Do you think that was true?' I exclaimed incredulously.

Griffith shrugged his shoulders.

'I've no means of forming a judgement. I've only been here five years. As far as I've ever seen, the Symmingtons were a placid, happy couple devoted to each other and their children. It's true that the boy doesn't particularly resemble his parents – he's got bright red hair, for one thing – but a child often throws back in appearance to a grandfather or grandmother.'

'That lack of resemblance might have been what prompted the particular accusation. A foul and quite uncalled-for bow at a venture.'

'Very likely. In fact, probably. There's not been much accurate knowledge behind these poison pen letters, just unbridled spite and malice.'

'But it happened to hit the bull's-eye,' said Joanna. 'After all, she wouldn't have killed herself otherwise, would she?'

Griffith said doubtfully:

'I'm not quite sure. She's been ailing in health for some time, neurotic, hysterical. I've been treating her for a nervous condition. It's possible, I think, that the shock of receiving such a letter, couched in those terms, may have induced such a state of panic and despondency that she may have decided to take her life. She may have worked herself up to feel that her husband might not believe her if she denied the story, and the general shame and disgust might have worked upon her so powerfully as to temporarily unbalance her judgement.'

'Suicide whilst of unsound mind,' said Joanna.

'Exactly. I shall be quite justified, I think, in putting forward that point of view at the inquest.'

'I see,' said Joanna.

There was something in her voice which made Owen say:

'Perfectly justified!' in an angry voice. He added, 'You don't agree, Miss Burton?'

'Oh yes, I do,' said Joanna. 'I'd do exactly the same in your place.'

Owen looked at her doubtfully, then moved slowly away down the street. Joanna and I went on into the house.

The front door was open and it seemed easier than ringing the bell, especially as we heard Elsie Holland's voice inside.

She was talking to Mr Symmington who, huddled in a chair, was looking completely dazed.

'No, but really, Mr Symmington, you must take something. You haven't had any breakfast, not what I call a proper breakfast, and nothing to eat last night, and what with the shock and all, you'll be getting ill yourself, and you'll need all your strength. The doctor said so before he left.'

Symmington said in a toneless voice:

'You're very kind, Miss Holland, but –'

'A nice cup of hot tea,' said Elsie Holland, thrusting the beverage on him firmly.

Personally I should have given the poor devil a stiff whisky and soda. He looked as though he needed it. However, he accepted the tea, and looking up at Elsie Holland:

'I can't thank you for all you've done and are doing, Miss Holland. You've been perfectly splendid.'

The girl flushed and looked pleased.

'It's nice of you to say that, Mr Symmington. You must let me do all I can to help. Don't worry about the children – I'll see to them, and I've got the servants calmed down, and if there's anything I can do, letter-writing or telephoning, don't hesitate to ask me.'

'You're very kind,' Symmington said again.

Elsie Holland, turning, caught sight of us and came hurrying out into the hall.

'Isn't it terrible?' she said in a hushed whisper.

I thought, as I looked at her, that she was really a very nice girl. Kind, competent, practical in an emergency. Her magnificent blue eyes were just faintly rimmed with pink, showing that she had been soft-hearted enough to shed tears for her employer's death.

'Can we speak to you a minute?' asked Joanna. 'We don't want to disturb Mr Symmington.'

Elsie Holland nodded comprehendingly and led the way into the dining-room on the other side of the hall.

'It's been awful for him,' she said. 'Such a shock. Whoever would have thought a thing like this could happen? But of course, I do realize now that she had been queer for some time. Awfully nervy and weepy. I thought it was her health, though Dr Griffith always said there was nothing really wrong with her. But she was snappy and irritable and some days you wouldn't know just how to take her.'

'What we really came for,' said Joanna, 'was to know whether we could have Megan for a few days – that is, if she'd like to come.'

Elsie Holland looked rather surprised.

'Megan?' she said doubtfully. 'I don't know, I'm sure. I mean, it's ever so kind of you, but she's such a queer girl. One never knows what she's going to say or feel about things.'

Joanna said rather vaguely:

'We thought it might be a help, perhaps.'

'Oh well, as far as that goes, it would. I mean, I've got the boys to look after (they're with cook just now) and poor Mr Symmington – he really needs looking after as much as anyone, and such a lot to do and see to. I really haven't had time to see much of Megan. I think she's upstairs in the old nursery at the top of the house. She seems to want to get away from everyone. I don't know if –'

Joanna gave me the faintest of looks. I slipped out of the room and upstairs.

The old nursery was at the top of the house. I opened the door and went in. The room downstairs had given on to the garden behind and the blinds had not been down there. But in this room which faced the road they were decorously drawn down.

Through a dim grey gloom I saw Megan. She was crouching on a divan set against the far wall, and I was reminded at once of some terrified animal, hiding. She looked petrified with fear.

'Megan,' I said.

I came forward, and unconsciously I adopted the tone one does adopt when you want to reassure a frightened animal. I'm really surprised I didn't hold out a carrot or a piece of sugar. I felt like that.

She stared at me, but she did not move, and her expression did not alter.

'Megan,' I said again. 'Joanna and I have come to ask you if you would like to come and stay with us for a little.'

Her voice came hollowly out of the dim twilight.

'Stay with you? In your house?'

'Yes.'

'You mean, you'll take me away from here?'

'Yes, my dear.'

Suddenly she began to shake all over. It was frightening and very moving.

'Oh, do take me away! Please do. It's so awful, being here, and feeling so wicked.'

I came over to her and her hands fastened on my coat sleeve.

'I'm an awful coward. I didn't know what a coward I was.'

'It's all right, funny face,' I said. 'These things are a bit shattering. Come along.'

'Can we go at once? Without waiting a minute?'

'Well, you'll have to put a few things together, I suppose.'

'What sort of things? Why?'

'My dear girl,' I said. 'We can provide you with a bed and a bath and the rest of it, but I'm damned if I'll lend you my toothbrush.'

She gave a very faint weak little laugh.

'I see. I think I'm stupid today. You mustn't mind. I'll go and pack some things. You – you won't go away? You'll wait for me?'

'I'll be on the mat.'

'Thank you. Thank you very much. I'm sorry I'm so stupid. But you see it's rather dreadful when your mother dies.'

'I know,' I said.

I gave her a friendly pat on the back and she flashed me a grateful look and disappeared into a bedroom. I went on downstairs.

'I found Megan,' I said. 'She's coming.'

'Oh now, that *is* a good thing,' exclaimed Elsie Holland. 'It will take her out of herself. She's rather a nervy girl, you know. Difficult. It will be a great relief to feel I haven't got her on my mind as well as everything else. It's very kind of you, Miss Burton. I hope she won't be a nuisance. Oh dear, there's the telephone. I must go and answer it. Mr Symmington isn't fit.'

She hurried out of the room. Joanna said:

'Quite the ministering angel!'

'You said that rather nastily,' I observed. 'She's a nice kind girl, and obviously most capable.'

'Most. And she knows it.'

'This is unworthy of you, Joanna,' I said.

'Meaning why shouldn't the girl do her stuff?'

'Exactly.'

'I never can stand seeing people pleased with themselves,' said Joanna. 'It arouses all my worst instincts. How did you find Megan?'

'Crouching in a darkened room looking rather like a stricken gazelle.'

'Poor kid. She was quite willing to come?'

'She leapt at it.'

A series of thuds out in the hall announced the descent of Megan and her suitcase. I went out and took it from her. Joanna, behind me, said urgently:

'Come on. I've already refused some nice hot tea twice.'

We went out to the car. It annoyed me that Joanna had to sling the suitcase in. I could get along with one stick now, but I couldn't do any athletic feats.

'Get in,' I said to Megan.

She got in, I followed her. Joanna started the car and we drove off.

We got to Little Furze and went into the drawing-room.

Megan dropped into a chair and burst into tears. She cried with the hearty fervour of a child – bawled, I think, is the right word. I left the room in search of a remedy. Joanna stood by feeling rather helpless, I think.

Presently I heard Megan say in a thick choked voice:

'I'm sorry for doing this. It seems idiotic.'

Joanna said kindly, 'Not at all. Have another handkerchief.'

I gather she supplied the necessary article. I re-entered the room and handed Megan a brimming glass.

'What is it?'

'A cocktail,' I said.

'Is it? Is it really?' Megan's tears were instantly dried. 'I've never drunk a cocktail.'

'Everything has to have a beginning,' I said.

Megan sipped her drink gingerly, then a beaming smile spread over her face, she tilted her head back and gulped it down at a draught.

'It's lovely,' she said. 'Can I have another?'

'No,' I said.

'Why not?'

'In about ten minutes you'll probably know.'

'Oh!'

Megan transferred her attention to Joanna.

'I really am awfully sorry for having made such a nuisance of myself howling away like that. I can't think why. It seems awfully silly when I'm so glad to be here.'

'That's all right,' said Joanna. 'We're very pleased to have you.'

'You can't be, really. It's just kindness on your part. But I am grateful.'

'Please don't be grateful,' said Joanna. 'It will embarrass me. I was speaking the truth when I said we should be glad to have you. Jerry and I have used up all our conversation. We can't think of any more things to say to each other.'

'But now,' I said, 'we shall be able to have all sorts of interesting discussions – about Goneril and Regan and things like that.'

Megan's face lit up.

'I've been thinking about that, and I think I know the answer. It was because that awful old father of theirs always insisted on such a lot of sucking up. When you've always got to be saying thank you and how kind and all the rest of it, it would make you go a bit rotten and queer inside, and you'd just long to be able to be beastly for a change – and when you got the chance, you'd probably find it went to your head and you'd go too far. Old Lear was pretty awful, wasn't he? I mean, he did deserve the snub Cordelia gave him.'

'I can see,' I said, 'that we are going to have many interesting discussions about Shakespeare.'

'I can see you two are going to be very highbrow,' said Joanna. 'I'm afraid I always find Shakespeare terribly dreary. All those long scenes where everybody is drunk and it's supposed to be funny.'

'Talking of drink,' I said turning to Megan. 'How are you feeling?'

'Quite all right, thank you.'

'Not at all giddy? You don't see two of Joanna or anything like that?'

'No. I just feel as though I'd like to talk rather a lot.'

'Splendid,' I said. 'Obviously you are one of our natural drinkers. That is to say, if that really was your first cocktail.'

'Oh, it was.'

'A good strong head is an asset to any human being,' I said.

Joanna took Megan upstairs to unpack.

Partridge came in, looking sour, and said she had made two cup custards for lunch and what should she do about it?

CHAPTER 6

The inquest was held three days later. It was all done as decorously as possible, but there was a large attendance and, as Joanna observed, the beady bonnets were wagging.

The time of Mrs Symmington's death was put at between three and four o'clock. She was alone in the house, Symmington was at his office, the maids were having their day out, Elsie Holland and the children were out walking and Megan had gone for a bicycle ride.

The letter must have come by the afternoon post. Mrs Symmington must have taken it out of the box, read it – and then in a state of agitation she had gone to the potting shed, fetched some of the cyanide kept there for taking wasps' nests, dissolved it in water and drunk it after writing those last agitated words, 'I can't go on . . .'

Owen Griffith gave medical evidence and stressed the view he had outlined to us of Mrs Symmington's nervous condition and poor stamina. The coroner was suave and discreet. He spoke with bitter condemnation of people who write those despicable things, anonymous letters. Whoever had written that wicked and lying letter was morally guilty of murder, he said. He hoped the police would soon discover the culprit and take action against him or her. Such a dastardly and malicious piece of spite deserved to be punished with the utmost rigour of the law. Directed by him, the jury brought in the inevitable verdict. Suicide whilst temporarily insane.

The coroner had done his best – Owen Griffith also, but afterwards, jammed in the crowd of eager village women, I heard the same hateful sibilant whisper I had begun to know so well, 'No smoke without fire, that's what *I* say!' 'Must 'a been something in it for certain sure. She wouldn't never have done it otherwise . . .'

Just for a moment I hated Lymstock and its narrow boundaries, and its gossiping whispering women.

II

It is difficult to remember things in their exact chronological order. The next landmark of importance, of course, was Superintendent Nash's visit. But it was before that, I think, that we received calls from various members of the community, each of which was interesting in its way and shed some light on the characters and personalities of the people involved.

Aimée Griffith came on the morning after the inquest. She was looking, as always, radiant with health and vigour and succeeded, also as usual, in putting my back up almost immediately. Joanna and Megan were out, so I did the honours.

'Good morning,' said Miss Griffith. 'I hear you've got Megan Hunter here?'

'We have.'

'Very good of you, I'm sure. It must be rather a nuisance to you. I came up to say she can come to us if you like. I dare say I can find ways of making her useful about the house.'

I looked at Aimée Griffith with a good deal of distaste.

'How good of you,' I said. 'But we like having her. She potters about quite happily.'

'I dare say. Much too fond of pottering, that child. Still, I suppose she can't help it, being practically half-witted.'

'I think she's rather an intelligent girl,' I said.

Aimée Griffith gave me a hard stare.

'First time I've ever heard anyone say that of her,' she remarked. 'Why, when you talk to her, she looks through you as though she doesn't understand what you are saying!'

'She probably just isn't interested,' I said.

'If so, she's extremely rude,' said Aimée Griffith.

'That may be. But not half-witted.'

Miss Griffith declared sharply:

'At best, it's wool-gathering. What Megan needs is good hard work – something to give her an interest in life. You've no idea what a difference that makes to a girl. I know a lot about girls. You'd be surprised at the difference even becoming a Guide makes to a girl. Megan's much too old to spend her time lounging about and doing nothing.'

'It's been rather difficult for her to do anything else so far,' I said. 'Mrs Symmington always seemed under the impression that Megan was about twelve years old.'

Miss Griffith snorted.

'I know. I had no patience with that attitude of hers. Of course she's dead now, poor woman, so one doesn't want to say much, but she was a perfect example of what I call the unintelligent domestic type. Bridge and gossip and her children – and even there that Holland girl did all the looking after them. I'm afraid I never thought very much of Mrs Symmington, although of course I never suspected the truth.'

'The truth?' I said sharply.

Miss Griffith flushed.

'I was terribly sorry for Dick Symmington its all having to come out as it did at the inquest,' she said. 'It was awful for him.'

'But surely you heard him say that there was not a word of truth in that letter – that he was quite sure of that?'

'Of course he *said* so. Quite right. A man's got to stick up for his wife. Dick would.' She paused and then explained:

'You see, I've known Dick Symmington a long time.'

I was a little surprised.

'Really?' I said. 'I understood from your brother that he only bought this practice a few years ago.'

'Oh yes, but Dick Symmington used to come and stay in our part of the world up north. I've known him for years.'

Women jump to conclusions that men do not. Nevertheless, the suddenly softened tone of Aimée Griffith's voice put, as our old nurse would have expressed it, ideas into my head.

I looked at Aimée curiously. She went on – still in that softened tone:

'I know Dick very well. . . . He's a proud man, and very reserved. But he's the sort of man who could be very jealous.'

'That would explain,' I said deliberately, 'why Mrs Symmington was afraid to show him or tell him about the letter. She was afraid that, being a jealous man, he might not believe her denials.'

Miss Griffith looked at me angrily and scornfully.

'Good Lord,' she said, 'do you think any woman would go and swallow a lot of cyanide of potassium for an accusation that wasn't true?'

'The coroner seemed to think it was possible. Your brother, too –'

Aimée interrupted me.

'Men are all alike. All for preserving the decencies. But you don't catch *me* believing that stuff. If an innocent woman gets some foul

anonymous letter, she laughs and chucks it away. That's what I –'
she paused suddenly, and then finished, 'would do.'

But I had noticed the pause. I was almost sure that what she had
been about to say was 'That's what I did.'

I decided to take the war into the enemy's country.

'I see,' I said pleasantly, 'so you've had one, too?'

Aimée Griffith was the type of woman who scorns to lie. She
paused a minute – flushed, then said:

'Well, yes. But I didn't let it worry me!'

'Nasty?' I enquired sympathetically, as a fellow-sufferer.

'Naturally. These things always are. The ravings of a lunatic. I
read a few words of it, realized what it was and chucked it straight
into the waste-paper basket.'

'You didn't think of taking it to the police?'

'Not then. Least said soonest mended – that's what I felt.'

An urge came over me to say solemnly: 'No smoke without fire!'
but I restrained myself. To avoid temptation I reverted to Megan.

'Have you any idea of Megan's financial position?' I asked. 'It's
not idle curiosity on my part. I wondered if it would actually be
necessary for her to earn her living.'

'I don't think it's strictly *necessary*. Her grandmother, her father's
mother, left her a small income, I believe. And in any case Dick
Symmington would always give her a home and provide for her,
even if her mother hasn't left her anything outright. No, it's the
principle of the thing.'

'What principle?'

'Work, Mr Burton. There's nothing like work, for men and
women. The one unforgivable sin is idleness.'

'Sir Edward Grey,' I said, 'afterwards our foreign minister, was
sent down from Oxford for incorrigible idleness. The Duke of
Wellington, I have heard, was both dull and inattentive at his books.
And has it ever occurred to you, Miss Griffith, that you would
probably not be able to take a good express train to London if little
Georgie Stephenson had been out with his youth movement instead
of lolling about, bored, in his mother's kitchen until the curious
behaviour of the kettle lid attracted the attention of his idle mind?'

Aimée merely snorted.

'It is a theory of mine,' I said, warming to my theme, 'that we owe
most of our great inventions and most of the achievements of genius
to idleness – either enforced or voluntary. The human mind prefers
to be spoon-fed with the thoughts of others, but deprived of such

nourishment it will reluctantly, begin to think for itself – and such thinking, remember, is original thinking and may have valuable results.

'Besides,' I went on, before Aimée could get in another sniff, 'there is the artistic side.'

I got up and took from my desk where it always accompanied me a photograph of my favourite Chinese picture. It represents an old man sitting beneath a tree playing cat's cradle with a piece of string on his fingers and toes.

'It was in the Chinese exhibition,' I said. 'It fascinated me. Allow me to introduce you. It is called "Old Man enjoying the Pleasures of Idleness."'

Aimée Griffith was unimpressed by my lovely picture. She said: 'Oh well, we all know what the Chinese are like!'

'It doesn't appeal to you?' I asked.

'Frankly, no. I'm not very interested in art, I'm afraid. Your attitude, Mr Burton, is typical of that of most men. You dislike the idea of women working – of their competing –'

I was taken aback. I had come up against the Feminist. Aimée was well away, her cheeks flushed.

'It is incredible to you that women should want a career. It was incredible to my parents. I was anxious to study for a doctor. They would not hear of paying the fees. But they paid them readily for Owen. Yet I should have made a far better doctor than my brother.'

'I'm sorry about that,' I said. 'It was tough on you. If one wants to do a thing –'

She went on quickly:

'Oh, I've got over it now. I've plenty of willpower. My life is busy and active. I'm one of the happiest people in Lymstock. Plenty to do. But I do go up in arms against the silly old-fashioned prejudice that women's place is always the home.'

'I'm sorry if I offended you,' I said. 'And that wasn't really my point. I don't see Megan in a domestic role at all.'

'No, poor child. She'll be a misfit anywhere, I'm afraid.' Aimée had calmed down. She was speaking quite normally again. 'Her father, you know –'

She paused and I said bluntly: 'I *don't* know. Everyone says "her father" and drops their voice, and that is that. What did the man *do*? Is he alive still?'

'I really don't know. And I'm rather vague myself, I'm afraid. But he was definitely a bad lot. Prison, I believe. And a streak of very strong abnormality. That's why it wouldn't surprise me if Megan was a bit "wanting."'

'Megan,' I said, 'is in full possession of her senses, and as I said before, I consider her an intelligent girl. My sister thinks so too. Joanna is very fond of her.'

Aimeé said:

'I'm afraid your sister must find it very dull down here.'

And as she said it, I learnt something else. Aimée Griffith disliked my sister. It was there in the smooth conventional tones of her voice.

'We've all wondered how you could both bear to bury yourselves in such an out-of-the-way spot.'

It was a question and I answered it.

'Doctor's orders. I was to come somewhere very quiet where nothing ever happened.' I paused and added, 'Not quite true of Lymstock now.'

'No, no, indeed.'

She sounded worried and got up to go. She said then:

'You know – it's got to be put a stop to – all this beastliness! We can't have it going on.'

'Aren't the police doing anything?'

'I suppose so. But I think we ought to take it in hand *ourselves*.'

'We're not as well equipped as they are.'

'Nonsense! We probably have far more sense and intelligence! A little determination is all that is needed.'

She said goodbye abruptly and went away.

When Joanna and Megan came back from their walk I showed Megan my Chinese picture. Her face lighted up. She said, 'It's heavenly, isn't it?'

'That *is* rather my opinion.'

Her forehead was crinkling in the way I knew so well.

'But it would be difficult, wouldn't it?'

'To be idle?'

'No, not to be idle – but to enjoy the pleasures of it. You'd have to be very old –'

She paused. I said: 'He *is* an old man.'

'I don't mean old that way. Not *age*. I mean old in – in . . .'

'You mean,' I said, 'that one would have to attain a very high state of civilization for the thing to present itself to you in that way – a fine point of sophistication? I think I shall complete your education, Megan, by reading to you one hundred poems translated from the Chinese.'

III

I met Symmington in the town later in the day.

'Is it quite all right for Megan to stay on with us for a bit?' I asked. 'It's company for Joanna – she's rather lonely sometimes with none of her own friends.'

'Oh – er – Megan? Oh yes, very good of you.'

I took a dislike to Symmington then which I never quite overcame. He had so obviously forgotten all about Megan. I wouldn't have minded if he had actively disliked the girl – a man may sometimes be jealous of a first husband's child – but he didn't dislike her, he just hardly noticed her. He felt towards her much as a man who doesn't care much for dogs would feel about a dog in the house. You notice it when you fall over it and swear at it, and you give it a vague pat sometimes when it presents itself to be patted. Symmington's complete indifference to his stepdaughter annoyed me very much.

I said, 'What are you planning to do with her?'

'With Megan?' He seemed rather startled. 'Well, she'll go on living at home. I mean, naturally, it is her home.'

My grandmother, of whom I had been very fond, used to sing old-fashioned songs to her guitar. One of them, I remembered, ended thus:

> *Oh maid, most dear, I am not here*
> *I have no place, no part,*
> *No dwelling more, by sea nor shore,*
> *But only in your heart.*

I went home humming it.

IV

Emily Barton came just after tea had been cleared away.

She wanted to talk about the garden. We talked garden for about half an hour. Then we turned back towards the house.

It was then that lowering her voice, she murmured:

'I do hope that that child – that she hasn't been too much *upset* by all this dreadful business?'

'Her mother's death, you mean?'

'That, of course. But I really meant, the – the unpleasantness *behind* it.'

I was curious. I wanted Miss Barton's reaction.

'What do you think about that? Was it true?'

'Oh, no, no, surely not. I'm quite sure that Mrs Symmington never – that he wasn't' – little Emily Barton was pink and confused – 'I mean it's quite untrue – although of course it may have been a judgement.'

'A judgement?' I said, staring.

Emily Barton was very pink, very Dresden china shepherdess-like.

'I cannot help feeling that all these dreadful letters, all the sorrow and pain they have caused, may have been sent for a *purpose*.'

'They were sent for a purpose, certainly,' I said grimly.

'No, no, Mr Burton, you misunderstand me. I'm not talking of the misguided creature who wrote them – someone quite abandoned that must be. I mean that they have been permitted – by Providence! To awaken us to a sense of our shortcomings.'

'Surely,' I said, 'the Almighty could choose a less unsavoury weapon.'

Miss Emily murmured that God moved in a mysterious way.

'No,' I said. 'There's too much tendency to attribute to God the evils that man does of his own free will. I might concede you the Devil. God doesn't really need to punish us, Miss Barton. We're so very busy punishing ourselves.'

'What I can't make out is *why* should anyone want to do such a thing?'

I shrugged my shoulders.

'A warped mentality.'

'It seems very sad.'

'It doesn't seem to me sad. It seems to me just damnable. And I don't apologize for the word. I mean just that.'

The pink had gone out of Miss Barton's cheeks. They were very white.

'But why, Mr Burton, *why*? What pleasure can anyone get out of it?'

'Nothing you and I can understand, thank goodness.'

Emily Barton lowered her voice.

'They say that *Mrs Cleat* – but I really cannot believe it.'

I shook my head. She went on in an agitated manner:

'Nothing of this kind has ever happened before – never in my memory. It has been such a happy little community. What would my dear mother have said? Well, one must be thankful that she has been spared.'

I thought from all I had heard that old Mrs Barton had been sufficiently tough to have taken anything, and would probably have enjoyed this sensation.

Emily went on:

'It distresses me deeply.'

'You've not – er – had anything yourself?'

She flushed crimson.

'Oh, no – oh, no, indeed. Oh! that would be dreadful.'

I apologized hastily, but she went away looking rather upset.

I went into the house. Joanna was standing by the drawing-room fire which she had just lit, for the evenings were still chilly.

She had an open letter in her hand.

She turned her head quickly as I entered.

'Jerry! I found this in the letter box – dropped in by hand. It begins, "You painted trollop . . ."'

'What else does it say?'

Joanna gave a wide grimace.

'Same old muck.'

She dropped it on to the fire. With a quick gesture that hurt my back I jerked it off again just before it caught.

'Don't,' I said. 'We may need it.'

'Need it?'

'For the police.'

V

Superintendent Nash came to see me the following morning. From the first moment I saw him I took a great liking to him. He was the best type of CID county superintendent. Tall, soldierly, with quiet reflective eyes and a straightforward unassuming manner.

He said: 'Good morning, Mr Burton, I expect you can guess what I've come to see you about.'

'Yes, I think so. This letter business.'

He nodded.

'I understand you had one of them?'

'Yes, soon after we got here.'

'What did it say exactly?'

I thought a minute, then conscientiously repeated the wording of the letter as closely as possible.

The superintendent listened with an immovable face, showing no signs of any kind of emotion. When I had finished, he said:

'I see. You didn't keep the letter, Mr Burton?'

'I'm sorry. I didn't. You see, I thought it was just an isolated instance of spite against newcomers to the place.'

The superintendent inclined his head comprehendingly.

He said briefly: 'A pity.'

'However,' I said, 'my sister got one yesterday. I just stopped her putting it in the fire.'

'Thank you, Mr Burton, that was thoughtful of you.'

I went across to my desk and unlocked the drawer in which I had put it. It was not, I thought, very suitable for Partridge's eyes. I gave it to Nash.

He read it through. Then he looked up and asked me:

'Is this the same in appearance as the last one?'

'I think so – as far as I can remember.'

'The same difference between the envelope and the text?'

'Yes,' I said. 'The envelope was typed. The letter itself had printed words pasted on to a sheet of paper.'

Nash nodded and put it in his pocket. Then he said:

'I wonder, Mr Burton, if you would mind coming down to the station with me? We could have a conference there and it would save a good deal of time and overlapping.'

'Certainly,' I said. 'You would like me to come now?'

'If you don't mind.'

There was a police car at the door. We drove down in it.

I said:

'Do you think you'll be able to get to the bottom of this?'

Nash nodded with easy confidence.

'Oh yes, we'll get to the bottom of it all right. It's a question of time and routine. They're slow, these cases, but they're pretty sure. It's a matter of narrowing things down.'

'Elimination?' I said.

'Yes. And general routine.'

'Watching post boxes, examining typewriters, fingerprints, all that?'

He smiled. 'As you say.'

At the police station I found Symmington and Griffith were

already there. I was introduced to a tall lantern-jawed man in plain clothes, Inspector Graves.

'Inspector Graves,' explained Nash, 'has come down from London to help us. He's an expert on anonymous letter cases.'

Inspector Graves smiled mournfully. I reflected that a life spent in the pursuit of anonymous letter writers must be singularly depressing. Inspector Graves, however, showed a kind of melancholy enthusiasm.

'They're all the same, these cases,' he said in a deep lugubrious voice like a depressed bloodhound. 'You'd be surprised. The wording of the letters and the things they say.'

'We had a case just on two years ago,' said Nash. 'Inspector Graves helped us then.'

Some of the letters, I saw, were spread out on the table in front of Graves. He had evidently been examining them.

'Difficulty is,' said Nash, 'to get hold of the letters. Either people put them in the fire, or they won't admit to having received anything of the kind. Stupid, you see, and afraid of being mixed up with the police. They're a backward lot here.'

'Still, we've got a fair amount to get on with,' said Graves. Nash took the letter I had given him from his pocket and tossed it over to Graves.

The latter glanced through it, laid it with the others and observed approvingly:

'Very nice – very nice indeed.'

It was not the way I should have chosen to describe the epistle in question, but experts, I suppose, have their own point of view. I was glad that that screed of vituperative and obscene abuse gave *somebody* pleasure.

'We've got enough, I think, to go on with,' said Inspector Graves, 'and I'll ask all you gentlemen, if you should get any more, to bring them along at once. Also, if you hear of someone else getting one – (you, in particular, doctor, among your patients) do your best to get them to come along here with them. I've got –' he sorted with deft fingers among his exhibits, 'one to Mr Symmington, received as far back as two months ago, one to Dr Griffith, one to Miss Ginch, one written to Mrs Mudge, the butcher's wife, one to Jennifer Clark, barmaid at the Three Crowns, the one received by Mrs Symmington, this one now to Miss Burton – oh yes, and one to the bank manager.'

'Quite a representative collection,' I remarked.

'And not one I couldn't match from other cases! This one here is as near as nothing to one written by that milliner woman. This one is the dead spit of an outbreak we had up in Northumberland – written by a schoolgirl, they were. I can tell you, gentlemen, I'd like to see something *new* sometimes, instead of the same old treadmill.'

'There is nothing new under the sun,' I murmured.

'Quite so, sir. You'd know that if you were in our profession.'

Nash sighed and said, 'Yes, indeed.'

Symmington asked:

'Have you come to any definite opinion as to the writer?'

Graves cleared his throat and delivered a small lecture.

'There are certain similarities shared by all these letters. I shall enumerate them, gentlemen, in case they suggest anything to your minds. The text of the letters is composed of words made up from individual letters cut out of a printed book. It's an old book, printed, I should say, about the year 1830. This has obviously been done to avoid the risk of recognition through handwriting which is, as most people know nowadays, a fairly easy matter ... the so-called disguising of a hand not amounting to much when faced with expert tests. There are no fingerprints on the letters and envelopes of a distinctive character. That is to say, they have been handled by the postal authorities, the recipient, and there are other stray fingerprints, but no set common to all, showing therefore that the person who put them together was careful to wear gloves. The envelopes are typewritten by a Windsor 7 machine, well worn, with the a and the t out of alignment. Most of them have been posted locally, or put in the box of a house by hand. It is therefore evident that they are of local provenance. They were written by a woman, and in my opinion a woman of middle age or over, and probably, though not certainly, unmarried.'

We maintained a respectful silence for a minute or two. Then I said:

'The typewriter's your best bet, isn't it? That oughtn't to be difficult in a little place like this.'

Inspector Graves shook his head sadly and said:

'That's where you're wrong, sir.'

'The typewriter,' said Superintendent Nash, 'is unfortunately too easy. It's an old one from Mr Symmington's office, given by him to the Women's Institute where, I may say, it's fairly easy of access. The ladies here all often go into the Institute.'

'Can't you tell something definite from the – er – the touch, don't you call it?'

Again Graves nodded.

'Yes, that can be done – but these envelopes have all been typed by someone using one finger.'

'Someone then unused to the typewriter?'

'No, I wouldn't say that. Someone, say, who can type but doesn't want us to know the fact.'

'Whoever writes these things has been very cunning,' I said slowly.

'She is, sir, she is,' said Graves. 'Up to every trick of the trade.'

'I shouldn't have thought one of these bucolic women down here would have had the brains,' I said.

Graves coughed.

'I haven't made myself plain, I'm afraid. Those letters were written by an educated woman.'

'What, by a lady?'

The word slipped out involuntarily. I hadn't used the term 'lady' for years. But now it came automatically to my lips, re-echoed from days long ago, and my grandmother's faint unconsciously arrogant voice saying, 'Of course, she isn't a *lady*, dear.'

Nash understood at once. The word lady still meant something to him.

'Not necessarily a lady,' he said. 'But certainly not a village woman. They're mostly pretty illiterate down here, can't spell, and certainly can't express themselves with fluency.'

I was silent, for I had had a shock. The community was so small. Unconsciously I had visualized the writer of the letters as a Mrs Cleat or her like, some spiteful, cunning half-wit.

Symmington put my thoughts into words. He said sharply:

'But that narrows it down to about half a dozen to a dozen people in the whole place!'

'That's right.'

'I can't believe it.'

Then, with a slight effort, and looking straight in front of him as though the mere sound of his own words was distasteful, he said:

'You have heard what I stated at the inquest. In case you may have thought that that statement was actuated by a desire to protect my wife's memory, I should like to repeat now that I am firmly convinced that the subject matter of the letter my wife received was absolutely false. I *know* it was false. My wife was a very sensitive woman, and – er – well, you might call it *prudish* in some respects. Such a letter would have been a great shock to her, and she was in poor health.'

Graves responded instantly.

'That's quite likely to be right, sir. None of these letters shows any signs of intimate knowledge. They're just blind accusations. There's been no attempt to blackmail. And there doesn't seem to be any religious bias – such as we sometimes get. It's just sex and spite! And that's going to give us quite a good pointer towards the writer.'

Symmington got up. Dry and unemotional as the man was, his lips were trembling.

'I hope you find the devil who writes these soon. She murdered my wife as surely as if she'd put a knife into her.' He paused. 'How does she feel now, I wonder?'

He went out, leaving that question unanswered.

'How does she feel, Griffith?' I asked. It seemed to me the answer was in his province.

'God knows. Remorseful, perhaps. On the other hand, it may be that she's enjoying her power. Mrs Symmington's death may have fed her mania.'

'I hope not,' I said, with a slight shiver. 'Because if so, she'll –'

I hesitated and Nash finished the sentence for me.

'She'll try it again? That, Mr Burton, would be the best thing that could happen, for us. The pitcher goes to the well once too often, remember.'

'She'd be mad to go on with it,' I exclaimed.

'She'll go on,' said Graves. 'They always do. It's a vice, you know, they can't let it alone.'

I shook my head with a shudder. I asked if they needed me any longer, I wanted to get out into the air. The atmosphere seemed tinged with evil.

'There's nothing more, Mr Burton,' said Nash. 'Only keep your eyes open, and do as much propaganda as you can – that is to say, urge on everyone that they've got to report any letter they receive.'

I nodded.

'I should think everyone in the place has had one of the foul things by now,' I said.

'I wonder,' said Graves. He put his sad head a little on one side and asked, 'You don't know, definitely, of anyone who *hasn't* had a letter?'

'What an extraordinary question! The population at large isn't likely to take me into their confidence.'

'No, no, Mr Burton, I didn't mean that. I just wondered if you knew of any one person who quite definitely, to your certain knowledge, has not received an anonymous letter.'

'Well, as a matter of fact,' I hesitated, 'I do, in a way.'

And I repeated my conversation with Emily Barton and what she had said.

Graves received the information with a wooden face and said: 'Well, that may come in useful. I'll note it down.'

I went out into the afternoon sunshine with Owen Griffith. Once in the street, I swore aloud.

'What kind of place is this for a man to come to lie in the sun and heal his wounds? It's full of festering poison, this place, and it looks as peaceful and as innocent as the Garden of Eden.'

'Even there,' said Owen dryly, 'there was one serpent.'

'Look here, Griffith, do they know anything? Have they got any idea?'

'I don't know. They've got a wonderful technique, the police. They're seemingly so frank, and they tell you nothing.'

'Yes. Nash is a nice fellow.'

'And a very capable one.'

'If anyone's batty in this place, *you* ought to know it,' I said accusingly.

Griffith shook his head. He looked discouraged. But he looked more than that – he looked worried. I wondered if he had an inkling of some kind.

We had been walking along the High Street. I stopped at the door of the house agents.

'I believe my second instalment of rent is due – in advance. I've got a good mind to pay it and clear out with Joanna right away. Forfeit the rest of the tenancy.'

'Don't go,' said Owen.

'Why not?'

He didn't answer. He said slowly after a minute or two.

'After all – I dare say you're right. Lymstock isn't healthy just now. It might – it might harm you or – or your sister.'

'Nothing harms Joanna,' I said. 'She's tough. I'm the weakly one. Somehow this business makes me sick.'

'It makes *me* sick,' said Owen.

I pushed the door of the house agents half-open.

'But I shan't go,' I said. 'Vulgar curiosity is stronger than pusillanimity. I want to know the solution.'

I went in.

A woman who was typing got up and came towards me. She had frizzy hair and simpered, but I found her more intelligent than the spectacled youth who had previously held sway in the outer office.

A minute or two later something familiar about her penetrated through to my consciousness. It was Miss Ginch, lately Symmington's lady clerk. I commented on the fact.

'You were with Galbraith and Symmington, weren't you?' I said.

'Yes. Yes, indeed. But I thought it was better to leave. This is quite a good post, though not quite so well paid. But there are things that are more valuable than money, don't you think so?'

'Undoubtedly,' I said.

'Those awful letters,' breathed Miss Ginch in a sibilant whisper. 'I got a dreadful one. About me and Mr Symmington – oh, terrible it was, saying the most *awful* things! I knew my duty and I took it to the police, though of course it wasn't exactly *pleasant* for me, was it?'

'No, no, most unpleasant.'

'But they thanked me and said I had done quite right. But I felt that, after that, if people were talking – and evidently that *must* have been, or where did the writer get the idea from? – then I must avoid even the appearance of evil, though there has never been anything at all *wrong* between me and Mr Symmington.'

I felt rather embarrassed.

'No, no, of course not.'

'But people have such evil minds. Yes, alas, such evil minds!'

Nervously trying to avoid it, I nevertheless met her eye, and I make a most unpleasant discovery.

Miss Ginch was thoroughly enjoying herself.

Already once today I had come across someone who reacted pleasurably to anonymous letters. Inspector Graves's enthusiasm was professional. Miss Ginch's enjoyment I found merely suggestive and disgusting.

An idea flashed across my startled mind.

Had Miss Ginch written these letters herself?

CHAPTER 7

When I got home I found Mrs Dane Calthrop sitting talking to Joanna. She looked, I thought, grey and ill.

'This has been a terrible shock to me, Mr Burton,' she said. 'Poor thing, poor thing.'

'Yes,' I said. 'It's awful to think of someone being driven to the stage of taking their own life.'

'Oh, you mean Mrs Symmington?'

'Didn't you?'

Mrs Dane Calthrop shook her head.

'Of course one is sorry for her, but it would have been bound to happen anyway, wouldn't it?'

'Would it?' said Joanna dryly.

Mrs Dane Calthrop turned to her.

'Oh, I think so, dear. If suicide is your idea of escape from trouble then it doesn't very much matter what the trouble is. Whenever some very unpleasant shock had to be faced, she'd have done the same thing. What it really comes down to is that she was that kind of woman. Not that one would have guessed it. She always seemed to me a selfish rather stupid woman, with a good firm hold on life. Not the kind to panic, you would think – but I'm beginning to realize how little I really know about anyone.'

'I'm still curious as to whom you meant when you said "Poor thing",' I remarked.

She stared at me.

'The woman who wrote the letters, of course.'

'I don't think,' I said dryly, 'I shall waste sympathy on her.'

Mrs Dane Calthrop leaned forward. She laid a hand on my knee.

'But don't you realize – can't you *feel*? Use your imagination. Think how desperately, violently unhappy anyone must be to sit down and write these things. How lonely, how cut off from human kind. Poisoned through and through, with a dark stream of poison that finds its outlet in this way. That's why I feel so self-reproachful. Somebody in this town has been racked with that terrible unhappiness, and I've had no idea of it. I should have had. You can't interfere with actions – I never do. But that black inward unhappiness – like a septic arm physically, all black and swollen. If you could cut it and let the poison out it would flow away harmlessly. Yes, poor soul, poor soul.'

She got up to go.

I did not feel like agreeing with her. I had no sympathy for our anonymous letter writer whatsoever. But I did ask curiously:

'Have you any idea at all, Mrs Calthrop, who this woman is?'

She turned her fine perplexed eyes on me.

'Well, I can guess,' she said. 'But then I might be wrong, mightn't I?'

She went swiftly out through the door, popping her head back to ask:

'Do tell me, why have you never married, Mr Burton?'

In anyone else it would have been impertinence, but with Mrs Dane Calthrop you felt that the idea had suddenly come into her head and she had really wanted to know.

'Shall we say,' I said, rallying, 'that I have never met the right woman?'

'We can say so,' said Mrs Dane Calthrop, 'but it wouldn't be a very good answer, because so many men have obviously married the wrong woman.'

This time she really departed.

Joanna said:

'You know I really do think she's mad. But I like her. The people in the village here are afraid of her.'

'So am I, a little.'

'Because you never know what's coming next?'

'Yes. And there's a careless brilliancy about her guesses.'

Joanna said slowly: 'Do you really think whoever wrote these letters is very unhappy?'

'I don't know what the damned hag is thinking or feeling! And I don't care. It's her victims I'm sorry for.'

It seems odd to me now that in our speculations about Poison Pen's frame of mind, we missed the most obvious one. Griffith had pictured her as possibly exultant. I had envisaged her as remorseful – appalled by the result of her handiwork. Mrs Dane Calthrop had seen her as suffering.

Yet the obvious, the inevitable reaction we did not consider – or perhaps I should say, I did not consider. That reaction was Fear.

For with the death of Mrs Symmington, the letters had passed out of one category into another. I don't know what the legal position was – Symmington knew, I suppose, but it was clear that with a death resulting, the position of the writer of the letters was much more serious. There could now be no question of passing it off as a joke if the identity of the writer was discovered. The police were active, a Scotland Yard expert called in. It was vital now for the anonymous author to remain anonymous.

And granted that Fear was the principal reaction, other things followed. Those possibilities also I was blind to. Yet surely they should have been obvious.

II

Joanna and I came down rather late to breakfast the next morning. That is to say, late by the standards of Lymstock. It was nine-thirty, an hour at which, in London, Joanna was just unclosing an eye-lid, and mine would probably be still tight shut. However when Partridge had said 'Breakfast at half-past eight, or nine o'clock?' neither Joanna nor I had had the nerve to suggest a later hour.

To my annoyance, Aimée Griffith was standing on the doorstep talking to Megan.

She gave tongue with her usual heartiness at the sight of us.

'Hallo, there, slackers! I've been up for hours.'

That, of course, was her own business. A doctor, no doubt, has to have early breakfast, and a dutiful sister is there to pour out his tea, or coffee. But it is no excuse for coming and butting in on one's more somnolent neighbours. Nine-thirty is not the time for a morning call.

Megan slipped back into the house and into the dining-room, where I gathered she had been interrupted in her breakfast.

'I said I wouldn't come in,' said Aimée Griffith – though why it is more of a merit to force people to come and speak to you on the doorstep, than to talk to them inside the house I do not know. 'Just wanted to ask Miss Burton if she'd any vegetables to spare for our Red Cross stall on the main road. If so, I'd get Owen to call for them in the car.'

'You're out and about very early,' I said.

'The early birds catches the worm,' said Aimée. 'You have a better chance of finding people in this time of the day. I'm off to Mr Pye's next. Got to go over to Brenton this afternoon. Guides.'

'Your energy makes me quite tired,' I said, and at that moment the telephone rang and I retired to the back of the hall to answer it, leaving Joanna murmuring rather doubtfully something about rhubarb and french beans and exposing her ignorance of the vegetable garden.

'Yes?' I said into the telephone mouthpiece.

A confused noise of deep breathing came from the other end of the wire and a doubtful female voice said 'Oh!'

'Yes?' I said again encouragingly.

'Oh,' said the voice again, and then it enquired adenoidally, 'Is that – what I mean – is that Little Furze?'

'This is Little Furze.'

'Oh!' This was clearly a stock beginning to every sentence. The voice enquired cautiously, 'Could I speak to Miss Partridge just a minute?'

'Certainly,' I said. 'Who shall I say?'

'Oh. Tell her it's Agnes, would you? Agnes Waddle.'

'Agnes Waddle?'

'That's right.'

Resisting the temptation to say, 'Donald Duck to you,' I put down the telephone receiver and called up the stairs to where I could hear the sound of Partridge's activities overhead.

'Partridge. Partridge.'

Partridge appeared at the head of the stairs, a long mop in one hand, and a look of 'What is it *now*?' clearly discernible behind her invariably respectful manner.

'Yes, sir?'

'Agnes Waddle wants to speak to you on the telephone.'

'I beg your pardon, sir?'

I raised my voice. 'Agnes Waddle.'

I have spelt the name as it presented itself to my mind. But I will now spell it as it was actually written.

'Agnes Woddell – whatever can she want now?'

Very much put out of countenance Partridge relinquished her mop and rustled down the stairs, her print dress crackling with agitation.

I beat an unobtrusive retreat into the dining-room where Megan was wolfing down kidneys and bacon. Megan, unlike Aimée Griffith, was displaying no 'glorious morning face.' In fact she replied very gruffly to my morning salutations and continued to eat in silence.

I opened the morning paper and a minute or two later Joanna entered looking somewhat shattered.

'Whew!' she said. 'I'm so tired. And I think I've exposed my utter ignorance of what grows when. Aren't there runner beans this time of year?'

'August,' said Megan.

'Well, one has them any time in London,' said Joanna defensively.

'Tins, sweet fool,' I said. 'And cold storage on ships from the far-flung limits of the empire.'

'Like ivory, apes and peacocks?' asked Joanna.

'Exactly.'

'I'd rather have peacocks,' said Joanna thoughtfully.

'I'd like a monkey of my own as a pet,' said Megan.

Meditatively peeling an orange, Joanna said:

'I wonder what it would feel like to be Aimée Griffith, all bursting with health and vigour and enjoyment of life. Do you think she's ever tired, or depressed, or – or wistful?'

I said I was quite certain Aimée Griffith was never wistful, and followed Megan out of the open french window on to the veranda.

Standing there, filling my pipe, I heard Partridge enter the dining-room from the hall and heard her voice say grimly:

'Can I speak to you a minute, miss?'

'Dear me,' I thought. 'I hope Partridge isn't going to give notice. Emily Barton will be very annoyed with us if so.'

Partridge went on: 'I must apologize, miss, for being rung up on the telephone. That is to say, the young person who did so should have known better. I have never been in the habit of using the telephone or of permitting my friends to ring me up on it, and I'm very sorry indeed that it should have occurred, and the master taking the call and everything.'

'Why, that's quite all right, Partridge,' said Joanna soothingly, 'why shouldn't your friends use the phone if they want to speak to you?'

Partridge's face, I could feel, though I could not see it, was more dour than ever as she replied coldly:

'It is not the kind of thing that has ever bèen done in this house. Miss Emily would never permit it. As I say, I am sorry it occurred, but Agnes Woddell the girl who did it was upset and she's young too, and doesn't know what's fitting in a gentleman's house.'

'That's one for you, Joanna,' I thought gleefully.

'This Agnes who rung me up, miss,' went on Partridge, 'she used to be in service here under me. Sixteen she was, then, and come straight from the orphanage. And you see, not having a home, or a mother or any relations to advise her, she's been in the habit of coming to me. I can tell her what's what, you see.'

'Yes?' said Joanna and waited. Clearly there was more to follow.

'So I am taking the liberty of asking you, miss, if you would allow Agnes to come here to tea this afternoon in the kitchen. It's her day out, you see, and she's got something on her mind she wants to consult me about. I wouldn't dream of suggesting such a thing in the usual way.'

Joanna said bewildered:

'But why shouldn't you have anyone to tea with you?'

Partridge drew herself up at this, so Joanna said afterwards and really looked most formidable, as she replied:

'It has never been the custom of This House, miss. Old Mrs Barton never allowed visitors in the kitchen, excepting as it should be our own day out, in which case we were allowed to entertain friends here instead of going out, but otherwise, on ordinary days, no. And Miss Emily she keeps to the old ways.'

Joanna is very nice to servants and most of them like her but she has never cut any ice with Partridge.

'It's no good, my girl,' I said when Partridge had gone and Joanna had joined me outside. 'Your sympathy and leniency are not appreciated. The good old overbearing ways for Partridge and things done the way they should be done in a gentleman's house.'

'I never heard of such tyranny as not allowing them to have their friends to see them,' said Joanna. 'It's all very well, Jerry, but they can't *like* being treated like black slaves.'

'Evidently they do,' I said. 'At least the Partridges of this world do.'

'I can't imagine why she doesn't like me. Most people do.'

'She probably despises you as an inadequate house-keeper. You never draw your hand across a shelf and examine it for traces of dust. You don't look under the mats. You don't ask what happened to the remains of the chocolate soufflé, and you never order a nice bread pudding.'

'Ugh!' said Joanna.

She went on sadly. 'I'm a failure all round today. Despised by our Aimée for ignorance of the vegetable kingdom. Snubbed by Partridge for being a human being. I shall now go out into the garden and eat worms.'

'Megan's there already,' I said.

For Megan had wandered away a few minutes previously and was now standing aimlessly in the middle of a patch of lawn looking not unlike a meditative bird waiting for nourishment.

She came back, however, towards us and said abruptly:

'I say, I must go home today.'

'What?' I was dismayed.

She went on, flushing, but speaking with nervous determination.

'It's been awfully good of you having me and I expect I've been a fearful nuisance, but I have enjoyed it awfully, only now I must go back, because after all, well, it's my home and one can't stay away for ever, so I think I'll go this morning.'

Both Joanna and I tried to make her change her mind, but she was quite adamant, and finally Joanna got out the car and Megan went upstairs and came down a few minutes later with her belongings packed up again.

The only person pleased seemed to be Partridge, who had almost a smile on her grim face. She had never liked Megan much.

I was standing in the middle of the lawn when Joanna returned.

She asked me if I thought I was a sundial.

'Why?'

'Standing there like a garden ornament. Only one couldn't put on you the motto of only marking the sunny hours. You looked like thunder!'

'I'm out of humour. First Aimée Griffith – ("Gracious!" murmured Joanna in parenthesis, "I must speak about those vegetables!") and then Megan beetling off. I'd thought of taking her for a walk up to Legge Tor.'

'With a collar and lead, I suppose,' said Joanna.

'What?'

Joanna repeated loudly and clearly as she moved off round the corner of the house to the kitchen garden:

'I said, "With a collar and lead, I suppose?" Master's lost his dog, that's what's the matter with you!'

III

I was annoyed, I must confess, at the abrupt way in which Megan had left us. Perhaps she had suddenly got bored with us.

After all, it wasn't a very amusing life for a girl. At home she'd got the kids and Elsie Holland.

I heard Joanna returning and hastily moved in case she should make more rude remarks about sundials.

Owen Griffith called in his car just before lunchtime, and the gardener was waiting for him with the necessary garden produce.

Whilst old Adams was stowing it in the car I brought Owen indoors for a drink. He wouldn't stay to lunch.

When I came in with the sherry I found Joanna had begun doing her stuff.

No signs of animosity now. She was curled up in the corner of the sofa and was positively purring, asking Owen questions about his work, if he liked being a GP, if he wouldn't rather have specialized? She thought doctoring was one of the most fascinating things in the world.

Say what you will of her, Joanna is a lovely, a heaven-born listener. And after listening to so many would-be geniuses telling her how they had been unappreciated, listening to Owen Griffith was easy money. By the time we had got to the third glass of sherry, Griffith was telling her about some obscure reaction or lesion in such scientific terms that nobody could have understood a word of it except a fellow medico.

Joanna was looking intelligent and deeply interested.

I felt a moment's qualm. It was really too bad of Joanna. Griffith was too good a chap to be played fast and loose with. Women really were devils.

Then I caught a sideways view of Griffith, his long purposeful chin and the grim set of his lips, and I was not so sure that Joanna was going to have it her own way after all. And anyway, a man has no business to let himself be made a fool of by a woman. It's his own lookout if he does.

Then Joanna said:

'Do change your mind and stay to lunch with us, Dr Griffith,' and Griffith flushed a little and said he would, only his sister would be expecting him back –

'We'll ring her up and explain,' said Joanna quickly and went out into the hall and did so.

I thought Griffith looked a little uneasy, and it crossed my mind that he was probably a little afraid of his sister.

Joanna came back smiling and said that that was all right.

And Owen Griffith stayed to lunch and seemed to enjoy himself.

We talked about books and plays and world politics, and about music and painting and modern architecture.

We didn't talk about Lymstock at all, or about anonymous letters, or Mrs Symmington's suicide.

We got right away from everything, and I think Owen Griffith was happy. His dark sad face lighted up, and he revealed an interesting mind.

When he had gone I said to Joanna:

'That fellow's too good for your tricks.'

Joanna said:

'That's what you say! You men all stick together!'

'Why are you out after his hide, Joanna? Wounded vanity?'

'Perhaps,' said my sister.

IV

That afternoon we were to go to tea with Miss Emily Barton at her rooms in the village.

We strolled down there on foot, for I felt strong enough now to manage the hill back again.

We must actually have allowed too much time and got there early, for the door was opened to us by a tall rawboned fierce-looking woman who told us that Miss Barton wasn't in yet.

'But she's expecting you, I know, so if you'll come up and wait, please.'

This was evidently Faithful Florence.

We followed her up the stairs and she threw open a door and showed us into what was quite a comfortable sitting-room, though perhaps a little over-furnished. Some of the things, I suspected, had come from Little Furze.

The woman was clearly proud of her room.

'It's nice, isn't it?' she demanded.

'Very nice,' said Joanna warmly.

'I make her as comfortable as I can. Not that I can do for her as I'd like to and in the way she ought to have. She ought to be in her own house, properly, not turned out into rooms.'

Florence, who was clearly a dragon, looked from one to the other of us reproachfully. It was not, I felt, our lucky day. Joanna had been ticked off by Aimée Griffith and Partridge and now we were both being ticked off by the dragon Florence.

'Parlourmaid I was for fifteen years there,' she added.

Joanna, goaded by injustice, said:

'Well, Miss Barton wanted to let the house. She put it down at the house agents.'

'Forced to it,' said Florence. 'And she living so frugal and careful. But even then, the government can't leave her alone! Has to have its pound of flesh just the same.'

I shook my head sadly.

'Plenty of money there was in the old lady's time,' said Florence. 'And then they all died off one by one, poor dears. Miss Emily nursing of them one after the other. Wore herself out she did, and always so patient and uncomplaining. But it told on her, and then to have worry about money on top of it all! Shares not bringing it what they used to, so she says, and why not, I should like to know? They ought to be ashamed of themselves. Doing down a lady like her who's got no head for figures and can't keep up to their tricks.'

'Practically everyone has been hit that way,' I said, but Florence remained unsoftened.

'It's all right for some as can look after themselves, but not for *her*. She needs looking after, and as long as she's with me I'm going to see no one imposes on her or upsets her in any way. I'd do anything for Miss Emily.'

And glaring at us for some moments in order to drive that point thoroughly home, the indomitable Florence left the room, carefully shutting the door behind her.

'Do you feel like a blood-sucker, Jerry?' enquired Joanna. 'Because I do. What's the matter with us?'

'We don't seem to be going down very well,' I said. 'Megan gets tired of us, Partridge disapproves of you, faithful Florence disapproves of both of us.'

Joanna murmured: 'I wonder why Megan *did* leave?'

'She got bored.'

'I don't think she did at all. I wonder – do you think, Jerry, it could have been something that Aimée Griffith said?'

'You mean this morning, when they were talking on the doorstep.'

'Yes. There wasn't much time, of course, but –'

I finished the sentence.

'But that woman's got the tread of a cow elephant! She might have –'

The door opened and Miss Emily came in. She was pink and a

little out of breath and seemed excited. Her eyes were very blue and shining.

She chirruped at us in quite a distracted manner.

'Oh dear, I'm so sorry I'm late. Just doing a little shopping in the town, and the cakes at the Blue Rose didn't seem to me quite fresh, so I went on to Mrs Lygon's. I always like to get my cakes the last thing, then one gets the newest batch just out of the oven, and one isn't put off with the day before's. But I am so distressed to have kept you waiting – really unpardonable –'

Joanna cut in.

'It's our fault, Miss Barton. We're early. We walked down and Jerry strides along so fast now that we arrive everywhere too soon.'

'Never too soon, dear. Don't say that. One cannot have too much of a good thing, you know.'

And the old lady patted Joanna affectionately on the shoulder.

Joanna brightened up. At last, so it seemed, she was being a success. Emily Barton extended her smile to include me, but with a slight timidity in it, rather as one might approach a man-eating tiger guaranteed for the moment harmless.

'It's very good of you to come to such a feminine meal as tea, Mr Burton.'

Emily Barton, I think, has a mental picture of men as interminably consuming whiskies and sodas and smoking cigars, and in the intervals dropping out to do a few seductions of village maidens, or to conduct a liaison with a married woman.

When I said this to Joanna later, she replied that it was probably wishful thinking, that Emily Barton would have liked to come across such a man, but alas, had never done so.

In the meantime Miss Emily was fussing round the room, arranging Joanna and myself with little tables, and carefully providing ashtrays, and a minute later the door opened and Florence came in bearing a tray of tea with some fine Crown Derby cups on it which I gathered Miss Emily had brought with her. The tea was china and delicious and there were plates of sandwiches and thin bread and butter, and a quantity of little cakes.

Florence was beaming now, and looked at Miss Emily with a kind of maternal pleasure, as at a favourite child enjoying a doll's tea-party.

Joanna and I ate far more than we wanted to, our hostess pressed us so earnestly. The little lady was clearly enjoying her tea party and I perceived that, to Emily Barton, Joanna and I were a big adventure, two people from the mysterious world of London and sophistication. Miss Barton spoke warmly of Dr Griffith, his kindness and his cleverness as a doctor. Mr Symmington, too, was a very clever lawyer, and had helped Miss Barton to get some money back from the income tax which she would never have known about. He was so nice to his children, too, devoted to them and to his wife – she caught herself up. 'Poor Mrs Symmington, it's so dreadfully sad, with those young children left motherless. Never, perhaps, a very strong woman – and her health had been bad of late. A brain storm, that is what it must have been. I read about such a thing in the paper. People really do not know what they are doing under those circumstances. And she can't have known what she was doing or else she would have remembered Mr Symmington and the children.'

'That anonymous letter must have shaken her up very badly,' said Joanna.

Miss Barton flushed. She said, with a tinge of reproof in her voice:

'Not a very nice thing to discuss, do you think, dear? I know there have been – er – letters, but we won't talk about them. Nasty things. I think they are better just ignored.'

Well, Miss Barton might be able to ignore them, but for some people it wasn't so easy. However, I obediently changed the subject and we discussed Aimée Griffith.

'Wonderful, quite wonderful,' said Emily Barton. 'Her energy and her organizing powers are really splendid. She's so good with girls too. And she's so practical and up-to-date in every way. She really runs this place. And absolutely devoted to her brother. It's very nice to see such devotion between brother and sister.'

'Doesn't he ever find her a little overwhelming?' asked Joanna.

Emily Barton stared at her in a startled fashion.

'She has sacrificed a great deal for his sake,' she said with a touch of reproachful dignity.

I saw a touch of Oh Yeah! in Joanna's eyes and hastened to divert the conversation to Mr Pye.

Emily Barton was a little dubious about Mr Pye.

All she could say was, repeated rather doubtfully, that he was very kind – yes, very kind. Very well off, too, and most generous. He had very strange visitors sometimes, but then, of course, he had travelled a lot.

We agreed that travel not only broadened the mind, but occasionally resulted in the forming of strange acquaintances.

'I have often wished myself, to go on a cruise,' said Emily Barton wistfully. 'One reads about them in the papers and they sound so attractive.'

'Why don't you go?' asked Joanna.

This turning of a dream into a reality seemed to alarm Miss Emily. 'Oh, no, no, that would be *quite* impossible.'

'But why? They're fairly cheap.'

'Oh, it's not only the expense. But I shouldn't like to go alone. Travelling alone would look very peculiar, don't you think?'

'No,' said Joanna.

Miss Emily looked at her doubtfully.

'And I don't know how I would manage about my luggage – and going ashore at foreign ports – and all the different currencies –'

Innumerable pitfalls seemed to rise up before the little lady's affrighted gaze, and Joanna hastened to calm her by a question about an approaching garden fête and sale of work. This led us quite naturally to Mrs Dane Calthrop.

A faint spasm showed for a minute on Miss Barton's face.

'You know, dear,' she said, 'she is really a very *odd* woman. The things she says sometimes.'

I asked what things.

'Oh, I don't know. Such very *unexpected* things. And the way she looks at you, as though you weren't there but somebody else was – I'm expressing it badly but it is so hard to convey the impression I mean. And then she won't – well, *interfere* at all. There are so many cases where a vicar's wife could advise and – perhaps *admonish*. Pull people up, you know, and make them mend their ways. Because people would listen to her, I'm sure of that, they're all quite in awe of her. But she insists on being aloof and far away, and has such a curious habit of feeling sorry for the most unworthy people.'

'That's interesting,' I said, exchanging a quick glance with Joanna.

'Still, she is a very well-bred woman. She was a Miss Farroway of Bellpath, very good family, but these old families sometimes *are* a little peculiar, I believe. But she is devoted to her husband who is a man of very fine intellect – wasted, I am sometimes afraid, in this country circle. A good man, and most sincere, but I always find his habit of quoting Latin a little confusing.'

'Hear, hear,' I said fervently.

'Jerry had an expensive public school education, so he doesn't recognize Latin when he hears it,' said Joanna.

This led Miss Barton to a new topic.

'The schoolmistress here is a most unpleasant young woman,' she said. 'Quite *Red*, I'm afraid.' She lowered her voice over the word 'Red.'

Later, as we walked home up the hill, Joanna said to me:

'She's rather sweet.'

V

At dinner that night, Joanna said to Partridge that she hoped her tea-party had been a success.

Partridge got rather red in the face and held herself even more stiffly.

'Thank you, miss, but Agnes never turned up after all.'

'Oh, I'm sorry.'

'It didn't matter to *me*,' said Partridge.

She was so swelling with grievance that she condescended to pour it out to us.

'It wasn't me who thought of asking her! She rang up herself, said she'd something on her mind and could she come here, it being her day off. And I said, yes, subject to your permission which I obtained. And after that, not a sound or sign of her! And no word of apology either, though I should hope I'll get a postcard tomorrow morning. These girls nowadays – don't know their place – no idea of how to behave.'

Joanna attempted to soothe Partridge's wounded feelings.

'She mayn't have felt well. You didn't ring up to find out?'

Partridge drew herself up again.

'No, I did *not*, miss. No, indeed. If Agnes likes to behave rudely that's her lookout, but I shall give her a piece of my mind when we meet.'

Partridge went out of the room still stiff with indignation and Joanna and I laughed.

'Probably a case of "Advice from Aunt Nancy's Column",' I said. '"*My boy is very cold in his manner to me, what shall I do about it?*" Failing Aunt Nancy, Partridge was to be applied to for advice, but instead there has been a reconciliation and I expect at this minute that Agnes and her boy are one of those speechless couples locked in each other's arms that you come upon suddenly standing by a dark hedge. They embarrass you horribly, but you don't embarrass them.'

Joanna laughed and said she expected that was it.

We began talking of the anonymous letters and wondered how Nash and the melancholy Graves were getting on.

'It's a week today exactly,' said Joanna, 'since Mrs Symmington's suicide. I should think they must have got on to something by now. Fingerprints, or handwriting, or *something*.'

I answered her absently. Somewhere behind my conscious mind, a queer uneasiness was growing. It was connected in some way with the phrase that Joanna had used, 'a week exactly.'

I ought, I dare say, to have put two and two together earlier. Perhaps, unconsciously, my mind was already suspicious.

Anyway the leaven was working now. The uneasiness was growing – coming to a head.

Joanna noticed suddenly that I wasn't listening to her spirited account of a village encounter.

'What's the matter, Jerry?'

I did not answer because my mind was busy piecing things together.

Mrs Symmington's suicide. . . . She was alone in the house that afternoon. . . . Alone in the house *because the maids were having their day out*. . . . A week ago exactly. . . .

'Jerry, what –'

I interrupted.

'Joanna, maids have days out once a week, don't they?'

'And alternate Sundays,' said Joanna. 'What on –'

'Never mind Sundays. They go out the same day every week?'

'Yes. That's the usual thing.'

Joanna was staring at me curiously. Her mind had not taken the track mine had done.

I crossed the room and rang the bell. Partridge came.

'Tell me,' I said, 'this Agnes Woddell. She's in service?'

'Yes, sir. At Mrs Symmington's. At Mr Symmington's, I should say now.'

I drew a deep breath. I glanced at the clock. It was half-past ten.

'Would she be back now, do you think?'

Partridge was looking disapproving.

'Yes, sir. The maids have to be in by ten there. They're old-fashioned.'

I said: 'I'm going to ring up.'

I went out to the hall. Joanna and Partridge followed me.

Partridge was clearly furious. Joanna was puzzled. She said, as I was trying to get the number:

'What are you going to do, Jerry?'

'I'd like to be sure that the girl has come in all right.'

Partridge sniffed. Just sniffed, nothing more. But I did not care twopence about Partridge's sniffs.

Elsie Holland answered the telephone the other end.

'Sorry to ring you up,' I said. 'This is Jerry Burton speaking. Is – has – your maid Agnes come in?'

It was not until after I had said it that I suddenly felt a bit of a fool. For if the girl had come in and it was all right, how on earth was I going to explain my ringing up and asking? It would have been better if I had let Joanna ask the question, though even that would need a bit of explaining. I foresaw a new trail of gossip started in Lymstock, with myself and the unknown Agnes Woddell as its centre.

Elsie Holland sounded, not unnaturally, very much surprised.

'Agnes? Oh, she's sure to be in by now.'

I felt a fool, but I went on with it.

'Do you mind just seeing if she has come in, Miss Holland?'

There is one thing to be said for a nursery governess; she is used to doing things when told. Hers not to reason why! Elsie Holland put down the receiver and went off obediently.

Two minutes later I heard her voice.

'Are you there, Mr Burton?'

'Yes.'

'Agnes isn't in yet, as a matter of fact.'

I knew then that my hunch had been right.

I heard a noise of voices vaguely from the other end, then Symmington himself spoke.

'Hallo, Burton, what's the matter?'

'Your maid Agnes isn't back yet.'

'No. Miss Holland has just been to see. What's the matter? There's not been an accident, has there?'

'Not an *accident*,' I said.

'Do you mean you have reason to believe something has happened to the girl?'

I said grimly: 'I shouldn't be surprised.'

CHAPTER 8

I slept badly that night. I think that, even then, there were pieces of the puzzle floating about in my mind. I believe that if I had given my mind to it, I could have solved the whole thing then and there. Otherwise why did those fragments tag along so persistently?

How much do we know at any time? Much more, or so I believe, than we know we know! But we cannot break through to that subterranean knowledge. It is there, but we cannot reach it.

I lay on my bed, tossing uneasily, and only vague bits of the puzzle came to torture me.

There *was* a pattern, if only I could get hold of it. I ought to know who wrote those damned letters. There was a trail somewhere if only I could follow it. . . .

As I dropped off to sleep, words danced irritatingly through my drowsy mind.

'No smoke without fire.' No fire without smoke. Smoke . . . Smoke? Smoke screen . . . No, that was the war – a war phrase. War. Scrap of paper. . . . Only a scrap of paper. Belgium – Germany. . . .

I fell asleep. I dreamt that I was taking Mrs Dane Calthrop, who had turned into a greyhound, for a walk with a collar and lead.

II

It was the ringing of the telephone that roused me. A persistent ringing.

I sat up in bed, glanced at my watch. It was half-past seven. I had not yet been called. The telephone was ringing in the hall downstairs.

I jumped out of bed, pulled on a dressing-gown, and raced down. I beat Partridge coming through the back door from the kitchen by a short head. I picked up the receiver.

'Hallo?'

'Oh –' It was a sob of relief. 'It's *you!*' Megan's voice. Megan's voice indescribably forlorn and frightened. 'Oh, please do come – *do* come. Oh, please do! Will you?'

'I'm coming at once,' I said. 'Do you hear? *At once.*'

I climbed the stairs as fast as I could and burst in on Joanna.

'Look here, Jo, I'm going off to the Symmingtons'.'

Joanna lifted a curly blonde head from the pillow and rubbed her eyes like a small child.

'Why – what's happened?'

'I don't know. It was the child – Megan. She sounded all in.'

'What do you think it is?'

'The girl Agnes, unless I'm very much mistaken.'

As I went out of the door, Joanna called after me:

'Wait. I'll get up and drive you down.'

'No need. I'll drive myself.'

'You can't drive the car.'

'Yes, I can.'

I did, too. It hurt, but not too much. I'd washed, shaved, dressed, got the car out and driven to the Symmingtons' in half an hour. Not bad going.

Megan must have been watching for me. She came out of the house at a run and clutched me. Her poor little face was white and twitching.

'Oh, you've come – you've *come*!'

'Hold up, funny face,' I said. 'Yes, I've come. Now what is it?'

She began to shake. I put my arm round her.

'I – I found her.'

'You found Agnes? Where?'

The trembling grew.

'Under the stairs. There's a cupboard there. It has fishing-rods and golf clubs and things. You know.'

I nodded. It was the usual cupboard.

Megan went on.

'She was there – all huddled up – and – and *cold* – horribly cold. She was – she was *dead*, you know!'

I asked curiously. 'What made you look there?'

'I – I don't know. You telephoned last night. And we all began wondering where Agnes was. We waited up some time, but she didn't come in, and at last we went to bed. I didn't sleep very well and I got up early. There was only Rose (the cook, you know) about. She said she was very cross about Agnes not having come back. She said she'd been before somewhere when a girl did a flit like that. I had some milk and bread and butter in the kitchen – and then suddenly Rose came in looking queer and she said that Agnes's outdoor things were still in her room. Her best ones that she goes out in. And I began to wonder if – if she'd ever left the house, and I started looking round, and I opened the cupboard under the stairs and – and she was there . . .'

'Somebody's rung up the police, I suppose?'

'Yes, they're here now. My stepfather rang them up straightaway. And then I – I felt I couldn't bear it, and I rang *you* up. You don't mind?'

'No,' I said. 'I don't mind.'

I looked at her curiously.

'Did anybody give you some brandy, or some coffee, or some tea after – after you found her?'

Megan shook her head.

I cursed the whole Symmington *ménage*. That stuffed shirt, Symmington, thought of nothing but the police. Neither Elsie Holland nor the cook seemed to have thought of the effect on the sensitive child who had made that gruesome discovery.

'Come on, slabface,' I said. 'We'll go to the kitchen.'

We went round the house to the back door and into the kitchen. Rose, a plump pudding-faced woman of forty, was drinking strong tea by the kitchen fire. She greeted us with a flow of talk and her hand to her heart.

She'd come all over queer, she told me, awful the palpitations were! Just think of it, it might have been *her*, it might have been any of them, murdered in their beds they might have been.

'Dish out a good strong cup of that tea for Miss Megan,' I said. 'She's had a shock, you know. Remember it was she who found the body.'

The mere mention of a body nearly sent Rose off again, but I quelled her with a stern eye and she poured out a cup of inky fluid.

'There you are, young woman,' I said to Megan. 'You drink that down. You haven't got any brandy, I suppose, Rose?'

Rose said rather doubtfully that there was a drop of cooking brandy left over from the Christmas puddings.

'That'll do,' I said, and put a dollop of it into Megan's cup. I saw by Rose's eye that she thought it a good idea.

I told Megan to stay with Rose.

'I can trust you to look after Miss Megan?' I said, and Rose replied in a gratified way, 'Oh yes, sir.'

I went through into the house. If I knew Rose and her kind, she would soon find it necessary to keep her strength up with a little food, and that would be good for Megan too. Confound these people, why couldn't they look after the child?

Fuming inwardly I ran into Elsie Holland in the hall. She didn't seem surprised to see me. I suppose that the gruesome excitement of the discovery made one oblivious of who was coming and going. The constable, Bert Rundle, was by the front door.

Elsie Holland gasped out:

'Oh, Mr Burton, isn't it *awful*? Whoever can have done such a dreadful thing?'

'It *was* murder, then?'

'Oh, yes. She was struck on the back of the head. It's all blood and hair – oh! it's *awful* – and bundled into that cupboard. Who can have done such a wicked thing? And *why*? Poor Agnes, I'm sure she never did anyone any harm.'

'No,' I said. 'Somebody saw to that pretty promptly.'

She stared at me. Not, I thought, a quick-witted girl. But she had good nerves. Her colour was as usual, slightly heightened by excitement, and I even fancied that in a macabre kind of way, and in spite of a naturally kind heart, she was enjoying the drama.

She said apologetically: 'I must go up to the boys. Mr Symmington is so anxious that they shouldn't get a shock. He wants me to keep them right away.'

'Megan found the body, I hear,' I said. 'I hope somebody is looking after her?'

I will say for Elsie Holland that she looked conscience-stricken.

'Oh dear,' she said. 'I forgot all about her. I do hope she's all right. I've been so rushed, you know, and the police and everything – but it was remiss of me. Poor girl, she must be feeling bad. I'll go and look for her at once.'

I relented.

'She's all right,' I said. 'Rose is looking after her. You get along to the kids.'

She thanked me with a flash of white tombstone teeth and hurried upstairs. After all, the boys were her job, and not Megan – Megan was nobody's job. Elsie was paid to look after Symmington's blinking brats. One could hardly blame her for doing so.

As she flashed round the corner of the stairs, I caught my breath. For a minute I caught a glimpse of a Winged Victory, deathless and incredibly beautiful, instead of a conscientious nursery governess.

Then a door opened and Superintendent Nash stepped out into the hall with Symmington behind him.

'Oh, Mr Burton,' he said. 'I was just going to telephone you. I'm glad you are here.'

He didn't ask me – then – why I was here.

He turned his head and said to Symmington:

'I'll use this room if I may.'

It was a small morning-room with a window on the front of the house.

'Certainly, certainly.'

Symmington's poise was pretty good, but he looked desperately tired. Superintendent Nash said gently:

'I should have some breakfast if I were you, Mr Symmington. You and Miss Holland and Miss Megan will feel much better after coffee and eggs and bacon. Murder is a nasty business on an empty stomach.'

He spoke in a comfortable family doctor kind of way.

Symmington gave a faint attempt at a smile and said:

'Thank you, superintendent, I'll take your advice.'

I followed Nash into the little morning-room and he shut the door. He said then:

'You've got here very quickly? How did you hear?'

I told him that Megan had rung me up. I felt well disposed towards Superintendent Nash. He, at any rate, had not forgotten that Megan, too, would be in need of breakfast.

'I hear that you telephoned last night, Mr Burton, asking about this girl? Why was that?'

I suppose it did seem odd. I told him about Agnes's telephone call to Partridge and her non-appearance. He said, 'Yes, I see . . .'

He said it slowly and reflectively, rubbing his chin.

Then he sighed:

'Well,' he said. 'It's murder now, right enough. Direct physical action. The question is, what did the girl know? Did she say anything to this Partridge? Anything definite?'

'I don't think so. But you can ask her.'

'Yes. I shall come up and see her when I've finished here.'

'What happened exactly?' I asked. 'Or don't you know yet?'

'Near enough. It was the maids' day out –'

'Both of them?'

'Yes, it seems that there used to be two sisters here who liked to go out together, so Mrs Symmington arranged it that way. Then when these two came, she kept to the same arrangement. They used to leave cold supper laid out in the dining-room, and Miss Holland used to get tea.'

'I see.'

'It's pretty clear up to a point. The cook, Rose, comes from Nether Mickford, and in order to get there on her day out she has to catch the half-past two bus. So Agnes has to finish clearing up lunch always. Rose used to wash up the supper things in the evenings to even things up.

'That's what happened yesterday. Rose went off to catch the bus at two twenty-five, Symmington left for his office at five-and-twenty to three. Elsie Holland and the children went out at a quarter to three. Megan Hunter went out on her bicycle about five minutes later. Agnes would then be alone in the house. As far as I can make out, she normally left the house between three o'clock and half-past three.'

'The house being then left empty?'

'Oh, they don't worry about that down here. There's not much locking up done in these parts. As I say, at ten minutes to three Agnes was alone in the house. That she never left it is clear, for she was in her cap and apron still when we found her body.'

'I suppose you can tell roughly the time of death?'

'Doctor Griffith won't commit himself. Between two o'clock and four-thirty, is his official medical verdict.'

'How was she killed?'

'She was first stunned by a blow on the back of the head. Afterwards an ordinary kitchen skewer, sharpened to a fine point, was thrust into the base of the skull, causing instantaneous death.'

I lit a cigarette. It was not a nice picture.

'Pretty cold blooded,' I said.

'Oh yes, yes, that was indicated.'

I inhaled deeply.

'Who did it?' I said. 'And why?'

'I don't suppose,' said Nash slowly, 'that we shall ever know exactly why. But we can guess.'

'She knew something?'

'She knew something.'

'She didn't give anyone here a hint?'

'As far as I can make out, no. She's been upset, so the cook says, ever since Mrs Symmington's death, and according to this Rose, she's been getting more and more worried, and kept saying she didn't know what she ought to do.'

He gave a short exasperated sigh.

'It's always the way. They won't come to us. They've got that deep-seated prejudice against "being mixed up with the police." If she'd come along and told us what was worrying her, she'd be alive today.'

'Didn't she give the other woman *any* hint?'

'No, or so Rose says, and I'm inclined to believe her. For if she had, Rose would have blurted it out at once with a good many fancy embellishments of her own.'

'It's maddening,' I said, 'not to know.'

'We can still guess, Mr Burton. To begin with, it can't be anything very definite. It's got to be the sort of thing that you think over, and as you think it over, your uneasiness grows. You see what I mean?'

'Yes.'

'Actually, I think I know what it was.'

I looked at him with respect.

'That's good work, Superintendent.'

'Well, you see, Mr Burton, I know something that you don't. On the afternoon that Mrs Symmington committed suicide both maids were supposed to be out. It was their day out. But actually Agnes came back to the house.'

'You know that?'

'Yes. Agnes has a boy-friend – young Rendell from the fish shop. Wednesday is early closing and he comes along to meet Agnes and they go for a walk, or to the pictures if it's wet. That Wednesday they had a row practically as soon as they met. Our letter writer had been active, suggesting that Agnes had other fish to fry, and young Fred Rendell was all worked up. They quarrelled violently and Agnes bolted back home and said she wasn't coming out unless Fred said he was sorry.'

'Well?'

'Well, Mr Burton, the kitchen faces the back of the house but the pantry looks out where we are looking now. There's only one entrance gate. You come through it and either up to the front door, or else along the path at the side of the house to the back door.'

He paused.

'Now I'll tell you something. That letter that came to Mrs Symmington that afternoon *didn't come by post*. It had a used stamp affixed to it, and the postmark faked quite convincingly in a lamp-black, so that it would seem to have been delivered by the postman with the afternoon letters. But actually *it had not been through the post.* You see what that means?'

I said slowly: 'It means that it was left *by hand*, pushed through the letter box some time before the afternoon post was delivered, so that it should be amongst the other letters.'

'Exactly. The afternoon post comes round about a quarter to four. My theory is this. The girl was in the pantry looking through the window (it's masked by shrubs but you can see through them quite well) watching out for her young man to turn up and apologize.'

I said: '*And she saw whoever it was deliver that note?*'

'That's my guess, Mr Burton. I may be wrong, of course.'

'I don't think you are. . . . It's simple – and convincing – and it means that Agnes knew *who the anonymous letter writer was.*'

'Yes.'

'But then why didn't she –?'

I paused, frowning.

Nash said quickly:

'As I see it, the girl *didn't realize what she had seen*. Not at first. Somebody had left a letter at the house, yes – but that somebody was nobody she would dream of connecting with the anonymous letters. It was somebody, from that point of view, quite above suspicion.

'But the more she thought about it, the more uneasy she grew. Ought she, perhaps, to tell someone about it? In her perplexity she thinks of Miss Barton's Partridge who, I gather, is a somewhat dominant personality and whose judgement Agnes would accept unhesitatingly. She decides to ask Partridge what she ought to do.'

'Yes,' I said thoughtfully. 'It fits well enough. And somehow or other, Poison Pen found out. How did she find out, superintendent?'

'You're not used to living in the country, Mr Burton. It's a kind of miracle how things get round. First of all there's the telephone call. Who overheard it your end?'

I reflected.

'I answered the telephone originally. Then I called up the stairs to Partridge.'

'Mentioning the girl's name?'

'Yes – yes, I did.'

'Anyone overhear you?'

'My sister or Miss Griffith might have done so.'

'Ah, Miss Griffith. What was she doing up there?'

I explained.

'Was she going back to the village?'

'She was going to Mr Pye first.'

Superintendent Nash sighed.

'That's two ways it could have gone all over the place.'

I was incredulous.

'Do you mean that either Miss Griffith or Mr Pye would bother to repeat a meaningless little bit of information like that?'

'Anything's news in a place like this. You'd be surprised. If the dressmaker's mother has got a bad corn everybody hears about it! And then there is this end. Miss Holland, Rose – they could have heard what Agnes said. And there's Fred Rendell. It may have gone round through him that Agnes went back to the house that afternoon.'

I gave a slight shiver. I was looking out of the window. In front of me was a neat square of grass and a path and the low prim gate.

Someone had opened the gate, had walked very correctly and quietly up to the house, and had pushed a letter through the letter box. I saw, hazily, in my mind's eye, that vague woman's shape. The face was blank – but it must be a face that I knew. . . .

Superintendent Nash was saying:

'All the same, this narrows things down. That's always the way we get 'em in the end. Steady, patient elimination. There aren't so very many people it could be now.'

'You mean –?'

'It knocks out any women clerks who were at their work all yesterday afternoon. It knocks out the school-mistress. She was teaching. And the district nurse. I know where she was yesterday. Not that I ever thought it was any of *them*, but now we're *sure*. You see, Mr Burton, we've got two definite times now on which to concentrate – yesterday afternoon, and the week before. On the day of Mrs Symmington's death from, say, a quarter-past three (the earliest possible time at which Agnes could have been back in the house after her quarrel) and four o'clock when the post must have come (but I can get that fixed more accurately with the postman). And yesterday from ten minutes to three (when Miss Megan Hunter left the house) until half-past three or more probably a quarter-past three as Agnes hadn't begun to change.'

'What do you think happened yesterday?'

Nash made a grimace.

'What do I think? I think a certain lady walked up to the front door and rang the bell, quite calm and smiling, the afternoon caller. . . . Maybe she asked for Miss Holland, or for Miss Megan, or perhaps she had brought a parcel. Anyway Agnes turns round to get a salver for cards, or to take the parcel in, and our lady-like caller bats her on the back of her unsuspecting head.'

'What with?'

Nash said:

'The ladies round here usually carry large sizes in handbags. No saying what mightn't be inside it.'

'And then stabs her through the back of the neck and bundles her into the cupboard? Wouldn't that be a hefty job for a woman?'

Superintendent Nash looked at me with rather a queer expression.

'The woman we're after isn't normal – not by a long way – and that type of mental instability goes with surprising strength. Agnes wasn't a big girl.'

He paused and then asked: 'What made Miss Megan Hunter think of looking in that cupboard?'

'Sheer instinct,' I said.

Then I asked: 'Why drag Agnes into the cupboard? What was the point?'

'The longer it was before the body was found, the more difficult it would be to fix the time of death accurately. If Miss Holland, for instance, fell over the body as soon as she came in, a doctor might be able to fix it within ten minutes or so – which might be awkward for our lady friend.'

I said, frowning:

'But if Agnes were suspicious of this person –'

Nash interrupted me.

'She wasn't. Not to the pitch of definite suspicion. She just thought it "queer". She was a slow-witted girl, I imagine, and she was only vaguely suspicious with a feeling that something was wrong. She certainly didn't suspect that she was up against a woman who would do murder.'

'Did you suspect that?' I asked.

Nash shook his head. He said, with feeling:

'I ought to have known. That suicide business, you see, frightened Poison Pen. She got the wind up. Fear, Mr Burton, is an incalculable thing.'

Yes, fear. That was the thing we ought to have foreseen. Fear – in a lunatic brain . . .

'You see,' said Superintendent Nash, and somehow his words made the whole thing seem absolutely horrible. 'We're up against someone who's respected and thought highly of – someone, in fact, of good social position!'

III

Presently Nash said that he was going to interview Rose once more. I asked him, rather diffidently, if I might come too. Rather to my surprise he assented cordially.

'I'm very glad of your co-operation, Mr Burton, if I may say so.'

'That sounds suspicious,' I said. 'In books when a detective welcomes someone's assistance, that someone is usually the murderer.'

Nash laughed shortly. He said: 'You're hardly the type to write anonymous letters, Mr Burton.'

He added: 'Frankly, you can be useful to us.'

'I'm glad, but I don't see how.'

'You're a stranger down here, that's why. You've got no preconceived ideas about the people here. But at the same time, you've got the opportunity of getting to know things in what I may call a social way.'

'The murderer is a person of good social position,' I murmured.

'Exactly.'

'I'm to be the spy within the gates?'

'Have you any objection?'

I thought it over.

'No,' I said, 'frankly I haven't. If there's a dangerous lunatic about driving inoffensive women to suicide and hitting miserable little maidservants on the head, then I'm not averse to doing a bit of dirty work to put that lunatic under restraint.'

'That's sensible of you, sir. And let me tell you, the person we're after is dangerous. She's about as dangerous as a rattlesnake and a cobra and a black mamba rolled into one.'

I gave a slight shiver. I said:

'In fact, we've got to make haste?'

'That's right. Don't think we're inactive in the force. We're not. We're working on several different lines.'

He said it grimly.

I had a vision of a fine far-flung spider's web. . . .

Nash wanted to hear Rose's story again, so he explained to me, because she had already told him two different versions, and the more versions he got from her, the more likely it was that a few grains of truth might be incorporated.

We found Rose washing up breakfast, and she stopped at once and rolled her eyes and clutched her heart and explained again how she'd been coming over queer all the morning.

Nash was patient with her but firm. He'd been soothing the first time, so he told me, and peremptory the second, and he now employed a mixture of the two.

Rose enlarged pleasurably on the details of the past week, of how Agnes had gone about in deadly fear, and had shivered and said, 'Don't ask me,' when Rose had urged her to say what was the matter. 'It would be death if she told me,' that's what she said, finished Rose, rolling her eyes happily.

Had Agnes given no hint of what was troubling her?

No, except that she went in fear of her life.

Superintendent Nash sighed and abandoned the theme, contenting himself with extracting an exact account of Rose's own activities the preceding afternoon.

This, put baldly, was that Rose had caught the 2.30 bus and had spent the afternoon and evening with her family, returning by the 8.40 bus from Nether Mickford. The recital was complicated by the extraordinary presentiments of evil Rose had had all the afternoon and how her sister had commented on it and how she hadn't been able to touch a morsel of seed cake.

From the kitchen we went in search of Elsie Holland, who was superintending the children's lessons. As always, Elsie Holland was competent and obliging. She rose and said:

'Now, Colin, you and Brian will do these three sums and have the answers ready for me when I come back.'

She then led us into the night nursery. 'Will this do? I thought it would be better not to talk before the children.'

'Thank you, Miss Holland. Just tell me, once more, are you *quite* sure that Agnes never mentioned to you being worried over anything – since Mrs Symmington's death, I mean?'

'No, she never said anything. She was a very quiet girl, you know, and didn't talk much.'

'A change from the other one, then!'

'Yes, Rose talks much too much. I have to tell her not to be impertinent sometimes.'

'Now, will you tell me exactly what happened yesterday afternoon? Everything you can remember.'

'Well, we had lunch as usual. One o'clock, and we hurry just a little. I don't let the boys dawdle. Let me see. Mr Symmington went back to the office, and I helped Agnes by laying the table for supper – the boys ran out in the garden till I was ready to take them.'

'Where did you go?'

'Towards Combeacre, by the field path – the boys wanted to fish. I forgot their bait and had to go back for it.'

'What time was that?'

'Let me see, we started about twenty to three – or just after. Megan was coming but changed her mind. She was going out on her bicycle. She's got quite a craze for bicycling.'

'I mean what time was it when you went back for the bait? Did you go into the house?'

'No. I'd left it in the conservatory at the back. I don't know what time it was then – about ten minutes to three, perhaps.'

'Did you see Megan or Agnes?'

'Megan must have started, I think. No, I didn't see Agnes. I didn't see anyone.'

'And after that you went fishing?'

'Yes, we went along by the stream. We didn't catch anything. We hardly ever do, but the boys enjoy it. Brian got rather wet. I had to change his things when we got in.'

'You attend to tea on Wednesdays?'

'Yes. It's all ready in the drawing-room for Mr Symmington. I just make the tea when he comes in. The children and I have ours in the schoolroom – and Megan, of course. I have my own tea things and everything in the cupboard up there.'

'What time did you get in?'

'At ten minutes to five. I took the boys up and started to lay tea. Then when Mr Symmington came in at five I went down to make his but he said he would have it with us in the schoolroom. The boys were so pleased. We played Animal Grab afterwards. It seems so awful to think of now – with that poor girl in the cupboard all the time.'

'Would anybody go to that cupboard normally?'

'Oh no, it's only used for keeping junk. The hats and coats hang in the little cloakroom to the right of the front door as you come in. No one might have gone to the other cupboard for months.'

'I see. And you noticed nothing unusual, nothing abnormal at all when you came back?'

The blue eyes opened very wide.

'Oh no, inspector, nothing at all. Everything was just the same as usual. That's what was so awful about it.'

'And the week before?'

'You mean the day Mrs Symmington –'

'Yes.'

'Oh, that was terrible – terrible!'

'Yes, yes, I know. You were out all that afternoon also?'

'Oh yes, I always take the boys out in the afternoon – if it's fine enough. We do lessons in the morning. We went up on the moor, I remember – quite a long way. I was afraid I was late back because as I turned in at the gate I saw Mr Symmington coming from his office at the other end of the road, and I hadn't even put the kettle on, but it was just ten minutes to five.'

'You didn't go up to Mrs Symmington?'

'Oh no. I never did. She always rested after lunch. She had attacks of neuralgia – and they used to come on after meals. Dr Griffith had given her some cachets to take. She used to lie down and try to sleep.'

Nash said in a casual voice:

'So no one would take her up the post?'

'The afternoon post? No, I'd look in the letter box and put the letters on the hall table when I came in. But very often Mrs Symmington used to come down and get it herself. She didn't sleep all the afternoon. She was usually up again by four.'

'You didn't think anything was wrong because she wasn't up that afternoon?'

'Oh, no, I never dreamed of such a thing. Mr Symmington was hanging up his coat in the hall and I said, "Tea's not quite ready, but the kettle's nearly boiling," and he nodded and called out, "Mona, Mona!" – and then as Mrs Symmington didn't answer he went upstairs to her bedroom, and it must have been the most terrible shock to him. He called me and I came, and he said, "Keep the children away," and then he phoned Dr Griffith and we forgot all about the kettle and it burnt the bottom out! Oh dear, it *was* dreadful, and she'd been so happy and cheerful at lunch.'

Nash said abruptly: 'What is your own opinion of that letter she received, Miss Holland?'

Elsie Holland said indignantly:

'Oh, I think it was wicked – wicked!'

'Yes, yes, I don't mean that. Did you think it was true?'

Elsie Holland said firmly:

'No, indeed I don't. Mrs Symmington was very sensitive – very sensitive indeed. She had to take all sorts of things for her nerves. And she was very – well, *particular*.' Elsie flushed. 'Anything of that sort – *nasty*, I mean – would have given her a great shock.'

Nash was silent for a moment, then he asked:

'Have you had any of these letters, Miss Holland?'

'No. No, I haven't had any.'

'Are you sure? Please' – he lifted a hand – 'don't answer in a hurry. They're not pleasant things to get, I know. And sometimes people don't like to admit they've had them. But it's very important in this case that we should know. We're quite aware that the statements in them are just a tissue of lies, so you needn't feel embarrassed.'

'But I haven't, superintendent. Really I haven't. Not anything of the kind.'

She was indignant, almost tearful, and her denials seemed genuine enough.

When she went back to the children, Nash stood looking out of the window.

'Well,' he said, 'that's that! She says she hasn't received any of these letters. And she sounds as though she's speaking the truth.'

'She did certainly. I'm sure she was.'

'H'm,' said Nash. 'Then what I want to know is, why the devil hasn't she?'

He went on rather impatiently, as I stared at him.

'She's a pretty girl, isn't she?'

'Rather more than pretty.'

'Exactly. As a matter of fact, she's uncommonly good looking. And she's young. In fact she's just the meat an anonymous letter writer would like. Then why has she been left out?'

I shook my head.

'It's interesting, you know. I must mention it to Graves. He asked if we could tell him definitely of any one who hadn't had one.'

'She's the second person,' I said. 'There's Emily Barton, remember.'

Nash gave a faint chuckle.

'You shouldn't believe everything you're told, Mr Burton. Miss Barton had one all right – more than one.'

'How do you know?'

'That devoted dragon she's lodging with told me – her late parlourmaid or cook. Florence Elford. Very indignant she was about it. Would like to have the writer's blood.'

'Why did Miss Emily say she hadn't had any?'

'Delicacy. Their language isn't nice. Little Miss Barton has spent her life avoiding the coarse and unrefined.'

'What did the letters say?'

'The usual. Quite ludicrous in her case. And incidentally insinuated that she poisoned off her old mother and most of her sisters!'

I said incredulously:

'Do you mean to say there's really this dangerous lunatic going about and we can't spot her right away?'

'We'll spot her,' said Nash, and his voice was grim. 'She'll write just one letter too many.'

'But, my goodness, man, she won't go on writing these things – not now.'

He looked at me.

'Oh yes, she will. You see, *she can't stop now*. It's a morbid craving. The letters will go on, make no mistake about that.'

CHAPTER 9

I went and found Megan before leaving the house. She was in the garden and seemed almost back to her usual self. She greeted me quite cheerfully.

I suggested that she should come back to us again for a while, but after a momentary hesitation she shook her head.

'It's nice of you – but I think I'll stay here. After all, it is – well, I suppose it's my home. And I dare say I can help with the boys a bit.'

'Well,' I said, 'it's as you like.'

'Then I think I'll stay. I could – I could –'

'Yes?' I prompted.

'If – if anything awful happened, I could ring you up, couldn't I, and you'd come?'

I was touched. 'Of course. But what awful thing do you think might happen?'

'Oh, I don't know.' She looked vague. 'Things seem rather like that just now, don't they?'

'For God's sake,' I said. 'Don't go nosing out any more bodies! It's not good for you.'

She gave me a brief flash of a smile.

'No, it isn't. It made me feel awfully sick.'

I didn't much like leaving her there, but after all, as she had said, it was her home. And I fancied that now Elsie Holland would feel more responsible for her.

Nash and I went up together to Little Furze. Whilst I gave Joanna an account of the morning's doings, Nash tackled Partridge. He rejoined us looking discouraged.

'Not much help there. According to this woman, the girl only said she was worried about something and didn't know what to do and that she'd like Miss Partridge's advice.'

'Did Partridge mention the fact to anyone?' asked Joanna.

Nash nodded, looking grim.

'Yes, she told Mrs Emory – your daily woman – on the lines, as far as I can gather, that there were *some* young women who were willing to take advice from their elders and didn't think they could settle everything for themselves offhand! Agnes mightn't be very bright, but she was a nice respectful girl and knew her manners.'

'Partridge preening herself, in fact,' murmured Joanna. 'And Mrs Emory could have passed it round the town?'

'That's right, Miss Burton.'

'There's one thing rather surprises me,' I said. 'Why were my sister and I included amongst the recipients of the anonymous letters? We were strangers down here – nobody could have had a grudge against us.'

'You're failing to allow for the mentality of a Poison Pen – all is grist that comes to their mill. Their grudge, you might say, is against humanity.'

'I suppose,' said Joanna thoughtfully, 'that that is what Mrs Dane Calthrop meant.'

Nash looked at her enquiringly, but she did not enlighten him. The superintendent said:

'I don't know if you happened to look closely at the envelope of the letter you got, Miss Burton. If so, you may have noticed that it was actually addressed to Miss Barton and the *a* altered to a *u* afterwards.'

That remark, properly interpreted, ought to have given us a clue to the whole business. As it was, none of us saw any significance in it.

Nash went off, and I was left with Joanna. She actually said: 'You don't think that letter can really have been meant for Miss Emily, do you?'

'It would hardly have begun "You painted trollop",' I pointed out, and Joanna agreed.

Then she suggested that I should go down to the town. 'You ought to hear what everyone is saying. It will be *the* topic this morning!'

I suggested that she should come too, but rather to my surprise Joanna refused. She said she was going to mess about in the garden.

I paused in the doorway and said, lowering my voice:

'I suppose Partridge is all right?'

'Partridge!'

The amazement in Joanna's voice made me feel ashamed of my idea. I said apologetically: 'I just wondered. She's rather "queer" in some ways – a grim spinster – the sort of person who might have religious mania.'

'This isn't religious mania – or so you told me Graves said.'

'Well, sex mania. They're very closely tied up together, I understand. She's repressed and respectable, and has been shut up here with a lot of elderly women for years.'

'What put the idea into your head?'

I said slowly:

'Well, we've only her word for it, haven't we, as to what the girl Agnes said to her? Suppose Agnes asked Partridge to tell her why Partridge came and left a note that day – and Partridge said she'd call round that afternoon and explain.'

'And then camouflaged it by coming to us and asking if the girl could come here?'

'Yes.'

'But Partridge never went out that afternoon.'

'We don't know that. We were out ourselves, remember.'

'Yes, that's true. It's possible, I suppose.' Joanna turned it over in her mind. 'But I don't think so, all the same. I don't think Partridge has the mentality to cover her tracks over the letters. To wipe off fingerprints, and all that. It isn't only cunning you want – it's knowledge. I don't think she's got that. I suppose –' Joanna hesitated, then said slowly, 'they are sure it is a woman, aren't they?'

'You don't think it's a man?' I exclaimed incredulously.

'Not – not an ordinary man – but a certain kind of man. I'm thinking, really, of Mr Pye.'

'So Pye is your selection?'

'Don't you feel yourself that he's a possibility? He's the sort of person who might be lonely – and unhappy – and spiteful. Everyone, you see, rather laughs at him. Can't you see him secretly hating all the normal happy people, and taking a queer perverse artistic pleasure in what he was doing?'

'Graves said a middle-aged spinster.'

'Mr Pye,' said Joanna, '*is* a middle-aged spinster.'

'A misfit,' I said slowly.

'Very much so. He's rich, but money doesn't help. And I do feel he might be unbalanced. He is, really, rather a *frightening* little man.'

'He got a letter himself, remember.'

'We don't know that,' Joanna pointed out. 'We only thought so. And anyway, he might have been putting on an act.'

'For our benefit?'

'Yes. He's clever enough to think of that – and not to overdo it.'

'He must be a first-class actor.'

'But of course, Jerry, whoever is doing this *must* be a first-class actor. That's partly where the pleasure comes in.'

'For God's sake, Joanna, don't speak so understandingly! You make me feel that you – that you understand the mentality.'

'I think I do. I can – just – get into the mood. If I weren't Joanna Burton, if I weren't young and reasonably attractive and able to have a good time, if I were – how shall I put it? – behind bars, watching other people enjoy life, would a black evil tide rise in me, making me want to hurt, to torture – even to destroy?'

'Joanna!' I took her by the shoulders and shook her. She gave a little sigh and shiver, and smiled at me.

'I frightened you, didn't I, Jerry? But I have a feeling that that's the right way to solve this problem. You've got to be the person, knowing how they feel and what makes them act, and then – and then perhaps you'll know what they're going to do next.'

'Oh, hell!' I said. 'And I came down here to be a vegetable and get interested in all the dear little local scandals. Dear little local scandals! Libel, vilification, obscene language and murder!'

II

Joanna was quite right. The High Street was full of interested groups. I was determined to get everyone's reactions in turn.

I met Griffith first. He looked terribly ill and tired. So much so that I wondered. Murder is not, certainly, all in the day's work to a doctor, but his profession does equip him to face most things including suffering, the ugly side of human nature, and the fact of death.

'You look all in,' I said.

'Do I?' He was vague. 'Oh! I've had some worrying cases lately.'

'Including our lunatic at large?'

'That, certainly.' He looked away from me across the street. I saw a fine nerve twitching in his eyelid.

'You've no suspicions as to – *who*?'

'No. No. I wish to God I had.'

He asked abruptly after Joanna, and said, hesitatingly, that he had some photographs she'd wanted to see.

I offered to take them to her.

'Oh, it doesn't matter. I shall be passing that way actually later in the morning.'

I began to be afraid that Griffith had got it badly. Curse Joanna! Griffith was too good a man to be dangled as a scalp.

I let him go, for I saw his sister coming and I wanted, for once, to talk to her.

Aimée Griffith began, as it were, in the middle of a conversation.

'Absolutely shocking!' she boomed. 'I hear you were there – quite early?'

There was a question in the words, and her eyes glinted as she stressed the word 'early'. I wasn't going to tell her that Megan had rung me up. I said instead:

'You see, I was a bit uneasy last night. The girl was due to tea at our house and didn't turn up.'

'And so you feared the worst? Damned smart of you!'

'Yes,' I said. 'I'm quite the human bloodhound.'

'It's the first murder we've ever had in Lymstock. Excitement is terrific. Hope the police can handle it all right.'

'I shouldn't worry,' I said. 'They're an efficient body of men.'

'Can't even remember what the girl looked like, although I suppose she's opened the door to me dozens of times. Quiet, insignificant little thing. Knocked on the head and then stabbed through the back of the neck, so Owen tells me. Looks like a boy-friend to me. What do you think?'

'That's your solution?'

'Seems the most likely one. Had a quarrel, I expect. They're very inbred round here – bad heredity, a lot of them.' She paused, and then went on, 'I hear Megan Hunter found the body? Must have given her a bit of a shock.'

I said shortly:

'It did.'

'Not too good for her, I should imagine. In my opinion she's not too strong in the head – and a thing like this might send her completely off her onion.'

I took a sudden resolution. I had to know something.

'Tell me, Miss Griffith, was it you who persuaded Megan to return home yesterday?'

'Well, I wouldn't say exactly persuaded.'

I stuck to my guns.

'But you did say something to her?'

Aimée Griffith planted her feet firmly and stared at me in the eyes. She was, just slightly, on the defensive. She said:

'It's no good that young woman shirking her responsibilities. She's young and she doesn't know how tongues wag, so I felt it my duty to give her a hint.'

'Tongues –?' I broke off because I was too angry to go on.

Aimée Griffith continued with that maddeningly complacent confidence in herself which was her chief characteristic:

'Oh, I dare say *you* don't hear all the gossip that goes round. I do! I know what people are saying. Mind you, I don't for a minute think there's anything in it – not for a minute! But you know what people are – if they can say something ill-natured, they do! And it's rather hard lines on the girl when she's got her living to earn.'

'Her living to earn?' I said, puzzled.

Aimée went on:

'It's a difficult position for her, naturally. And I think she did the right thing. I mean, she couldn't go off at a moment's notice and leave the children with no one to look after them. She's been splendid – absolutely splendid. I say so to everybody! But there it is, it's an invidious position, and people will talk.'

'Who are you talking about?' I asked.

'Elsie Holland, of course,' said Aimée Griffith impatiently. 'In my opinion, she's a thoroughly nice girl, and has only been doing her duty.'

'And what are people saying?'

Aimée Griffith laughed. It was, I thought, rather an unpleasant laugh.

'They're saying that she's already considering the possibility of becoming Mrs Symmington No. 2 – that she's all out to console the widower and make herself indispensable.'

'But, good God,' I said, shocked, 'Mrs Symmington's only been dead a week!'

Aimée Griffith shrugged her shoulders.

'Of course. It's absurd! But you know what people are! The Holland girl is young and she's good looking – that's enough. And mind you, being a nursery governess isn't much of a prospect for a girl. I wouldn't blame her if she wanted a settled home and a husband and was playing her cards accordingly.'

'Of course,' she went on. 'Poor Dick Symmington hasn't the least idea of all this! He's still completely knocked out by Mona Symmington's death. But you know what men are! If the girl is always there, making him comfortable, looking after him, being obviously devoted to the children – well, he gets to be dependent on her.'

I said quietly:

'So you do think that Elsie Holland is a designing hussy?'

Aimée Griffith flushed.

'Not at all. I'm sorry for the girl – with people saying nasty things! That's why I more or less told Megan that she ought to go home. It looks better than having Dick Symmington and the girl alone in the house.'

I began to understand things.

Aimée Griffith gave her jolly laugh.

'You're shocked, Mr Burton, at hearing what our gossiping little town thinks. I can tell you this – they always think the worst!'

She laughed and nodded and strode away.

III

I came upon Mr Pye by the church. He was talking to Emily Barton, who looked pink and excited.

Mr Pye greeted me with every evidence of delight.

'Ah, Burton, good-morning, good-morning! How is your charming sister?'

I told him that Joanna was well.

'But not joining our village parliament? We are all agog over the news. Murder! Real Sunday newspaper murder in our midst! Not the most interesting of crimes, I fear. Somewhat sordid. The brutal murder of a little serving maid. No finer points about the crime, but still undeniably, news.'

Miss Barton said tremulously:

'It is shocking – quite shocking.'

Mr Pye turned to her.

'But you enjoy it, dear lady, you enjoy it. Confess it now. You disapprove, you deplore, but there *is* the thrill. I insist, there *is* the thrill!'

'Such a nice girl,' said Emily Barton. 'She came to me from St Clotilde's Home. Quite a raw girl. But most teachable. She turned into such a nice little maid. Partridge was very pleased with her.'

I said quickly:

'She was coming to tea with Partridge yesterday afternoon.' I turned to Pye. 'I expect Aimée Griffith told you.'

My tone was quite casual. Pye responded apparently quite unsuspiciously: 'She did mention it, yes. She said, I remember, that it was something quite new for servants to ring up on their employers' telephones.'

'Partridge would never dream of doing such a thing,' said Miss Emily, 'and I am really surprised at Agnes doing so.'

'You are behind the times, dear lady,' said Mr Pye. 'My two terrors use the telephone constantly and smoked all over the house until I objected. But one daren't say too much. Prescott is a divine cook, though temperamental, and Mrs Prescott is an admirable house-parlourmaid.'

'Yes, indeed, we all think you're very lucky.'

I intervened, since I did not want the conversation to become purely domestic.

'The news of the murder has got round very quickly,' I said.

'Of course, of course,' said Mr Pye. 'The butcher, the baker, the candlestick maker. Enter Rumour, painted full of tongues! Lymstock, alas! is going to the dogs. Anonymous letters, murders, any amount of criminal tendencies.'

Emily Barton said nervously: 'They don't think – there's no idea – that – that the two are connected.'

Mr Pye pounced on the idea.

'An interesting speculation. The girl knew something, therefore she was murdered. Yes, yes, most promising. How clever of you to think of it.'

'I – I can't bear it.'

Emily Barton spoke abruptly and turned away, walking very fast.

Pye looked after her. His cherubic face was pursed up quizzically.

He turned back to me and shook his head gently.

'A sensitive soul. A charming creature, don't you think? Absolutely a period piece. She's not, you know, of her own generation, she's of the generation before that. The mother must have been a woman of a very strong character. She kept the family ticking at about 1870, I should say. The whole family preserved under a glass case. I do like to come across that sort of thing.'

I did not want to talk about period pieces.

'What do you really think about all this business?' I asked.

'Meaning by that?'

'Anonymous letters, murder . . .'

'Our local crime wave? What do you?'

'I asked you first,' I said pleasantly.

Mr Pye said gently:

'I'm a student, you know, of abnormalities. They interest me. Such apparently unlikely people do the most fantastic things. Take the case of Lizzie Borden. There's not really a reasonable explanation of that. In this case, my advice to the police would be – study *character*. Leave your fingerprints and your measuring of handwriting and your microscopes. Notice instead what people do with their hands, and their little tricks of manner, and the way they eat their food, and if they laugh sometimes for no apparent reason.'

I raised my eyebrows. 'Mad?' I said.

'Quite, quite mad,' said Mr Pye, and added, 'but you'd never know it!'

'Who?'

His eyes met mine. He smiled.

'No, no, Burton, that would be slander. We can't add slander to all the rest of it.'

He fairly skipped off down the street.

IV

As I stood staring after him the church door opened and the Rev. Caleb Dane Calthrop came out.

He smiled vaguely at me.

'Good – good-morning, Mr – er – er –'

I helped him. 'Burton.'

'Of course, of course, you mustn't think I don't remember you. Your name had just slipped my memory for the moment. A beautiful day.'

'Yes,' I said rather shortly.

He peered at me.

'But something – something – ah, yes, that poor unfortunate child who was in service at the Symmingtons'. I find it hard to believe, I must confess, that we have a murderer in our midst, Mr – er – Burton.'

'It does seem a bit fantastic,' I said.

'Something else has just reached my ears.' He leaned towards me. 'I learn that there have been anonymous letters going about. Have you heard any rumour of such things?'

'I have heard,' I said.

'Cowardly and dastardly things.' He paused and quoted an enormous stream of Latin. 'Those words of Horace are very applicable, don't you think?' he said.

'Absolutely,' I said.

V

There didn't seem anyone more I could profitably talk to, so I went home, dropping in for some tobacco and for a bottle of sherry, so as to get some of the humbler opinions on the crime.

'A narsty tramp,' seemed to be the verdict.

'Come to the door, they do, and whine and ask for money, and then if it's a girl alone in the house, they turn narsty. My sister Dora, over to Combeacre, she had a narsty experience one day – Drunk, he was, and selling those little printed poems . . .'

The story went on, ending with the intrepid Dora courageously banging the door in the man's face and taking refuge and barricading herself in some vague retreat, which I gathered from the delicacy in mentioning it must be the lavatory. 'And there she stayed till her lady came home!'

I reached Little Furze just a few minutes before lunch time. Joanna was standing in the drawing-room window doing nothing at all and looking as though her thoughts were miles away.

'What have you been doing with yourself?' I asked.

'Oh, I don't know. Nothing particular.'

I went out on the veranda. Two chairs were drawn up to an iron table and there were two empty sherry glasses. On another chair was an object at which I looked with bewilderment for some time.

'What on earth is this?'

'Oh,' said Joanna, 'I think it's a photograph of a diseased spleen or something. Dr Griffith seemed to think I'd be interested to see it.'

I looked at the photograph with some interest. Every man has his own ways of courting the female sex. I should not, myself, choose to do it with photographs of spleens, diseased or otherwise. Still no doubt Joanna had asked for it!

'It looks most unpleasant,' I said.

Joanna said it did, rather.

'How was Griffith?' I asked.

'He looked tired and very unhappy. I think he's got something on his mind.'

'A spleen that won't yield to treatment?'

'Don't be silly. I mean something real.'

'I should say the man's got *you* on his mind. I wish you'd lay off him, Joanna.'

'Oh, do shut up. I haven't done anything.'

'Women always say that.'

Joanna whirled angrily out of the room.

The diseased spleen was beginning to curl up in the sun. I took it by one corner and brought it into the drawing-room. I had no affection for it myself, but I presumed it was one of Griffith's treasures.

I stooped down and pulled out a heavy book from the bottom shelf of the bookcase in order to press the photograph flat again between its leaves. It was a ponderous volume of somebody's sermons.

The book came open in my hand in rather a surprising way. In another minute I saw why. *From the middle of it a number of pages had been neatly cut out.*

VI

I stood staring at it. I looked at the title page. It had been published in 1840.

There could be no doubt at all. I was looking at the book from the pages of which the anonymous letters had been put together. Who had cut them out?

Well, to begin with, it could be Emily Barton herself. She was, perhaps, the obvious person to think of. Or it could have been Partridge.

But there were other possibilities. The pages could have been cut out by anyone who had been alone in this room, any visitor, for instance, who had sat there waiting for Miss Emily. Or even anyone who called on business.

No, that wasn't so likely. I had noticed that when, one day, a clerk from the bank had come to see me, Partridge had shown him into the little study at the back of the house. That was clearly the house routine.

A visitor, then? Someone 'of good social position.' Mr Pye? Aimée Griffith? Mrs Dane Calthrop?

VII

The gong sounded and I went in to lunch. Afterwards, in the drawing-room I showed Joanna my find.

We discussed it from every aspect. Then I took it down to the police station.

They were elated at the find, and I was patted on the back for what was, after all, the sheerest piece of luck.

Graves was not there, but Nash was, and rang up the other man. They would test the book for fingerprints, though Nash was not hopeful of finding anything. I may say that he did not. There were mine, Partridge's and nobody else's, merely showing that Partridge dusted conscientiously.

Nash walked back with me up the hill. I asked how he was getting on. 'We're narrowing it down, Mr Burton. We've eliminated the people it couldn't be.'

'Ah,' I said. 'And who remains?'

'Miss Ginch. She was to meet a client at a house yesterday afternoon by appointment. The house was situated not far along the

Combeacre Road, that's the road that goes past the Symmingtons'. She would have to pass the house both going and coming . . . the week before, the day the anonymous letter was delivered, and Mrs Symmington committed suicide, was her last day at Symmington's office. Mr Symmington thought at first she had not left the office at all that afternoon. He had Sir Henry Lushington with him all the afternoon and rang several times for Miss Ginch. I find, however, that she did leave the office between three and four. She went out to get some high denomination of stamp of which they had run short. The office boy could have gone, but Miss Ginch elected to go, saying she had a headache and would like the air. She was not gone long.'

'But long enough?'

'Yes, long enough to hurry along to the other end of the village, slip the letter in the box and hurry back. I must say, however, that I cannot find anybody who saw her near the Symmingtons' house.'

'Would they notice?'

'They might and they might not.'

'Who else is in your bag?'

Nash looked very straight ahead of him.

'You'll understand that we can't exclude anybody – anybody at all.'

'No,' I said. 'I see that.'

He said gravely: 'Miss Griffith went to Brenton for a meeting of Girl Guides yesterday. She arrived rather late.'

'You don't think –'

'No, I don't think. But I don't *know*. Miss Griffith seems an eminently sane healthy-minded woman – but I say, I don't *know*.'

'What about the previous week? Could she have slipped the letter in the box?'

'It's possible. She was shopping in the town that afternoon.' He paused. 'The same applies to Miss Emily Barton. She was out shopping early yesterday afternoon and she went for a walk to see some friends on the road past the Symmingtons' house the week before.'

I shook my head unbelievingly. Finding the cut book in Little Furze was bound, I knew, to direct attention to the owner of that house, but when I remembered Miss Emily coming in yesterday so bright and happy and excited . . .

Damn it all – excited . . . Yes, excited – pink cheeks – shining eyes – surely not because – not because –

I said thickly: 'This business is bad for one! One sees things – one imagines things –'

'Yes, it isn't very pleasant to look upon the fellow creatures one meets as possible criminal lunatics.'

He paused for a moment, then went on:

'And there's Mr Pye –'

I said sharply: 'So you have considered him?'

Nash smiled.

'Oh, yes, we've considered him all right. A very curious character – not, I should say, a very nice character. He's got no alibi. He was in his garden, alone, on both occasions.'

'So you're not only suspecting women?'

'I don't think a man wrote the letters – in fact I'm sure of it – and so is Graves – always excepting our Mr Pye, that is to say, who's got an abnormally female streak in his character. But we've checked up on *everybody* for yesterday afternoon. That's a murder case, you see. *You're* all right,' he grinned, 'and so's your sister, and Mr Symmington didn't leave his office after he got there and Dr Griffith was on a round in the other direction, and I've checked up on his visits.'

He paused, smiled again, and said, 'You see, we *are* thorough.'

I said slowly, 'So your case is eliminated down to those four – Miss Ginch, Mr Pye, Miss Griffith and little Miss Barton?'

'Oh, no, we've got a couple more – besides the vicar's lady.'

'You've thought of *her*?'

'We've thought of *everybody*, but Mrs Dane Calthrop is a little too openly mad, if you know what I mean. Still, she *could* have done it. She was in a wood watching birds yesterday afternoon – and the birds can't speak for her.'

He turned sharply as Owen Griffith came into the police station.

'Hallo, Nash. I heard you were round asking for me this morning. Anything important?'

'Inquest on Friday, if that suits you, Dr Griffith.'

'Right. Moresby and I are doing the P.M. tonight.'

Nash said:

'There's just one other thing, Dr Griffith. Mrs Symmington was taking some cachets, powders or something, that you prescribed for her –'

He paused. Owen Griffith said interrogatively:

'Yes?'

'Would an overdose of those cachets have been fatal?'

Griffith said dryly:

'Certainly not. Not unless she'd taken about twenty-five of them!'

'But you once warned her about exceeding the dose, so Miss Holland tells me.'

'Oh that, yes. Mrs Symmington was the sort of woman who would go and overdo anything she was given – fancy that to take twice as much would do her twice as much good, and you don't want anyone to overdo even phenacetin or aspirin – bad for the heart. And anyway there's absolutely no doubt about the cause of death. It was cyanide.'

'Oh, I know that – you don't get my meaning. I only thought that when committing suicide you'd prefer to take an overdose of a soporific rather than to feed yourself prussic acid.'

'Oh quite. On the other hand, prussic acid is more dramatic and is pretty certain to do the trick. With barbiturates, for instance, you can bring the victim round if only a short time has elapsed.'

'I see, thank you, Dr Griffith.'

Griffith departed, and I said goodbye to Nash. I went slowly up the hill home. Joanna was out – at least there was no sign of her, and there was an enigmatical memorandum scribbled on the telephone block presumably for the guidance of either Partridge or myself.

'If Dr Griffith rings up, I can't go on Tuesday, but could manage Wednesday or Thursday.'

I raised my eyebrows and went into the drawing-room. I sat down in the most comfortable armchair – (none of them were very comfortable, they tended to have straight backs and were reminiscent of the late Mrs Barton) – stretched out my legs and tried to think the whole thing out.

With sudden annoyance I remembered that Owen's arrival had interrupted my conversation with the inspector, and that he had just mentioned two other people as being possibilities.

I wondered who they were.

Partridge, perhaps, for one? After all, the cut book had been found in this house. And Agnes could have been struck down quite unsuspecting by her guide and mentor. No, you couldn't eliminate Partridge.

But who was the other?

Somebody, perhaps, that I didn't know? Mrs Cleat? The original local suspect?

I closed my eyes. I considered four people, strangely unlikely people, in turn. Gentle, frail little Emily Barton? What points were there actually against her? A starved life? Dominated and repressed from early childhood? Too many sacrifices asked of her? Her curious horror of discussing anything 'not quite nice'? Was that actually a sign of inner preoccupation with just these themes? Was I getting too horribly Freudian? I remembered a doctor once telling me that the mutterings of gentle maiden ladies when going off under an anæsthetic were a revelation. 'You wouldn't think they knew such words!'

Aimée Griffith?

Surely nothing repressed or 'inhibited' about her. Cheery, mannish, successful. A full, busy life. Yet Mrs Dane Calthrop had said, 'Poor thing!'

And there was something – something – some remembrance . . . Ah! I'd got it. Owen Griffith saying something like, 'We had an outbreak of anonymous letters up North where I had a practice.'

Had that been Aimée Griffith's work too? Surely rather a coincidence. Two outbreaks of the same thing.

Stop a minute, they'd tracked down the author of those. Griffith had said so. A schoolgirl.

Cold it was suddenly – must be a draught, from the window. I turned uncomfortably in my chair. Why did I suddenly feel so queer and upset?

Go on thinking . . . Aimée Griffith? Perhaps it was Aimée Griffith, *not* that other girl? And Aimée had come down here and started her tricks again. And that was why Owen Griffith was looking so unhappy and hag ridden. He suspected. Yes, he suspected . . .

Mr Pye? Not, somehow, a very nice little man. I could imagine him staging the whole business . . . laughing . . .

That telephone message on the telephone pad in the hall . . . why did I keep thinking of it? Griffith and Joanna – he was falling for her. . . . No, that wasn't why the message worried me. It was something else . . .

My senses were swimming, sleep was very near. I repeated idiotically to myself, 'No smoke without fire. No smoke without fire. . . . That's it . . . it all links up together . . .'

And then I was walking down the street with Megan and Elsie Holland passed. She was dressed as a bride, and people were murmuring:

'She's going to marry Dr Griffith at last. Of course they've been engaged secretly for years . . .'

There we were, in the church, and Dane Calthrop was reading the service in Latin.

And in the middle of it Mrs Dane Calthrop jumped up and cried energetically:

'It's got to be stopped, I tell you. It's got to be stopped!'

For a minute or two I didn't know whether I was asleep or awake. Then my brain cleared, and I realized I was in the drawing-room of Little Furze and that Mrs Dane Calthrop had just come through the window and was standing in front of me saying with nervous violence:

'It has got to be *stopped*, I tell you.'

I jumped up. I said: 'I beg your pardon. I'm afraid I was asleep. What did you say?'

Mrs Dane Calthrop beat one fist fiercely on the palm of her other hand.

'It's got to be stopped. These letters! Murder! You can't go on having poor innocent children like Agnes Woddell *killed*!'

'You're quite right,' I said, 'But how do you propose to set about it?'

Mrs Dane Calthrop said:

'We've got to do something!'

I smiled, perhaps in rather a superior fashion.

'And what do you suggest that we should do?'

'Get the whole thing cleared up! I said this wasn't a wicked place. I was wrong. It is.'

I felt annoyed. I said, not too politely:

'Yes, my dear woman, but what are you going to *do*?'

Mrs Dane Calthrop said: 'Put a stop to it all, of course.'

'The police are doing their best.'

'If Agnes could be killed yesterday, their best isn't good enough.'

'So you know better than they do?'

'Not at all. *I* don't know anything at all. That's why I'm going to call in an expert.'

I shook my head.

'You can't do that. Scotland Yard will only take over on a demand from the chief constable of the county. Actually they *have* sent Graves.'

'I don't mean *that* kind of an expert. I don't mean someone who knows about anonymous letters or even about murder. I mean someone who knows *people*. Don't you see? We want someone who knows a great deal about *wickedness*!'

It was a queer point of view. But it was, somehow, stimulating.

Before I could say anything more, Mrs Dane Calthrop nodded her head at me and said in a quick, confident tone:

'I'm going to see about it right away.'

And she went out of the window again.

CHAPTER 10

The next week, I think, was one of the queerest times I have ever passed through. It had an odd dream quality. Nothing seemed real.

The inquest on Agnes Woddell was held and the curious of Lymstock attended *en masse*. No new facts came to light and the only possible verdict was returned, 'Murder by person or persons unknown.'

So poor little Agnes Woddell, having had her hour of limelight, was duly buried in the quiet old churchyard and life in Lymstock went on as before.

No, that last statement is untrue. Not as before . . .

There was a half-scared, half-avid gleam in almost everybody's eye. Neighbour looked at neighbour. One thing had been brought out clearly at the inquest – it was most unlikely that any stranger had killed Agnes Woddell. No tramps nor unknown men had been noticed or reported in the district. Somewhere, then, in Lymstock, walking down the High Street, shopping, passing the time of day, was a person who had cracked a defenceless girl's skull and driven a sharp skewer home to her brain.

And no one knew who that person was.

As I say, the days went by in a kind of dream. I looked at everyone I met in a new light, the light of a possible murderer. It was not an agreeable sensation!

And in the evenings, with the curtains drawn, Joanna and I sat talking, talking, arguing, going over in turn all the various possibilities that still seemed so fantastic and incredible.

Joanna held firm to her theory of Mr Pye. I, after wavering a little had gone back to my original suspect, Miss Ginch. But we went over the possible names again and again.

Mr Pye?

Miss Ginch?

Mrs Dane Calthrop?

Aimée Griffith?

Emily Barton?

Partridge?

And all the time, nervously, apprehensively, we waited for something to happen.

But nothing did happen. Nobody, so far as we knew, received any more letters. Nash made periodic appearances in the town but what he was doing and what traps the police were setting, I had no idea. Graves had gone again.

Emily Barton came to tea. Megan came to lunch. Owen Griffith went about his practice. We went and drank sherry with Mr Pye. And we went to tea at the vicarage.

I was glad to find Mrs Dane Calthrop displayed none of the militant ferocity she had shown on the occasion of our last meeting. I think she had forgotten all about it.

She seemed principally concerned with the destruction of white butterflies so as to preserve cauliflower and cabbage plants.

Our afternoon at the vicarage was really one of the most peaceful we had spent. It was an attractive old house and had a big shabby comfortable drawing-room with faded rose cretonne. The Dane Calthrops had a guest staying with them, an amiable elderly lady who was knitting something with white fleecy wool. We had very good hot scones for tea, the vicar came in, and beamed placidly on us whilst he pursued his gentle erudite conversation. It was very pleasant.

I don't mean that we got away from the topic of the murder, because we didn't.

Miss Marple, the guest, was naturally thrilled by the subject. As she said apologetically: 'We have so little to talk about in the country!' She had made up her mind that the dead girl must have been just like her Edith.

'Such a nice little maid, and so willing, but sometimes just a *little* slow to take in things.'

Miss Marple also had a cousin whose niece's sister-in-law had a great deal of annoyance and trouble over some anonymous letters, so the letters, also, were very interesting to the charming old lady.

'But tell me, dear,' she said to Mrs Dane Calthrop, 'what do the village people – I mean the townspeople – say? What do *they* think?'

'Mrs Cleat still, I suppose,' said Joanna.

'Oh no,' said Mrs Dane Calthrop. 'Not *now*.'

Miss Marple asked who Mrs Cleat was.

Joanna said she was the village witch.

'That's right, isn't it, Mrs Dane Calthrop?'

The vicar murmured a long Latin quotation about, I think, the evil power of witches, to which we all listened in respectful and uncomprehending silence.

'She's a very silly woman,' said his wife. 'Likes to show off. Goes out to gather herbs and things at the full of the moon and takes care that everybody in the place knows about it.'

'And silly girls go and consult her, I suppose?' said Miss Marple.

I saw the vicar getting ready to unload more Latin on us and I asked hastily: 'But why shouldn't people suspect her of the murder now? They thought the letters were her doing.'

Miss Marple said: 'Oh! But the girl was killed with a *skewer*, so I hear – (very unpleasant!). Well, naturally, that takes *all* suspicion away from this Mrs Cleat. Because, you see, she could ill-wish her, so that the girl would waste away and die from natural causes.'

'Strange how those old beliefs linger,' said the vicar. 'In early Christian times, local superstitions were wisely incorporated with Christian doctrines and their more unpleasant attributes gradually eliminated.'

'It isn't superstition we've got to deal with here,' said Mrs Dane Calthrop, 'but *facts*.'

'And very unpleasant facts,' I said.

'As you say, Mr Burton,' said Miss Marple. 'Now *you* – excuse me if I am being too personal – are a stranger here, and have a knowledge of the world and of various aspects of life. It seems to me that you ought to be able to find a solution to this distasteful problem.'

I smiled. 'The best solution I have had was a dream. In my dream it all fitted in and panned out beautifully. Unfortunately when I woke up the whole thing was nonsense!'

'How interesting, though. Do tell me how the nonsense went?'

'Oh, it all started with the silly phrase, "No smoke without fire." People have been saying that *ad nauseam*. And then I got it mixed up with war terms. Smoke screen, scrap of paper, telephone messages – No, that was another dream.'

'And what was that dream?'

The old lady was so eager about it, that I felt sure she was a secret reader of Napoleon's Book of Dreams, which had been the great stand-by of my old nurse.

'Oh! only Elsie Holland – the Symmingtons' nursery governess, you know, was getting married to Dr Griffith and the vicar here was reading the service in Latin – ("Very appropriate, dear," murmured Mrs Dane Calthrop to her spouse) and then Mrs Dane Calthrop got up and forbade the banns and said it had got to be stopped!'

'But that part,' I added with a smile, 'was true. I woke up and found you standing over me saying it.'

'And I was quite right,' said Mrs Dane Calthrop – but quite mildly, I was glad to note.

'But where did a telephone message come in?' asked Miss Marple, crinkling her brows.

'I'm afraid I'm being rather stupid. That wasn't in the dream. It was just before it. I came through the hall and noticed Joanna had written down a message to be given to someone if they rang up. . . .'

Miss Marple leaned forward. There was a pink spot in each cheek. 'Will you think me *very* inquisitive and *very* rude if I ask just what that message was?' She cast a glance at Joanna. 'I *do* apologize, my dear.'

Joanna, however, was highly entertained.

'Oh, I don't mind,' she assured the old lady. 'I can't remember anything about it myself, but perhaps Jerry can. It must have been something quite trivial.'

Solemnly I repeated the message as best I could remember it, enormously tickled at the old lady's rapt attention.

I was afraid the actual words were going to disappoint her, but perhaps she had some sentimental idea of a romance, for she nodded her head and smiled and seemed pleased.

'I see,' she said. 'I thought it might be something like that.'

Mrs Dane Calthrop said sharply: 'Like what, Jane?'

'Something quite ordinary,' said Miss Marple.

She looked at me thoughtfully for a moment or two, then she said unexpectedly:

'I can see you are a very clever young man – but not quite enough confidence in yourself. You ought to have!'

Joanna gave a loud hoot.

'For goodness' sake don't encourage him to feel like that. He thinks quite enough of himself as it is.'

'Be quiet, Joanna,' I said. 'Miss Marple understands me.'

Miss Marple had resumed her fleecy knitting. 'You know,' she observed pensively. 'To commit a successful murder must be very much like bringing off a conjuring trick.'

'The quickness of the hand deceives the eye?'

'Not only that. You've got to make people look at the wrong thing and in the wrong place – Misdirection, they call it, I believe.'

'Well,' I remarked. 'So far everybody seems to have looked in the wrong place for our lunatic at large.'

'I should be inclined, myself,' said Miss Marple, 'to look for somebody very sane.'

'Yes,' I said thoughtfully. 'That's what Nash said. I remember he stressed respectability too.'

'Yes,' agreed Miss Marple. 'That's *very* important.'

Well, we all seemed agreed.

I addressed Mrs Calthrop. 'Nash thinks,' I said, 'that there will be more anonymous letters. What do you think?'

She said slowly: 'There may be, I suppose.'

'If the police think that, there will have to be, no doubt,' said Miss Marple.

I went on doggedly to Mrs Dane Calthrop.

'Are you still sorry for the writer?'

She flushed. 'Why not?'

'I don't think I agree with you, dear,' said Miss Marple. 'Not in this case.'

I said hotly: 'They've driven one woman to suicide, and caused untold misery and heartburnings!'

'Have you had one, Miss Burton?' asked Miss Marple of Joanna.

Joanna gurgled, 'Oh yes! It said the most frightful things.'

'I'm afraid,' said Miss Marple, 'that the people who are young and pretty are apt to be singled out by the writer.'

'That's why I certainly think it's odd that Elsie Holland hasn't had any,' I said.

'Let me see,' said Miss Marple. 'Is that the Symmingtons' nursery governess – the one you dreamt about, Mr Burton?'

'Yes.'

'She's probably had one and won't say so,' said Joanna.

'No,' I said, 'I believe her. So does Nash.'

'Dear me,' said Miss Marple. 'Now that's *very* interesting. That's the most interesting thing I've heard yet.'

II

As we were going home Joanna told me that I ought not to have repeated what Nash said about letters coming.

'Why not?'

'Because Mrs Dane Calthrop might be It.'

'You don't really believe that!'

'I'm not sure. She's a queer woman.'

We began our discussion of probables all over again.

It was two nights later that I was coming back in the car from Exhampton. I had had dinner there and then started back and it was already dark before I got into Lymstock.

Something was wrong with the car lights, and after slowing up and switching them on and off, I finally got out to see what I could do. I was some time fiddling, but I managed to fix them up finally.

The road was quite deserted. Nobody in Lymstock is about after dark. The first few houses were just ahead, amongst them the ugly gabled building of the Women's Institute. It loomed up in the dim starlight and something impelled me to go and have a look at it. I don't know whether I had caught a faint glimpse of a stealthy figure flitting through the gate – if so, it must have been so indeterminate that it did not register in my conscious mind, but I did suddenly feel a kind of overweening curiosity about the place.

The gate was slightly ajar, and I pushed it open and walked in. A short path and four steps led up to the door.

I stood there a moment hesitating. What was I really doing there? I didn't know, and then, suddenly, just near at hand, I caught the sound of a rustle. It sounded like a woman's dress. I took a sharp turn and went round the corner of the building towards where the sound had come from.

I couldn't see anybody. I went on and again turned a corner. I was at the back of the house now and suddenly I saw, only two feet away from me, an open window.

I crept up to it and listened. I could hear nothing, but somehow or other I felt convinced that there was someone inside.

My back wasn't too good for acrobatics as yet, but I managed to hoist myself up and drop over the sill inside. I made rather a noise unfortunately.

I stood just inside the window listening. Then I walked forward, my hands outstretched. I heard then the faintest sound ahead of me to my right.

I had a torch in my pocket and I switched it on.

Immediately a low, sharp voice said: 'Put that out.'

I obeyed instantly, for in that brief second I had recognised Superintendent Nash.

I felt him take my arm and propel me through a door and into a passage. Here, where there was no window to betray our presence to anyone outside, he switched on a lamp and looked at me more in sorrow than in anger.

'You *would* have to butt in just that minute, Mr Burton.'

'Sorry,' I apologized. 'But I got a hunch that I was on to something.'

'And so you were probably. Did you see anyone?'

I hesitated. 'I'm not sure,' I said slowly. 'I've got a vague feeling I saw someone sneak in through the front gate but I didn't really *see* anyone. Then I heard a rustle round the side of the house.'

Nash nodded.

'That's right. Somebody came round the house before you. They hesitated by the window, then went on quickly – heard *you*, I expect.'

I apologized again. 'What's the big idea?' I asked.

Nash said:

'I'm banking on the fact that an anonymous letter writer can't stop writing letters. She may know it's dangerous, but she'll have to do it. It's like a craving for drink or drugs.'

I nodded.

'Now you see, Mr Burton, I fancy whoever it is will want to keep the letters looking the same as much as possible. She's got the cut-out pages of that book, and can go on using letters and words cut out of them. But the envelopes present a difficulty. She'll want to type them on the same machine. She can't risk using another typewriter or her own handwriting.'

'Do you really think she'll go on with the game?' I asked incredulously.

'Yes, I do. And I'll bet you anything you like she's full of confidence. They're always vain as hell, these people! Well, then, I figured out that whoever it was would come to the Institute after dark so as to get at the typewriter.'

'Miss Ginch,' I said.

'Maybe.'

'You don't know yet?'

'I don't *know*.'

'But you suspect?'

'Yes. But somebody's very cunning, Mr Burton. Somebody knows all the tricks of the game.'

I could imagine some of the network that Nash had spread

abroad. I had no doubt that every letter written by a suspect and posted or left by hand was immediately inspected. Sooner or later the criminal would slip up, would grow careless.

For the third time I apologized for my zealous and unwanted presence.

'Oh well,' said Nash philosophically. 'It can't be helped. Better luck next time.'

I went out into the night. A dim figure was standing beside my car. To my astonishment I recognized Megan.

'Hallo!' she said. 'I thought this was your car. What have you been doing?'

'What are you doing is much more to the point?' I said.

'I'm out for a walk. I like walking at night. Nobody stops you and says silly things, and I like the stars, and things smell better, and everyday things look all mysterious.'

'All of that I grant you freely,' I said. 'But only cats and witches walk in the dark. They'll wonder about you at home.'

'No, they won't. They never wonder where I am or what *I'm* doing.'

'How are you getting on?' I asked.

'All right, I suppose.'

'Miss Holland look after you and all that?'

'Elsie's all right. She can't help being a perfect fool.'

'Unkind – but probably true,' I said. 'Hop in and I'll drive you home.'

It was not quite true that Megan was never missed.

Symmington was standing on the doorstep as we drove up.

He peered towards us. 'Hallo, is Megan there?'

'Yes,' I said. 'I've brought her home.'

Symmington said sharply:

'You mustn't go off like this without telling us, Megan. Miss Holland has been quite worried about you.'

Megan muttered something and went past him into the house. Symmington sighed.

'A grown-up girl is a great responsibility with no mother to look after her. She's too old for school, I suppose.'

He looked towards me rather suspiciously.

'I suppose you took her for a drive?'

I thought it best to leave it like that.

CHAPTER 11

On the following day I went mad. Looking back on it, that is really the only explanation I can find.

I was due for my monthly visit to Marcus Kent. . . . I went up by train. To my intense surprise Joanna elected to stay behind. As a rule she was eager to come and we usually stayed up for a couple of days.

This time, however, I proposed to return the same day by the evening train, but even so I was astonished at Joanna. She merely said enigmatically that she'd got plenty to do, and why spend hours in a nasty stuffy train when it was a lovely day in the country?

That, of course, was undeniable, but sounded very unlike Joanna.

She said she didn't want the car, so I was to drive it to the station and leave it parked there against my return.

The station of Lymstock is situated, for some obscure reason known to railway companies only, quite half a mile from Lymstock itself. Halfway along the road I overtook Megan shuffling along in an aimless manner. I pulled up.

'Hallo, what are you doing?'

'Just out for a walk.'

'But not what is called a good brisk walk, I gather. You were crawling along like a dispirited crab.'

'Well, I wasn't going anywhere particular.'

'Then you'd better come and see me off at the station.' I opened the door of the car and Megan jumped in.

'Where are you going?' she asked.

'London. To see my doctor.'

'Your back's not worse, is it?'

'No, it's practically all right again. I'm expecting him to be very pleased about it.'

Megan nodded.

We drew up at the station. I parked the car and went in and bought my ticket at the booking office. There were very few people on the platform and nobody I knew.

'You wouldn't like to lend me a penny, would you?' said Megan. 'Then I'd get a bit of chocolate out of the slot machine.'

'Here you are, baby,' I said, handing her the coin in question.

'Sure you wouldn't like some clear gums or some throat pastilles as well?'

'I like chocolate best,' said Megan without suspecting sarcasm.

She went off to the chocolate machine, and I looked after her with a feeling of mounting irritation.

She was wearing trodden over shoes, and coarse unattractive stockings and a particularly shapeless jumper and skirt. I don't know why all this should have infuriated me, but it did.

I said angrily as she came back:

'Why do you wear those disgusting stockings?'

Megan looked down at them, surprised.

'What's the matter with them?'

'Everything's the matter with them. They're loathsome. And why wear a pullover like a decayed cabbage?'

'It's all right, isn't it? I've had it for years.'

'So I should imagine. And why do you –'

At this minute the train came in and interrupted my angry lecture.

I got into an empty first-class carriage, let down the window and leaned out to continue the conversation.

Megan stood below me, her face upturned. She asked me why I was so cross.

'I'm not cross,' I said untruly. 'It just infuriates me to see you so slack, and not caring how you look.'

'I couldn't look nice, anyway, so what does it matter?'

'My God,' I said. 'I'd like to see you turned out properly. I'd like to take you to London and outfit you from tip to toe.'

'I wish you could,' said Megan.

The train began to move. I looked down into Megan's upturned, wistful face.

And then, as I have said, madness came upon me.

I opened the door, grabbed Megan with one arm and fairly hauled her into the carriage.

There was an outraged shout from a porter, but all he could do was dexterously to bang shut the door again. I pulled Megan up from the floor where my impetuous action had landed her.

'What on earth did you do that for?' she demanded, rubbing one knee.

'Shut up,' I said. 'You're coming to London with me and when I've done with you you won't know yourself. I'll show you what you can look like if you try. I'm tired of seeing you mooch about down at heel and all anyhow.'

'Oh!' said Megan in an ecstatic whisper.

The ticket collector came along and I bought Megan a return ticket. She sat in her corner looking at me in a kind of awed respect.

'I say,' she said when the man had gone. 'You are sudden, aren't you?'

'Very,' I said. 'It runs in our family.'

How explain to Megan the impulse that had come over me? She had looked like a wistful dog being left behind. She now had on her face the incredulous pleasure of the dog who has been taken on the walk after all.

'I suppose you don't know London very well?' I said to Megan.

'Yes, I do,' said Megan. 'I always went through it to school. And I've been to the dentist there and to a pantomime.'

'This,' I said darkly, 'will be a different London.'

We arrived with half an hour to spare before my appointment in Harley Street.

I took a taxi and we drove straight to Mirotin, Joanna's dressmaker. Mirotin is, in the flesh, an unconventional and breezy woman of forty-five, Mary Grey. She is a clever woman and very good company. I have always liked her.

I said to Megan. 'You're my cousin.'

'Why?'

'Don't argue,' I said.

Mary Grey was being firm with a stout Jewess who was enamoured of a skin-tight powder-blue evening dress. I detached her and took her aside.

'Listen,' I said. 'I've brought a little cousin of mine along. Joanna was coming up but was prevented. But she said I could leave it all to you. You see what the girl looks like now?'

'My God, I do,' said Mary Grey with feeling.

'Well, I want her turned out right in every particular from head to foot. *Carte blanche*. Stockings, shoes, undies, everything! By the way, the man who does Joanna's hair is close round here, isn't he?'

'Antoine? Round the corner. I'll see to that too.'

'You're a woman in a thousand.'

'Oh, I shall enjoy it – apart from the money – and that's not to be sneezed at in these days – half my damned brutes of women never pay their bills. But as I say, I shall enjoy it.' She shot a quick professional glance at Megan standing a little way away. 'She's got a lovely figure.'

'You must have X-ray eyes,' I said. 'She looks completely shape-less to me.'

Mary Grey laughed.

'It's these schools,' she said. 'They seem to take a pride in turning out girls who preen themselves on looking like nothing on earth. They call it being sweet and unsophisticated. Sometimes it takes a whole season before a girl can pull herself together and look human. Don't worry, leave it all to me.'

'Right,' I said. 'I'll come back and fetch her about six.'

II

Marcus Kent was pleased with me. He told me that I surpassed his wildest expectations.

'You must have the constitution of an elephant,' he said, 'to make a come-back like this. Oh well, wonderful what country air and no late hours or excitements will do for a man if he can only stick it.'

'I grant you your first two,' I said. 'But don't think that the country is free from excitements. We've had a good deal in my part.'

'What sort of excitement?'

'Murder,' I said.

Marcus Kent pursed up his mouth and whistled.

'Some bucolic love tragedy? Farm lad kills his lass?'

'Not at all. A crafty, determined lunatic killer.'

'I haven't read anything about it. When did they lay him by the heels?'

'They haven't, and it's a she!'

'Whew! I'm not sure that Lymstock's quite the right place for you, old boy.'

I said firmly:

'Yes, it is. And you're not going to get me out of it.'

Marcus Kent has a low mind. He said at once:

'So that's it! Found a blonde?'

'Not at all,' I said, with a guilty thought of Elsie Holland. 'It's merely that the psychology of crime interests me a good deal.'

'Oh, all right. It certainly hasn't done you any harm so far, but just make sure that your lunatic killer doesn't obliterate *you*.'

'No fear of that,' I said.

'What about dining with me this evening? You can tell me all about your revolting murder.'

'Sorry. I'm booked.'

'Date with a lady – eh? Yes, you're definitely on the mend.'

'I suppose you could call it that,' I said, rather tickled at the idea of Megan in the role.

I was at Mirotin's at six o'clock when the establishment was officially closing. Mary Grey came to meet me at the top of the stairs outside the showroom. She had a finger to her lips.

'You're going to have a shock! If I say it myself, I've put in a good bit of work.'

I went into the big showroom. Megan was standing looking at herself in a long mirror. I give you my word I hardly recognized her! For a minute it took my breath away. Tall and slim as a willow with delicate ankles and feet shown off by sheer silk stockings and well-cut shoes. Yes, lovely feet and hands, small bones – quality and distinction in every line of her. Her hair had been trimmed and shaped to her head and it was glowing like a glossy chestnut. They'd had the sense to leave her face alone. She was not made up, or if she was it was so light and delicate that it did not show. Her mouth needed no lipstick.

Moreover there was about her something that I had never seen before, a new innocent pride in the arch of her neck. She looked at me gravely with a small shy smile.

'I do look – rather nice, don't I?' said Megan.

'Nice?' I said. 'Nice isn't the word! Come on out to dinner and if every second man doesn't turn round to look at you I'll be surprised. You'll knock all the other girls into a cocked hat.'

Megan was not beautiful, but she was unusual and striking looking. She had personality. She walked into the restaurant ahead of me and, as the head waiter hurried towards us, I felt the thrill of idiotic pride that a man feels when he has got something out of the ordinary with him.

We had cocktails first and lingered over them. Then we dined. And later we danced. Megan was keen to dance and I didn't want to disappoint her, but for some reason or other I hadn't thought she would dance well. But she did. She was light as a feather in my arms, and her body and feet followed the rhythm perfectly.

'Gosh!' I said. 'You can dance!'

She seemed a little surprised. 'Well, of course I can. We had dancing class every week at school.'

'It takes more than dancing class to make a dancer,' I said.

We went back to our table.

'Isn't this food lovely?' said Megan. 'And everything!'

She heaved a delighted sigh.

'Exactly my sentiments,' I said.

It was a delirious evening. I was still mad. Megan brought me down to earth when she said doubtfully:

'Oughtn't we to be going home?'

My jaw dropped. Yes, definitely I was mad. I had forgotten everything! I was in a world divorced from reality, existing in it with the creature I had created.

'Good Lord!' I said.

I realized that the last train had gone.

'Stay there,' I said. 'I'm going to telephone.'

I rang up the Llewellyn Hire people and ordered their biggest and fastest car to come round as soon as possible.

I came back to Megan. 'The last train has gone,' I said. 'So we're going home by car.'

'Are we? What fun!'

What a nice child she was, I thought. So pleased with everything, so unquestioning, accepting all my suggestions without fuss or bother.

The car came, and it was large and fast, but all the same it was very late when we came into Lymstock.

Suddenly conscience-stricken, I said, 'They'll have been sending out search parties for you!'

But Megan seemed in an equable mood. She said vaguely:

'Oh, I don't think so. I often go out and don't come home for lunch.'

'Yes, my dear child, but you've been out for tea and dinner too.'

However, Megan's lucky star was in the ascendant. The house was dark and silent. On Megan's advice, we went round to the back and threw stones at Rose's window.

In due course Rose looked out and with many suppressed exclamations and palpitations came down to let us in.

'Well now, and I saying you were asleep in your bed. The master and Miss Holland' – (slight sniff after Miss Holland's name) – 'had early supper and went for a drive. I said I'd keep an eye to the boys. I thought I heard you come in when I was up in the nursery trying to quiet Colin, who was playing up, but you weren't about when I came down so I thought you'd gone up to bed. And that's what I said when the master came in and asked for you.'

I cut short the conversation by remarking that that was where Megan had better go now.

'Good night,' said Megan, 'and thank you *awfully*. It's been the loveliest day I've ever had.'

I drove home slightly light-headed still, and tipped the chauffeur handsomely, offering him a bed if he liked. But he preferred to drive back through the night.

The hall door had opened during our colloquy and as he drove away it was flung wide and Joanna said:

'So it's you at last, is it?'

'Were you worried about me?' I asked, coming in and shutting the door.

Joanna went into the drawing-room and I followed her. There was a coffee pot on the trivet and Joanna made herself coffee whilst I helped myself to a whisky and soda.

'Worried about you? No, of course not. I thought you'd decided to stay in town and have a binge.'

'I've had a binge – of a kind.'

I grinned and then began to laugh.

Joanna asked what I was laughing at and I told her.

'But Jerry, you must have been mad – quite mad!'

'I suppose I was.'

'But, my dear boy, you can't do things like that – not in a place like this. It will be all round Lymstock tomorrow.'

'I suppose it will. But, after all, Megan's only a child.'

'She isn't. She's twenty. You can't take a girl of twenty to London and buy her clothes without a most frightful scandal. Good gracious, Jerry, you'll probably have to marry the girl.'

Joanna was half-serious, half-laughing.

It was at that moment that I made a very important discovery.

'Damn it all,' I said. 'I don't mind if I do. In fact – I should like it.'

A very funny expression came over Joanna's face. She got up and said dryly, as she went towards the door:

'Yes, I've known that for some time. . . .'

She left me standing, glass in hand, aghast at my new discovery.

CHAPTER 12

I don't know what the usual reactions are of a man who goes to propose marriage.

In fiction his throat is dry and his collar feels too tight and he is in a pitiable state of nervousness.

I didn't feel at all like that. Having thought of a good idea I just wanted to get it all settled as soon as possible. I didn't see any particular need for embarrassment.

I went along to the Symmingtons' house about eleven o'clock. I rang the bell and when Rose came, I asked for Miss Megan. It was the knowing look that Rose gave me that first made me feel slightly shy.

She put me in the little morning-room and whilst waiting there I hoped uneasily that they hadn't been upsetting Megan.

When the door opened and I wheeled round, I was instantly relieved. Megan was not looking shy or upset at all. Her head was still like a glossy chestnut, and she wore that air of pride and self-respect that she had acquired yesterday. She was in her old clothes again but she had managed to make them look different. It's wonderful what knowledge of her own attractiveness will do for a girl. Megan, I realized suddenly, had grown up.

I suppose I must really have been rather nervous, otherwise I should not have opened the conversation by saying affectionately, 'Hallo, catfish!' It was hardly, in the circumstances, a lover-like greeting.

It seemed to suit Megan. She grinned and said, 'Hallo!'

'Look here,' I said. 'You didn't get into a row about yesterday, I hope?'

Megan said with assurance, 'Oh *no*,' and then blinked, and said vaguely, 'Yes, I believe I did. I mean, they said a lot of things and seemed to think it had been very odd – but then you know what people are and what fusses they make all about nothing.'

I was relieved to find that shocked disapproval had slipped off Megan like water off a duck's back.

'I came round this morning,' I said, 'because I've a suggestion to make. You see I like you a lot, and I think you like me –'

'Frightfully,' said Megan with rather disquieting enthusiasm.

'And we get on awfully well together, so I think it would be a good idea if we got married.'

'Oh,' said Megan.

She looked surprised. Just that. Not startled. Not shocked. Just mildly surprised.

'You mean you really want to marry me?' she asked with the air of one getting a thing perfectly clear.

'More than anything in the world,' I said – and I meant it.

'You mean, you're in love with me?'

'I'm in love with you.'

Her eyes were steady and grave. She said:

'I think you're the nicest person in the world – but I'm not in love with you.'

'I'll make you love me.'

'That wouldn't do. I don't want to be *made*.'

She paused and then said gravely: 'I'm not the sort of wife for you. I'm better at hating than at loving.'

She said it with a queer intensity.

I said, 'Hate doesn't last. Love does.'

'Is that true?'

'It's what I believe.'

Again there was a silence. Then I said:

'So it's "No", is it?'

'Yes, it's no.'

'And you don't encourage me to hope?'

'What would be the good of that?'

'None whatever,' I agreed, 'Quite redundant, in fact – because I'm going to hope whether you tell me to or not.'

II

Well, that was that. I walked away from the house feeling slightly dazed but irritatingly conscious of Rose's passionately interested gaze following me.

Rose had had a good deal to say before I could escape.

That she'd never felt the same since that awful day! That she wouldn't have stayed except for the children and being sorry for poor Mr Symmington. That she wasn't going to stay unless they got another maid quick – and they wouldn't be likely to do that when there had been a murder in the house! That it was all very well for that Miss Holland to say she'd do the housework in the meantime. Very sweet and obliging she was – Oh yes, but it was mistress of the house that she was fancying herself going to be one fine day! Mr Symmington, poor man, never saw anything – but one knew what a widower was, a poor helpless creature made to be the prey of a designing woman. And that it wouldn't be for want of trying if Miss Holland didn't step into the dead mistress's shoes!

I assented mechanically to everything, yearning to get away and unable to do so because Rose was holding firmly on to my hat whilst she indulged in her flood of spite.

I wondered if there was any truth in what she said. Had Elsie Holland envisaged the possibility of becoming the second Mrs Symmington? Or was she just a decent kind-hearted girl doing her best to look after a bereaved household?

The result would quite likely be the same in either case. And why not? Symmington's young children needed a mother – Elsie was a decent soul – beside being quite indecently beautiful – a point which a man might appreciate – even such a stuffed fish as Symmington!

I thought all this, I know, because I was trying to put off thinking about Megan.

You may say that I had gone to ask Megan to marry me in an absurdly complacent frame of mind and that I deserved what I got – but it was not really like that. It was because I felt so assured, so certain, that Megan belonged to me – that she was my business, that to look after her and make her happy and keep her from harm was the only natural right way of life for me, that I had expected her to feel, too, that she and I belonged to each other.

But I was not giving up. Oh no! Megan was my woman and I was going to have her.

After a moment's thought, I went to Symmington's office. Megan might pay no attention to strictures on her conduct, but I would like to get things straight.

Mr Symmington was disengaged, I was told, and I was shown into his room. By a pinching of the lips, and an additional stiffness of manner, I gathered that I was not exactly popular at the moment.

'Good morning,' I said. 'I'm afraid this isn't a professional call, but a personal one. I'll put it plainly. I dare say you'll have realized that I'm in love with Megan. I've asked her to marry me and she has refused. But I'm not taking that as final.'

I saw Symmington's expression change, and I read his mind with ludicrous ease. Megan was a disharmonious element in his house. He was, I felt sure, a just and kindly man, and he would never have dreamed of not providing a home for his dead wife's daughter. But her marriage to me would certainly be a relief. The frozen halibut thawed. He gave me a pale cautious smile.

'Frankly, you know, Burton, I had no idea of such a thing. I know you've taken a lot of notice of her, but we've always regarded her as such a child.'

'She's not a child,' I said shortly.

'No, no, not in years.'

'She can be her age any time she's allowed to be,' I said, still slightly angry. 'She's not twenty-one, I know, but she will be in a month or two. I'll let you have all the information about myself you want. I'm well off and have led quite a decent life. I'll look after her and do all I can to make her happy.'

'Quite – quite. Still, it's up to Megan herself.'

'She'll come round in time,' I said. 'But I just thought I'd like to get straight with you about it.'

He said he appreciated that, and we parted amicably.

III

I ran into Miss Emily Barton outside. She had a shopping basket on her arm.

'Good morning, Mr Burton, I hear you went to London yesterday.'

Yes, she had heard all right. Her eyes were, I thought, kindly, but full of curiosity, too.

'I went to see my doctor,' I said.

Miss Emily smiled.

That smile made little of Marcus Kent. She murmured:

'I hear Megan nearly missed the train. She jumped in when it was going.'

'Helped by me,' I said. 'I hauled her in.'

'How lucky you were there. Otherwise there might have been an accident.'

It is extraordinary how much of a fool one gentle inquisitive old maiden lady can make a man feel!

I was saved further suffering by the onslaught of Mrs Dane

Calthrop. She had her own tame elderly maiden lady in tow, but she herself was full of direct speech.

'Good morning,' she said. 'I hear you've made Megan buy herself some decent clothes? Very sensible of you. It takes a man to think of something really practical like that. I've been so worried about that girl for a long time. Girls with brains are so liable to turn into morons, aren't they?'

With which remarkable statement, she shot into the fish shop.

Miss Marple, left standing by me, twinkled a little and said:

'Mrs Dane Calthrop is a very remarkable woman, you know. She's nearly always right.'

'It makes her rather alarming,' I said.

'Sincerity has that effect,' said Miss Marple.

Mrs Dane Calthrop shot out of the fish shop again and rejoined us. She was holding a large red lobster.

'Have you ever seen anything so unlike Mr Pye?' she said – 'very virile and handsome, isn't it?'

IV

I was a little nervous of meeting Joanna but I found when I got home that I needn't have worried. She was out and she did not return for lunch. This aggrieved Partridge a good deal, who said sourly as she proffered two loin chops in an entrée dish: 'Miss Burton said specially as she was going to be *in*.'

I ate both chops in an attempt to atone for Joanna's lapse. All the same, I wondered where my sister was. She had taken to being very mysterious about her doings of late.

It was half-past three when Joanna burst into the drawing-room. I had heard a car stop outside and I half expected to see Griffith, but the car drove on and Joanna came in alone.

Her face was very red and she seemed upset. I perceived that something had happened.

'What's the matter?' I asked.

Joanna opened her mouth, closed it again, sighed, plumped herself down in a chair and stared in front of her.

She said:

'I've had the most awful day.'

'What's happened?'

'I've done the most incredible things. It was awful –'

'But what —'

'I just started out for a walk, an ordinary walk — I went up over the hill and on to the moor. I walked miles — I felt like it. Then I dropped down into a hollow. There's a farm there — a God-forsaken lonely sort of spot. I was thirsty and I wondered if they'd got any milk or something. So I wandered into the farmyard and then the door opened and Owen came out.'

'Yes?'

'He thought it might be the district nurse. There was a woman in there having a baby. He was expecting the nurse and he'd sent word to her to get hold of another doctor. It — things were going wrong.'

'Yes?'

'So he said — to *me*. "Come on, you'll do — better than nobody." I said I couldn't, and he said what did I mean? I said I'd never done anything like that, that I didn't know anything —

'He said what the hell did that matter? And then he was *awful*. He turned on me. He said, "You're a woman, aren't you? I suppose you can do your durnedest to help another woman?" And he went on at me — said I'd talked as though I was interested in doctoring and had said I wished I was a nurse. "All pretty talk, I suppose! You didn't mean anything real by it, but this *is* real and you're going to behave like a decent human being and not like a useless ornamental nit-wit!"

'I've done the most incredible things, Jerry. Held instruments and boiled them and handed things. I'm so tired I can hardly stand up. It was dreadful. But he saved her — and the baby. It was born alive. He didn't think at one time he could save it. Oh dear!'

Joanna covered her face with her hands.

I contemplated her with a certain amount of pleasure and mentally took my hat off to Owen Griffith. He'd brought Joanna slap up against reality for once.

I said, 'There's a letter for you in the hall. From Paul, I think.'

'Eh?' She paused for a minute and then said, 'I'd no idea, Jerry, what doctors had to *do*. The nerve they've got to have!'

I went out into the hall and brought Joanna her letter. She opened it, glanced vaguely as its contents, and let it drop.

'He was really rather wonderful. The way he fought — the way he wouldn't be beaten! He was rude and horrible to *me* — but he *was* wonderful.'

I observed Paul's disregarded letter with some pleasure. Plainly, Joanna was cured of Paul.

CHAPTER 13

Things never come when they are expected.

I was full of Joanna's and my personal affairs and was quite taken aback the next morning when Nash's voice said over the telephone: '*We've got her*, Mr Burton!'

I was so startled I nearly dropped the receiver.

'You mean the –'

He interrupted.

'Can you be overheard where you are?'

'No, I don't think so – well, perhaps –'

It seemed to me that the baize door to the kitchen had swung open a trifle.

'Perhaps you'd care to come down to the station?'

'I will. Right away.'

I was at the police station in next to no time. In an inner room Nash and Sergeant Parkins were together. Nash was wreathed in smiles.

'It's been a long chase,' he said. 'But we're there at last.'

He flicked a letter across the table. This time it was all type-written. It was, of its kind, fairly mild.

'*It's no use thinking you're going to step into a dead woman's shoes. The whole town is laughing at you. Get out now. Soon it will be too late. This is a warning. Remember what happened to that other girl. Get out and stay out.*'

It finished with some mildly obscene language.

'That reached Miss Holland this morning,' said Nash.

'Thought it was funny she hadn't had one before,' said Sergeant Parkins.

'Who wrote it?' I asked.

Some of the exultation faded out of Nash's face.

He looked tired and concerned. He said soberly:

'I'm sorry about it, because it will hit a decent man hard, but there it is. Perhaps he's had his suspicions already.'

'Who wrote it?' I reiterated.

'Miss Aimée Griffith.'

II

Nash and Parkins went to the Griffiths' house that afternoon with a warrant.

By Nash's invitation I went with them.

'The doctor,' he said, 'is very fond of you. He hasn't many friends in this place. I think if it is not too painful to you, Mr Burton, that you might help him to bear up under the shock.'

I said I would come. I didn't relish the job, but I thought I might be some good.

We rang the bell and asked for Miss Griffith and we were shown into the drawing-room. Elsie Holland, Megan and Symmington were there having tea.

Nash behaved very circumspectly.

He asked Aimée if he might have a few words with her privately.

She got up and came towards us. I thought I saw just a faint hunted look in her eye. If so, it went again. She was perfectly normal and hearty.

'Want me? Not in trouble over my car lights again, I hope?'

She led the way out of the drawing-room and across the hall into a small study.

As I closed the drawing-room door, I saw Symmington's head jerk up sharply. I supposed his legal training had brought him in contact with police cases, and he had recognized something in Nash's manner. He half rose.

That is all I saw before I shut the door and followed the others.

Nash was saying his piece. He was very quiet and correct. He cautioned her and then told her that he must ask her to accompany him. He had a warrant for her arrest and he read out the charge –

I forget now the exact legal term. It was the letters, not murder yet.

Aimée Griffith flung up her head and bayed with laughter. She boomed out: 'What ridiculous nonsense! As though I'd write a packet of indecent stuff like that. You must be mad. I've never written a word of the kind.'

Nash had produced the letter to Elsie Holland. He said:

'Do you deny having written this, Miss Griffith?'

If she hesitated it was only for a split second.

'Of course I do. I've never seen it before.'

Nash said quietly: 'I must tell you, Miss Griffith, that you were observed to type that letter on the machine at the Women's Institute between eleven and eleven-thirty p.m. on the night before last. Yesterday you entered the post office with a bunch of letters in your hand –'

'I never posted this.'

'No, *you* did not. Whilst waiting for stamps, you dropped it inconspicuously on the floor, so that somebody should come along unsuspectingly and pick it up and post it.'

'I never –'

The door opened and Symmington came in. He said sharply: 'What's going on? Aimée, if there is anything wrong, you ought to be legally represented. If you wish me –'

She broke then. Covered her face with her hands and staggered to a chair. She said:

'Go away, Dick, go away. Not you! Not *you*!'

'You need a solicitor, my dear girl.'

'Not you. I – I – couldn't bear it. I don't want you to know – all this.'

He understood then, perhaps. He said quietly:

'I'll get hold of Mildmay, of Exhampton. Will that do?'

She nodded. She was sobbing now.

Symmington went out of the room. In the doorway he collided with Owen Griffith.

'What's this?' said Owen violently. 'My sister –'

'I'm sorry, Dr Griffith. Very sorry. But we have no alternative.'

'You think she – was responsible for those letters?'

'I'm afraid there is no doubt of it, sir,' said Nash – he turned to Aimée, 'You must come with us now, please, Miss Griffith – you shall have every facility for seeing a solicitor, you know.'

Owen cried: 'Aimée?'

She brushed past him without looking at him.

She said: 'Don't talk to me. Don't say anything. And for God's sake don't *look* at me!'

They went out. Owen stood like a man in a trance.

I waited a bit, then I came up to him.

'If there's anything I can do, Griffith, tell me.'

He said like a man in a dream:

'Aimée? I don't believe it.'

'It may be a mistake,' I suggested feebly.

He said slowly: 'She wouldn't take it like that if it were. But I would never have believed it. I *can't* believe it.'

He sank down on a chair. I made myself useful by finding a stiff drink and bringing it to him. He swallowed it down and it seemed to do him good.

He said: 'I couldn't take it in at first. I'm all right now. Thanks, Burton, but there's nothing you can do. Nothing *anyone* can do.'

The door opened and Joanna came in. She was very white.

She came over to Owen and looked at me.

She said: 'Get out, Jerry. This is my business.'

As I went out of the door, I saw her kneel down by his chair.

III

I can't tell you coherently the events of the next twenty-four hours. Various incidents stand out, unrelated to other incidents.

I remember Joanna coming home, very white and drawn, and of how I tried to cheer her up, saying:

'Now who's being a ministering angel?'

And of how she smiled in a pitiful twisted way and said:

'He says he won't have me, Jerry. He's very, *very* proud and stiff!'

We sat there for a while, Joanna saying at last:

'The Burton family isn't exactly in demand at the moment!'

I said, 'Never mind, my sweet, we still have each other,' and Joanna said, 'Somehow or other, Jerry, that doesn't comfort me much just now . . .'

IV

Owen came the next day and rhapsodized in the most fulsome way about Joanna. She was wonderful, marvellous! The way she'd come to him, the way she was willing to marry him – at once if he liked. But he wasn't going to let her do that. No, she was too good, too fine to be associated with the kind of muck that would start as soon as the papers got hold of the news.

I was fond of Joanna, and knew she was the kind who's all right when standing by in trouble, but I got rather bored with all this high-falutin' stuff. I told Owen rather irritably not to be so damned noble.

I went down to the High Street and found everybody's tongues wagging nineteen to the dozen. Emily Barton was saying that she had never really trusted Aimée Griffith. The grocer's wife was saying with gusto that she'd always thought Miss Griffith had a queer look in her eye –

They had completed the case against Aimée, so I learnt from Nash. A search of the house had brought to light the cut pages of Emily Barton's book – in the cupboard under the stairs, of all places, wrapped up in an old roll of wallpaper.

'And a jolly good place too,' said Nash appreciatively. 'You never know when a prying servant won't tamper with a desk or a locked drawer – but those junk cupboards full of last year's tennis balls and old wallpaper are never opened except to shove something more in.'

'The lady would seem to have had a *penchant* for that particular hiding-place,' I said.

'Yes. The criminal mind seldom has much variety. By the way, talking of the dead girl, we've got one fact to go upon. There's a large heavy pestle missing from the doctor's dispensary. I'll bet anything you like that's what she was stunned with.'

'Rather an awkward thing to carry about,' I objected.

'Not for Miss Griffith. She was going to the Guides that afternoon, but she was going to leave flowers and vegetables at the Red Cross stall on the way, so she'd got a whopping great basket with her.'

'You haven't found the skewer?'

'No, and I shan't. The poor devil may be mad, but she wasn't mad enough to keep a blood-stained skewer just to make it easy for us, when all she'd got to do was to wash it and return it to a kitchen drawer.'

'I suppose,' I conceded, 'that you can't have everything.'

The vicarage had been one of the last places to hear the news. Old Miss Marple was very much distressed by it. She spoke to me very earnestly on the subject.

'It isn't *true*, Mr Burton. I'm sure it isn't true.'

'It's true enough, I'm afraid. They were lying in wait, you know. They actually *saw* her type that letter.'

'Yes, yes – perhaps they did. Yes, I can understand *that*.'

'And the printed pages from which the letters were cut were found where she'd hidden them in her house.'

Miss Marple stared at me. Then she said, in a very low voice: 'But that is horrible – really *wicked*.'

Mrs Dane Calthrop came up with a rush and joined us and said: 'What's the matter, Jane?'

Miss Marple was murmuring helplessly:

'Oh dear, oh dear, what can one *do*?'

'What's upset you, Jane?'

Miss Marple said: 'There must be *something*. But I am so old and ignorant, and I am afraid, so foolish.'

I felt rather embarrassed and was glad when Mrs Dane Calthrop took her friend away.

I was to see Miss Marple again that afternoon, however. Much later when I was on my way home.

She was standing near the little bridge at the end of the village, near Mrs Cleat's cottage, and talking to Megan of all people.

I wanted to see Megan. I had been wanting to see her all day. I quickened my pace. But as I came up to them, Megan turned on her heel and went off in the other direction.

It made me angry and I would have followed her, but Miss Marple blocked my way.

She said: 'I wanted to speak to you. No, don't go after Megan now. It wouldn't be wise.'

I was just going to make a sharp rejoinder when she disarmed me by saying:

'That girl has great courage – a very high order of courage.'

I still wanted to go after Megan, but Miss Marple said:

'Don't try and see her now. I do know what I am talking about. She must keep her courage intact.'

There was something about the old lady's assertion that chilled me. It was as though she knew something that I didn't.

I was afraid and didn't know why I was afraid.

I didn't go home. I went back into the High Street and walked up and down aimlessly. I don't know what I was waiting for, nor what I was thinking about. . . .

I got caught by that awful old bore Colonel Appleton. He asked after my pretty sister as usual and then went on:

'What's all this about Griffith's sister being mad as a hatter? They say she's been at the bottom of this anonymous letter business that's been such a confounded nuisance to everybody. Couldn't believe it at first, but they say it's quite true.'

I said it was true enough.

'Well, well – I must say our police force is pretty good on the whole. Give 'em time, that's all, give 'em time. Funny business this anonymous letter stunt – these desiccated old maids are always the ones who go in for it – though the Griffith woman wasn't bad-looking even if she was a bit long in the tooth. But there aren't any decent-looking girls in this part of the world. Except that governess girl of the Symmingtons. She's worth looking at. Pleasant girl, too. Grateful if one does any little thing for her. Came across her having a picnic or something with those kids not long ago. They were romping about in the heather and she was knitting – ever so vexed she'd run out of wool. "Well," I said, "like me to run you into Lymstock? I've got to call for a rod of mine there. I shan't be more than ten minutes getting it, then I'll run you back again." She was a bit doubtful about leaving the boys. "They'll be all right," I said. "Who's to harm them?" Wasn't going to have the boys along, no fear! So I ran her in, dropped her at the wool shop, picked her up again later and that was that. Thanked me very prettily. Grateful and all that. Nice girl.'

I managed to get away from him.

It was after that, that I caught sight of Miss Marple for the third time. She was coming out of the police-station.

V

Where do one's fears come from? Where do they shape themselves? Where do they hide before coming out into the open?

Just one short phrase. Heard and noted and never quite put aside: 'Take me away – it's so awful being here – feeling so wicked . . .'

Why had Megan said that? What had she to feel wicked about?

There could be nothing in Mrs Symmington's death to make Megan feel wicked.

Why had the child felt wicked? Why? Why?

Could it be because she felt responsible in any way?

Megan? Impossible! *Megan* couldn't have had anything to do with those letters – those foul obscene letters.

Owen Griffith had known a case up North – a schoolgirl . . .

What had Inspector Graves said?

Something about an *adolescent mind . . .*

Innocent middle-aged ladies on operating tables babbling words they hardly knew. Little boys chalking up things on walls.

No, no, not *Megan*.

Heredity? Bad blood? An unconscious inheritance of something abnormal? Her misfortune, not her fault, a curse laid upon her by a past generation?

'I'm not the wife for you. I'm better at hating than loving.'

Oh, my Megan, my little child. Not *that*! Anything but that. And that old Tabby is after you, she suspects. She says you have courage. Courage to do *what*?

It was only a brainstorm. It passed. But I wanted to see Megan – I wanted to see her badly.

At half-past nine that night I left the house and went down to the town and along to the Symmingtons'.

It was then that an entirely new idea came into my mind. The idea of a woman whom nobody had considered for a moment.

(Or had Nash considered her?)

Wildly unlikely, wildly improbable, and I would have said up to today impossible, too. But that was not so. No, not *impossible*.

I passed through the Symmingtons' gate and up to the house. It was a dark overcast night. A little rain was beginning to fall. The visibility was bad.

I saw a line of light from one of the windows. The little morning-room?

I hesitated a moment or two, then instead of going up to the front door, I swerved and crept very quietly up to the window, skirting a big bush and keeping low.

The light came from a chink in the curtains which were not quite drawn. It was easy to look through and see.

It was a strangely peaceful and domestic scene. Symmington in a big armchair, and Elsie Holland, her head bent, busily patching a boy's torn shirt.

I could hear as well as see for the window was open at the top.

Elsie Holland was speaking.

'But I do think, really, Mr Symmington, that the boys are quite old enough to go to boarding school. Not that I shan't hate leaving them because I shall. I'm ever so fond of them both.'

Symmington said: 'I think perhaps you're right about Brian, Miss Holland. I've decided that he shall start next term at Winhays – my old prep. school. But Colin is a little young yet. I'd prefer him to wait another year.'

'Well of course I see what you mean. And Colin is perhaps a little young for his age –'

Quiet domestic talk – quiet domestic scene – and a golden head bent over needlework.

Then the door opened and Megan came in.

She stood very straight in the doorway, and I was aware at once of something tense and strung up about her. The skin of her face was tight and drawn and her eyes bright and resolute. There was no diffidence about her tonight and no childishness.

She said, addressing Symmington, but giving him no title (and I suddenly reflected that I never had heard her call him anything. Did she address him as father or as Dick or what?):

'I would like to speak to you, please. Alone.'

Symmington looked surprised and, I fancied, not best pleased. He frowned, but Megan carried her point with a determination unusual in her.

She turned to Elsie Holland and said:

'Do you mind, Elsie?'

'Oh, of course not.' Elsie Holland jumped up. She looked startled and a little flurried.

She went to the door and Megan came farther in so that Elsie passed her.

Just for a moment Elsie stood motionless in the doorway looking over her shoulder.

Her lips were closed, she stood quite still, one hand stretched out, the other clasping her needlework to her.

I caught my breath, overwhelmed suddenly by her beauty.

When I think of her now, I always think of her like that – in arrested motion, with that matchless deathless perfection that belonged to ancient Greece.

Then she went out shutting the door.

Symmington said rather fretfully:

'Well, Megan, what is it? What do you want?'

Megan had come right up to the table. She stood there looking down at Symmington. I was struck anew by the resolute determination of her face and by something else – a hardness new to me.

Then she opened her lips and said something that startled me to the core.

'I want some money,' she said.

The request didn't improve Symmington's temper. He said sharply:

'Couldn't you have waited until tomorrow morning? What's the matter, do you think your allowance is inadequate?'

A fair man, I thought even then, open to reason, though not to emotional appeal.

Megan said: 'I want a good deal of money.'

Symmington sat up straight in his chair. He said coldly:

'You will come of age in a few months' time. Then the money left you by your grandmother will be turned over to you by the public trustee.'

Megan said:

'You don't understand. I want money from *you*.' She went on, speaking faster. 'Nobody's ever talked much to me about my father. They've not wanted me to know about him. But I do know that he went to prison and I know why. It was for blackmail!'

She paused.

'Well, I'm his daughter. And perhaps I take after him. Anyway, I'm asking you to give me money because – if you don't' – she stopped and then went on very slowly and evenly – 'if you don't – *I shall say what I saw you doing to the cachet that day in my mother's room.*'

There was a pause. Then Symmington said in a completely emotionless voice:

'I don't know what you mean.'

Megan said: 'I think you do.'

And she smiled. It was not a nice smile.

Symmington got up. He went over to the writing-desk. He took a chequebook from his pocket and wrote out a cheque. He blotted it carefully and then came back. He held it out to Megan.

'You're grown up now,' he said. 'I can understand that you may feel you want to buy something rather special in the way of clothes and all that. I don't know what you're talking about. I didn't pay attention. But here's a cheque.'

Megan looked at it, then she said:

'Thank you. That will do to go on with.'

She turned and went out of the room. Symmington stared after her and at the closed door, then he turned round and as I saw his face I made a quick uncontrolled movement forward.

It was checked in the most extraordinary fashion. The big bush that I had noticed by the wall stopped being a bush. Superintendent Nash's arms went round me and Superintendent Nash's voice just breathed in my ear:

'Quiet, Burton. For God's sake.'

Then, with infinite caution he beat a retreat, his arm impelling me to accompany him.

Round the side of the house he straightened himself and wiped his forehead.

'Of course,' he said. 'You *would* have to butt in!'

'That girl isn't safe,' I said urgently. 'You saw his face? We've got to get her out of here.'

Nash took a firm grip of my arm.

'Now, look here, Mr Burton, you've got to *listen*.'

VI

Well, I listened.

I didn't like it – but I gave in.

But I insisted on being on the spot and I swore to obey orders implicitly.

So that is how I came with Nash and Parkins into the house by the back door which was already unlocked.

And I waited with Nash on the upstairs landing behind the velvet curtain masking the window alcove until the clocks in the house struck two, and Symmington's door opened and he went across the landing and into Megan's room.

I did not stir or make a move for I knew that Sergeant Parkins was inside masked by the opening door, and I knew that Parkins was a good man and knew his job, and I knew that I couldn't have trusted myself to keep quiet and not break out.

And waiting there, with my heart thudding, I saw Symmington come out with Megan in his arms and carry her downstairs, with Nash and myself a discreet distance behind him.

He carried her through to the kitchen and he had just arranged her comfortably with her head in the gas-oven and had turned on the gas when Nash and I came through the kitchen door and switched on the light.

And that was the end of Richard Symmington. He collapsed. Even while I was hauling Megan out and turning off the gas I saw the collapse. He didn't even try to fight. He knew he'd played and lost.

VII

Upstairs I sat by Megan's bed waiting for her to come round and occasionally cursing Nash.

'How do you know she's all right? It was too big a risk.'

Nash was very soothing.

'Just a soporific in the milk she always had by her bed. Nothing more. It stands to reason, he couldn't risk her being poisoned. As far as he's concerned the whole business is closed with Miss Griffith's arrest. He can't afford to have any mysterious death. No violence, no poison. But if a rather unhappy type of girl broods over her mother's suicide, and finally goes and puts her head in the gas oven – well, people just say that she was never quite normal and the shock of her mother's death finished her.'

I said, watching Megan:

'She's a long time coming round.'

'You heard what Dr Griffith said? Heart and pulse quite all right – she'll just sleep and wake naturally. Stuff he gives a lot of his patients, he says.'

Megan stirred. She murmured something.

Superintendent Nash unobtrusively left the room.

Presently Megan opened her eyes. 'Jerry.'

'Hallo, sweet.'

'Did I do it well?'

'You might have been blackmailing ever since your cradle!'

Megan closed her eyes again. Then she murmured:

'Last night – I was writing to you – in case anything went – went wrong. But I was too sleepy to finish. It's over there.'

I went across to the writing-table. In a shabby little blotter I found Megan's unfinished letter.

'My dear Jerry,' it began primly:

'I was reading my school Shakespeare and the sonnet that begins:

"*So are you to my thoughts as food to life*
Or as sweet-season'd showers are to the ground."

and I see that I am in love with you after all, because that is what I feel. . . .'

CHAPTER 14

'So you see,' said Mrs Dane Calthrop, 'I was quite right to call in an expert.'

I stared at her. We were all at the vicarage. The rain was pouring down outside and there was a pleasant log fire, and Mrs Dane Calthrop had just wandered round, beat up a sofa cushion and put it for some reason of her own on the top of the grand piano.

'But did you?' I said, surprised. 'Who was it? What did he do?'

'It wasn't a he,' said Mrs Dane Calthrop.

With a sweeping gesture she indicated Miss Marple. Miss Marple had finished the fleecy knitting and was now engaged with a crochet hook and a ball of cotton.

'That's my expert,' said Mrs Dane Calthrop. 'Jane Marple. Look at her well. I tell you, that woman knows more about the different kinds of human wickedness than anyone I've ever known.'

'I don't think you should put it quite like that, dear,' murmured Miss Marple.

'But you do.'

'One sees a good deal of human nature living in a village all the year round,' said Miss Marple placidly. Then, seeming to feel it was expected of her, she laid down her crochet, and delivered a gentle old-maidish dissertation on murder.

'The great thing is in these cases to keep an absolutely open mind. Most crimes, you see, are so absurdly simple. This one was. Quite sane and straightforward – and quite understandable – in an unpleasant way, of course.'

'Very unpleasant!'

'The truth was really so very obvious. *You* saw it, you know, Mr Burton.'

'Indeed, I did not.'

'But you did. You indicated the whole thing to me. You saw perfectly the relationship of one thing to the other, but you just hadn't enough self-confidence to see what those feelings of yours meant. To begin with, that tiresome phrase "No smoke without fire." It irritated you, but you proceeded quite correctly to lable it for what it was – a smoke screen. Misdirection, you see – everybody looking at the wrong thing – the anonymous letters, but the whole point was that there *weren't* any anonymous letters!'

'But my dear Miss Marple, I can assure you that there *were*. I had one.'

'Oh yes, but they weren't real at all. Dear Maud here tumbled to that. Even in peaceful Lymstock there are plenty of scandals, and I can assure you any *woman* living in the place would have known about them and used them. But a man, you see, isn't interested in gossip in the same way – especially a detached logical man like Mr

Symmington. A genuine woman writer of those letters would have made her letters much more to the point.

'So you see that if you disregard the smoke and come to the fire you know where you are. You just come down to the actual facts of what happened – Mrs Symmington died.

'So then, naturally, one thinks of who might have wanted Mrs Symmington to die, and of course the very first person one thinks of in such a case is, I am afraid, the *husband*. And one asks oneself is there any *reason*? – any *motive*? – for instance, *any other woman*?

'And the very first thing I hear is that there is a very attractive young governess in the house. So clear, isn't it? Mr Symmington, a rather dry repressed unemotional man, tied to a querulous and neurotic wife and then suddenly this radiant young creature comes along.

'I'm afraid, you know, that gentlemen, when they fall in love at a certain age, get the disease very badly. It's quite a madness. And Mr Symmington, as far as I can make out, was never actually a *good* man – he wasn't very kind or very affectionate or very sympathetic – his qualities were all negative – so he hadn't really the strength to fight his madness. And in a place like this, only his wife's death would solve his problem. He wanted to marry the girl, you see. She's very respectable and so is he. And besides, he's devoted to his children and didn't want to give them up. He wanted everything, his home, his children, his respectability and Elsie. And the price he would have to pay for that was murder.

'He chose, I do think, a very clever way. He knew so well from his experience of criminal cases how soon suspicion falls on the husband if a wife dies unexpectedly – and the possibility of exhumation in the case of poison. So he created a death which seemed only incidental to something else. He created a non-existent anonymous letter-writer. And the clever thing was that the police were certain to suspect a *woman* – and they were quite right in a way. All the letters *were* a woman's letters; he cribbed them very cleverly from the letters in the case last year and from a case Dr Griffith told him about. I don't mean that he was so crude as to reproduce any letter verbatim, but he took phrases and expressions from them and mixed them up, and the net result was that the letters definitely represented a woman's mind – a half-crazy repressed personality.

'He knew all the tricks that the police use, handwriting, typewriting tests, etc. He'd been preparing his crime for some time. He typed all the envelopes before he gave away the typewriter to the

Woman's Institute, and he cut the pages from the book at Little Furze probably quite a long time ago when he was waiting in the drawing-room one day. People don't open books of sermons much!

'And finally, having got his false Poison Pen well established, he staged the real thing. A fine afternoon when the governess and the boys and his stepdaughter would be out, and the servants having their regular day out. He couldn't foresee that the little maid Agnes would quarrel with her boy and come back to the house.'

Joanna asked:

'But what did she *see*? Do you know that?'

'I don't *know*. I can only guess. My guess would be that she didn't see anything.'

'That it was all a mare's nest?'

'No, no, my dear, I mean that she stood at the pantry window all the afternoon waiting for the young man to come and make it up and that – quite literally – she saw *nothing*. That is, *no one* came to the house at all, not the postman, nor anybody else.

'It would take her some time, being slow, to realize that that was very odd – because apparently Mrs Symmington *had* received an anonymous letter that afternoon.'

'Didn't she receive one?' I asked, puzzled.

'But of course not! As I say, this crime is so simple. Her husband just put the cyanide in the top cachet of the ones she took in the afternoon when her sciatica came on after lunch. All Symmington had to do was to get home before, or at the same time as Elsie Holland, call his wife, get no answer, go up to her room, drop a spot of cyanide in the plain glass of water she had used to swallow the cachet, toss the crumpled-up anonymous letter into the grate, and put by her hand the scrap of paper with "*I can't go on*" written on it.'

Miss Marple turned to me.

'You were quite right about that, too, Mr Burton. A "scrap of paper" was all wrong. People don't leave suicide notes on small torn scraps of paper. They use a *sheet* of paper – and very often an envelope too. Yes, the scrap of paper was wrong and you knew it.'

'You are rating me too high,' I said. 'I knew nothing.'

'But you did, you really *did*, Mr Burton. Otherwise why were you immediately impressed by the message your sister left scribbled on the telephone pad?'

'I repeated slowly, '"Say that *I can't go on* Friday" – I see! *I can't go on*?'

Miss Marple beamed on me.

'Exactly. Mr Symmington came across such a message and saw its possibilities. He tore off the words he wanted for when the time came – a message genuinely in his wife's handwriting.'

'Was there any further brilliance on my part?' I asked.

Miss Marple twinkled at me.

'You put me on the track, you know. You assembled those facts together for me – in sequence – and on top of it you told me the most important thing of all – that Elsie Holland had never received any anonymous letters.'

'Do you know,' I said, 'last night I thought that *she* was the letter-writer and that that was why there had been no letters written to her?'

'Oh dear me, no. . . . The person who writes anonymous letters practically always sends them to herself as well. That's part of the – well, the excitement, I suppose. No, no, the fact interested me for *quite* another reason. It was really, you see, Mr Symmington's one weakness. He couldn't bring himself to write a foul letter to the girl he loved. It's a very interesting sidelight on human nature – and a credit to him, in a way – but it's where he gave himself away.'

Joanna said:

'And he killed Agnes? But surely that was quite unnecessary?'

'Perhaps it was, but what you don't realize, my dear (not having killed anyone), is that your judgement is distorted afterwards and everything seems exaggerated. No doubt he heard the girl telephoning to Partridge, saying she'd been worried ever since Mrs Symmington's death, that there was something she didn't understand. He can't take any chances – this stupid, foolish girl has seen *something*, knows something.'

'Yet apparently he was at his office all that afternoon?'

'I should imagine he killed her before he went. Miss Holland was in the dining-room and kitchen. He just went out into the hall, opened and shut the front door as though he had gone out, then slipped into the little cloakroom. When only Agnes was left in the house, he probably rang the front-door bell, slipped back into the cloakroom, came out behind her and hit her on the head as she was opening the front door, and then after thrusting the body into the cupboard, he hurried along to his office, arriving just a little late if anyone had happened to notice it, but they probably didn't. You see, no one was suspecting a *man*.'

'Abominable brute,' said Mrs Dane Calthrop.

'You're not sorry for him, Mrs Dane Calthrop?' I enquired.

'Not in the least. Why?'

'I'm glad to hear it, that's all.'

Joanna said:

'But why Aimée Griffith? I know that the police have found the pestle taken from Owen's dispensary – and the skewer too. I suppose it's not so easy for a man to return things to kitchen drawers. And guess where they were? Superintendent Nash only told me just now when I met him on my way here. In one of those musty old deed-boxes in his office. Estate of Sir Jasper Harrington-West, deceased.'

'Poor Jasper,' said Mrs Dane Calthrop. 'He was a cousin of mine. Such a correct old boy. He would have had a fit.'

'Wasn't it madness to keep them?' I asked.

'Probably madder to throw them away,' said Mrs Dane Calthrop. 'No one had any suspicions about Symmington.'

'He didn't strike her with the pestle,' said Joanna. 'There was a clock weight there, too, with hair and blood on it. He pinched the pestle, they think, on the day Aimée was arrested, and hid the book pages in her house. And that brings me back to my original question. What about Aimée Griffith? The police actually *saw* her write that letter.'

'Yes, of course,' said Miss Marple. 'She did write *that* letter.'

'But why?'

'Oh, my dear, surely you have realized that Miss Griffith had been in love with Symmington all her life?'

'Poor thing!' said Mrs Dane Calthrop mechanically.

'They'd always been good friends, and I dare say she thought, after Mrs Symmington's death, that some day, perhaps – well –' Miss Marple coughed delicately. 'And then the gossip began spreading about Elsie Holland and I expect that upset her badly. She thought of the girl as a designing minx worming her way into Symmington's affections and quite unworthy of him. And so, I think, she succumbed to temptation. Why not add one more anonymous letter, and frighten the girl out of the place? It must have seemed quite safe to her and she took, as she thought, every precaution.'

'Well?' said Joanna. 'Finish the story.'

'I should imagine,' said Miss Marple slowly, 'that when Miss Holland showed that letter to Symmington he realized at once who had written it, and he saw a chance to finish the case once and for all, and make himself safe. Not very nice – no, not very nice, but he was frightened, you see. The police wouldn't be satisfied until they'd got the anonymous letter-writer. When he took the letter down to the police and he found they'd actually seen Aimée writing it, he felt he'd got a chance in a thousand of finishing the whole thing.

'He took the family to tea there that afternoon and as he came from the office with his attaché case, he could easily bring the torn-out book pages to hide under the stairs and clinch the case. Hiding them under the stairs was a neat touch. It recalled the disposal of Agnes's body, and, from the practical point of view, it was very easy for him. When he followed Aimée, and the police, just a minute or two in the hall passing through would be enough.'

'All the same,' I said, 'there's one thing I can't forgive you for, Miss Marple – roping in Megan.'

Miss Marple put down her crochet which she had resumed. She looked at me over her spectacles and her eyes were stern.

'My dear young man, *something* had to be done. There was no evidence against this very clever and unscrupulous man. I needed someone to help me, someone of high courage and good brains. I found the person I needed.'

'It was very dangerous for her.'

'Yes, it was dangerous, but we are not put into this world, Mr Burton, to avoid danger when an innocent fellow-creature's life is at stake. You understand me?'

I understood.

CHAPTER 15

Morning in the High Street.

Miss Emily Barton comes out of the grocer's with her shopping bag. Her cheeks are pink and her eyes are excited.

'Oh dear, Mr Burton, I really am in such a flutter. To think I really am going on a cruise at last!'

'I hope you'll enjoy it.'

'Oh, I'm sure I shall. I should never have dared to go by myself. It does seem so *providential* the way everything has turned out. For a long time I've felt that I ought to part with Little Furze, that my means were really *too* straitened but I couldn't bear the idea of *strangers* there. But now that you have bought it and are going to live there with Megan – it is quite different. And then dear Aimée, after her terrible ordeal, not quite knowing what to do with herself, and her brother getting married (how nice to think you have *both* settled down with us!) and agreeing to come with me. We mean to be away quite a long time. We might even' – Miss Emily dropped her voice – '*go round the world*! And Aimée is so splendid and so practical. I really do think, don't you, that everything turns out for the *best*?'

Just for a fleeting moment I thought of Mrs Symmington and Agnes Woddell in their graves in the churchyard and wondered if they would agree, and then I remembered that Agnes's boy hadn't been very fond of her and that Mrs Symmington hadn't been very nice to Megan and, what the hell? we've all got to die some time! And I agreed with happy Miss Emily that everything was for the best in the best of all possible worlds.

I went along the High Street and in at the Symmingtons' gate and Megan came out to meet me.

It was not a romantic meeting because an outsize Old English sheepdog came out with Megan and nearly knocked me over with his ill-timed exuberance.

'Isn't he *adorable*?' said Megan.

'A little overwhelming. Is he ours?'

'Yes, he's a wedding present from Joanna. We *have* had nice wedding presents, haven't we? That fluffy woolly thing that we don't know what it's for from Miss Marple, and the lovely Crown Derby tea set from Mr Pye, and Elsie has sent me a toast-rack –'

'How typical,' I interjected.

'And she's got a post with a dentist and is very happy. And – where was I?'

'Enumerating wedding presents. Don't forget if you change your mind you'll have to send them all back.'

'I shan't change my mind. What else have we got? Oh, yes, Mrs Dane Calthrop has sent an Egyptian scarab.'

'Original woman,' I said.

'Oh! Oh! but you don't know the best. *Partridge* has actually sent me a present. It's the most hideous teacloth you've ever seen. But I think she *must* like me now because she says she embroidered it all with her own hands.'

'In a design of sour grapes and thistles, I suppose?'

'No, true lovers' knots.'

'Dear, dear,' I said. 'Partridge *is* coming on.'

Megan had dragged me into the house.

She said:

'There's just one thing I can't make out. Besides the dog's own collar and lead, Joanna has sent an extra collar and lead. What do you think that's for?'

'That,' I said, 'is Joanna's little joke.'